Somersault

Kenzaburo Oe's prolific body of work, which includes *A Personal Matter, Teach Us to Outgrow Our Madness, The Crazy Iris, A Quiet Life,* and *Rouse Up O Young Men of the New Age!* has won many international literary honours, including the Prix Europalia and the Nobel Prize for Literature.

Also by Kenzaburo Oe

Kenzaburo Oe

SOMERSAULT

Translated from the Japanese by
Philip Gabriel

ATLANTIC BOOKS
London

First published in the United States of America in 2003 by Grove/Atlantic Inc., New York.

Originally published in the Japanese language as Chkgaeri by KMdansha, Tokyo.

First published in Great Britain in 2003 by Atlantic Books, an imprint of Grove Atlantic Ltd.

This paperback edition published by Atlantic books in 2004.

The publisher gratefully acknowledges the following for permission to quote from the poetry of R. S. Thomas in 'Chapter Four: Reading R. S. Thomas':

The Orion Publishing Group for permission to quote from R. S. Thomas, *Collected Poems 1945–1990*, J. M. Dent (London), 1993, for the following poems: 'Correspondence' (pp. 67–68 of *Somersault*), 'Suddenly' (p. 73), 'Balance' (p. 75), and 'Sea-watching' (p. 79).

Kunjana Thomas for permission to quote from *Between Here and Now*, Macmillan London Limited, 1981, for the poem 'Threshold' (pp. 70–71).

The prose quotation on page 72 is from R. S. Thomas, *Selected Prose*, published by Poetry Wales Press, 1983. The prose quotation on page 76 is from *The Page's Drift: R. S. Thomas at Eighty*, edited by M. Wynn Thomas, published by Seren Books/Poetry Wales Press, 1993.

All biblical quotations are taken from *The New International Version Study Bible*, Zondervan Publishers, Grand Rapids, Michigan, 1985.

9 8 7 6 5 4 3 2 1

A CIP catalogue record for this book is available from the British Library.

1 84354 081 9

Printed in Great Britain by Mackays of Chatham plc, Chatham, Kent

Atlantic Books
An imprint of Grove Atlantic Ltd
Ormond House
26–27 Boswell Street
London WC1N 3JZ

Prologue
Beautiful Eyes in a Doglike Face

A small figure was making its way forward—a man, it appeared, with extraordinarily well-developed muscles yet reduced in scale. Chest thrust out, he advanced into the gloom, clutching in his outstretched arms a structure made of two boomerang-shaped wings, one on top of the other. Narrow banners hung down in front of him; beyond that was a brightly lighted stage. Just as he bent down to pass by a switchboard that jutted out into the passageway, one tip of the wing of the structure plunged under the tutu of a dancer who was hurrying past.

The small man and the young dancer froze. The girl, bent forward, shifted her weight to her right leg, leaving her wide-open left leg defenseless, elevated in midair, yet somehow she was able to keep her balance. She glared at the small man, her anger evident at having been forced into this helpless position. Her little face turned bright red, like a sunlit plum. But what looked back at her wasn't a small man. It was a boy—forehead, mouth, and ears protruding like those of a dog—yet with a strangely beautiful gaze.

The boy looked at her for the briefest of moments. In order to rescue the structure he supported in his outthrust arms, the boy tried to lift it up above the framework sticking out from the wall to his left, twisting the joint connecting the two wings in an attempt to slide one half upward. For her part, the girl, through her billowed-out skirt, shifted the structure toward her abdomen to absorb some of its weight, all the while keeping her left foot raised and balancing on the right one. From in front and behind the unfortunate pair, men in black leaned forward and jostled one another. At that instant, a flash of determination swept across the boy's doglike face and he flung his structure straight down, scattering hundreds of multicolored plastic pieces.

Now free, the girl pressed down her bell-shaped skirt and flew off in tears to join the group of dancers beside the stage.

The young boy pushed forward with his narrow yet strong shoulders, shoving aside the taller black-suited men. Like a very small model of someone who's just completed a grand project, he strode off into the dark of the passage behind the stage, a dignified exit undeterred by the shouts of the men. The dance troupe members halfheartedly consoled the girl, who was late, but they were concerned with their own costumes, and, besides, they'd missed their big chance that day to appear. The young boy, favored to receive the grand prize in the awards ceremony, had smashed to bits both his creation and any reason for him to make an appearance and had now disappeared.

Did destroying the model city he'd taken a year to create afford him a precocious, lawless sense of confidence—this boy who often fled from the center of Tokyo? Did seeing his creation as something whose sole purpose was to be broken to pieces make him wonder if even this huge metropolis could be razed if one wanted it to? But to what end? He had no idea, but there was plenty of time in life to try to answer that, or at least to formulate the question. This dog-faced boy, with his combination of breathtaking ugliness and beauty, must have been convinced of this, deep inside his still-forming body.

This episode took place at a public exhibition of imaginary landscapes of the future created from small plastic blocks, an event sponsored jointly by an American educational materials company and a Japanese firm that imported stationery supplies. In later years, Kizu, who had been on the screening committee, often recalled the boy who had arrogantly removed himself from the competition. Kizu could never forget how, when he first saw the boy at the exhibition, the word *child* didn't come to mind, but rather the term *small man*. He recalled the boy's moment-to-moment movements and expressions—at once so ugly you could barely bring yourself to watch, yet so lovely you felt your chest constrict—and the extraordinary vitality evident behind them. Because he was a painter, it was second nature to Kizu to want to scrutinize, over time, the details of the object of his gaze, so he was struck by a desire to watch each stage of development of this strangely compelling little lump of a child: childhood, adolescence, and youth. He felt sure that someday he'd be able to do this yet equally certain it would never happen, for even when the boy was right in front of his eyes, it had all felt like a dream. . . .

The autumn when the exhibition was held had marked a new start in Kizu's life. Already in his late thirties, his major accomplishment was to be short-listed for the Yasui Prize, but he had actually won several awards, which had led to talk of a "Kizu style" being mentioned in the same breath as that of the work of an artist who specialized in reproductions of classic paintings, the kind found hanging in European galleries. Even so, some people still continued to compare Kizu's painting with the American Urban School, which led to his receiving a Fulbright to study at an American university on the East Coast well known in the field of art education. As with the majority of Japanese artists, this should have been nothing more than a simple rite of passage, but Kizu was genuinely interested in art education methods, and, in his typically intense and focused way he decided to go back to graduate school. This took five years, during which he divorced the wife he'd left behind in Japan. Now, several years later and PhD in hand, Kizu decided to say goodbye to life in the States and return to Japan.

Kizu had been asked to join the selection committee by its head, who'd been delegated the job by the corporate headquarters of the American company; the man had helped Kizu both during his Fulbright stay and after he extended it, and Kizu naturally felt obligated to him.

The creation the dog-faced boy came up with at the contest was amazingly inventive, yet what affected Kizu most was what radiated not from the work but from the boy's looks and attitude—his entire *being*. It pained Kizu to realize that he himself lacked the archetypal aura the boy possessed. Even when he was living in America he'd felt his style of painting had reached a dead end, a feeling that surfaced in the conviction that he had no ground to stand on as an artist.

After an assistant professor in Kizu's department at the American university failed to receive tenure and moved on to another institution, Kizu's mentor invited him to take the departed man's position. Kizu had spiritedly given up on having a career as an artist in his own country—a move spurred on by the deeds of that *small man*—so he accepted the mentor's invitation and returned to live more or less permanently in the United States. Kizu went on to spend the next fifteen years in the states on the East Coast, receiving tenure along the way. As part of academic life, Kizu had taken sabbaticals, and now for the first time he chose Japan for his sabbatical leave. An urgent reason lay behind this choice. Four years before, he had been operated on for colon cancer. The examinations and surgery he'd undergone after the first symptoms appeared were almost unbearable. What's more, his elder brother had undergone surgery for the same condition before Kizu; two years ago the disease had spread to his liver, and after one awful operation followed another, he passed away. Even though he felt unwell himself, Kizu refused to be examined further.

The previous autumn at a dinner party at his university's research institute, an oncologist of note commented that Kizu didn't look at all well and recommended he get a thorough checkup; he gave in to the sense of resignation he'd long held inside and had the doctor write a letter of introduction for him to a former student who ran his own clinic in Tokyo. Sick as he knew he was with cancer, though, the last thing Kizu wanted was any more painful poking and probing or operations.

Before Kizu left for Tokyo, a visiting scholar of Japanese literature in the East Asian studies department (with a doctorate from Tokyo University, according to his business card) said to Kizu, "Ah, so you'll be the mendicant pilgrim returning to his ancestral shores?" It was just an offhand comment and Kizu took it as a playful remark. Nevertheless, it hit home—things were much more serious than that.

Still, out of these negative prospects surrounding his impending stay in Tokyo, Kizu was able to discover one positive goal—the desire to find the boy he'd run across at the exhibition some fifteen years before, the boy so ugly you couldn't bear to look at his face, yet who'd shown a flash of aching beauty. Kizu wanted to meet him and see how the boy's life had taken shape in the intervening years. He grasped at a prescient feeling, akin to the dialectic of dreams, that this reunion could never come to pass, yet somehow—it most definitely *would*.

Soon after settling into the apartment house in Akasaka owned by his U.S. university, Kizu asked an arts reporter who had come to interview him on the state of art education in America to dig up the newspaper article on the events of that day fifteen years before. Even though the reporter's newspaper had been one of the sponsors of the contest, Kizu discovered, when the reporter sent him the article on the awards ceremony—for models constructed out of the kind of plastic blocks so popular both in America and this side of the Pacific—that it was surprisingly short and matter-of-fact. It didn't even mention the name of the boy who'd destroyed his creation just before taking it onstage for the final judging. A small sidebar on the same page, though, reported on the self-sacrificing actions of the boy and the courageous stance of the young girl, who suffered while trying to keep the model from being destroyed.

Kizu called up his contact again and was able to get in touch with the reporter who'd written the sidebar. This man himself, now an executive of the newspaper company, had been curious about the boy, who of course by now was a grown man, and had tried without success to do a follow-up interview four or five years ago.

At the time of the contest the boy was ten years old, in fifth grade in a private elementary school; he went on to graduate from the affiliated junior and senior high schools and entered Tokyo University. Until the time he enrolled in the department of architecture there, his name was still in his high school's annual alumni directory. He hadn't responded to the questionnaire the following year, however, and the high school listed his address as unknown. Inquiries at his university revealed that the boy had voluntarily withdrawn. He hadn't been in touch with his parents for quite some time, and even though they assumed he was all right, he might very well have been living a vagrant sort of life.

On the plus side, the reporter told him he knew how to get in touch with the young girl, now also an adult. When he'd written the original sidebar, his first inclination had been to focus on the young boy, but requests for an interview were turned down—whether by the boy or his parents was unclear. So the reporter based his article on what the girl told him. He'd even gotten a New Year's card from the girl's mother in Hokkaido. The card was sent a few years ago, when the girl had gone to Tokyo in hopes of becoming a dancer; if Kizu wanted to get in touch with her he could start with the residence listed on the card.

Kizu wasn't surprised to hear that the boy, with his amazing sense of the three dimensional, had studied architecture, even if only for a short time. Kizu remembered thinking when he saw the model the boy had been carrying, just before one wing of it got caught up under the girl's skirt, that its whole structure—the two boomerang-shaped wings, one on top of the other—must be an architectural design for a futuristic space station.

Kizu could understand, too, how when he got older, the boy dropped out of college. What sort of youth could be more appropriate for this boy, with his frightening canine face and beautiful, expressive eyes? This was the kind of person, after all, who could smash his own creation, something so big he could barely carry it—a creation that he must have constructed over what would have seemed like an endless year.

Since his current whereabouts were unknown even to his own family, it was probably impossible to track down the young man. Still, Kizu couldn't shake the optimistic feeling that during his special year in Tokyo he would somehow run across the boy.

One other person couldn't forget that day's meeting with the boy: the young dancer who'd been impaled by the boomerang model. She had a compelling reason for never forgetting that day, for the plastic tip of the model had robbed her of her virginity. She made this discovery during the long winter of her junior year in high school in Asahikawa, where her father had been transferred. She was having sex with the PE teacher who'd been teaching her dance, and the whole operation went so smoothly the teacher got upset, thinking she must be more sexually experienced than she'd made out, though truthfully it also put him at ease. She didn't say anything to him, but she recalled that abortive awards ceremony. When she had returned home the day of the ceremony, she'd extracted a yellow thumb-size plastic piece from the crotch of her panties, a piece covered with rust-colored blood.

The young girl knew that the way the newspaper article had portrayed events—the boy sacrificing his work in order to rescue the hapless girl from her predicament—was not what really happened. According to the article, as he was about to mount the stage with his already well-received model for the final judging, the boy had boldly taken action to save the girl from pain and embarrassment. But the girl knew that, with her stage costume on, it was a simple matter for someone to lift up her skirt, roll down her underwear, and remove the plastic wing that had inconveniently wormed its way underneath; even with all the people around, she wouldn't have been embarrassed. The wing tip intruding on her groin had indeed been painful, but she knew that the way she held her body, uncomfortable as it had been, kept the edge of the wing from causing even more pain.

For an instant there had been an entirely different, violent kind of pain, brought on by the boy's movement in powerfully flinging down the model. The whole thing was a kind of attack—an intentional attack, the girl sensed, that this boy directed against *himself*. Frightened by its cold-blooded barbarity, the girl had burst into tears.

These three people, whose lives crossed briefly some fifteen years before, were to meet again. The story about to unfold begins with their reunion. As the alert reader will already have noticed, up to this point the viewpoint has been that of Kizu. The eyes that saw the young boy as a small person with the musculature and symmetry of a grown man could only have been those of an artist.

Part I

1: A Hundred Years

1

Young Ogi's new acquaintances had recently dubbed him the Innocent Youth, an appellation he didn't really mind, seeing that these people, except for the young girl, were nearly his father's age. The girl, he knew at a glance, was far less innocent than himself. Ogi recalled reading about the two elderly men—Patron and Guide, as they were called—in the newspaper some ten years before; they were central characters in a scandalous religious incident they called a Somersault. From Ogi's perspective, then, they were not only participants in an episode from the past but also men still in the prime of life— though reports of the incident a decade before had portrayed them as getting on in years.

The two men's unusual names came about in the following way. At the time of the incident, when the two severed their ties with the religious organization they led, *The New York Times* had substituted these playful names, and the two men decided to adopt them. Later on, they created a similarly playful name for the young girl who assisted them in their life together, christening her *Dancer.*

When Ogi first found out that the two men had maintained a strict silence in the years following the incident, he was deeply impressed. Other than the minimum connections needed to survive, they'd lived in total isolation from the outside world. Ogi was further amazed at Patron's enormous energy, despite the fact that he was the older of the two and wasn't so physically robust. Patron spent his days tucked away from society yet in high spirits, as if surrounded by matters of the utmost urgency. But Ogi had also caught a glimpse of the deep depression to which he was prone.

For his part, Guide was always calm and self-possessed and was clearly, even to an outsider, Patron's valued companion. When the two of them conversed they reminded Ogi, straining to come up with an appropriate metaphor from his limited reading, of Kanzan and Jittoku, the legendary Tang dynasty monks. Peeking in on their amiable chats, Ogi inevitably found Dancer already with them, and after dealing with the two men became part of his regular job, he saw something unnatural, even irritating, in the way the girl related to these two elderly men. All these emotions vanished, however, when Dancer revealed to Ogi her mother's dream that her daughter study education at the university in Asahikawa where her father taught science and become a middle school or high school teacher in Hokkaido. If I'd listened to her, Dancer told him, my life would have been very different. I never would have experienced the fulfilling days I've spent with these two men, who are, in every sense of the words, my true Patron—in the sense of teacher—and Guide. Ogi had to agree with her assessment. There was indeed something special in the relationship between this young woman and the two older men.

Employing another youthful metaphor gleaned from his scanty reading experience, Ogi saw these two men in their fifties as a pair of grizzled sailors pulling into port after a grand ocean voyage. The image was prosaic, yet it had a sense of reality, despite the fact that placid, chubby little Patron and tall, muscular, hawk-profiled Guide wouldn't strike anyone as fellow sailors on a ship. Once this metaphor came to mind, though, Ogi tried it out on Dancer. Her reply left him flustered.

"Patron and Guide haven't yet made landfall but are still in the midst of a gigantic storm," Dancer replied. "In the not-too-distant future, as the waves and wind build up higher, even you will begin to see the gale and the downpour. Until then, I suggest you find a safe harbor where you can take shelter."

"What about you?" Ogi asked.

"I'll hitch my star to the captain and the chief navigator," the girl said, nearly whispering, her mouth slightly open, her moist pink tongue visible.

Despite what this physical description might imply, there was a simple reason why Ogi did not at first feel entirely comfortable with Dancer. Granted she had a unique personality and was young and pretty enough to attract most young men. Viewed from a different angle, her habit of antagonizing him might very well be part of her charm.

Her voice and the way she spoke, as if she were whispering secrets, were alluring, her slim, lithe body right up next to you, as if she wanted to hold you close and start dancing. That intimate voice, though, was rarely restrained from adding some sharp, critical comment.

For innocent young Ogi, the combination of Dancer's whispery way of speaking and the way her mouth always seemed half open—which oddly enough didn't make her come across as dull; indeed, it appeared to him merely as a punctuation mark in an otherwise intelligent and alert expression—wasn't something he could view dispassionately.

2

As part of his present job, Ogi got in touch with Dancer, Patron and Guide's private secretary, once every other month. Since he'd taken the job, not once had it been the other way around—Dancer phoning him. But now here she was, suddenly contacting him with the message that Patron urgently wanted to see him. The phone message was relayed to him by fax from the Tokyo head office of the International Cultural Exchange Foundation, for which Ogi worked—the post that kept him in touch with Patron as part of his job. The fax arrived in Sapporo, where Ogi was escorting a French physician and his wife to a conference of the Japan Dermatological Association:

Someone named Dancer called—she's Japanese, I'm pretty sure—saying she had to get in touch with you immediately. She said Guide has collapsed from a hemorrhage and Patron has to see you right away. I assume these are nicknames? I asked for their real names, but she said you'd understand. Since it would cause more trouble than it's worth for the conference to give her your hotel and phone number, I requested that she get in touch with you through us here. The woman seemed almost possessed. Dancer, Guide, Patron—what kind of people have you got yourself mixed up with?

Ogi's main assignment at the time was to escort the doctor and his wife, both from Lyons, to an office at the hotel that had been booked for the conference; the doctor was to deliver the keynote address. After making a long-distance call to Patron's residence, Ogi escorted the French couple to the mammoth preconference dinner reception, where the head of the Association, a longtime research collaborator of the French doctor's, sat waiting at the table with his wife to greet them. This accomplished, Ogi explained his situation to the conference staff, rushed by taxi to the Chitose airport outside Sapporo, and boarded the Tokyo-bound plane. Ogi realized he'd never before acted so rashly. It made him feel uncomfortable, yet this emotion alternated with a definite delight at having taken such a bold step.

The next morning, the foundation—or rather Ogi, as its representative—was to take the French doctor's wife around Sapporo by car while her husband was giving his speech. On the way back from the Chitose airport, Ogi might very well get stuck in traffic and not make it back in time, but still he decided to fly to Tokyo without arranging for someone to fill in for him. Ogi was normally a person with a strong sense of responsibility, and though this word can easily take on a negative connotation, he was even something of a perfectionist. Despite all this, he found skipping the next day's work profoundly gratifying.

This feeling of satisfaction was certainly in keeping with his youthful innocence, but such behavior couldn't be measured by the yardstick he'd lived his life by up to this point. A premonition even struck him that this hasty act might end up destroying the self-image he'd so carefully crafted. Why Ogi made such an out-of-character decision at such a critical time, though, was quite simple. It was that gentle whispery voice, that half-open mouth like an eel moving through water. Even over the phone, when he called, Dancer's breathless and intimate way of speaking had grabbed him. Without letting him get a word in edgewise, she explained the situation.

"Guide was invited to a gathering of former members of the church, and he collapsed there, apparently from a brain aneurysm. Before Guide spoke, while they were still eating, he complained of a headache. After this he felt bad and vomited in the bathroom. Fortunately there was a doctor at the meeting, and he arranged for Guide to be taken right away to a university hospital where a friend of his works. They operated on him for eight hours, and at this point things look promising. But he lost a lot of blood. Patron's been saying that ever since Guide took on the responsibilities of helping lead the church he's suffered from chronic collagen disease. Patron was worried that he's been battling illness for so long his blood vessels may have become weakened. He started crying after he said this. I can't handle all this alone. I need you to come back!"

Ogi told her he was scheduled the next morning to take the French doctor's wife, herself a tree specialist with some books to her name, to see the Tokyo University experimental tree farm, but Dancer brushed that aside.

"Don't wait till tomorrow. Take a plane to Haneda airport tonight and come straight to our headquarters. There's no one else nearby who can help. Patron's miserable, like a stonefish shot by a spear gun."

Ogi pictured Dancer's slim, muscular shoulders and upper arms, and the imagery she employed made him wonder for a moment if she maintained her physique through a little scuba diving thrown in on top of her dancing. He was convinced, though, of the urgency of the situation.

Arriving at Patron and Guide's office in Setagaya, Ogi walked through thick trees that gave way to a hedgerow toward the single-story building, all the while gazing up at the night sky. The stars were bright, the sky as clear as it had been in Hokkaido.

Before he could ring the front doorbell, Dancer opened the door from inside and stood there on the brick walkway, as if staring right through him.

"You should always ring the bell at the gate. Sometimes we have the Saint Bernard loose in the garden." Her always-sweet whisper contained a warning.

Dancer led the way into spacious connected living and dining rooms and, leaving Ogi in the faint glow of a lamp on a low bookshelf between a sofa and an armchair, strode off down the dark corridor leading to Patron's study-cum-bedroom.

Ogi sat down on the edge of the sofa nearest the entrance and recalled the time he'd delivered smoked turkeys from the foundation at the end of last year. He had had a lot of stops to make, and the chairman had instructed him to finish by Christmas Eve, so it was late at night by the time he reached Patron and Guide's home. At an intersection two streets away from the house he ran across Patron out walking his dog. Sleet was falling, the streetlights barely illuminating the road, and the short stocky man walking slowly down the street in a rain poncho reminded Ogi of the wooden toy soldier his father had brought back for him as a present from Germany when he was a child. The man was accompanied by a Saint Bernard whose body was as long as the man's torso. At first Ogi found his gaze drawn solely to the man's quiet footsteps, the way his body stayed completely level as he walked. The dog walked in exactly the same way. The hood on the man's poncho covered his face, and the dog's body was covered in the same material, which lent them a further air of similarity. After he passed them, it took a moment for Ogi to realize that the man was Patron, but he hesitated to turn and call out to him. The majestic and solemn way that Patron and his dog walked, like two brothers, kept him from saying anything.

Ogi recalled all this as he waited in the dimly lit room; he stood up and gazed out through a break in the curtain on the broad glass door at the darkened garden and its dense growth of trees. From behind a stealthy voice, Dancer's, addressed him.

"Are you checking out the doghouse? Why do that? He's inside it. You needn't worry that he'll attack you."

Used by now to her chiding, Ogi said nothing and merely looked down at the brick walkway below his feet. On both sides of the room, running the entire length, was a complicated sort of European shutter system, not now being used. Guide had explained why they were there to Ogi not long ago, as he stood on this very spot.

When Patron and Guide first moved into this house they had a terrible persecution complex and believed many people hated them. Fearful that these people would throw rocks at them, they decided to install sturdy shutters for protection. They were afraid that rocks thrown from outside would shatter the windows, so the sensible thing would have been to put the shutters on the *outside* of the fixed glass, but Patron had insisted on having them as close to him as possible as he lay reading on the sofa, so they put up these *interior* ones with their complex system of rails and wooden doors. Eventually the world lost interest in the two men, and once that happened Patron finally was willing to have this strange contraption removed someday. For whatever reason, Guide explained all these details to Ogi. On that day, Patron happened to be in the throes of one of his bouts with depression and did not come out of his room, so it was Guide who dealt with Ogi, visiting as usual on foundation-related business.

"Patron's awake now, and you can see him by his bedside. But no silly questions, okay?" Dancer continued, in an overbearing manner that made Ogi instinctively recall her entreaties to him over the phone.

Dancer spun around, pivoting from the waist. In the instant as she turned away, and just before following her down the corridor, Ogi was sure he caught a glimpse of a thread of saliva deep in her mouth, glinting silver in the light of the low lamp. But the youth could only grasp in a conceptual way what might be sensual to another.

Patron was lying on his low bed facing them, in a room even darker than the hallway. Dancer led Ogi to a bedside table with a lamp on it; when he saw Patron's face in the lamplight, Ogi was pierced to the quick. Patron, so much older than he was, lay there looking up at Ogi with tearful imploring eyes, the kind of gaze you just couldn't hold. Ogi stared off into space and listened to his sad complaints.

"I don't have all that much goodness in the past to remember," Patron said, "and now I feel like I've lost the future as well. Even if I were to fall into a trance again and go over to the other side, anything I might say about my experiences there would just be so much nonsense. Guide is the only one who can make my words intelligible, so for the first time people on this side can understand me. Without Guide to listen to me, my words are like a feverish delirium, and afterward I have no memory of them at all. All that remains is the empty husk where the fruit of meaning once resided.

"Without Guide, my words are nonsense. Looking back now on our life together, I see with great clarity how true that is. Even if I were to write my memoirs, without him I couldn't say a thing. The same holds true for the Somersault. Guide put everything in order and created memories for me. But now that he's collapsed, what can possibly remain? I'm no better than a corpse.

"Nothing of substance will remain from my life, not even words. This is especially true when it comes to my concept of the future. Only through Guide can the visions I have be put into recognizable words and these concepts made possible. Without him I'm left with no past and no future. If all I have is the present, that's the same as saying that all I have left is this present hell! Why in the world did this *happen* to me?"

With this pitiful question—Ogi knew he wasn't really expecting an answer—Patron fell silent. Despite the impassioned words, his long, enervated, deeply still face maintained a passive look, demanding nothing of his listeners. The only relevant thought that passed through Ogi's mind was that he'd never in his life before encountered such a deeply peaceful yet despairing adult. An aged child with the despairing soul of a youth.

Ogi said nothing. Beside him, also silent, Dancer nodded a couple of times, like a mother soothing her child. *I hear you, things will be fine,* her nods conveyed, not seeking any solutions to the problem. How could she be so calm when she'd pleaded with him to rush back to Tokyo?

While Ogi stood there, unresponsive, Dancer got up and bustled briskly about the room. From the darkness beyond the circle of light cast by the lamp, somewhere over near the wall, she fetched a chair, one lower than a normal chair and the same height as the bed; next to that she placed a cushion for her own use. Ogi sat down in the chair, legs straight out in front of him; he smelled a powdery leather odor as Dancer plopped her rump down on the cushion. This way the two of them were on the same level as Patron, who was leaning in their direction.

Ogi glanced over at Dancer, her half-open mouth glistening faintly in the light, then turned his gaze to Patron, waiting expectantly for his tearful voice to resume its tale of woe. There had to be a special reason why Dancer chose *him* to be her partner here, he thought, trying to compose himself.

In the west corner of the bedroom/study, just outside the curtain and the glass door, there was the movement of some large beast. That had to be where the doghouse was. The Saint Bernard's restless stirrings overlapped in Ogi's mind with Patron's black spacy eyes, and once again the image came to him of that sleety night, man and dog in identical rainwear, out for a walk.

3

Patron didn't say anything more that night; he fell asleep, and Dancer told Ogi—who ended up spending the night—to go back to the living room. When the housekeeper they'd hired after Guide fell ill arrived the next morning, Ogi left with Dancer to visit Guide in the university hospital in Shinjuku.

Seated behind the wheel of her Mitsubishi Pajero, glaring down on the road as if she were driving a tank, Dancer was a fearless driver. She handled the car like the agile danseuse she was, with a no-nonsense approach to maneuvering it through the maze of city streets.

Until they came out onto Koshu Boulevard, Dancer carefully chose one back road after another, avoiding traffic jams. The highway might take even more time, she said, almost making Ogi carsick each time she skillfully changed lanes. She added, in a burst of self-criticism, "Of course, this might save us ten minutes at most."

Dancer told him that after their talk Patron had slept soundly the whole night but was still in shock about what had happened to Guide. She said nothing more about Guide's condition, perhaps feeling she'd already discussed it enough when she called Ogi in Sapporo. Again Ogi sensed Dancer's matter-of-fact style. There was something about her lithe body and childlike expression with its half-open mouth that made Ogi feel he had to be on his guard, yet her way of speaking was still whispery and vague. Beyond this, though, he sensed a strong reliable core. Even in a business setting, Ogi found it hard to maintain a proper reserve. Once negotiations began, he quickly took an interest in the person he was dealing with, making a real attempt to understand the other's point of view. All of which might support Dancer's calling him Innocent Youth, even though they still didn't know each other all that well. Ogi could equally well be labeled just a straightforward, affable young man. Sometimes, though, he would puzzle his listeners by abruptly denying what they said; this would happen when he decided, while listening in all sincerity, that what he was hearing was a waste of time.

Sitting in the car beside Dancer, listening to her whispery voice, Ogi knew that never once had anything she said been a waste of time. Never once had she upset him with a vapid repetition of the obvious.

Dancer dropped him off at the reception desk of the hospital, parked quickly in the lot in front, and eagerly tripped back inside. In her white Lycra sweater and narrow pair of pink trousers, she radiated youthful efficiency; Ogi wasn't surprised to see she already had on a visitor's badge. Getting the badges was such a simple matter it made him worry about how secure the hospital was. Ten years ago Patron and Guide, the latter now lying helpless in a hospital bed, were the focus of a major dispute within the ranks of their church, and the matter still remained unresolved.

They rode the elevator to the intensive care unit on the fifth floor, where the door opened inward after Dancer, her efficiency unfailing, used a phone high on the wall beside the entrance to phone for permission to enter.

Once inside the ICU they washed their hands with a liquid disinfectant soap, Dancer instructing Ogi not to wipe his hands on anything. Following her lead, Ogi held his hands in front of him, watching as the volatile soap dried before his very eyes; they came to a second set of automatic doors and entered the inner recesses of the ICU. On the floor was a three-yard strip of sticky tape spanning the width of the hallway, and again, following Dancer, Ogi stepped heavily on the strip, letting it grab his shoes. He was a large fly caught on a huge piece of flypaper, a typically shallow metaphor he came up with as the grip on his shoes tightened.

They passed by the nurses' station and, in the first of the row of private rooms, ran across a depleted, dejected patient clad in a robe lying there staring vacantly into space. Ogi understood quickly this wasn't Guide's room, but it was still a shock. Guide's room turned out to be a large one at the end of the corridor, a room with three or four beds partitioned off with white curtains; Guide lay in the nearest one, even worse off than the patient Ogi'd just seen. He was hooked up to IV tubes, and a larger pleated tube was joined to an artificial respirator, his arms and legs restrained by sturdy rope. An electric monitoring system the size of a medium-sized TV was set up at the head of the bed, with green, red, and yellow lines flashing parabolas across the screen.

Even lying flat, Guide was obviously a big-boned man; the bed was a bit too short for him. His head was covered with a white hood, his eyes were closed, and the upper lid of his closed right eye was darkly congested with blood. His breathing was labored, hence the respirator tube running out of his mouth. His magnificently sturdy face was red, like an overly robust child's.

A nurse led Dancer and Ogi to his bedside, briefly checked the drip on the IV, and left without a word. As soon as she was gone, Dancer, standing with Ogi alongside the bed, where Guide's rough legs stuck out beyond the blanket, swiftly occupied the spot the nurse had vacated. She began rubbing Guide, from one shoulder, the top of which was outside his robe, down to his muscular chest.

"His nostrils are nicely formed, don't you think? He was able to breathe on his own until yesterday. And he had enough strength to kick off his covers. . . . They've intentionally lowered his body temperature. Touch his hand and see; it's strange how cold it is."

Ogi did as she asked. The hand was far colder than his own. It didn't possess the strength to squeeze back, but its heft and feeling still made him feel like Guide was moving it.

Dancer stroked all of Guide's exposed skin so intently that it seemed like she might crush the tubes strung out of him. Leaning over the bed, she cast an upward glance at Ogi, disappointed, it seemed, that he hadn't denied her observation. Then, as if to lift her own spirits before she strode off to the nursing station, Dancer said, "I'm going to find the physician in charge and get the latest update. You stay here, and if Guide comes around, be gentle with him, okay? If he were to regain consciousness surrounded by people he doesn't know well, he might have a fit and burst another blood vessel. And that would be the end."

Left alone, Ogi's mind wandered. Whenever Ogi had looked in on the three of them—Dancer, Patron, and Guide—Dancer always seemed to be paying sole attention to Patron and was even cold to Guide. With Guide, too, you could detect an occasional sense of reverence toward Patron, but whenever Dancer tried to enter the scene he unhesitatingly ignored Patron's wishes and shooed her away. But now that Guide had collapsed, wasn't there a distinctly sexual undertone in the way she caressed his skin?

These thoughts began to take him in a different direction, and in order to crush out the stirrings they provoked, he considered again the way Dancer was nursing Guide. Ogi had, half jokingly, gone along with the name Patron when referring to him, but was this man really mankind's Patron? And Guide—this man he both respected and felt a strong aversion to—could he really be the one to guide all the world? And was it only now, with Guide's suffering an aneurysm and losing consciousness—indeed, being on the verge of death—that Ogi came to this realization?

By the time Dancer returned, Ogi was sunk in a state of sad self-pity. She had a sullen look on her face and her upturned nose wrinkled as she gave Ogi a cool glance and turned without a word for the ICU's exit. Experiencing again the uncomfortable sensation of the adhesive tape sucking at his heels, Ogi came to a halt at the double doors that should have opened in toward them; he froze for a moment, unable to think, as Dancer roughly reached out and punched the automatic button.

"What a grouch that doctor is. He's so pessimistic. He talked about brain death," Dancer said, unable to hide her displeasure, as she came to a halt in front of the bank of elevators. "Guide's brain is still swelling, he told me. At this rate the dark opening you could see in the middle of his brain in the CT scan might very well burst. I asked if they were taking any steps to reduce the swelling, but he didn't say a thing."

Dancer drove her Pajero out toward the intersection of Koshu Boulevard, and Ogi glanced at his watch; he should be able to make it over to the foundation's headquarters before it closed for the day, he thought. He didn't have the courage to tell Dancer to turn left and take him to Shinjuku Station; instead, he just asked her to stop the car up ahead somewhere. But Dancer's reaction was convulsively severe; she was furious. "Where do you think you're *going*? You're going to run away? You see what shape he's in, and you want to leave me to take care of him *all by myself*?"

Just before the intersection the Pajero came to a stop, horns blasting behind it; the engine had stalled, quaking like a person with something stuck in his throat. Her face downturned, barbs of hatred shooting out in all directions, Dancer struggled to get the car moving again and managed to pull onto the shoulder. Ogi realized with a start that she was crying, her shoulders under her white sweater quivering as she sobbed. Ogi didn't know what to do, so he just sat tight, as he usually did in cases like this. Then he got out and, more horns blaring at him, eased around to the other side of the car and got in on the driver's side. Dancer obediently moved over and, sinking back in her seat, covered her face with her lovely fingers, as Ogi started the car and moved into the traffic.

A mere ten minutes later, though, she had pulled herself together, wiped away her tears, and faced straight ahead. In her usual whispery voice, now a bit husky, she told Ogi the following, the whole thing striking him as a bit overly logical.

When Dancer had made up her mind to leave Asahikawa for Tokyo to pursue dancing, her father introduced her to his good friend Guide, who'd been his classmate in the science department in college. Her father was aware that Guide and Patron had been founders of a religious group but saw no reason to change his opinion that Guide was a trustworthy person. Dancer had seen TV reports on the religious group and was a little anxious, but she also decided to trust Guide and moved to Tokyo. Guide and Patron gave her a room in the office where they lived—albeit an inactive office—and in return she did housework for them. Around the time they started calling her Dancer, her duties smoothly shifted over to also being their personal secretary.

While she still lived in Hokkaido, Dancer had held her own recital, and a newspaper reporter in Sapporo had written a glowing review of it that had, in fact, been the push she needed to come to Tokyo. When she told the reporter where she was now living, he wrote to tell her that not only had Patron and Guide renounced their church, they had made their whole religious doctrine a laughingstock. They'd sold out to the authorities the radical faction in the church that had moved away from religious to political activities.

Dancer wasn't fazed. She didn't care what philosophy or beliefs the two might have had or what had become of it all; instead, she cherished the warm feelings she had for these two elderly men who welcomed her into their home and allowed her the freedom to do as she pleased. And when she listened to them talk to her about religious matters—either the doctrines they'd renounced or some entirely new ideas; she had no idea which—she found herself drawn to them even more.

At this point Dancer was still unaware that Patron used to fall into unusual, deep trances. One time Patron fell into a deep melancholy, the first time it had happened since she'd moved into their office, and those few dark days left a lasting impression on her, as did the general relief when this central figure in their lives was finally able to shake free of his melancholy. After this episode, when Patron was excitedly talking with Guide, Dancer overheard what he said as she did some ironing on the divider separating the living and dining rooms.

"What I just went through," Patron told Guide, "wasn't like the trances I used to have. That's all I'm going to say about it for now, but I will say this: If only we had insisted from the beginning that our church was trying to accomplish something a hundred years in the future—in other words, that we were preparing for events that would occur at the end of the twenty-first century—we wouldn't have had to go through that unfortunate confrontation with the radical faction. Anybody can see that a hundred years from now all mankind will be forced to repent. It's obvious that mankind won't be able to avoid a total deadlock. And yet here we are, the advanced countries with their booming consumer culture and third-world countries lusting after the same, like something straight out of the Old Testament—pleasure-seeking cities like Sodom and Gomorrah on the eve of destruction.

"What we *should* have done was emphasize the need for mankind to repent in the face of this ultimate trial awaiting us a hundred years from now. *That's* the foundation on which we should have built our church and prepared for the battles ahead. We should have preached that people should prepare *over the next hundred years* for the total repentance and salvation of mankind. 'When you consider the two thousand years since Jesus, a hundred years isn't such a long time. During the next hundred years we'll see new technology that will dominate over the next millennium. We have to begin now, not slack off; we have to continue our efforts.' *That's* what we should have said."

Guide impressed Dancer as a decisive person, but she'd never seen him speak his mind clearly, and though he was always kind to her she found him taciturn and hard to approach. But now he responded promptly, and Dancer could understand how very apt his name was.

"A hundred years, though, *is* a long time," Guide said. "I agree we should preach that a mere century separates us from inevitable destruction; nevertheless, if you actually live through a hundred years, it *is* a long time. I'm always reminded of the group of women who viewed our Somersault as a descent into hell. They will face the next hundred years ever mindful of our fall. In the commune they live in, they're keeping the faith, patiently striving to make it through one year after another toward the hundred. But how do they instill this in their members—a way of living a hundred years one year at a time? How to keep the faith and not be taken advantage of by the radical faction?"

After this, Dancer began to pay close attention to Patron and Guide's conversations, she told Ogi, and even now, when they weren't engaged in religious activities, just working in their office helped her find the kind of happiness a true believer must feel. But now, just when she sensed that Patron was about to revive his religious activities for the first time in a decade, Guide collapses with a brain aneurysm and loses consciousness, and Patron goes into shock. Other than myself and Guide, who's ill, she told him, you're the one person who's closest to Patron. How can you abandon him and go back to your job?

4

Ogi would never forget the strange event that took place when he had introduced Patron to the chairman of the board of directors of the foundation he worked for. As the two men exchanged business cards, Patron hit the Chairman sharply on top of the head. The Chairman had Caucasian-like skin, and after receiving this blow to his right temple, most likely the first time in his more than seventy years that someone had hit him on the head, his large, oxen eyes looked on the verge of tears. As for the perpetrator of this blow, he himself maintained a stolid wooden expression.

On this particular day, Ogi had accompanied Patron to the Kansai area factory of the pharmaceutical company that was the Chairman's main business. It was autumn, and as they left the Osaka Station and headed out of the city, they followed a course that took them through a tunnel dug out at the base of the mountain pass that formed a shortcut connecting two parts of the old highway. The autumn foliage was magnificent. Patron was already clothed for winter, dressed in an overcoat with a rounded collar, buttoned all the way to his throat, and a pear-shaped fedora, altogether like a dubious imitation of the Tohoku poet Kenji Miyazawa.

The factory and research facility were housed in a chalkstone building in the midst of rustic surroundings. As you went inside from the imposing façade there was a large entrance hall, and below the vaulted ceiling an ancient-looking marble statue of Hermes. The jovial Chairman came out to greet them. Patron was barely able to mumble a greeting, and right after this came the startling blow to the head. Afterward Ogi read a book translated into Japanese about the god Hermes and found out that he was both the god of medicine—fitting for the research center of a pharmaceutical company—and also the god of commerce, as well as a Trickster symbol. These memories came back to him now that he'd decided to leave the International Cultural Exchange Foundation to work for Patron's religious organization and was on his way to report to the Chairman, who was attending a meeting at the headquarters of the foundation.

Ogi was ushered into the waiting room next to the large conference room and cautioned by the head of operations of the pharmaceutical company that the Chairman could spare five minutes and no more. The Chairman strode in robustly, clad in a navy blue suit and yellow necktie, shooed away this underling, and sank his sturdy frame into an armchair.

"Well, let's take our time, shall we?" he began. "That's why I had you come in. I have to report to Dr. Ogi, after all." (Ogi's father, a medical doctor, had business connections with this company.) "I hope your father's well? I haven't seen him since last year at the ceremony when he won that international prize."

"Thank you for asking. I think he's well, though it's probably been longer than that since I've seen him myself," Ogi replied, a bit nervously.

He hoped to avoid having the conversation turn to the troubles between himself and his father, especially since there was a different, more pressing question he needed to solve. "Through my work with the International Cultural Exchange Foundation, mostly work in Japan I've been involved with," he went on, "I've begun to have dealings with a man I know you are aware of, called Patron. Just as Patron was beginning to firm up plans for a new movement, something terrible's happened and he's found himself short-handed and asked me to help out. I'm not a follower of the man, and I don't know much about the troubles that took place ten years ago involving Patron, his colleague—the one who's fallen ill now—and the church he led up to that point, but after discussing things with Patron and his secretary, I decided that I want to do what I can. I know the foundation will view this as irresponsible, but that's what I'd really like to do. My father helped pave the way for me to work here, and you were generous enough to accept me, and I'd like to be the one to report directly to him about my decision."

Ogi paused. The atmosphere between them had changed suddenly. Ogi was sure he had no way of convincing the Chairman to understand his views, yet something about his vague arguments seemed to take hold of the older man. The appointed five minutes had passed, and his head of operations opened the heavy oak door leading into the reception-sized conference room and stuck his head in, only to be directed by the Chairman in a loud voice to tell the other executives to wait. He then told Ogi something quite unexpected.

Befitting the longtime industrialist he was, the Chairman quickly dealt with the business matters at hand. He accepted Ogi's resignation from the main company, which had had him on loan to the foundation. Ogi would not receive any severance pay, the Chairman said, but he wanted Ogi to continue to work as a liaison between himself and Patron. Since Ogi would become one of Patron's men, the Chairman made arrangements to continue to pay him a part-timer's salary.

"Now that's settled, I'd like to ask you something. Have you ever read Balzac? Balzac's not exactly in fashion here—it's been twenty years or more, I believe, since a publisher put out his collected works—but if you've read much of him, I'm sure you've run across the notion of Le Treize. I read this myself a long time ago. The idea behind Le Treize is that there's a group of thirteen powerful men who control France during one generation, including the underworld.

"When I was young I was fascinated by the idea. I wanted to form my own Japanese Treize, with myself as the head. Of course, that was a mere pipe dream. Now that I've reached my present age, though, when I look back at what I've accomplished I see the shadow of Le Treize behind it all. Or something like it. At one time I was one of the main backers of a veteran politician who became prime minister and is still head of the most powerful political faction. Before Japan opened up diplomatic relations with China, I helped some of the more ambitious and resourceful politicians and business leaders of both countries carry on actual trade. And the International Cultural Exchange Foundation that you've worked for, with its emphasis on the medical field—by not sparing any funds to back the most outstanding talent from China and France—reflects the deep influence of Le Treize.

"These are of course unconscious influences, and I never actually thought to create my own group. Now, through the auspices of the foundation, we've made this personal connection with Patron. Whenever I think of him, I feel a wave of nostalgia. I've never met anyone like him before, which makes it contradictory to speak of nostalgia, I suppose, but what I mean is I get the same sort of feeling from him as when I read Balzac and imagined my very own Treize.

"Just when I was considering all this, I received a communication from the foundation's secretary, saying you'd grown closer to Patron and had been sloughing off your work for the foundation. She had so many complaints I had to check into things myself. I've confirmed what you told me—that Patron's right-hand man has collapsed, and that he plans to start a new movement. As a matter of fact, I was just mulling over what a difficult situation this is.

"I find this absolutely fascinating! Isn't Patron the very image of Le Treize? At least I'd like to think so. Amazingly, just when I felt this way, here you come along saying you want to work for him. I'll do what I can to help you out."

5

Ogi returned to the office from Hibiya and reported excitedly to Dancer about his conversation with the Chairman. She herself had just returned from the hospital, where she'd spent time with the still-unconscious Guide, massaging him to improve his circulation, none too good after lying so long in a hospital bed. This weekend, after tests to determine if he was able to withstand it, he would undergo an operation to prevent hydrocephalus. When he heard this, Patron had taken to his bed again.

As Ogi reported on his meeting with the Chairman, Dancer's attitude was noncommittal. He found it easy to talk with her—that is, until he mentioned, jokingly, the Chairman's talk about Le Treize, which he'd omitted up till then, thinking it irrelevant. Dancer got suddenly irritated, and before he knew it things escalated to the point where she threw some fairly scathing remarks his way. Too late, he listened carefully, reflected on what she said, and realized that although he'd taken the Chairman's story of Le Treize as so much boastful talk, Dancer saw it as part of a serious evaluation of Patron and Guide.

"Are you really such an ineffectual person?" she asked him. "When I was a child I couldn't stand boys like you, I couldn't believe people could be that indecisive! You're like one of those boys all grown up. Don't think the name Innocent Youth that Patron and Guide gave you is entirely positive. I don't know what to do with people like you!"

Ogi was startled and couldn't help asking why.

"Don't you get it?" Dancer went on. "What you said isn't just weak, it's irresponsible!"

She wasn't so much disappointed as angry. Ogi felt confused but also sensed that she wasn't about to release him from the cage that surrounded him, but was tightening the rope that bound them together, showing the kind of displeasure you find only between family members. For even in a situation like this, though her voice grew ever more emphatic, he could detect a kind of trembling in her sad, whispery voice.

"Patron is shut up inside himself, in no shape whatsoever to give directions, and even if Guide regains consciousness the chances are slim that he'll return to normal. You're the only one we can rely on!

"You knew how worried I was, so you put your assignment in Sapporo on hold and flew down here. These past ten days you've devoted yourself to helping us, and I'm grateful. You know very well the situation we're in, which is why you quit the foundation to work full time as a staff member in our office. When I heard you were quitting, I finally stopped worrying about you being a police spy."

"A police spy?" Ogi parroted.

"*Really!* You're beyond innocent. You know what happened ten years ago, right? I got this position because my father was a classmate of Guide's in college. So it wouldn't have been so strange that they might have thought *me* a police spy. But Patron and Guide welcomed me, provided me with a place to live in Tokyo, and let me develop my dancing. I'll never forget that. I have no idea what plans they have for the future, so I don't think I can be of much use to them as they restructure their religious movement. But I want to work for Patron. I want to be a believer.

"This is getting kind of personal, but I wanted more than anything to continue dancing, and when I came to Tokyo without any plans it was Patron who showed me what I really want to do most. Guide, too. Neither of them have said much to me about religious matters. You've only seen the severe side of Guide. It might be hard for you to imagine, but when you're a part of the peaceful relationship between the two of them, before you realize what's happening you find them leading you in new directions. Every day with them is simply amazing. I enjoy my dancing more, now, and I want to become one of Patron's followers. But suddenly, in the middle of all this, Guide's seriously ill.

"With Guide unconscious and Patron in shock, all I can do is try my best to get Patron back on his feet, right? Since I have no one else to rely on, I phoned you in Sapporo and insisted that you come here, and you've been more of a help than I ever expected.

"This is what I think: Patron and Guide know I'm not very smart and don't have even a basic knowledge of religion, and that's why they never discussed it with me. But I know how special the two of them are, and I've always done my very best for them. Now you're one of my colleagues and you know things I don't; you can teach me a lot, and I'm looking forward to it. This may well be the chance for *you* to become my new mentor."

Dancer had never spoken so much before, but what surprised Ogi most was her final declaration. He'd been looking down as he listened to her, but now he glanced up and saw her staring right at him, mouth slightly open as usual, a steady stream of tears flowing down her cheeks. He knew he was a young man without much experience, yet at this moment Dancer struck him as even more wet behind the ears. Observing her in a detached way he never had before, he found her silly, even a bit unattractive, yet he went ahead and did something quite unexpected. Well, what else can I do? he asked himself, a generous sense of resignation coursing through him.

Ogi wrapped his arms around Dancer's slim yet solid neck and shoulders and drew her to him. He eased her crying face closer and kissed her thin lips.

At first Ogi was the initiator, but then Dancer leaned forward from the edge of the armchair she was sitting in and deliberately returned his kiss; she placed her left knee on the floor, nudged Ogi back in that direction, and rested her left leg on top of his right thigh. Their long kiss continued, Dancer restlessly rubbing her firm belly against Ogi's thigh; her fragrant breath grazed his neck for a moment. Dancer became an unexpectedly heavy weight, straining his awkwardly bent back.

After a while she roused herself and gazed down abashedly at Ogi, lying there in an unnatural pose. "Not to worry," she said. "It won't be easy, but if we work together we can protect Patron!" With this she disappeared into the bathroom and then went off to Patron's room.

After a while Ogi sat up on the sofa and went to relieve himself in the guest toilet next to the front door. He gazed down steadily at his engorged, tormented penis. Then he picked up the hand mirror hanging by a ribbon next to the sink and examined a large blood blister that had developed inside his cheek.

"How did that all happen? This is too much!" he said pointedly to himself.

But a light feeling, a desire to be productive, welled up in him and he returned to the living-dining room to check out the way things were arranged in the corner where, starting today, he would work. Guide had his own residence in a separate annex and apparently did all his work there. Since Ogi would be a member of Patron's office staff, the only place he could possibly work was here in the living room. Ogi checked out the telephone and fax, set up on a low wide partition separating the dining room from the living room. Below this was a generous amount of storage space and a bookshelf for storing fax equipment. In the east corner of the dining room was a mammoth desk twice the size of an ordinary study desk, and opening the drawers he found some brand-new disposable fountain pens, neatly sharpened soft lead pencils, and a set of thick German-made colored pencils. He'd seen Dancer seated there, busy at work.

On the west side of the living room the bookshelf above the sofa still had plenty of space in it, and between the back of the sofa and the partition were filing cabinets and a level board that could be used as a sideboard. Next to the wall on the east side of the living room, beside the TV and VCR, slightly removed from the side facing the garden, was an oblong object with a cover over it; Ogi discovered it was a copy machine.

"All *right*!" he said aloud, energy coursing through him as he stood in the middle of the living room, arms folded, surveying his surroundings. Move that desk over to the space on the east side of the living room, he thought, line up my chair and Dancer's facing each other across the two desks, and we'll have a nice little workstation. That would definitely be—all right!

Ogi's shout of joy wasn't just because he'd figured out how to arrange his office. It was as if his renewed sexual energy, missing an outlet for its discharge, had called out. He had no idea what he'd be able to accomplish here, working on Patron's staff, though he felt relieved to know the foundation would still be paying him something. He wouldn't be working here as a fresh-faced new believer—it was just a job, after all—but even so he was filled with an enthusiastic desire to shout for joy. All *right*!

6

Without rearranging any of the office equipment, Ogi moved the office desk by himself, figured out how he and Dancer would both sit, checked the electrical outlets, and adjusted the height of his chair. He brought a rag and a bucket of water from the kitchen and cleaned the unused desk and shelves, generally getting his new workplace in order. As he did, the unkempt garden with its flowering dogwoods, camellias, and magnolias grew darker as the June twilight came on. The limpid blue sky stayed light for the longest time. Finished with his straightening up and with no work to do yet in the newly settled office, he sat on the side of the sofa nearer the garden, lost in thought, gazing out the window at the gathering gloom. Dancer suddenly appeared from the dark corridor. She had changed into a sleeveless linen shirt and a long light-colored skirt. With her hair pulled back, she reminded Ogi of an attractive Chinese girl he'd seen once in San Francisco's Chinatown.

"Patron would like to talk with you," she said, her voice hard; Ogi understood she wanted him to act as if nothing had happened. Ever resigned, he played along. He realized that for the last two hours he'd been enjoying the afterglow of those lips and tongue, the movement of that belly.

Dancer waited for him to stand up, switched on the light in the corridor, and deftly explained things to him.

"We'll tell him about your conversation with the Chairman. If there's something you'd like to add, be sure to make it short. Patron may have some questions for you. . . . By the way, you've done a good job of arranging your workstation."

The drapery with its design of groves of trees was half drawn, and a faint lustrous golden light shone through the lace curtains against the glass; in the western side of the room, at a what looked like a small ornamental desk, Patron's heavy form sat at an angle. On top of the desk were some envelopes—too small for mailing letters—and Patron, half turned in their direction, held a fountain pen in his pudgy fingers. The light wasn't conducive to writing letters, though.

Dancer and Ogi couldn't find any chairs to sit on, so they stood together facing Patron. Patron's face still looked swollen, but he seemed to have recovered from his earlier emotional turmoil as Ogi reported on how he'd changed jobs, unable to resist touching on what the Chairman had told him about Balzac. Just as it had with Dancer, this brought on an irritable reaction.

"I can't believe Le Treize was such a simplistic idea. I think the Chairman has his own preconception about it," Patron said, inclining his overly large head and casting a gloomy look at Ogi. "For someone like him who's lived such a focused life, no matter how imaginative the notion he's always got to bring it back down to earth. I'm flattered that he thought of Guide and me when he came up with these ideas, though I can't imagine how what we've done or are about to do might correspond to some modern-day Thirteen. What do you think, Ogi?"

Ogi understood that Patron's question to him was nothing more than a rhetorical device he used when delivering a sermon, but he went ahead and replied. Although he was not a particularly voluble person, it was Ogi's nature that once he had something to say, he didn't hold back.

"The foundation holds regular conferences, one of which you attended, as you recall," Ogi said. "I used to be in charge of making the arrangements. The members included such people as the French ambassador, chairmen of large corporations, advisers to banks and brokerage firms, even a novelist who'd won the Order of Cultural Merit—to put it bluntly, all people whose careers in their respective fields are basically drawing to a close.

"There was some discussion about making you a member, and they decided to invite you once as a guest. Ever since the time I escorted you to the Kansai research facility, the Chairman has recommended you to the conference. Being a clever group of men, they did not oppose having you participate one time. To tell the truth, though, some of them acted as if they were receiving a jester into their midst. Several of the members' secretaries reported happily to me later that their bosses enjoyed your talk enormously. These secretaries also asked me, in their employers' stead, whether it was true that you and Guide had actually severed all ties with your church, or whether that was merely a diversionary tactic aimed at the upcoming trials.

"In other words, from the very beginning it's been just a pipe dream for those movers and shakers to join forces with an eccentric such as yourself. They're cautious people; they were just amusing themselves at your expense. Even if you had become a member, as soon as they knew you were about to begin leading a new religious movement you can be sure they'd have voted you out."

Patron listened carefully. Instead of adding a comment, though, he wound up their conversation by directing Ogi and Dancer to undertake a new job. The two young people withdrew and began preparing a late dinner. In the kitchen next to the dining room, they took out what was available in the refrigerator and set to work.

"Patron looks well, don't you think?" Dancer said to Ogi, as they divided up the work. "It's hard to believe, after how hopeless he said he felt once Guide looked like he wouldn't recover. Now, ten days later, with you working as a secretary, here he is already set on starting a new movement. He's an amazing personality, don't you think? Though that's nothing new to me."

Sautéing a thinly sliced onion in butter, Ogi wanted to say, If that's nothing new to you, why don't you keep quiet? But Dancer, ever sensitive, ended her thoughts with a meaningful remark. "I think it was good for both of you that Patron opened up so honestly." She was slicing a chunk of beef into thin strips in preparation for making a quick gourmet curry, her mouth half open as usual, revealing a tongue glistening with saliva that brought a painful twinge of nostalgia to Ogi.

Patron had told them as he outlined the task he wanted them to begin, "I only rely on a very few of my followers, which isn't surprising, seeing as how I couldn't even rely on myself!"

This struck Ogi as a bit of a non sequitur, but Dancer gave a cute, nonchalant laugh.

"Ogi's working for us now as kind of an extension of his earlier job," Patron added, "but I don't think he's made the leap over to our side yet. Well, just so that we all agree on that, starting tomorrow I'd like you do this for me. It's the reason I called you both in here. I have a number of handwritten cards making up a name list. First I'd like Dancer to make two complete copies and return the originals to me."

Patron gathered up the papers on his desk that were too small for stationery and handed them over to Dancer, who promptly disappeared into the living room and was back in the blink of an eye.

"What I'd like the two of you to do," Patron continued, "is to get in touch with my supporters on this list, mainly those in Tokyo and surrounding areas, but also some in outlying regions."

Patron was at the age when he should be wearing reading glasses, but he took the originals of the cards Dancer had returned to him, holding them at arm's length from his large face as he studied them. Dancer had been standing next to Ogi, but now she moved closer to Patron; knitting her brow in a line of fine wrinkles, she attentively examined the copies, for all the world like a schoolgirl reading a handout of her lines for the school play. For Ogi, the handwriting of this man who'd been schooled in the precomputer age was surprisingly unimpressive, even childish. He felt compelled to question Patron about this rather audacious list.

"About Guide and your Somersault—I'm using the term the media used at the time—weren't you criticized by some of the followers in your church? I heard that the radical faction was arrested and prosecuted, though not every member was caught, and while they didn't have a chance to make any public declaration against you, some terrible things were said during the trial. Even more moderate members who made up the core of your church denounced you, didn't they?

"What's the connection between the new supporters on this list and those earlier members of the church? Are these supporters sympathizers who still remained within the church? If so, then you didn't completely renounce the church but only cut off connections at a superficial level, maintaining a relationship with certain key members. Putting aside your statements on television directed at society at large, doesn't this mean that you lied to the Chairman of the foundation? I told him your Somersault meant you completely cut all ties with the church, and in fact had become its enemy."

For the first time that day Patron turned to face Ogi. He straightened up, his head held high, no longer a vulnerable old man but now like a large, combative animal asserting its dignity.

"I did not lie," Patron said, in a strong voice. "All the names on the list are people who've sent us letters in the ten years since we apostatized. I've omitted anyone who had a connection with our earlier activities.

"Through our Somersault, Guide and I renounced the church and our doctrine. Now we're about to step into a new stage. Some people view our renunciation as our fall into hell. According to Guide, after we left the church this was how a group of women followers who also left the church and now live an independent communal life interpreted it. Before a savior can accomplish the things he has prophesied—before he can free this fallen world and lead the people into a transcendent realm—he first has to experience hell. That sort of notion. Before the Somersault, those same people called us Savior and Prophet, you'll recall.

"Be that as it may, through our Somersault, Guide and I seceded from the church. Since then the church has continued its activities, with Kansai headquarters leading the way, but the two of us have nothing to do with them. Now that Guide has collapsed we're faced with the worst crisis—the biggest trial we've gone through since our secession.

"So I thought of contacting those who have nothing to do with the church who've sent us letters of support. As far as I remember, I've never met any of these people on the list. They became interested in us after Guide and I left the church and were spurned by society and became public laughing-stocks. I've started considering these new supporters just recently, and I'd like you to work at getting in touch with them, Ogi, together with Dancer, of course. This will be your first job here."

"I think we need to start off by checking your list against the letters people sent," Dancer said. "Some of them might be trying to deceive us. We'll have you check our letters before we send them out, of course. Ogi, we can discuss this in the other room. Patron needs to rest."

Dancer helped Patron, clad in his dressing gown, get up from the small chair. Heavy head sunk between his soft shoulders, he shuffled back to his bed on weak, sickly legs.

That evening Ogi waited while, in the already darkened garden, Dancer went out to feed the Saint Bernard, who made sounds that were at once generous and bighearted, unmistakably those of a large beast. Patron had gone to bed without eating. Ogi and Dancer finally had a late supper, and as they ate they reviewed their instructions.

"As I was listening to Patron," she said, "I couldn't help but wonder why—when you aren't a devotee of Patron's teachings—you're supporting him and working to help him. I know I asked you to, but I feel a little bad about it."

"I don't know . . . he has a sort of strange appeal," Ogi replied. "I've never met another man of his age quite like him."

2: Reunion

1

The story now shifts to the reunion of the artist Kizu and the dog-faced boy with the beautiful eyes fifteen years after their first meeting. In the interim one can safely assume that innocent young Ogi spared no pains as he worked with Dancer to carry out the task Patron assigned them. The account that unfolds now will shortly wind up at Ogi's place of work, and the two stories will merge into one.

By coincidence, Kizu was able to meet the young man whose growth he had been so obsessed by, though it took some time after the two of them grew close before he realized that the young man and the boy he'd seen so many years before were one and the same.

Back in his homeland on sabbatical, Kizu was living in an apartment in Akasaka; a former student introduced him to an athletic club in Nakano, where he became a member and began going twice a week to swim. One might not expect a person who's had a relapse of cancer to be so active, yet it was this very relapse that spurred him on. Soon after joining, Kizu began to take notice of a young man at the club, someone he caught sight of every once in a while but had never spoken to, let alone heard anyone else talk about. Kizu was drawn to this twenty-four or -five-year-old young man's beautiful body and his unique sense of style, all of which connected up, in Kizu's mind, with his plan to take up oil painting once again during his year in Tokyo. In the United States he'd been so involved in running the research institute, giving lectures and seminars, and taking care of a thousand and one other related tasks that he'd drifted away from creative art. Deciding to return to painting was one thing, settling on the subject matter was another, and Kizu was still without a clue, though he did find the idea of painting a young man more attractive than that of a female nude.

Kizu watched the young man leading grade-school children in warm-up exercises by the poolside and correcting their form once they were in the water. Another scene stayed with him too, one that took place when the young man was doing his own personal training. One weekday, early in the afternoon, the pool on the first floor of the athletic club was relatively uncrowded, with just two children's classes and one adult group, the last made up mostly of women with a couple of elderly men thrown into the mix. In the lanes set aside for full members to swim laps there were only two or three swimmers, Kizu among them, as he paddled back and forth in the unusually cool transparent water.

Soon it was time for classes to change, and in the wide space between the main pool and the one used for synchronized swimming practice, a large class of children were going through their warm-up routine. Kizu had finished his exercise for the day and was just leaving when he ran across a strange sight. At the bottom of the stairs, in a corner where there were showers and sinks for rinsing your eyes, there was a six-foot-square pool. Kizu had always thought it was just some special water tank, but now he understood it was for training people to hold their breath underwater. Three young girls stood there, leaning against the brass railing and looking down at the little pool; their high-cut swimsuits exposed the smooth skin of their muscular thighs.

A head wearing a white rubber swim cap bobbed straight up, breaking the surface, the shoulders following next in a quiet yet grandiloquent movement. In a moment the person turned to face the opposite direction, rested one hand on a depression in the wall just above the surface of the water, and took a deep breath. The body rising high above the water was that of a young man without an ounce of fat, his body stretched taut, but what caught Kizu's interest was how the body looked naturally strong, not the result of training. The rubber swim cap he had on was one worn by swimming instructors, and just after the young man broke the surface from deep underwater Kizu had recognized him, for not many of the instructors had such a muscular build. The tall girls gazing down into the pool were quite muscular, too, the base of their necks swelling up in an arc, interrupting the line of their shoulders. Once more the young man sank straight down beneath the water. Effortlessly, he let go of the inner wall of the pool, looked down, put his arms by his sides, and sank, leaving behind barely a ripple. And after a while, longer than one might expect, he forcefully yet quietly resurfaced, bobbing up past his shoulders, and took a huge gulping breath.

Soon the young man, gripping the trough that ran around the pool, lifted his face to look at Kizu; the young man didn't have goggles on, and his face showed nothing of the heightened vitality one might expect after such exertion. He completely ignored the young girls. His forehead was like a turtle's, the eyes sunken, the nose wide, lips full; the flesh down to his chin was like taut leather, the chin itself quite manly. Kizu thought he had never seen a Japanese with a face like this before, though it was most definitely of Mongolian stock: a fierce face yet one that looked, overall, refined. And from this very masculine face large eyes gazed out, a gaze that made Kizu feel he was being stared at by an obstinate woman.

Walking away, Kizu felt agitated. The wisdom gained with age allowed him to avoid trying to pin down this nameless unease; Kizu realized that diverting his attention was a better course of action. After this, whenever he saw the young man leading an adult swimming class, a disquiet jolted him, and he averted his eyes.

The first time Kizu spoke to the young man was in the athletic club's so-called drying room. Things changed quickly at this club, with a third of the training equipment, for instance, being replaced within the first six months after Kizu joined. Still, there was one place that was clearly a holdover from the past, a dim room about fifteen by eighteen feet that had just one small door and, in the middle, an elliptical wooden enclosure, in complete contrast to the ultramodern facilities on the other floors of the club. Inside the enclosure, dark stones were piled up and heated, like a sauna. In fact it was a kind of sauna room, though kept at a lower temperature than the modern saunas next door to the public baths.

Members sat on wide two-tiered wooden levels, leaning back against the unpainted wooden wall, drying their chilled bodies after swimming. Children in the swimming school, of course, used the drying room, but veteran members plopped themselves down on oversized yellow towels and sweated in the room before they went swimming, loosening up their muscles this way instead of doing warm-up exercises.

The first time the young man spoke to Kizu, the two of them, as long-time members were wont to do, were already stretched out for some time in the darkened drying room. In the dull light, Kizu didn't realize that the person lying down in the far corner was this young man because—no doubt to increase the amount he sweated—he was completely wrapped in a towel from his head on down, with just his knees and the lower half of his legs sticking out.

Kizu had been in the drying room for quite some time when seven or eight young girls in their late teens took over the upper and lower tiers on the right side, directly opposite the entrance. The girls chattered away boisterously; Kizu was already aware that they were members of the swim team at a Catholic girls high school. They were discussing the program they were preparing for their school's festival, based on the book of Jonah. They were already in a lively mood as they voiced their opinions and complaints in loud voices. One small girl, apparently an underclassman, spoke out in an especially conspicuous way.

"We're the swim team," she complained, "so we should have been allowed to do the scenes where Jonah's thrown into the water, or where he's spit up from the whale's belly and swims to shore. But Sister's script has us doing the part in the storm where Jonah's grilled by all the sailors, and where he builds that hut on the outskirts of Nineveh and complains to God. What's a castor oil plant, anyway? Sounds pretty weird to me! We have to construct the set without even knowing what it looks like!"

Kizu finally spoke up. It had been through the auspices of the girls' swim coach, also an instructor of art and design, that Kizu had been introduced to the athletic club and joined for a year, and the girls had surely heard from their coach about his work in the United States.

Kizu told them how he had done the illustrations for a children's version of Bible stories. As part of his research for the book, he traveled to the Middle East, where he saw actual castor oil plants growing. "Come here this time next week," Kizu told them, "and I'll bring a colored sketch for you to look at. In the book of Jonah," he went on, "the castor oil plant is an important minor prop—no, maybe a major prop—expressing God's love." The students welcomed his proposal.

This decided, the occupying force of girls, their clumsy attempts at working up a good sweat over, left the drying room with hearty farewells more befitting an athletic meet. A jostle of muscular legs was visible just outside the cloudy heat-resistant glass of the door's window.

At this point the young man, oversized towel heavy with sweat wrapped around his waist, spoke up, his voice different from the times Kizu had overheard it in the club.

"Professor, you seem to be quite well versed in the Bible."

Kizu was seated on the lower tier, in the back left-hand corner, the young man on the upper tier directly facing him. Perhaps not wanting to look down on Kizu, the young man clambered down to the lower tier and turned his face, the same color as a boiled crab's shell, toward Kizu, who replied, "Not at all—it's just as I told the girls. It's not like I attend church."

"I was about to tell the girls, but in the bookshelf in the third-floor members' lounge there's a copy of your children's book," the young man said. "The club's Culture Society collects and displays books written by the club's members. When I was a child—and until much later, in fact—I was amazed at how realistically people and objects are depicted in Renaissance paintings, and I find your illustrations in the children's book very similar. Children find this especially appealing, I imagine. When I read your book, I could get a clear picture of how big Nineveh was and what the boat that went to Tarshish looked like."

The artist found the young man's observations interesting—since Kizu was young at the time he did these illustrations he'd been very conscious of his painting style, insisting on its anachronistic character—but what most impressed him was the young man's way of talking. Kizu recalled a certain Mexican stage actor with unusual looks. You would normally expect anyone aware that they had such extraordinary features to be a bit more reticent.

Kizu was silent and the young man went on. "I'm not a Christian either. But ever since I was a child, the book of Jonah has bothered me."

"Since you've read my children's book it's obvious to you," Kizu said, "that I made the book of Jonah the centerpiece of the project."

"If I went to a church," the young man went on, "I'm sure I could hear a detailed explanation, but I don't get on well with clergy, so I've never found an answer to my concerns."

"Maybe it's not my place to ask, but what exactly are these concerns?"

Kizu didn't ask this expecting any specific answer to issue from the youth's somewhat cruel-looking mouth, but the young man responded eagerly, as if he'd been waiting for the chance.

"I don't know, I just feel anxious, wondering if the book of Jonah really ends where it does. I know it's a childish question, but I can't help wondering if the Jonah we have now is complete, or whether it might originally have had a different ending."

"That's an interesting point," Kizu remarked. "Now that you mention it, I've felt somewhat the same, as if it's vague and doesn't go anywhere."

Cutting to the chase, the young man said, "Would it be possible, Professor, for me to come over to your home to hear more about this? The club office manager told me you have American citizenship and are living in extraterritorial, non-Japanese housing."

"It's not extraterritorial; I'm not a diplomat. But if you're interested in the book of Jonah, I do have a few reference works, and I'd be happy to show them to you. I'm here at the club on Tuesdays and Fridays, but most other afternoons I'm free. Tell the office I said it's all right for you to get my address and phone number."

The young man was clearly elated by the news.

"I'm sorry to be so forward; you must think I'm pushy. I'll phone you later this week."

The sauna wasn't especially hot, but Kizu had reached his limit and decided to leave. He made his way around the heat source in the center of the room, pushed the unpainted door open, and went outside. Through the heat-resistant glass his eyes met those of the young man, who was leaning in his direction as if bowing. A faint smile came to Kizu's face, and he looked down and descended to the swimming pool.

2

The reader already knows why Kizu, teaching in the art department of an American East Coast university, decided to take a sabbatical in Tokyo. The same reason accounts for his not planning a terribly strenuous schedule during his sabbatical year. The university provided housing for him in an apartment building that had been acquired during the Occupation, changed management several times, was rebuilt, but continued to be owned by the university. The building was not solely for the use of faculty sent by Kizu's university—Japanologists from other universities were housed there as well—but as a faculty member from the home institution, Kizu had been given priority and provided with an apartment on the top floor, a two-bedroom apartment with four rooms altogether. He made the spacious living room and dining-kitchen into one large room, setting up beyond his dining table a space that became his studio. Between these he placed a sofa and armchair, and this became the spot where he spent most of his time.

Three days later, in the morning, the young man phoned, but Kizu was confused for a few moments, unable to recall who he was when he gave his name. At the athletic club, though the way he spoke and the topics he talked about were intelligent enough, one couldn't separate his voice from the forceful physicality of his brawny features. On the phone, though, his voice came across as gentle and clear.

Once the young man was in the apartment, Kizu had him sit on the sofa that formed the boundary of the studio, and he sat down on the matching armchair, next to which was a table on which he'd placed the reference materials. Ikuo—the young man's name—was dressed in jeans, T-shirt, and a cotton shirt with rolled-up sleeves over it; dressed, he looked much younger than when he'd been nude in the drying room. From Ikuo's unease as soon as he entered the apartment, though, Kizu had the feeling that these nondescript clothes were not his usual style and the young man felt ill at ease in this plebeian setting.

After Ikuo began coming to Kizu's place to model for him, he explained why, on this first day, he had gazed so intently at everything around him in the apartment. The ceilings, he said, were much higher than those in his own place in Tokyo. Not just the inside of the apartment, but the elevator area and the first-floor lobby with the residents' mailboxes were larger and had a rough-hewn no-nonsense look to them. Listening to Ikuo explain his sense of incongruity with the surroundings, Kizu understood why, in contrast, he had felt so quickly at home. The apartment was an exact replica of the faculty housing in New Jersey he'd lived in as a new instructor for seven or eight years.

With Ikuo posing questions, Kizu showed him the research materials he'd promised and talked about what he'd learned about the book of Jonah while doing research for the children's books on the Old Testament.

"These are notes I copied from a translation of a book by someone named J. M. Meyers," Kizu said. "Meyers says that Nineveh was the capital of Assyria and a very large place, though saying that 'It took three days to go all around the city' has to be an exaggeration. Still, it's estimated that the population was 174,000. The Bible says, 'There were more than 120,000 people who cannot tell their right hand from their left, and many cattle as well.' I realized that apart from the livestock the focus is on the children. Experts probably don't make much of this, however. In short, what God feels most sad about are the children and the livestock—the innocent. After all, the ones who have sinned are the adults.

"One other point Meyers makes is that the citizens of Nineveh are Gentiles. According to the words of God that Jonah conveyed, what stopped God from destroying the people of Nineveh was that these Gentiles truly repented. Meyers says this must have been quite a shock to the Israelites, who were convinced they were the chosen people. The problem was, these chosen people were obstinate, while the people of Nineveh were obedient.

"The town of Tarshish that Jonah set sail for from Joppa was a port in Sardinia with a huge blast furnace—probably the farthest destination for any ship from Palestine. So Jonah was on a ship carrying steel or steel products. Jonah thought that God's power extended only as far as the borders of the land of Israel. That makes sense, right? The storm hits the ship, and only Jonah is unperturbed. 'How can you sleep?' the captain wonders. But it's no wonder Jonah can sleep soundly. Gentiles might not understand it, but Jonah is convinced he's escaped God's wrath, which makes any storm look like the proverbial tempest in a teacup.

"After this comes the part where he's thrown into the sea, enters the stomach of the whale, and finally goes to Nineveh. Then God's wrath is explained, and it all ends, with Meyers commenting that Jonah 'wanted to restrict God and his saving love to himself and his people. Jonah thought he had failed and would be the object of ridicule.'"

"The part about the children is interesting, isn't it," Ikuo replied in a dreamy voice, a voice etched in Kizu's memory of this first day. "This might be off the subject, but what a terrible thing it must have been to destroy the whole city of Nineveh. For us now, mightn't it be equivalent to destroying a city the size of Tokyo?"

They didn't take this thought any further. Kizu didn't have any reason to empathize with the young man's vision of the destruction of the entire population of a city like Tokyo. And from this commentary on the book of Jonah alone, he couldn't answer the question put to him in the drying room about whether the story of Jonah in the Bible is actually the whole story.

Ikuo quickly detected Kizu's confusion and neatly changed the subject. Ikuo walked around the studio, looking at the sketches and oil paintings Kizu had begun now that he was painting again. He was clearly pleased to see the same distinctive style as that in the children's book; the color of the original paintings, he commented, is so much brighter, and looks like the use of color you find in modern American paintings. Kizu found these comments right on target. It was during this time that Ikuo proposed that if Kizu needed a nude male model he'd be happy if he'd hire him; while he was painting, Ikuo could learn more from Kizu—two birds with one stone and all that.

This decided, Kizu saw Ikuo out. This young man, he mused, might very well have already had the idea of posing in mind before he came to visit. Still, Kizu found the same sort of faint smile he had outside the drying room once again rising to his lips.

That weekend Kizu woke up while it was still dark out. He noticed something about the way he held his body in bed. Probably because he felt the cancer had spread to his liver, these days he always slept with his left elbow as a pillow. It was a position based on a distant memory, a memory of himself at seventeen or eighteen, in the valley in the forest where he was born and raised, lying on the slope of a low hill. Sometimes this vision of himself appeared in dreams as a richly colored reality, Kizu seeing this as his own figure in the *eternal present*. And in the predawn darkness, in a dream just before waking, he returned to his *eternal present* body.

Kizu was at the point where his hair, to use the American expression, was salt and pepper, yet his mental image of himself was always that of this seventeen- or eighteen-year-old. Emotionally, he knew he hadn't changed much from his teen years. He was aware, quite graphically, of a grotesque disjuncture within him, a man with an over-fifty-year-old body attached to the emotions of a teenager. Kizu recalled the thirteenth canto of Dante's *Inferno,* the scene in which a soul on the threshold of old age picks up its own body as a seventeen- or eighteen-year-old and hangs it from some brambles.

Beginning a week later, Ikuo began posing to help Kizu with a series of tableaus he'd only vaguely conceived. As he drew, Kizu, influenced by what Ikuo had said that first day, lectured as he used to do in classrooms—though of course in American universities if a professor did all the talking he'd receive a terrible evaluation from the students at the end of the semester. Sometimes Kizu would respond promptly to the questions Ikuo asked as he posed; other times he gave himself until the following week to answer. Kizu recalled in particular one question from early in their sessions.

"Last time," Kizu said, "you asked me what it means for a person to be free. I think I struggled with the same question when I was young. So I gave it some thought. An anecdote I once read about a painter came to mind.

"In order to give you an idea of how I understand it, I need to give you another example, not from some book I read but a quote I heard from a colleague of mine who teaches philosophy, which is: A circle in nature and the concept of a circle within God are the same, they just manifest themselves differently.

"The anecdote took place during the Renaissance, when an official in charge of choosing an artist to paint a mammoth fresco requested one particular artist (an artist I was quite taken with when I was young) to submit a work that best displayed his talents. The response of the artist—which became famous—was to submit a single circle he had drawn.

"An artist draws a circle with a pencil. And that circle fits perfectly with the concept of a circle that resides within God. The person who can accomplish this is a *free man.* In order to arrive at that state of freedom, he has had to polish his artistry through countless paintings. It was as if my own life work I had dreamed about was contained in this. When I was young, I mean."

Ikuo continued to hold his pose, gazing at the space in front of him, listening attentively, his expression unchanged, his rugged features reminding Kizu of Blake's portrait of a youthful Los, likened to the sun—Kizu feeling he was brushing away with his crayon the shadows of Blake's colored block prints that shaded Ikuo's nude body.

Ikuo was silent until their next break. "I've been thinking about something very similar to what you said, Professor. People say young children are free. Okay, but if you get even a little self-conscious you can't act freely, even though you might have been able to a few years before. When I was no longer a child, I fantasized about a freedom I could attain. And not just talking about it like this, either. . . .

"I've been thinking about Jonah, too. He tried to run away from God but couldn't. He learned this the hard way, almost dying in the process. Made me think how much the inside of a whale's stomach must stink!" Kizu couldn't keep from smiling faintly.

"Finally he gave up and decided to follow God's orders. Once he made that decision he stuck to his guns. Jonah complained to God that he'd changed his original plan. Aren't you supposed to finish what you first decided to do? he implored. Isn't the way Jonah acted exactly the way a free person is supposed to act? Of course it's God who makes this freedom possible—and correct me if I'm wrong—but if God doesn't take into account the freedom to object to what He wants, how can He know what true unlimited freedom is? That's why I'd like to read what happens next in the book of Jonah."

Instead of a reply, a faint smile on Kizu's face showed he understood what the young man meant.

3

It was the beginning of autumn in Tokyo. Near the faculty housing where Kizu had lived in New Jersey, there was a so-called lake, actually a long muddy creek used for rowing practice, and every year as autumn arrived he used to hear from the far shore of the lake a cicadalike call; his African roommate, an art history major, insisted it was a bird. Now in his Tokyo apartment he could see a mammoth *nire* tree that stood about five yards from his south-facing terrace. The soft broad rounded leaves reminded him of the stand of trees that lined the campus grounds back in New Jersey; he guessed it was a type of elm. He didn't stop to think that elms in Japan are, indeed, classified as *nire*. The first time Ikuo had removed all his clothes to pose nude, he looked off at the far-off buildings through the leafy branches of the tree and remarked, "That *akadamo* screens us well here, though it won't after the leaves fall."

"*Akadamo?*"

"That's the name I heard it called when I was wandering around Hokkaido," Ikuo replied. "Most people call it a *harunire*—a wych elm—but it's different. I imagine it'll be blossoming soon. You can tell it from a wych elm by when it blooms, according to what my father told me. . . ."

Ikuo's face, reminding Kizu of a carnivore's snout, was soon lost in reverie; Kizu too was lost in thought. Ikuo hadn't had any contact with his family in a long time and had never said anything about the home he grew up in. His face was so unusual that Kizu felt sure Ikuo must have had a comical appeal when he was a boy and been a favorite in his family. After he grew up and began wandering in Hokkaido and elsewhere around the country, his family surely must have felt a profound sense of loss.

The wych elm near his terrace began to take on erotic connotations for Kizu. One morning, his gaze was drawn to the lush foliage of the tree, for it was swaying and shaking with unusual force. Soon he saw a pair of squirrels leaping about on a bare branch, disappearing in the shadows, their power concentrated in the base of their thick tails. Kizu could sense that the squirrels were preoccupied with mating, and as their movements made the leaves shake exaggeratedly he felt familiar stirrings deep in his loins. Kizu could imagine, in the deep green shadows of the tree, Ikuo's slim waist, the muscles of his butt underneath the tough outer layer of skin softly expanding and contracting. For the first time in quite a while, Kizu's penis grew almost painfully erect.

As Kizu watched, the swelling peacefully subsided. He was lying naked, sunbathing opposite the wych elm, whose foliage covered a broad expanse. It was 9 A.M., and Kizu had spent an hour in the light of the sun, now behind the wych elm's branches. He'd spread a bed cover on the terrace floor and was lying down, his legs spread wide toward the window. This was his new habit, a sentimental yet possibly effective way to warm the insides of his cancer-ravaged body.

Today, though, with his abdomen bare in the sunlight, his pose called to mind a baby having his diapers changed. And an even more laughable image occurred to him: a racial memory, if you can call it that, of long ago, when he existed as genetic material in a monkey, and that monkey—himself—was presenting his anus to the sun. Even within this gentle sunbathing, then, sexual yearnings brewed and bubbled. . . .

Before long, in the shadows of the wych elm, this time much closer to the terrace, a much more explicitly erotic movement began. On this canvas made up of the shadings of green and gentle waves, Kizu stretched out an imaginary pencil and traced the line of Ikuo's body, thighs slightly spread, from his waist to his rump viewed diagonally from behind. Once again he felt a rush of heated blood spread from his abdomen to his waist, his penis became rigid, and he began fondling his genitals with his left hand while sketching in the air. When he ejaculated, Kizu heard a powerful sigh—his own—calling out, "Ikuo, Ikuo! Ah—Ikuo!"

Kizu now knew what it was he'd been seeking from Ikuo ever since that day in the club's drying room. A man in his fifties only now awakening to the fact that he was gay, he realized that what he wanted was simply to have sex with this young man with the strong beautiful body.

After this Kizu eagerly anticipated the days when Ikuo posed for him. Many a session passed, though, with nothing out of the ordinary happening. When he was alone, Kizu had no idea how to make his daydreams a reality, and Ikuo, oblivious to Kizu's desires, said things that were painful for him to hear.

"Sometimes this studio smells like a bachelor my own age is living here!" Ikuo said one day. "I blushed when I was modeling 'cause I thought it was because I hadn't bathed in a couple of days! I haven't been to the pool either, for a while."

Kizu wasn't embarrassed, but he did feel confused about his masturbation, a habit now revived after a long dormancy.

Ikuo also said to Kizu, and not as mere flattery, "They say when artists create they get younger—and in your case it's true!"

4

It was a dark day, as dark as if the sun had already set, the wind gusting out of the north. The *hygiene cure,* a dated term that made him wince—his sunbathing, in other words—which Kizu had continued entirely on his own since the middle of July, was out of the question on a day like this. The glass door was cold against his forehead as he gazed at the shadowy leaves of the wych elm rustling in the wind. The leaves were dry and dull, their undersides, exposed when the wind curled them up, even more dry and whitish. Until now, the only yellowish leaves he'd seen were those on branches broken by the wind or by squirrels, but now there were clumps of lemon-colored leaves on several more recessed branches. Kizu spent the morning, till past noon, in a state of agitation. Ikuo was supposed to come in the morning, but he didn't show up. Two weeks before, on a Monday, he'd called and said he couldn't model that day. Thursday came, and again he didn't show up, this time not even phoning. The same thing happened both days the following week. On this particular day Kizu phoned the athletic club and was told that

Ikuo wasn't out sick, in fact was at that very moment teaching an adult class. Kizu said to tell Ikuo he'd called.

Finally, on a sunny Thursday morning, Ikuo appeared at his door, without giving any explanation for having taken two and a half weeks off. His reticence wasn't the result of some self-centered insecurity, but a willful decision to keep what he wanted to say within him, a stance that made Kizu all the more concerned. To top this off, something about Ikuo's nude body seemed unfamiliar. As artists are wont to do, Kizu looked at him intently as if he were listening to some strange sound. In contrast to his attitude when he came into the apartment, Ikuo was now quick to react. With the luxuriant foliage of the wych elm behind his right shoulder as he posed, the strong sunlight, which they hadn't seen in a while, above him, Ikuo kneaded the tight skin around his washboard abdomen.

"These past two weeks I've been training like crazy," he said. "Coaching recreational swimmers doesn't keep me in shape. My stomach's gotten pretty buff, but I'm worried the lines won't be the same as the last time I modeled."

"That's not a problem," Kizu replied. "Right now I'm concentrating on the swell of the shoulders. Your whole body does look quite toned."

Still seeming concerned, Ikuo kneaded the flesh of his abdomen, pulling it toward his navel. The movement pulled his soft but heavy penis away from his thick pubic hair and over toward his thigh.

Feeling Kizu's gaze, Ikuo fidgeted the muscles of his buttocks and tried, without success, to hide his genitals in the shadow of his thick thigh. Soon his penis started curving to the right, pointing toward the wych elm outside the glass door as it swelled to life. This was different from Kizu's recent erections, reminding him of the uncontrollable, autonomous erections of his younger days.

Finally, Ikuo relaxed his pose and covered his penis with both hands, decisively turning a stern but blushing face to Kizu and looking straight at him for the first time that day.

"Actually, there's something I need to talk with you about," Ikuo said, "and thinking about it got all these personal emotions welling up. And now look what's happened. You'll have to pardon my confusion. Calling it *personal emotions* might sound a little strange, but you've taught me so many things. Sometimes I can't believe how kind you've been to me. These past few months I've felt less lonely than I have for years. I know it'll seem ungrateful, but I've given it a lot of thought and I've decided to quit my job in Tokyo.

"When we first met in the pool drying room I was already thinking of doing this. I've worked there a full two years already. Fortunately, that allowed me to meet you, to get this modeling job, and to be able to study with you. I'm thankful, but if I just continue as a swimming coach, I'm never going to be able to solve any of the problems I'm facing—problems connected with what we were talking about last time, about being a free person.

"So the past two weeks I've been training like crazy and doing some thinking, and I came to the conclusion that I've got to leave. Yesterday I submitted my resignation to the athletic club. Since I didn't give them two weeks' notice I won't be getting any severance pay, though."

Kizu felt as if the cells of his body were being surrounded by an overwhelming force of invaders, and he was choked by a visceral sense of grief. At the same time he was convinced that this is how people are abandoned. Now that he'd reached his fifties, he wondered, confused, was this all life had in store for him?

"Well," he said, "you're an independent spirit. I never imagined you'd be a swimming instructor for the rest of your life, let alone an artist's model. Wanting to set off for somewhere is perfectly natural. Though it does make me wistful, I guess you'd say, or regretful."

As he said this, Kizu heard ill will mixed in with the sound of his pumping blood. Ikuo turned fervent eyes toward him, and with one totally unexpected question, laid bare all of Kizu's recent fantasies.

"Professor, are you gay? Sometimes I've wondered whether you've been kind to me just to try to have a relationship with me, and whether the whole thing might not end with me having to beat the crap out of you. But I don't have those hostile feelings anymore, and, since this is the last time, if you'd like to do some kind of gay thing to me, I wouldn't hate you or anything. That's what I was thinking about, and—well, you can see the result."

Kizu was struck by an unexpected emotion: This must be what they used to call heartrending grief, he thought. He stood up. Ikuo reacted defensively by protecting his genitals with his cupped hands. His pride wounded, Kizu said in a parched voice, nearly shouting, "That's not what's going on here! I don't know anything about homosexuality; I don't have any experience with it. Still, you have a beautiful body, and I do feel some sort of urges. I haven't been planning anything, but sadly, I do feel a kind of yearning. Maybe it's that time in my life. I don't know.

"This may sound like sour grapes, but why do you have to leave? Are you sure you'll never come back here again? Can't you seek your goal of being free together with me?"

Kizu fairly groaned this out. Not knowing how to continue, he collapsed in his chair, burying his face in his hands. He was crying. Through the spaces between his fingers, he could see Ikuo get down from the dais he'd been posing on, pressing down with one hand the bounding movements of his penis as he walked over to stand uncertainly in front of him, his waist slightly jutted forward. Kizu took himself by surprise, releasing his tear-stained hands to grasp Ikuo's buttocks, aiming for the anarchically moving penis and grasping it in his mouth. He opened his mouth wide, taking care not to hurt it with his false teeth, unsure how much pressure he could apply, getting the energetic penis to come to rest against his upper palate, wrapping his tongue around it as Ikuo held his head tightly with both hands.

Kizu acted like some old veteran, and when Ikuo ejaculated for what seemed like forever, Kizu couldn't have been happier. He let go his fingers from where they'd dug into the muscle and dimples on Ikuo's rump, and Ikuo's penis, still too large to be held in one hand, hung down next to Kizu's lips. Ikuo asked, vaguely, if there was some way he could repay him for all his kindness. Kizu gently shook his head, hoping to show that this was enough, and wiped away the excess semen dripping from the corners of his mouth with the back of his hand.

Kizu and Ikuo lay down side by side on wicker lounge chairs, the venetian blinds half drawn to shut out the intense sunlight as they gazed up at the brilliant outline of the leaves of the wych elm against the cloudless autumn sky. They discussed how they would live now in Tokyo, after Ikuo quit his athletic club job and continued as Kizu's model. They decided not to make any quick decisions about the details. Occasionally they fell silent, simply enjoying the feeling of closeness. Ikuo was stretched out fully beside Kizu, who reached out to trace with his fingernails the circuit-board design of the skin—skin like the finest paper—on Ikuo's concave belly. Ikuo gazed down at this as if he were watching a drawing develop. Kizu saw how the movement of his fingernails made Ikuo's penis rub against his thigh. The head of the penis was dry, with fine reddish wrinkles, but looked wet. Embarrassed because it was starting to glisten again, Ikuo covered it with his dark shiny palm, and Kizu laid his own wrinkled palm on top.

Kizu dozed for a while and then awoke, as if his consciousness had been speared by a gaff, to see Ikuo still stretched out beside him. Ikuo's muscular shoulders—their layers like seams of armor—and his waist and buttocks were covered with droplets of sweat. Kizu raised himself up, choking with excitement, picked up the tissue paper box from the side table, and, lying so close to Ikuo he could feel the warmth of his body, began to masturbate. As he ejaculated a small amount of semen into the tissue, a light brownish color mixed in, Ikuo, whom he thought was asleep, reached over without moving to lay a sweaty hand on the artist's wizened thigh. Eyes closed, Ikuo shifted around, wrapped Kizu's weak-looking body in his strong arms, and lovingly kissed

Kizu's shoulders. Kizu guessed it was a gesture to assuage his guilty conscience at not wanting to fellate him. But Ikuo's face, close up as he gently kissed Kizu, showed a rapturous satisfaction.

5

Kizu spread out on the floor the drawings he'd done for his as-yet still inchoate tableau with Ikuo modeling for him; Ikuo, Kizu's worn-out dressing gown draped over his naked body, came over close to him to stare intently at one drawing in particular, a design Kizu had done on a separate sheet of paper and then attached to the bottom of one of the sketches of Ikuo. After a moment, uneasy, Kizu looked up and saw that, as often happened when he was concentrating on something, Ikuo had the clever, severe expression of a hawk or a falcon. He spoke in dreamy voice, his eyes glazed.

"A strange thought occurred to me that I've experienced this before. I can't really remember, but something in my childhood. . . ."

At first Kizu was startled. Around the time he determined he had had a relapse of cancer, he decided to take his sabbatical in Japan in order to search for that young man from long ago. When this desire had been at its height, he'd even drawn up a sort of wanted-poster sketch of the boy's plastic model under the girl's skirt. Now, without any particular idea in mind, he'd attached this sketch to the drawing he'd done of Ikuo. Kizu looked at this, then turned his gaze to the real Ikuo beside him. Memories of fifteen years before suddenly zoomed in, and in an instant he saw in Ikuo the fierce canine face and beautiful eyes of that young boy. Once he realized this, Kizu also understood how, ever since they'd first met in the drying room at the club, a voice had been nagging at him, berating him for not seeing the obvious.

In the midst of their now exultant conversation, Kizu laughed out loud a few times, while Ikuo fell into deep thought. Ikuo had arrived in the morning and didn't leave until sunset; in the afternoon, a powerful cloud bank blew in from the southeast, forming into cirrus clouds with a reddish lower layer. Reflecting back on how full these hours had been, Kizu felt that everything that had happened to him over the past two or three weeks was a godsend.

"You've really captured that scene well in your sketch," Ikuo had said repeatedly, unable to contain himself. "I don't have any memory of how I actually appeared as a child myself, but this scene of the bulky model I busted my butt to make getting caught in that girl's skirt, and her comically trying to keep her balance, is exactly as I remember it. And her little angry face glaring back at me—her whole pose seemed to be making fun of me."

"I can't forget it either, even a mediocre painter like myself, " Kizu said, remembering how it was seeing that scene that convinced him he didn't have any talent.

"I've been self-consciously drawing since I was fourteen or fifteen, and even allowing for the time when I didn't paint, living as an artist has become— to use the expression you've used several times—an ingrained habit. You sketch on paper, synchronizing the speed of your hand movements, so that even if you aren't holding a pencil you retain the scenery, objects, and people in a purely visual memory."

Ikuo listened carefully to Kizu's excited words, at the same time staring entranced at the drawing of the young girl balancing strangely on one leg. Kizu came back to reality.

"I know where this young girl is now," he said. "The newspaper company told me. I even phoned once, trying to check it out on my own."

"What did she sound like?"

"As you might expect, she's a unique young woman. There's a certainty in her voice, the way she talks, that you don't find in young Japanese girls these days. And when I remember how she clutched your model, trying her hardest not to lose her balance and let it fall, she's definitely not an average sort of girl. I don't have many memories as clear as that one. It's not just because of her, but she holds a treasured spot in my mind—along with the memory of the light I saw in a very special young boy who destroyed his own creation."

"Up to that age I was just an ordinary child," Ikuo said slowly, still lost in his own memories. "I was crazy about making all kinds of models, from preformed plastic pieces or from pieces of wood I carved with a knife; sometimes I'd go for days with hardly any sleep. Constantly making something made me feel like I was telling a story in words.

"What I remember is that the girl was a strange one. When she got caught up by the model it was like she was challenging me. I remember hating her because I lost the chance to win the top prize and get a free trip to Disneyland in California."

"But now aren't you a little nostalgic when it comes to her?" Kizu asked excitedly. "You want to start a new life, right? Aside from the question of being a *free man,* this might be a good opportunity for you. Think about it. It's pretty extraordinary for that one day in the past to come back to life at a single stroke for three people. Why don't we invite her for dinner? Considering the dramatic way you two first met, how could she pass up the chance for a reunion? We can use this sketch as a thank-you present."

3: Somersault

1

The young girl, who fifteen years before had been pierced by Ikuo's plastic model and yet managed painfully to maintain her balance, was now of course a grown woman, and when Kizu's invitation came she readily accepted. Kizu was overjoyed to hear her say that after his first phone call to her she had remembered everything that happened on that long-ago day. She hastened to add that she was working now in the office of a religious movement and wouldn't be able to spare much time. She asked if they could meet during her lunch break, near the Seijo Gakuenmae Station, not far from her office.

The way she responded was so typical of this new generation of Japanese, Kizu mused, for when he invited her out for a meal she immediately asked if she could go ahead and make a reservation in a French restaurant she knew. They decided on a date and time, and the next day a fax arrived for Kizu with a map indicating landmarks such as an old Catholic church and the route the buses take to Shibuya, as well as a photo of the restaurant itself, an old-style former Japanese residence with a large zelkova tree in front.

On Friday the three of them settled into their seats at the restaurant under a clear plastic roof and the lush foliage of the zelkova branches. The young woman sat by the window on one side, with Kizu seated across from her and Ikuo by his side.

"The way I remember you," Kizu said to her, unwrapping the sketch from its cardboard cover, "is shown in this sketch, but I can still see traces of the young girl in you."

The young woman, glistening chestnut hair cascading past her shoulders, gazed at the sketch, her mouth exactly as Ikuo remembered it, lips slightly parted. She straightened her thin cylindrical neck and looked at Ikuo.

"As soon as we met today," she said, "I knew you were that frightening young boy. I remember you very well."

Ikuo was overwhelmed, and Kizu interceded.

"Ikuo's looks were definitely special from the time he was in grade school. When I met him again for the first time in fifteen years, it took me a while to recognize him, though subconsciously I think I was aware of who he was."

Ikuo, blushing, turned his face from both of them. Kizu was reminded of the head of a young bull. The young woman, too, seemed to enjoy looking at him. The waiter came to tell them the lunch specials, and Kizu, constantly amazed at the high prices of wine in Tokyo, studied the wine list and ordered a California brand.

"I know you were a member of the ballet team that was going to perform at the awards ceremony," Kizu said, "and I understand, from what someone at the newspaper told me, that you're still involved in dance."

"I study under a teacher in India, but I'm only able to go once a year for five weeks. I've given a few recitals in Tokyo, but mainly I'm just doing it for my own amusement."

"Then how do you know when you're making progress?" Ikuo asked, his large eyes fixed on her face.

Kizu was astonished at the unexpected question, but the young woman was unfazed. It had been sprinkling when they entered the restaurant, and now the rain was coming down hard on the zelkova.

The young woman looked up at the water dripping off the clear roof. "It's true my dance teacher lives far away," she said, "but right next to me I have two teachers who instruct me in much more important things. They're kind enough to make time each day to talk with me, though one of them is sick right now. . . . I'm sure you heard from the reporter about the people I work for now, Patron and Guide?"

She directed this question to Kizu. He nodded. The waiter poured him a glass of Napa Valley white wine, a type he'd often had in America, and turned a curious look at the young woman when she mentioned these unusual names. Ikuo, face red, shot him an intentionally cruel, violent look that made Kizu shudder when he imagined the potential for violence underlying his own relationship with Ikuo these past two months. However, the one who most clearly felt the danger inherent here was the waiter, Ikuo's contemporary; after he finished pouring the wine he scurried off as if he had a sail attached to him and the wind at his back.

Only the young woman seemed unperturbed. She must have sensed the unusual roughness in Ikuo and seen the way the waiter acted, like a beaten dog with his tail between his legs, yet she didn't flinch or even seem tense.

"The names Patron and Guide *are* a little unusual," she said calmly, "and people who don't know about the incident they were involved in tend not to want to have anything to do with them. People who actually meet them, though, find them quite extraordinary. To give you an example, my Indian dance teacher doesn't dance himself anymore, but once he accompanied a dance troupe he used to choreograph, a troupe that's become one of the mainstays of Indian dance, on a trip to Japan. I'd been going to his dance seminar in Madras since I was in high school, and my teacher was worried when he heard I wasn't studying under a dance teacher here but was living with these religious leaders. When he came to see Patron, Guide, and me at our place, though, he was impressed."

"By Patron?" Ikuo asked, his face no longer red.

"By both of them. He said that in Indian mythology there's a duo much like them."

"You mean playing the roles of Patron and Guide?"

"Not exactly. I think he meant their faces, bodies, the way they talk and move and walk. The combination of the two of them."

"Since your teacher's a dance teacher then, he can perceive the secrets hidden behind physical movement?"

"Physical expression, you might call it," the young woman answered. "He can detect the inner being of people by how they move. He showed a lot of respect for Patron and Guide and even danced for them in the annex they built for me to practice dance in. The teacher's students, the musicians who accompanied him, were quite bowled over. They hadn't seen him dance for ages."

"Did those students accompany him?" Kizu asked. "Maybe they had some premonition that he was going to dance."

"When I saw that they'd brought their instruments, I had a feeling that maybe he would dance. I mean, what with meeting Patron and Guide and all. Maybe he sensed this and had his students prepare for it."

Several varieties of intricate dessertlike hors d'oeuvres were brought to their table. Ikuo polished off one dish in a single bite and turned to the next. The young woman possessed a healthy appetite too, assimilating the fuel she needed like an automatic machine.

Next they were served foie gras topped by a dark wine-colored sauce. The waiter had made a point of emphasizing that it was flown in from France. Ikuo gobbled his up quickly, and Kizu transferred his own to Ikuo's plate, eating instead some warmed vegetables he'd covered with the sauce. The young woman gazed at this, her mouth slightly open in what seemed to be her usual expression as she pondered things.

"I don't like Patron eating rich foods either," she said.

After this, they ate the final dish in silence—a moose steak that, by chance, they had all ordered from the two choices on the menu. Kizu followed the young people's lead. Ikuo must have been mulling over things to say while they ate, for just as they began their after-dinner coffees he burst out again with an unexpected question.

"The names Patron and Guide—have they used these names ever since they first started the church?"

"I don't think so," she answered. "In the church they used others."

"So even though they left the church they still maintain the ties they made to it and use those names. In other words, the game continues?"

The young woman took her coffee cup from her still slightly parted lips and returned it to the saucer. She stared fixedly at Ikuo. Kizu found it hard to separate his imagination from his memory of events, but he was sure that fifteen years before he'd seen the same look in her eyes.

"It's not a *game,*" she said. "If you define a game as *play,* something done for fun, then no, these two men weren't playing a game these past ten years— they suffered too much for that. True, they left the church, and Patron is as we speak planning to begin a new movement. And Guide's collapse has been a major shock to him. . . . Anyhow, to start a religious movement you need a committed core of followers. We're that first core of people now who are committed to Patron. Do you really imagine such a small group has the leisure to play *games?*"

"What kind of teacher of mankind will Patron be in this new movement? And where will Guide lead humanity?"

"The world is on a path to destruction," the young woman said. "Patron is planning to be mankind's teacher in these perilous times. And Guide, assuming he recovers, will be his right-hand man. They've suffered the past ten years in order to discover this new way. . . .

"Now it's *my* turn to ask a question. You asked what roles Patron and Guide will play in this new movement. Why did you want to know this? Or is this just your own game to pass the time while we're eating?"

Ikuo turned red again but spoke with conviction. "I've been living my whole life with the idea that the end of the world isn't that far off," he said, "and I always wanted to be there to experience it. So why is it strange for someone like me to be interested in what the Patron and Guide of mankind are planning to do?"

"It's true," Kizu broke in. "He *has* been thinking about the end of the world for a long while. Remember, he's the child who destroyed the plastic model of a megalopolis he'd so carefully constructed. After he smashed that model to bits, isn't it understandable for him to have a vision of the destruction of Tokyo? Though I suppose you could label that just a child's game."

"I'm sure it wasn't a game," the young woman answered Kizu, "since any kind of event—once it takes place in reality—leaves traces behind, especially with children." He found himself staring at her waxlike ears as she turned and focused on Ikuo. "I understand you gave a lot of thought to the end of the world, but have you ever belonged to any group that actually dwells on the end time? Any Christian denominations, for example?"

"I've put out a few feelers."

"What to do you mean by *that*?" she retorted.

"I mean I don't belong to any religious group now, but that doesn't mean I haven't tried out a few."

Kizu expected the young woman to feel rebuffed and pursue the matter more, but she didn't. Instead she looked at Ikuo with interest and said calmly, "I'd say you didn't meet me again just out of nostalgia for something that happened fifteen years ago. I think you're seriously checking out Patron and Guide. How about visiting our office as a next step? Meeting Guide's out of the question now, but I'd be happy to introduce you to Patron. I know I'm repeating myself, but he's gone through so many trying experiences that I can't be too careful."

2

Ikuo and Kizu stood under the eaves of the restaurant, the zelkova tree dripping copiously, and said goodbye to the girl. She flipped open her umbrella, and the two men ran out into the pouring rain and made a dash for the nearby parking lot. If Kizu had been alone he would have had one of the waiters bring his car around, but he decided to keep pace with his young companion's way of doing things.

"It seems to me that having a religious leader's office in a residential area like this might make the residents upset enough to force him out— not the old-time residents, maybe, but the nouveau riche. But she seems pretty carefree."

Ikuo said this as they drove past a crowded intersection, hemmed in by a bank on one side and a train station on the other, and caught sight of the girl and her practiced dancer's gait.

"Maybe it's because they're not holding any religious activities there now," Kizu speculated. "She said they were in the planning stages of a new movement. When this so-called Patron and Guide were involved in the scandal where they apostatized, they did have their headquarters downtown, as I recall. I remember reading about it in *The New York Times*. After they renounced their faith they must have wanted a quiet place to live. They call it an office, but apparently it's also their residence."

Two days before—to the kidding of his apartment's super, who chided him for his pointless faithfulness to the American economy—Kizu had purchased a brand-new Ford Mustang, the same car he drove in the States, and had promised to let Ikuo do the driving, but since he wasn't used to a steering wheel on the left, today Kizu took the wheel. Besides, Kizu figured that part of Ikuo's forwardness at lunch was the wine talking.

As they headed toward Shibuya, Kizu asked Ikuo about something he hadn't quite understood during his conversation with the girl.

"As I explained earlier, Ikuo, I really do believe you've been thinking about the end of the world ever since you were a child. And that what happened fifteen years ago is not unrelated to that.

"What strikes me as odd, though, is that you don't seem to recall much about the Somersault incident ten years ago. I read about it in the papers in the United States, so it must have been big news in Japan. The *Times* said it was widely reported on Japanese TV, and that Patron's remarks on television also played a major role."

"At the time it was called the Church of the Savior and the Prophet," Ikuo said. "I realized today when I was talking with that girl that I heard about it through the media."

"Then why didn't you put out feelers, as you put it, to that church? Because it wasn't that well known before the leaders' renunciation?"

"For me, at least, it wasn't," Ikuo said. "I first heard of it when the leaders publicly announced they weren't saviors or prophets after all, and everything they'd preached was a bunch of bull. I watched the reports afterward that made fun of them and just felt contempt for people who'd do what they did. I really wanted to know what mankind should do, faced with the end of the world, and—I don't know—perhaps I felt betrayed."

Kizu glanced at Ikuo's face. His tone of voice indeed contained a hint of a grudge.

"So what about the young lady? Seeing her after fifteen years—"

"I was surprised she was just as I remembered her," Ikuo said, his voice now calm. "It was like looking at your painting; her eyes were still like faded India ink, her mouth still open as if that were the correct way to breathe."

"Ha! She does seem to like to keep her mouth open, doesn't she. And her eyes!" Kizu said, as if ever the artist, continuing the sketch. "When they look at you they turn even darker."

"I also had a feeling of déjà vu, as if I knew exactly how she would turn out when she grew up."

Kizu understood exactly what he meant. Déjà vu neatly summed up his own feelings when he met Ikuo again and discovered he was the young boy from so long ago.

"She's definitely unique, isn't she?" Kizu said. "I knew that the first time we talked on the phone. Her job—her lifestyle choice, I guess you'd say—is pretty extraordinary, too."

"Do you think she believes in the new teachings of that old leader who did a Somersault?" Ikuo asked. "For the sake of her dance, even though he hasn't restarted his religious movement yet?"

"Are you going to accept her challenge and go meet this Patron?"

"I haven't really thought about it," Ikuo said. "First of all, I really don't know much about this Somersault."

"Shall I give a little lecture, then, based on what I know from *The New York Times*? The media over here treated the leaders' recantation entirely as a scandal, and I think that's what you remember. The *Times* correspondent, though, was really fascinated by the story. The religious group had been founded by two middle-aged men. One of them formulated their basic doctrine based on his mystical experiences. Over time he refined this. The second man's job was verbal expression of the mystical experiences the first man had. He was also the one who took care of the day-to-day running of the church.

"The *Times* correspondent reported on their church for a year. He got to know the two leaders well; he's the one, in fact, who dubbed them Patron and Guide. I imagine he used these names because calling them Savior and Prophet would have provoked some serious negative reactions from his American readers. After the Somersault the two of them adopted these names themselves; they weren't fond of their earlier names, anyway.

"Anyhow, just around the time the correspondent was wrapping up his reporting, the Somersault incident occurred. What happened was that the two leaders negotiated with the authorities to inform on some potentially dangerous activities of a radical faction within their church.

"It was on a much smaller scale than Aum Shinrikyo, but the research facility they owned in Izu became the focal point of the radical faction's activities, the cornerstone of which was their plan to occupy a nuclear power plant. One of the people at the research center had a PhD in physics. They wanted to turn a nuclear plant into an atomic bomb to force the leaders' teachings on all Japanese, or at least to preach the need for universal repentance now that the end of the world was drawing near. Or maybe by blowing up two or three nuclear plants they felt they could make everyone experience how very near the end of the world was. Their entire plan for repentance was based on this. Radical political groups all have the same basic idea, don't they— pushing the country into crisis? But here the target was nuclear power plants. From the beginning this was an apocalyptic teaching.

"The church's leaders found they couldn't suppress the radical faction that had sprung up among them, so they went to the police. Sensing this might happen, the radical faction dispersed throughout the country. No one knew when or where they might attack a nuclear plant. At this point the leaders asked to hold a press conference. They indicated ahead of time what they planned to do and asked for full-scale coverage. I'm sure the authorities helped out in this as well.

"The first leader—Patron, as he's called now—sat in front of the cameras on live TV and told the church's radical faction members scattered throughout the country to abandon their plans to occupy a nuclear plant. We are neither saviors nor prophets, he said. Everything we've preached till now has been one big joke. We abandon the church. Everything we've said and done was a silly prank. Now that we've confessed, we want you to stop believing.

"Especially you members of the radical faction, he went on. I want you to understand that our church is a sand castle built as a lark. We enjoyed playing the savior of the world and the prophet at the end time, using all those high-sounding phrases and acting solemn and grave. Thanks to all of you we had a wonderful time, especially getting incorporated as a religious foundation two years ago and receiving tons of money for our playacting. But this is as far as we'll take it. It's all a big farce, get it? *Look* at me, here on TV. How could you possibly believe *I'm* the savior of mankind? How can this scornful-looking partner of mine sitting here really be the prophet of the end of the world?

"Through this TV performance, the nation learned all about their Somersault, to use the term coined by the *Times* correspondent. The word became a popular expression in Japan for a time.

"To tell the truth, I don't know the scale of this event in Japan. I know that the news shows on commercial networks followed up on the story, treating it as slapstick comedy, though I heard that NHK didn't report on it at all. Didn't you see this when you were a child? What interested me while I was in the United States was the correspondent's follow-up article on the aftermath of the incident. 'The Japanese have a psychological aversion to recantations,' he wrote, 'so with this announcement that everything they preached was just a joke, this false savior and false prophet came under severe attack.' The correspondent also reported the outrage of ordinary Japanese citizens, who heaped abuse on the two men, and he included letters from people unconnected with the church who complained about its immorality.

"The correspondent found this one-sided attack rather strange. 'Through the Somersault of this false savior and false prophet,' he wrote, 'it is possible that several cities were spared a nuclear holocaust. The authorities insisted it was impossible for a nuclear power plant to be invaded and said a bunch of young amateurs would never be able to convert it into a stationary nuclear weapon. But how true was this? The people of Japan didn't give any credit to the church's two leaders who'd risked everything to defuse the crisis, concentrating instead on a moral critique of their recantation. This criticism became even more intense once it was known at the trial of the radical faction that, because of the deal they'd made with the authorities, the two leaders were going to avoid prosecution.' The correspondent ended by saying that the Japanese were certainly a strange race.

"Ikuo, I'm sure you saw these reports on TV and elsewhere about public opinion in Japan at the time, right? You wanted to be there to see the end of the world, after all. What did you think about it?"

"As I said before, I had nothing but scorn for them," Ikuo replied, "especially when those afternoon women's talk shows kept playing the so-called savior of mankind's recantation speech ad nauseam. Even though I was only a kid, it made me laugh. Deep down inside, though, I think I was disappointed."

3

Having talked for so long, Kizu drove in silence for a while. From Ikuo's continued silence, Kizu could sense something he couldn't quite lay a finger on, something he hadn't been conscious of recently. His liaison with Ikuo had given him back his self-confidence, though he sometimes felt their relationship was different from that of gay couples he used to see in his university community. Maybe it was the same with those couples, but Ikuo didn't seem to accept the kind of closeness you'd expect to arise from physical intimacy and made it clear he wanted to maintain a certain distance from Kizu.

Ikuo seemed genuinely interested in the reunion with the girl he'd had such a strange encounter with fifteen years ago, an interest mixed with curiosity about the former religious leaders she was now working for. Ikuo's comments after listening to Kizu made him sense both how strong his interest was in Patron and Guide and also that he was hiding something.

Kizu turned to slowly look at Ikuo; the latter's face had lost its wine-induced flush and again looked like a statue with skin covering the indentations and protruding bones. Shake it a bit, and the heavy lump of a head looked like it would tip right over.

The next day, though, after modeling for Kizu in the morning, Ikuo himself brought up the subject of the girl, as if filling in all his previous silence.

"The girl met Patron and Guide after their Somersault, yet she believes in them totally. The world's going to end, she said, and Patron and Guide will show us the way to deal with that. What they said and did during their Somersault doesn't seem to faze her."

"She puts more emphasis on their suffering over the past ten years," Kizu said. "I wonder if that's the basic approach the two of them will take as they start over. This new beginning means a great deal to her. That's why she got so angry when you used the word *game*."

"Was I wrong to say that?" Ikuo turned his dark, affectionate eyes to Kizu, who felt a surge of desire race through him. "Like I said yesterday, I'm serious about the end time. But she changed the subject. I wish I could have heard more about Patron.

"This morning when I woke up, I regretted not asking for more details about what these leaders' ten years of suffering was all about. All I remember from watching TV was this frivolous old guy blabbing on and on."

"Maybe this new beginning for them is a casual somersault in the opposite direction," Kizu remarked.

"Gymnasts sometimes move forward by doing one somersault after another," Ikuo said. "Unless we talk to them directly, though, we're merely tossing metaphors around."

"In other words," Kizu said, "even if they're phonies you want to meet this self-styled savior of mankind and his prophet, right? Well, you have a standing invitation from her. And I think I'd like to go with you."

"Let me get in touch with her first."

Kizu couldn't read anything in Ikuo's expression, but as he looked at Ikuo's muscular chest and neck, exposed at the loose collar of the robe he'd thrown on over his nude body, Kizu found himself less interested in pursuing the meaning behind Ikuo's expression than simply standing in awe at this young man's magnificent physique. What a waste, he thought, for such a fertile body to be given to someone who has so much still to attain spiritually.

No doubt Kizu was so involved in drawing Ikuo, preparing to create his tableau, because he wanted to capture this young man—for himself alone—before he leaped to the next stage, where that wonderful body would go hand in hand with spirituality. Kizu loved to imagine that Ikuo's body was already lending a sense of solemnity to the privileged thoughts that lay within him. And what convinced Kizu that something special lay in Ikuo's inner being was none other than what he had witnessed fifteen years before: beautiful eyes in the wildly ferocious face of someone who looked less a child than a small man.

After he met Ikuo again, Kizu had remembered a paper presented at a symposium his institute had sponsored that used as its text etchings based on old French prints depicting the stages through which a human face evolves out of wild animals' muzzles. When he first heard this presentation, showing how the cruelest of human faces developed from the line that began with the muzzle of a bear, Kizu had thought of the young boy carrying his plastic model. However, the bear-man's eyes were sunken and expressionless, while the young man's, equally sunken, had been full of suggestive feeling.

Kizu gazed steadily at his young friend. Ikuo sensed he was being looked at, stood up, threw his robe aside on the chair he'd been sitting on, and laid his naked suntanned body on the sofa. He spread his legs wide and beckoned to Kizu with a shy look. Though he was sunk back deep on the sofa, his long bountiful penis was clearly visible, already raising its head. Kizu went off to the bathroom first. Ikuo seemed ready to thank him for his help in bringing him together with the girl and Patron. Still, though, as he stood there, touching his own penis, which was already so hard he could barely get it out of his pants, Kizu allowed himself a feeling of unalloyed pleasure.

In the afternoon, after Ikuo had gone home, Kizu was cutting his nails in the sunny spot beside the wide glass sliding doors. As he clipped the fourth toe of his right foot, he thought unexpectedly that it was like some good little beetle larva dug up from a mound of fallen leaves, very different from the other toes. The toe of his left foot, he found, was exactly the same. He'd lived with these toes for over half a century. Why was it only now that he found them so funny?

Thinking it over, he paused in his clipping. It wasn't that his powers of observation were fading, but rather—as the last vestiges of youth disappeared from every corner of his body—that his toes had really begun to *change.* These are the toes, he thought, of someone whose cancer is back, who's going to end up an elderly corpse. If it hadn't been for his sexual relationship with Ikuo, though, he never would have noticed.

4

On Saturday, Kizu attended an international awards ceremony for a Japanese architect who had, during Kizu's time in the United States, garnered a worldwide reputation. He thought about inviting Ikuo, the former architecture student, but the girl they'd met had asked him to take care of something for her and he wouldn't be back until evening, so Kizu went alone. Arriving at the hotel in Shimbashi, he found that only those involved in the actual ceremony were dressed formally, and he felt out of place in his tuxedo. There were no other familiar faces at the party, either, and Kizu's relationship with the architect himself was superficial. When he had given a public lecture at the architecture department at Kizu's university, Kizu had served as discussant when the architect showed slides of the art museum he'd designed in Los Angeles.

Kizu greeted the architect and his wife and made an early retreat from the reception; next to the escalator, he ran across an American newspaper reporter he knew who wrote about the arts and architecture. The man, an old acquaintance, was also decked out in a tuxedo, and Kizu called out to him, kidding him he was going to stand out dressed like that. The reporter had been invited to a small dinner after the ceremony, but decided to bow out, instead inviting Kizu, whom he hadn't seen in a long time, out for a chat. He led Kizu to a basement-level bar, and they settled in at the counter.

They'd just finished one glass of white wine each and were about to order another when the reporter's long-winded commentary on architecture connected up with the religious leader the girl was working for. It all started when the reporter mentioned an extraordinary place he ran across in the forests of Shikoku.

"The area is like a solitary island," he said, "in the hills about a two-hour drive from the airport. Makes you feel like you're being shown around the remnants of Japanese mythology. You arrive at this dead end with a sea of trees blocking the way. And in a village of fifteen hundred souls, can you believe it, there's an ultramodern chapel and dormitory!

"Makes you wonder how there could be such large new buildings in a depopulated mountain village. What happened was a new religion arose in the village, and they hired one of Japan's leading architects to build a headquarters. But the new religion broke up and disappeared. The village didn't know what to do. They tried to find someone to take over the chapel for them. Then they came up with a plan to convert it to a village junior high school, but that would have been too expensive, so it came to nothing. I suppose they wanted to keep the headquarters building as it was, since it was designed by such a famous architect.

"Finally a different religious organization expressed interest in the building, a group with a really unusual background. The Tokyo correspondent for *The New York Times* told me that"—at this point Kizu could guess what was coming—"ten years ago the two leaders had renounced their faith. They denounced all their own teachings, which was apparently a major shock! The religious organization itself, though, kept on going, with quite a few believers still involved. Followers who left the church maintained their own divisions, ranging from a group of radical revolutionaries to a co-op of gentle Quaker-like women. Sort of an interesting case—and not very Japanese, when you think about it.

"Right now the activities of this church center around another headquarters, in the Kansai region, where they've kept their name and religious foundation status. Most of the followers work in Osaka or Kobe and donate their pay, minus a small amount for living expenses, so they were able to purchase this chapel. And during the last ten years they completed the dormitory, according to the architect's original plans. Some Japanese certainly don't give up, do they?

"The religious organization, though, hasn't moved to this chapel and dorm. Small groups of them visit, staying in the monastery, which is what they call the dorm, and praying in the chapel. They also work for a week, taking care of the building and grounds, before they leave.

"I paid a visit to the building's caretaker, a local woman, and asked if these poor little lost sheep, whose leaders had renounced the faith, still believe that the beloved pair will make a comeback. Her answer took me totally by surprise. (The old lady, by the way, was born in the village but spoke better English than the interpreter I brought with me.) 'Outsiders to the church, myself included, don't really understand this,' she said, 'but when believers pray in the chapel and raise their eyes upward, they say they see the souls of the two former leaders, separated from their suffering bodies so far away, hovering up in the air.' It's gotta be true—'cause how else can you explain their keeping the faith for ten years after their leaders denied it?"

Kizu didn't let on that he'd just met a girl who worked for these two former leaders. The reporter, for his part, didn't go into much detail about this place with the modern buildings. The caretaker, afraid that tourist buses might start showing up, was wary of outsiders coming to visit. Through an introduction from an architecture journal, the reporter was able to view the inside of the chapel, but the woman never left his side and made sure he didn't take any photos.

Kizu, of course, had himself originally learned of the savior and the prophet of the end time through an interesting article in *The New York Times*. The leaders' renunciation, their Somersault, he imagined, must have left an indelible impression on the two thousand or more followers they left behind, but even now, after meeting the young woman who worked for them, he couldn't shake the notion that it was all rather comical.

After hearing this reporter's story of how the abandoned followers had worked hard to collect enough money to buy and add on to the building, however, the story of this church took on a sharpened sense of reality. These leaders must really be something extraordinary, to motivate their followers so highly after they'd abandoned them.

And the followers who came to the building to pray, with great awe and sadness, insisted that the two leaders, after their Somersault, suffered so much that the souls of the two men took leave of their bodies and floated beside them as they prayed.

"Who knows?" Kizu said to the American reporter. "Maybe the souls of those two men really *do* fly all the way to those woods and into that modern building." And he sighed.

4: Reading R. S. Thomas

1

On the day Ikuo phoned the office in Seijo, the young woman's reaction was different from when he met her in the restaurant. Sounding tense, she asked him to come alone.

During the morning of the Saturday awards ceremony Kizu attended, Ikuo had moved his things into Kizu's spare bedroom. He whiled away the rest of the morning without unpacking and then drove Kizu's car over to the young woman's office.

At four in the afternoon, Ikuo had phoned Kizu and told him the girl had had a car accident the day before yesterday at the entrance to the parking area of the hospital when she went to pay Guide a visit. She wanted badly to go see Guide that evening, but the young man she worked with was busy with preparations for starting Patron's new movement. With her car still in the repair shop she'd have to rely on Ikuo driving her in Kizu's car. Kizu still had to get ready to go to the architect's reception—and get the tuxedo prepared he'd convinced himself he had to wear—so he had ended up calling a cab.

Ikuo returned home late that night and told Kizu that the young woman wanted him to work as their official driver. His first assignment would be to pick up her car when the repairs were finished the beginning of next week. He'd already quit his job at the athletic club, and the office would pay him a salary, so Ikuo was enthusiastic about the idea. The working hours were open-ended, he said—though later on they proved not to be—he'd just go over whenever they needed a driver. It shouldn't interfere with his modeling for

Kizu. One more reason Ikuo was so drawn to this job offer was that driving for Patron would give Ikuo the opportunity to talk with him—although Patron had yet to say a word to him of any spiritual matters.

Ikuo began to go every day for a full day's worth of training at the office. Guide had still not regained consciousness, Ikuo reported, but in other respects was recovering nicely. Patron mostly stayed in his room; Ikuo had only been able to speak directly with him a couple of times but found him fascinating. "And the girl is called Dancer at the office," Ikuo added, "so that's what I'm going to call her."

A week passed, and word came that Patron wanted to meet Kizu, so he and Ikuo left for the office together. Kizu could sense Dancer at work behind the scenes to make this invitation possible. Ikuo had not yet had a good long talk with Patron, but starting on this day Kizu was able to.

Patron's voice was low but resonant. "I hear you're an artist," he said right off, skipping the usual formalities. "Even if I hadn't known that, I could have guessed." Patron was sunk deep into an unusually low armchair, his chubby, round face full of childlike curiosity. "It feels like you're tracing the outlines of my face and body with a pencil."

Kizu was flustered and didn't know how to respond. He and Ikuo had first been escorted to Patron's combination study and bedroom by Dancer. Patron was still in bed. Dancer helped him over to the armchair and brought over a chair to face Patron for Kizu to use; Ikuo glided smoothly out of the room as if by previous arrangement. Kizu was introduced by Dancer to Ogi, "whom Patron calls our Innocent Youth," she said, who was working in the office at the front of the house.

"While you're observing me using your professional skills," Patron went on, "I've been doing the same. I sense you're undergoing a major change in your life right now, on a scale you've seldom experienced before."

Kizu found it comical that Patron would adopt the strategies of a fortune-teller on a crowded street, yet confronted with this man's dark eyes—steady, surprised-looking beady eyes, the whites showing above and below almond-shaped lids—the thought occurred to him that he might very well end up kneeling before him to confess his innermost thoughts. Considering his cancer relapse and his emotional and physical relationship with Ikuo, Patron's fortune-telling was right on target.

At any rate, to distance himself and give a neutral reply, Kizu relied on the skills he'd acquired teaching in an American university and brought up a poet he was familiar with.

"When you reach my age," he said, "the sort of change you've mentioned is inevitably linked with death, though I try not to think about it. In this regard I've grown fond of a certain Welsh poet. I hope I can face death with the attitude found in his poetry."

Kizu went on spontaneously to translate a verse he'd memorized in the original:

"'As virtuous men pass mildly away/ and whisper to their souls to go,' the poet writes, showing dying humans calling out to their souls as they are left with just the physical body. I think this fits me to a T."

"Usually it's the opposite, isn't it?" Patron said. "If one could make such a clean break with the soul, imagine how soundly the body would sleep. I've read John Donne myself. One of his other poems goes like this, doesn't it? 'But name not Winter-faces, whose skin's slack;/ Lank, as an unthrift's purse; but a soul's sack.' If an elderly person's body is like a withered sack, it should be easy for the soul to make its exit, I imagine."

Kizu was embarrassed at having his superficial knowledge exposed. Instead of reproving him, though, Patron seemed to want only to show Kizu that he too was enamored of poetry.

"I haven't read any poetry for years, Japanese or foreign," Patron said. "You've recently run across a new poet who has impressed you, have you?"

"It seems like everything about me is coming to light, bit by bit. But you're right," Kizu answered honestly. "Last summer I attended a symposium on art education in a town called Swansea in Wales. The organizer of the seminar presented me with a volume of poetry by a local poet. That evening, as I leafed through it in our cliffside hotel it encouraged me so much—physically and mentally—that I couldn't stay lying down." (As he said this, Kizu realized that he'd always associated this restlessness with the relapse of his cancer; now he was pleased to interpret it as presaging his relationship with Ikuo.)

"Despite my age, my face grew red and I paced back and forth in the small hotel room. Even if I were to meet this poet, I almost moaned, I don't have the energy or time left to respond to him, do I? You might suppose this marked some major change in my life, but I'm afraid I'm too wishy-washy a person for that."

"You said it was Wales, but the poet wasn't Dylan Thomas, I assume? Since you said you've just recently discovered him." Patron asked this quickly, like some teasing child.

"The poet's name is R. S. Thomas."

"What kind of poems were they? Can you remember a verse, any at all?" Patron asked, even more impatiently.

"I'm afraid I can't memorize verses like I used to. . . . About his themes, though, maybe because his name is Thomas, he wrote several poems about

Doubting Thomas. He wrote from Thomas's viewpoint, discussing the reasons why he had to touch Jesus' bloody wounds before he believed in the resurrection."

Patron's almond-shaped eyes were unusually intense as he listened.

"I wonder if you would read to me from his poetry collection?" he asked, making it clear this was not a passing wish. "Even if just once a week. Ikuo will be working in our office, and he's told me you have an interest in our activities too. For the past ten years I've needed to do this kind of study but haven't been able to."

Thus Kizu's meeting with Patron was so successful they decided that once a week Kizu would come and give Patron lectures on R. S. Thomas—something that, considering his art background, was way outside his field of expertise. As they drove home, Kizu found it strange that things had turned out the way they did, but Ikuo seemed to have expected it all along.

Kizu already had a paperback edition of Thomas's poems, the one he received in Wales, but he bought a volume of his collected works at the university co-op, along with a reference work on his poetry, and had them delivered to his apartment. His own copy was filled with notes, and he wanted to present Patron with a clean and complete edition.

Instead of giving private lectures to Patron, Kizu planned just to read the poems together and discuss them, though two or three days later, when he was up far into the night, preparing, Dancer called him, and he headed off to their office despite the late hour. She explained to him that Patron's depression was back and he was staying up late and sleeping through the mornings. Kizu was led into the bedroom study; Ikuo, who'd driven him over, stayed out in the office beside Dancer and Ogi.

Kizu had selected as their first poem one from the collection *Between Here and Now* that was written when the poet was about the same age as Kizu and Patron:

> "You ask why I don't write.
> But what is there to say?
> The salt current swings in and out
> of the bay, as it has done
> time out of mind. How does that help?
> It leaves illegible writing
> on the shore. If you were here,
> we would quarrel about it.
> People file past this seascape
> as ignorantly as through a gallery

of great art. I keep searching for meaning.
The waves are a moving staircase
to climb, but in thought only.
The fall from the top is as sheer
as ever. Younger I deemed truth
was to come at beyond the horizon.
Older I stay still and am
as far off as before. These nail-parings
bore you? They explain my silence.
I wish there were as simple
an explanation for the silence of God."

Patron had a lot to say about the poem. It occurred to Kizu that Patron's insomnia was due less to depression than to the recent intellectual stimulation that had entered his life and was cutting down on his hours of sleep. Patron's large, moist eyes reminded Kizu of a photo he'd seen of a nocturnal marsupial from Tasmania.

"*'You ask why I don't write./ But what is there to say?'* That line makes me recall a very pressing matter," Patron blurted out, for all the world like a bright yet rash child. "I've never written a thing, ever since I was young. In a way, though, I guess what I did up to the Somersault was a kind of writing. Guide helped me in this, of course. The things I experienced in my trances I couldn't put into clear words, but I told them to Guide and he'd translate them into something intelligible.

"After the Somersault, I wasn't able to fall into any major trances, which Guide was aware of. This last half year, though, I could tell Guide wanted to say something to me, something like the first two lines of the poem. 'Why don't you fall into any trances? And why don't you tell me your visions?' But if, for instance, I were to fall into a trance now, I know I wouldn't come into contact with anything transcendental. Which is why I don't make the effort. That's all I can say, if *'you ask why. . . .'*

"*'But what is there to say?'*" he continued. "I'm holed up in this place as in a hideout, not looking at the tides in the bay every day. But for a long time I have been letting time flow from my heart—the movement the poet compares to the tides. These past ten years I've been doing nothing, merely observing the flow of the tides in my own heart.

"Time . . . the flow of the tides move indeed. *'How does that help?'* That's exactly right. *'It leaves illegible writing/ on the shore. If you were here,/ we would quarrel about it.'* Guide was by my side, but I never spoke to him of that writing. When it flows out of my heart, what does time inscribe? Even if it could be deciphered, I know it would be meaningless. There would be nothing to quarrel about.

"But people live their lives for all they're worth, knowing nothing. '*I keep searching for meaning.*' That's the truth. I didn't expect that everything would be thrilling in life. If someone accused me of just sitting on the beach, staring vacantly before me, I couldn't deny it. Sometimes when I feel in good spirits, that is still '*in thought only,*' just climbing the stairs of waves.

"That's so painfully true! '*The fall from the top is as sheer/ as ever.*' It's true. Every single day and night, all I've thought about is what happened ten years ago. The way I fell then, I continue to fall, moment after moment, in my mind.

"The next stanza expresses exactly how I feel right now. '*Younger I deemed truth/ was to come at beyond the horizon./ Older I stay still and am/ as far off as before.*' What does '*these nail-parings*' really point to? At any rate, here I am, sitting here blankly staring at the horizon. It's no wonder Guide got angry and asked *why.*

"This is what I should have said to him: '*They explain my silence./ I wish there were as simple/ an explanation for the silence of God.*' That hits it right on the head."

Patron's dark glistening eyes were no longer aimed at Kizu but were fixed steadily on an invisible companion only he could see.

The mid-October sky was threatening rain, the gloomy road beginning to lighten in the approaching dawn, as they sped toward home, Ikuo at the wheel. Kizu, meanwhile, ruminated on what Patron had said regarding Thomas's poem and his accompanying translation. '*Younger I deemed truth/ was to come at beyond the horizon,*' he mused. I think that's true. Isn't that why I set out for America? And what was the result? I ended up never really investigating that truth.

Ikuo got out of the car for a moment. As Kizu opened the side door next to the main entrance with the same key he used for his apartment, he heard Ikuo's voice, almost apologetically, from behind.

"I wish I could come up to my room now, but Ogi and Dancer have this plan we need to work on."

Kizu turned around and nodded.

"Yesterday, after I drove you and went back to the office," Ikuo went on, "Dancer told me that Patron would like you to donate something he needs, something of great value. Did you talk about this? Religious leaders might seem unworldly, but they have a practical side too, don't they?"

Kizu suspected that Ikuo and Dancer were behind this pronouncement of Patron's. But he merely nodded again, pushed open the solid American-type steel door, and went in alone.

2

This year Kizu sensed that the seasons were changing quickly. Even on days when the morning light shone into his room above the branches of the wych elm, the position of the light was changing, no longer reaching the spot where he sunbathed in the nude.

Kizu's sunbathing, his middle-aged-man's habit, wasn't something he wanted others to see. Ikuo might be living with him and modeling in the nude, but even if Kizu often lounged nude on the sofa he never invited Ikuo to join him. Not that there were many chances to do so, with Ikuo now so busy at the office.

When he was alone, Kizu spent his time painting and preparing his readings of R. S. Thomas for Patron. He reread his note-filled paperback copy of Thomas's poems, gathered books of Thomas's prose writings, and read the theses and monographs that young Welsh scholars had written, like good conscientious sons. He faxed the assistant in his office back in the States a request to look for these books. Coincidentally, the assistant's father happened to be an immigrant from Wales, from Thomas's own parish, in fact. Though he wasn't an Anglican but a member of a minor denomination, her father remembered seeing Thomas, a clergyman, walking through the fields wielding a walking stick like some kind of sports equipment. She added a note in the package of books saying how surprised she was to find that even the Japanese were reading Thomas's poetry.

At one of their late-night readings, Kizu quoted the following Thomas poem.

> "I emerge from the mind's
> cave into the worse darkness
> outside, where things pass and
> the Lord is in none of them.
>
> "I have heard the still, small voice
> and it was that of the bacteria
> demolishing my cosmos. I
> have lingered too long on

> "this threshold, but where can I go?
> To look back is to lose the soul
> I was leading upwards towards
> the light. To look forward? Ah,

> "what balance is needed at
> the edges of such an abyss.
> I am alone on the surface
> of a turning planet. What"

Kizu and Patron always began with Kizu reading aloud from his paperback copy, Patron following along in the hardbound copy in his lap. Kizu's translations served as reference. Then they would discuss the poem, stanza by stanza. On this particular day when Kizu had read to this point, Patron thought the poem ended there, an understandable mistake since the poems in the collected works edition he was using were almost all complete on one page.

"That's exactly right." He sighed in admiration. "Only someone who's desperate, driven into a corner, could write a poem like that."

This didn't sit well with Kizu, the longtime teacher.

"Thomas divides his stanzas in unusual ways," he cautioned his pupil. "The last word in this stanza, *'What,'* is the first word in the next stanza, actually. The meaning of the line doesn't end there."

Patron's response was unexpected.

"But the next stanza isn't really necessary, is it?" he said confidently. "How did you translate the next line? What comes after *'What'*?"

> "to do but, like Michelangelo's
> Adam, put my hand
> out into unknown space,
> hoping for the reciprocating touch?"

"I see! But even though he triumphantly produced this smart stanza, if you look at the whole poem it's an unnecessary addition, don't you think?"

"Don't you believe at all in this kind of *'reciprocating touch'*?" Kizu questioned him.

"These past ten years I've been in the dark," Patron said, "but I haven't relied on a reciprocating touch. *'I emerge from the mind's/ cave into the worse darkness/ outside, where things pass and/ the Lord is in none of them.'* I've experienced this more often than I can recall, but I never attempted to find

God as I passed through there. Doesn't Thomas at times try to be overly suggestive?

"Do you really need to keep your balance on the edge of the abyss? When I made my noisy reversal in front of the media, falling even farther into the abyss, it was like a Ping-Pong ball trying to sink down by itself into a tub of water. Even without the last stanza—no, even *with* it—I agree that this is an outstanding poem."

Kizu felt a slight maliciousness from Patron as he smiled at him in the gloom. Trying to control his rising displeasure, Kizu took out a volume of Thomas's prose writings and showed the following to Patron.

> The ability to be in hell is a spiritual prerogative, and proclaims the true nature of such a being. Without darkness, in the world we know, the light would go unprized; without evil, goodness would have no meaning. Over every poet's door is nailed Keats's saying about negative capability. Poetry is born of the tensions set up by the poet's ability to be "in uncertainties, mysteries, doubts, without any irritable reaching after fact and reason."

When he'd finished reading, Patron looked serious again.

"He's entirely correct," he said. "Thomas is a clergyman, but I think he says more telling things about poetry than about religion. In the final analysis, I should say, he's a poet."

Once more, Kizu felt he'd been given the slip. He said nothing. Compared to the craftiness of Patron, a man of about his own age, Kizu felt himself rather naive.

Patron continued, trying to soothe Kizu. "Of course there's nothing of the poet about me, but I can sympathize with this particular one. This calm *ability to be in hell* and, as Keats puts it, the ability to be 'in uncertainties, mysteries, doubts, without any irritable reaching after fact and reason'—these would be wonderful mottoes for my old age!"

Under the light of the lamp stand, Patron's head jutted forward as he read, and Kizu could see saliva glistening on both sides of his dark cocoonlike lips. His voice had risen in pitch, and Dancer, sensing in this a sign of excitement and exhaustion, quickly and stealthily stepped to his side, gave him medicine directly from her hand, and held a glass of water to his lips. Patron gave himself up to Dancer's practiced movements. She then transferred the cup to her left hand and wiped the saliva away from Patron's lips with the back of her other hand.

* * *

It was morning again when Kizu went home, but this time, instead of Kizu's Mustang, Ikuo drove a minivan, a present from Kizu for Patron to use for meetings he planned to hold in sites outside Tokyo. Expecting that he would be attending these meetings, Ikuo was doing his best to get used to driving the van.

"I think reading that Welsh poet with you is having a good psychological effect on Patron," Ikuo said. "For the first time in a while he came out to the front of the house, to the office, and chatted with the three of us, and he used an English phrase he said was from Thomas that he'd heard from you— *quietly emerge*. He read the poem to us. It was in the translation that you did, and I think it's wonderful."

Kizu reached into the briefcase on his lap, pulled out the copy he was using as a text, sandwiched in between his notes, angled it up in the pale, cloudy light, and read.

> "As I had always known
> he would come, unannounced,
> remarkable merely for the absence
> of clamour. So truth must appear
> to the thinker; so at a stage
> of the experiment, the answer
> must quietly emerge. I looked
> at him, not with the eye
> only, but with the whole
> of my being, overflowing with
> him as a chalice would
> with the sea."

Ikuo nodded. "Patron said, 'If once again God is going to *quietly emerge* to me, I want to welcome him calmly, without flinching. I take this poem as a sort of sermon, and when I can accomplish this and I am able to '*quietly emerge*' before you as mankind's Patron in the end time, I hope you too can welcome me as just calmly, without hesitating.' That's the last thing Patron said." And Ikuo clenched his mouth, in a way that reminded Kizu of a shallow-water fish he'd seen on TV ripping apart a turban shell, and stared fixedly at the lights of the oncoming cars.

Kizu wasn't sure what Ikuo was thinking, but he went ahead and spoke. "I want to believe that Patron is a man of great charisma."

Ikuo drove on in silence for a while, his mouth still set in that strange

way. And then he spoke, quietly, of something he'd apparently been considering ever since he was getting the minivan ready to take Kizu home.

"Yes, Patron certainly does have charisma. But is he planning to lead
people using that charisma? That's the question. I used to think he used the
media to appeal to the dispersed radical faction when he did his Somersault,
but now I have the feeling that the Somersault was necessary for *him*. Once
again, he said, God would *quietly emerge*.

"That's why," Ikuo continued, "though I feel his charisma, I have no real
sense of what kind of person he is. I'm not sure whether I should get more deeply
involved. Since you're well grounded and have a relationship with him that
maintains a certain distance, I think it might be best for me to rely on that."

3

During the week Kizu was able to talk with Dancer, who came to his
apartment just as Ikuo was setting out for the office. Ikuo hadn't told him in
advance, but he'd urged Dancer to pay Kizu a visit.

The only person who had sat on Kizu's sofa since he'd been in Tokyo was
Ikuo, so now, as Dancer sat on it—teacup and saucer resting on her shapely
thighs, watching Kizu as he spoke, her eyes barely blinking, the pink inside her
mouth showing as she sipped her tea—she looked incredibly delicate.

Appearance aside, Kizu already knew she never hesitated to speak her
mind. Today, too, she broached a topic that took him completely by surprise.

"There still is a lot of criticism of Patron," she said. "So much it makes
me realize how much more vicious the attacks must have been ten years ago.
Every time some article lambasting him was sent to us I always asked Guide
for his opinion, but now with things the way they are. . . .

"One famous retired journalist writes the most abusive, scathing things,
but I don't pay him any mind. I'd say the problem's more with the person
who's writing than with anything to do with Patron. Recently we received a
copy of a university bulletin that contained an interview between a Protestant theologian and an associate professor who'd just joined the same church.
Overall it was typical overbearing criticism of Patron, the main point being
their agreement that since Patron had abandoned his own church, the only
way he'd be saved was to join a proper church.

"I told Patron about this, and he said he wants to keep apart from all
established churches, Protestant, Catholic, or whatever. Every person has that
right, he said. If he were to share the same certainty in an objective external
God with the other members of a church, his critics included, he said, he might

very well lose his faith entirely. Instead of climbing into the same bed of faith with these people, he said he much preferred a gnashing of teeth and the uncertainty of belief, lying over seventy thousand fathoms, where he could taste the reason he was living in this world. . . .

"What I wanted to ask you, Professor, was what did he mean by *over seventy thousand fathoms*? I asked him, but he just said you mentioned it in one of your talks. Is the phrase from one of Thomas's poems?"

Dancer stopped speaking, her lips slightly parted as usual, and gazed at the artist.

"It's originally from Kierkegaard," Kizu replied, "though Thomas used it several times. I do remember linking the phrase with the poetry and discussing Kierkegaard with Patron. This wasn't directly from Thomas's poetry collections, but something from a volume published to commemorate the poet's eightieth birthday . . . *this* book, in fact. The author of the text I chose discusses the metaphorical uses Thomas has in his poems for the desolate farmland and sea in Wales. . . . The author quotes two poems; the latter, entitled "Balance," directly mentions Kierkegaard. Let's take a look at it."

> No piracy, but there is a plank
> to walk over seventy thousand fathoms,
> as Kierkegaard would say, and far out
> from the land. I have abandoned
> my theories, the easier certainties
> of belief. There are no handrails to
> grasp. I stand and on either side
> there is the haggard gallery
> of the dead, those who in their day
> walked here and fell. Above and
> beyond there is the galaxies'
> violence, the meaningless wastage
> of force, the chaos the blond
> hero's leap over my head
> brings him nearer to.
>   Is there a place
> here for the spirit? Is there time
> on this brief platform for anything
> other than the mind's failure to explain itself?

"After this poem of Thomas's, the author quotes at length from Kierkegaard's writings. Shall I translate it for you?"

Without risk there is no faith. Faith is precisely the contradiction between the infinite passion of the individual's inwardness and the objective uncertainty. If I am capable of grasping God objectively, I do not believe, but precisely because I cannot do this I must believe. If I wish to preserve myself in faith I must constantly be intent upon holding fast the objective uncertainty, so as to remain out upon the deep, over seventy thousand fathoms of water, still preserving my faith.

"So that's what it means. Patron was quoting Kierkegaard," Dancer said, sounding for all the world like the intelligent heroine in some drama. "Patron jokes around at the most unexpected times, so often I don't know what he's really getting at. But even when he's joking, I think he's suffering over questions of faith. I get the same feeling from those words of Kierkegaard. Thank you for helping me understand. I'm so happy I had a chance to talk with you."

Despite his years, Kizu felt buoyant—the same sort of happiness he felt when students had come to his office back at the university to ask pointed questions and then listen in rapt awe as he gave a detailed response.

Kizu had Dancer stay a little longer and showed her Thomas's collection of poems to accompany a series of paintings, from Impressionist paintings to the work of the Surrealists. This book, a birthday present sent by the head assistant back at his home office, differed from both the paperback and collected works edition, for it contained vivid full-color plates of the paintings. Kizu found it odd as he watched her, the contrast between the way she gazed, open-mouthed, at the plates, and the nimbleness and efficiency with which she had earlier bustled about wiping away Patron's saliva. She still had a touch of the child about her, he realized.

In the evening, uncertain about when Ikuo was to return, Kizu went ahead and began preparing a stew. As he'd learned to do in America, he'd bought various cuts of beef and frozen the unused portions. Now, to use these leftovers, he cut them up and put them in a pot with water, celery, carrots, and onions—leftover vegetables from the bottom shelf of his refrigerator. The stew was just beginning to bubble when Kizu tasted it and decided that, all things considered, it could do with a pinch more salt. His chipper feelings from talking with Dancer were still with him as he tapped the plastic salt shaker smartly against the cutting board to loosen the lumps of salt inside. The salt shaker, it turned out, wasn't plastic but glass, and it shattered, a shard of glass cutting deeply into his right wrist.

The only doctor Kizu could think of was the well-known cancer specialist his institute had introduced him to so, at his wits' end, he called the apartment superintendent, who advised him to go to a hospital in Roppongi where Kizu's university had a special arrangement. Kizu rushed off to the hospital in a taxi and, for the first time since his operation for intestinal cancer, had stitches taken in his skin. If this were your *left* wrist, the blunt physician remarked, hoping to be funny, you'd have some explaining to do.

Ikuo was still out when Kizu returned to his apartment. The pain in his wrist bothered him—making him consider the deeper pain that was sure to come from his cancer—so he went about cleaning up the kitchen to take his mind off it. Inside the brass sink there was one large pinkish drop of his blood.

Kizu couldn't shake off thoughts of his cancer, his mind drifting to how fragile his body was. When you consider the eternal soul, though, he thought, which links humanity's past, present, and future, the fragility of the body is of little consequence. Instead, it should be a sign pointing the way for people to overcome the individual ego. The eternal soul, connecting the far-off Stone Age with some perhaps purgatorylike future Electronic Age. But did he have faith in the soul? The closest thing to faith he had, he decided, with a sinking feeling, were the thoughts that arise from these very emotions.

In the end he gave up on the stew, making do with a can of Campbell's tomato soup and some large crackers that he ate in the living room. The illustrated poetry collection and the research books he'd shown Dancer were still on top of the small table. He picked up the book with the essay comparing Thomas and Kierkegaard, and flipped through an essay by a woman scholar on the poetry collection.

In a pedantic tone the woman noted that the word *ingrowing* was a key term for Thomas, that he was well aware that if one thought too long about something, there was the danger of one's thoughts becoming too narrow and closed in. As Yeats puts it, she wrote, "Things thought too long can be no longer thought, for beauty dies of beauty, worth of worth."

Thomas, then, wrote the poems that accompany the paintings in order to rescue himself from his own narrow way of thinking as a poet. At this point the author embarked on her main theme, an analysis of Thomas's poem on the famous René Magritte painting showing a boot changing, at the tip, into a human foot.

Kizu returned to his own closed-in, ingrown nail-parings. In the kitchen, too, this thought had arisen in his mind—a mental image of Tokyo hit by some catastrophe, too many dead bodies for anyone to do anything about, a favor only for the crows (this area didn't have any stray dogs)—the leftover bodies rotting, shriveling up, and himself among the dead. In the face of thoughts like these, how can one believe in the eternal soul?

"Well, maybe that's a kind of sign?" Kizu said aloud, as if to make certain that these thoughts were *ingrowing* within him.

Starting with Dancer's visit, the day had been a busy one for him. And it turned out to be an important day for Patron's new movement. Dancer had dropped by Kizu's apartment on the way back from visiting Guide in the hospital, and when she was still on the way back to the office the news came in that Guide had regained consciousness. Ogi drove Patron over to the hospital right away, with Ikuo driving the minivan, Dancer aboard, close on their heels. This time they were all able to see Guide. In the evening, Patron wanted to discuss something with Kizu, so Ikuo called the apartment several times, but there was no reply. Kizu was out getting his injured wrist treated. When Ikuo returned to the apartment late that night, Kizu was still up, so they headed off to the office once again.

Kizu and Ikuo both knew very little about Guide's condition, so there wasn't much to talk about as they drove. When they arrived at Seijo, they learned that Ogi had stayed behind in the hospital waiting room on Guide's floor in case there were any changes. Dancer led Kizu inside. Patron was crouched down, head hanging on his chest, in the low armchair beside his bed. But as soon as Kizu sat down across from him, he looked up and a torrent of words gushed forth.

"Professor, Guide has regained consciousness! I don't know how his rehabilitation will go, but I know he'll be all right. He was asleep when I went into his room, but he opened his eyes right away and looked at me. He didn't say anything, which is understandable, seeing as how he'd only been conscious for two hours. But I saw in his eyes exactly what you talked about. I saw him *quietly emerge*.

"Guide closed his eyes after this, but I could tell he wasn't asleep since he blinked over and over. I stood beside his bed and couldn't contain my excitement. And I remembered some lines of poetry you had talked with me about, not Thomas's poetry but a Greek poem translated by E. M. Forster that Thomas apparently loved. You'll have to remind me of the exact wording."

"That was Pindar's ode:

> Man is the dream of a shadow, But when the
> god-given brightness comes

A bright light is among men, and an age that is
gentle comes to birth."

"Thank you, that's it exactly," Patron said, his eyelids swelling reddish, his eyes turning tearful. "In our last lecture I think I spoke a bit too
openly and hurt your feelings, and I apologize. The reason I've asked you
over tonight is for you to lecture one more time on Thomas. With Guide
recovering now, our movement will regain momentum. This is all well and
good, but I might get too caught up in things to have time for any more
poetry lectures. So tonight I was hoping you could read one of his more
deeply contemplative poems."

Kizu complied right away. He picked from his notes one that he had
already translated.

Grey waters, vast
                as an area of prayer
that one enters. Daily
                over a period of years
I have let the eye rest on them.
Was I waiting for something?
                                Nothing
but that continuous waving
                that is without meaning
occurred.
                Ah, but a rare bird is
rare. It is when one is not looking,
at times one is not there
                that it comes.
You must wear your eyes out,
as others their knees.
                I became the hermit
of the rocks, habited with the wind
and the mist. There were days,
so beautiful the emptiness
it might have filled,
                its absence
was as its presence; not to be told
any more, so single my mind
after its long fast,
                my watching from praying.

Kizu first read the original poem and then his translation, and afterward Patron turned his eyes—no longer the tearful eyes of a child, but soft, the edges of the eyelids red—toward Kizu and spoke in a calm voice.

"How wonderful it would be if Guide continues to recover, his rehabilitation goes well, and we could be like the *hermit of the rocks*. But now that he's awakened, I don't imagine he'll want to live that way. Our tranquil days are over."

5: The Moosbrugger Committee

1

Ogi began organizing the name list from Patron the day after he got it. He input all the information into the computer and then started writing each person individually, asking whether he or she would like to receive a letter of greetings from Patron now that he was on the verge of starting a new movement. (One of the reasons that Ikuo was asked to work at the office, not incidentally, was that Ogi was now spending all his time in this outreach task.) Ogi informed the recipients that their names and addresses were in Patron's notebook and asked them to respond on an enclosed postcard. Nearly 30 percent wrote back to say they were looking forward to Patron's message.

Ogi crossed off the names of those who either didn't respond or said they weren't interested; when the names were those of celebrities he wondered whether the name list might be Patron's own concoction. Still, those who responded were all ordinary people, people who, after the Somersault, had written to express sympathy and encouragement. Patron seemed to have cherished these expressions of goodwill in response to all his critics in the media.

Individual names on the list were no problem, but in cases involving the name of an organization, if the person who was listed as the head of the group didn't respond to the initial letter, Ogi, a perfectionist in such matters, called on the phone. In some cases, quite frankly, it was more curiosity that drove him than anything else.

In a new university town constructed in the outskirts of Tokyo, at the farthest end of a private railway line, there was one such organization in a multipurpose building rising among all the new housing subdivisions, a building set aside, among other things, for various cultural and sporting activities. The name of the organization was the Moosbrugger Committee. Ogi wondered who in the world Moosbrugger might be. He'd sent the initial query to a man listed as the organization's contact person, but when he phoned the group it was a woman who answered. The woman sounded older than himself, and her cheery, cartoony voice made Ogi suspect that this was merely a group of people who'd sent Patron a fan letter for fun. However, she turned out to be the officer in charge of overseeing the study groups who used the cultural center's facilities.

"I'd like to ask you about the Moosbrugger Committee," Ogi began, unsure of how to pronounce this Germanic-sounding name.

"Moosbrugger Committee? Aha! Yes, there *was* a group that went by that name here, but they're inactive now. Are you selling something?"

"No, I'm not a salesman, I'm working for a person we call Patron, and he received a letter from this committee."

"Patron? I see! They were a rather eccentric group, so I wouldn't put it beyond them. But that must have been several years ago. Why in the world would you be calling now?"

"I'm working for Patron, helping with his new movement. I apologize, but I don't know anything about the committee. Patron is now formulating new plans, and after a ten-year period of inactivity he's sending out greetings to individuals and groups who supported him ten years ago."

"You sound young, but you do seem to be on the ball," the woman said, in a voice quite different now from her earlier outrageously cheery laughter. "Looking at our list of organizations, I see that the Moosbrugger Committee hasn't been active much, but since most of the members also belong to other study groups I imagine some of them are still coming to our center. I'll look into it, and if I run across some of them I'll give you a call. Would you tell me your telephone number please? My name is Nobuko Tsugane, and I work here at the center. The center itself receives funding from the Tokyo metropolitan government."

Ogi felt sure that after this phone call he could cross one more name off his list, but the next day the woman called him back and told him two members of the Moosbrugger Committee wanted to hear more about Patron's new plans. As they talked, Ogi decided to go visit them to discuss it, something he hadn't done before. So on the weekend, he took the Chuo Line train from Shinjuku and, after a couple of transfers, arrived at this university town an hour away from the city.

Ogi was born and raised in Tokyo during the Japanese economic boom and had graduated from college at the height of the Bubble Economy, but he still had no idea what scale this Culture and Sports Center—built jointly by Japanese Railway and a private railroad line—would be. As he climbed the stairs running between the two railroad stations, he was taken aback at the mammoth building rising in front of him. According to a pamphlet he picked up, the center contained a large concert hall boasting a pipe organ brought over from Germany, a medium-size theater and some smaller ones, and, in a separate building, a hotel with an international conference center with facilities for simultaneous interpreting. The two identical postmodern buildings were linked, and the connecting office, outfitted with a kitchen, was where he found the woman he'd talked with, Mrs. Tsugane.

Ogi proffered one of his old business cards, explaining that though he was working now for Patron, he had ties to the foundation on the card. Mrs. Tsugane stared fixedly at him, a searching look on her face. Ogi felt a wave of nostalgia looking at this woman's narrow face, which despite its finely chiseled features had a soft profile. Even more so, her dark, damp hair, falling in a gentle wave, sent a clear memory of something, he wasn't sure what, running through him.

Mrs. Tsugane, noticing him looking at her hair, casually explained that she'd been for a swim during her lunch hour. She seemed a bit embarrassed at her own vitality, the lithe way she moved her body, clearly trained in high school or college sports—all of which fit perfectly her open laughter on the phone. Overall she seemed a well-brought-up intelligent woman.

Mrs. Tsugane said that the two women Ogi wanted to meet would be a little late, so she'd go ahead and tell him what she knew about the Moosbrugger Committee. "The committee began as a reading circle set up to discuss Musil's *A Man Without Qualities,*" she began, "and took its name from the name of a character in the novel, a strange person involved in sex crimes. The members included people with backgrounds in sociology and psychology as well as housewives who loved literature.

"When the committee was formed, they planned mainly to have talks with a retired member of the police force who had been involved in a major sex crime investigation. Soon they were able to directly hear from the criminal himself, which made the name of the committee all the more fitting.

"However, relations with rather peculiar individuals brought about some difficult problems. At one point it became necessary to give an honorarium to one of the guests they'd invited. Because the committee itself didn't have the funds, they made do with a contribution by one individual, but this gave rise to all sorts of complications. As these mounted, the Moosbrugger Committee found itself at a standstill. The two members who are on their way to see you now—one of whom was the woman who made that contribution—were the members who, after Patron and Guide incurred the censure of society with the Somersault, began to be interested in them and planned to invite them as guests. As I said earlier, the two women are members of other cultural groups besides the Moosbrugger Committee, so don't worry if you don't arrive at any definite conclusion talking with them today—it's not like they're going out of their way to come here."

Just as Mrs. Tsugane concluded her neat summary, the two women entered the office, one of them a modest yet obviously strong-willed woman in her thirties, the other, younger, a large, ashen-faced woman who, perhaps because of her makeup, Ogi found hard to characterize. Mrs. Tsugane introduced them, the first woman as Ms. Tachibana, the second as Ms. Asuka. Mrs. Tsugane drew out the older of the two women to talk about what led her to send a letter to Patron. Mrs. Tsugane handled this in a considerate yet efficient manner that increased Ogi's admiration for this experienced career woman.

Ms. Tachibana looked straight at Ogi through egg-shaped glasses; she sounded as if she'd prepared her remarks in advance.

"When the Moosbrugger Committee was originally formed—I wasn't yet a member then—their first guest speaker was a member of Patron's church. He was quite a strange character, which made him perfect for the committee: so much so they dubbed him 'Our Own Moosbrugger.' After he heard Patron's sermons, this man came to the outrageous conclusion that, with the world about to end, it didn't matter what sort of terrible things you did— in fact, those acts might even be of value—and he committed a crime. He'd served his time in jail and was out at this point, and we paid him an honorarium to speak to us about his experiences. I became a member the third time he spoke to us. I think he got the nickname Our Own Moosbrugger because he appeared so many times.

"At our meetings, someone raised the idea that it would be interesting to hear from the leader of the church the man belonged to, to hear his opinion about all this. We discussed it further, and this being a time when media reports on the Somersault were still fairly fresh in people's minds, we put two and two together and realized that the church leader on TV and the leader of Our Own Moosbrugger's church were one and the same. Maybe from the beginning it was unrealistic to ask this former leader who'd renounced his own church to come speak to us, seeing as how it'd be difficult for him to compare the radical faction that caused him so much trouble and a person like Our Own Moosbrugger.

"Still, the committee began to make preparations for his visit, came to me for advice, and that's how I ended up a member. The reason they came to me was that I'd talked to Ms. Asuka here, whom I'd met at the documentary film society at the center, and told her that I'd heard Patron give a sermon to a small gathering—this was before the Somersault, of course—and had been quite moved. Ms. Asuka makes films; actually, she's making her own documentary about the main speaker at the committee, Our Own Moosbrugger. She's a very self-assured woman and has a job that ordinary people would never think of doing, in order to earn the funds needed to finance her film. She's the person who contributed the honorarium. At any rate, I was the one who sent the letter to Patron, using the name of the man who was the representative of the committee. You might think I thought that with Patron out of the church he might consider coming to talk with our group, but that wasn't my motivation at all; I just wanted to meet him myself."

"Did Patron write back?" Ogi asked.

"They waited a long long time and only now have a reply," Mrs. Tsugane put in.

"That's right. Over a thousand days. So—would it be possible for him to visit our group?"

"Patron's restarting his religious activities for the first time in a decade," Ogi said, "and he's contacting those people who wrote to him during that time. So it might be possible."

"If he were to come, we'd have to get our committee up and running again. Not to bother him with old tales of Our Own Moosbrugger but to listen to one of his wonderful sermons."

"I'd like to film his sermons too, since you've told me, Ms. Tachibana, how powerful a figure he is." Though her name had come up in the conversation, Ms. Asuka had remained silent, her flat face impassive in its greasepaintlike makeup. Now her remarks went immediately to the point.

Though her tone and voice were more affable than the other two women's, Mrs. Tsugane's next remarks brought Ogi up short.

"I understand that this Patron, as you call him, is getting back into religious activities," she said, "but if your visit here to the Moosbrugger Committee is for the purpose of recruiting converts, we can't allow the committee to use any of the conference rooms at the center. Outside of the meeting, of course, anyone is free to become a member."

It finally struck Ogi, whose innocence was in keeping with the nickname his colleagues had given him, what his role had become—a religious canvasser.

"Just as when I wrote that letter," Ms. Tachibana said, "that isn't the reason why I want him to visit us. And I don't think that's where the interests of the other members lie, either." In the overly hot central heating, strands of loose hair were plastered to her sweaty, pale forehead.

Ms. Asuka nodded in silent agreement.

"It's just that if we're going to have a relationship from now on," said Mrs. Tsugane, "I need you to understand that the Culture and Sports Center is a public facility."

Mrs. Tsugane said something next that, in one stroke, clarified the vaguely familiar feeling Ogi'd had ever since he met her; her face, too, was filled with a bright, wistful smile.

"When you were still a fresh-faced boy, Mr. Ogi, I sometimes saw you at your family's summer cottage in the Nasu Plateau. I tried to be friendly toward you, and according to your sister-in-law you liked me, too . . . and now look at you—grown into a wonderful young man."

After Ogi arrived back at his apartment, one station beyond the office at Seijo on the Odakyu Line, and began preparing dinner, the vivid memories Mrs. Tsugane's remarks revived in him suddenly hit home. In the summer after his first year of high school, at their summer cottage in the Nasu Plateau, Ogi's whole family, from his father—head of the medical department at a public university—on down, were friends with a designer of hospital furniture who often came to stay with them. This year the man brought along his young wife Mrs. Tsugane. Her family had a summer home in the same area, and she and her husband were friends of Ogi's brother and sister-in-law. Ogi wasn't part of the two young couples' activities, since he was younger.

One day, when the young couples had changed into swimsuits at the house and gone to a nearby heated pool, Ogi went into the rest room connected to the bath and discovered the designer's wife's discarded white tank top, soft denim skirt, and a pair of panties with a flowery watercolor design in a laundry hamper. Seized by a sudden impulse, Ogi stuffed the skimpy pair of panties in his pocket. That night he easily slipped the panties—two pieces of cloth connected by bits of elastic—onto his skinny body, and slept with them on, enveloped in a warm comfortable feeling, as if once more he were a happy baby. The next day, though, feelings of remorse clutched at him, and knowing that this panty thievery would not go unnoticed, he returned alone to Tokyo.

Every summer after that, Ogi begged off going to the summer cottage, saying he was busy with extracurricular activities.

2

When Ogi told her about the Moosbrugger Committee's proposal, Dancer said that while it might be possible for Patron to visit the committee, she wanted to wait before she broached the topic. For the time being, Patron had to concentrate on his discussions concerning their new plans with Guide, who had quickly recovered and had been released from the hospital. Ogi, always meticulous when it came to their office work, wanted to get in touch with the Culture and Sports Center to let them know not to expect a quick reply. But he had another, more emotional, motive for calling: Mrs. Tsugane's voice on the phone, he had to admit, gave him a tingly feeling all over.

"I think you should get in touch with Ms. Tachibana directly," Mrs. Tsugane told him, and gave him the telephone number; Ms. Tachibana worked in the library of a Jesuit university in Yotsuya.

"She's a very capable woman," Mrs. Tsugane went on, "and has been living for a long time with her handicapped younger brother. She isn't doing this as an act of self-sacrifice but because she feels it's the best way she and her brother can become more independent. Ms. Asuka is also a free spirit, with her own special way of putting that freedom into practice. As Ms. Tachibana implied, Ms. Asuka is involved in adult entertainment, saving up the funds she needs to make her own films. . . . They're such opposites it makes me wonder how they've come to rely on each other so much as members of the committee. . . .

"Well, now that you know all this background, I'm sure you'll find plenty to talk about. After you do I'd like you to come see *me*. You do owe me something, right? Ha!"

Ogi got in touch that day with Ms. Tachibana's office, and they met the following day, after she finished work, outside the side gate to the university. They sat down for a talk on a bank that overlooked a moat, amid a line of cherry trees whose leaves had turned.

Ms. Tachibana had on a white and navy blue suit too subdued for her age, and, in contrast to her introspective demeanor, she strode toward him with firm, determined steps.

Ogi began by explaining to her about the young woman they all called Dancer, how she took care of Patron's daily needs and was responsible for many of the activities they had planned for the future, and then he gave her the message Dancer had asked him to relay. He apologized for his ambivalent reply the other day. Ms. Tachibana wasn't interested in talking about the Moosbrugger Committee, but wanted to explain why it was important for her, as an individual, to meet with Patron. Ogi readily agreed. Despite his youth, he was an excellent listener.

"I was once a student at this university," Ms. Tachibana began, "and a little more than ten years ago, just before the Somersault, when my brother and I were still living with our parents, an acquaintance invited me to a small gathering where Patron spoke.

"I wasn't a believer at the time, and though his sermon really moved me, it didn't convert me. At any rate, I'd become friends with the mother of a mentally challenged child who worked at the same welfare office where I took my brother, and she was the one who took me to the gathering. This mother wasn't a believer either.

"Life wasn't easy for me then, because of my brother. He could only use a few words, and has the cognitive ability of a four- or five-year-old, his motor skills about the same. But he has perfect pitch and composes music. He'd already begun composing at the time. Once there was a concert at the Welfare Center and the volunteer pianist advised me to send copies of my brother's compositions to a famous composer, which I did right away. The composer wrote back, saying the melodies were exquisite, and also sent me a copy of a book he wrote. I brought the book with me. Here's what it says."

Ms. Tachibana took out a small hardcover book from her oversized handbag. Ogi motioned her over to some concrete seats shaped like tree stumps.

When one thinks, it's impossible to escape the agency of language. Even when one thinks in the medium of sound, there's an inevitable connection with language. In my case, in order to form a framework in which my thoughts can be clearly expressed in the overall structure of my music and also in the details, I find it necessary to verify things in language. And I leave it up to a decision of the senses. I discover the themes of my music, too, through this sort of process. It has nothing to do with a poetic mood or anything like it.

"This made me think my brother's music has limitations. It's like there's a bar set up very low, and the music can't get over that hurdle. Perhaps the composer didn't want to hurt my feelings by telling me that directly, and that's why he sent me his book.

"My brother lies on the floor of our apartment, in our public housing apartment, and writes his compositions on music sheets. When he makes a mistake he erases it and then writes down the right notes. It's as if he already has the music in his head and just needs to get the notes down on paper.

"He can't explain in words what kind of music he's trying to compose, and I doubt he's even thinking in words when he does compose. As the composer put it, he's unable *to verify things in language.*

"I started thinking about the limits of my brother's music, and I became quite sad and depressed as I realized what a dead end it was. I was feeling so down the woman I knew at the Welfare Center took me to hear Patron's sermon.

"It took place long ago, but I still remember it well; it was as if his sermon reached out and grabbed me right where I live.

"I took notes on his sermon in my notebook here; it was based on the words of a seventeenth-century philosopher:

> God revealed himself in Christ and in Christ's spirit, not following the words and images the prophets had given.
>
> When the true spirit of things is grasped, apart from words and images, then and only then are they truly understood. . . . Christ actually, and completely, grasped this revelation.

"As I listened to him read each sentence aloud and then comment on it, I couldn't contain myself. I had to ask a question. The meeting was held in a small shop converted into a residence, which because of rising land prices was about to be sold; fifteen or sixteen believers filled this dim room near the entrance, and we were seated just behind them. I raised my hand, leaned forward, and nearly shouted out my question. 'Sir,' I asked, 'I don't know anything about this special person named Christ, but could this be applied instead to someone else—say, an unfortunate person? A person who doesn't even know he's unfortunate and has a pure heart? Is it possible that God could reveal himself directly, not through words, but through *music?*'

"After I said this, Patron wove his way on unsteady legs through the narrow space between the people sitting in front and came and held my hand and whispered to me, '*That's exactly right!*' I was still a young girl, and those words stayed in my heart. I felt as if my body and heart were filled with light."

As if to calm the tide of excitement, Ms. Tachibana was silent for a time, staring at the black trunks of the cherry trees in front of her. Ogi turned his gaze not on the shadows of the cherry leaves but toward the deep-hued autumn foliage of the mistletoe, even now turning darker as night approached. So even a woman like this, he thought, a serious, modest person who calmly goes about doing her own job and living her own life, was encouraged by

Patron. And now, even ten years after the Somersault, that emotion still remains alive inside her.

"I've been thinking about this for a long time," she went on, "but if Patron can come to the Moosbrugger Committee, I want to bring my brother along as a kind of test—to see whether Patron would reveal God in him, directly, without words or images. In the past, when my brother listened to music, you could see light filling his body and heart. That was when my parents were still alive. But now he's more like an old man; his head droops. I want him to meet Patron and be filled again with light, the way he used to be. Wouldn't that be a sign of God's revelation? I know my idea is a little wild, but after all the trouble you've gone through I just had to tell you. I'm sorry to have kept you so long—I appreciate your listening to me."

"No, I'm the one who should thank *you*," Ogi said. "I'm glad to hear that Patron has such power, even after the Somersault. Once his plans crystallize, you can expect a letter from him."

Ms. Tachibana nodded and stood up, made a slight bow, and walked off alone down the stone pathway in the direction of the Yotsuya Station. Ogi could imagine her taking walks here during her lunch break, with an invariably gloomy, serious look on her face. With her stolid way of walking, which took one's attention away from her features or manners, she disappeared down the path, her heels clicking against the stone paving.

So that he wouldn't seem to be following her, Ogi had set off in the opposite direction, down the path through the cherry trees. The farther he went the darker it became, and the only way he could reach the paved road lined with streetlights was to stray off the path and head toward the grassy slope. The moment he stepped off the path that sloped down through the trees, a thick branch of a cherry tree raked across his eyes and nose.

Holding his face, he plopped down on the withered lawn and grumbled a complaint directed less at his own pain than at something beyond.

"Why do there have to be so many unhappy people in the world? No wonder someone like this self-styled Patron of Humanity appears. What in the world is happening to life on this planet?"

3

When Dancer asked Ogi to report on his progress in contacting people, he submitted a revised name list to her, but he decided to approach Patron directly about Ms. Tachibana.

"Do you happen to recall," he asked Patron, "a small gathering about ten years ago when a young girl, whose younger brother was mentally challenged, asked you a question? She wasn't one of the followers of the church. This girl, still in her teens at the time, listened to your sermon and said her whole body was filled with light."

Patron's pensive face, which looked like it was covered with a thin sheen of oil, came alive, the color rising.

"I *do* remember that," he said, his voice so suddenly transformed that Ogi nearly regretted his words, thinking they'd been too much of a shock. "The girl told me her body and heart were filled with light, and I could see that her skin, even the part covered by her clothes, was glowing."

Ogi recalled Ms. Tachibana's forehead, perfect for the kind of crown that adorned a Girls' Day doll, her tiny lips and chin. An image of her face as a youngster—not a particularly attractive girl—flashed through Ogi's mind. And of light flooding through her thin, pale skin from *within*.

"That woman belongs to a group called the Moosbrugger Committee, which is on our list. In fact, she's the one who wrote to you. She wants to invite you to visit them. Before things become too busy with your new activities, would it be possible to fit a short meeting with the members of the committee into your schedule? She said she wanted to bring her mentally challenged brother along, too."

Ogi made up his mind to report to Ms. Tachibana that, although Patron couldn't make a firm commitment at this time, he did get the feeling he was leaning in that direction. The university library was closed, though, for a Founder's Day holiday. He phoned Mrs. Tsugane, and she told him her husband had received an award given in northern Europe for his designs for improved furniture for elderly patients. He was in Europe now to attend the awards ceremony, and she was bored and asked Ogi to come over to see her. She had something she wanted to talk with him about, she added. Her voice had a force in it that couldn't be denied, so Ogi agreed to meet her Saturday afternoon at the entrance to the Culture and Sports Center.

On the appointed day, though, when she alighted from the elevator, Mrs. Tsugane wore a cold, serious expression completely in contrast with her voice on the phone. Silently, she led Ogi along a stone path heading toward the top of a hill right before them crowded with various cultural facilities and stores. Sculptures lined the narrow path, Ogi taking particular note of a combination of slabs of metal with complex reflections of the light and one mounted on a concrete base like an egg sliced in half. Elderly couples and small groups of young girls especially seemed to enjoy shaking the movable metal parts of some of the statues and stroking an almost comically old-fashioned realistic statue of an infant.

With no rhyme or reason to the way the level areas and steps were adjoined, it was a tiring walk up the slope, and Mrs. Tsugane, lost in thought, eventually led the way to an outdoor amphitheater surrounded by a horseshoe-shaped ring of sunken stone seats; she went halfway around and began descending the south side of the hill. Without a word to Ogi, she strode off quickly toward a colony made up of a small group of residences and an apartment building rising up from slightly below.

She stopped at the brick entrance of the nearest residence, surrounded by yew trees, and for the first time seemed to relax. She had Ogi wait at the foyer as she went in, bustling noisily just past the door and then inviting him in. A spacious living room/kitchen greeted Ogi, a sparse woods visible on a steep slope outside. The lace curtain on the inset window was drawn, blocking the unusually strong sunlight that had made them both perspire on the walk over. Ogi sat down on a sofa, his position affording him an angled view of the scenery to his right, and gazed at the framed picture hanging on the wall in front of him, a colored print of a railroad station constructed of iron, viewed from the front, and a plan, drawn in pencil, that continued on the same paper.

"This is where I escape to," said Mrs. Tsugane, catching what Ogi was looking at as she brought in a liter bottle of Evian and two fluted glasses. "My husband picked that up in France. He has a number of sketches of railway bridges too, all of which have a pagoda on them, obviously not of practical use but more as a type of monument."

"It's from the end of the nineteenth century, around the time the Eiffel Tower was built," Ogi said, noting the date on the print.

"That was the age when metal structures had a religious feel to them," Mrs. Tsugane said. She sat down on the sofa, waiting for Ogi's gaze to move from the print to her. "It's been so many years, but I wonder what happened to my missing panties? How about telling me the details?"

Ogi blushed, and felt like he was left dangling stupidly in the air. He fingered the Evian bottle on the low table, wondering how he should begin, as Mrs. Tsugane leaned forward and stretched out her hand as if she were about to slap his knee. Instead, she leaned back and said, in an intelligent, serious tone, "Please don't get angry, but just hear me out. I'm not doing this to have fun at your expense. It's just that recently I feel anxious, as if I'm stuck in a rut, and I feel a lot of nostalgia for those old days, and for the high school student who was so curious about my panties. I can imagine how tough it must have been for you, with your brother and his wife always leaving you out of their activities. And I wonder why I didn't do anything to help include you."

"The other day, after I got back to my apartment, I thought a lot about that," Ogi said. "Back then I just put your panties on and felt a gentle calm come over me and went to sleep . . . but I can't remember at all what happened the next morning."

His words felt forced to him, a sense of reality missing from them. He blushed even more, afraid she might think he wasn't telling the truth, and took a sip of water. But Mrs.Tsugane seemed to accept everything he said. She even inclined her head coyly to one side.

"This might be a naive question, but when a young man wears a woman's panties—assuming everything's normal with him—don't things get out of hand?"

"Not for me. Everything settled down nicely. It felt like my whole body was cocooned in a fluffy softness, and I slept soundly."

As she listened to Ogi, a yawn came to her flushed, small, round face, taking Ogi by surprise. Despite this, she appeared still to be deep in thought, and finally said, in a low voice, "Maybe you wanted to become a girl, you poor thing."

That certainly made sense, Ogi mused, when you consider how his genitals subsided and how calmly he slept after putting the panties on. Having confessed, his face red and drooping, Ogi realized that he might seem to be enjoying a kind of masochistic solace in all this, which made him blush all the more.

Mrs. Tsugane stared steadily at him for a time, then gulped and, steeling herself, made a decisive announcement.

"Certainly you don't strike me as girlish now. The subconscious desires you had as a young boy are still with us, inside your trousers. And the girl I used to be and the woman I am right now are very happy, I can tell you. Your brother and sister-in-law teased me no end about the panty incident, but it also brought on some erotic dreams. Why don't we reward our formerly naive selves? What do you say? Let's do it!"

Up the spiral staircase with its metal banister that ascended from the entrance with its vaulted ceiling, there was just one large bedroom, with a toilet and bath attached. The room contained little more than a vanity mirror and chair, an oak sideboard, and a double bed spilling over and occupying the rest of the space. Mrs. Tsugane turned down the bedspread and light blanket and, standing firmly on the rug, legs set apart, took off her skirt, shrugged off her silk slip, and let it drop to the floor. After carefully removing her stockings, she was taking off her panties when a faint smile spread lines from her flushed eyelids to her cheeks. Ogi didn't like that particular look, which was directed at him, but not to be outdone, he enthusiastically sloughed off his clothes.

Only three minutes into sex, as Ogi was moving vigorously up and down, his passion rising, Mrs. Tsugane pushed up her slim arms against his chest. Ogi was annoyed, but she modestly explained that she felt she was going to come first, and wanted him to get off her. She turned around, face down, hoisting up to a comical height the two white globes of her rump and the reddish slit between. She had all the seriousness of purpose of a little girl absorbed in play and Ogi, once again in a good mood, couldn't suppress a smile, feeling proud that such an intelligent older woman would openly show him such passion.

Ogi enjoyed remembering their sexual activities for many days thereafter. Even when he was taking care of the inquiries related to Patron's name list—and the number of replies they received exceeded a hundred—he'd be possessed by fragmentary mental pictures of Mrs. Tsugane's body, and of her fingers, and of his as they moved over her. He made out a schedule of visits to the university town Mrs. Tsugane lived in, taking care of all the business at hand up to the last possible moment—sending out Patron's letters, getting in touch with people by e-mail, fax, and, when necessary, by phone. For her part, Mrs. Tsugane, with her insatiable desire and stamina—at least from the viewpoint of an inexperienced youth—responded to Ogi's every need. What's more, she displayed the kind of good sense appropriate to an older woman.

One day between bouts of sex as they lay sprawled out, resting their weary bodies, Mrs. Tsugane, puffing on a cigarette, said, sounding less like she was addressing Ogi than reciting lines from a one-man play, "Please don't tell anyone about what's going on between us. After my husband gets back from abroad, we won't be able to meet as frequently, and we'll both have time to do some soul-searching. In my experience, even if you try very hard to analyze a physical relationship, one that's just begun, you'll find it meaningless to do so."

Innocent, and at the same time moralistic, Ogi listened to her, dead serious. A moment later, though, as Mrs. Tsugane, lying face down, slid up and reached out for the ashtray, Ogi's attention was riveted by the red lines on the outer part of her small buttocks attached to thick thighs, and by her anus, like a dried jujube-tree fruit, the only part of the sweaty flushed inner flesh of her skin that wasn't soaked, like an ornamental button amid the pubic hair surrounding it.

In the end, innocent young Ogi put these words of a most discreet and experienced older woman on a back burner and didn't pursue their implications. After three weeks of bliss, though, the day came when he had to face an inevitable reality, on the heels of which he was ambushed by jealousy and ended up angry and miserable: Mrs. Tsugane's husband was coming back from Europe the following day.

Ogi learned that they wouldn't be seeing much of each other since she was going to take some time off from her job and spend a week with her husband at their cottage in South Izu before he reported back to his design center. When he heard this, Ogi felt like breathing a sigh of relief for his penis, which had never had such a workout. Perhaps eager to reward him for the time they'd have to be apart, when Ogi arrived at her refuge on this final day Mrs. Tsugane had laid out a plastic sheet on the rug at the foot of the bed, as well as a professional-size bottle of body lotion Ms. Asuka had given her.

Ogi had heard that Ms. Asuka worked in "adult entertainment," but it was only when he saw this bottle that he fully understood what this meant. According to what he'd heard, the Our Own Moosbrugger fellow had used some of Ms. Asuka's contributions to pay a visit to her massage parlor.

They spread the lotion over each other's bodies and went through the same routine they normally performed on the bed. But this time Mrs. Tsugane didn't let Ogi pin her down; instead she got up on his chest and straddled him, facing away from him and bending over. As he knew it would, his penis trembled from this new workout as her head bobbed up and down on it. Thinking to return the favor, Ogi stuck his neck out like a turtle, but with the rapid movement of her tight little rump, his tongue couldn't quite reach the red slit right before his eyes. He grabbed on to her glistening white butt, a hand on each hemisphere to hold it still, and relaxed his neck. But as Mrs. Tsugane became more absorbed in performing fellatio, the bobbing movements of her head led her butt to rise and fall; Ogi touched his right index finger to the jujube fruit between her buttocks, and it slid in smoothly. As if to encourage the movements of his fingers, her rump gracefully slid down deeper and the young man's finger came to rest on a soft cocoon like a tiny ball of finely dried hay. . . .

After he returned to his apartment, Ogi finally realized what that had all been about. A few days before, as they took a break in bed, Mrs. Tsugane had mentioned that her furniture-designer husband had an interest in scatology and had shown interest in her urine and feces. Once it was out of the body it was dead, as far as she was concerned, and though she had urinated on him once, she didn't let him touch anything else, she said.

Mrs. Tsugane had given Ogi the body lotion bottle to throw away in the garbage cans outside the station on his way home, but as she did so she poured the remaining lotion into a small bottle of a generic brand of make-up, and put the apparently new container in her purse. Now when he recalled this he understood he'd been nothing more than a guinea pig in an experiment prepared for her returning husband's new sexual proclivities. And this became the trigger for the jealousy that consumed him the following week.

4

After a truly miserable week alone, when Ogi showed up at Mrs. Tsugane's office she was on the phone, speaking slowly and deliberately. She motioned to him to take a seat. Apparently she was talking with the PR department of a company regarding travel funding for a Polish avant-garde troupe that was scheduled to appear at the drama festival sponsored by the Culture and Sports Center the following spring. She had on a beige suit and, around her neck, a scarf of horizontal light green and grass-colored stripes. On his trip to Europe to the awards ceremony, Mrs. Tsugane had told Ogi proudly, she'd asked her husband to attend a famous scarf designer's show of his new collection.

As he listened to her endless phone call, Ogi remembered that long-ago summer day, her tank top, and her lush heavy hair cascading down her back. Her hair now, bangs as well as the hair down the nape of her neck, was thinner and piled up on top of her head. He had learned that the wrinkles that ran from her eyes to the upper part of her cheeks grew darker as she got sexually aroused, but now they were merely an indicator of aging skin; in her profile, as she quietly but persistently made her case over the phone, Ogi could see exhaustion seeping through.

She finally finished her call and hung up, a self-deprecating look on her face at having someone else witness her struggle over the phone.

"No matter how much I plead, they won't contribute the funds. Before the economic bubble burst, companies used to give money before they even heard what it was for. Nowadays, with the recession getting worse, they feel they've done their duty merely by listening."

Ogi nodded at her. He broached the topic he'd been thinking about all the way over on the Chuo Line train, his words sounding unnatural to him as he spoke.

"It seems it's impossible for Patron to come to a meeting of the Moosbrugger Committee. Not that he has no interest in Ms. Tachibana and her brother—quite the opposite. He wants to invite them to come to his own office. I called her to convey the news and she seemed quite taken with the idea."

"If that's the case," Mrs. Tsugane said, staring fixedly at Ogi as if finally noticing him, "there's no reason for Ms. Tachibana to attend the Moosbrugger Committee anymore. She has a close friend in Ms. Asuka, and the other people on the committee are really not her type. This would mean too, wouldn't it, that you have no more business here? When we talked this morning, though we haven't seen each other for ten days, you didn't seem too enthusiastic about meeting me.

"Does this mean our relationship is over, now that my husband's back in the country? Did your sense of morality drive you to this decision? Surely you're not suddenly afraid of my husband?"

Ogi decided he'd best say nothing. Angry emotions welled up inside, but if he let her storm of words sweep over his head, this troublesome matter he didn't know how to begin to approach would simply resolve itself. The ten days of misery he'd experienced had made him think things out in a more adult way. It was worse than cowardly to put all the blame on her.

"I don't know if I can say anything about morality. But I *do* know that jealousy's made me miserable these past ten days, and there's no way out. If I said I was going to snatch you away from your husband, you'd be the first to laugh at me. But I still went ahead cooking up all kinds of silly schemes. Finally, I decided that I couldn't keep on as I am, suffering from a jealousy that has me bent out of shape. In other words, the only way is to make a clean break."

"Isn't there some less drastic way?" Mrs. Tsugane asked. "Maybe we could go on as we are, for a while, and then say goodbye with only a minimum of pain."

"The pointless suffering I've been through made me realize that I can't stand being in this kind of pain anymore. If we keep on, my head will explode. There's no other way. If we cut things off here I'll suffer for a time, but I can tough it out."

Mrs. Tsugane's small figure shrank farther into her chair, as she turned her pinked-rimmed eyes to Ogi. She licked her upper lip and the skin above it with her peach-colored tongue, which Ogi found, all over again, alluring.

"You're basically a very serious person, aren't you?" she asked. "Your parents are probably bemoaning the fact that, of all your brothers, you're the one who's gone bad and doesn't have a decent job, but you're still as serious as the high school boy I remember, jogging for all he was worth on the Nasu Plateau. So serious you just had to steal my panties, didn't you?

"I understand, so let's say goodbye. I'd like you to have a keepsake— and don't think a new pair of panties is what you want—so I'd like to give you a brand-new cassette player. With a cassette tape, too: music that

Ms. Tachibana's younger brother composed. I listened to it a little this morning, and it made me so sad I couldn't listen anymore. After your phone call, I had a premonition of what was going to happen. And now that it has, you can't expect me to listen to that music, can you? Farewell. Horseman, pass by!"

For about thirty minutes on the train to Shinjuku, Ogi sat with his head hanging down, but then he switched on the tape recorder and listened to the tape from the point where Mrs. Tsugane had stopped it. Each of the short pieces was made up of simple chord structures and melodies, but the music felt like the cries of a bared soul. So this is how a person lives with a mental handicap, Ogi thought, and how an unfortunate woman takes care of him all on her own. Heedless of the pair of high school girls who stared at him, Ogi felt tears coursing down his cheeks.

If Patron can make a light shine in someone like that, not just in their hearts but inside their very *bodies,* Ogi thought, I want to do my utmost to help him. He was crushed by a lump of grief, but even if he wasn't aware of it at the time, at the far end of his sorrow was a ray of light, and the dark monster of his jealousy was even now in retreat.

6: Guide

1

Kizu had heard from Dancer about the separate annex in the compound where their office was located, but he'd never seen it. Almost immediately after he was released from the hospital, though, Guide let Kizu know that he'd heard about him from Patron and wanted him to come over to visit, so they set a date and time.

In the minivan on the way over, Kizu learned from Ikuo that while Ogi was spending all his energies in laying the groundwork for Patron's new movement, Dancer was spending all her time taking care of Guide's day-to-day needs.

"Guide says he wants to participate in the new movement, but Dancer told him that after managing to survive a burst brain aneurysm his number-one priority should be getting back on his feet.

"And Guide retorted, 'If I'm going to die anyway with my skull full of blood, I might as well work while I can for that slipshod friend of mine!'"

They walked around back of the main building, a half-Japanese half-Western affair under the dense foliage of a camphor tree, and came upon a building with white walls and Spanish-style roof tiles. The walls were thick, like the ones Kizu had seen in farmhouses in Mexico; the whole thing was built like a jail, with double-pane windows. They opened the heavy front door, and Kizu waited with Ikuo for Dancer. The sound of a similar heavy door was heard upstairs, a band of yellowish light shone on the white walls, and Dancer appeared, dressed in black tights and an ice-hockey shirt.

As he and Ikuo followed her, Kizu noticed that the steep stairs seemed out of character with the sense of open space the building imparted, and once they were upstairs and he looked back, the entrance where they'd removed their shoes seemed strangely far away. The spacious room that Kizu and Ikuo were shown into, lined as it was with bookshelves, looked like an academic's study. Guide was at the other end of the room, lying back on a raised chaise longue.

Dancer had Kizu and Ikuo sit down on a shiny white wooden platform with cushions on top. Guide's chaise longue, writing desk, and chair were all made of the same material. They were all simple yet solid looking.

After the initial introductions, Kizu looked around the room, and Guide, whose color looked perfectly healthy, said, " Professor, you're in charge of the art education department, I understand. I'm curious. What grade would you give this room, B minus? C plus?"

"Nothing that low. It's clear what you had in mind, and I like that."

"Guide designed the whole thing," Dancer put in, "and supervised the construction too. My dance studio's on the first floor."

"Architects were mostly all members of their high school art clubs and good with their hands, correct? I just helped out a bit in calculating construction costs."

"Shall I make the room brighter so you can see the details better?" Dancer asked as she stepped to the half-opened curtain.

"No," Guide said, stopping her. "It's fine the way it is."

"Is strong light bad for you?" Kizu asked.

"No, it's not that. I just thought you'd rather not see the scars from my operation."

Guide seemed to have a dark gray hood over half his forehead, though it may have just been a scarf wrapped around his head, the ends touching the collar of his sweater in back. He was a stylish man, belying what Kizu had heard. His features included a strong yet not too broad nose and a straight mustache that occupied a willful upper lip. A pair of equally neat eyebrows were raised upward, toward his covered forehead. He turned his large black shining eyes, the whites visible on both sides and below, toward Kizu.

"I understand from Ikuo, Professor, that you read about our apostasy in the newspapers in America. I find this interesting, since I've never heard the reactions of intellectuals to what we did."

"*The New York Times* reporter who wrote the articles about Patron and you is Jewish—you can tell from the name," Kizu said. "I don't want to oversimplify his level of knowledge, but he did bring up the name of Sabbatai Zevi, a seventeenth-century figure who announced he was the Jewish Messiah but who ended up being forcibly converted to Islam by the Turks. A colleague of mine, a historian of religions, told me that, despite Zevi's apostasy, his followers continued to believe in his teachings for many years afterward, in an area stretching from Turkey and Eastern Europe to Asia Minor all the way to Russia. This made me start to wonder whether, after your Somersault, there were followers who still believed in the teachings you'd renounced and, if so, whether you and Patron were able to ignore them."

"This is precisely the area I wanted to ask you about, Professor," Guide said, in a calm, strong tone. "Ten years ago Patron and I discarded not only our followers but our teachings. On national television Patron told our followers that what we preached was rubbish and he wanted them to stop their foolishness.

"Even when he's joking around, Patron is the kind of person who only speaks what he believes is the truth. We may have been driven into a corner by circumstances, but he wasn't compelled to say things he didn't believe were true.

"I was at his side as Patron frantically considered what to do, and I racked my brain as well. And I came to the conclusion that that's all we *could* do. We drove ourselves to the point where there was no other possible outcome. We were dead men then, you might say. Having done our Somersault, we were like the living dead.

"Everything before the Somersault vanished for us. It was as if we were amnesiacs, bereft of any traces of our former lives. Since we'd abandoned our faith, we were nothing more than living puppets. But even puppets suffer, you know. Patron felt this, and so did I. He called it falling into hell. I agree, but at no time during these ten years did we discuss what this hell consisted of. We lived together all that time but never spoke of what was really most important.

"After our Somersault we were, as I said before, like the living dead, but you might say we were hibernating. Like sick bears who may die in their cave at any moment. Patron is a complex person, and perhaps his inner experience was different. But I have never in my life experienced such a lazy decade, perhaps too lazy for our own good. If mental activity gets rid of cholesterol, our lack of activity alone was enough to make the blood vessels inside our brains so clogged they'd burst."

Dancer was standing beside Guide like a well-trained waiter, holding a flower-patterned tray level with her chest, on the tray a cup of water and various medicines. As Guide spoke about laziness, she shook her head ever so slightly from side to side. And when he paused and turned to pick up the cup of water, she rotated the tray so the pills were in front of him, as if to say, No water for you unless you take your medicine.

"What you said, Professor, is quite true," Guide said. "There are still some people who remain in the church, and some who've formed their own communal groups and continue to maintain their faith. Just before I went into the hospital, some of them got in touch with me; I had planned to meet with one group that's still within the church. I didn't tell Patron about this, but when I was released from the hospital I found out that he was communicating too, on a private level, with small groups who had written directly to him.

"We haven't talked about it yet, but it would seem that, now that a decade has gone by, Patron's thought processes and mine are leaning in the same direction. It makes me realize what happens when two people live so closely for so long.

"At the time of our Somersault, both Patron and I hoped that the church would disappear. But soon the Kansai branch became a nonprofit foundation and took over. They didn't pour their energy into attacking us for our apostasy. Instead, they concentrated on defending the organization by refuting all the criticisms and ridicule put out by the media. But one other group that became independent after the Somersault *did* denounce us. And some followers were left on their own and joined groups like Aum Shinrikyo and fundamentalist Christian groups. We received communications from those men and women, too, trying to win us over to their views.

"Understandably, those people's interest in us has dissipated over the past decade, and they've stopped writing. I have no idea what's become of them. The ones we know the most about are those who formed groups outside the church. One group, made up of women, continues to believe in Patron's teachings and, rather than criticize us, these women are trying to share our sin, if you view it as that, and the suffering that accompanies it. In fact, they see us as apostates falling into hell in order to atone for the sins of all mankind and thus summon forth salvation. They're praying for the day when we can escape our hell and return. Their prayers, I believe, consist of an attempt to visualize and truly comprehend this hell we're in. I don't know whether Patron was influenced by them to speak of us as falling into hell, or whether it was his original concept and they happened to hear of it and that's how they started speaking of it in those terms.

"Anyway, after ten years I was slowly but surely opening lines of communication with former believers, but I collapsed just as this opening became significant. Now that I've managed to survive and come home, I find Patron is beginning some new activities. The people he's plugged into, though, aren't former members, but people who got in touch with him only *after* the Somersault. What I find interesting is that both Patron and I see this ten-year period as a kind of turning point.

"I'm also fascinated by the idea of people continuing to believe in a false Messiah who's renounced his faith. There's the Kansai branch that's been going strong for a decade, and another group that wants to go back to the time of the Somersault and erase everything that happened. And then there are people eagerly awaiting Patron's return from the hell of apostasy. After all this time we can't just deny a connection with these men and women or with those who developed an interest in us more recently.

"I'd like to hear much more from you about this seventeenth-century Messiah and his apostasy. Would you talk to me as you did with Patron about English poetry? I know you'll need time to prepare; I'm in no hurry. It takes longer than ten years for our time in hell to end."

2

In the car on the way home, Kizu asked Ikuo, who'd been silent the whole time, what his impressions were.

"Even after I started working at the office I never had much chance to talk with Patron," Ikuo replied. "I'd heard him talk with Dancer and with Ogi, of course. When Guide was released from the hospital, though, and Dancer stayed behind to take care of the paperwork, I was alone with Guide, and later on I was asked to rearrange his room, and both times I was able to talk with him. He doesn't treat me merely as a driver hired to work there. Since he came home from the hospital he and Patron don't seem to be doing much together, but listening to him today it's clear how important Patron is to him.

"I'd rather ask you, Professor, what *you* think about them, since you've had good long talks with both of them. You said Patron has a lot of charisma, but what do you make of the way he doesn't resist being called *Patron?* Guide, I can understand—he's Patron's *guide,* and the guide for those who approach him."

Kizu admitted he did feel Patron was very charismatic, yet even though they were still continuing their discussions of R. S. Thomas, he didn't have enough to go on to give a proper response. As if he anticipated this, Ikuo continued, not waiting for the stammering Kizu to finish his reply.

"I believe you approached Patron, and later Guide, because you think it's risky for me to be working in their office. Which means it's nonsense for me to ask you this kind of question, I know. Still, I feel that by working alongside them I'm getting deeper into Patron, which is why I wanted to get your opinion. It's a spoiled streak in me, I know: getting more deeply involved with them because *I* want to and then making *you* get involved and relying on *you.*

"This is what I've been thinking: Ten years ago, Patron and Guide lost their faith. They said that all they'd taught up till then was one big joke. If we assume this wasn't some strategy or tactic directed against the authorities or the media, but was something they had to admit from the heart, will this new unexpected movement they're starting create a new kind of doctrine? Or will they say they were wrong to deny their old teachings, and then repent and go back to square one? It seems to me that the people waiting for Patron's next move aren't unanimous in their attitudes."

"I wonder," Kizu said. "At this moment I really can't say. It may seem a little standoffish of me, but to be perfectly frank my ulterior motive in coming to their office was so I could be with you. They're not men who will let me get away with that for long. But I am going to try to find out an answer to your questions, especially about Patron."

The day after this conversation with Ikuo, Kizu, egged on by his own words, went over to the office for the first time without being invited. He didn't accompany Ikuo in the minivan—Ikuo had left early in the morning—but drove over in his Mustang after finishing his daily quota of painting.

It was past the dinner hour when Kizu arrived at the office, but when he parked his car in the hollow of shrubbery next to the gate, the front door was already open and someone was looking out at him. When Kizu went in, he found Ogi standing there, the front door wide open.

"You're expecting someone?" Kizu said in greeting. Ogi nodded and, though they hadn't spoken very loudly, motioned for Kizu to keep his voice down.

Ogi's voice was subdued. "Ikuo drove Dancer to get the doctor."

That's all he said. He slipped past Kizu to shut the front door noiselessly. Having lived in America so long, Kizu didn't pay much attention to the sound of doors opening and closing, but he realized Ogi was taking care not to slam it.

Guide had come over to the front office from his attached building. He wore an expensive cardigan with a frayed collar over his shirt and sat on the sofa on the garden side of the room, lost in thought. Ogi went back to the office to take care of some e-mail, and Kizu settled down on the edge of the sofa at a right angle to Guide.

As if Kizu were someone who belonged in this room and he himself did not, Guide nodded a tentative greeting. Then, noticing that Kizu was at loose ends, Guide turned his hood-covered bird-of-prey head to him.

"Patron is in a kind of state right now. It's not one of his deep trances, but something close to it. In the past we would have considered this a preliminary. Perhaps it's a prelude to his first deep trance in ten years, I don't know. It started early this morning, so it's been going on for over ten hours now. He hasn't been this way for so long, we thought it best to send for the doctor. Dancer has gone to fetch him."

Kizu had heard about these trances, and just learning that Patron might be close to being in one was enough to put him on edge. He said nothing, just looked at Guide as he continued.

"Would you agree to see him in this condition? Dancer has some plan for you to draw his portrait, so it could also be of help. Anyhow, it's something you'll never see anywhere else."

"I barely know him. Do you think it's all right?" Kizu asked.

"As long as you don't make any noise, it'll be okay. Loud sounds seem to hurt him. In his condition now he's not completely gone over to the other side, but even so . . . Dancer had never seen him in this condition before and was beside herself; she couldn't drag herself away so I thought it best to send her for the doctor." Ogi looked up in their direction, and Guide said to him, "I'm going to take Professor Kizu in."

Guide led the way down the dim hallway and instructed Kizu to sit down next to the empty bed in his usual spot on the wooden chair, lit in the faint glow of a bedside lamp; Guide himself sat down on the middle of the bed. His actions were matter-of-fact, yet Kizu thought that even if this wasn't a deep trance Patron must be absorbed in something heavy and mystical that he'd never been privy to before. Still, when his eyes adjusted to the darkness he was shocked at what he saw.

Kizu knew there was a low chair Patron used for reading, and a straight-backed chair across from him that he himself used whenever they read poetry together. What he saw now on the low chair was Patron, legs resting on a stool the height of two shoe boxes, head stuck deep between his widespread knees, arms hanging straight down on each side, unmoving.

Patron's face was hidden, the delicate nape of his neck covered tightly with a white collar, a jacket half slipping down his rounded back. Kizu remembered seeing that gray jacket during their midnight poetry sessions, but the clothes he had on now were brand new. Perhaps he had several sets. Wearing fine clothes must be a habit he picked up in his former days as an eager missionary. Another thought struck Kizu; namely, that Patron wore these brand-new clothes because he *knew* a deep trance was coming on.

Could this state really be only a preliminary? Patron seemed totally absorbed. He held his body in a way you would never expect from a living human being. He sat there, utterly still, every semblance of humanity gone, as if he were carved out of wood or wrought out of metal.

"He's held this position for over ten hours?" Kizu whispered. "Isn't it painful?"

"He doesn't seem to feel any pain. But physically there may be some damage. You know, like when kids bite their lips before the anesthetic wears off at the dentist."

"Why isn't this considered a deep trance?"

"He's too calm. In a deep trance his body moves. Before he goes into a deep trance he acts like this for a short while, and then it's as though he's tossing and turning in his sleep. That's the usual pattern. Only when something prevents him from going into a deep trance is he like this, as if he's in a chrysalis, for such a long time."

The two of them kept their voices down. Even after they stopped talking, they stayed leaning close to each other, gazing at this unnatural shape in front of them, an object it would be difficult to call a living thing. Guide cleared his throat as if sighing and spoke in a low yet distinct voice. Once, he said, they had had a doctor, a specialist, measure Patron before and after a trance using some specialized equipment. This was twelve or thirteen years ago, done at the request of a TV network. Patron's brain waves and EKG were incredibly calm, his breathing and pulse barely detectable. For a person to have readings at this level and still be alive, the specialist explained, was truly remarkable.

"What about when he's in a trance?" Kizu asked.

"We couldn't attach any measuring instruments," Guide said. "His movements are so violent that after a deep trance he's completely spent, physically and emotionally. After he's come back, he says all sorts of complex things, as if he's possessed. He says he's standing in front of a kind of three-dimensional mesh, a display screen on which a blur of light is continuously changing, receiving information.

"Patron seems to confront some kind of white glowing object. When you look at him when he's like this, it's as if his body is reacting to each bit of information he's receiving, moving constantly, never static. It's too much to bear. When I try to help him interpret all this, I realize the amount and quality of information he receives is amazing. That's one of his real trances. His fate is to have this very rare ability. This might sound exaggerated, but Patron can freely view the entire course of human history and experience every last detail. He traces it all with his own body. He conveys to us what he's learned about the history of mankind and even its future, speaking to us—in the *present*—of the end time."

"What is this blur of light you mentioned?"

"As someone who's listened to what Patron says after he returns from his trances, transmitting what that's all about is my job." Saying this, Guide, who'd been listening to some inner voice, now lifted his head as if to turn his ear to sounds from the world outside.

Kizu heard a car pull up and stop in the road beyond the garden, and several people came quietly into the residence.

"Dancer will take over now," Guide said. "I'll see you home, Professor. Ikuo will have to come back later, so I can ride with you and we can talk some more."

Guide turned once again to the thing, sitting there like a strangely twisted statue, and then faced Kizu. His eyes now adjusted to the dark, Kizu could read the strong emotions rising to the surface in Guide's face. His expression held, at one and the same time, a fierce penetrating look and a look that could have been either pity or love.

Kizu was about to stand up after Guide when a small, sunburned energetic old doctor came in—a *minitank of a man,* to use a phrase that Kizu and his friends had used when they were boys—together with Dancer. Ignoring their bows, the doctor strode right up to Patron, peered at him, and faced Dancer.

"It's exactly the same as in the past," the doctor said, in a nostalgic tone. "If he's been this way until now, he'll be okay. But he might have one of his deep trances, so I'll sleep here tonight in his bed. I'll keep an eye on him, but I'm sure he'll be fine."

3

"About these deep trances again, you said that Patron sees a net that shows the entire history of the human race?" Kizu had had them park his Mustang in the garage and was now in the minivan, with Ikuo at the wheel and Guide alongside him. "No matter how big this white blur of light is, wouldn't individual people, and the groups they form, be no bigger than a cell? Or is this just some kind of metaphor, a model for a certain historical perspective?"

"It's neither a metaphor nor a model," Guide replied. (At that instant, Kizu caught an unexpected whiff of alcohol. Later, when asked, Ikuo said Guide only drank occasionally.) "No matter how minute something might be, Patron actually *sees* it. A cell can't be seen by the naked eye, but can you use physical parameters to measure what the visionary eye detects? Patron sees the entire world, from the beginning of time to the very end, as *one whole vision*.

"Inside that would be included, as one particle, you, on the verge of making an important decision about your life, and me, talking here with you. Both present as eternal moments."

"If I were counting on death to help me escape myself," Kizu said, "that net would indeed be a kind of hell."

"I don't believe Patron is viewing hell in his visions," Guide replied seriously. "It's not as if he chooses what to see, as if he's purposefully interpreting a satellite photograph, but rather that he's grasping the entire structure of this huge net of blurred white light. That's the stance he takes, I think, when he's in a trance.

"After one of his major trances, Patron talked with me about that. It's not like the blur of light is projected out in space but more like a bottomless hollow. The entire hollow is a kind of spinning and weaving net, and the net with its countless layers is a screen that reveals human existence in one fell swoop, from its beginning to its end, and each point on that net is moving forward. It covers everything from the origins of time—nothing other than the first signs of the Big Bang to come—to the time when everything flows back to the one ultimate being. That whole huge spinning hollow, Patron told me, you could call God. In other words, as he sits there with his head between his knees like a weighed-down fetus, he's about to embark on a trance in which he'll come face-to-face with that God."

"If that's what God is, it's just another way of saying there *is* no God." Ikuo's eyes looked straight forward as he drove, his taut shoulders, twice the size of Patron's, filled with the tension of his remark.

"What do you mean, there is no God?" Guide asked him back.

"Saying that God is this hollow of the whole world is the same thing as saying there isn't any God, right?"

"But by saying that God is this hollow you're admitting there *is* a God."

"That might be true of people who accept that huge hollow and think it's enough," Ikuo said, "but for people who don't, it's the same as saying there is no God."

"For *you*, in other words."

"That's right. For me there is no God."

"I detect here something other than an abstract debate over the existence of God. What really concerns you is whether God is actively working *in your life* or not."

"That's right, you got it," Ikuo admitted candidly, still stubborn.

Guide didn't say anything. Kizu couldn't intervene in their argument. For a while Ikuo drove on, the three of them silent. Kizu caught another whiff of alcohol and noticed that Guide was hiding a small flask of whiskey in his coat pocket. Guide cleared his throat lightly and spoke.

"One sure thing, though, is that the white blur of light Patron confronts in his trances has decided the course of his life."

"If I confronted a God who's some huge hollow," Ikuo said, "well, I can tell you I wouldn't accept his deciding my life."

"Isn't this God that Patron senses in a holistic way, then, also the God you believe can speak to you directly?" Kizu asked. "Soon after I met you, Ikuo, I felt you were thinking about God as the power to grasp *yourself*. And I hoped that your notion of God would be like a passage enabling you to find an entrance to Patron's vast deep vision: namely, the God he confronts in his trances. Is the God that Ikuo's thinking of just one part of the all-embracing God that Patron sees?"

"It wouldn't fit Patron's definition of God to say one *part* of God," Guide said. "I spoke of a passage, but I think of it as a bundle of fiber-optic lines, with Ikuo on this side, at the terminus of one line, wondering if he can send a signal to the other side, the terminus of all the lines—in other words, to the enormous structure that is God."

"If there's a terminus on the other side, and an infinite number of them on this side, is it really possible that God would send a message directly to me?" Ikuo asked.

Guide was silent as he thought about it. The swaying of the speeding minivan made his head rock back and forth. Kizu could see he was fairly drunk by now, though he didn't let his drunkenness take over when he spoke.

"This might be a self-centered way of approaching it," Ikuo said, "but I think the only way to experience God is when the signal comes from his side to ours. Once his voice came to me and I did what it said, but afterward, when there was no response, there was no other way to meet God but to wait for his signal."

Ikuo stared straight ahead as he drove, his voice no longer angry, as it was a moment before, but filled with a sorrow that pierced Kizu to the quick. Guide might have felt the same way, for he spoke now in a more formal way. "Ikuo, have you spoken to Patron about this?"

"No. I've only just started working as his driver, and I haven't had a chance. Also, I think if I don't prepare myself before I talk with him, he'll end up having nothing more to do with me."

"But you came to work for Patron because you expected someday he might fulfill this longing you have toward God, right?"

"That's right. I met Dancer through a connection we had from before, but I felt Patron has the power to help us transcend our limits—something not unrelated to God."

Ikuo's words were not entirely unexpected, yet as he listened to this earnest confession Kizu was surprised and sympathetic.

"If that's the case, you should tell Patron exactly how you feel," Guide said to Ikuo, speaking the exact words of encouragement Kizu had been about to use. "Right now it would appear that Patron is laying the groundwork for a major vision, the kind that has eluded him for so long. At the next opportunity he may be able to interpret God's message to you in that blurred net of light. I'll call it *your God* for the time being, but there's no contradiction between that and Patron's all-inclusive God."

Kizu didn't quite follow Guide's final words. Ikuo went back to the first remarks, to make sure of what was most critical to him.

"Why would that be significant for me? Is it okay for me to think that he's interpreting a message from the God who once called out to me and was silent afterward?"

"What's wrong with that? With Patron trying to undergo a deep trance for the first time in so long, this may be an encouragement to him. Your questions to Patron may spur him on."

"But if that happened, would it be a good thing?"

"If *what* happened?"

"If I happened to give him a push that affected the way he's living his life."

"You're afraid as an outsider you may have an influence on Patron? Rather than an old person like *me* influencing him, it may very well need to be a young person who's struggling, working beside him, searching for the way. *The poor in spirit.* That would be you, all right. Though I've always seen you as the opposite type."

Guide was clearly drunk by now, but Ikuo pressed on.

"I don't want to hear Patron telling me some story just to make me happy."

"Patron isn't that clever," Guide said. "It's more likely the opposite. If you help him find his direction and give him a shove, that'll be his way of putting his life back together. Right now Patron's beginning a new movement. It's actually been my hope that with his newfound desire to be active again, a young person like yourself who takes these things to heart would give him a shove in the right direction. Speaking from experience, though, once you get deeply involved with Patron, you won't come out unscathed. There's no way to avoid being influenced."

"So what should I do?" Ikuo asked. "If I were to sit down face-to-face with him, I wouldn't be able to say a thing. Committing a terrorist act would be a whole lot easier."

"Summon up the courage to appeal to him," Guide said. "Right now, Patron is awakening from his preparations for a vision, and the physical and emotional aftereffects will last for some time. But once he's over that, let's tell him your thoughts. Professor Kizu will help us too, won't you?"

Even though he was speeding along in the dark at eighty miles an hour, Ikuo turned around to Kizu and spoke in an urgent, almost pushy, tone.

"Please write a letter for me, explaining why I need to talk with Patron. I haven't revealed everything to you, Professor, but still I'd like you to write the letter."

7: A Sacred Wound

1

Patron had taken to his bed to recuperate and now, five days later, he was allowed to return to normal activities. In the evening, while Dancer was helping him take a bath, Ogi took a phone call from Guide in his annex.

Patron's bathroom was like a greenhouse, a brightly lit wing built onto the north side of his bedroom study. Patron liked to take long soaks in his roomy Western-style tub. Cordless phone in hand, Ogi called to him from just outside the changing room. There wasn't any sound of running water, but no one seemed to have heard him, so he stepped inside the changing room and stood facing the open door to the bathroom, going too far to turn back.

The first thing Ogi saw was Patron stretched out in the bottom of the nearly empty tub that lay at right angles to his line of sight. Dancer abruptly cut off his view as she slipped in from the side and leaned her nude body over the edge of the tub; she had a detachable shower hose in her right hand. Her head seemed bulky with her hair piled high, and she cast a piercing glare at Ogi from upside down. She didn't try to hide anything; her legs were spread wide on the tiles. With her magnificent body, then, she was trying to hide Patron's naked form. Ogi placed the phone down on the threshold and retreated. Guess even the changing room's off limits to me! he thought, finding it comical and yet disturbing.

Dancer soon appeared, neatly dressed, in front of Ogi's desk.

"I guess there's nothing we can do now that you saw it," she said, in a sort of affected calm, "but I would appreciate your not saying anything to Ikuo, Ms. Tachibana, or, of course, Professor Kizu."

She turned her back on him, her rump tightly sheathed in her skirt, and walked to the kitchen; after a time, she came back, her tongue visible between her slightly parted lips.

"You saw the wound in Patron's side, right? When I said *you saw it* a moment ago, what did you think I was talking about?"

Dancer said this very quickly and then gazed at Ogi silently, her face flushed with anger.

"When you wash a man's body, you have to undress yourself, right? If you think I was reproaching you for looking between my legs, I don't know what to say! When animals aren't in heat, their genitals aren't even genitals really, are they? Which goes double for humans! You're no longer the innocent you once were. I thought you'd grown up a little!"

Dancer twirled her high waist in an about-face to the right and set off again to the kitchen to prepare a late dinner for Patron, Guide, Ogi, and herself.

Ogi felt numbed with a vague coldness as he rested his face in his hands. He lowered his eyes to some documents on his desk, but he couldn't concentrate on the words. I *saw* it, he thought, and I *did* turn away as fast as I could, didn't I? Didn't I try to erase what I saw as much as I could? Despite what went on with Mrs. Tsugane, I set my gaze on Dancer's fleshy genitals! But I did see it, and can see it still—that reddish dark *thing* on the upper part of Patron's chubby white left side.

Back when Patron was made the leader of the church, did he already have that red gouged-out pomegranate-shaped wound in his side? That wasn't a scar but an open *wound*, with fresh blood oozing out. Ten years ago when he did his Somersault, was the wound like that? Or did it appear in the decade that followed? Or maybe it opened up only now that he's starting a religious movement again? At any rate, Ogi thought, now I've seen something I never imagined I would—the strangest of wounds.

2

The following week was a busy one for Ogi. The reason lay in that phone call he'd answered from Guide to Patron, the urgent call that led to all those complications. Guide had told him over the phone that he wanted to have a chance to talk with Patron.

The doctor had recommended, as part of his recovery, that Patron take a short trip for a change of scenery, so Patron decided to take the three young people, Ikuo, Dancer, and Ogi, on a trip outside Tokyo. Preparations fell to

Ogi. He got in touch with his mother for the first time in a long while and had her send him the keys to their cottage in Nasu Plateau—the place where he first saw Mrs. Tsugane. Ms. Tachibana dropped by the office on a day off from work at the library—she was planning to quit the job someday—and Ogi decided their trip should take place on Saturday and Sunday, when Ms. Tachibana could take care of the office for them the whole day.

They set off from Tokyo in the minivan, Ikuo at the wheel, late on Friday night. They'd chosen this late departure to avoid any traffic jams, but soon found themselves side by side with eighteen-wheelers that monopolized the highway. The minivan was comically puny compared to these mammoth trucks, but with Ikuo's bold driving, not once did any trucker behind them blare his horn to hound them to let him by. Even when they left behind the satellite cities that ringed Tokyo, the highway was still lit by streetlights, the inside of the minivan darker than the outside. Patron was sitting directly behind Ikuo, Dancer beside him, with Ogi in the rear seat, which allowed him to view everyone else from the back.

Ogi wanted to take a good long look at these three people, the core group of Patron's new movement—minus Guide, of course—and as he looked at their shoulders and the backs of their heads, he was struck by emotions he'd never felt before, a combined sense of how strange it all was and how thrilling.

Ogi was indeed drawn to this elderly man, fast asleep like a worn-out teddy bear, his large head fallen back; even though Ogi was working for him, he still didn't understand the part of Patron that was on a quest for spiritual matters. Ten years ago, Patron had denied all the teachings he was working so hard to disseminate and had renounced his church. And now, even though he was starting a new movement, he still hadn't shown them any new teachings to take the place of the old. And here was this unknown factor—Ikuo —seeking to talk about spiritual matters with Patron. What sort of fate could possibly have brought Ogi together with these people as fellow voyagers? That he was with them was a fact, but each day it was one unexpected thing after another. Add eccentric Dancer to the mix, and Ogi had a premonition that this group was about to take him on the ride of his life.

The country house to which Ogi was taking Patron and the others was part of a large parcel of land his grandfather had originally obtained when the Nasu Plateau area was first developed, which had remained in their family ever since. When they arrived at dawn it was still dark, with low-lying clouds, and through a line of barren trees they could see two or three other villas. The Ogi family's place, though, a large Western-style home, stood alone in a desolate spot. It seemed different from his memories of childhood summer vacations. . . .

They decided that Ogi would go up to the villa alone to open it, while Patron and the others stayed in the minivan they'd parked on the road below; the ground rose up on either side of the road, which lay below a dried-up grassy slope. After checking the lights and the water and switching on the propane gas heater next to the stove, Ogi looked down through the cloudy window. The barren forest surrounding the building was an old one, with huge gnarled trees; some trunks that had been cruelly felled by a typhoon were scattered about. Ogi began to regret bringing Patron to such a cold, forbidding place.

Before long Dancer ran up to the house to get it ready and told him she'd give a signal when the house was warm, so Ogi walked back down to the minivan. For the first time ever, he found Patron and Ikuo engaged in a friendly conversation. Ogi boarded the warm minivan in time to hear Patron say, "It's not exactly a desolate wilderness, but with the woods like this, after the leaves have fallen and before the snows, it does have that feeling. The place I went to in my visions was like this."

Ikuo seemed surprised. "Guide told me it was more like a dreamy atmosphere."

"Guide was almost always the first person I talked to when my visions were finished and I returned to this side, so his impression of what it was like may very well be just as accurate. The sense *I* had of it, though, was like being in a desolate place like this, confronting that blurred white light. Since it was painful to go from the *other side* back to this side, as painful as dying, I imagine, I suppose it's a bit of a contradiction to say that the *other side* is a more bitter, desolate place than this side."

"I had the impression that Guide always spoke of your visionary world in bright, cheery terms."

"Whenever I come back from the *other side* I talk about what I saw there in a kind of delirious way, and Guide listens and explains it all in a logical way. What he says stuns me."

"How could that be possible? You're stunned by hearing your own experiences told back to you?"

"It's entirely possible," Patron replied spiritedly, turning an amused look first at Ikuo, then at Ogi.

"You take leave of reality, go over to the *other side,* and accept the spiritual, right?" Ikuo said. "How can you be stunned by hearing about what you yourself saw?"

"Maybe that's the fate involved in using language to speak and to listen, especially when you're dealing with transcendental matters. There's no direct connection between the visions I see in my trances and our language on this side. If I wanted to go over to the *other side* permanently, all I'd have to do would be to immerse myself in experiences that have nothing to do with language on this side. Being immersed like that is how God reveals Himself; it's everything to me.

"Still, I suffer tremendously to return to this side. There wouldn't be any problems if I stayed silent after I came back, but that would be as if what I experienced on the *other side* never took place. Guide's the one who told me I couldn't leave it at that and encouraged me to put my experiences into words. Often when I listen to Guide retelling my experiences, though, I feel he's unearthed deeper meaning to them than I ever realized. He definitely is my guide when it comes to making this mystical world clear to me. But I do sometimes feel uncomfortable with it. That's what I mean by saying I feel stunned."

There was more they seemed to want to say, but they fell silent for a time. Ogi sensed a movement out the van window and discovered Dancer out on the porch, doing a pirouette leap—her signal that the villa had warmed up enough to come inside.

3

The living room had the very latest propane heater—a device with self-regulating temperature and a gas leak detector—as well as a wood-burning fireplace, and it was there the three young people had a breakfast of ham, bacon, eggs, and vegetable salad the next morning. Dancer put away as much as the two young men. Patron's breakfast consisted of liquid food, appropriate to an elderly convalescent, that Dancer had brought along from Tokyo in a thermos. Once they were free of the day-to-day routine of the office, Ogi was struck by how very simple a matter it was to satisfy Patron's worldly desires. The same, of course, could be said of Guide.

After eating, they all went out for a walk. Before they left the villa, Dancer made Patron prepare for the winter cold by wearing an overcoat over his sweater and a long muffler that trailed down to his knees. The clouds hung lower than one would expect on a high plain, and it felt like the first snow of the season was just around the corner. Ogi took Patron's arm to help him along, but Patron soon said he needed time alone to think and strode aloofly off ahead of them.

The three young people walked behind Patron, keeping their distance, Ogi first, with Ikuo and Dancer side by side after him. Ikuo had taken out a folding wheelchair from the minivan and, with the chair still folded up, pushed it along, Dancer helping him.

Dancer had recommended that they buy the wheelchair after Guide had collapsed and it looked like he wouldn't soon recover. After he left the hospital, though, Guide had no need of it, and it had been stored in the outbuilding and then loaded into the minivan. Patron was descending the gentle slope now with a healthy stride, but coming back he'd have the uphill slope to face and might be glad to use the chair. Dancer took all possible precautions when it came to Patron's health.

"I felt closer to Guide at first, but there was something I couldn't quite grasp about him," Dancer said to Ikuo, loud enough for Ogi, two or three paces ahead, to hear. "I don't know anything about what happened more than ten years ago. I've been thinking about this since I came to live with Patron and Guide and observe them up close. Guide always seems to be urging Patron to do things, but once it seems that his words and actions are actually influencing Patron's judgment and actions, he immediately pulls back. I find his hesitation hard to fathom.

"I don't have anything to base this on, but I came up with a guess. I'm not saying that Patron was led into doing the Somersault by Guide, but maybe Guide did have an influence on Patron's decision. With this talk you're planning to have with Patron, didn't you say you wanted to talk without Professor Kizu and Guide around? Even if Professor Kizu couldn't make the trip because of his health, I wonder if Guide didn't think it better that he not be there since you and Patron had some important things to discuss. That must be the reason he didn't come, despite that long phone call and the fact that he urged you to go ahead and talk with Patron."

"It was Guide who encouraged me to bring my main concerns directly to Patron," said Ikuo, who had been silent up to this point.

Ogi sensed something, turned around, and saw Dancer twist to turn around to face Ikuo, who was a head taller than she was. In a very sharp tone of voice she said, "You're free to voice your own concerns, but whatever Patron tells you should be shared with all of us. Patron isn't going to give you a hint for you alone; he will indicate the direction *all* of us should be taking. Don't forget that!"

Dancer had clearly had her say; she began to walk more quickly in order to shorten the distance between herself and Patron. Urged on, Ogi and Ikuo picked up the pace. It was a simple matter for the young men and Dancer, with her gymnastic training, to catch up with Patron. He had stopped at the side of the road where raised earth marked the boundary of the older residential section of the area; across from him was a paved road and a slope running downhill and, even farther down the slope, a newer residential area that he was now gazing at. Dancer may have cut her conversation with Ikuo short because she noticed where Patron was standing.

A broad deep expanse of snow-covered mountains lay before them. On this side ran the line of woods that this morning had seemed desolate; bathed in the faint sunlight, the woods now had a gentle reddish-yellow tinge. The whole scene gave the impression that both people and trees had finished their preparations for the day, fast approaching, when snow would blanket ground and woods, and the far-off mountains would become one continuous stretch of white.

As the three of them reached the bundled-up Patron, he turned grace-fully toward them in his expensive boots at the sound of Dancer's voice and she briskly helped him into the wheelchair. Standing at the tip of that old road sloping down, their backs to it, they could feel the wind whipping up the slope, carrying with it a hint of cold air from the snow-covered mountains in the distance. At this season this was an appropriate spot to end their walk, and all of them understood it was the proper time to begin pushing Patron back up the hill. With her quick, unsparing way of working, Dancer was the per-fect attendant.

4

By six it was already dark. Patron had slept during the day and then eaten dinner in bed, and Dancer urged him to stay in bed for the time being. Their group discussion, then, began at little after seven. The young people lit the wood in the fireplace, set an armchair in front of it for Patron, and settled down directly on an electric blanket they placed on the rug. They didn't face Patron directly, and as he stared into the fireplace, they followed suit, listen-ing intently and gazing at the flames. Ikuo had used a saw to cut up some of the pine, light brown birches, and cherry trees that had toppled over in the typhoon into six-foot-long logs, but couldn't find a hatchet to chop them into smaller pieces.

"I understand Guide suggested that you talk directly with me, Ikuo," Patron began. "He phoned me from his annex to tell me this. The fact that he didn't come to see me directly is a sign that he has something in mind. Professor Kizu, too, sent me a letter outlining the background to your ques-tions, that your motivation for getting close to Guide and me can be traced to a desire you've had ever since you were a young boy. He wrote that you're a young man with something very special inside, and that if talking with me is needed to bring that to the surface, he wants to do what he can to help out.

"So it's obvious that Professor Kizu thinks you're a pretty special person. Dancer tells me that my answers to you shouldn't be for you alone, but for all of you, Dancer and Ogi included. In other words, whatever I say is connected to the movement I'm about to launch. In Guide's case, however, there's a separate issue at stake. Guide sympathizes with you, Ikuo, and the difficult questions you have, which is why he's advising you. I know him very well, though, and I know that can't be all there is to it.

"Guide is making the following proposal to me *through* you, Ikuo: *In the past, God called to this young man. And I want you, for the sake of this young man, to act as intermediary to revive God's call to him.*

"Guide is throwing up a challenge to me. He's also proposing that we try once more to do an important job that he and I weren't able to complete in the past. How this will come about, he's leaving up to me. According to Professor Kizu's letter, the God that appeared to you, Ikuo, told you to *do* something, and though you were still a child then, you waited with all your might to see what God wanted you to *do*. But you waited in vain.

"This is similar to the time before our Somersault, when Guide wanted me to act as intermediary between God and the radical sect he created. Around the time our church was getting established and really beginning to grow, he gathered a group of elite young people and created a place where they could freely conduct their research—his own special vanguard, in other words. Doesn't it seem now as if he's singling you out, hoping to raise you up as a firm believer, as a kind of replacement for the sect? What I need to know is what fundamental difference Guide sees between then and now, between you and the radical faction in Izu.

"In the past we used to have these kinds of heavy discussions as he tried to grasp the vision I saw in my trance. Right now I've come back from an unsuccessful attempt to enter into a deep trance—my first in a decade. Guide tells me this is a preliminary to the return of those trances of old.

"I don't know yet what form it will take, but I've taken the first steps toward starting a new movement. Guide is essential to this, but you young people are also crucial. This is why I responded to Ikuo's appeal and asked you three to travel with me.

"I'd like to tell you young people about what Guide and I used to do in the old days and how our Somersault came about. Until we abandoned our movement, what was it I preached to our followers? In a nutshell, it was my hope that the world be filled with people who repent what's happened to our world, because that is the only way for life to be restored to our planet. In the visions I had in my trances, I grasped how to do this. The sect that Guide created came up with tactics for accomplishing this, tactics that would forcibly drag people with us until everyone realized the kind of future mankind was facing.

"I can't deny that that's the direction in which I led the church. *Those who can envision the end of the world, the end time, will, in the near future, create an actual crisis that will be a productive opportunity for repentance; those people are out there,* I said in my sermons. This is the point at which the sect Guide created rose to prominence within the church—working to bring about a crisis that would lead everyone to immediate repentance and preparing the methods and shock troops to carry it out.

"Up till the stage where the ideology behind this young elite sect in Izu was set, Guide and I worked in harmony. Once the whole body of believers accepted the Izu sect's ideas, and the shock troops that would initiate a crisis grew until they had the power to destroy an entire city, then my sermons anticipating a crisis would take on a real sense of power. Guide wasn't the only one who believed this; I did too.

"The reason I preached about making my visions of the end of the world a reality is that I wanted the people who live on this planet to have the courage to face that crisis, while they still had the energy to be restored to life out of the ruins that, even then, were already appearing. What would be the point of having the human race repent en masse if they didn't have the courage or energy to *do* anything about it? That was my doctrine, and this was supposed to be the source of the orders for whatever actions the church was about to take."

This is a sermon in itself, Ogi thought. The sense of emotional tension that came across struck him as incongruous, so much so that he felt like interrupting Patron to say, *Hey! I'm not one of your believers, I just work here!* Though he was, of course, up to his ears in helping Patron restart his religious activities. What did Dancer think about all this? Just as this thought occurred to Ogi, Dancer interrupted Patron, though what she said didn't answer Ogi's unspoken question.

"Ogi and I have heard all this before from Guide," she said. "He painted a vivid picture of what the end of the world looks like in visions. Isn't that right?" Ogi, suddenly urged to agree, nodded but felt uneasy about how Patron would interpret his assent. "We've all read newspaper articles about overpopulation, our lack of resources, and the destruction of the environment, but the images that Guide painted for us really struck us to the core. They were heartrending. Guide told us you have profound visions, which you describe in a torrent of words. He also told us he feels a great anxiety as he interprets these visions, anxiety about whether or not he's getting them right."

"It's not that I *see* visions," Patron said, "but rather that I'm *assaulted* by them, and the question then is how to convey this to people. The only way I could put them into some sort of logical language was through Guide's help. He's the one who understands better than I—at the linguistic level—what my visions are all about."

"But it seems to me *you're* the one who established the basic system of the church," Dancer said. "Guide told me, too, that it might be impossible to convey the whole of your visions in language people can understand. Mankind faces a cruel future, is at a dead end, staring at a wall; as long as people don't have a way to scale that wall, they'll never understand the depths of the crisis they're in. People are really good at ignoring danger. The task for your church was to bring the end of the world closer, to let people actually *see* it. How was this supposed to happen? The only alternative was to present a model of this crisis to force people to repent. The tactics of the Izu radical faction were to precipitate this crisis, radically and concretely. That's what Guide said. Patron has just spoken of this, but the point I'm trying to make is that the two of them were in agreement at that time."

Ogi decided that Dancer's long interruption was a tactic of her own to give Patron a break from doing all the talking. But it also worked to encourage the others to speak up, and now Ikuo raised a question.

"Setting aside the issue of the Izu radical faction and their gaining power in the church, if Patron's visions were the basis for the church's teachings, wasn't that doctrine correct and isn't it *still* correct? I mean, during the past ten years this crisis hasn't been resolved, has it? So why was it necessary at the time of the Somersault to deny these teachings? You and Guide announced that it was all nonsense, right?"

Sitting in a faded purple chair that Ogi remembered from childhood, Patron shifted to face Ikuo. As if to put a stop to this, Dancer spoke up.

"If you're going to talk about Patron's state of mind at the time of the Somersault, then all of us—since we weren't present at the time—need to consider the background. Don't you agree, Ikuo? The elite group that Guide created was already acting on its own, trying to bring ordinary people face-to-face with what Patron envisioned in his trances. When they got the idea to move the whole church body in that direction, the radical sect went ahead and took action, attempting to get the entire church implicated. Although the church's attitude wasn't yet set, the radical faction went ahead with its adventurist schemes."

Ikuo still didn't give up trying to speak directly to Patron. "I was still basically a child," he said, "when I saw the whole Somersault affair on TV. Your announcement seemed like one more in a long string of jokes. This was right after Chernobyl, and I remember being upset, thinking it was absolutely insane to intentionally try to cause an accident like that. But I was also agitated by the thought that God had told the radical faction to *Do it*."

"If it was really God telling the radical faction to act, they wouldn't have collapsed so easily," Dancer said, not giving Patron a chance to respond. "With the information that Patron and Guide gave the authorities at the time of their Somersault, the radical faction's shock troops were arrested on their way to the nuclear power facility at Mount Fuji and their intentions for the plant came to light; the authorities, though, downplayed the scale of what they were planning. Once power was brought to bear on the situation, in other words, the whole thing was treated as a farce. Guide told me that since it would have been too much for the government to admit the existence of a sophisticated plan to blow up nuclear power plants, they treated it as a crude, childish idea as a way of defusing any concerns the public might have. And what was particularly effective in this effort to downplay and mock the plans—as you are well aware, Ikuo—was Patron and Guide's Somersault, that comical TV performance."

As Ogi saw it, Ikuo's question to Patron was at the heart of what really concerned the young man. He didn't think Patron, having undertaken this short trip to the cottage, could very well refuse to answer, nor could he understand why Dancer insisted so strongly on blocking Patron's reply. Ogi was just about to summon up his courage and tell Dancer to let them hear what Patron had to say when the phone rang.

The phone was in the dining room, next to the spacious living room with its fireplace; to keep the heat in during the winter the glass door between the two rooms was kept closed. The ringing startled them. It was not yet 9 P.M., but all the surrounding houses were shut up and the silence of the high plain was more like the middle of the night. Ogi stood up to answer the phone and noticed that Patron looked particularly tense.

The caller wasn't unexpected—Ms. Tachibana, who was taking care of things back at the office—but what she had to say *was*. Several former members of the church were scheduled to visit Guide that evening, and he'd told Ms. Tachibana not to prepare any meal for them but to just serve tea; if they showed up after she went home she should lay out the tea things before leaving. He also told her that if Dancer called on their way to Nasu Plateau, Ms. Tachibana wasn't to say anything about Guide's having visitors.

The visitors didn't come while Ms. Tachibana was at the office, so she went ahead and followed the recipes Dancer left her and made dinner for Guide, whose diet had been restricted ever since he fell ill. After arranging the dinner on the dining table, Ms. Tachibana left to return to the college town where her brother was waiting in their apartment. Around eight o'clock she began to worry about the visitors and phoned the annex to tell Guide to leave the dirty cups and dishes for her to wash later, but there was no response. She called the office in the main building, but still no answer. She was so worried she thought she would go back to Seijo, despite the late hour.

Ogi hesitated to report what Ms. Tachibana had told him where Patron could overhear it. Patron—pressed to respond to Ikuo—was still excited in a cold, melancholy way. He didn't ask Ogi about the call but was obviously preoccupied with some unfortunate things that could happen, or might have already happened, to Guide. Patron watched silently as Ikuo rearranged the remaining logs in the fireplace.

It was impossible now to continue their discussion, so Ogi just waited for another phone call as Dancer gave Patron some sleeping pills and tranquilizers and went with him to his bedroom. Ikuo was dissatisfied, of course, at having to cut their conversation short, but since Patron had not fully recovered from his physical and emotional exhaustion, there was nothing they could do.

Dancer had her hands full taking care of Patron, so it was left to Ogi to get Ikuo's bedding ready in the second-floor bedroom. The heat of the fireplace didn't reach this room, and it was as cold as Tokyo in the middle of the winter. "You'll be fine if you use an electric blanket," Ogi told him, but Ikuo still seemed preoccupied after his discussion with Patron had fallen apart, and a bit suspicious of Ogi's practical advice.

Ogi went downstairs, banked the fire with ashes, and was getting his own futon ready on the floor when Dancer appeared and asked him to wake up Ikuo. Patron insisted on continuing his earlier talk with Ikuo in his bedroom, and wouldn't hear otherwise.

Dancer obviously wasn't too happy about it but did as Patron asked. While they waited for Ikuo to dress and join them downstairs in front of the fireplace, she whispered to Ogi, "Patron was trying to get to sleep, but he seems upset, not just about Guide but about painful memories that our earlier talk brought to mind. He said tonight he wanted to finish talking about all the things he was going to say to Ikuo.

"I told him the medicine was going to take effect and tried to persuade him to wait until tomorrow morning. If Ikuo looks like he's going to start debating him, please caution him not to, okay? I'll be right beside you."

"Are you planning to censor his questions and give answers in Patron's place?" Ikuo asked, entering the room in time to hear Dancer's last words.

The fire had burned down to embers and the only light was that filtering in from the dining room; Ikuo's face was darkly flushed and his rough reaction was enough to make Dancer wince.

"Well, then, would you go with him instead of me, Ogi?" Dancer asked, in an edgy, teary voice. "If he doesn't find Patron's answers to his liking and starts to get violent, there's nothing I'd be able to do. I'll wait by the phone."

Ogi led Ikuo into the master bedroom. The room was large, Western style, with a high bed that Ogi's mother had said was just like one she'd seen in a photo of an American farmhouse in an interior design magazine. Both the overhead lights and the nightstand lamp were turned off. In the glow of an electric space heater set up at the foot of the bed, the two young men could make out an old chest of drawers but no chairs for them to sit on. They had to stand looking down at Patron, whose head was resting on the high pillows, and couldn't even tell if his eyes were open. Ogi thought optimistically that he was asleep, but he wasn't. Soon, eyes closed, he began to speak, his words to Ikuo quite thoughtful.

"Professor Kizu told me in his letter that he was surprised when he heard you say that you heard the voice of God when you were a teenager, that ever since then you've been waiting to hear God's voice again, and that right now you want me to act as intermediary so the voice of God will speak to you again."

Patron's voice was different from his earlier eloquent sermonizing tone; his tone was unclear, his tongue slurred, the words seemingly pushed up from deep inside his throat. Ogi was favorably impressed, though, that despite his poor physical and emotional state and his worries over Guide, Patron was bent on fulfilling his promise to Ikuo. On the same wavelength, Ikuo responded in an entirely natural tone of voice.

"I was convinced, as a child, that I had heard the voice of God, though I never told Professor Kizu the details surrounding this event. At any rate, I believed God spoke to me, and I've been waiting expectantly ever since for that voice to speak to me again. I quit college, never had a steady job, didn't make any friends, and never lived long in any one place, always waiting and waiting. But God was silent.

"This year, however, after I met Professor Kizu—or had a reunion with him, I should say—I felt that things were changing. And then I was able to meet you, Patron. And I knew that you of all people would understand what it means to a person to hear the voice of God. I know I'm just dreaming, but I hope that you can help me hear the rest of what God wants to tell me. I've also started to get interested in the radical faction that Guide created, since they're the very people who, through you, heard the voice of God telling them to get on with it! And just when that voice was about to be heard, you and Guide snuffed it out."

Ikuo finished speaking, as if this was what he'd been thinking of earlier when he asked about the Somersault, and Patron was silent for a time. To Ogi the silence seemed too long, but finally Patron did speak. His speech was slower than before, and more disjointed. Ogi tried to put it in some kind of order so he could remember it. Since there was sufficient power in what Patron said to frighten an innocent youth like Ogi, he listened very carefully, trying to pick out what Patron mumbled, so his memory of it was reliable.

"Though Guide and I had begun a movement to show people a model of what the end of the world would be like and bring them to repentance, with the Somersault we abandoned it all. You asked me why Guide and I, particularly, denied our teachings then. You also said I served as an intermediary and made them wait in a place where they could hear God's voice to get on with it! Well, not only did I make them wait in vain, I announced to the world how stupid they were to be waiting at all.

"For ten years afterward we were the laughingstock of Japan, but in our inner being we felt even more driven into a corner–like the living dead, as I've put it. And now I've been raised up out of the pit of hell to where I must proclaim the words of God: *Do it!* I've resigned myself to living out this fate. If I'm the intermediary again for God's voice, this time I won't take back what he tells us to do. I promise you that, Ikuo.

"The reason we denied our teachings at the time of the Somersault is precisely because that's what a Somersault's all about. Whatever I do in this new direction I'm embarking on, I'll do as a person who has *Somersaulted*. Someone who Somersaults also has to participate, in a personal way, in the call for repentance. If you think about it, it's all too clear how the end of the world will come about in a hundred years. Is a hundred years so far off?

"Ikuo, you said you want me to act as intermediary so you can hear God's voice. But the relevant question is, Is it possible for someone who's done a Somersault to confront God again? I've only just returned to the point of preparing for a deep trance, but I think the answer is *yes,* it *is* possible. Would God abandon a person who's gone so far as to do a Somersault? God wouldn't allow himself to be left a fool, would he? You have the conviction that you'll hear again the voice of God, and that's what's brought you to me. I'm sure for someone as young as you it must have been hard to maintain that conviction. You—or I should say you *too*—have received a wound that never heals. But Ikuo, that is a *sign. . . .*"

Patron's voice grew lower and ever more slow. Finally he fell silent, his quiet breathing no longer a voice, and then he began to snore peacefully. The two young men stood there, straining their ears. Soon, from behind them, they sensed something only slightly louder than Patron's snores. Backlit by the light from the dining room, Dancer stood in the doorway motioning to them. They went out into the hallway. As she shut the heavy door behind them Dancer leaned her small slim body against Ikuo and whispered, "Patron told you something very important, didn't he?"

Before Ikuo could respond, she relayed a message from Ms. Tachibana, who had finally telephoned again. Guide was missing. When she called the police, they came to the residence and found Patron's beloved Saint Bernard poisoned. First thing tomorrow morning, Ms. Tachibana told her, they had to return to Tokyo with Patron to deal with this emergency.

They had dug up the glowing coals from underneath the ashes and re-kindled the blackened firewood when Ms. Tachibana called a third time. He had had another stroke, she reported. Guide had been held prisoner in a secret hiding place, subjected to a rough interrogation, and then abandoned; the perpetrators had phoned in his whereabouts, and the ambulance crew had discovered Guide lying there alone.

8: A New Guide

1

After Ikuo returned to Tokyo from their trip to the Nasu Plateau, he slept over in the office, phoning Kizu to tell him how freezing cold it had been in the mountains. Tokyo was in the midst of Indian summer, but by the next day it suddenly began to feel more like winter. The cold continued for a week. One day, when it felt like it might snow, Ms. Tachibana called Kizu. She had quit her job at the library earlier than she'd planned and was now working in Patron's office. She told Kizu that Patron was going to be visiting Guide in the hospital and wondered if Kizu would accompany him.

Kizu had already heard that Guide was expected to survive but that the chances he would regain consciousness were slim. Nor had Kizu seen Patron in quite some time. Ikuo, who was now diligently handling most phone calls, had told him that Patron was in a blue funk and had holed up in his bedroom study. Since it was members of the former radical faction who had interrogated Guide to the point where he had a stroke, the incident obviously stemmed from the Somersault, so it was natural enough that Patron felt responsible. Once more the media's attention was focused on Patron, Guide, and the events of a decade before.

Kizu headed off for the hospital in Ogikubo that Ms. Tachibana directed him to, and when he arrived at the nurses' station of the cerebral surgery department he found Patron waiting there in his high collar, looking for all the world like a servant in some Chekhov play. Patron set off without even giving Kizu a chance to say hello. Kizu watched him from behind, his fleshy shoulders and chubby body walking briskly as he led Kizu to the ICU. Patron told him he was a bit concerned at how much simpler all the preliminaries were here at this hospital, compared to the hospital in Shinjuku; security here was, as Kizu could see, minimal. Patron and Kizu went into the five-person intensive care unit. Kizu had vaguely imagined what his own hospital room would look like later on, when he himself was on the verge of death, but this room was very different—much noisier than he'd expected.

Guide was lying in the bed on the far right, his head swathed in bandages, two nurses bustling about him. Apparently they were having trouble getting the phlegm to drain correctly from the hole that had been opened in his throat. The head nurse spoke to the unresponsive Guide while she fixed the connection between the plastic tube and the machine it was attached to. The inhalation sounds were now louder, the patient's breathing more pronounced, and Patron leaned his head back to look out the window. Kizu, too, gazed at the heavy clouds in the sky. The nurses finally unclogged the phlegm and, speaking words of encouragement to Guide, who of course couldn't respond, began putting away the machine.

Patron and Kizu were left alone with Guide, but before Kizu could walk over to stand at Guide's left side, Patron went over, leaned close to Guide's right cheek, and spoke to him.

"Guide! Guide! Professor Kizu's here. There's so much more you wanted to discuss with him, didn't you? Try to remember. Even if you can't speak, try to remember! It'll be good practice for when you *can* speak and can talk with him once more!"

This struck Kizu as a bit theatrical. Still, he felt a power flowing out of Patron as he moved Guide's hand closer to him, a power that might very well help in his recovery. The elbows of the two men were sticking out at angles, half their palms resting diagonally on the other's, and when Kizu saw Guide's large, dark, sinewy fingers wrap themselves around Patron's fleshy pale ones, he knew that—at least in part—Patron's message was getting across.

Guide's salt-and-pepper hair and skin gleamed cleanly from under the bandages that had been wrapped around him after his second operation. The wound from before was visible, his complexion flushed, his right eye engulfed in wrinkles. His left eye, in contrast, was wide open, but the pupil was unfocused. Guide's usual darkly sharp dignity was gone; he looked like some clownish old man from the countryside.

"Guide! Guide! Though your consciousness is asleep, the words are waiting to find a voice. If only you could interpret for me now! You put the visions I saw into words, but I can't do a thing for you! You do realize Professor Kizu's come to see you, don't you? Guide?"

Kizu could picture words stacked up like out-of-focus, blood-smeared playing cards inside Guide's head. Before long a large teardrop ran down Guide's right cheek.

At the same moment as Kizu, Patron noticed these tears. And the physical vitality that Kizu had found disconcerting in Patron disappeared, like thin ice melting away. Now his large face revealed a deep exhaustion, his unblinking eyes fixed on Guide's tears. Again he spoke. "Guide, Guide," he said, in a low, soothing voice, too preoccupied to worry about Kizu anymore.

Patron's complexion darkened suddenly, like the sun disappearing behind clouds. His previous vitality and ceaseless speech were now hidden, a transformation that struck Kizu as odd.

Guide's reddened, comical face twitched sporadically, and he slowly licked his chapped lips. Soon he fell asleep and began to snore lightly, the white of his left eye showing. Patron's large head hung heavily; Kizu could see the thinning hair on top.

Dancer, who'd come in unnoticed and was standing behind Kizu, reached out the ball of her thumb, wet with saliva, and closed Guide's one open eyelid. Drawn by Patron's pitiful look, Kizu turned around and watched as, still gazing down at Guide, she stuck her wet thumb in her mouth again and sucked it.

Soon Dancer wiped her wet thumb on the paper apron each visitor was given, and straightened the clothes around Guide's bare chest and legs. A steel ball the size of a tennis ball dropped down from the hem of his *yukata*, startling Patron and Kizu, but without a word, Dancer picked it up and showed them how it was used to strengthen one's grip.

She then spoke to Patron, whose back was hunched up.

"Let's all go back to the office now," she whispered, and then explained things to Kizu in a composed voice. "Yesterday he was much better, and when the nurses called to him he made a V-for-victory sign, something he never does. Patron was ecstatic. But even today the doctors are amazed how strong his grip is. Try gripping his hand."

She looked alertly at the mister that was spraying disinfectant near the entrance of the ward. Kizu stuck his hands out toward it and misted his hands wet again. Guide's right hand did squeeze Kizu's hand back with a crude strength. Patron reached out and laid his plump palm on top of where the sharp joints of the two men's hands touched.

After this, they all headed back to the office. As Ikuo pulled up the minivan in front, Dancer, clearly the one in charge of their little group, straightened Patron's muffler and coat collar.

"You've been up and about since morning," she said to Patron, "so I'd like you to rest for a while. I know you have things to talk about with Profes-

sor Kizu, but I want you to wait a little. Professor, you don't mind waiting
for a while in the living room, do you? Ikuo, you'll give him a ride home later,
right?"

Patron acquiesced silently. If meeting Patron for the first time in so long
wasn't going to lead to any substantive discussion, Kizu felt he might as well
have hailed a cab in front of the hospital and gone home alone. He didn't mind
waiting for a time, though.

Since Guide suffered his calamity, the front gate of their residence had
been bolted, so when he heard the van pull up Ogi came out to greet them
and let them in. Supported on both sides by Dancer and Ogi as he walked
into the house, Patron had none of the vitality he'd displayed in front of the
nurses' station; watching him leaning his entire weight on the two young
people, Kizu was cut to the quick.

2

In the corner office, Ms. Tachibana was sorting the letters they'd received
from people who'd learned of Patron's new movement through newspaper
reports of the incident involving Guide. When Kizu stopped by to ask her
how the work was going, she merely said she'd taken over because Ogi was
busy, her eyes remaining glued to the computer screen.

After leading Patron to his bedroom study and letting Dancer take over
from there, Ogi came back and stood beside Ms. Tachibana's desk, but he
didn't seem to have anything new to report. Ikuo had parked the car in the
garage, reset the bolt in the gate, and come to sit down beside Kizu, silent, his
arms folded over his massive chest.

Not long after, Dancer appeared in the office, leaned over, and whispered something into Ogi's ear. Usually Ogi played the role of younger brother
to Dancer, but now she seemed to rely on him more than the other way around.
After listening to her, Ogi shared her confusion. Before long he spoke up.

"If that's what Patron wants, there's nothing you or I can do about it.
Why don't you just tell him exactly what Patron said?"

Dancer looked like a little girl who had been slapped in the face as she
walked over to Kizu. "Patron says he wants you to be the new Guide," she said.

"New *Guide*? That's pretty unexpected!" Rather than replying to Dancer,
Kizu seemed to be muttering to no one in particular. His words were like a
pebble thrown down a deep well without response, but after some time Dancer
finally spoke up.

"Whether you accept or not, you need to tell Patron yourself. I tell you, it's been one surprise after another. I have no idea what to do."

Dancer's voice was different from its usual piercing whisper, more muffled now; Kizu could catch a hint of her Hokkaido accent seeping through. Most likely this was the way she spoke when, years before, she was struggling to convince her family to let her study modern dance. At the same time, Kizu felt Ikuo's tense gaze clinging to him.

The person waiting for him, lying in bed, blanket and down comforter up to his chest, was neither the unusually vigorous person of the first half of their hospital visit nor the plainly exhausted person of the second half. Patron had a sort of composed strength about him now. He looked up at Kizu with distant eyes and, with a solemn movement of his head, motioned for Dancer to leave them.

"In my new church," he said, "I'd like you to succeed Guide in his work. To repay you, I'll help you overcome the terrible thing that's assailing you spiritually and physically."

Kizu answered at once, "If you have that kind of power, then you should fix Guide's brain!"

Patron didn't react to these mean-spirited words but lamented instead, in a voice so full of grief it was comical, "Ah—if only I *could*!"

Taken aback by Patron's directness, Kizu felt deflated. Having lost his chance to continue by Kizu's interruption, Patron looked away, a dark look on his brow. Then he pulled himself together and began to speak in a more prosaic way, quite the opposite of the enthusiasm with which he'd invited Kizu to take Guide's place.

"With Guide the way he is now, maybe I'm just an old man who can't do a thing, and maybe I should just forget about this new movement and spend the rest of my days taking care of Guide. Isn't that what you're thinking? When we read R. S. Thomas that topic came up, as I recall. I'd like to talk with Guide about it, though I have no idea if he'd understand what I say. At the time of the Somersault we'd already imagined that sort of future for us.

"But Professor, with Guide in the hospital, I can't just abandon my role as Patron and spend my time pushing him around in his wheelchair as he goes through rehabilitation; Guide was injured facing up to a group that held him against his will and put him through a trumped-up trial to get him to admit that the Somersault was a mistake.

"I don't think he'll ever be able to communicate with us again. But even if he were to die without regaining full consciousness or the ability to talk, he's fulfilled his mission in life. He has suffered as a true prophet.

"But *I* have to live on. Having done the Somersault and now unable, without Guide, to put my visions into words, I still have the audacity to keep on living. But if I just grow decrepit and senile and die, my life will have been in vain. And then what would being Patron amount to? Nothing—just one big joke.

"Only after I've lived a life befitting Patron do I want to die. Those people held Guide prisoner, gouging out what wounded him most, a more abominable act than actually killing him. That being the case, I want to rise up again to the point where they have to choose *me* as their target."

Patron turned sharp birdlike eyes to Kizu.

"Professor, *please*. You don't need to say a thing. You can be a Guide who just paints!" Patron implored. "You can express things in a way I cannot. Your painting can clarify what my visions mean. If you turn your eyes in the direction of my beliefs, that's enough. With Guide in the shape he's in now, can you really refuse? I have only a handful of young people around me. Other than you, what mature person can I count on?"

"I don't know if I'll be able to fill the role, but I'll do my best until he recovers," Kizu replied, overcoming his nervousness. "I've been stopping by the office every once in a while, but I'll come more often. I can be your partner."

"Ikuo can drive you back and forth," Patron said, his eyes sleepy like those of a contented bird. "Now, would you mind asking Dancer to bring me my sleeping pills?"

Kizu returned to the living room and told Dancer, who was still standing beside the desk with Ogi, what Patron had said to him. As the young man and woman listened, he noticed for the first time a shared expression on their faces, like brother and sister. Kizu also noticed, in Ikuo's attitude as he looked up at him, that all three of them agreed with the decision Kizu had come to. Ms. Tachibana, too, in her unobtrusive way, looked content.

As powdery snow swirled around him, Kizu stood on the pavement waiting for Ikuo to bring the minivan around. The snow was different from the light flakes that had fallen in the United States at his East Coast university and had the soft, easy-melting quality of snow he remembered from his childhood. He felt a tinge of nostalgia. He got in beside Ikuo and looked up at the snowy sky, his heated mind reviewing his conversation with Patron.

Patron had said that if Kizu undertook the role of Guide he would help him overcome his spiritual and physical crisis; Kizu smiled coolly at the thought. He's not just dealing with my soul, he mused, but maybe sensed the reoccurrence of my cancer as well. He felt his cheeks tense up, though, at the memory of his huffy, mean response.

"There's something different about you," Ikuo said. "You seem—I don't know—cold, I guess. I've never seen you smile like that before. Have you changed your mind?"

"I'm smiling at myself, not at other people," Kizu replied.

"If you see Patron's proposal as too painful, I can understand that," Ikuo said, "but I was really keeping my fingers crossed you'd accept. I know you weren't too enthusiastic about the idea when Dancer first brought it up, and I was afraid it was going to be a problem. I was afraid you'd feel forced to go back to America, and I didn't want to end up having to choose between you. If you left Japan, Patron would lose his new Guide, but we'd be completely lost as well."

"But I don't have any of the qualities to make Patron want to rely on me," Kizu said. "I don't know anything about his earlier teachings, even if he has renounced them. And when I think of Guide, still such a unique spirit despite his condition, I don't think I understand him, either."

"You've only known Patron a short time, but the two of you have had some pretty deep conversations," Ikuo said. "Knowing you, Professor, I imagine that if you take on the role of the new Guide you'll use the opportunity to study Patron more. I've been thinking about this for a while now, but I really want you to ask Patron why he began calling himself the *savior* of mankind—whether fake or otherwise. I wanted to ask him myself, but our trip to Nasu Plateau was cut short."

"If it's so important to you, I'll do it. I need to ask Patron about Guide, too, why he called himself the *prophet* of mankind—fake or otherwise."

In the faint light of the snowy sky, an unexpected smile rose, like a cheerful mask, to Ikuo's angular, deeply chiseled features. Kizu had no idea how he was interpreting his response but didn't pursue it further. Staring out at the thickening snow lashing the windshield, he began to feel a decided softness coming from Ikuo. Not that Ikuo's soldierly frame or muscles softened, it was rather that something inside was seeping out. When he turned to Ikuo, the young man's faint smile was gone, replaced by a relaxed, youthful expression.

Ever since he had first met Ikuo at the athletic club and invited him to pose for him at his apartment, and even more so after they began a sexual relationship, Kizu sensed the tension draining from the young man from time to time. But still Ikuo's attitude toward him, and probably toward everyone, contained, deep down, something hard and unrelenting; when Kizu had been about to write the letter to Patron for him, he had thought about how the incident he'd talked about, about God calling him as a child, had affected his life ever since.

Not that Kizu believed everything that Ikuo revealed to him. Kizu didn't believe that in this day and age there was a God who would let a young boy have such a mystical experience—not that, for God, such a concept as *this day and age* was relevant. Nevertheless, it was true that after Ikuo quit college, the conviction that he'd had this experience was the cornerstone of his life. When Kizu first saw Ikuo at the athletic club he had the look of a lone jungle fighter. In his rugged features and hard body, Ikuo's expression was far removed from the soft, gentle look Kizu had often seen in people of the same age after he returned to Japan. This didn't mean that Ikuo had anything in common with the dry and prosaic Vietnam vets that Kizu sometimes taught in the United States; this young man's heart was full of a yearning that wouldn't allow him to settle for being dull and ordinary.

At first Kizu had sensed something of the wild animal in Ikuo. A true loner, he drew no one else to him, but his exterior, which rejected everyone and everything, hid something quite extraordinary. Even though they were lovers the hard armor that was very much a part of Ikuo was still in place. But now, with Kizu's acceptance of the role of new Guide, came that faint smile, that unexpected softness. He remembered that Dancer had looked displeased at Patron's proposal, but later, after Kizu had emerged from the bedroom study, both she and Ogi accepted the idea.

Kizu considered again what it would mean to be the new Guide. And when he recalled something Patron had said, it was almost enough to revive the faint smile Ikuo said he'd never seen before: *You don't need to say a thing. You can be a Guide who just paints!* But hadn't Patron said Guide was a man of language, who fulfilled his role by *speaking*? How could Kizu possibly convey Patron's visions to others through *painting*?

Kizu tried to imagine serving as the new Guide, but he couldn't imagine himself taking a proactive stance. He'd follow Patron's lead and do what he could as a painter. But painting what? Surely Patron didn't think he would do *kamishibai* illustrations for a storytelling session, did he?

Eventually, the agitation he'd felt talking to Patron died down, though there was no doubt in his mind that he was beginning a new stage of his life, a stage that, thankfully, included Ikuo.

3

The next morning when Kizu awoke, it had stopped snowing. It was not yet seven, but he was too excited to stay in bed. With Ikuo busy every day in the office, housecleaning duties were once more his, and he spent time straightening up the living room. He didn't use the powerful American-made vacuum cleaner that came with the apartment, though, for fear that it would disturb the neighboring residents. Sensing a flutter outside, he turned to look and saw that the powdery snow had begun to fall again. Kizu's sensitivity to peripheral movement seemed to him a good indicator of his present state of mind, though he had no idea why he felt this way.

After cleaning up his studio for a while, he looked out past the veranda to where, down the grassy slope, the surface of the pond had turned white. A thin layer of ice had covered the pond, with snow now piled on top. Snow lay, too, on the thick branches of the leafless, darkly exposed wych elm. A flock of wild birds that normally would have been chased off by even a sprinkle of rain were oblivious to the powdery snow, occasionally shaking their bodies as each protected its spot on the branch. Kizu realized that the snow had had something to do with the stirring he felt deep inside himself.

The sun came out in the afternoon and the snow that had been clinging to one side of the wych elm's trunk and the nearly horizontal parts of the thick branches melted away. All the snow on the pond's surface had disappeared, but no ripples disturbed the pond, so it was still frozen. The snow was gone from the lawn, too, just some white spots here and there on the withered grass between the trees. During the morning the awareness he felt inside him was mixed with darkness, and he recalled, for the first time in a long while, the phrase *tingle with excitement,* but in the afternoon the clarity of the sky and the clouds seeped into his heart.

He couldn't help but consider the new and difficult task that confronted him, but he felt he had sufficient energy saved to face up to it, so his feelings were, to use the term his students in New Jersey used, entirely *positive.* The clouds spreading outside his window were not the beginnings of a storm but rather a watercolor painted across the bright sky.

In the upper third of a Wattman F6 sketch pad he held vertically, Kizu sketched glittering white clouds and a light blue sky infused with light; in the lower fourth of the paper a totally leafless woods and a range of twiglike branches. He left the middle of the page blank. He wasn't clear about this space at all, but his years of experience as an artist told him it was significant; this sketch, still five-twelfths empty, would only become a work of art when this blank area was filled in. He wasn't going to use what he saw outside his window, though. The space was just the right size for his imagination to fill in with something suited to the sky above and the woods below.

After a while Kizu began filling in the remaining areas with a soft pencil sketch of two standing figures facing away from the viewer. He switched to watercolors for the figures and added many vertical banks of clouds to the light-blue sky.

What Kizu had drawn was himself and Ikuo standing there and, in a way somehow not unnatural for two grown men, holding each other's hand. In the painting Kizu was dressed as he was now, in faded black cotton trousers, a wool shirt, and a wine-colored sweater. Ikuo wore jeans and an oversized blue shirt with sleeves that were too long. On their feet were something you'd never need in this city, the kind of ankle-high lace-up winter boots you might find a U.S. artist in the Northeast wearing.

In a much more natural way than the fanciful images conjured up by run-of-the-mill surrealists, the figures of Ikuo and Kizu in the painting were walking off into the bright sky. Kizu realized he'd been taking Patron's trance world quite optimistically, hoping that he and Ikuo could stroll off into it in the near future. Even if you viewed this vision as his unconscious rising up to support his decision to become the new Guide, it was such a simplistic view he knew he himself, not Ogi, was the innocent one.

Construction work outside the apartment building that afternoon prevented people from parking in front, so Ikuo called him from down the road where he had parked. Kizu walked one block, to where Ikuo was waiting outside the car, and rested his hand on the young man's shoulder in lieu of a greeting, only to feel an inorganic coldness rising up at his touch, as if denying any affinity between them. Even if the young man's body was only transmitting the outside temperature, Ikuo was more taciturn than the day before. Intermittently in the course of their relationship Kizu had felt that they were going backward, to the time when they first met—and today was one of those days. Ordinarily he would have taken the watercolor he'd painted that day out of its cardboard tube and shown it to Ikuo while they were waiting for a light to change. But today the timing was off.

"When you called a while ago, you said you'd just driven Dancer to the hospital for Guide's rehabilitation. Is he strong enough to undergo rehabilitation? Is there a chance he'll recover his strength?"

Ikuo didn't respond right away to Kizu's question but just stared straight ahead. Finally, reluctantly, he answered.

"Dancer's doing her best, going to the hospital every day, but she doesn't believe he'll recover enough to take on his role as Guide again. The only thing she talked about in the car was what we can expect from you."

Kizu was escorted into the bedroom study by Ogi and sat down in a chair facing Patron, who was sunk deep in his armchair; Ikuo brought in a backless chair from the office for himself and sat down too. As they had gotten out of the car, Kizu had passed him the cardboard tube with the watercolor painting in it; now Ikuo laid it in his lap and rested a hand on one end.

"We haven't done this before, but I'd like Ikuo to join us this time in hearing what you have to say, and Ogi tells me you've agreed," Kizu said.

"It's more proper now for *me* to say I'll listen to *you*," Patron said, his words brisk but his expression pensive. "Actually, I'd been hoping that we could both talk with Ikuo. There's also another reason for this meeting today. Often just after I wake up I'm in a kind of half-awake, half-asleep state, and when that happened again this morning I envisioned a scene before me. I interpreted this as a sign that you would take on the role of being the new Guide with Ikuo beside you. I wanted to talk with you about this, and that's why I called you here without much warning.

"What I saw was you and Ikuo, hand in hand as I watched over you, stepping into space, each of you a sturdy support to the other in case one of you was about to fall. That was the scene I saw."

Kizu thought he was being taken in by some elaborate trick; at the same time he felt drawn in by those gentle, trusting eyes. He tried to resist.

"In this scene that you saw, was the place where you said Ikuo and I were walking—a space, you called it—was it the sky? If so, what was the weather like?"

"It was sunny," Patron replied. "I saw newly formed clouds gleaming whitely between the two of you and me, who was waiting to receive you. The clouds were shaped like a baby whale without a tail. The whale's head was three-dimensional; you could sense its weight, and the force of this weight made it move diagonally downward."

Kizu turned to look at Ikuo, who, before a word could pass between them, handed Kizu the cardboard tube on his lap. Kizu stuck two fingers inside the open end of the tube and extracted the watercolor painting, along with the cotton paper that was wrapped around it.

Patron took the painting and held it up to the light on the bedside table. Kizu knew he often listened to classical CDs in this room, everything from ancient to modern music. The feeling rose up in Kizu that he was in the presence of a considerable connoisseur of art.

After a while Patron lifted his eyes from the painting and laughed aloud, a simple, innocent burst of laughter. He nodded at Kizu, then passed the painting, its edges curling up on its own, over to Ikuo, who had been leaning over hesitantly to catch a glimpse. Patron didn't say a word about the congruence between the dream or vision he'd had and the scene depicted in the painting; his hearty laughter expressed it all. He evidently saw no need for any verbose explanation for himself, or for Kizu, or for Ikuo, who was poring over the painting.

It was Kizu, rather, taken in by Patron's laughter and unable to suppress a smile, who felt that the painting cried out for interpretation. Kizu gazed at the painting in Ikuo's hands, as did Patron, Ikuo angling the painting so it was easier for them to see, and once more he found himself unable to suppress a smile.

"This light-blue sky is what I saw from my apartment window this morning, and I painted it as it was," Kizu said. "The same with the grove of trees. The clouds, though, are something else. I'm amazed how accurate your description of them is—like a baby whale without a tail. These were clouds I saw outside the window of my university office in the States. Especially after I just took the job and was a little anxious about it, the clouds comforted me, so I added them nostalgically to the painting."

"That cloud-filled sky is the world on the other side toward which your soul is heading," Patron said. "It makes sense to see it as a nostalgic place."

"I wonder if I was thinking those kinds of things while I was painting it. It's a little vague to put it this way, I suppose, but I think I was envisioning Ikuo and me walking off into the bright sky as the two of us entered the world on the other side, the one you see in your trances. Rather than it being us entering *my* own trance."

"In a sense, though, they're one and the same," Patron said. "When you're so absorbed in your work, you break through to the other world of my trances. That's the ideal working relationship between patron and guide. Guide once said that's what he was aiming at.

"Another important thing is that you and Ikuo are holding hands. Through trances, we experience the world on the other side. But as Guide always told me, because this great flow itself is God, you can't let yourself get caught up in the flow of ecstasy on the other side. Getting carried away by that flow means becoming one with God, and the ecstasy is a premonition of this.

"Of course, you could argue that getting caught up in it is actually the most natural thing to do. However, inside us all we have particles of light or resonance that are bestowed upon us by the One-and-only, the Almighty, or, in more prosaic terms, by God. For an individual, coming to faith means we take these particles of light or resonance so they're not some vague concept but are resituated in a more favorable environment in our own body and spirit. Those particles of light or resonance are *inside* us, but they don't *belong* to us. Even less are they *created* by us. They're put in our care by the Almighty. Finally—and by this I don't mean just the inevitable result of the passage of time but also through training—we have to return these particles of light or resonance to the Almighty, where they originated. This is why we must keep them alive, unsullied. Not for a single moment must we forget these particles of light or resonance, which we take care of in our own bodies and spirit, are the source of *life,* which we must in the end return to the Almighty.

"If we get drunk on the ecstasy of the trance and are swallowed up by this deep drunkenness, we won't be able to return from that huge flow back to *this* side. But one of the conditions of being a living human being is that you do not stay forever over *there.* In other words, if you are mechanically returned to this side, you'll never again be able to discover the particles of light or resonance within your body and spirit.

"No matter the level of the trance you're in, you have to wake up within it. You have to gaze at that huge flow with your eyes wide open. You have to let your body and spirit be transparent and gaze at those particles of light or resonance reflected in the mirror of that massive flow. This has nothing to do with what we might look like from the outside while in a trance.

"You recall Guide said that when I'm in a trance I confront a huge glowing structure? That's how he understood what I described, what I see when I'm gazing at this huge flow with open eyes. What I see and what he describes are one and the same. From the start, what you experience in a deep trance is something that can't be categorized in words. Which means that if you *do* attempt to transform it into words, there'll be many different ways of expressing it—all of them accurate.

"To get back to your painting, you can't let feelings of ecstasy draw you into that massive flow. So what do you do to prevent it? Mystics in Europe used lections, sacred phrases—the words of a prayer—as a kind of handrail to keep from falling into the abyss of ecstasy. They'd tie sacred phrases around their waists as a kind of lifeline.

"In this painting, Professor, you're walking off into the depths of the sky holding on to Ikuo's hand. Ikuo's hand linked with yours is your handrail, your lifeline. Led by me, you've made the decision to go into the world on the other side. But from the first you refuse to be inundated by it. You won't allow yourself to be swallowed up in that massive flow. You've decided to protect the particles of light or resonance inside your body and spirit.

"Ikuo is your handrail, or lifeline, but by the same token if I were to lead him into a deep trance you want to keep him from sinking into that flow. And you did this painting of you and Ikuo holding hands in order to make this clear to yourself. Looking at this painting, I think Ikuo, too, can mentally prepare himself."

Patron turned from Kizu to look at Ikuo—Kizu found he couldn't help but do the same with a forceful shift of weight—and Ikuo nodded so decisively that Kizu was overjoyed.

4

Kizu still wasn't sure exactly what a guide was supposed to be or do, though it was clear Patron viewed him as both a personal adviser and an adviser to his new movement. Like Ikuo, Kizu was determined to absorb all Patron had to tell him. When he'd given Patron talks on the Welsh poet, Patron had been far from just a student. A new dynamic was at work here, with Patron now endeavoring to educate Kizu. Patron was attempting to revive the doctrine that he and the sick Guide had created—despite having denied it all by doing their Somersault.

"When Guide and I were young," he told Kizu, "there was a time when our youthful unease and energy drove us to devour books in order to find out more about mysticism. There was a great inherent difference, though, between our reading abilities. Guide would read books I'd never pick up on my own and then underline or circle in red those parts he thought I'd be interested in. I'd read more than just those parts, of course, but never the entire book. I'd read the chapters that caught his attention enough for him to mark up. And if I didn't understand that chapter, I'd read the ones that bracketed it.

"Guide would use different-colored pencils to indicate the chapters that were for reference. Once he began to drink (which didn't happen all that often) he couldn't stop. He'd adopt this overbearing attitude that he was the one in charge of educating the leader of the church. He's a detail person, so he made a distinction between what he was teaching me and what was originally within me, something on a different plane from what we usually think of as educating or being educated. Rather, he said he was led by what was inside me to find those kinds of books and read them.

"Does this make me sound pretty full of myself? Guide didn't treat me as someone with special privileges. He just *happened* to choose me as the Savior—at that point we weren't using the names Patron or Guide—but he could easily have chosen someone else. What's most important exists in *every* person, the particles of light or resonance that flow out from the Almighty, the one Being that was there at the beginning, the Always-already who includes the entire universe. The only difference is that in some people those particles of light are clearer and give off a much more intense resonance. *Yours are extraordinarily clear and intense,* Guide told me when we met; that's where he found his surety that I was the one.

"At that time, Guide was still teaching mathematics and science in night school. All the various students in his gloomy classroom, he said, each had these particles of light or resonance. He told me he actually got the whole concept of these particles from one of the more progressive textbooks he used for his students.

"Most of us are convinced we're each active subjects who happen to contain DNA, but most scholars now agree that since the dawn of mankind humans have been little more than containers, vehicles to transport the DNA that determines our individuality.

"Guide taught me his basic doctrine: that the world was created by light radiating from the Almighty, that each of us contains within our bodies and spirits these particles of light or resonance, and eventually these will return to their Creator.

"People tend to believe that each of us as individuals are the center of things, but we really *are* nothing more than vehicles for these particles of light or resonance: just portable containers, until the time when each and every particle of light returns to the Almighty and *becomes* the Almighty. This flowing out and return takes place in a different way from the events that we're used to thinking about as happening in historical time. Both happen in an instant yet are also occurring eternally.

"I can't say I really understood what Guide meant at the time. When those particles of light or resonance return to the Almighty, they'll cast off the body they've occupied. They'll also separate themselves from the spirit, but this doesn't mean that our individuality is discarded like a used container. Each of our individual souls will become particles of light or resonance and return to the Almighty. I didn't entirely understand it, but I was drawn to the idea.

"I've never prayed in a Christian church—let alone in an Islamic mosque or even a Buddhist temple, for that matter—and what I know about this may be the kind of random knowledge one picks up from movies, TV, and novels, but the faithful do say, don't they, *Thy will be done?* There's a scene in the Koran where Abraham and Isaac pray together as one, and you can find the same sort of thing in Buddhist tales. *Thy will be done,* I believe, is a universal element of prayer.

"Even in our own church, *Thy will be done* was the basis of everything we did. I didn't interpret God in an anthropomorphic way but as the light that penetrates the world, the universe, the whole, and all the details, each and every one. I said these particles of light or resonance are in me, and I'm just one speck in an infinite number, but these particles of light, like salmon swimming upstream, become part of countless other particles to create one enormous entity as they return to the Almighty. The faithful imagine this One-and-only in an anthropomorphic way, as the originating ultimate Almighty. Call it God, if you wish.

"This being called out once to you, Ikuo, and now you say you want to face that voice again and have me act as intermediary. There was a time, apparently, when you viewed God as something like God in the Old Testament, and I think it's all right that you want me to be a mediator for you. What the Almighty makes clear through me is directed at *me,* but all you need to do, Ikuo, is press the SHIFT key to change it to the voice of God *you* heard in your late teens. My God and the God you heard calling to you are one and the same, since the Almighty penetrates every detail in this world and in the entire universe. There can be *no other God.*

"You can't forget the voice of God you heard as a teenager. You staked your entire youth on waiting to hear the voice again. Even so, when Guide urged you to ask me to serve as intermediary between you and the Almighty, you hesitated—wondering whether it was right for you, as just one little individual, to do something that might affect *Thy will be done* in the world, in the universe. Guide told me how impressed he was by this young man, so poor in spirit.

"I think Guide knew exactly what he urged you to do. Recently he ran across some words in a sixteenth-century book by a Sufi mystic that supported this belief. '*The process of all creation, which is from God, being restored to its true state,*' the book said, '*requires more than simply a propulsive force from God; it also requires a propulsive force found in the religious activities of the created.*' The book goes on to say that '*this is why the prayerful hold a tremendous power in the inner world, and at the same time a tremendous responsibility to realize their messianic mission.*'

"I believe Guide wanted to make this idea the basis for our new movement. And he started by encouraging you, Ikuo. I can imagine how dejected you must have been when he collapsed, but now—with Professor Kizu taking over—you must feel as though you've been revived. And when I looked at this painting, I felt exactly the same way!"

9: The Book Already Written

1

When Patron was a child he learned of a book he knew he had to spend his entire life searching for. "How old were you at the time?" Kizu asked, but Patron neatly dodged the question.

It all began when Patron was attending a piano concert in place of his father, who was busy elsewhere; he was seated in special box enclosed in marble next to the main aisle that ran parallel to the stage. Right after the house lights dimmed, a tall skinny man approached him like the shadow of a bird flitting by and said, "You are a unique person, and there's something written about you in. . . ."

The man leaned over the enclosure as he spoke and then left swiftly, bent over from the waist like someone late to the concert trying to not bother those already seated, walked quickly to a seat in the rear of the hall, and disappeared.

"It bothered me that I didn't catch the title of the book," Patron said. "The concert was an all-Bach program and I was soon carried away by the music, but I found myself wondering whether the music was conveying to me the contents of that book. In other words, the man's words had an immediate effect, though what sort of content was being communicated, I couldn't have said. It was as if a surgical laser beam were shining on each word of that book inside me, and it was impossible to read it consciously—at least now that's how I look at it."

"I'm sure as you were growing up you read a lot of books," Kizu said, "but did you ever run across a book and think *This is it?*"

Patron let the question pass by like a breath of wind grazing him, not letting it interrupt the rhythm of his narrative. "I never thought I'd run across an actual book. Still, sometimes I felt like I was reading it and knew all the words in it. If someone made a concordance based on that book, you'd find listed in it all the words I'd ever spoken. Still, my fate as described in that book was something that I created myself over a long period of time.

"I was always searching through large bookstores and libraries for that book, even thinking maybe I should write it myself. Indeed, it was by constructing that book that I ended up living the life I've led. Before I could write such a book, I had to live in a way befitting its author. So there was no need to put things down on paper, and I didn't become an actual writer."

Patron said no more. While he mulled over his words a thought struck Kizu, a thought so overpowering that if he didn't suppress it he might burst out with it: Wasn't the title of that book *Somersault*? he wanted to shout.

He realized right away how flippant this would have been and breathed a sigh of relief that he hadn't actually voiced the question.

Later on he discovered another reason why he was happy he hadn't said this at the time; he was no longer convinced that the word *Somersault* could sum up Patron's whole life. After Patron and Guide admitted the way in which the term had been used to ridicule their actions, Kizu couldn't quite understand its new connotations. Another thought struck him: that if there was a book called *Somersault* he wanted to read it because it would contain something written about *him*.

With all this as background, Kizu was able to draw out from Patron a more focused response about his special book. On this particular day they were all discussing the mystical experiences Patron had had that Guide had described to Kizu and Ikuo. Deepening his understanding of this was, for Kizu, of the utmost importance. As the person chosen by Patron to be his new adviser, Kizu wanted to take over Guide's responsibilities as much as he could. But ever since he'd agreed to assume the role, Patron had been somewhat casual about it, never pressing him. Still, he felt increasingly anxious.

"Guide told us once," Kizu began, "that when you are in a trance you're standing in front of a whitely glowing object, like a net that shows the entire past, present, and future of the world. I always assumed that mystical experiences meant you were communicating directly with God, which is why I thought this netlike structure must *be* God. The structure also struck me as a fantastic model of the world's whole past, present, and future. But the other day the idea came to me that perhaps this whitely glowing model itself is that one-of-a-kind book you told us about. So when you're in your trance you're focused entirely on reading that book."

"I agree," Patron said, his response so matter-of-fact that Kizu had doubts about what he'd just said. "But if I'd told Guide, when I related my visions to him, that it was the same as reading that book he wouldn't have accepted it. Books are limited in all kinds of ways, aren't they? A book has words printed in it. While you read it you can't change it. Reading can't be the same as living in the real world. Guide insisted on this rather simplistic line of reasoning.

"If you look carefully at that whitely glowing structure, you'll see that inside the net there are rapidly moving minute particles. Since it's structured this way, you can read your own present, Guide said, and you can live it and change your future. What I meant by a special book was exactly this type of new-style book."

"So," Kizu began, summoning up his courage, "was the Somersault, then, a kind of misreading the two of you had, as leaders of the church and, more specifically, of the activities of the radical faction? And didn't you and Guide notice this?"

"A *misreading*?" Patron gave it some thought.

Just as Kizu was about to withdraw his careless comment, Patron answered him with unexpectedly honest words.

"In this large book there's one thing that can't be misread, and that is the fact that, if mankind fails to repent, an irreversible time is fast approaching. Truthfully, though, if I were to describe for you the scene of the end of the world that I spoke about in the afterglow of my trance, and that Guide heard in the context of words on this side and then related to me, you'd be discouraged by how very ordinary it is. It's a picture of a medium-sized provincial city here in Japan. The afternoon is shining down on the scene, but it's entirely desolate. No dogs wandering around, no napping cats. The streets are filthy with garbage, but the amount remains the same; no garbage has been freshly discarded. All manufacturing facilities have stopped. The people haven't been completely eliminated yet but are living off the remains of what's been manufactured and not replacing them once they're used up. There's no electricity, no running water, no public transportation. Everyone's waiting for death in inconspicuous corners of this city, lying there, curled up, helpless babies once again, bereft of the skills needed to live.

"Why did things reach this state? Was a neutron bomb dropped that spared the buildings but is killing the people and animals through radiation? Has a hitherto unknown epidemic broken out? It would still have been fine if this was just one medium-sized city that the outside world kept isolated, waiting for the radiation or epidemic to run its course. But if the exact thing is happening everywhere around the globe, doesn't this scene show us the human race becoming extinct?

"What I was surely doing was reading one page of this heretofore unknown kind of book to Guide. How was this going to take place? Could it be halted? And what was God trying to tell us? I was supposed to read on, a Herculean task. Guide and I were agreed that we were standing at that very starting point."

2

"Looking back on it, I see this is where, for the first time since we'd begun our movement, a crack developed in our sense of oneness. Back at the very beginning, Guide discovered in me the person he'd been searching for and shaped me in that image. I have already told you what happened after that. At the same time, I discovered in him someone I could lean on. I pressed him hard, too, to make him become that support.

"He dubbed me Savior, but I didn't have any confidence that I *was* one, though he was way too strict to let me joke around about being a false savior or anything.

"Sad to say, I didn't think he'd always stay with me as my prophet. He took the words I spouted out when the effects of my deep trances were still with me and translated them into proper language. But every moment I was afraid that someday he'd find it too much trouble and get up and leave. If that happened, I'd be nothing. I'd still babble out delirious nonsense after my trances, but what would be the point?

"I had the feeling that maybe Guide didn't really need me. And this made me fearful of two things. First, I was afraid I was forcing him to work for me, and this might cause him to leave the church. Second, I was afraid that, as he became a more experienced prophet, he'd find me inadequate as a savior and look for someone more suited to the role.

"So a fissure opened up between us. By this time our church was already registered as a nonprofit religious foundation, which immediately made tax matters easier to handle and gave our followers legal protection. Up to this point, Guide, who'd studied mathematics, was our accountant, but after this some followers he'd trained took over the finances. This freed him up to do other things, and he used this free time to organize within the church a group of hand-picked followers, bright athletic young people. Since we started the church, I've always wanted all members to be equal. That's why I didn't create any official positions. After some time passed I told him my concerns about expanding his elite group any further. But he told me to let him have his way; having been a teacher for so many years, he said, he found it a real psychological boost to be able to have young people in his charge again.

"I haven't really said anything about my own position in the church, have I? Anyway, the basis for our teachings was this: that we should all be conscious that the end of the world was approaching, and be more open to it, on both an emotional and an intellectual level. And most importantly, we should *repent*. Isn't it a tragedy for this planet to be destroyed—a planet that has sustained so many countless lives—because only a small minority are truly repentant? (Though some people would argue that the only thing that's destroyed is the environment needed for mankind to survive, not the planet itself.)

"With these feelings in mind, Guide and I began spreading our message to the world. That's all it was, really. To tell the truth, I would have been happy dealing with the end of the world and repentance just on my own personal level. If I had my own time connected with God I'd be able to face death without any regrets or fears. I wasn't thinking about the afterlife or the salvation of the soul, just that I'd be able to survive for a certain time. During that time, as the end time drew near, I'd have a clear understanding that it *was* the end, I would repent as one, individual human being, and, as far as possible, I would end my days in a personal relationship with God, like some mystical hermit. That was my dream. And it could have come true.

"Why did someone like me, then, become the leader of a religious organization? Why did I come to have so many people call me Savior, and why did I let them? The reason is that I didn't train myself enough, like the hermits of old had. Ultimately I couldn't free myself from the one basic element of humanity—language. During this time, my trances steadily became more profound. I was also able to expand the visions I encountered and make them more real. And I couldn't keep silent about it. I was awed by the magical power of language.

"There are two aspects here. The first is connected with the contents of my trances. I'd fall into a deep trance and enter the world beyond. After returning to our world, I couldn't keep from mulling over the visions I'd had there. And here, the role Guide played was decisive. I'd turn to him and talk about the visions I had but couldn't understand. Words just spilled out. He'd put what I said into some sort of logical order, and I'd tell him his words weren't like the experience. And once again, he and I would try to get closer to what I saw in my trances. The visions and these new words would illuminate each other. That's how I learned the irreplaceable power that words can have.

"The second aspect of language was this: When, through Guide's help, we were able to narrate from what I'd read in that book in my trances, people began to come to listen to us. Before I met Guide I'd been doing something similar. At first it was just one or two people who'd listen to my solitary tales and then use the details as a kind of fortune-telling to figure out their future. The number of people gradually increased until there was a set group of about fifteen who'd gather together. And then new people would come, men and women with pressing concerns of their own. A woman would ask how she could get her runaway drug-taking son to come home. A man would say he treated his father-in-law so coldly it's practically like he committed suicide, and how can he deal with this? As I got a reputation for being able to give people hints to solve their personal problems, more and more people began to gather around me. I was able to live on their offerings. Up to then I'd eked out a living writing record reviews for a music magazine.

"As I've told you, it was at this point that I met Guide. He came to a gathering to get my advice on a very personal problem; his wife and autistic son were afraid of him and had run away from home. Even if we can't get back together right away, he said, he wanted to find out where they were and whether they were okay.

"And he did get some results, so afterward he still kept coming to see me. He'd come alone and we'd have long talks. One day he happened to be there when I went into a trance, and he took care of me for several days. After I was back to a normal state of consciousness, Guide told me, in clear language, what my mutterings had meant. I can never forget how surprised and happy I was when my visions were revived like that. That's how our relationship began.

"Before long he began seeing me as a savior. I don't know whether, in the beginning, he believed that or not. Maybe he thought it was an amusing nickname. But I began calling him Prophet, because of how he interpreted my visions. Those names helped our relationship run more smoothly. That was the turning point at which what had been a private gathering turned into a religious organization.

"Our church grew overnight. We started out with fifteen people, and in less than two years over five hundred people had renounced the world to join us. Having people renounce everything to join wasn't Guide's idea. One old lady did it and others followed suit. Since becoming a renunciate meant selling your house and land and donating all your assets to the church, our financial situation improved by leaps and bounds. Guide took care of the bookkeeping, as well as of the steps needed to make our church nonprofit. As I mentioned before, at that point we had over two thousand members.

"At this stage my own personal prayers and teachings were simple. I remember being questioned once by a Belgian reporter who was writing a piece on our church. I have trances, I told him, in order to gain a deeper understanding of the approaching end of the world. This helps me be more open to it, intellectually and emotionally. My goal is complete repentance. As the power of the repentant grows, our connection with God will exceed the level of each individual and may even influence society.

"Suspicious of why the interpreter was silent, the Belgian reporter asked, 'Is that all?' just to make sure. 'Are your teachings really that simple?' The way he said it implied he was trying to unearth some secret teachings that had to exist in a church like ours, with over two thousand renunciates and funds exceeding two billion yen. To tell the truth, though, that was all there was to it.

"It was after our church became a religious foundation that Guide created his group of the best and the brightest of our young people. He expanded this group at a feverish pace. He bought some resort facilities in Izu that had belonged to a printing company and showed them how to fix it up; when it was finished it was quite a nice research facility. He created research teams to carry out inquiries in many fields—chemistry, biology, and physics—sparing no expense. At first the team members were selected from among our followers and were allowed to carry out the kind of research they had been doing in their former graduate schools and research labs. Over time, though, these members began to ask that former colleagues be allowed to join them. As they did their research together, the new people would usually become believers, a development that took off quickly.

"Guide was always so excited when he reported to me on the activities of the Izu center. Those researchers who joined the church had all had some spiritual unease, and some people had dropped out of the competitive world of graduate school and research labs. Others couldn't get along with their academic advisers. Once these young people found our state-of-the-art research facility, they cooperated with their fellow researchers and immersed themselves in their research.

"The results they came up with at the research facility were good enough to present at international academic conferences, but in Japan once you leave your research lab it's difficult to get another job. These young researchers were oblivious to that, though, and went at their research with all the enthusiasm of young people training for a soccer match. Their attitude toward their work might very well be a model for how young people today should repent. All fired up, Guide told me he dreamed about organizing the education of this kind of young people.

"However, among this elite group, whom I'd left up to him for the most part and whom he mostly trained, a special sort of movement arose concerning our religious activities. In other words, what the press later dubbed the radical faction. This radical faction grew so quickly that it forced Guide and me to do our Somersault, but at first I had no misgivings about them whatsoever. Rather, I felt a childish sense of relief. With this elite corps going at their research with such zeal, Guide wasn't likely to leave the church anytime soon. That's what I hoped."

3

"Before long, Guide began running religious seminars at the Izu center and invited me to lecture. As I'm sure you know, Professor, from your years of teaching, seminars are an interesting forum for teaching because of the interaction between people involved. I was used to speaking about my religious experiences as the visions I'd emotionally and physically experienced, with Guide helping to interpret them, but at the seminar the young people challenged me, and I discovered a new light shining on the page I'd seen in my vision. I found myself rereading this in front of them. That was how I discovered the way to proceed.

"I remember the first seminar well. Guide picked me up at headquarters and accompanied me to the Izu research center; our headquarters had begun as just a single rented room in Asukayama, where we used to meet, but soon we purchased the land and the whole apartment building and made a headquarters appropriate for this period of growth in the church.

"I had little academic background, and I thought it was a bother to have to go to Izu to appear in front of these former students from science departments and medical schools. But something beyond this bothered me. The research facility, once a company resort, looked like an old deserted house from the outside, but once inside you could see how the members' devotion had made it into a pleasant place. To my surprise when I actually saw them all together, I found Guide had assembled over forty of these men and women.

The seminar began in a conference room right after we arrived, as we ate lunch. I was scared to death, but soon I was completely absorbed and found myself saying things I never would have normally said aloud. Guide, seated beside me, sometimes tilted his head to one side in disbelief, but still he viewed the proceedings happily.

"This elite group at the Izu research center was much more alert and active than the young followers at our usual gatherings. They sat at these old-fashioned long tables, no doubt left over from the days when the center was a recreational facility, and leaned forward toward me in rapt attention. I wasn't used to such attentive expressions and shining eyes. It gave me the kind of happy feeling you get when you see something completely new and unexpected. Finally Guide spoke.

"'This isn't the first time you all have met Savior, is it? Most of you have heard him talk before, at various branch gatherings. I assume you're all pleased to have this opportunity to ask him questions directly?'

"They responded with youthful laughter, and one young woman spoke up and said it was the first time she'd actually seen me. She was part of a little five-person group that was seated in the front row, on the right. As soon as I entered the conference room I'd felt something was different about that group. The young woman's hair was pulled back so tightly her forehead looked stretched, and though the color of her eyes was not pure Japanese, she was a type of person you might run across on the streets of Tokyo. Gesticulating in an offhand way that was different from people raised in Japan, she made the following statement:

"'This is the first time I've met Savior,' she said. 'My mother became a follower first. My parents were divorced when I was little and I grew up with my father, who's of Irish extraction, in California. But my mother in Japan got very sick and wanted to see her ex-husband and daughter. She was having a terrible time trying to track us down when Savior gave her a hint that allowed her to locate us. After she got in touch with my father, he went to see her, quit his job, and decided to live in Japan. That's how our family was reunited.

"'I looked for a university I could transfer to from the one I was going to in the States. After I started school here I ran across an old friend from when I was a student in the American School in Yokohama, who was a follower of the Savior. When we graduated he was asked to come to the center here, and I came with him.

"'I was only able to nurse my mother for a short time, but throughout she told me about your teachings, so when I came here I wasn't completely ignorant. Hearing about how you helped my mother find us and, though she didn't recover, how my father changed after meeting her—all this made me believe in the power you possess. And now that I have met you I'm as happy as I imagined I'd be.'

"Still worked up after she finished speaking, the young woman covered her face with her silver-nailed hands and the boy with round glasses next to her, also a Eurasian, gave her a hug. The young women and men around them gave her an enthusiastic round of applause.

"Guide turned to me—he was really speaking to everyone there—and by way of introduction explained that the group this girl was in felt more comfortable speaking English than Japanese. Including this girl, three of them had attended high school at the American School, and two more had lived in English-speaking environments in Fiji and Western Samoa and then returned to high school in Tokyo. Guide explained how these young people were a task force he'd created to deal with the foreign media. That wasn't their only job, of course; they'd all majored in computer science or engineering in college and were going to continue their work here at the center.

"After this bilingual group presented testimonies of how they came to faith, we had a question-and-answer period about the future of the church. They had all swiftly devoured their lunch in the healthy way young people do and were waiting for me to respond to their questions, which I had to do alone, and I remember looking down impatiently at the food that was still on my plate, which I couldn't finish because of all the questions."

4

Patron continued reminiscing to Kizu about the meeting while flipping through a stack of cards that Dancer had brought to him from their office workstation; the cards were ones she'd made by copying out passages from church publications that predated the Somersault.

"One young man who asked some questions was trained in experimental physics. Guide had great hopes for him. This is what the young man said:

"'I'd been taking medicine for many years to control my epileptic seizures. Because of the medicine my head was always in a fog, and I worried that I wouldn't be able to handle the delicate elements of my research. As I feared, I was forced off the research team just when we were reaching the final stages of the research. I'd been on this team ever since I entered the department, so this was a terrible shock. I couldn't get over it and quit the university before I graduated. Despite these problems, soon after I joined the church I was allowed to work in the prophet's research center and I felt—I'd like to check this English word with the bilingual group—*overjoyed*.

"'In the university I was too preoccupied with my own research project and couldn't recognize obstacles along the way, but after I started my research again here I felt I could understand the feelings of my former professor, the one who fired me, and why I wasn't allowed to be a part of the final critical stage of the project. Some of my former colleagues later joined me here, and we enjoy our research to the full every day. Hallelujah! If things continue as they have, I predict some good results before too much longer, and we'll be able to outwit all those colleagues of mine still in the university. The bilingual group has been kind enough to translate some of our research papers into English, and it's as if all the burdens and problems I used to face are gone.

"'But am I making a big mistake all over again? The impetus for joining the church was my frustration, my suffering, but what drew me further in was the Savior's teachings. The world is fast approaching its end, a point that my field of research confirms too. But even if our research team's efforts bear fruit—and I have no doubt they will—that's not going to do anything to stave off the end of the world, is it?

"'Is it really all right for us to just enjoy doing our research in this wonderful environment? The Prophet told us if our research gets results that become known abroad, people won't confuse our church with a cult. That's good, but even if people hold us in higher regard and we get more members, aren't we just doing the same thing that established religious organizations do?

"'There's a list in this little almanac here of the official numbers of members of various religious groups, many of which have huge numbers of followers. Tenrikyo, for instance, has 1.84 million members, Kongokyo has 440,000, Omotokyo has 170,000, Reiyukai 3.2 million, Seicho no ie 840,000, Sekai Kyuseikyo 840,000, Perfect Liberty Church has 1.26 million, Risho Kyosei Kai has 6.35 million, and Sokka Gakkai has more than any of these. If all these churches got together to repent and parade, there'd be 20 million people flooding the streets. But no one ever attempts to do that. Even if our church grows bigger, won't it just become like all the others? If that's the case, my present happiness rests on dubious ground! What I'd like to hear from you are the concrete goals you have in mind for this church you lead.'

"I think what Guide said in response to this was important.

"'It would be even more fitting,' Guide said, 'if you included the large traditional Buddhist sects, as well as Catholics and Protestant denominations, though we're not planning to imitate any of them. If there's anyone here optimistic enough to think that you'll just spend your days leisurely doing research, you're very much mistaken.

"'The Savior has communicated many visions that he's had. The majority of you here have heard his sermons and, as they make clear, the Savior has a comprehensive understanding of the end of the world.

"'The Savior's connection with God is personal, as will be ours as we repent. As our church grows more active, though, and as we call for true repentance and raise society's consciousness of the end of the world, we'll transcend that personal relationship with God. That's the basis of the Savior's teaching. And as for myself, as Prophet, I founded this research center because I wanted to improve the minds of those who were repentant.

"'As the question you've raised indicates, this center has become a solid research facility. It's obvious to me that each researcher here, as a firm believer, has his eyes set on the realistic goals set forth by the Savior. The urgent question you've raised springs directly from that. I'm happy my efforts haven't been in vain. However, don't close your eyes to the problems inherent in your question, problems that characterize the intellectuals in our church. How should we advance toward our goals? Isn't this a question each person must try to answer individually? In this community you're in now, where you can concentrate on both research and prayer, won't all your individual goals eventually meld into one? That's my response as Prophet.'

"After this it was my turn, as Savior, to respond, which I did to some incidental questions; the responses I gave are all on these cards Dancer's putting together, which summarize the opinions I gave through the course of the discussion.

"'On a very basic level, I'm not the kind of person who can deal with society by myself,' I told them. 'When the visions I have in my trances are translated, though, I *am* driven by their power to speak out to you all. Those of you gathered here are all quite young, most of you having joined the church after it was already established; the first person who spoke today, I believe, is the son of one of my followers from the earliest days. I preached that one should cut one's worldly ties in order to repent, but when I see a case like this in which the bonds of family lead one to join the church, I stand in awe.

"'I used to live a hermit's life, like someone living in a cave—my own private life, with my own private trances, and private prayers—until the Prophet forced me to face my followers, whose number had swelled to form a real church, and to confront the outside world. However, as the Prophet has often said, my faith rests solely on the foundation of my trances. I have no set notions of the future, or any concrete plan as to how to proceed. That is the truth.

"'When I am in one of my trances, I'm on the *other side*. When I'm there I don't have a consciousness of standing in front of it—this only comes after I've awoken and mulled over the experience—but what I come face-to-face with is everything in miniature: past, present, and future, every person, thing, and event. It all forms a glowing structure that I'm standing in front of. I'm led to read and understand this structure by a *will* moving horizontally and vertically at the speed of light. If you wish to use the word God, then that *will* is God, that structure itself is God, an understanding I come to only after I've returned.

"'To use a simpler metaphor, it's a book unlike any other, a book within a book, which includes the entire world, the entire universe. I'm on the other side, reading it. This means being conscious of things that transcend the real world, that tie together past and future. Reading this book also means I'm alive in this world, and by living I'm writing new sections of it. If I distance myself even a little, I realize that the words already written in the book, and the new words written in it, are not merely about my own individual inner life. They're not just about my own individual actions, and the limited range of influence these might have in the real world. What I read in that book is the entire past and future of the world—indeed, of the universe—but what happens is that even my own insignificant individual actions, my own passing thoughts, very subtly rewrite the whole. And in this I find evidence that my trifling individual self is one of the saviors of humanity.

"'I think the problem can be summarized this way. All the followers in this church want to take some decisive practical action, with the Prophet and myself leading them. These actions are already written in the book I read in my trances and can be written anew. But I cannot, ahead of time, tell you what they are. When it becomes absolutely necessary for me to speak, when something that transcends us pushes me forward in order to speak, be assured that my vision will take the form of words at the most opportune moment and you'll be the first to know. That time hasn't arrived yet, but it isn't far off.'

"After I finished saying this, the Prophet—for the first time since I met him—swept away the distance he'd always maintained between us. He faced me, gave a slight yet truly heartful bow, and then turned toward the assembled group of hand-picked young people who filled the conference room.

"'Everyone, let us pray! Let us pray! Hallelujah! Let us have faith that even the prayers of the weak and helpless such as ourselves may write one new line in that massive book. And let us all have hope in the Savior's trying task of seeing that in his vision! Let us pray that we may discover what sort of actions are possible for us. Let us await, as we pray, ideas that come to us of our own accord yet are also written in that book. Let us pray for understanding. The end of the world is fast approaching. As we repent, what can we do? What *must* we do? Let us also pray that through the mediation of the Savior, this massive book on the *other side* will reveal the actions we must take. In his presence, and relying on him alone, let us pray. Hallelujah!'"

Kizu had never before heard Patron so excited, or speak about Guide being so worked up. As a person getting on in years, Kizu knew that if this excitement infected him as well, later on, retrospectively, it would leave behind a quite ambiguous emotion. So he adopted an artist's strategy, taking a step back from his subject and reexamining it.

"Did Guide talk to you before all this about why he put forth such a theory? I'm sure the two of you must have discussed it thoroughly beforehand."

A childish, prankish expression crossed Patron's face. "I think Guide must have been worried that I was going to sidestep those zealous young people. I think he was afraid that at my advanced age I wouldn't have anything to say to them and might end up with a few curt words of greeting and call it a day. Looking back on it now, I think the temptation for a Somersault grazed by me at that moment, and Guide must have sensed it."

"I've only spent a short time with him," Kizu said, "but I got the impression that he's not the type who opens up to others. On the other hand, when Ikuo expressed an interest in questioning you directly, Guide was kind enough to make the arrangements. Were Guide's sermons always this emotional?"

"I never saw Guide so excited in front of the followers again, though he could be pretty emotional when we talked privately.

"Another issue was raised that day at the research center. One researcher stood up, a naïve-looking man but actually one tough customer. 'You keep saying the end of the world is near,' he said, 'and I agree. As the earth's population increases, human dignity will go down the drain. But how will the world end? As one who quietly awaits this with a repentant heart, I'd be happy if you'd say a few words about *how* it will end.'

"A few of his fellows heckled him pretty severely for asking this. 'What good is asking that going to do? That's not important!' That sort of thing. The young man turned on his detractors and shouted in an even louder voice than theirs:

"'You all are repenting and praying because the approaching end of the world is important, right? If that's all it is, how is this any different from the apocalyptic teachings of traditional religions?' Why did you choose this particular church to join?

"'I entered this church,' he went on, 'after I heard about the real, concrete visions the Savior had about the end of the world in his trances. I wanted to know more. The more we know, in case the approaching end time gets stalled we can give it a push with our own hands.'

"A young woman wearing glasses as round as two tennis balls, a lively, intelligent sort who looked like she came from a good family, responded to this; she wasn't irritated, exactly.

"'But just because the momentum toward the end of the world comes to a halt,' she said, 'isn't it going a little too far for us to help it along? I'm just a simple person who works with computers, so maybe I haven't grasped the full extent of what you mean. What bothers me about the way you said it is the hint of cynicism. Not that I'm saying you're enjoying the idea of the world ending. Through the Savior's teaching I do want to repent, as the world comes to an end, and gain a deeper acceptance of what's going to occur. There's no room for cynicism or curiosity.'

"Guide broke in at this point to urge me to respond. Based on Dancer's cards, here is the gist of what I said.

"'My vision of the end of the world is limited to a view of a small-sized provincial city, a city on the verge of death. The end has not yet arrived but is surely on its way. Yet not a single voice arises in prayer. The citizens have lost all vitality. That's the scene I envision. What I want to do is to insert a group of repentant, prayerful people in the midst of this scene. My hope is that this will become the model for all human cities.

"'As I said earlier, in the beginning I was just a hopeless recluse who only thought about the salvation of his own soul. As I began to share my individual visions with other people—visions I had in trances that resulted from prayer— I couldn't stay hidden away any longer. And the spot where I ended up was so high it made me dizzy, a place where I also felt I was forced into a dead end.

"'I believe there are many like me now. Compared to two thousand years ago, many more people are leading mankind toward the final day, which I interpret as a sign that indeed the end time is drawing near. I stand before you as one of those people. Because I am, I hope to relate a vision that responds to the question I was just asked in a clearer, more inclusive way.

"'The next time one of my trances comes over me, that's what I plan to do. Striving to answer this ultimate question will add new sentences to the book in which everything, from the beginning to the end, is already written.

"'Today what we've done is confirm this. Everything has gone according to what's been written in the design, from the Prophet preparing this research facility, to his choosing all of you, to finally having me come here. Let's pray, not forgetting to thank the Prophet for what he's done. Hallelujah!'"

Patron's style of speaking, his pauses and his tone of voice, were just like his sermons; once he came to an end, he changed gears, a faint smile arising from something Kizu could only guess at.

"If you look at this first sermon I gave at the Izu research center, it would be irresponsible of me to insist that Guide was solely responsible for training the radical faction. As the new Guide, didn't you think the same thing as you listened to me? Anyhow, that's how it began, and though there were all sorts of complicated situations within the church at the time, my visions were what sparked the radical faction to develop its so-called *Threshold Crosser* device."

Noticing Kizu's suspicious look, Patron said with his fixed Cheshire cat smile, "It's a device to convert a nuclear power plant into a nonportable nuclear bomb. And if this had spread, you'd better believe mankind would have crossed a threshold it was never meant to."

10: Wake Mania Without End (I)

1

The ceiling of the prewar Western-style kitchen was strangely low, the window smeared, and the putty around the frame greasy. Outside, large wet snowflakes were falling; Kizu watched them out to the edge of the faint light illuminating the scene.

It was after dinner. Patron was listening to the CD version of Furt-wängler conducting Bach's St. Matthew Passion on the sound system set up next to the dining table. Soon a cold look came to his face, and without concerning himself with Kizu he shut off the music halfway through. Outside, beyond Patron's drooping shoulders, sleet was changing to snow. Kizu felt uneasy, as if his sense of hearing had suddenly been stripped away from him, and he imagined Patron must be even more sensitive to the sudden silence. Patron went into the kitchen to start washing up, and Kizu followed after him.

There was a huge pile of dirty dishes. At the beginning of the week Guide had taken a turn for the worse and been put in a private room, and Dancer, who'd been with him the whole time, had returned in the late afternoon for the first time to report on his condition. After dinner with Ogi, Ikuo, and Ms. Tachibana, the young people set off for the hospital. Ms. Tachibana, living with her younger brother, had to be home by a fixed time, so it was left to Kizu and Patron to clean up.

With his long years living alone in New Jersey, and now in his Tokyo apartment, Kizu was used to cooking and cleaning up on his own, but Patron was a compete novice when it came to washing dishes. It might have been easier if Kizu had done it alone. Patron, though, seemed genuinely afraid of withdrawing to his bedroom study. At Dancer's insistence there were no chemical cleansers in the kitchen, so it took quite some time to wash the filthy dishes the young people had left using only a large bar of coconut oil soap rubbed into a sponge. Kizu soon took over washing the dishes, Patron the drying. As he dried one dish after another, Patron began a long monologue.

"A while ago I told you how I came to know Guide, and how I was making a living as a fortune-teller. Guide's wife and autistic son ran out on him. His wife had left a note. She said he worried so much and was so overly solicitous toward their son she felt stifled, and they couldn't take it anymore. 'If you come after us and try to get us to come home,' she said, 'we'll kill ourselves. Just leave us alone.'

"When Guide brought this letter to me he was beside himself. A woman whose son was going to night classes at the high school equivalency school felt she just couldn't stand by without doing anything and brought Guide to one of our meetings. He wasn't hoping his wife and son would come back, he just wanted to know they were all right. Instead of trying to search for them, he thought I should read the letter, go into a trance, and tell him how they were. I had two different types of trances, and this required the shallow kind, which I could go into and out of at will.

"The scene I saw in my trance was clear enough but hard to pin down. A middle-aged woman was sitting on a bus, a bulky bag beside her. From the shadows a young man leaped into the picture, and when he reached the front row of seats he rested his hand on the shoulder of a man sitting there and, in a quiet voice, asked him if he was getting off at the next stop.

"When I'd said this much, Guide began to tremble. 'That's definitely my wife and son,' he said. What he said next was the very first of his interpretations of my visions, one might say. 'My son likes buses,' he said, 'especially the front row. My wife or I tell him not to, but he always sidles up to the front and asks whoever's sitting there that question. My wife's people live in Boso and earn their living farming and fishing, so they must be carrying fish and vegetables into Tokyo to sell. Seeing as how they make a round trip every day into the city on trains and buses, my son must be happy.'

"Even after Guide had determined where his family was, he still came sometimes to our meetings; before long his wife filed for divorce. His wife was afraid of him and didn't show up in family court, so the divorce wasn't finalized, but Guide just left it at that. He said the reason he didn't get divorced was like the idea you had, Professor Kizu, of you and Ikuo grasping hands and heading off to the *other side*. When his autistic son was to head off to the *other side*, Guide wanted to be there to help him. Guide had been over-zealous in educating his son so the boy had rebelled. When Guide had tried to suppress the rebellion, the mother felt sorry for the boy and the two of them ran away from home.

"Still, though, Guide's dream was to be able to help his son on the *other side,* to mediate between his son's soul and God. He couldn't give up this idea. Guide was able to interpret my visions, and finally that became his full-time role. But behind his becoming a pillar of the church lay these personal emotional motives.

"And now Guide is unconscious, his body reacting only mechanically. On the one hand is the brain of the autistic son, closed to the world outside; on the other, the brain of the father, struck down by an aneurysm. I'm haunted by a scene of endless sky and far-off horizon, with two oval-shaped dishes like these lying there. And a human brain on each one."

Patron held a large plate to the lacy apron at his chest, and while Kizu pictured what was happening in a far-off building surrounded by snow, he almost burst out laughing. With Patron's combination of the tragic and the comic, his solemn seriousness and his occasional doubtfulness, Kizu couldn't help but know he was in the presence of someone quite special.

"What really hurts most when I think of Guide is what he told me after he had his first attack, when he recovered and came home from the hospital. When the blood vessel in his forehead burst, he said, he didn't get confused right away. He felt bad, got up go to the rest room to try to throw up, and was halfway there when he suddenly found himself not inside a building but standing in a wilderness at twilight. And with a great noise, this whole wilderness was rolling up from the edges at the horizon. And then he lost consciousness. Guide used this expression, which makes it seem that the vision I had that I just told you about was something *he* told *me.* That's how strong a relationship we'd built up over such a long time.

"What comes to me now is that during his second attack there must have been a short period when his mind was still clear. Guide knew what was going on. How frightened he must have been, wondering whether the group that took him captive was hoping he'd collapse. He must have felt a terrible sadness too, knowing he'd lost forever his chance to find his son and escort him to the *other side.*

"That's how I imagined Guide's experience. And the conclusion I came to, Professor, is that although Guide wanted to be a mediator for his autistic son, in fact it was the son who was *his* railing, *his* lifeline."

Patron ran out of words. His spiritless face, poised between his bent left hand, about to grasp a plate, and his right, holding out a dish towel, fairly glinted with sorrow.

As he had never done before to anyone, Kizu placed his arm around Patron's apron-wrapped shoulder and led him out of the kitchen. The curtains were still open, and in the darkness of the garden the snow began to swirl silently. The two elderly men, in their loud aprons, faintly reflected in the windowpane, looked just like two children in a nursery school Christmas pageant who had stood rooted to one spot until, years later, they'd grown old.

2

Kizu planned to take Patron to his bedroom study and then wait in the office in case there was an emergency call from the hospital. But as they rounded the corner in the hallway Patron came to a halt and refused to go farther. Reluctantly, Kizu led him to the living room sofa, but again he protested wordlessly and sat down in the armchair facing away from the glass door leading to the garden.

"Would you like to listen to Bach again?" Kizu asked.

Looking back at him, Patron shook his head.

"Well, then," Kizu said, "maybe I can use this opportunity to ask you something Ikuo wants me to ask."

"Dancer already told me," Patron said. "She came to me all excited and said Ikuo had just asked you to put this question to me: *Whether false savior or genuine, how did you start thinking you were the savior?* Isn't this what he wanted you to ask?" Kizu nodded. "Since he used these exact words with Dancer, I think that even before Ikuo talked to you he knew exactly what he wanted to say.

"The best way to answer is, once again, to begin by talking about Guide. When I asked him to take on the job of Prophet, I didn't have a clear sense of myself as Savior. It was only after I forced him into the role of Prophet that he began to see my trances as mystical experiences and convinced me that I could use them to lead him and other people.

"Ever since I was a certain age I knew I couldn't avoid having these experiences. Over time they jolted me out of the everyday. Every time I had a mystical experience I suffered and was worn out, though afterward I felt totally energized. After I returned to this side, I was driven to tell people what I'd seen over there. Before Guide was with me I experimented with all sorts of ways to do this, but no one took me seriously, except for the predictions I made after I reluctantly starting earning a living as a fortune-teller.

"Soon I'd fall into depression again and begin to regret the stupid things I was doing. As I became more and more depressed, I had a premonition that when I hit bottom I'd be thrust into another mystical experience. So I realized depression wasn't going to make me kill myself.

"I was repeating this cycle over and over when I first met Guide. A true man of science, no doubt he was eager to uncover this fortune-teller as a fraud. But the scene I saw in the trance portrayed—quite accurately, it turned out—his wife and autistic son.

"Since he was a scientist, Guide placed a high value on the scientific method and believed the only valid theory was one that grew out of this. He studied my trances with great inquisitiveness and soon experienced one of my deep trances. He made a distinction between the two kinds and concentrated on the more intense ones, with their visions I couldn't comprehend yet couldn't let slip away.

"Guide wasn't the kind of person to be satisfied with a halfhearted response, so I felt cornered and for the first time got serious about these visions myself. He took care of me when I had my trances, and I did my best to tell him the visions that remained like echoes in my mind. As if I had no other choice, I talked for about an hour, and gradually the roles of speaker and listener were reversed. He connected the fragments of my vision and began talking to me, convincing me that yes, indeed, what he was saying was what I saw in my trance.

"Since he could describe what I saw in my visions, I began to rely on him more and more. I would fall into one of these painful trances and have a vision, and during its aftereffects, when my psyche was still half destroyed, I'd blurt out some nonsense. He helped me link up the person I became in moments like that with the person I was after I'd recovered. I felt I could pull together the shattered personality I'd believed to be lost for over a decade.

"As I said a while ago, right after my trances I was always worked up. I had to tell people what I'd seen. I knew what I said was mostly nonsense, but I just had to say *something*. And then I'd deeply regret having spoken and become depressed. Still, through that process I couldn't deny the mystical experiences I had. It was all so unspeakably painful.

"The difference now was that after I awoke from a trance and recovered from the unsettled emotional state that always followed, I had a patient listener who would put my scattered words in order. He gave meaning to the disaster that had ruined half my life, and through his help I discovered a new whole sense of self. What he made whole was me, the Savior, *whether false or genuine.* That was how it began."

Patron's monologue came to a halt. A long but not unnatural silence descended on them. With all other sounds absorbed by the falling snow, the sound of the gate outside being pushed open suddenly rang out loud and clear.

Dancer came into the living room, surrounded by the cold iron smell of the snow she'd brushed off at the entrance. Silently, she looked reprovingly at Patron and, ignoring Kizu, walked over to the armchair.

"I'll talk with you after you've gone to your room," she said, nimbly getting Patron up.

Kizu watched her propel Patron into his bedroom study, a clump of snow clinging to her skirt. Ikuo, coming in a moment later, plopped down without a word in the chair facing away from the dining room, the one at a right angle to the sofa. The scent Kizu sniffed out from his large body was the metallic smell of snow Dancer had brought with her, overlaid with sweat. Ikuo held Kizu's questioning gaze and nodded gravely, his expression showing small signs both of a deep exhaustion and a renewed vigor.

"I see. . . . He's gone. That is really a shame," was all Kizu could muster. "So the two of you walked back all the way in the snow?"

"The train was stopped at Kyodo so we walked from there. Dancer's done so much serious training she barely broke a sweat. Ogi stayed at the hospital to deal with the police and make funeral arrangements. The newspapers seem to have caught wind of it, and reporters have been snooping around the night reception desk. I thought it would be a pain to have phone calls coming in here so I switched the office phone over to fax when we left—which is why we couldn't call you—and came back instead. Dancer in particular wanted to report directly to Patron."

Dancer had led Patron into the back, as if scolding a child for staying up too late, but now no voices could be heard. Kizu fixed his gaze on the carved vine-covered clock on the wall, which hung next to the watercolor he'd presented to Patron. It was already past three.

"When people die . . . even if it's from illness, it's a terrible thing," Ikuo said. "Guide may have been brain dead, just an *object,* but when I saw him sweep aside his IV tube and sit up halfway in bed to vomit, trying not to soil his bed, I knew this wasn't just some inanimate thing."

They suddenly noticed that Dancer had come out from Patron's room and was standing at the corner of the dining room, looking down at Kizu and Ikuo.

"Patron told me again that he wants you to be Guide," she said to Kizu.

3

The next morning dawned clear, not a cloud in the sky. Over a foot of snow piled up in the branches and treetops, and the trees in the garden leaned over at anarchic angles. The line of potted wild plants looked like deep-dish pot pies. The layer of snow covering the ground twinkled in dead silence. The morning was still early. Kizu and Ikuo had slept in the annex, and Kizu left Ikuo there, deep in the enduring sleep of a healthy young man, and went over to the main house. Dancer was already up, planted in the chair that Ogi normally used, hard at work. When she saw Kizu she reported that last night she'd recorded Patron's statement on the death of Guide. She was letting Patron sleep in and was getting things ready for what was likely to prove a busy afternoon.

The small lamp on her desk just illuminated the documents on top of it, and in contrast to the bright snow coming from the north and south sides of the garden, in this darkly shadowed interior Dancer's face looked pale and swollen. Her nostalgic little-girl-with-a-cold face at the same time showed the pain of one who's been abandoned. Kizu wondered when Patron was planning to visit the hospital and how they planned to get there if the snow prevented them from taking the car.

"Patron isn't going to the hospital," Dancer replied. "Point-blank, without any emotion, he said there was no need, now that Guide has passed away."

"But he will have to bid farewell to the body, won't he? Is Ogi going to bring the body back here?"

"We've made an appointment at the crematorium; Ogi will take care of everything. We'll just wait for the ashes to be brought back here. In the afternoon we'll be inundated with reporters, and Patron plans to hold a press conference. We'll all be pretty busy. Ms. Tachibana will be bringing one of her colleagues but will have to wait until the trains are running again."

"How were Guide's wife and son told?"

As if wondering how much Kizu already knew about Guide's family, Dancer assumed her typical expression, mouth slightly open, for the first time this morning.

"I think Ogi contacted them last night, before dinner," she replied. "When we got back to the hospital, his wife and son were already there. His wife seemed to think it was very important for her to see him once before he died—even if he wasn't able to realize she was there. When the doctors were performing heart massage and ordered everyone out of the room, she insisted on staying there and did so, along with her son. When we went back into the room, she looked devastated, as if it had been her chest they'd been massaging.

"All things considered, she held up well; she kept repeating to her poor son that his father had died repentant. Ogi's supposed to escort them to the crematorium. Guide's wife wanted to go back to Boso as soon as she could and told us that though her husband had been a big man and there would be a lot of bones left after the cremation, they need only bury a small portion."

"So his wife said he died repentant, did she?" Kizu said, his voice full of regret for the bereaved family.

Dancer leaped in adroitly. "I wonder how his wife and son understood the word. Ikuo and I discussed it on the way back, whether what she said about repentance is the same thing as the term Patron uses in his teaching, or whether she meant your garden variety of repentance."

"Do you mean Guide repenting what he did to his family?" Kizu asked her. "Maybe all repentance leads in the same direction."

"When Patron heard this, he cried," Dancer said, looking at Kizu closely to gauge his reaction.

"It must be a complex thing for Patron."

"Don't be so standoffish—like it has nothing to do with you," Dancer protested mildly. "Instead, as your first task as the new Guide, would you transcribe the tape of Patron's announcement?"

Dancer leaned forward to pass him the tape, still in its Walkman, her eyes as she did so overflowing with light reflected from the snow on the north side of the house like some alien on a TV movie. Dancer had a dignity that wouldn't take no for an answer, and her obvious exhaustion—she'd only managed to grab a few hours' sleep—did nothing to diminish the energy with which she took care of the work she had to do. Still, though, she showed her concern, saying, "If you'd like to have breakfast before you get to work, I'll make it."

"No, I don't want to bother you with those kinds of chores," Kizu said, borrowing a ballpoint pen and loose-leaf notebook. "Ikuo should be up soon. I'll ask him to fix it."

Kizu settled down in the armchair Patron had recently occupied, put on the headphone, and pushed the PLAY button on the Walkman.

Patron was muttering, so at first Kizu couldn't understand him. He was about to turn up the volume but the switch was taped over. He looked up and Dancer, who'd been watching him all the while, nodded, her eyes like melted pools of ice. She seemed to be telling him to listen to the tape as it was, until Patron's low murmur itself changed in tone.

Headphones still on, Kizu turned to look at the snowy garden outside. The small leaves of the azalea hedge shivered under the thick layer of snow; the snow-covered stems of the withered hydrangea leaves shook with the wind. Kizu noticed one clear difference between this scene and the one that greeted him on snowy mornings back in the States. At the thick base of the winter camellia, with its large white flowers, the snow was sticking to one side only. The snow was piled up on the branches and clumps of leaves, but the wind didn't budge it. At his apartment at the university the day after it snowed, the piled-up snow, as high as the roof and the trees, would blow up in the air and swirl around in dry and powdery flakes.

Gradually, though it was still muffled and at the same volume level, he could make out what Patron was saying. As he came to the end of the tape, one phrase in particular stood out: *Thy will be done.*

Kizu transcribed Patron's talk on the tape into the notebook. As he did so he felt a force pushing him back, interrupting the flow of the sentences, a force that had its roots in the quiet, calm measures in which Patron spoke. Kizu couldn't reproduce this style in writing, and he was amazed all over again at the depth and intimacy that Patron and Guide had shared. Still, Kizu managed to finish a first draft, which he tore out of the notebook and placed beside the computer where Dancer was working.

"This is pretty flat and doesn't reflect Patron's tone of voice at all," Kizu explained timidly.

Guide has died of a brain aneurysm that was deliberately brought on by those who held him captive and, for a long time, harassed him in a kangaroo trial. The people in this group who victimized him were members of the radical faction of our church at the time, ten years ago, when we did our Somersault. Several of these people belonged to the group that actually committed subversive activities. As a result these people, including ones who were legally sanctioned, took revenge on Guide and carried out their lynch-mob justice.

They were trying, after a ten-year delay, to make Guide take responsibility for the Somersault. But the Somersault was mostly my responsibility, something Guide did along with me. The relationship between Guide and myself continued all the while, from when it was just the two of us training ourselves spiritually, through when we formed a church, to the time when we undertook large-scale religious activities. The Somersault, too, took place as part of our longtime relationship. But I took the lead. It's illogical for the radical faction to kill Guide while not pursuing me.

If they were aware of this inconsistency yet still went ahead with it, it must be part of their strategy for the future. Their intention is to provoke me—but to what end? To direct me to perform another Somersault, this time without Guide backing me up?

What we did, though, makes that impossible. Having done our Somersault, the two of us fell into hell, where we stayed for ten years. Just when we found the strength to crawl out of this hell, Guide was tortured to death by those people who, clinging to their one-dimensional viewpoint, tried to force him into a backward Somersault. Now that he's been killed, all I have is a handful of trusted companions to help me begin my new movement.

This is what the people who killed Guide planned from the start. They weren't really aiming at a reverse Somersault. Guide's refusal—unto death—to take a backward Somersault showed them exactly where we stood, stumbling up out of the abyss of our own private hell to begin again.

I'm announcing this to those who did not distort our Somersault and who patiently awaited our rebirth from hell. I am also appealing to those who only just learned about what happened to Guide and who want to hold him dear in their memory. Guide has been lost to us, but I, Patron, am taking a bold new step forward.

First of all, though, I will hold a memorial service for Guide. I would like to pray together with my new companions. Hallelujah! Thy will be done!

4

Dancer read Patron's announcement that Kizu had transcribed and, without expression, went to Patron's room to deliver it to him. Ikuo was up by this time and came over, and Kizu told him about the job he'd just completed, urging him to listen to the Walkman. Ikuo, too, had a hard time at first in trying to turn up the volume. After he was finished listening, he said, excitedly:

"Patron seems to be focusing on those who still believe in him and people who individually got in touch with him. But wouldn't this include people left over from the radical faction? Won't they respond to Patron's announcement too? Not those who were directly responsible for Guide's death, of course; that's out of the question. But don't some of these former faction members still want to take radical action?"

"You really seem to be interested in what moves that group is going to make," Kizu asked. "This meeting that Patron's going to hold is his way of memorializing Guide."

"Patron announced he's starting a new movement," Ikuo said, "so after the service there's no way he can retreat back into the hell he fell into after the Somersault. Not that I understand much about this hell or anything—"

Dancer rejoined them, interrupting Ikuo, who was about to say more. "Patron says the announcement is fine," she said to Kizu. "He told me once that when he and Guide used to be engrossed in work together they'd invariably argue. Guide's task, as you know, was to take from Patron what could not be put into human language and somehow make it understandable, right? I imagine, Professor, that as you listened to the tape you struggled with the same thing."

"But what I did was different from what Guide used to do," Kizu said, "which must have been an amazingly difficult undertaking. There's a context behind the nuances of what Patron says that I can't quite grasp, and I'm afraid I had to content myself with writing the sort of humdrum sentences anybody can come up with."

"I was talking with Ogi about creating a home page on the Internet for our new movement," Ikuo cut in. "People could access that and listen directly to Patron's announcement. What do you think?"

"Please don't get our Innocent Youth involved in all kinds of extraneous work," Dancer replied, sidestepping his question. "While he's busy at the hospital and crematorium, I'd like you to take care of the business here that needs to be done. I want to pass this announcement to the media, so I'd like you to input it into the computer."

Ikuo stretched out a long muscular arm to take the loose-leaf pages and began running his eyes over them.

"Patron said it's fine the way it is."

Undeterred by the way Dancer had flared up at him, Ikuo began intently working under Kizu's attentive gaze. Did the tension between these two young people have its origin in their conversation during their forced march through the snow the night before? Kizu wondered.

Less than an hour later the front doorbell rang, and since Dancer and Ikuo were engrossed in their work it was left to Kizu, ensconced on the sofa, to answer it. He stepped down onto the concrete floor of the entrance, unlatched the lock Ikuo had fastened, and found Ms. Tachibana and a young woman standing just outside the front door. The snow-covered garden behind them was excessively bright. Backlit by this, the pale young woman was introduced to him by Ms. Tachibana as her friend Ms. Asuka; Ms. Asuka merely nodded her head in greeting. Ms. Tachibana continued.

"There's someone outside the main gate who says he made a TV program about Patron before the Somersault," she said. "He hasn't seen Patron in fifteen years, and asked if Patron would be willing to meet him."

The three of them went to the office and found Dancer on the phone. She soon held the receiver out for Ikuo.

"It's Ogi," she told him. "He says a bunch of people showed up at the hospital who are causing trouble. But he doesn't want the hospital to call the police to clear them out."

Ikuo took the receiver and began to talk, and Dancer, in her unaffected way, went over to stand beside Ms. Tachibana and Ms. Asuka, and the three of them went into the kitchen. Ikuo finished his phone call and told Kizu what it was all about.

"As Dancer said, a few members of the former radical faction saw the news on the morning TV show and came to the hospital. Ogi says he doesn't know if they have any connection with the ones who killed Guide, but he doesn't think they're the ones the police are looking for. Since the former radical faction consisted of people hand-picked and trained by Guide, it's only natural, I guess, that some of them would grieve over his death. Anyway, Ogi had them wait in a corner of the hospital waiting room while he was busy taking calls and greeting other visitors. He told them someone from our office would be coming in an hour and asked them to wait at a coffee shop between the hospital and the subway station."

"I'd like the Professor to stay here, so you go alone, Ikuo," Dancer said, sticking her face out from the kitchen; she and the other two women had been doing something in there. "I'll go talk with the TV reporter outside."

Kizu expected Ikuo to object to Dancer's unilateral orders, but he seemed instead to accept them wholeheartedly.

"What about breakfast? Would you like something before you go?" Ms. Tachibana said, as she too stuck her head out from the kitchen.

Ikuo picked up his down jacket and muffler from the two Windsor chairs in a corner of the office that he and Dancer had used to drape their clothes over the previous night and, unconcerned about whether they were dry or not, prepared to leave.

"I'll pick up something at the McDonald's near the station," Ikuo said.

"I've made up these expense forms, so be sure to sign one before you go," Dancer said, holding out the envelope. She hurried to catch up with him and walked outside to talk with the reporter, who was waiting beyond the still snow-covered gate.

After some time, Dancer returned. The TV van to be used in a live remote was parked at the large railroad crossing, already cleared of snow, she reported, and they'd discussed how the media crowd was to be handled and the arrangements for the afternoon. The van driver told her about traffic conditions after the snowfall, and Dancer was optimistic that the road from the hospital to the crematorium and then back to headquarters with the remains would be passable. Preparations for breakfast were finished. Dancer went again to help Ms. Tachibana and Ms. Asuka and then took Patron's meal and her own into his bedroom study.

Kizu was quite dazzled by these young women's brisk way of working. The meal they laid out on the dining table was a kind of brunch, a word now even used in Japan, and Kizu found himself unexpectedly nostalgic for life in America. Seeing Japanese homestyle meals becoming, in an entirely natural way, so close to ones in America made him realize how long he'd been away from his homeland.

Ms. Asuka, with her round forehead and long thin eyebrows, sat across from Kizu, looking quite aloof. She was adroitly eating ham with a slice of soft-boiled egg on top, and this, too, struck Kizu as part of a new Japanese way of eating. Unexpectedly, she asked him a direct question.

"There'll be TV cameramen at Patron's press conference this afternoon, won't there? If Patron is starting up his movement again, I'd like to record his sermon on video. I mentioned this to Ogi, and he sounded out Patron. I know a press conference and a sermon are different, but when I asked Dancer if I could start filming today for practice, she said I should ask *you*."

"I think it would be all right, though I'm sort of feeling my way into this new role," Kizu ventured timidly.

"If Patron is officially launching his new movement, I'd like to bring my brother with me," Ms. Tachibana said.

"I have no idea how Patron plans to develop this new movement. One thing he did say in his announcement was that it's not a reverse Somersault. And it's clear that he's appealing to new participants like you," Kizu said.

"We're really looking forward to it," Ms. Asuka said calmly, and Ms. Tachibana nodded in agreement.

"Ikuo and I, too, have decided to follow Patron, but honestly speaking, that's all there is to it. There's no way I could replace Guide."

The three sat there silently, lost in their own thoughts. Their conversation may have come to a halt, but the dining area was filled with unusual vitality.

5

Only a handful of reporters showed up for Patron's afternoon press conference, representing one national newspaper, one national wire service, one Nagasaki newspaper—Kizu wondered why Nagasaki, but Patron said that was where Guide was from—and two weekly magazines. In addition to the reporters, a few photographers also showed up for the conference, which was set up by connecting the dining room and the living room. Though there were so few participants, with the sofas pushed off to one side next to the sliding glass door leading to the garden, and TV cameras from the TV station set up, it did have the feeling of a genuine press conference.

The reporters were asked to sit directly on the carpeting. Flanking them were Kizu and Ms. Tachibana. Ikuo, who had returned with Ogi, was holding the urn that contained Guide's remains. In addition, there were three brawny men in their late thirties who had not given their names to Ms. Asuka, who was in charge of having people sign in, insisting instead that they'd already cleared things. The men wore humble-looking outfits not in keeping with their robust physiques. As they settled down hesitantly into seats behind the TV crew, Ikuo watched them carefully but didn't acknowledge them.

Kizu could sense that Ogi, who as the emcee made a few opening remarks before Patron appeared, was nervous about the presence of these men. Ikuo, in contrast, couldn't have appeared more nonchalant.

Patron came into the room, accompanied by Dancer. The partition between the dining room and the living room, which was one level lower, was set up for use as a table, and they had placed a chair there for Patron. He was dressed in navy blue cotton slacks and a paisley collared shirt, with a black denim shirt over it. Dancer, her arm around his back as they walked, wore a form-fitting green dress, adding a bit of accent to Patron's conservative appearance.

Patron sat down in the chair and Dancer stood to one side behind him. Ogi had already taken up a similar position on Patron's other side. Kizu noticed how Dancer kept her eyes on the young men sitting behind the TV crew. Previously somber, the young men were now suddenly rejuvenated as they trained their attention on Patron. For his part Patron swept the assemblage with his eyes, without paying attention to anyone in particular. He looked at Ogi and began speaking, sounding less like he was holding a press conference than just having a private conversation.

"I'm planning to hold a memorial service and give a sermon to pay tribute to Guide's suffering. . . . I assume you all have a copy of my announcement?"

Patron paused and looked out, head raised, as if to make sure the television crew had set up their camera in a good position for a view of his face and torso. Ms. Asuka stood beside the TV crew, video camera in hand. Kizu noticed a faint smile on her lips.

Before the reporters showed up, Kizu had expressed his misgivings to Dancer about allowing Patron to appear, defenseless, in front of the media.

She didn't answer him directly but did say that when she told Patron the name of the TV producer she'd met with he was relieved and seemed to be planning to talk to the TV camera rather than the newspaper reporters.

"Is Ogi sending out invitations to the memorial service to people who said they'd like to attend?" Patron asked. "Ever since Guide's disaster was reported, he's been receiving e-mails and other communications. I'd like to hold the service within three weeks, and I'd like you to start thinking about a venue. We need to consider the scale of the meeting, and how many invitations to send out, so you'll need to confirm by checking Ogi's list. So far he has over two hundred names.

"We'll expand from this base of two hundred people. I plan to give a major sermon at the memorial service. I'm not expecting all the people who attend the service to want to participate in my new movement, but with that many people assembled I do want to announce the restarting of our up-till-now dormant movement. I'm also hoping people in the media will cover this announcement.

"At the start of our new movement, I want to make one position clear. As our church expands—starting with Japan but including the entire world— we will never again compromise. I will call on every single person on this planet to repent. I want our church and all our activities to be permeated with this urgent call for universal repentance.

"After the Somersault, Guide and I fell into the abjectness of hell, where I was forced to ponder the salvation of mankind. Guide was the one pilot we could rely on. Just as we resurfaced, though, he was cruelly murdered. At the same time, this proved to me that the time to take action was near. I want to appeal again to people to repent at the coming end of the world. In order to carry this out, I will fight the final battle against the entire human race on this planet. My church does not possess nuclear weapons, nor does it manufacture chemical weapons. People might wonder how we can possibly carry out a such a battle, and laugh at us for trying, but I believe we *can* and *must* fight. At the cost of his own life, Guide protected mankind's Patron—in other words, me. His death has revealed my legitimacy. In the end, people like us will emerge victorious."

When Patron ended there was applause, which startled Kizu. His surprise was also due in part to the strange feeling he got from what Patron had just said. Stretching themselves upward, the three vigorous young men behind the TV crew were among those clapping. Patron looked in their direction for the first time and appeared to be searching his memory.

Seeing that Patron was not about to begin speaking again, a small dark-skinned man stood up to ask a question. He was the city section reporter from the national newspaper. He had been exchanging whispered comments with the woman beside him, a colleague by the look of it, as they eyed the three men in back.

"You just stated your determination to fight the final battle on earth," the reporter said, "which is a pretty frightening prospect when you think about it. You also said that you possess neither nuclear nor chemical weapons, and I can tell you that those of us in the secular world are thankful to hear that!"

He paused for a moment, apparently expecting laughter, but none of his colleagues laughed.

"Further, you have given us a surprisingly open view of the inner workings of your new movement and stated that you plan to restart your religious movement starting with just two hundred people. How can that be enough people to fight this final battle?"

The reporter paused again, waiting for a merry response, but this didn't work out as he'd hoped either. Kizu sensed it had something to do with the attitude of the three men who had earlier applauded.

"I'm assuming that what you told us is based on the principles of the movement you are about to begin," he went on, "but there's something that bothers me. Recently there was another religious group in our country that advocated an Armageddon fight to the finish, a group that committed indiscriminate terrorist acts against ordinary citizens by releasing sarin gas in the Tokyo subway. No one in Japan has forgotten this.

"The founder of this group, Aum Shinrikyo, was trained in India, and at the point where he first declared himself to be the Final Liberated One he had only thirty-five followers. By the next year this had grown to fifteen hundred. Later, a core leadership joined that committed several terrorist acts. The following year, the year their Mount Fuji headquarters was completed, they reached thirty-five hundred followers and became a religious corporation. Two years later they ran candidates in a national election, and even the one billion yen they spent in the effort didn't seem to faze them, so great were their financial resources by this time. Finally, they made contacts with sources in the collapsing Soviet Union and purchased some large helicopters, all the while developing the capability to produce seventy tons of sarin.

"So they started with thirty-five people and got to this point in less than ten years. If they'd really been able to carry out their Armageddon battle, the four thousand people killed and injured in the sarin attack on the subway would have been nothing in comparison. The people of Tokyo already know this all too well, wouldn't you agree, that this religious group steadfastly did not *compromise*—not with Japanese society and not with mankind?

"You were the leader of a religious organization that was also recognized as a religious nonprofit organization. You have the experience and, as we've heard today, the faith to be that type of leader. I'm not saying that the Anti-Subversive Act should be applied to your church as you begin a new movement, but as someone whose job it is to report to the public, I don't want to be just a mouthpiece to publicize your group either. We in the media need to be self-critical. At a certain stage of Aum's rapid growth, the media actually helped popularize it; this played well with the boom in interest in supernatural powers that the media also instigated. Even if we knew our articles were nonsense when we wrote them, many people began serious training in order to achieve supernatural powers, then became renunciates, abandoning their studies in college or their positions in society.

"Ten years ago, you yourself, fearing new developments that the radical faction was instigating, abandoned your followers. As the leader you went on national television and revealed that nothing you'd done and said should be taken seriously. And you did your Somersault. This was absolutely necessary to abort the plans of the radical faction to take over a nuclear power plant. And the remnants of this radical faction have now taken your companion captive and killed him.

"This is what we understand from police reports. However, here, at a press conference to announce a gathering to mourn the death of this victim, you make these antisocial pronouncements. What's going on here? I really find it hard to fathom—"

At this point Dancer cut off both the reporter and Patron, who was about to respond, and turned decisively to the assembled members of the media.

"Please consider the gentleman's words as more like a commentary on what Patron said than a question. For the rest of our time, we'd like to have a genuine question-and-answer session. Keep your questions concise, if you would. Since Guide met his untimely end, Patron has been exhausted both mentally and physically, so we'd like to keep this to a maximum of thirty minutes."

"All right, then, I'll rephrase it as a question," the reporter who'd just spoken said, raising his hand. "What do you mean when you say you'll fight the final war with the world? What was the Somersault all about? Its aftereffects have not disappeared even after ten years, as we see from this recent tragic turn of events—"

Dancer wasn't about to let Patron take over.

"Why are you asking what the Somersault was all about?" she said. "Patron and Guide went through that painful experience because the Somersault was necessary at that time. And they fell into hell, didn't they? Since you already know all this, I want to ask *you* how you could possibly ask what the Somersault meant."

The three vigorous young men clapped loudly and Dancer glared at them. To Kizu her stance looked like a *mie,* one of those frozen dramatic moments in kabuki when the actor assumes an exaggerated pose.

"Then I'll ask a different question," the reporter persisted. "Since the direction you'll be taking your church is toward a final war with the world, how do you differ from Aum Shinrikyo, which preached an apocalyptic vision of Armageddon?"

Dancer looked ready to snap at him again, but Patron, the sleeves of his oversized denim shirt flapping, stopped her. To Kizu this action was yet another of Patron's gestures he'd perfected over time.

"In the past," Patron said, "both Guide and I believed that only through our own deaths would we be able to send out a clear message for people to repent. The idea of occupying a nuclear power plant and using it as a nuclear weapon that didn't need a delivery system was based on this. When our shock corps went into action, it would mean that Guide and I were going to die— together with these young people who, through their actions, repented, cleansed their souls, and were headed toward rebirth.

"However, what would we do if—in this suffering world—some people decided that they alone would survive? Realizing that what we'd said and done was being used to justify this erroneous way of thinking, we did the Somersault. This new church we're starting, however, is not at all like that."

At this point Dancer, who was there to support Patron physically, skillfully took over. The three men seated behind the TV crew seemed about to protest—not at Patron's words but over the reporter's attitude—but Dancer raised her hands to stop both them and the reporters and helped Patron to his feet. By the time Ogi announced that the press conference was over, the two of them had already disappeared down the darkened hallway.

Kizu watched as Ikuo stepped in to smooth things down among the three men as they shouted at the dark-skinned reporter, who had been the sole interlocutor at the press conference. Freed by Ikuo's intervention, the reporter walked over to talk with Kizu.

11: Wake Mania Without End (II)

1

In the end, the indomitable reporter talked Kizu into going with him to a coffee shop on the road back to the station from the office. The owner of the shop, busy brewing some coffee through a siphon, took their orders and slipped back behind the antique counter, while the reporter turned to Kizu and reintroduced himself.

"I originally worked for an economics trade paper, but soon after I shifted over to a regular newspaper I began covering the story of those men; in my first article I called them the Don Quixote and Sancho Panza of new religions. Using the names the people in the church used at the time, the Prophet, tall and thin, was Don Quixote, while roly-poly Savior was Sancho Panza. But my editor complained that readers would get confused unless I called the founder of the church Don Quixote, so they reversed the names.

"I'm not just saying this to butter you up, but I find it interesting that you also, as Patron's new adviser, are a fairly large-boned man."

Without any indication that he was absorbing this, Kizu asked a question of his own. "Have you been gathering material on the two men all this time?"

"In our paper I'm mainly the one who covered them."

"I'd like to help you as much as I can," Kizu said, "but I don't have a lot of background knowledge. Could you fill me in on Guide's childhood and the background to his joining the religious movement? I've been asked to take over his job—only a part of it, of course—but it bothers me that I know next to nothing about my predecessor."

The reporter's dark skin and features put Kizu in mind of a *karasu tengu*, a legendary goblin with a crow's beak.

"Guide was born in Nagasaki City," the reporter began, as he stared back at Kizu, "and as an infant survived the atomic bombing. His mother died; his father, an army doctor, was at the front; he was rescued by his uncle, also a physician, who came back for him in the chaos following the bombing. A dramatic sort of childhood, I'm sure you'd agree. His family had been Catholic for generations, and Guide was baptized as an infant. He ended up leaving the church when he was in high school, though, when he read in the paper that a famous Catholic man of letters was granted an audience by Emperor Hirohito. That was enough reason for him to bid Catholicism adieu.

"Guide admitted this was a childish reaction, but at the time he concluded that he couldn't continue in his faith. This relates to the dilemma that's been around since the Meiji period, when Christianity swelled in influence at the same time that nationalism came to the fore. You know the old saw: Who is greater, Jesus Christ or the Emperor?

"As a young man, Guide decided that Christ could never have real authority in this country. So he spent the following years cut off from the church, entered the science department at the university, and became obsessed with a new idea—that it was exactly in a country like Japan that Jesus Christ *must* appear in the Second Coming. Guide started attending Protestant churches with only one goal in mind. When he found a minister who was open to him, he would confront him: Who is greater, Jesus Christ or the Emperor?

"Our country's Emperor was no longer the god people thought he was before and during the war. The new constitution defined him as a symbol of the state, with no actual power. This is what the minister told Guide. Stubborn young man that he was, though, Guide insisted: Who is greater, Jesus Christ or the Emperor? And this led to a falling-out between him and the Protestant church.

"His dream was for Jesus' Second Coming to take place in Japan so he could finally answer the question of who was greater. But since it didn't look like Christ was going to appear, he came up with the radical idea of people creating a substitute with their own hands.

"In Guide's heart, then, someone like Patron was necessary, and from early on he had the idea of creating that sort of figure. I think the explanation for the two of them getting together might lie in this, don't you think?"

"I can see you're a real reporter, since you've cut right to the core of what I've been concerned about. You've given me a lot to think about concerning Guide's background," Kizu honestly admitted.

The reporter smiled, a friendly, shy smile.

"Saying I'm a real reporter also points out my weak points. When I interviewed Guide he explained things in great detail. He's quite well read and had some interesting ideas. One concerned the nature of symbols, which came from something he'd read by a Jewish scholar. The work he read discussed the Star of David, the symbol of the state of Israel. Some people insist that the Star of David calls to mind the Jewish people's road to the gas chamber and that a new symbol of *life* would be more fitting for a new country. After reviewing these arguments, the scholar insisted on the exact opposite interpretation. For his generation, the Star of David was a holy symbol born of their suffering and death. And precisely for this reason, it's valuable to light the path toward life and rebuilding. Next, in somewhat cryptic language, he wrote that before ascending to the heights the road descends into the darkest abyss, and what had been a symbol of utter humiliation thus achieves greatness.

"Using this scholar's work as a reference, Guide began to have doubts about whether the symbolic Emperor for Japan and the Japanese defined in the postwar constitution was like the sort of symbol the Jewish scholar had discussed. What Guide and others were searching for was a holy sign or symbol for their generation created from suffering and death, something they could hold up as lighting the way to life and regeneration.

"I couldn't write this in my article, but that's what I concentrated on. Right after I heard this, however, Guide and Patron did their Somersault. 'Everything we've said and done has been one big joke,' they said, as their parting shot. I was thoroughly disappointed, even angry. In other words, with the Emperor greater than Patron, this would be just a repetition of the same old cycle the Japanese people have experienced since the creation of the Meiji constitution.

"After the Somersault I gave up reporting on them. But then, ten years later, suddenly Guide is murdered, which explains why I'm here today. Patron didn't criticize his own actions in the Somersault, though, and even though he says he's starting up the movement again he doesn't seem to have any idea where he's headed. In place of the murdered Guide, you'll be a member of the leadership. What do you think: Has Patron picked up on Guide's ideas about life and regeneration?"

"I have no idea either of the direction Patron's renewed movement will take," Kizu replied. "I started working for Patron simply because a young friend of mine was drawn to him. I've only known Patron for a short while, but I'm very impressed by him. I want him to be resurrected as a spiritual leader, and I plan to do whatever I can to help him. I guess my viewpoint is that of a father who can't just sit by idly and watch his son take on some dangerous task but has to leap in and share the responsibility. Also, Patron asked me to replace the murdered Guide. A strange request, and equally strange for someone like me to accept, but I did, though I don't have the foggiest idea of what he wants me to do."

"To use Patron's phrase for it, with Guide—his companion in the fall into hell—suddenly taken from him, things must look pretty uncertain for him, now that he's alone. Even so, I imagine it must have been a shock to be told you'd be the new Guide." The reporter's eyes behind his glasses softened somewhat as he smiled.

"From what you've told me, I'm convinced that Guide was a religious man," Kizu said. "The words he quoted, too, are in keeping with what I know of him. I also understand the intensity with which Patron considered Guide, through his suffering and death, the holy *symbol* of this generation. When I consider the ten years following Patron and Guide's Somersault, I think I understand even better both the idea of falling into a dark place before you ascend to the heights and the idea of a symbol of utter humiliation."

The reporter sat mulling over what Kizu said. Then he nodded, snatched up the check on the table, and signaled the owner of the coffee shop.

"A lot to think over before the memorial service," he said. "One thing's clear, though: Patron's found himself an excellent new Guide."

2

The next day when Kizu and Ikuo showed up at the office, Dancer and Ogi were huddled together in the midst of a dispirited discussion. Several newspapers were spread out on the office desk. Kizu imagined they were depressed because the only article on the previous day's press conference was written by the single persistent reporter. That morning Kizu had checked all the newspapers in the below-ground meeting room of his apartment building. When Ikuo came in the minivan, he reported that the morning TV news anchors had showed a scene of Patron talking at the press conference and made comments on the death of Guide that touched on the Somersault ten years ago.

When Kizu mentioned this to Dancer and Ogi, however, it turned out they were discussing something completely different.

"I'm not surprised, since all the newspapers are definitely anti-Patron," Dancer answered. "What's unfortunate is that the attitude of the media has spread to society in general. All the halls and conference sites have turned us down. This is a memorial service for someone killed by terrorists, right? Why won't they let us use their hall? What a bunch of spineless idiots!"

A hand bell rang out from Patron's room, and Dancer leaped to her feet. Once again her generous response impressed Kizu as she disappeared down the darkened corridor, a worried look on her face. The hand bell, Ogi explained, was originally used in Patron's church to signal the beginning and end of prayer time. After the Somersault, neither Patron nor Guide had touched it, but since Guide's death, Patron had sought it out.

As was his wont, though, Ogi didn't explain any further, instead taking up where Dancer had left off. "None of the people we've been negotiating with over possible venues has criticized Guide for being responsible for terrorist acts. And they remember Patron and his Somersault very well. All the early reports in the papers touched on the former radical faction that held him captive and drove him to his death. Could they be afraid of an attack on Patron?"

As he listened to Ogi, Kizu thought of the lounge in his apartment building where he'd read the newspapers that morning. If you removed the partition between it and the dining room, it could easily seat four or five hundred people, even allowing for a small temporary stage. The dining room was closed, and the apartment bulletin had reported that very few people used the lounge. It shouldn't be hard, should it, to rent that room?

"The underground lounge of my apartment building is built in American style and would seat five hundred people for a meeting," Kizu said. "Why don't you try there. The building manager is an American, so I doubt he'd react the way Japanese do. There's no parking lot, but it's close enough from the Akasaka–Mitsuke subway to walk."

After Ikuo parked the minivan in the garage, he and Ogi spread out a map of Tokyo and began examining it. Dancer came back in. As soon as Kizu had explained his idea to her, she nearly yelled at the young men.

"Why are you wasting time checking out the location? Every other hall has turned us down, so that's our last hope. Have the Professor call right away and begin negotiations!"

The apartment manager responded that as long as it wasn't some openly anti-American political meeting he didn't see a problem. Thus the first hurdle regarding Guide's memorial service was overcome.

Ikuo was put in charge of coordinating initial arrangements for the service, as well as organizing a security team. Considering how kind the manager had been, they wanted to do their utmost to see that no acts of violence took place in the confines of this American-owned property. As far as preparations for the service, everyone, from Kizu on down, pinned their hopes on Ikuo. Ikuo's plan of attack, however, remained secret, and he said nothing about the lineup he had in mind for the security team. Kizu recalled the three young men at Patron's press conference, and how Ikuo had, if only for a short while, dealt with them. At any rate, Ikuo was out of the office on related matters when Kizu stuck his head in and spoke with Dancer. Ogi, too, was out helping arrange the service, so Dancer and Ms. Tachibana were left to run the office.

"Professor, you know Ikuo best, right?" Dancer said. "He's such a male chauvinist that if you or Patron aren't there and I ask him how arrangements are going, I barely get a response."

"You have to admit he's reliable, though," Ms. Tachibana added.

Dancer and Ms. Tachibana were hard at work addressing individual invitations to the memorial service, using the list of names Ogi had come up with, lumping together those who had founded their own special groups after leaving the church. Patron had hoped to invite the church's Kansai headquarters, if there was enough space in the improvised meeting room. Dancer reread the letters they'd received from individuals, as well as the replies sent in to Ogi's inquiries, checking to see that there wasn't some hidden leg-pulling in the letters. For her part, Ms. Tachibana addressed the envelopes in a tranquil, beautiful script.

"Neither Patron nor Ogi can detect simple malice in others," Dancer explained, "but I can sniff out people who aren't up front. Due to my bad upbringing, perhaps."

"Patron took great care with letters from people he didn't know," Ms. Tachibana added, ever serious. "I was quite moved to find he'd kept the note I sent him years ago about my younger brother, folded up all nice and neat."

"Such a heartfelt letter must have been a great encouragement to him," Dancer said. "There are several letters that respond to Guide and Patron's having fallen into hell. Patron and Guide have always been kind to me, and I've never properly expressed my thanks. I did and said some things to Guide I wish I could take back now, but I can't."

"I'm sure that's not true," Ms. Tachibana said, looking straight at Dancer so intently through her oval glasses that Dancer could only look down.

"I'd like to explain to Patron about the place we're going to use for the memorial service," Kizu said. "Could I see him now?"

"I'll go see if he's up. He hasn't been sleeping well lately and has been taking medicine during the day."

Soon after Dancer left, the sound of the hand bell ringing from Patron's room told them he was awake.

3

When Kizu went in, Patron was standing beside the armchair waiting for him, wearing what looked like a brand-new light-colored gown. To Kizu he seemed quite lively.

"I understand you negotiated with the people from the American university," Patron said.

Kizu proceeded to tell him about the underground lounge at his apartment. The building's main entrance was at the basement level, with the first floor facing an expansive garden in back with a pond; the gently sloping garden had a calmness about it you wouldn't expect to find in the heart of Tokyo. The participants would walk down from the right side of the building and enjoy the vista as they headed toward the memorial service.

Kizu finished his explanation, but still Patron stayed beside him. He didn't seem to have anything he wanted to talk about but just cheerfully enjoyed gazing at Kizu. Kizu broached the topic of Guide's background and what he'd heard from the newspaper reporter, and Patron filled in even more of the details. Guide's uncle—who'd found the infant Guide beside his dead mother at a collection spot in Nagasaki for bodies of people killed in the bombing and taken him home—was a man of strong faith. As he grew up, Guide mourned his absent mother; though he knew how she had died, he had no actual memories of her. He felt his mother's death and his father's disappearance after the war were part of God's plan for him and had led to his good fortune in being taken in by his kind, naively optimistic uncle, but still he struggled with a sense of guilt toward his parents whenever he went to church.

Guide's father was at the front in China when Nagasaki was hit by the atomic bomb. After he was repatriated, he made one visit to his brother-in-law's family, in the Goto Islands off the coast of Nagasaki, where they'd been evacuated. He didn't reclaim his son, and even after Guide's uncle had rebuilt the clinic and moved back to Nagasaki City, he didn't get in touch. The one time he was at his brother-in-law's in Goto, this repatriated officer was obviously greatly disturbed. He drank to excess and told them how in China, he'd witnessed unspeakable atrocities committed by Japanese troops. He had planned to resist if they tried to force him to massacre peasants and rape women, but he knew it wasn't enough just to sit by passively while others killed and looted.

The fact that he was an officer, a doctor, also weighed heavily on him, because of what the Chinese novelist Lu Shun had written: *If you're going to war, it's best to go as a doctor. . . . It's heroic, yet safe.* You can't avoid being tested. Was this the will of God? Ever since he was a child, Guide had thought often about God's will, no doubt because of his father's stories, as told to him by his adopted father.

The Nagasaki that his father saw after he was repatriated was utterly destroyed by an atomic bomb, the second to fall on Japan. Nagasaki had the highest concentration of Catholics in Japan. He'd committed no atrocities himself, yet his own wife, a woman of strong faith, was killed and her youthful body destroyed, leaving a baby behind. This had to be God's will, God's plan, he concluded. A sin is committed in a certain place, and just by being in that place aren't those who didn't participate equally guilty? Further, when God punishes us, he doesn't distinguish between the sinful and the blameless. We're punished for the simple fact that we're *human.*

Guide's father understood this through his experience. He realized that to live is to suffer and through this he could find repentance. Nagasaki must be filled with people who feel the same way. Together with them, he wanted to make Nagasaki a shining example in Japan of a place filled with the repentant, and he began to work to see this happen. This was a huge undertaking, well beyond him no matter how much time he devoted to it. I won't be able to come see my son very often, he told his brother-in-law, but I hope you'll forgive me, as someone who shares my faith.

His brother-in-law, also a doctor, was much more of a realist. He was resigned to the repatriated officer's never regaining his mental stability and leading a steady life. Ever since he'd made his way through the still radioactive rubble of Nagasaki searching for his younger sister and his nephew, he knew that even a tragedy of this magnitude would lead only a small minority of people to repent. If someone were to stand at the ruins of Urakami Cathedral, show a charred Pietà to all the survivors milling about, and shout at them to repent, he might very well be stoned to death.

Guide's father disappeared after that, but his brother-in-law began to hear reports about him. They weren't detailed, but the outlines were clear enough. He didn't hear about any repatriated officer being stoned to death after shouting to people to repent in the nuclear wasteland of Nagasaki, but he did hear news of a young leader walking a tightrope separating the legal from the illegal in regard to concessions at the occupation force's base in nearby Sasebo. Had his young brother-in-law done a complete about-face? Was he doing his best to commit sinful acts, testing God's will and God's plan in an utterly un-Catholic way? After a while these rumors of a young leader in Sasebo faded away. This wasn't a time when the Japanese *yakuza* gangs were able to fight the MPs and survive.

So Guide was raised by his stepfather, who himself drank as he related these stories. Kizu wondered how, because of Guide's past, the Somersault reverberated differently within his inner being from within Patron himself.

"I know even less about the Somersault than I do about Guide's background, but I guess I'm digging into what makes me most anxious," Kizu said, summoning up his resolve. "Guide considered you his Patron, too, and the names you used were perfect for the kind of relationship you had. Didn't you take turns being the leader?"

"That's right," Patron replied. "Actually when it comes down to church doctrine and activities, I think Guide was much more the leader than I ever was."

"Which is exactly why I can't fill his shoes," Kizu insisted. "You're a unique person, and I know Guide must have been too. But *I'm* not. I want to help you out, but the one great hope of my life, my one and only desire for the future, is to be with Ikuo. Ikuo is absorbed in working for you, so here I am.

"Although I'm aware I can never measure up to Guide, I still want to do whatever I can. I was hoping you'd teach me what role you envision this new Guide playing. Otherwise I'll be lost. At my age it's not easy to take on new responsibilities without understanding what you're supposed to be doing. It's very hard for me, a lovesick old man who wants more than anything else to hang out with a certain young person, to just slouch around the office with nothing to do."

After he said this, Kizu felt the blood rise to his face. And he felt Patron gazing at his hot, fleshy face—at first with a flash of surprise, then with a sense of sympathy tinged with sad resignation. Kizu knew that what he blurted out was considered beyond the pale here in Japan, but it did reveal his true feelings. And when he spoke with Patron, more than anything else Kizu wanted to show how he really *felt*.

After a moment of silence, Patron said, "Professor, I'd like you to undertake something that goes in a different direction from what Guide did but that's also absolutely essential to our movement. If I say this you might get upset, thinking it's something I just came up with on the spur of the moment, but as someone once said, a historian is a prophet who looks backward. The late Guide was a forward-looking prophet, and I've been thinking of having you be a *backward*-looking one. I'd like you to play the role of historian concerning the entire process of my constructing a new church."

"Historian?" Kizu echoed.

"I haven't hurt your feelings, I hope?" Patron asked timidly, even fearfully.

"No. I appreciate your thought."

"Before I met the late Guide," Patron went on, "whenever I had visions, I thought they were symptoms of an illness. As I began to awaken from trances

I couldn't control, I blurted out delirious things—the kind of things I never imagined would be intelligible. While I still had a family, my wife took care of me while I was in my trances; she was convinced that they were attacks of mental illness. She called it—my spouting all this nonsense after I awoke— *the return of the wobbles.*

"I mentioned this before, but it was Guide who took this delirious talk and made sense of it. This enabled me to relate my experiences on the *other side.* The accumulation of all this became the teachings of the Savior and the Prophet. Alone, I never would have been able to do a thing."

"But first you had those trances and visions, right?" Kizu said. "Guide wasn't creating anything new, he was just telling you what you yourself had said. You said the words, delirious though they might sound, and he just rearranged them into something logical. Like Guide did, I sense in you a strange and wonderful power to inspire. I'm not good with words; it's only when I paint that the things influencing me come out smoothly. Take that watercolor of Ikuo and me walking in the sky—it's not so much that what I painted happened to correspond to what you envisioned but rather that the silent words inside of you took hold of me, inspiring me to paint that picture. But being your historian would involve words more than painting, wouldn't it?"

Patron held his heavy-looking head upright, took a deep breath, and then spoke.

"I want you to paint a picture of me too. I have a hunch that it will convey something very important."

Patron's eyes—the pupils distinctly separate from both top and bottom lids—looked straight at Kizu. He nodded once and answered the question Kizu had posed earlier.

"I want you to do the opposite of what Guide used to do. Guide fulfilled his role of Prophet by having me relate the future. But with our Somersault we denied all that. We made the doctrine of interpreting my visions one big joke, and the two of us unhesitatingly apostatized. For Guide and me, our Somersault was the truth. And the ten years of hell that followed were not meant to erase this. Quite the opposite: The truth of our Somersault was etched into us, which is the very reason that, even though he was interrogated by the former radical faction to the point where he suffered mightily, bursting a blood vessel, Guide did not denounce our Somersault. And then he died. You understand, then, another reason why I can't do another Somersault? This is why I said Guide's death legitimized me.

"I've told you, Professor, much more about Guide than I've ever told anyone else. And about the Somersault and our descent into hell. I've done this so you can record them. The same holds true for the new movement I'm about to launch. Put in these terms, don't you think the term *historian* makes sense here? My hope for you as an artist is for much more than this, actually. . . . Anyway, that's what I wanted to tell you."

As Kizu was leaving the room, Patron's solemn expression softened so unexpectedly it was almost comical. "I didn't know you were so attached to Ikuo. He's quite a special young man, and if his charm has led you to us, I'd say he's already made a major contribution to our church!"

Kizu felt, anew, that he was seeing Patron's complex nature, something he had to be on guard for. Dancer, passing him as he went out of the room, had obviously heard Patron's words, her mouth, with its pearlescent luster, open even wider than usual as she gazed steadily at Kizu. Kizu turned around once more and saw a satisfied look on Patron's face.

4

The next day when Kizu broached the subject of going back to the United States, Ikuo exploded. These days Kizu had found something humorous in Ikuo's face, with its prominent cheekbones, but his words now brought out only anger and malice in the young man.

"How can you do that?" Ikuo barked out. "You're going to abandon us and run away—*now,* when we're on the verge of beginning something new and important? How can you just hightail it to America and put an end to *us*?"

Kizu was startled, but he didn't feel like responding emotionally. Despite how busy he'd become, he was well aware that his physical ailments and deep exhaustion had fenced him in, pushing him away from the young man.

"Of course, I'd like you to come with me if you can get away from the office," he explained. "You don't need to get a visa these days. . . . But I know you're busy arranging for the memorial service.

"I'm planning to put all my affairs in order in the States and come back again to Japan. It's also the time of year when they're making the schedule for the next academic year. After that I plan to return to Tokyo and devote myself to Patron's church. I think it's best if I resign from the university. It could be a major problem for the university if one of their tenured professors helped lead a religious organization in Japan.

"I'm going to settle my estate, have a lawyer divide my wife and children's portion, take care of the taxes and everything else; the balance I'll transfer to the church. Since I'll be a part of Patron's new religious movement, this strikes me as the proper way to handle my affairs. With all the things to take care of, I imagine it will take me about ten days. At my age, jet lag really hits you hard, but I feel I have to get going."

Ikuo was dumbfounded. He couldn't even manage an apology. The area around his eyes reddened, and he withdrew without a word to begin preparing dinner with the ingredients Kizu had purchased. Every once in a while the kitchen was utterly silent, Ikuo undoubtedly pausing in his cooking to ponder what he'd heard, and Kizu felt sorry about the young man's depressed and troubled feelings. Meanwhile, until Ikuo called him to the dinner table he had set in the kitchen, Kizu packed for his round trip to the United States.

The meal Ikuo made consisted of a mound of french fries with steaks, a vegetable salad, and canned minestrone. That was all, but Kizu happily enjoyed the meal, knowing how carefully Ikuo had prepared it. Ikuo remained silent, sitting across from him as they ate, his puffy eyes turned downward. Kizu felt bad about how upset he looked. That night, still without a word, Ikuo performed his sexual services so completely that Kizu forgot all about his illness and exhaustion. In each and every thing Ikuo did, though, Kizu could catch a glimpse of someone who was voluntarily prostituting himself.

Returning to his university in New Jersey, Kizu was confronted with something else unexpected: The female head of his research institute announced he'd been accused of sexual harassment.

A year before his sabbatical, one of the students in Kizu's fall seminar was a woman exchange student from Japan who had an unusually confrontational attitude. Kizu became really aware of her when, as they were approaching the end of the fall term without her having said anything of substance in the seminar, he asked her if she might make a presentation at their next class. He asked this in front of the mailboxes at the institute's office where he ran across her; one of his colleagues was right beside them, using the copy machine. She replied in English in a loud voice, as Kizu noticed a moment too late, so that the American professor wouldn't misunderstand their discussion.

"I'm an auditor in your class, Professor, so I'm not obliged to write reports or make presentations. Please don't mistake me for one of your lazy students!"

The young woman was twenty-seven or twenty-eight, of medium height but well built, someone who—at least from the perspective of Kizu's generation—represented a completely new type of Japanese. Her face, though, with its dark hair, pouty little lips, and Fuji-shaped brow, was definitely old school. Kizu had published a paper once in the university bulletin on women's faces in *ukiyoe* prints, classifying them as unassuming plain types and demoness types, and he was once again drawn to this woman and her classic features.

The next semester she didn't sign up for Kizu's seminar, but one day when there was still snow on the campus she showed up at his office during lunch break; she explained that one of the male students was bothering her, which is why she couldn't attend his seminar, but she had some of her own artwork in her apartment that she'd like to show him, she said, inviting him with a modesty quite unlike her previous outburst. Kizu happened to be free that afternoon, so he went with her in her Citroën to her place, where she lived with a roommate; Kizu was surprised to find it was an apartment in the center of town, outfitted with a concierge. The living room and kitchen weren't so big, but on the ceiling of her bedroom was a tempera painting in arabesque style of flowers and birds she'd done herself, which meant that even if she hadn't purchased the apartment she was living there under a long-term lease. Her roommate was out on a date until late, so Kizu enjoyed the *chirashizushi* she prepared for him and looked over several tableaus. These also depicted birds and flowers. Kizu sat on the cloth-covered sofa while the young woman sat in front of him on the floor, holding the paintings she wanted to show him, dressed in a black wool outfit with a short skirt that revealed her fleshy thighs, though he pretended not to notice.

That was all that happened. Soon after, Kizu happened to be in New York City, and since the university had been unable to procure a model for him, he stopped by an adult store to buy a video so he could get an eyeful of young black and Hispanic men. He spied a three-pack of condoms for sale in a box near the register, mixed in with aphrodisiacs and sex toys, and bought it. But the woman never invited him back to view her artwork.

The particulars in the sexual harassment charge were these: First, that he came over to her apartment on a night her roommate was out, saying he'd take a look at her paintings; second, having carelessly mentioned the painting on her bedroom ceiling, she was forced to show it to him; third, he made a suggestive joke about the uncensored book of *ukiyoe* prints she had on a bookshelf; fourth, as Kizu sat on the sofa, he looked at her inner thighs as she crouched on the floor in front of him; and fifth, during this time, he intended her to see that something was coming alive in his trousers.

As Kizu sat opposite the head of his research institute, he not only had to read the e-mails the young woman had submitted, he had to listen to the tape recording she'd secretly made of their conversation that night.

Kizu was so deflated that the institute head, who at first had had a fretful look on her face, burst out laughing; listening to Kizu's constrained way of talking on the tape, she said, and the woman's relaxed voice, he hardly came across as overly macho.

In fact, what really gave Kizu a shock was how pitifully immature he sounded. He was seeing himself as a precocious child talking with adults about grown-up topics, the tape mercilessly revealing how, deep down, he hadn't matured at all since those early postwar days back in his home village.

If that fidgety middle-aged character on the tape had had an ounce of courage and propositioned the woman, Kizu knew he would have been turned down flat. Suddenly, sitting there in front of the institute head, Kizu found a new self springing up, a new Kizu who acted as he never would have before. He admitted that everything the young woman had listed had probably taken place, agreed he was in the wrong as far as what she'd interpreted as sexual harassment, and announced his decision to resign his teaching position.

The head of the institute, originally sympathetic, now turned indignant. As Kizu left her office, the feeling struck him that he had come back to the university from Tokyo for the sole purpose of receiving this punishment, and he said to himself, silently, *I've done an act of repentance!*

A second event awaited Kizu in America, one that took place in the hotel he was staying at in New York the night before his flight back to Tokyo. That morning Kizu woke with his usual uncomfortable feeling in his gut, exhausted from having forced himself to get back to sleep any number of times. In order to suppress what this exhaustion had triggered—the headlong rush of his mind into darkness—one of the pieces of wisdom he'd picked up in his advancing old age was that it was best to get up and get his body moving.

So Kizu got up out of bed, as if hurrying off somewhere, and went into the sitting room of his hotel suite, a room partitioned off simply from the bedroom by a white-framed door with a square mirror set on it—the Japanese owner had come up with double-door construction, which had proved quite popular, according to what Kizu had heard from a woman in a painting class for expatriate Japanese he used to teach. Beyond the curtain, which he'd left open the night before, a seventy-story high-rise building with a green-and-white crown structure on top blocked his view. Below a broad layer of clouds that covered the sky, darker clouds moved, and a fine rain was falling. The raindrops fell a long, long way down. What would it look like if it snowed? Kizu wondered. And just then he discovered that it *was* snowing, fine flakes swirling in the air. This wasn't a particularly remarkable scene. The snow lacked force, as if it might peter out at any moment. But Kizu saw in the movements of his heart and the appearance of the snow a synchronicity he took as a sign. Inside his chest he felt something, like a bulb sprouting.

Two men—one given the suspicious name Savior, the other called Prophet, abandoned their followers, did a Somersault, and for ten years languished in what they termed hell. And now one of them was restarting a movement calling on people to repent: to make them deeply aware of, and prepared for, the end of the world.

He and Ikuo had joined the movement. And now Kizu had even settled his estate and given up his job. But hadn't this duo of Patron and Guide misunderstood their roles? The real Patron was actually *Guide,* who'd been taunted by his former followers and tortured until he died an agonizing death. The surviving Patron had been nothing but a puppet, a springboard for Guide's mystical philosophy. Didn't this account for the awful shock that Guide's misfortune and death brought on?

If that were true, it meant the new movement they were starting was without a leader, only this person called Patron and himself, a makeshift new Guide without the least hint of mysticism about him. Bereft of their true leader, they weren't even able to comprehend the meaning of Guide's sacrifice and could only stagger about pointlessly.

The snow had stopped. The flakes had fallen past the fortieth floor, where Kizu stood, but by street level had changed to rain. With the blanket of clouds lightening and the darker clouds gone, the rain, too, seemed about to clear up. To the left of the narrow building directly across from him there was a smaller building, clouds of steam rising from it, beyond which he could see the trees in Central Park, with their fresh spring foliage. Moving his eyes as if following along with a soft-tipped watercolor brush, Kizu continued to gaze at the clumps of leaves propped up by the young, uncertain trunks of the trees.

12: Initiation of New Believers

1

The reporter who covered the memorial service press conference had sent Kizu a fax telling him where to find a group of women believers who had left the church after the Somersault and were now living a communal life in the southwest part of Kanagawa Prefecture. So on a Saturday afternoon near the end of April, Kizu set off for this suburban bedroom community, one that still had a scattering of rice fields, about an hour from Shinjuku on the Odakyu express train.

The believers occupied a closed elementary school they'd converted into a residence. They numbered some forty people, mothers and children as well as single women, all living a quiet, bucolic life. Thinking he'd just check out the environment these women lived in, Kizu set off with Ikuo at the wheel of his Ford Mustang. The wooden schoolhouse was at the base of a line of low gentle hills, but three-quarters of the school grounds had been dug up and was enclosed as a large-scale plastic-covered greenhouse. Kizu and Ikuo parked their car on the road that ran along the former school grounds and set off on foot.

In the narrow space left in front of the school building, some children were playing in a sandbox outfitted with a horizontal exercise bar, a scene that brought on a nostalgia that pierced Kizu to the quick. There were seven or eight children, upper elementary school or junior-high kids by the look of them, all of them dressed in simple plain clothes—very different from the aggressive, gaudy colors Kizu was used to seeing each time he returned to Japan—as if a half century had been ignored and he was swept back into the colors he remembered from his childhood.

"It's like a black-and-white movie," Ikuo said.

The children played without saying a word. Ikuo strode from the path beside the greenhouse over to the sandbox, and Kizu, hesitating, followed suit. As he got closer he noticed that the children were gazing at a line of ants in the corner of the box. Very different from the usual overbearing attitude of kids who haven't quite decided whether or not to squash a bug, tormenting it until they did, these children showed an unexpected reverence for small living creatures.

The children didn't seem on their guard at the approach of these two strangers, nor did they show any friendly interest. The older children especially seemed to be purposely ignoring them. After a while Ikuo rested his hands on the horizontal bar, too low for him, and pulled himself upright on it. He tucked in his legs, pushed his elbows tight against his chest, and slowly rotated around the bar five or six times. The younger children looked at him with open admiration. Kizu, too, found himself looking with appreciative eyes at Ikuo, from his thighs to the tips of his feet, as he held his body stationary, stretched out vertically upside down. Beyond Ikuo's upside-down body, Kizu caught sight of flower petals fluttering down from the tops of hills; looking more carefully, he saw they were wet snowflakes.

Kizu remembered the scene from his hotel window high above the New York streets, snow vanishing in the air. Sometimes he wondered what he'd been thinking about that morning. Now that he considered it again, he felt that maybe he'd made this journey here to the countryside to grope for some meaningful clue. If the snow across the ocean had been a sign, this out-of-season snow here in Japan must be one too. The children were now looking up at the snowy sky. The older children stood off to one side in a clump, but even the younger kids standing close by were calm and well mannered. All of them looked entirely relaxed as they gazed up at the swirling snow.

Ikuo silently lowered himself from the bar—his controlled landing as casual as the attitude of the children—and he and Kizu walked back toward the car, leaving the children behind, all gazing up at the snowy sky, some of the older children whispering among themselves.

"Boy, oh, boy," Ikuo murmured.

Kizu knew he didn't mean the unexpected snow. Ikuo felt oppressed by the children's natural dignity. Kizu was about to express his agreement when they found, standing next to their car and waiting for them, oblivious to the snow, a short, solidly built middle-aged woman. Continuing their own conversation was out of the question.

Kizu surmised that it was one of the children's mothers, a representative of this commune that, while he'd only caught a glimpse of it, was obviously quite tidy and organized, who'd come out to challenge these suspicious-looking intruders.

Kizu didn't catch sight of anyone looking out the line of first- or second-story windows of the schoolhouse, glass windows whose gleaming well-polished look contrasted with the old window frames, but apparently the report of their presence had spread among the residents. As Kizu and Ikuo walked on against the blustery wind and snow, the woman stood there at a corner they had to turn. She'd been looking down until they approached, but now, quite suddenly, she spoke out in a charged, emotional voice.

"This is a private road. The land was originally donated to the town by my husband's grandfather, and after the school closed it was sold. I'm paying taxes on it. And I can't have you parking your car here."

"I'm very sorry," Kizu said. "I thought it was a public road."

"If it were a public road there'd be even more reason not to park!" the woman said vehemently. With stubby fingers she brushed away the snow-flakes that clung to her curly reddish-brown hair and her flushed face. "I saw you watching the children. If you try to take any photographs, my husband says he's going to come over; he's been watching you from the farm. Rubberneckers and the media have stopped coming here, and the mothers and children don't want to be bothered. But now you TV people come trying to stir things up! Why can't you leave us alone? We've never bothered the people in this neighborhood. The constitution guarantees freedom of religion, you know!"

Kizu was finally able to get a word in edgewise. "So you share the same beliefs?"

With a look that was neither surprise nor fear, the woman stared directly at him for the first time. "*What?* Don't come around making false accusations! I've lived here most of my life—why would I adopt the religion of people who're just temporary residents?"

The woman sputtered to a halt, and Kizu himself was so flustered Ikuo intervened.

"The Professor and I are working for the gentleman who used to be the leader of this little community. We're not connected with any TV station or weekly magazine. Their former leader is concerned about what kind of life the group has been living after they became independent of the church. We just came to observe, not to bother anyone."

"By former leader, you mean the one who did the Somersault? These women aren't angry about that anymore. There are some profound reasons for this, apparently, though I have no idea what. . . . So he's worried about them, is he?"

Her words were somewhat feeble now. Apparently a basically kind-hearted person, she seemed to regret having scolded these people who had come from so far away, and shook her lightly snow-covered head to get her pluck back.

"Well, if that's the case, with this unexpected snow and all, why don't you just rest here for a while? This is a private road, so your car will be fine! They're packing lilies in boxes inside the greenhouse. Maybe you'd like to take a look?"

She seemed so apologetic it would have been rude to turn down her suggestion. Kizu hadn't planned to stay, but he looked at the woman, her skin roughened by gooseflesh, and nodded, so she hurried ahead. By the time they arrived at the greenhouse closest to the road, the children in the sandbox who'd been gazing up at the snow had formed a line and were quietly filing toward the building.

The old woman went in a step ahead of them, past what looked like the door of a warehouse, and Kizu and Ikuo followed, brushing the already melting snowflakes from their heads, chests, and shoulders. The children stood at one corner of the greenhouse in swirling snow that was coming down harder than ever. If they'd been seeking shelter from the snow, the only place to find it around the greenhouse, a structure made of thick metal piping covered with tough tentlike plastic sheeting, was under the eaves at the entrance. The children, though, didn't seem to have come over in order to get out of the snow. As he watched them standing there through the steadily falling snow, their expressions and even the outlines of their faces now blurred, a slight sense of the unearthly was added to Kizu's earlier impression. Ikuo, too, had to look away.

2

They went inside the greenhouse, only slightly warmer than outside, and found that they had to walk quite some distance to where the packing operation was under way, watching their step as they moved through a maze of obstacles. All sorts of objects, large and small, were arbitrarily piled up on the path. They stumbled over what at first appeared to be small empty boxes but turned out to be as heavy as bricks. On both sides of the path the equipment required to grow the plants wasn't just laid out flat; they bumped their heads and shoulders on various pipes. For outsiders it was a veritable labyrinth. Kizu found himself concerned, too, about the strange little line of children who followed their movements through the three-tiered window in the plastic covering the greenhouse.

People were working in the greenhouse in a clearing cut out of the long line of cultivated plants. Hemmed in on both sides by equipment, some twenty women were seated, busy at work, on top of a platform covered with mats. This particular greenhouse seemed to be in an in-between stage between cultivation and harvesting; all that could be seen in back were several lines of dark green leaves forming a frame in the cultivating apparatus used to grow flowers. On this side were the women, seated in a large circle with mounds of lilies in front of them that they were packing into long cardboard boxes.

Kizu had been raised in the country and was used to the customs of farmers, but when he first saw farm women in the Tokyo area working in the fields with cloth head coverings, he found it a bit suspect. The women here, too, worked with their heads covered, in this case with simple knitted hats. The women were of all ages, yet they all shared the same pale faces, the same quiet look.

More noticeable than anything else, though, was the overpowering, animal-like odor of the lilies. Kizu noticed how Ikuo's sturdy face recoiled from the smell. The women worked so silently that Kizu and Ikuo found themselves tiptoeing, and this heavy scent wafting over from the silent women made for a grotesque sense of incongruity.

Kizu and Ikuo had come close to the women, but they kept on working without showing the slightest bit of interest. With relaxed yet swift motions, they packed away the lilies, while Kizu and Ikuo stood there, overwhelmed. The woman who accompanied them had already gone behind the circle of working women, stuck her head in between the boxes of packed lilies and the mound of unpacked flowers, and begun speaking to the women.

Before long a man's head popped up above the piled boxes of lilies—a close-cropped white head with white whiskers—and stared at Kizu and Ikuo. Approaching from the side, before the woman who'd accompanied them returned, this man, the farm's owner, dressed in a white collared shirt and wine-colored vest, walked in front of the working women, their bare arms full of lilies, distributing empty boxes. Then he lifted a box that was larger than the others and lowered it to the ground; he was making a place on the platform for Kizu and Ikuo to sit. The woman led them up onto the mats, while the man went back to his original position; whether through innate shyness or because he was the type who kept people at arm's length, he merely nodded slightly to greet them. The women went on working, oblivious to the two men, who'd now become part of their group.

Not that the women were rejecting these unexpected visitors. The farm woman who'd led them in, after glancing at the farm owner, sitting off to one side, began addressing the other women, who cheerfully stopped and paid attention.

"I'll pass around the business card I received from this gentleman, who tells me he's working for the former leader of the church you all used to belong to. I know we've talked recently about the man who was with this leader at the time of the Somersault, the one we read about in the paper who was tortured to death.

"It seems the former leader is concerned about what sort of life all of you have been living. This gentleman wasn't really planning to meet you and talk with you today, he said, and maybe I'm butting in where I don't belong, but I thought it would be nice for you to meet him, seeing as how he's also a professor at an American university. I'm sure you heard my husband scold me for my rash assumptions."

The woman stopped speaking and bowed her head, and the company fell silent. Kizu wondered if they were waiting for him to introduce himself but realized that the woman had essentially covered what needed to be said. While Kizu was hesitating, the farm woman whispered to an old woman sitting opposite her.

For an old lady, this second woman was unusually erect, though something was wrong with her legs, and she sat differently from the rest of the women, her feet splayed out to one side. For a woman of her generation she was quite large, with fine features, putting Kizu in mind of someone from a good family who happened to live near the sea.

"If you don't mind, I'll speak first," the old woman said. "Do you think the children watching us are all right? The snow looks like it's letting up, so maybe there's no need to tell them to go inside."

There was no response from those around her, and the old woman shook her head magnanimously at the children outside the window. She turned to glance at the buds on the oak tree growing toward the high windows and then, taking her own sweet time, went on.

"We heard rumors that the Savior and the Prophet had emerged from their shut-in life and were beginning a new movement. We read later in the newspaper about the Prophet's awful death, which grieves us terribly. We also talked about what this new movement will be about, didn't we? However, he's the one who cut his ties with the church, and we're just a little group here, suffering in our own way. Still, knowing he's concerned about us might possibly move our own group in a different direction."

The woman stopped speaking and looked up at the branches of the dark oak through the melting snow on the top of the window, and all the women in the circle turned their eyes in that direction. Kizu sensed that the other women were quite used to her style of speaking.

"Actually I've been thinking for a while about the scope of our group— I should add that not everyone's here today—and I thought it might be compared to that clump of leaves out there. Today we have this unseasonable snow, but the buds have already started to come out, haven't they, on the oaks and zelkovas? Not long ago they were just dark trunks—even the tips of the thinnest branches looked old and withered—and it made me feel sorry, thinking that when trees get big every part of them ages.

"Once a tree starts budding, though, it takes off with such energy that the whole tree is revitalized, not just the branches but even down to the trunk. It makes me think about whether our little group has the vigor of those buds sprouting out on the oak tree. Just to make sure, I counted them, and discovered there are about forty buds on every three feet of branch, which really brings home to me how small our group is. Even when the Savior's church was at its peak, if you compare it to the buds, it was made up of fewer members than the number of buds on that single oak tree. And our group is just one very small branch.

"I'm afraid I've strayed off the topic, as I often do, but as we've talked in our small group, this is how we think about what happened after the Somersault: Though the Savior and Prophet survived, they descended into hell. The Prophet either stayed in hell or was killed just as he was crawling out— either way, it's a great tragedy. My husband was a classmate in medical school of the man who adopted him as an infant, so I've heard things about him from that source too. What a cruel, painful thing to have happened. . . .

"The Savior and the Prophet fell into hell, and that was where they atoned. I can only imagine how incredibly painful it was for both of them to suffer such disgrace for ten years. When you look back on something once it's over, one's life seems to have passed by in an instant, though of course it all depends on the quality of that particular time. Having spent the last ten years living together with all of you, I feel that quite strongly.

"What do you say? How about talking to these gentlemen about our past ten years? The weekly magazines have treated us like eccentrics abandoned by Savior and Prophet. But we have our own thoughts about life here. Why don't we share something of them. Anybody? Ms. Takada, how about you?"

Kizu glanced around at the women listening to the old lady and came across one whose unusual features riveted his attention. Her face had a terrible scar, as if maybe when she was a baby she'd been slashed with a hatchet from one ear down to her cheek. More than the scar, though, one of her eyes was completely covered over by a smooth layer of skin. She looked around thirty, and as she'd been listening to the old lady speak she didn't make any attempt to hide the side of her face with the skin-covered eye. This was the Ms. Takada the old lady had named. The woman responded right away, turning unflinchingly to face Kizu and the others.

"It's only natural that I felt a pain in my heart when the Savior and the Prophet did their Somersault, but in my case physically I couldn't deal with the pain; I vomited every day. Some people were concerned I was having morning sickness, though that was impossible.

"Over and over I'd go to sleep and dream that the Somersault never took place and feel relieved, only to awaken to the awful truth. This happened day after day. At first I felt as if the Savior had betrayed me. It was like being covered with ants that were biting me, but I'd been anesthetized and couldn't feel anything. But I could sense that the anesthesia would wear off and suddenly I'd be hit by this enormous pain, which led to my vomiting all the time.

"Never once, in all my life, have I run across a person as kind as Savior was, and that's why I felt betrayed. After I joined the church, many people were kind to me, but Patron's kindness—I'm sure all of you would agree— was on a whole other level.

"This happened after my unhappy marriage broke up, soon after I renounced the world. The church had a house in Yokohama in a brand-new subdivision—remember?—on a high piece of land, from which you could see the ocean. A lot of times I'd gaze out absently at the ocean from the big window on the second floor where we had a meeting room. There was a large horse chestnut tree outside, too. One day Savior, who happened to be staying there, was sitting beside that big window when he called me over and told me to come closer and look deep into his eyes. He was sitting in his usual armchair where he liked to read, beside the window. So I knelt down in front of him and gazed into his eyes. It was the time of year when the horse chestnut's leaves were still soft, a fine clear morning when I was left in charge of cleaning and answering the phones while everyone else was out working.

"I was afraid he was going to make a pass at me. But he said it so casually I couldn't resist, and though I was wary, I went ahead and knelt in front of him. He told me to look once inside his eyes, and what I saw was this: my own face, *beautiful, completely unscarred.* The face of a young woman, her eyes wide open in surprise.

"Next he told me to smile, since then I'd see my own face smiling. I tried to smile, but I was so happy I burst into tears. My eyes were so full of tears I couldn't see a thing, and the thought occurred to me that since my face was reflected in his eyes like that, unscarred, that was exactly how he saw me.

"He'd encouraged me so much that when he did his Somersault and said everything he'd done and said was a joke, I couldn't accept it. He looked totally insincere when he was talking in front of the TV cameras, which may have been the way the camera caught him, but the words were definitely his.

"The way he acted ridiculed us, trampled down our desire for salvation and all the efforts we'd made to reach it. We were suffering and unhappy and needed salvation more than anything, yet he was laughing in our faces. On top of that, the whole world was laughing at this silly Savior and Prophet who were ridiculing their followers, which made me feel as if we were being doubly mocked. I think we all felt that way, angry at what had happened. We kept the faith, though, and felt we had to settle the score with those apostates. Some people even gave sermons advocating revenge."

3

"I was probably angrier than anyone else, but I still couldn't forget how the Savior had used his own eyes as a mirror to show me my real face. Every time I remembered that, new rage would well up within me. Was what he'd said just a bad joke?

"As time passed, though, I calmed down, and began to think that the Somersault might have been a childish prank, without any malice behind it. I realized how I'd been moved by him and how happy that made me. And I became convinced that the beautiful face I saw reflected in the Savior's eyes was my *real* face, the one my soul possessed before I was born, so I was able to forgive him and think of him with fondness. That's how I was able to keep my faith during these ten years of living together with all of you."

When Ms. Takada finished speaking, her companions surrounded her with an empathetic silence. The wife of the owner of the greenhouses, her upper body stiff, pushed up her glasses with a small calloused palm to wipe away the tears. Her husband shot her a look of rebuke and turned away. After her tears were over, the woman—as if it was her wont to speak up despite the patriarchal authority over her—cleared her throat with a little cough and broke the circle of silence.

"He wasn't hypnotizing you when you saw your beautiful face with two eyes. You *were* seeing your real face!"

The farm owner inclined his head, which reminded Kizu of the profile of General Nogi on playing cards he used as a child, and poked his wife's shoulder. She twisted away to avoid his hand and continued unhesitatingly.

"I don't really know what kind of person the Savior was, but if as you say he's come back from hell, you should have him show you your real face once more. This time try to keep from crying and give him a big smile!"

"If he has returned, that's enough for me," the one-eyed woman said, calmly yet passionately. "But more than my own healing, *everything* will be healed, since he's atoned for all our sins in hell. Actually, in the past ten years, I don't hate this face so much anymore."

"That's the way to think about it!" the farm owner shouted, his voice filled with both indignation and self-reproach. "My unthinking better half said some stupid things, but you have your real face now! Why do you have to hate it?"

"I think that's quite enough of your little marital spats and solutions to the problem, Mr. Sasaki. These two men have come all this way to see us. Shouldn't we let them speak?" The speaker here was a woman around forty or so who looked like she'd been an athlete in her younger days.

Saying this, the woman turned a somewhat sullen smile toward Kizu and Ikuo. With her lightly tanned face and strong look, she stood out among all the pale faces. The woman seemed frankly surprised that the doctor's widow, the woman with the congenital defect in her face, and all the other women who had listened so intently to their stories had opened up so much to these two strangers who had suddenly appeared in their midst. Only this woman who had just spoken seemed to have some complicated psychological barrier.

"The Savior—Patron, as the newspapers now call him—well, if he truly is to return to us, I expect he'll make a direct appeal. Since the two of you just planned to take a look at how we're living, I don't expect you have any sort of message for us from him, do you?"

"No, we don't," Kizu said, feeling a bit wretched as he said it. "We didn't even tell Patron we were coming."

"You haven't been believers very long, have you?" the woman asked. "Apart from these young people here, I know the faces of most of the believers above a certain age. My job in the church kept me in contact with them."

As he turned a searching look at Kizu, the farm owner had now calmed down from his earlier pronouncement, his skin color fading back to match his white hair and whiskers.

"The Professor and I are much newer believers than all of you," Ikuo answered in Kizu's stead. "I know this might sound a little vague to you. Even though I say we're followers, we haven't done much yet to help Patron with his religious activities. We got to know Patron and Guide just before they restarted their religious activities—years after the Somersault, of course. It's clear, though, that Patron will be relying a lot on the Professor in the days to come. I only knew the late Guide for a short time, but he was someone I respected very much. And Patron—well, I've never met a person like him before, a leader like that."

"What are your feelings about the Somersault?" the woman asked. "I ask because all of us are somewhat fixated on it. . . . We gathered a small group together, after we were abandoned by our leaders, and lived as if in the wilderness for ten years. And we suffered—which made Guide's death all the more painful. They didn't take us with them when they descended into hell, but now that they came back after atoning, and are starting this new movement, I think we'll be waiting for a call."

Kizu was apprehensive about how Ikuo would reply, but he answered quite seriously. "I'm sure you've read this in the newspaper, and I don't know much more than what Patron said at the press conference for Guide's memorial service. I read about the Somersault in the papers and saw it on TV, though I was still a child at the time.

"As I've been working alongside Patron, though, I've learned this: Since the police had figured out what the radical faction was up to, if Patron and Guide hadn't abandoned the church the authorities would have come down hard on the entire movement. The whole thing would have exploded—maybe to the point where politicians would be up in arms trying to enforce every word of the Anti-Subversive Activities Law.

"But as long as the leaders discarded their church, the whole thing could be dismissed as some petty scandal. And that's exactly what happened. It was the Somersault that the TV news shows had such great fun with. There was a pitfall in this, though, because the authorities and the police were under the impression that they'd uncovered all the activities the radical faction was involved in. But the investigation didn't go as smoothly as they hoped. The church avoided self-destructing, and a core remained active.

"In a sense what was emphasized was what I saw as a child and what the Professor saw reported abroad—namely, Patron's Somersault pronouncements on TV. But after I had a chance to talk with Patron and Guide, and meet all of you here, I understand a lot more about how much you all have suffered, and especially Guide, before he was murdered."

"What's the motivation behind Patron's deciding to start a new movement?" the woman asked. "I understand he was thinking of doing this even before Guide was killed."

"I'm not in a position to say, really," Ikuo replied, "but my opinion is that if this crisis hadn't ended with a small bang as it did, Patron and Guide—and the whole church—would have taken things as far as they possibly could. The Somersault prevented this, but somewhere along the line the idea of repentance as the end of the world approaches disappeared. Maybe I shouldn't say this, but hasn't the true mission of the church remained alive only among those people Patron abandoned? And now isn't Patron—as someone who's experienced hell—trying once more to take on this mission? Well, those are my thoughts. Please understand that my generation is pretty ignorant of what went on in the past. After the collapse of Aum, young people who were searching for salvation lost a forum to carry out this search. What are they supposed to do? Patron and Guide felt a sense of responsibility toward this situation, and that's what motivated them. And, as if waiting for this chance, some people killed Guide."

"You can call it a return or a resurrection or whatever, but what I want to know is what are his immediate plans? Now that Guide isn't with him anymore." This was asked by the old lady who was sitting up erect, her legs out to one side.

"I think Patron wants to take responsibility for the gap in time after he and Guide fell into hell," Ikuo said. "Because he abandoned people like yourselves who continued to keep the faith. Actually, you should be getting a message from him quite soon.

"At the time of the Somersault, Patron stated that everything he'd said and done up till then was all a joke, a big gag. I don't know anything about the real substance of this, so what I did was read through the transcripts of his sermons that predated the Somersault that were among the documents my colleagues have been looking at. In one of the sermons, Patron remarked on the increase in the number of people who need to be saved. This latent power of the soul's thirst now, he said—and this was ten years ago—exists on a large scale, from urban areas like Tokyo to provincial cities, even reaching to disintegrating farming communities. In my visions, Patron said, these countless young people, filled with anxiety and pained frustration, all take on one face. And this face, he said, raises a silent cry: *The flames are coming*! Was this, too, just a joke? I think he'll be taking action that gives us the answer to that."

From over toward the mountains the same hand bell Kizu had heard at their office rang out, startling him. He looked out through the three-level window, and in the shafts of twilight sun shining through breaks in the wind-tossed clouds he saw the children who had earlier been gazing into the green-house all filing away, led by a tall girl ringing the bell.

"It's five o'clock," one strong-looking woman said, "time that we set aside for prayer. I don't know how you all pray with this man you call Patron, but it would be nice if you would join us, like Mr. and Mrs. Sasaki do, in silent meditation.

"Today it's my turn to say a few words as we pray. I'd like to express my thanks at having these unexpected visitors and being able to listen to what they have to say. As I listened to them, something welled up in me I'd like to talk about. A person told us once, also just before our prayer time, that the reason we felt close to each other when we were in the church was that we all share similar weaknesses. These are the kind of people who ran off and formed this group, yet to me it was only a very short time during which we suffered after being crushed by the crisis of the Somersault.

"Soon after the Somersault, we wanted to accompany Savior and Prophet to hell, to take care of them, but we knew that that was beyond our endurance. If it was something we *could* endure, why did the two of them take on the Somersault *alone*?

"And so our communal life here continued. Every moment, we had engraved on our minds the fact that those two had fallen into hell to atone for our sins and were humiliated and suffered, and we prayed for them. We believed that when they were resurrected, they would lead a huge procession calling for repentance at the end of the world and we could join them once again.

"But just on the eve of this procession—just as the Savior was struggling to be resurrected—the Prophet passed away. I feel we've been very fortunate to be here these ten years, living a prayerful life. Just as Patron's decision to be resurrected gelled, Guide suffered that terrible death—a death to atone for us all—not just us but for all people on this planet. And it was this act of atonement that gave Savior the strength to take the final step toward resurrection.

"So, through the intercession of the Savior, who is alive among us, let us pray for our dear departed Prophet!"

4

As Kizu closed his eyes and began to pray, he discovered something laughable about himself. Patron had dubbed him the new Guide, yet he'd never been in the habit of praying and no words of prayer came to him now. At a loss, he began mentally sketching a full-length drawing of Patron. He gave himself up to the feeling of moving a charcoal pencil, tracing Patron's face, his body, and the way he held himself, and as he did so his imaginary Patron sprang to life. It was quite realistic, yet it overlapped with what the reporter had told him, his mental image of Patron suddenly decked out in Spanish farmer's dress from the Middle Ages. A round and chubby figure, certainly nothing martial about him, casual, yet surprisingly nimble. Come to think of it, didn't Sancho Panza, too, get lost in thought sometimes just like Patron?

And Guide as Don Quixote—his upright posture and thin figure and his long scrupulous face were perfect for the role. That morning in the hotel in New York came back to him once again, when the snow turned to rain before it reached the ground. Was he now supposed to join the antics of this man pretending to be mankind's Patron by performing antics of his own as the newly chosen Guide? Could a clowning pair really lead these praying women, with so much suffering behind them, in a march toward repentance at the end of the world? Wasn't this asking the impossible?

Kizu felt a burning sensation run up his back. He opened his eyes. He'd participated occasionally in silent prayer in America, but nothing that lasted as long as this. It was already ten minutes since they began, with no sign from the circle of women that they were nearing the end.

Eyes closed, heads held straight, the women looked totally transformed from when they had been packing lilies into boxes. And very different, too, from the way they were earlier today, listening to their colleagues' stories and to the replies of Kizu, Ikuo, and the husband and wife who owned the farm. The women, their hats off now, looked irretrievably tired, as if they were pieces of machinery suffering from metal fatigue and about to break apart. The face of the one old lady who, from the waist up had such good posture, reminded him of a death mask. And looking at the young woman with the scar running from her ear, over where one eye should be, and down her cheek, Kizu was shocked all over again.

"It's a good time for us to leave, don't you think?" the farmer's wife whispered into Kizu's ear. "Sometimes their silent prayers go on for more than twenty minutes. Occasionally we do overtime till six, but five is their prayer time and after that they usually clean up and call it a day."

The farmer's wife had already stood up and was making her way through the cultivation equipment. Kizu followed after the farmer, bent over as he walked, with Ikuo bringing up the rear. There was no reaction from the praying women as they walked out. Despite the lighting inside, as they came out of the greenhouse it was like emerging from a dark cave into the brilliance of the snow. They felt liberated by the light and invigorating air— refreshing after the oppressive odor of the lilies. With the old school building as a backdrop in the twilight, they could see the shaggy young leaves of an oak tree they hadn't noticed before. For a moment the leaves were rustled by a strong wind. Blue sky was visible through a few cracks in the clouds, which tumbled violently across the sky.

The farm owner turned his white-sideburned sallow face toward the hills and said, "There's going to be a storm, though it'll pass quickly. I'd better go check on the rest of the farm."

As her husband walked briskly away, the farm wife bowed to them, her red hands held to her face for warmth, and followed him toward where the blackened earth was filled with the brilliant green of mustard plants. Kizu and Ikuo continued on to the road where they'd parked their car. The new leaves of the beech trees on the school grounds sparkled like gold paper, but when they passed by them the sun was blocked out by the clouds and the leaves turned dark. Right beneath the tree several of the younger children were squatting, drawing on the ground or otherwise amusing themselves, no doubt, while waiting for their mothers to finish work. But they were so motionless; could they really be playing? And then it struck Kizu: These children, as well as the older children who were standing off at some distance, were *praying*.

The wind blew down to ground level, blowing straight toward Kizu and Ikuo. Thunder roared, and large drops of rain began to fall. Looking around, Kizu saw that the children had all sought shelter in the school building. This was the first time today anyone had moved quickly.

Lightning flashed in the dark. As he watched the wind blowing the rain, Ikuo carefully pulled out onto the road. Kizu, too, gave himself up to watching the force of the wind and rain. As the farm owner had said, the storm was soon over, but as they got onto the highway it was littered with broken tree branches and their new leaves. The Ford Mustang continued down the silent, thickly wooded dark slope, flicking aside the branches.

"Those women's prayers were pretty powerful, weren't they?" Ikuo said, after a long spell of silence.

"You and I have both spoken directly with Patron and Guide, and everyone's counting on us to help out with Patron's new movement. But I don't think that we—or myself, at least—can ever approach the depth of the prayers we just witnessed."

"There are lots of ways to contribute to Patron's new movement," Ikuo replied. "Never forget that Patron is counting on you. But yes, I'd agree—their prayers are pretty amazing."

"Did you notice that the children were praying too?"

"In his Somersault, Patron made fun of everything he'd done, right? The thought just struck me for the first time that if he hadn't done that he would have had a lot more worries."

"You mean about what people who pray so intensely would do after they'd been abandoned?" Kizu asked.

"Right. When I was watching those women praying, I was thinking how extraordinary it is for them to live like this for ten years. And I was also thinking that it was very possible they might not have put up with things passively but taken a different tack entirely. I know it must have been tough emotionally for Patron when he thought about having to abandon followers like these. But isn't that why he had to make such a big joke about things—so these prayerful women would be shaken to the core?"

"I guess so, and yet he wasn't able to shake them," Kizu said. "Still, the worst-case scenario Patron feared didn't take place. For ten years they lived like we just saw, praying ceaselessly. I suspect if we met the radical faction who murdered Guide, who've lived their own kind of life of faith over the last decade, we'd find them pretty formidable too.

"I really don't have a mental picture of what the hell Patron and Guide fell into was like, but for Patron, who survived alone and was resurrected, I can't imagine life will be very easy from now on."

That evening, on the drive back to Tokyo, Ikuo said one more thing.

"I think the road ahead is going to be bumpy for you too, Professor, now that you've decided to be with Patron. But I really want to thank you for coming back from America!"

13: Hallelujah

1

The day of the memorial service dawned clear and sunny, a typical end-of-spring morning. Since Kizu, officially a professor until the end of the academic year, was the only one among the participants privileged to use the American university–owned facilities freely, he set out diligently that morning to walk around the grove of trees and sloping lawn by the pond on the southeast side of the garden and see if there were any weak points through which outsiders could crash the service.

From his room Kizu couldn't tell, but the young trees bordering the grounds were slippery elms, the same as the young trees planted on the campus of his New Jersey university to replace larger trees destroyed by insects. These days he hadn't seen much of the squirrels from last summer, the ones whose vigorous movements among the green leaves of the wych elm had aroused him. They might very well have shifted over to these younger trees in order to eat the soft seeds or the young buds, for the branches had definitely been gnawed. The ground was littered with twigs that had quickly dried up.

Kizu picked up one little branch, and in a flash of inspiration, while he was checking out its withered flowers, he solved a riddle that had bothered him ever since he moved to the United States. Within layers of anthers the color of dried sunflowers, a dark-colored stigma poked out rigidly. It looked like a *hanko,* the kind of personal-name seals Japanese used instead of signatures. The word *stigma* came from the Latin for *mark,* or *brand,* which came in turn from a Greek word for *tattoo,* similar to a seal. One semester, Kizu had even lectured on the history of European seals.

Up till now, whenever Kizu had been teaching students to sketch flowers and spoke about the pistil he'd always wondered why the tip of this part of the flower was called the stigma. Whenever Kizu examined the pistil of a daffodil, he would rack his brain trying to figure out why the stigmata, the plural of stigma, shared its name with the stigmata of Jesus, the crucifixion wounds on his hands and feet. But suddenly he realized that the sacred wounds were like seals impressed on Jesus' body, and the riddle was easily solved. Feeling this was a good omen for the upcoming memorial service, Kizu placed the small branch back on the soft young grass.

They had arranged for the front gate of the apartment building to be closed while the memorial service was in progress. Dancer and Ogi would be on the tiled carport just outside the main entrance, protected by the security force Ikuo was leading, as they checked their list of invitees against the invitation each person brought.

It was imperative that all participants come on time. After the start of the service the security guards planned to shut the side door and stand guard. Patron would wait in Kizu's apartment, and then Kizu and Dancer, after she'd finished checking all the invitations, would escort him to the service. The other participants would enter the hall on the building's south side, through a corridor below the veranda on the first floor, while Patron would take an elevator to the basement and proceed to the meeting room down a corridor between the bicycle racks and the laundry room.

Ikuo's task was to bring Patron from the office in Seijo to the apartment building; when he and his three security guards had arrived in the minivan with Patron, then and only then would the front gate be opened. Kizu and the building manager had already sent out a letter to the other residents, Kizu's university colleagues, asking their cooperation in not using their cars from 10 A.M. to 3 P.M.

After Kizu had checked the grounds, he walked up to the front gate, where Ikuo was just getting out the minivan to go pick up Patron. Ikuo left the security guards inside, thirtyish men dressed in light charcoal-gray pullovers and dark gray trousers—a kind of uniform for those organizing the memorial service—and got out of the driver's seat; he was dressed similarly. Kizu explained to him how the grounds of this building, which had served as the Cultural Affairs Section during the Occupation, was still, as in the old days, surrounded by a high, sturdy chain-link fence.

Ikuo listened attentively. "The security guards have all had military training," he said, "so unless we're attacked by a huge force, the front gate should hold. It's hard to imagine an attacking force of that size moving about the center of Tokyo, though, don't you think?"

The three uniformed guards inside, who didn't greet Kizu, nodded to one another at Ikuo's confident words. Ikuo had from the first been openly enthusiastic as he made the security preparations, and perhaps his bluster was for their ears.

Ikuo returned to the minivan. Kizu watched as he raced off; then he helped the guard close the front gate. The guard was an old Filipino man over seventy who claimed he'd been working there since the Occupation; far from looking put out at having to do something beyond his job description, the old man seemed positively buoyant. Kizu guessed this was due to Ikuo's influence. Despite his dark, forbidding looks, the young man could be sunny and charming beyond belief.

A long table was set up next to the side entrance, where Ogi sat with the list of attendees; he nodded to Kizu, who walked over to him and said, "Ikuo's security squad seems to be doing a good job."

Ogi agreed, and looked out over the porte cochere. Right next to him were three more guards, also in their thirties and dressed in uniform; on the other side of the pavement, five guards stood at set intervals. Ogi didn't seem to mind that the guards who'd gathered at one end of the table heard him as he explained things to Kizu, who had dimly sensed the situation.

"The members of the security squad are all followers from the Izu research center, before the Somersault," Ogi said. "The radical faction, in other words. . . . At that time the police intervened in everything they did, so they left the church, formed their own group, and continued to keep the faith. . . . The ones who kidnapped Guide and caused his death were one element of this group, not the ones cooperating with us, of course; they didn't approve of that. Since the people who took Guide are being held in custody, there's no chance they'll be coming here."

"Aren't some of the members of the former radical faction who joined the security squad the ones who attended Patron's press conference?" Kizu asked.

"I believe so. It was afterward that Ikuo started getting in touch with members of the faction. He didn't act alone; he had Dancer's help in finding out how to locate them. I'm a naive person—hence my nickname—but if they'd asked me I would have advised them to discuss things with Patron first. I was left out of the loop, but now that I see the security squad he put together I think Ikuo made the right decision."

The men, who were within earshot of Kizu and Ogi's conversation, casually moved away to stand beside the concrete wall of the entrance and, bunched together, began smoking. They had a sophisticated air about them.

"Still," Kizu said, "even if they criticized how their colleagues let Guide die, they used to be part of the radical faction, so aren't they still upset because of the Somersault? If Patron doesn't apologize for the Somersault at the memorial service, and doesn't criticize his own actions, then what . . . ?"

"When I heard the guards for the service were former members of the radical faction the thought occurred to me too," Ogi said, "that if Patron plays dumb regarding the Somersault there might very well be trouble. When I mentioned that to Ikuo, he went over to discuss things with them, and apparently they came to some kind of understanding."

"I know bringing this up won't get us anywhere, but what if their understanding with Ikuo is just a ruse and they're planning to take over the memorial service and lynch Patron?" Kizu said, as he glanced around inside the side gate. "We'd be playing right into their hands. I mean, they're the only potentially violent group at the service."

"Dancer asked Ikuo the same thing. He said if it came to that, he'd stand up to them and defend Patron himself, and she was satisfied. What I'm hoping is that Patron's sermon will go over well, not just with the former radical faction but with the women's group you and Ikuo visited. We have limits on the number of participants, so we weren't able to invite anyone from the Kansai headquarters, the group that continued to run the religious corporation. The rest of the people coming are individual participants. Professor, did you help prepare Patron's sermon for today?"

"I did," Kizu replied, "but I imagine he'll end up mostly improvising, even though his meetings with me have been like miniature model sermons. The only thing I've done consciously to help him is to check some of the quotes from the Bible and elsewhere."

One of the men smoking by the wall took a walkie-talkie out of his pocket, spoke into it, and came back. In the broad street outside, a single large tourist bus was slowly pulling up to the curb with one of the security staff guiding it, also with a walkie-talkie in hand. He walked over to where Ogi and Kizu were and asked if they'd allow these participants, who had overestimated the amount of time they'd be stuck in traffic, to come in early. As Ogi refused their request, Kizu saw a side of him he'd never seen before. "Have them find a place near the moat to park and let them eat their lunches a bit early," Ogi instructed the guard.

The tourist bus started off again, the clump of children in front looking out the window at them. It was the women's group Kizu had visited with Ikuo. The older girl who had led the line of children off after their prayers was among them, waving something that looked like a lily as it caught the faint white light. It was a hand bell. Her fingers rested on the inside to keep it from ringing.

2

In the meeting hall for the memorial service, a room combining the lounge and the dining room of the apartment building, there were already over three hundred and fifty participants, including the organizers. The women's group were the only ones who had brought their children with them. Only they and the former members of the radical faction in the security detail were followers from before the Somersault; the rest were new converts from the past ten years, people Ogi had contacted after they had sent individual letters to Patron. One example of the latter was Ms. Tachibana, who'd brought along her mentally challenged younger brother. Ms. Asuka was there as well, recording the proceedings with her video camera.

After escorting Patron to his apartment and going down to check on the meeting hall, Kizu was asked by Ogi to take still photos of the event. Ogi clearly wanted to give him a role that would allow him to walk freely about the hall, not under the restrictions imposed by the security detail. Ogi added that, if things got out of hand, he and the others would whisk Patron to safety, while Kizu was to take refuge as quickly as he could in his apartment.

During their short exchange, the participants had lined up in the corridor beside the lawn on the south side of the building and were filing inside. Ms. Tachibana was there, along with her brother, his handsome, even solemn features set off by fixed eyes behind thin-framed glasses; a rather flamboyant woman in her mid-thirties was walking with them. When Ogi spotted her he flushed red in apparent consternation.

Kizu and the others were in the unused laundry room, watching the line of people through the frosted glass window. Dancer quickly noticed Ogi's reaction. It was clear she was interested.

The time was soon approaching for the service, so Kizu and Dancer escorted Patron down to the elevator lobby. Kizu noticed that Patron was dragging his right leg ever so slightly, and as they descended to the basement, Dancer supported Patron's back. They walked past the bicycle racks and the laundry room. When they came to the heavy door leading to the meeting room, they could sense the mass of people waiting there, even though there were no voices coming from the other side. All the participants had taken their seats, but they knew that Ogi, who was in charge of the itinerary, would want to stay on track, and it was five minutes before the scheduled start.

Kizu turned to Patron and asked about an attack of gout that had begun a week before.

"No, it doesn't hurt anymore," Patron replied, pulling himself away from some other thought that preoccupied him. "The inflammation's gone, just the embers left. . . . A long time ago, when I had my first attack of gout, Guide explained—very coldly, I thought—how it starts with the base of your big toe, moves to your shin, goes to your waist, and then reaches your heart. It's already gotten to my shin. At first it doesn't hurt so much, but at the end it spreads quite fast. I don't have much time."

Patron straightened up from the concrete wall he'd been leaning against to take the weight off his leg. Dancer, her paper-thin skin pale from excitement, took out a brush and tidied the collar of his midnight-blue jacket. Ogi opened the door to greet them, and Patron walked into the meeting hall, not dragging his leg at all.

Looking at Patron from behind, Kizu saw a relaxed man used to public speaking but with a touch of nerves. Perhaps out of concern for Patron's bad leg, Dancer had set up the podium on the same level as the seats. Head down, Patron proceeded past the front row of chairs that pressed up close. Dancer and Kizu went over to stand in front by Ogi and Ikuo. Patron rested both hands on the podium, apparently taking a moment in prayer. Then he raised his head. A deep sigh wafted over the packed assembly.

Patron thrust his chest out and stood silently facing the audience. With a brusque but dignified movement he turned to gaze at the photograph of Guide and the high vase with its branches of dogwood flowers in full bloom that were behind him. Then he turned back to face the audience and spoke for the first time.

"Thank you all for coming here to this service in memory of Guide. In the years after the Somersault, until Guide was cruelly murdered, he and I were always together. For Guide and myself this was a time when we fell into hell. The most painful aspect of our hell was that during those ten years I never once had a major trance, and as a consequence Guide was unable to interpret any visions for me. We existed in a silent darkness. The kind of scene displayed here was over. Without recovering his health, Guide was lost to me."

Patron fell silent again and turned back to the photograph behind him. It was a snapshot of the two of them sitting in armchairs in Patron's study. Patron looked absentminded, as if recovering from an illness, while Guide, his hair dark and luxuriant, was leaning toward Patron.

Kizu looked around the hall. The group of women he'd visited on the hilly district along the Odakyu Line occupied seats in the center, a few rows back from the front, their quiet children with them.

"Why were the two of us together during those ten years of hell?" Patron went on. "Because each of us had had his own hell decided for him, I believe. We did the Somersault together and fell into hell together. One of the aftereffects—or, I should say, legacies—of the Somersault was that, as one condition of our respective hells, we had to see each other day after day. Then, after ten years passed and we were considering climbing up out of the abyss—in other words, when we were starting to grope toward a new beginning—Guide was killed. This was also exactly the time when I began to find signs that my trances were about to return.

"Once more I felt banished to the wilderness. Even if in the near future my painful deep trances were to return, without Guide's intervention I wouldn't be able to put these visions into words. All my suffering would be in vain. Now I believe I've found a new Guide, though I am not saying that I've discovered someone to translate my visions. The Guide who was murdered was a unique individual, which indeed was one of the reasons he was killed.

"Without him, when I return from my trances, emotionally and physically drained, I'm unable to extract information from the other side from my dark, muddled brain. A fear seizes me each and every day that, if I am unable to unravel it, this lump of information will disappear.

"Once I lost Guide, I started reading, desperately searching through books that might show me how to create a line of communication between this side and the other, which is what I want the new Guide to help me do. One thing I read was the description from the Bible of Jesus on the cross. As long as Jesus could complete his work on the cross, he could leave the resurrection entirely up to God.

"I quote from the gospel according to Mark.

"At the sixth hour darkness came over the whole land until the ninth hour. And at the ninth hour Jesus cried out in a loud voice, 'Eloi, Eloi, lama sabachthani?'—which means, 'My God, my God, why have you forsaken me?'

"When some of those standing near heard this, they said, 'Listen, he's calling Elijah.'

"One man ran, filled a sponge with wine vinegar, put in on a stick, and offered it to Jesus to drink. 'Leave him alone now. Let's see if Elijah comes to take him down,' he said.

"With a loud cry, Jesus breathed his last.

"The curtain of the temple was torn in two from top to bottom."

"I just can't get the face of Jesus out of my mind, crying out in a loud voice as the earth turns dark. I realize it's a tasteless parody, but if I use the name that the old-timers among you are used to and imitate Jesus, in this dark situation I'm in right now, I imagine in my shock and anger I would raise up a loud voice and cry, *My Prophet, my Prophet, why have you for-saken me?*"

Resting both arms on the podium, Patron leaned backward, his face to the surprisingly large space above the underground lounge, and vehemently shouted this out. The windows facing the lawn were bright, and with the lights on at the other side of the room it felt to the participants as if an opaque membrane was hanging over them. The children sitting right in front of Patron all tucked in their chins as if something quite scary was about to happen.

"I would like to quote once more from the Bible. This is from the first letter of John:

> "Dear children, this is the last hour; and as you have heard that the antichrist is coming, even now many antichrists have come. This is how we know it is the last hour. They went out from us, but they did not really belong to us. For if they had belonged to us, they would have remained with us; but their going showed that none of them belonged to us."

"This particular passage has caused me great pain. In the last trial, you did not leave us, and though you continued to belong to us, neither Guide nor I remained with you. And I became the antichrist—both when I fell into hell, and even now that I have resurfaced. Is there so much misery and pain for mankind that this is the only alternative—that I must be seen as the antichrist?

"Guide was the only other person who agreed that I must tread this path. Together with me he did the Somersault and accompanied me to hell. This was his choice, I think, because he insisted to the end on the necessity of the Somersault. It was a Somersault where the antichrist appears, which signals the end of the world. That is the way I understand it now."

3

Dancer, her narrow profile tucked in tightly, was whispering in Ogi's ear. As if he'd been waiting for this, Ogi nodded. Both arms thrust out, he held out a sign that said THE FIRST HALF OF THE SERMON IS FINISHED AND THERE WILL NOW BE A COFFEE BREAK. Patron let his arms fall to the sides of the podium, and Dancer held her hand out and led him out of the hall for a while. By the time the audience had risen to their feet, tables had been set up in front and on both sides, with Styrofoam cups filled with coffee and small packets of cream and sugar, all done by the security squad, which had also stood guarding both sides of the door through which Patron had entered. The communal women's group helped pass out coffee cups to the rest of the participants. The tall doctor's widow with the unusual walk directed this operation.

Kizu knew it was now customary in Japan for meetings and seminars to include a coffee break, but still he found it quite a sight to see things go so smoothly at a memorial service, especially one with over three hundred and fifty attendees. He looked around for the young woman with the facial scar and spotted her still sitting with the children, who were waiting patiently as she handed out little cartons of coffee from a large cardboard box.

"They're very well organized, aren't they?" said the newspaper reporter Kizu knew from the press conference as he passed Kizu a Styrofoam container of coffee; standing by the wall, Kizu had been unable to take photographs of the goings-on or squeeze into line for coffee. "It turned out to be a good idea to have former radical-faction members work the security detail," the reporter added, "though I admit I was skeptical when I first heard about it."

"It's a lovely and solemn gathering, isn't it?" said a woman beside him, dressed in subdued clothes and also sipping coffee. She was the woman who had been beside the dark-skinned reporter at the press conference. Today she had pinned to her chest the white flower given to distinguish the twenty people from the media who were in attendance.

"I was quite surprised by how austere Patron was when he spoke," the reporter said, "because during the Somersault he wasn't that way at all. Guide was the gloomy one then, and Patron the clown."

"For a newspaper reporter, you talk too much," the woman said reprovingly. "It doesn't give us a chance to hear him speak."

Kizu sensed that she had heard something from her colleague about himself, so before she could ask for his take on the memorial service, he headed off to the door behind which Patron was waiting, receiving a nod from the ladies collecting the coffee cups. The guards standing there recognized Kizu and let him pass.

Kizu cut through the bicycle rack area and went over to the elevators, where he found Ikuo leaning against the door of the elevator to keep it propped open and available. Ogi stood in front of him, showing him a pile of documents, with a pair of scissors on top, and Ikuo seemed to be checking something. Patron was sitting in a round chair next to the wall opposite. Dancer stood protectively close behind him, so he could lean back against her. She was telling him some of her ideas about how the second half of the sermon should go.

"I understand how important the past is, but haven't you said enough about it? I'd like you to talk about the *future*, what your plans are. The followers are hanging on your every word. Even the children are listening intently."

Patron didn't directly respond to her, his eyes wide open as if he were attempting to see underwater. As Kizu approached, Patron asked him, "Professor, what do you think the audience thinks about the Somersault?"

Kizu was at a complete loss. Patron was looking up, waiting for his answer, when Dancer stuck her head next to his shoulder and intervened.

"Let's begin the second half and talk about that later. You have to talk about your future activities now. Speak with confidence."

"Ladies and gentlemen," Patron began again, "with the ideas I mentioned in the first half of my sermon, I'm planning to begin a new movement. Having lost Guide, I feel even more compelled to get started without a moment's delay. I can only hope and pray that something will take the place of Guide's interpretations of my visions—an ability we'll never see again—as things appear to me through this movement.

"No longer will I have a partner who can arrange into words the darkness of a human being's soul—my own. I can only reach inside my slit-open belly and yank out something—I have no idea what—and preach the most nonsensical, incoherent ideas.

"However, Guide taught me this: The only way I'll find a path is by sticking my hands into that dark place. That memory itself has been lost along with everything else we accumulated, and I can hear him accusing me of being nothing but a scarecrow filled with straw, which thoroughly discourages me.

"Speaking of the word *straw,* when I was quite young, about the age of the children who've come here to remember Guide, I thought about this word. Since all of you little ones are listening carefully to what I say, I'd like to direct this to you. When I was a child, I was told the expression *like a drowning man clutching at a straw.* And this expression bothered me. To tell the truth, I hated it. It made me feel awful.

"Imagine there's a poor child who's drowning in the river. And for whatever reason there are some adults standing on the bank just casually looking on. The child grasps at straws floating by. The adults burst out laughing. And finally, they step into the river and save the drowning child. That's the scene I imagined. A long time afterward, I told Guide about this and he told me that he imagined it this way: When you open a drowned child's hand you find he was clutching straw. He said he felt as if he'd actually seen this occur when he was a child.

"Ladies and gentlemen, that's the kind of person Guide was. If anything, it made me feel that *I* was the drowned child he saw, that he saw my cold wet hand clutching the straw and took pity on me. I have decided to restart my movement and build a new church. But if Guide is now like the drowning child, then through our new church I intend to discover the straw *his* fingers were clutching.

"By unraveling the words of the visions I had in my trances, Guide created our theology. At the time of the Somersault when I said it was all nonsense, this is what I meant. The basic idea is that God is the totality of nature that created this world. Living a life of faith for us means being accurately and fully aware of this fact. When we achieve this, we realize that our awareness itself is, from the very start, made possible by God. What flows from God into us makes this awareness possible, making us able to verbalize it.

"At the time of the Somersault, what was at work inside me when I said that our theology was nonsense was another theology just starting to sprout, a miserable theology that toyed with the first. Nature, which makes up the totality of this planet—the environment we humans live in, in other words—is steadily falling apart. We've gone beyond the point of no return. God as the totality of nature—including human beings—is decaying bit by bit. God is terminally ill.

"Moreover, our awareness of God as being destroyed, of God with an incurable illness, is itself a part of God. Our crumbling God, our God who's sick, is the one who makes us aware—just like a mother teaching her baby to speak: a mother who is falling apart, who's dying from an incurable disease and is talking to her baby, who is fading away along with her, telling the baby what she knew from the start would happen.

"What I'd like to say right now, based on my new theology at the time of the Somersault, is this: From our viewpoint, as infants whose fate is to die around the same time as our mother, we have the right to stand up to God and say that this wasn't part of his plan! The dying mother hears the nonsensical words of the feverish baby, puts them in the proper context, and returns them to the baby's mouth. It is in that mother–child dialogue that we should find mankind's true repentance, because the ones who made this happen, who destroyed the natural world, who destroyed God and gave him an incurable disease, are none other than *mankind itself.* Isn't this how the church of the one who will lead them to repentance, the church of the antichrist, should be constructed: through protesting to God?

"Having lost Guide I've lost the way to interpret my visions, and now—dragging the Somersault along with me—here I stand. And I have decided to restart my movement focusing on leading people to this kind of repentance.

"Just as there is no doubt that Christ's humiliating death had meaning, there must be meaning in the desperate struggle of the antichrist who has stepped into hell. Otherwise, in that first consciousness of God as He created the world, why did He structure it so that there would appear so many

antichrists at the end? God is the very one who, among all the things of creation, cannot be dismissed by a joke, the one existence that has absolutely no
reason ever to turn a Somersault."

After finishing, Patron propped his hands on the podium, and let his
shoulders relax and his head hang down as he looked absently around the
audience. Dancer approached and spoke to him, but Patron shook his head
and pointed listlessly with his left hand at Ogi. Ogi responded to this, and
looked at Dancer, who nodded back at him. Ogi went over to stand between
Dancer and Patron. Calling forth all his strength, Patron leaned forward and,
looking straight ahead toward the assembled multitude, cried out, "Ladies
and gentlemen, please pray for Guide. *Hallelujah!*"

4

Patron hung his large head down and began silently praying, and
Dancer and Ogi closed their eyes and followed suit. The people in the audience shifted in their seats and began to pray silently; the sound of this mass
movement of bodies was surprisingly peaceful. Kizu closed his eyes, too, and
prayed. Filtered through an image of Guide in his mind, he prayed for Patron. *Lord, please help this person. And give me strength.*

Just as at the farm along the Odakyu Line, Kizu found the lengthy
prayer a little too much to take, and he opened his eyes to find Ikuo standing
by the door Patron had used. Ikuo stood with legs apart as if he were about to
start a fight, facing the quiet, praying crowd, all them with their eyes closed.

If intruders had wanted to throw the service into chaos, it would have
been easy and now would have been the time. So Ikuo had a very good reason
for not joining them in prayer. Kizu could sense in Ikuo, standing there like
a rock that could at any moment swing into action, something menacing that
outweighed the usual affinity he felt for him.

Please help this young man too, Kizu thought; I don't really know much
about who he is, but he's in the grip of something that took hold of him when
he was a child, that propels him forward—toward *something.* Kizu bowed
his head and resumed his fervent prayers. I don't know what Ikuo is so fired
up about, he prayed, but if this is, as Patron said, a small part of Your consciousness of the world, isn't that something to smile about? I pray that You
help this young man so busily moving in that direction.

Here I am calling out to You, Kizu prayed, yet truthfully I'm not sure
about You. But through this young man I am leaving my whole life up to You.
I know that I have, inside me, an incurable illness that's fairly common for

someone my age. But as long as this doesn't come to the surface and steal away my ability to participate in the movement, please help me contribute in some fashion—for the sake of this young man who doesn't care what means he uses to realize this strange idea of his. I suspect the physical love he allows me might just be one more means to an end for him, though even my suspicion is sweet.

When Ogi announced the end of the silent prayer time, several hands shot up in the row of reporters—a show of hands from those who wanted to question Patron about his sermon. Patron was standing behind the podium, gathering himself together, and Dancer leaned toward him to ask for instructions. Patron gave a short reply. Reconfirming this, Dancer told Ogi what Patron had said.

"This is the time when we'd like to hear your responses to the sermon," Ogi said in a high voice, "and Patron said he would like to select the speakers. The person Patron has selected is Mrs. Shigeno, from the women's group that during these ten years was independent of the church and organized a communal life of faith. Mrs. Shigeno is also the person who, on the death of her husband, contributed the large hospital her family ran, as well as the land, to the church, as a special contribution to commemorate the church's becoming a religious corporation.

"In the early period of the church, Guide was in charge of finances, and he was not inclined to accept contributions from followers who had renounced worldly possesions, which meant the church's financial situation was unstable. It was Mrs. Shigeno who convinced Guide to accept these monetary donations, and it was through her that the church finally got on firm financial ground."

The old woman whom Kizu had noticed before, working despite her bad legs, was dressed the same as the other women around her, though her upper body, especially with the light gray scarf she had wrapped stylishly around her neck, took a backseat to none. Being careful of her legs, she rose serenely to her feet and took the wireless microphone that Dancer brought over. Her dignified face was full of tension, but the way she started her speech was appealing.

"That introduction is a bit overblown, I'm afraid. My money was going to be taken away in taxes anyway, so it's different from those followers who give up everything they own. Though I must admit that at my age having such a handsome young man say nice things about me isn't a bad feeling at all!

"I do have a few things I'd like to ask about the sermon, but I don't want to take up too much valuable time so I'll just touch on the one basic thing I've been thinking about these past ten years.

"When Patron and Guide turned their Somersault, to use the names you use now, I had the feeling that I'd already experienced that before.

"This happened at the time of our defeat in World War Two—ancient history, I'm afraid, for the young people here today. I was a student in a girls' school in a provincial town and was mobilized to work in a parachute factory. The representatives from each class were called to the main office and told that work would stop a half hour before lunchtime that day. We were to assemble with our teachers in the auditorium to listen to the radio.

"What really shocked us students was that the Emperor spoke in an entirely human voice, just like ours. This was the era when pictures of the Emperor and Empress hung like pictures of God in the chapel next to the auditorium.

"We learned about Patron and Guide's Somersault, too, through reports in the media—which reminded me of hearing the Emperor on the radio so many years ago.

"For us members of the church, Guide was like someone special selected from congregation. But Patron was different—he was directly connected to God. During the Somersault, though, here was Patron saying that all the mystical things he'd said and done were a joke. It was less like God's son becoming human than finding out he was, from the beginning, just an ordinary person. Wasn't this Patron's equivalent of the Emperor's speech, this time not on radio but on TV, with Patron adding all these comical gestures as he renounced his divinity?

"Wanting to understand Patron's Somersault, I took another look at the Emperor's renunciation speech. After the Somersault the young people became quite emotional, but I was too old for that. And after giving it a lot of thought I arrived at the following conclusion.

"The Emperor certainly did renounce his divinity then, but for the people of this country, in the hearts of its citizens, he didn't change at all, did he? It's a long story so I'll leave out the details, but what I ended up thinking about Patron is something similar. He announced that he's not directly connected with God, and there's not much we can do about that. He'll have to live the rest of his life cut off from God, but that doesn't affect *my* faith in him, or the faith of my companions. We are still fully prepared to follow him.

"It's been years since I heard his sermons, but it brings back many memories. We heard rumors about how Patron and Guide were living, and it was painful to hear him speak today about the ten years he suffered in hell. How awful this must have been for Patron, alienated from God, shut up day after day with Guide, with whom he still had such strong emotional ties. I can only imagine how ghastly this must have been. And Guide, still fallen in hell, was murdered, unable ever again to help Patron with his visions. How dreadful!

"When I think about it, isn't Patron even now pushed into a corner, suffering every day? Though my image of him is still that of a younger man, I'm so happy he didn't make some frivolous statement in today's sermon about how he'd regained his connection with God. The ever-suffering Patron has returned to us and has put out the call for a new movement. After ten years of suffering, there is no better master of the church to welcome back. Patron is fine just the way he is.

"I've been a little outspoken, I'm afraid, but the fact is, we *were* all shaken by the Somersault. The thought has even crossed my mind that losing Guide was retribution for our unfaithfulness. But Patron's fall and suffering have made him the perfect leader of our new church—and we mustn't lose him. I am overjoyed to follow Patron's new movement."

A hand bell rang out. The packed auditorium absorbed some of the sound, but with the windows closed the sound fairly snapped in the air. The row of children in front all stood up and in loud spirited voices shouted out, *"Hallelujah, hallelujah, hallelujah!"*

Urged on by the hand bell, which led the chorus, the children vigorously—and without any sound of scraping chairs—sat back down as one. Leaning with his elbows on the podium and all his weight shifted onto it, Patron raised his head. His lusterless face was exhausted, his eyes teary. Even so, in a hoarse voice he spoke words of encouragement.

"I would like to say this in response to what I've heard. When I fell into hell, my connection with God was severed. This was part of my hell because I did the Somersault. I've lost my connection with God and have nothing to do with visions I might see in trances anymore, but I still find myself burning with a desire to communicate the words from the other side. So where does that leave me? The reason I quoted from the first letter of John was to answer this: *Dear children, this is the last hour; and as you have heard that the antichrist is coming, even now many antichrists have come. This is how we know it is the last hour.*

"As a sign that the end time is here, antichrists are popping up all over the world, and I am one of them. I am going to be building a new church, and I want you to be clear on this: I'm starting this church as one antichrist among many. Why would you follow a leader, knowing full well he's an antichrist? With the exception of the children, it's because you, too, are all sinners. You're the ones who've destroyed God as the totality of nature and given him an incurable disease. It is for your sake, you who have committed these sins, and for my sake, as one himself who has sinned, that Guide died in such an excruciating, horrible way."

Patron stopped speaking. Kizu picked up now on how Dancer thrust her right arm slightly forward and made a twisting motion with her wrist. At one end of the row of children one of the older girls, her head raised high to watch Dancer intently, got the signal and rang the hand bell, and the children all stood as one and shouted out, *"Hallelujah, hallelujah, hallelujah!"*

After they stopped and had returned to their seats, Patron's voice continued over the faint reverberation. "This parade led by an antichrist will, in the end, reach the path to salvation—because this is a parade of the repentant, and even if I die a death befitting an antichrist, one more horrid even than Guide's, your march must go on. In order that the harvest gained by Guide's death will not be in vain, each one of us must play his part. *Hallelujah!*"

The hand bell rang out once more, and the children's voices filled the hall like a loud aria. With the exception of the reporters, all the participants joined in: *"Hallelujah, hallelujah, hallelujah!"*

In the midst of this chorus, Ogi and Dancer leaped forward to grab the lectern that, together with Patron's upper body leaning so heavily against it, seemed on the verge of tipping over, helped turn him around, and hurried him off to the elevator. Reporters who pushed forward trying to question Patron were met by a line of security guards who formed a human wall.

14: Why Patron? And Why Now?

1

An hour after the announcement that the memorial service was over, the partition between the dining hall and the lounge was back in place, the metal folding chairs piled up and stored away. Tables and chairs were returned to their original places in the lounge, where a press conference was to take place, the result of objections by representatives of the media. Some reporters were upset by Patron's absence from the press conference, but most accepted that he was too exhausted to attend. A long table was set up beside the window that looked out on the lawn. The members of Patron's newly announced church sat on one side, and the reporters sat across from them on the other.

Ogi and Dancer appeared first. Ikuo was still directing the security staff even at this press conference and sat off to one side, leaving enough space beside him so he could move if he needed to. One more member of the security staff was there, a fortyish man named Koga who looked, to Ogi's eyes, a bit of an anachronism with his rigid, possibly military-trained posture. Kizu had heard from Ikuo that this man, with his lively intelligent eyes, had been the only medical doctor at the Izu research center.

Ms. Tachibana and her younger brother were there as well, as was Ms. Asuka, who, as she had done at the memorial service, stood behind the row of reporters to film the event with her handheld video camera. The group of women living communally had taken their chartered bus back home, having turned down Dancer's request that one of them stay and take part.

The press conference began with a question from the dark-skinned reporter for the national newspaper.

"Last month at the press conference with Patron, quite frankly I felt it strange to see Dr. Koga there, since he was on the side that was at odds with Patron and Guide over the Somersault. Not that I'm saying he had anything to do with Guide's death, mind you! At any rate, I'm happy he's able to join this question-and-answer session. The first thing I'd like to ask is whether the people on the security staff today, in other words the former radical faction, have reached a reconciliation with Patron's church?"

Dr. Koga gazed at the questioner with a youthful expression that belied his years—though before he replied, his eyes clouded for just a moment and a solemn look came over his face.

"You've called us the *former* radical faction, and it was you in the media who originally dubbed us the *radical faction,*" Dr. Koga said, in a sonorous voice. "As I wanted to say at the time, it wasn't as if we just went off on our own and created a sect. We all worked at our research under Guide's supervision at the facility provided for us. Before long the entire research center was unified as the cutting edge of Patron's teachings. And our activities began to confirm this. You asked whether we've reconciled with Patron's church. Well, right now I think of Patron and the church as separate entities. The headquarters of the church exists in Kansai, and this church is active as a religious corporation. If there's going to be a reconciliation with the church, *Patron* should be the one seeking it.

"Some of you just laughed at this, but I think that shows you don't know much about the Somersault ten years ago. Patron and Guide *did* turn a Somersault. To say that the motivation for the Somersault lay in the activities of the so-called radical faction is a one-sided, solely political view. I reserve comment, but probably most people see it this way.

"It was Patron and Guide who announced the Somersault and left the church. Those of us in the church had our beliefs ridiculed and were abandoned by the founder. But in the sermon that he gave to eulogize Guide today, Patron reached out to all believers. That's how I see it, and frankly I was quite moved by his words."

"True, Patron did say he wants to make peace with you," the reporter said, "and you accept that, which seems auspicious. Does this mean, then, that Guide was executed because he didn't accept a reconciliation?"

"Calling it an execution isn't correct," Dr. Koga shot back. "I wasn't there until the very end, but as a doctor I think I know more about what happened than you do. In his sermon a short while ago Patron used the term *murdered,* and I understand his feelings, but it's an overly sentimental view. It's flat-out inaccurate. I'm confident that the charges will be dropped. And I expect the media to make a full apology.

"This is what really happened. Putting together all we'd been thinking about over the last ten years, we asked Guide whether he could make a fresh start together with us. Guide was willing to discuss it, but in the deliberations that followed we couldn't reach an agreement. And while this was happening my understanding is that an accident took place."

The reporter wanted to pursue this further but a woman beside him with a classic oval face interrupted with a question for the doctor. "Patron announced that he will restart his movement and has made up with you people in the former radical faction. He also told us he is one of the antichrists. What I'd like to make sure I understand is how you feel about the violent adventurism of the former radical faction?"

"If we put the two together," Dr. Koga said, "Patron's being the antichrist and the violent adventurism you spoke of, that would make for one terrible misfortune, certainly. That's what you're implying, right? You have to understand, though, that even with the *former* radical faction, violence and destruction were never the goals. We were using our own means to make society aware that the human race had to atone for its sins. The time of trial at the end time was fast approaching, and no matter how the Almighty's will might manifest itself, we wanted to help make that will come true by repenting. That's what inspired us.

"The so-called radical faction's designs were destroyed by the Somersault of the two leaders who had provided us with our basic vision. Despite being betrayed and abandoned, though, the faction deepened its understanding of the Somersault and their thinking and has stayed together to this very day. And now Patron, who has suffered more than we have—something we understood more about in our talk with Guide—is starting this new movement that we have great hopes for. As for this term *antichrist,* I don't think Patron wants us to interpret it as an evil figure who will cause confusion and disaster at the end time; rather it should be viewed as part of the painful, hard look he's taken of himself.

"Even for those of us who once opposed Patron and Guide with all our might, Patron remains an indispensable person. What I've said here is not just an answer to your question but a response to Patron's sermon from those members of the radical faction who participated in today's memorial service."

2

After speaking with so much emotion, Dr. Koga's expression indicated he was finished, yet the woman reporter wasn't about to let him off so easily.

"At the memorial service I noticed you too prayed silently for Guide," she remarked. "But being a doctor, don't you feel some responsibility for what happened? You must have known that Guide had had a brain aneurysm before, and it must have been common knowledge among your circle that they would interrogate him for that long."

Dr. Koga had been sitting up straight, but now, like a weasel, he raised his head even higher as he answered. "I believe what you're asking is, Do I feel responsible for the results of things done by a group I've been associated with for a long time? As you said, I am a physician, but even if I were a brain specialist it would be difficult to know, just by looking at a person, if he were likely to have a burst aneurysm. In fact, it might be impossible."

"Could you answer the question more directly?"

"I don't know if this is what you're looking for," Dr. Koga replied, "but as someone who knew Guide for a long time, I feel more sadness at his death than responsibility. Guide responded to the former radical faction's invitation to talk because he believed that even if he were destroyed, his death would directly link up with what came afterward: his hopes for Patron's restarting his movement. Which led me to want to participate in it."

The woman reporter was clearly unsatisfied, but the other reporter took over the questioning.

"At the time of the Somersault," he said, "in the television announcement—or perhaps I should say *performance*—what impressed me most about what Patron said was this: Although they continued their movement with the idea that the end time was coming in two or three years, he said that nobody seriously believed it. And while they were trying to get humanity to repent, those two or three years passed and people decided they were just a bunch of dummies and laughed at them like it was a joke that took forever to get to the punch line.

"I think it's important for the former radical faction members, as well as everyone who plans to join this new movement of Patron's, to remember his argument in the Somersault. Even now, as an antichrist, if Patron once again declares that the end of the world is near, can you go along with this?"

Dancer responded. "It's true that in the past Patron predicted the end of the world in two or three years and called for repentance. At the time of the Somersault he said this was a joke, that the end was greatly delayed. Does starting the new movement mean he's once again setting back the timetable for the end of the world? That's what you're laughing at, right? But is that what he preached at today's memorial service?

"After all that time he spent in hell, I don't think he's saying there should be another Somersault and we should all pretend the earlier one never took place. He was talking about a much more important problem than the amount of time that will elapse before the end of the world. We found his ideas quite moving, and we've recommitted ourselves to following him. And not just those of us who work with him every day. That's essentially what the women's group said as well."

"We'll have to wait to see what your new movement is all about before we can give an objective opinion about whether this is another Somersault or not," the reporter said. "I'd like to ask one more brief question, if you don't mind, and I'd appreciate it if you'd respond briefly so we can quote it in the newspaper: Why now—after Aum Shinrikyo—has Patron returned?"

Dancer motioned for Ogi to answer.

"Patron believes that if there hadn't been a Somersault ten years ago," Ogi said, "the church, with the radical faction leading it, would have ended up just like Aum. And if that happened our church, again like Aum, would have been attacked and destroyed. Patron needed to send out a message of healing for his followers. Also, he wants to put into practice a teaching that will soothe all the young people hurt by Aum Shinrikyo. *That's* one reason why now, after the Aum affair, Patron has revived his movement."

"Do you plan to reach out directly to people belonging to Aum?"

"No. When I say young people hurt by Aum, I'm not just referring to members of the cult. Our movement will have a broader appeal."

"Logically, then," the reporter persisted, "your broad appeal *would* allow former Aum members to join. And if that happens, wouldn't they be involved in a joint struggle with former radical-faction members who've helped Patron restart his movement, which would only put the authorities on edge?"

Dr. Koga fielded this one. "Maybe I shouldn't poke my nose into this, but since you said former radical-faction members are helping Patron and I'm one of them, I'll try to respond. I have no way of knowing how the authorities or the police feel. But the Aum Shinrikyo's understanding of Armageddon and our own concept of armed struggle are completely different. We were calling on society—the country—the world—to repent. One step in doing this was to occupy a nuclear power plant and get the attention of those who weren't listening.

"One clear difference between us and Aum was that, as our movement calling for repentance progressed and we blew up a nuclear plant, it would be very obvious that those participating in the operation did not intend to survive. Even if young people from Aum had participated, as long as they still accepted the teaching that they would survive Armageddon, I doubt they'd have gone along with our ideas. Because we put our own lives on the line."

"If the plan by the radical faction to occupy a nuclear power plant had been realized, wouldn't this have been even more dangerous than the Aum sarin gas attack?" This was asked, in a fit of indignation, by another reporter who up till then had remained silent. "If neither side takes a good hard look at their past, and the radical faction takes part in Patron's new movement, people won't stand for it. Haven't we learned anything from Aum? There's no way this should be allowed."

"*Who* won't stand for it? And what are they going to do?" Ikuo declared. Ogi could feel the mood of the gathering change. Ikuo didn't speak rudely or in a loud voice, but there was something in the way he delivered these questions that flouted the basic rules of this gathering.

Ikuo fell silent, his strong neck thrust out as he awaited a reply. As if he'd been treated in a violent, outrageous manner, the reporter turned bright red behind his oval-framed glasses. He may also have been feeling some pressure from the room next door, separated from this lounge by only a thin plywood wall, for at the same time as this press conference was going on there was a banquet in the dining room for those who'd helped prepare and run the memorial service, one that included many members of the security squad.

At times Ogi felt Dancer's plans were overly clever, but he had to admit that using the two rooms in this way was a stroke of genius. Actually he found it strange that after the memorial service, when the reporters were dissatisfied—in a fighting mood, even—about having their question-and-answer session attenuated, things had proceeded so peacefully that a question like Ikuo's stood out. The reporters' reticence might very well have been affected by the knowledge that among the people next door, who were trying to keep their voices down and not laugh, were those whose intimate companions had murdered the very man they were gathered to commemorate.

3

After a period of silence, Ogi was surprised again when Ms. Tachibana stood up, showing what must have been unusual fortitude on her part. Her younger brother, the one with mental disabilities, sat next to her, his face as tense as if he were the one about to speak.

"My brother and I were not followers of the church," Ms. Tachibana began. "At the time of Patron and Guide's Somersault we merely watched from outside with great concern. Still, we were surprised by what they said. In the Somersault, Patron said he wasn't serious about the world ending in two or three years. Are you saying, then, it'll come sooner? someone asked, making fun of him. For me it's rather that question itself which I found unexpected.

"With Patron in the lead, we're facing the end of the world and doing all we can to repent. Even now I am constantly thinking of my soul and my brother's. The timing of when the end comes isn't as important as the fact that we are—*right now*—repenting as the world draws to an end.

"Before a chance meeting opened my eyes to Patron's teachings, my brother and I went to a different church, a church founded on Saint Peter's having seen and talked to the resurrected Jesus. After we attended this church for several years I began to feel that the people there didn't have a genuine sense of repentance. My brother and I—I understand very well what my brother is thinking, by the way—sought a deeper level of repentance and found we couldn't stand being there, because people didn't see repentance as a pressing concern.

"After a time something happened that led us to distance ourselves from the church. A Bible study class for beginners started and I asked special permission for my brother and me to attend. My brother couldn't really understand how, three days after his crucifixion, Christ rose again. When he stubbornly persisted in this, he was scolded by the priest.

"I gathered my courage and told the priest that I believe it's true that on a certain day in history Jesus rose again, but also in myself, right now, I feel he's arisen. That's what I feel as I pray. My brother can't put this into words, I went on, and perhaps doesn't even think in terms of words, but every time I have a friend play the music he's composed, I can see Jesus risen right now in his heart.

"When I said this the priest looked shocked and told me the two of us are Gnostic heretics. The religious aficionados there started laughing. My brother hates this—it's literally painful for him, actually: people laughing at something he doesn't understand—and he slammed the desk, scandalizing everyone. We never went back.

"My brother and I both feel that the end of the world is the same as Jesus' crucifixion and resurrection—it's both something that happens at a certain point in time in history and also an event that is *always with us*. If not, then the inevitable end of the world will have meaning for those who experience it but none for those who died beforehand.

"When my brother and I feel repentance, we feel as if we're seeing the end of the world clearly right in front of our eyes. And we see Patron, looking down on the frightening scene at the end of the world, holding our hands as we ascend into heaven. I'm not much of a speaker, and I don't think I can convey what I feel, but if you listen to the composition my brother wrote called

'Ascending to Heaven,' I believe you'll be able to feel the joy of passing away as Patron holds your hand.

"This joy is not an intellectual exercise for my brother. He's a simple soul, but he expresses with great vividness the joy of ascending to heaven. He's able to do this, I think, because at the very moment of composition he's ascending to heaven hand in hand with Patron."

Ms. Tachibana touched the shoulder of her brother, who didn't have binocular vision and whose eyes, while wide open, were wall-eyed. Her brother picked up a medium-sized cassette recorder he'd had on his lap and, with unexpectedly graceful movements of his surprisingly beautiful fingers, set it in motion.

Until the music actually started, Ogi was anxious. If the music was childish, he thought, that would be understandable, but if it turned out to be something incredibly dull that would be even worse. But the low but piercing piano music invited one to smile with unalloyed joy.

When the tape was finished, the bug-faced reporter whose pronouncements had been interrupted by Ikuo—now with an even more insectlike, poker-faced look on his face—made the following comment.

"I understand that this music depicts the feeling of having Patron lead one by the hand into heaven, but it's a very short piece, isn't it, taking less than two minutes for the ascent? At any rate, I'm not given any space in the music review section of the paper, but I think it'd be difficult to convince readers if I wrote that a mentally handicapped person had had a mystical experience while he strung together bits of Bach or Mozart."

Ogi watched as Ikuo rose to his feet, as if he were danger incarnate.

"It's obvious that, along with your reference to his being mentally handicapped, you look down on the composer, Mr. Morio Tachibana. You said he's using bits of Bach or Mozart—well, which is it? And from which works?"

The reporter again ignored Ikuo's questions. Ms. Tachibana's brother, undaunted by Ikuo's earsplitting delivery, looked as if he was straining to hear the reporter's reply.

4

Thus the press conference fizzled to a close. On the way out, Ogi overheard the dark-skinned reporter speak to Dancer, whom he'd gotten to know, and what he said struck Ogi as entirely reasonable.

"I understand that Patron will be restarting his movement," the reporter said, "but there doesn't seem to be any shared point of view among his followers. Though I suppose if I put Patron's sermon and the comments of the communal women's group together I can come up with some sort of article."

After seeing the members of the press to the side entrance, and thanking the security staff, who, along with Dr. Koga, were about to leave, Ogi stuck his head in the dining hall. The partition was back in place, and in a corner of the wall next to the window there was an upright piano. Ms. Tachibana and her brother had brought over folding chairs and sat facing each other. Ikuo was standing beside them, talking with Ms. Tachibana's brother.

"That man was an unintelligent, stupid man, wasn't he?" Ikuo said, slowly, pausing between phrases. As proof that his words got through, Ms. Tachibana's brother, one eye fixed on Ikuo's mouth, nodded.

"The newspaper reporter gave his opinion about your music, didn't he?" Ms. Tachibana added. "Ikuo's saying that that was the opinion of an unintelligent, stupid man."

"I could sense that Morio was surprised by how ridiculous that guy's opinions were. Or was he angry? Somehow it seems that way."

"When people laugh at my brother," Ms. Tachibana said, "or show they don't take him seriously, he does get angry, but he just looks like he has a stomachache. Most people don't realize he's angry."

"Just a moment ago when I saw Morio's expression, it reminded me so much of myself as a child," Ikuo said, with such fervor it took Ogi by surprise. "When I got angry it felt like the space between my chest and stomach was being wrung in a knot. It was such a strong feeling that people misunderstood and thought I was crying, and I ended up lashing out at the arrogant bullies around me, which got me in a lot of trouble."

"Well, I never!" Ms. Tachibana's brother said, with a sigh of criticism.

"Morio knows exactly what you're talking about," Ms. Tachibana said. "He doesn't do anything violent, but when he's angry it's painful for him, and sometimes he even vomits."

"You don't need to!" Morio said, evidently meaning she didn't need to explain things that far, but it was clear he was wasn't upset.

"That asinine reporter mentioned Bach and Mozart," Ikuo said. "Would you let me listen to that tape again? I want to check to see what part of the piece he means by that."

Morio stood up, took the tape recorder out of a paper bag beside him, placed it on the table, and switched it on. As the music filtered out, Ikuo listened intently. He was silent, but, sensing his request, Morio rewound the tape and played it again.

Ogi was surprised at what happened next. Ikuo pulled a chair out from under the piano that was by the window, sat down, unlocked the keyboard, and played a phrase from the music. His playing was confident, not the hesitant touch of someone feeling his way through a piece. After a pause he began to play a short melody that, to Ogi's ears, sounded similar but different. After this, adding chords as he went, he painstakingly repeated Morio's composition.

"It's not Bach, and certainly not Mozart either," Ikuo said to Morio, after carefully closing the piano lid. "It's entirely your own music." His quiet voice contrasted with the tone of the piano he'd just played.

"I think so too," Morio said in a low voice, sounding as if he meant to encourage Ikuo more than himself.

Ikuo locked the piano—he'd borrowed the key for this very reason from the building superintendent—and turned his fierce-looking face, all angles and depressions, to gaze out the window. With smooth motions, Ms. Asuka filmed the scene with her video camera, first shooting Ms. Tachibana and Morio, then Ikuo's profile and the large trunk of the wych elm and the expanse of lawn. Before her camera turned in his direction, Ogi hurriedly wiped away a tear.

It was getting late, so the three young people—Ogi, Ikuo, and Dancer—returned to the office in Seijo, where Dancer put Patron, who was tired and didn't feel like eating anything, to bed, and then they set off for a Chinese restaurant in a narrow street along the Odakyu Line.

Inside the restaurant was a staircase on the left leading to the second floor and a kitchen that jutted out to just below the staircase going off into the back of the restaurant; on the other side of the counter, on the right-hand side, were four tables along the wall. There were no other customers, and the three of them chose the table farthest from the entrance. Ogi and Dancer sat on one side of the table, Ikuo on the other, his bulk overwhelming them.

Dancer had asked the reporters at the memorial service to fax her copies of their reviews for the next morning's papers. Inside a paper bag she carried faxes from those who'd conscientiously kept their promise. As she examined them, they ordered beer to celebrate the successful conclusion of the service. Ogi began to talk about the piano with Ikuo. Ogi was surprised to know that Ikuo played, since there was an Ibaha piano in the annex where Guide had lived but Ikuo had never once shown any interest in it.

Ikuo talked about his musical background, starting with how he took piano lessons from his mother, a graduate of Tokyo Arts Institute who'd been a music teacher in high school. His mother hadn't encouraged him to take music further, though. Ever since he was small he'd shown an aptitude for science, always making models and conducting experiments of one kind or another. One other reason was the scary look he had had ever since he was a child, a face that was bound to unsettle any panel of judges if he were to take the stage as a pianist.

"Ikuo, I think one can say you're certainly a pianist in your fingers, they have such strength and beauty," Dancer said; she'd just finished looking over the faxes and had caught only the tail end of the conversation.

She passed around three articles about the memorial service that were to appear in the morning papers. Two of them were just short pieces discussing the obvious, how this church gained notoriety ten years ago when its leaders renounced its teachings and how at a memorial service to one of the leaders who had suddenly passed away the surviving leader had declared that he was starting his religious movement again.

On the other hand, the dark-skinned reporter's article appeared in the second section of the general news pages as a five-column sidebar. The headline read AFTER AUM SHINRIKYO, WHY HAS PATRON RETURNED? First there was an explanation of the Somersault by the two men, named Savior and Prophet at the time, and how this nipped in the bud the terrorist plans of the church's radical faction. However, ten years later, while the two men, now known as Patron and Guide, were formulating their program for restarting their movement, the former radicals had kidnapped Guide, held him against his will, and roughed him up to the point of death.

Yesterday, the article went on, a memorial service was held for Guide at which two noteworthy events took place: Patron announced that he was restarting his religious movement, and two groups of followers who had continued in the faith even after being abandoned by their leaders had both expressed their desire to participate. Among these was part of the former radical faction. Patron's explanation for starting a new religion in the climate of intense criticism after the Aum Shinrikyo affair was quoted:

> When there is a great desire on the part of young people for spiritual salvation, nothing will be solved by crisis-management measures taken to crush new religious groups just because one group that absorbed these young people committed a blunder. Our attitude is to be open to any and all young people searching for salvation. With none of the established religions, including Buddhism and Christianity, offering this, I believe there is a place for us to care for these young people.

"At any rate," Ogi said, "I think he's done a good job by focusing on the question of why now, after Aum, Patron is starting again."

"I talked afterward with the reporter who wrote this article," Dancer said.

"But there's not a single line about what Patron said about the antichrist," Ikuo said.

"I made very sure he *didn't* add that," Dancer retorted. "As I spoke with the reporter on my cell phone, Patron was right beside me and he didn't admonish me at all."

"But that was the most interesting part of the whole sermon," Ikuo insisted.

"We have to make sure Patron doesn't have the rug pulled out from under him by the media, don't we? I want to avoid having them use a word like *antichrist*."

This said, Dancer drained her glass of beer and poured herself another. Their order of *gyoza* rice came just at that moment and she tucked into it with relish. Before the three of them were half finished, she got up and went over to the counter to order a late-night snack to take home for Patron. But when she returned to their table her spirits were dampened.

"The cook asked me if only one order of noodles and vegetables was enough. Because we always got two orders, one for Patron and one for Guide. Even though it was in all the papers, he still didn't realize that Guide was murdered. And it was for people like him that Guide died!"

Dancer didn't even try to keep her voice down.

5

It was late at night by the time they got back to the office. Dancer checked to see that Patron was still up, and while she was reheating the food she'd brought back—taking care of his stomach before giving him his sleeping pills—Ogi printed out the e-mails they'd received. Ikuo read through them too. Ms. Tachibana wanted Ikuo, more than anyone else, to read the e-mail from her. It said:

I think my brother was hurt by what happened at the press conference. We get these comments a lot, where people casually say that something he composed is like somebody else's—they're meant as praise for people with mental handicaps, but he finds them hard to comprehend. For him music just wells up naturally in him, like a birdcall, the sound of the wind, or a heartbeat.

These days he doesn't like letting other people listen to his music. The reason I urged him to play his tape, which he had a pianist record, was because of how important that piece is to both of us.

Ever since we went to that small gathering with Patron so long ago when he spoke with such caring words about my brother, Patron's been one of the main topics of conversation between us. My brother's vocabulary is poor, but his grammar is correct and if you listen carefully you realize what he's saying makes a lot of sense.

Once, actually more like a memory coming back to me, I suddenly told Morio about one of his compositions, "Morio, it's like we're going into heaven, with Patron leading us by the hand." And my brother said, very emphatically, "That's right!" This was the piece that, even though Patron couldn't join us, Morio was so excited about letting you all hear—only to be rewarded with those snide comments by the reporter.

Ikuo, when you asked, on my brother's behalf, which pieces of Bach or Mozart the reporter meant exactly, you can't imagine how tense my brother was! My own heart was beating a mile a minute. And that cowardly reporter couldn't say a thing.

Because of what you did, though, for the first time in our lives our honor has been redeemed. What's more, Morio really enjoyed the style in which you play. He can't put it into words, but he likes a powerful performance that doesn't have room for anything vague. More than anything else he dislikes playing that pussyfoots around. After we got home my brother was gazing for the longest time at his handwritten manuscript of that piece.

Speaking for both of us, we couldn't be happier that you're working to help Patron. Hallelujah, hallelujah!

Along with the e-mail came a fax of five handwritten compositions by Morio, each of them a page or two in length. Written in light pencil, the notes looking like a series of bean sprouts that were hard to decipher in places, and written over here and there in pen, the whole thing apparently had been checked by Ms. Tachibana. *My brother really enjoyed your playing, so he's sending over some other of his compositions,* she noted.

Ikuo carefully studied the sheets of music. "All three times I couldn't catch it and just played that section in my own way, as anyone who's studied music might. For Morio, of course, I wasn't getting it. He was kind enough to overlook that, but that's why he sent me the sheet music. All the pieces take off from that one piece, and if you study them together you can see there is a clear, connecting structure to them. Ms. Tachibana may think the music just seems to well up in him naturally, but in each successive piece the theme is developed in a carefully structured way."

Dancer had returned to the office and read the e-mail Ikuo had received, but just stood there without a word, her mouth slightly open, gazing off into space. What concerned her most among the messages was an e-mail from the person who had run the church after Patron and Guide stopped. He was an executive at one of the largest construction firms in the Kansai region, and though the headquarters didn't send a group delegation to the memorial service he wrote that he was quite moved by what he heard by phone from members who had attended individually.

His e-mail soon moved on to more practical matters, saying that, though he didn't know the direction Patron's newly founded movement would take, he assumed it would be based on a communal lifestyle. Perhaps, he suggested, the church could make use of some buildings in the woods of Shikoku that the Kansai headquarters owned. He added that he would be in Tokyo soon on business and could discuss it with Patron or, if that was out of the question, with members of his staff. All the Kansai people—who helped obtain the buildings, participated in refurbishing them, and were even now taking care of them—were hoping that Patron and Guide would rise again and make use of the facilities. *We pray that our dream will become a reality,* he wrote. *Once more, let me express my deepest condolences on the passing of Guide.*

Their schedule for this very long day was now over, and Dancer, whose bed was in the small room diagonally across the hall from Patron's—Ogi slept beside the entrance, Ikuo on the second floor of the annex—suggested that, since the studio was soundproof, Ikuo might like to try playing Ms. Tachibana's brother's compositions on Guide's piano. Up till now Dancer had only shown an interest in the next morning's newspaper articles and the e-mail from the church headquarters, and Ogi was surprised by her suggestion. Ikuo, too, seemed unsure if she was serious or not.

But Dancer, straightening up the documents on the desk, along with the PC and other devices on it, turned to Ikuo, who hadn't said anything and was about to leave, and repeated her offer, then went on to say, "When I met you when you were a child, I already felt there was something special about you. That model you made and were so gingerly carrying when it got caught in me—you didn't know what to do. Those eyes that glared back at me weren't the eyes of an ordinary child. A long time later the word came to me to describe what they looked like, and I thought: This was a person who expresses *dreadful* things. Even so, meeting you fifteen years later, I'm disappointed to find you aren't trying to express anything now. That's why, now that I've learned you play the piano, I want to hear you."

After she said this, Ikuo didn't hesitate. He took out Morio's music, which he'd put on a bookshelf, and stood up, grasping it in his huge hand. He strode off outside along the path that, despite the streetlight in the stand of trees, was dark, with Dancer walking in his footsteps as if leaping from one stepping-stone to the next. Following at some distance, Ogi felt as if he were viewing a ballet: a sprite dancing in the shadow of some giant beast.

Ikuo's playing threw cold water on Ogi's excitement. After running through the five short pieces, with brief intervals between them, he remained very still in front of the piano, while Dancer stood motionless in the center of the dance floor. Ogi felt the two of them had just shared something very special—something from which he was excluded.

15: Years of Exhaustion

1

A few days after the memorial service, Kizu awoke in the morning to the sound of a feeble sigh—his own voice, he realized—and knew it wasn't the first time this had happened. Snuggled in his blanket, he felt a balance deep within him collapse, giving rise to this voice that circumvented his consciousness. This time it had come out as a protracted *ahhhh,* and he knew he was shouldering an exhaustion that had hardened and would never dissipate. That sigh, then, echoed with a sense of his own body trying to comfort itself.

After a while he got out of bed to use the bathroom. Before he sat down on the toilet, Kizu looked out the window at the wych elm; strangely enough, it had regained the vivid softness it had had a week or two before, possibly as a result of the drizzle that had fallen all through the night. As he stood up, the large American-style toilet bowl looked—to use the first words that came to him—as if it were dyed a *shining vermilion* that dissolved the large pile of tarlike feces. Had all the energy he'd accumulated in his anus and intestines by exposing them to sunlight last summer now made his feces shine? No. It's come at last, Kizu thought. A thin sad smile came to his face. He avoided looking at himself in the mirror and flushed away the contents of the bowl.

As he walked back to his bed, Kizu looked out at the wych elm again; though the rain continued, beyond the branches he could spy a patch of light blue sky. But this blue sky, over the soft leaves washed by the rain, didn't have the usual effect on him. His cancer was back. He had long since come to terms with the fact that it was only a matter of time. And knowing this he'd come to Japan to start a new life. But up till now he'd tried to avoid facing any tangible signals his body might be sending him. Or at least, he realized, he'd postponed acknowledging them.

But now he could no longer ignore the cancer. For quite some time he'd felt something wrong inside him; was it now going to accelerate? Would he soon be racked with unspeakable pain? What held Kizu's attention was less the thought of pain—though of course this too was one way to avoid thinking about it—but thoughts of how much, as long as he was able to be up and about, he wanted to continue his physical relationship with Ikuo—at the same time, of course, not doing anything to dampen Ikuo's enthusiasm for working for Patron. He wanted to be close to the track Ikuo was running along, while still accomplishing his own goals. What was necessary now was getting a sense of how many days he had left to live his new life with Ikuo and Patron, as well as the best ways to cope with the pain once it began.

The director of Kizu's research institute had written him a letter of introduction to a local doctor, so Kizu telephoned the clinic and made an appointment. What he was really hoping for, though, was less a physical checkup than for the doctor to grasp the principle he'd committed himself to—the decision to live in a symbiotic relationship with his disease. Knowing the director of the institute would be a definite advantage here.

When he went in for his appointment, Kizu spoke to the doctor about his own past illnesses and then about his brother's cancer, all the details from the first occurrence to his death. He also told the doctor how, from the time his own cancer was first detected, he felt swept along by an unstoppable course of treatment, something he now wanted at all costs to avoid. Could you possibly, he asked, just ascertain that it's cancer by using traditional methods and then help me live with it at home?

Kizu was full of apprehension as he related his somewhat self-centered desires, but to his surprise the doctor agreed. Or at least he consented to examine him as his patient wanted.

Once the doctor had listened to his hopes, Kizu grew mellow and said, as he got dressed, "I think my dark mood of the last few years may have been a psychological expression of my cancer. It may sound like I'm exaggerating, but for the past six months I've felt so utterly positive it's as if I'm a young man all over again. I want to hold on to that feeling for the time I have left. For a year, if that's possible. Just to live a normal life for a year—without any operations, taking medicine when the pain gets to be too much, and, if I can, continuing to paint. Even if I can't do that, I want to live on my own and watch the activities of my young friend. Do you think I have a year left?"

The doctor was evasive, saying that it was possible, as far as today's checkup showed. But he wasn't at all indifferent to Kizu's hopes.

"You are an American citizen, so after the pain starts I can be more free in prescribing medicine for you than I would be with a Japanese," the doctor said. "I'll be getting in touch with the surgeon who first operated on you in New Jersey. That's where I met your friend the professor who introduced you to me." After saying this, the doctor, who was much younger than Kizu, began addressing him as Professor too. "You may not have a lot of time left, Professor, but you should be able to enjoy it to the fullest. Keep your spirits up! I feel like *you've* taught *me* that."

Kizu wondered about the childish enthusiasm of this statement. If my cancer can be fought through an operation or radiation therapy or medicine, he thought, even if it just means letting the doctor get his way, shouldn't he have challenged me to put up a good fight against my disease? Isn't he giving in too easily to my requests, implying—after just a simple examination—that my case is hopeless and the cancer will never go into remission?

"When you palpated my rectum your finger didn't seem to reach to the place where the cancer is," Kizu said, in a mischievous, sour-grapes sort of way. "Does this mean that when I have anal sex the penis won't hit the part that hurts?"

"Well, you can see how long my finger is," the doctor said, his earlier openness to Kizu now vanished.

In the taxi on the way home, though, Kizu couldn't forget what he'd said to tease the doctor. Well, he told himself, at least the hospital didn't grab me in its claws! But then he felt peeved: Was it really all right to announce so casually that he had terminal cancer? Not that he wanted to pin his hopes on some doctor newly returned from America and his latest high-tech machinery who might tell him that no, he didn't have cancer. Before long his own words came back to haunt him. There was no reason for him to suppress them.

Soon after he started teaching at the university in New Jersey, he had had an affair with a Jewish woman whom he later married. Her name was Naomi, and she'd lived with her former husband in Kobe; when he met her she had moved to New York and was writing her dissertation on the history of comparative art, and Kizu helped her decipher some of the brush writing in an illustrated Muromachi-period book. To celebrate finishing that work they had dinner together, with some wine, and when he was waiting at the bus stop under an enormous hickory tree to see her off on her bus back to New York, they kissed. Kizu took the first step, but she responded enthusiastically. Naomi was a large woman, taller than Kizu, and she held his head to steady it as they kissed intimately—not the other way around.

Kizu was still young and his penis soon rose up and pressed against her belly. As they waited for the bus on the boulevard in front of the university Naomi told him, after giving it a lot of thought, that she wouldn't mind going back to his apartment again.

He put clean sheets on the bed—not the right size ones, it turned out— and she began to, painfully, kiss his penis; he twisted to one side and began licking her strongly fragrant genitals; then, as he tried kissing her slightly reddish, cute little anus, Naomi called out in a small voice. After intercourse she told him about how her alcoholic ex-husband, when he did want sex, which wasn't too often, usually wanted anal sex. Taking this as a cue, Kizu tried it himself for the first time. She pulled apart her generous reddish buttocks to help him, and Kizu, although his penis wasn't quite hard enough, was able to penetrate her. Afterward she told him, happily, that it was all so *intense* she wasn't even sure if she came or not. After they got married, though, their sex turned more solemn, and never again did they stray like this into forbidden fields.

In the taxi, Kizu remembered the way Naomi's fingers moved and became possessed by the idea of doing the same thing for Ikuo. He fantasized about being penetrated by Ikuo's penis in a similarly *intense* way, positive that if the two of them weren't able to reach that level of feeling, until the day death came to take him he never would.

If such thoughts were motivated by the fact that he had a clear case of cancer, couldn't this be seen as a positive response to his illness? But Kizu couldn't help feeling he was being silly about the whole thing and laughed at himself for acting like some doddering old geezer. Still, he couldn't shake the notion from his mind.

2

Ikuo was kept busy after the memorial service, and it was a week before he was able to return to Kizu's apartment. He came with Dancer to express their thanks to the building superintendent for allowing them to use the facilities, and the two of them went together with Kizu to the man's office. The super was in a good mood, since the meeting place had been left so spic-and-span he didn't have to pay an extra fee to their regular janitorial company to clean up.

Dancer left, so Kizu and Ikuo were able to lounge on the sofa in Kizu's atelier and talk. Perhaps concerned because they hadn't seen each other in a week, Ikuo tried to humor Kizu.

"Patron told me what you said to him: that you don't know what direction his movement will take but as long I stay with it you'll stick with him."

"That's right," Kizu responded. "I really am interested in his new movement. You've helped me enter a new world I never would have found alone."

"That seems especially true since you came back from America."

"After all the trouble I'd taken to make a life over there, it wasn't easy giving up my home. I'd gotten far, I thought, but it didn't feel as if my life had taken a completely unexpected path. After coming back to Japan I felt really excited; for the first time in my life I didn't know what to anticipate. At my age, though, such positive emotions are always counterbalanced by a sense of unease. At any rate, I'm not going to back down."

"I can sense that."

"Those feelings, though, don't guarantee I'll do a good job of succeeding in Guide's position. He was one of a kind."

"It's like there are two people inside Patron," Ikuo said, "one who has visions, the other who interprets them. Guide's role was to make that second person inside Patron speak. As I was listening to Patron at the memorial service, it came to me how much he had suffered after Guide's death. And I wondered whether, as he suffered, the person inside him who interprets the visions may have taken on a different *form*. Taking that a step further, I began to wonder whether Patron might not be able to put his visions into ordinary language now, without any outside help. If he can, maybe Guide's death was necessary for Patron to begin his new movement."

Kizu felt something was wrong with this and brought up a point he'd noticed a while back. "It's logical, what you said. Not that I mean you've been illogical up till now, it's just that the logic you're using here is different. I'm wondering whether some of the radical faction's way of thinking has rubbed off on you as you worked with them."

Ikuo gazed back with a watchful, penetrating gaze, as if staking out some prey he was about to pounce on.

"I've learned a lot by talking with them," he said. "Working with them at the memorial service taught me how capable they are and how strongly they feel their convictions. Patron's movement has been able to take shape through proposals that the Kansai headquarters has made, and there's been discussion about including them in the new movement in order to firm up the support base—along with the group of women we visited. It would be hard to make a go of this new church relying solely on the participation of individuals. This will mean, though, that the list Ogi compiled of contributors after the Somersault won't be of much use—"

Ikuo stopped speaking, no doubt thinking that he'd gotten too far ahead of himself, and stood up.

"I've been too busy to take a shower these days, so if you don't mind—"

Ikuo's smile seem to be humoring Kizu, as he'd done before. But something welled up within Kizu, a thrill just like the day when, as a child, he'd first walked along the seashore and spotted a manateelike lump on the beach. The same rush of excitement he felt the first time he and Ikuo had sex. His throat felt parched.

Kizu took out the sheets he'd gotten back from the laundry and made up the bed. He went in to take a shower himself, passing Ikuo, who was wearing a dressing gown as he came out of the bathroom. But how should he bring it up to Ikuo? He racked his brain as he thoughtlessly scrubbed himself too hard and felt his body tighten with pain. Since the clear signs of cancer had appeared, Kizu had been careful about touching his belly, but now he'd forgotten.

Broaching the subject turned out to be easier than he had thought. "Let's try something a little different this time," Kizu said in an experienced tone, half playfully, and Ikuo, as casually as a chess player making a necessary strategic move, said that he'd already had a bit of experience playing the man, if that's what Kizu wanted.

With an eager movement out of keeping with his age, Kizu flipped himself over on his belly and, as Naomi had done, propped himself up on his chin and shoulders as he added some spit and pulled aside the folds of his buttocks. Ikuo struggled to penetrate, and Kizu felt a sharp pain that nearly made him cry out, but all for naught. Kizu remembered how it felt when, as he stroked the milky, flushed skin of Naomi's buttocks, he playfully had inserted first one finger and then a second as he roughly spread her sphincter. But he couldn't tell Ikuo to do the same, and he didn't have the nerve to do it himself.

Finally, as if the energy level he'd strained to keep up proved too much, Ikuo collapsed. Kizu sat up and noticed tears forming in Ikuo's large, sunken eyes. Kizu took Ikuo's still-engorged penis in his mouth to console it for all its struggles, but Ikuo remained passive and couldn't come.

After Ikuo went home, Kizu thought about the tears in Ikuo's eyes and how he'd instinctively turned away to try to hide them. What kind of tears were those? As he and Ikuo had talked that day he tried not to worry about the new situation with his cancer. With Patron's new movement beginning, he'd have to talk with Ikuo about his illness, now that it had taken a sudden turn for the worse, but it didn't seem fair to bring it up just as he was attempting to get their sexual relationship to enter a new phase.

Kizu wondered whether the sexual behavior of an old man, unconcerned with appearances, might not, in the eyes of someone much younger, go beyond the ugly and comical to arouse feelings of pity and sorrow. But late that night, as he once again climbed into bed and touched a wide, wet spot on the sheets, the thought struck him that he had been so hard on the young man he had made him cry. Shocked, Kizu tried to brush the thought aside.

3

Kizu was the type, once he started something, to persist—his character molded by his experiences in America, where he often felt terribly isolated and found that once he gave up, things got even worse—and he wasn't about to get discouraged by a couple of failed experiments. A motivating factor behind his persistence, Kizu was well aware, was the jealousy aroused in him when Ikuo revealed that he'd played the man before. As one failure followed another, this jealousy for some unknown past rival turned into a burning rage.

As a far-off memory, Kizu recalled reading Plato's words to the effect that human beings cannot hold two different emotions within them at the same time. This idea served to protect the emotions that—at the conscious level—he'd already prevented from making a comeback: the fear that his strong jealousy of Ikuo would accelerate the spread of the cancer within him, and his regret at having run from the advice he'd received in America to have himself get a thorough examination.

Dancer phoned him, asking him, if it was possible, to come over to discuss something with Patron. Recently Kizu had caught a ride two or three times with Ikuo when he went back to the office, but each time he found everyone rushing around like mad and had left without speaking with Patron.

Today, though, as he entered Patron's bedroom study, he spied a plan of the buildings in Shikoku that Dancer had prepared. As was his wont, though they hadn't seen each other since the memorial service, Patron didn't greet Kizu; instead, he seemed to be watching him closely. Finally Patron spoke up, explaining how he wanted to move his office to the building in the woods shown in the plan and start his church there. Kizu mentioned he'd heard from the newspaper reporter that the buildings were unusual modern structures and were being taken care of very thoroughly—but Patron cut him short.

"After they purchased these buildings, the followers apparently took turns staying in them for short periods of time," Patron said, "and things went smoothly between the people from the Kansai headquarters and the local people. Which isn't to say that if we move there to build our church there won't be friction. We need to understand this before we begin, and I think as Ikuo said the first step is to have an organized vanguard group of followers move to Shikoku. I'd planned to start the new movement with people who contacted me after the Somersault, but what Ogi's done will eventually be of use."

Patron went on to explain what Kizu was aware of how the Kansai headquarters had directed his attention to this woods surrounded by mountains and how things had developed since then.

"The Kansai headquarters, which essentially means the whole church that's been active till now, has proposed to give these buildings over to me in order for me to build a new church. While Guide and I were in hell and completely unproductive, the Kansai headquarters built up quite a sound financial base. Sometimes I even wonder whether it's right to accept all they've accomplished."

"If the church will again be centered around you and these people will be absorbed into it," Kizu said, "their proposal makes perfect sense. You might even say that after your Somersault the Kansai headquarters anticipated a day like this and prepared accordingly."

"I imagine that to them my actions in the Somersault must have seemed pretty shallow."

"But when you look at all the groups that have been able to maintain themselves independently," Kizu said, "the Kansai headquarters, the women's commune, and the former Izu radical faction, that must mean your teachings had an underlying and enduring strength."

"But Guide and I completely denied those teachings. And I'm not about to reverse my position."

"When I listen to you I get the impression you want to reach out first of all to the followers you abandoned. What with all those fights the local government had to get Aum Shinrikyo to evacuate their *satyan,* I imagine our job from now on won't be easy."

"Indeed it won't," Patron said, a glint in his eye. "Can I ask you, too, Professor, to move to our new headquarters in Shikoku?"

"Ikuo is very enthusiastic about your plan for the church and, as I've told you, I go where he goes."

Still looking Kizu straight in the eye, Patron said, "Of course, I'll also be counting on you to be the new Guide. Anyway, the reason I asked you to come over today is that Dancer feels anxious. She thinks you've changed somehow. Now that I see you myself I see something's troubling you. I haven't asked Ikuo about this, but I feel there's something going on with you physically that isn't encouraging."

Kizu was surprised, but at the same time he found this completely natural. "At the beginning of this month I started to show some clear symptoms," he began. "And I had a specialist confirm what I thought. It's not at a stage where an operation would help much, and actually I left America because I didn't feel like having one. It's terminal cancer. My doctor was very sympathetic to my viewpoint and said he'll help me control the pain so I can remain active on my own.

"As time goes on it'll be harder and harder for me to be the Guide, but as long as I'm not a burden, I want nothing more than to help Ikuo. At my checkup I wasn't given a definite amount of time I have left, but I'm counting on a year."

Patron leaned forward toward Kizu, his head tilted to one side. Kizu saw his intent eyes fill with a sorrow deeper than any he'd ever seen in a living person, let alone in any painting. In the very depths of this, like another eye, Patron gazed with great curiosity at this being named Kizu before him.

"Since you were told you have a year to live by someone with experience in these matters, I imagine that's the way it'll turn out. You may be going through a physical crisis, but spiritually you're strong. While I'm still able to count on your help, I want to make very clear again the significance behind my starting this church. If the historian doesn't have much time left, the ones creating history can't afford to dawdle. . . . I expect that within this year, sooner rather than later, you will see a *sign* I give, or a sign I *become,* and then you'll be able to write your history. I'll say it once again—*that* will be your task as the new Guide."

Patron lowered his eyelashes—thick lashes for a man his age. Eyes closed, he remained silent, as if he'd forgotten Kizu was there. Noiselessly Kizu stood up, left the room, and reported to Dancer what had just taken place. With a look that said she realized something very important had transpired in their discussion, she disappeared down the darkened corridor.

In the minivan on their way back to Kizu's apartment, Kizu told Ikuo about Patron's comments about looking for a sign—and *becoming* a sign—within a year. And related to this he told him all about his cancer. As always, Ikuo kept his eyes on the road as he drove. Kizu looked straight ahead too, even after he finished, but he could sense that Ikuo was deeply moved by what he'd heard. After a long stretch of silence, Ikuo finally spoke.

"When I was at a turning point in my life, you gave me a clue as to where to go, even though it meant a personal sacrifice on your part. We still haven't known each other that long, but you've done this for me any number of times.

When Patron heard you had cancer and only a year left, he must have come to a decision. I don't know what he means about giving a *sign,* but I do know you should take it seriously."

When they arrived at the apartment, as if by unspoken agreement they put off making dinner and went directly to bed. Ikuo diligently kneaded and massaged Kizu's buttocks and gave them some light slaps. Other than a few words to make sure that he wasn't putting too much weight on Kizu's abdomen—that it wasn't painful—Ikuo was silent. Soon, as if making a comfortable breakthrough in Kizu's body, Ikuo's penis penetrated him at a single stroke, and he stopped moving. Taking his time, Ikuo caressed Kizu's testicles and penis, as well as the area around his own penis that was so snugly buried. With Ikuo's penis deep within him, Kizu came. It was exactly the kind of internal *intense* feeling that Naomi had spoken of.

Soon, making sure that his penis wasn't pushed out, Ikuo, gingerly pushing his weight forward and asking Kizu again if it hurt him, slowly penetrated deeper into Kizu's now relaxed body. After a short spell of smooth in-and-out, with a youthful sigh Ikuo came. Kizu felt a damp heat spread through him, and experienced again the same sensation, but on a gentler scale. Ikuo's now half-limp penis slowly, then at the end more quickly, exited his body, and Kizu knew exactly what Naomi meant when, after that first sexual encounter, she'd pronounced it *lovely.*

Kizu experienced a deep sense of fulfillment now that their sexual love had been consummated. Lying face down, he was unable to see Ikuo as, back turned to him, he carefully wiped himself and Kizu down with a towel—his only regret in an otherwise satisfying encounter.

4

With their sexual relationship now cemented, the circle complete, Kizu no longer felt as compelled as he had before to have sexual relations with Ikuo. And the same was nearly true of Ikuo. They were sexually calm, like an experienced middle-aged couple.

Kizu had finished the technical preparations for the oil tableau he'd begun in Tokyo, and though he hadn't yet settled on a major theme, he worked in tandem on several works that were vaguely leading him in that direction, all of which kept him occupied. Ikuo spent most of his time on preparations for the move to Shikoku, and even when he could return to the apartment to model for Kizu, more often than not he had to rush off without any sexual interludes. Free of any sexual frustration or psychological turmoil, though,

Kizu saw his young lover off and found himself rather enjoying the free time and quiet to continue his painting. Along with the years of exhaustion he'd felt ever since his cancer had resurfaced, a lingering sense of weariness after such *intense* sexual intercourse also had something to do with this.

For their part, after creating a model of the new church in Shikoku, Patron and Dancer were hoping that Kizu would come to the office. Ogi and Ikuo were both busy with their respective groups—the communal women's group that lived along the Odakyu Line for Ogi, the remnants of the Izu research group for Ikuo—trying to get some concrete plans nailed down for the groups to move to Shikoku, and Patron, Dancer, and Ikuo spent much time in the office discussing these matters.

Two weeks after revealing his disease to Patron, Kizu caught a ride to the office after Ikuo had spent the night. Ikuo had an appointment to finalize some plans with Dr. Koga, so Kizu got out in Shibuya and hailed a cab from there. Hearing this, Dancer said, "Ikuo's pretty cold, isn't he," knowing all the while that Ikuo needed to concentrate on his work and that preparations with the former radical faction were on track.

Dancer had heard from Patron about Kizu's illness and already had made known to Patron her concerns about his health, yet now that she was face-to-face with him she didn't express her sympathy. Trusting in Patron's healing power, though, she made sure that when he was in the office Kizu sat nearest to Patron. When they went into Patron's room to talk, they established a pattern of lining Kizu's chair up beside Patron's armchair, with Dancer facing them as she took notes. Sitting like this, Kizu felt a definite heat radiating from Patron that spread from his side, to his waist, and then even deeper.

Dancer rearranged the entire office as they prepared for the move to Shikoku. Previously there'd been a low bookshelf for LPs and documents in front of the large glass door leading out to the garden, but this had been moved to the annex and the space it once occupied was wide open. The rainy season had yet to begin, and one sunny luxuriant day followed another, the long-untended garden a cheerful scene now, bursting with young leaves and shoots of grass growing where the doghouse of the poisoned Saint Bernard had once been.

Along with the new arrangement of the chairs, there was now a couch set out behind them, next to the bathroom. It was newly purchased, something they planned to take with them to Shikoku, and on the day Kizu took the cab to the office and was escorted into Patron's room, he found Morio Tachibana lying on the couch, reading a small yellow book of musical scores. When Patron, calling Ms. Tachibana's brother by his first name, asked him to put on a CD, the brevity of the response made Kizu realize that this wasn't the first time Morio had spent time here.

Patron discussed his basic plans for moving the new church to Shikoku, an explanation that was connected with Morio's being here. "The model that we'll base our new church on will be the women's commune near Odawara and the safe house of the former Izu Research Institute group. First of all we'll have these two groups move to Shikoku—groups that Dancer now calls the Quiet Women and the Technicians. After that we'll gradually move the other individuals with whom Ogi's been in touch.

"It's also necessary to have a reliable core of office staff. Dancer is increasingly busy, so I've had Ms. Tachibana come to take care of my day-to-day needs. She's the only one who wasn't a follower from before the Somersault that we'll be taking into our inner circle. Morio can't live apart from Ms. Tachibana. I considered this in light of the fact that the men in the Shikoku church are all renunciates who've cut their ties with their families, and I reached the conclusion that I'll have Morio come with us to Shikoku to assist me in my work. Just looking at him so absorbed in music does my heart good. He's also good at finding the CDs I want to hear right away."

As soon as he heard his name, Morio—who had a keen ear—raised his head and looked in Patron's direction. Patron nodded gently to him, and he went back to reading the score.

"Having quit my teaching position in America, I need to move out of my apartment in Tokyo anyway," Kizu said. "As I've said several times, I'm planning to go with Ikuo to Shikoku. I'm hoping to be able to live with him there with a modicum of privacy. If possible, I'd like to use the money I saved in the States to purchase a house next to the church. I'll use the house for myself, but the house itself and any remaining money I'll donate to the church."

"I'm very grateful to you," Patron said. He gave instructions to Dancer. "Please contact the people taking care of the buildings there and see that it's done. I'm hoping nothing will interfere with your private life there, Professor. Please consult with Ogi and Ikuo about what sort of tasks you'll be doing."

"Ikuo says he wants to use Morio's music to accompany the sermons and other church ceremonies in Shikoku. Maybe we could propose this to Dancer and Ogi."

"That would be fine," Patron said emphatically. "This will be Morio's work in the church, apart from what he does to help me. I heard Ikuo play Morio's depiction of his sister and himself ascending to heaven holding my hand, and I'd like to begin using that piece in a variety of ways, just as Ikuo has proposed. The composer himself likes Ikuo's work, so we'll record Ikuo's playing of the piece."

"I like it," Morio said in clear, refined child's voice.

Dancer added, "Ikuo heard that the chapel has good acoustics, and he's planning to hold a recital of Morio's works. Ms. Tachibana's quite encouraged by this. So Morio won't just be accompanying Ms. Tachibana; each of them will have their own role to play in the church—and I expect that'll serve as a good example for the others."

Morio, a look of concentration on his face, nodded at Dancer's words.

5

As Patron had said, Ikuo had one concrete proposal regarding a job for Kizu as they prepared to move the church to Shikoku. While rushing here and there, laying the groundwork for the move, Ikuo discovered that the art supply firm that had sponsored the contest he'd entered when he was a child, the contest for which he'd made his complex plastic model, still had an office and store in the heart of Tokyo. With Kizu a specialist in art education, and this company having pioneered a market in Tokyo, Ikuo came up with a plan for having the company provide art supplies to Kizu, who would then open a model art school for children in Shikoku.

Legally, the buildings the church was to occupy belonged to the Kansai headquarters. The village where these buildings were located had merged with other communities to become a town, and the people from the Kansai headquarters in charge of the buildings met with officials from the town to discuss the transfer. With the outstanding way the Kansai church had maintained the buildings, plus the fact that the elderly woman supervising their upkeep was from an old established family in the area, the two sides soon reached an official agreement allowing Patron's church to use the buildings as its base of operations.

Memories of the troubles with Aum Shinrikyo around its *satyan* at the base of Mount Fuji were still fresh in people's minds, however. The local people also couldn't forget that the buildings had originally belonged to another religious organization, which had started there and then disbanded, causing a huge uproar. Even with the agreement, then, Patron's people had to prepare themselves, once they actually began moving in, for possible resistance from the townspeople. As one way of smoothing the path, Ikuo proposed holding concerts of Morio's music and having Kizu teach art classes.

Kizu found out the address of the art supply company and set off for the Ginza. The first and second floors of the building were a spacious gallery; the atmosphere of the place was unlike any stationery shop or art supply store you'd normally find in Japan, and to Kizu it felt like the kind of supermarket you'd find in a college town in the United States. He stood there for a while, nostalgically taking in the scene. He noticed some American women among the customers, residents of Tokyo. In one corner near the watercolor paper and painting supplies he saw a rheumatic-looking woman sitting on the floor, legs to one side, checking out various types of sketchbooks; for a moment Kizu was struck by the illusion that she was someone he knew in New Jersey.

Among the Japanese customers were everyone from stylish-looking private junior high students, with their mothers, to younger children, all leisurely enjoying the paintings on exhibition. Kizu found them totally different from the students he'd taught in Japan some thirty years before. They were so obviously affluent and, even if you brushed close to them, they showed no interest in others around them.

The American general manager was still quite young; he said he'd first come to Japan as a Mormon missionary. Not to imply, he went on, that he was solely a Japanophile; he was interested in developing markets in China, too, and was studying Mandarin. He was a pleasant, serious young man, and since Kizu was well-known in art education circles, he said that as long as the head office gave the okay he could supply, free of charge, the twenty watercolor sets Kizu wanted, each with over a hundred colors, as well as a hundred inexpensive sketchbooks for children. He promised to ship these to Kizu's new address in Shikoku.

When they'd reached this stage, Kizu felt a bit anxious. He'd already explained that he belonged to a new religious organization, soon to be established in the countryside, and was planning to hold art classes for the local children. But as he listened to Kizu, the manager seemed blasé.

"Believe me," Kizu said, "I'm not trying to use these painting sets and sketchbooks as inducements to convert new followers."

The manager wasn't perturbed.

"I take the subway to work that was gassed with sarin gas," he said, "and I'm pretty interested in these new Japanese religions. As long as the church you belong to isn't like some fundamentalist sect in the States where everyone commits mass suicide with their leader, I don't see how it could be negative publicity for my company. But even with things like this sarin gas attack, don't you think that in general Japanese aren't very religious? When I was doing Mormon missionary work I already had that impression. Our company aims its goods at the children of well-heeled urban families. But I want to branch out beyond that. That's why I like your idea of opening an art school for children in the countryside."

They exchanged a firm handshake, something Kizu experienced rarely in Japan, and said goodbye, and Kizu strolled off toward the Ginza subway station—also something he hadn't done in a while—pleasantly anticipating his new art school. The children he'd teach probably had never seen such paints, and when he went through the names of the colors with them this simple process would be a real education about the world around them. The countryside they'd be moving to was near the central mountain range in Shikoku, and as the children looked at the changing seasons in the forest, giving the name of a particular color to what they saw and then reproducing the scene on paper, their awareness of the forest that surrounded them would be transformed. They'd come to know and grasp the world in a way they'd never experienced before.

Kizu realized that his life as an art instructor, which had begun in a high school in the countryside near a forest, was now about to end in a similar way, opening an art class in a place surrounded by a deep forest, albeit a place he'd yet to lay eyes on. He was deeply moved that his life was coming full circle.

Together with a strangely calm sense of fulfillment, he found himself in high spirits as he accepted the fact that he was about to be thrust into a life that promised some startling twists and turns. As long as cancer didn't floor him, he knew he could make it.

Kizu's subway car passed one of the stations that had been attacked with sarin gas.

6

With the scheduled move to the buildings in the forests of Shikoku fast approaching, the one urgent personal matter that Kizu had to solve was the question of finding a replacement in Shikoku for the doctor who had taken on the responsibility of overseeing his own self-centered way of dealing with his cancer. This was Kizu's one concern about leaving Tokyo for good. Completely at a loss as to what he should do, he went again to the clinic in Akasaka.

Kizu hadn't mentioned it before, but now he told his doctor how he had no intention of returning to his university in the United States, and would be moving to the forests of Shikoku as a member of a church; the doctor seemed surprised to hear this but didn't ask any questions. He seemed to be weighing the connection between the new signs of cancer and Kizu's dramatic lifestyle changes. Done with that, he questioned Kizu in detail about practical matters such as the distance between this village in the woods and the nearest city hospital, the conditions of the nearest clinic, and so on. But Kizu hadn't gathered any such information. Hard put to reply, he told him there would be one doctor, a Dr. Koga, among the followers, who'd all be living a communal life. "I'm not sure if he's still practicing," Kizu added, "but he's fairly well known."

"Kanau Koga?" said his doctor. "He is indeed a well-known clinician. Of course he's still practicing medicine. If he's going to quit his practice and move, it'll be a blow to whatever hospital he's been working for. You're very lucky to have him with you."

Surprised, Kizu listened as the doctor ardently talked on, his face with his rimless glasses looking down as Kizu watched him.

"I once read in the papers that Dr. Koga was involved with a religious group," the doctor said; though not looking in Kizu's direction, his reactions were precise. "But wasn't that a long time ago? We don't belong to the same academic society, but he was just a year ahead of me in university and I've known him ever since. Even now I hear news about him, but nothing about any religious group."

The doctor's next words showed he'd given this some thought and was trying to express his interest.

"That must be a very interesting religious group to make Dr. Koga quit his post in a Tokyo hospital and go live in a commune in the woods. And here you are too, participating despite your cancer."

"My case is different from Dr. Koga's," Kizu said hurriedly. "At any rate, this will be the last job of my life. Besides, I'm sort of a lukewarm participant—I don't even know much about the doctrines of the church."

"I'm not about to ask anything personal about the church," the doctor said, and looked down again as before, "but being with Dr. Koga is a definite plus for you. I haven't received the medical records yet from the hospital in New Jersey—we'll take care of that later—but for now I'll collect all the records I do have and hand them over to Dr. Koga. I'll write a letter to him, too, outlining the plan we discussed for administering morphine."

The thought suddenly came to Kizu that if he were to choose an adviser for Ikuo after his death this doctor would make a fine choice, and he realized he'd never considered who he could trust to be Ikuo's counselor after he was gone, a sure sign that he was trying to avoid thinking about his approaching inevitable demise.

The doctor half turned away from Kizu, who was sitting on a stool, and began writing a letter at his plain desk. After gathering together the documents he'd mentioned—Kizu's health record he'd brought from America, plus copies of the charts of his last examination—the doctor was no doubt writing a letter to Dr. Koga. This straightforward way of taking care of business forced Kizu to reflect on his own vague attitude toward life despite the short time left to him.

The doctor put the letter inside a plain business envelope printed with the name of the clinic and passed this, along with a larger envelope of medical records, over to Kizu.

"You tend to downplay the value of things you do, but I'm very interested to see people like you and Dr. Koga working on a joint project. It's quite refreshing, since intellectuals of your caliber in Japan very rarely do joint work outside their own fields."

"I don't know Dr. Koga very well," Kizu said, "but I know that through the events of ten years ago, and even now, he's a fanatically confident follower. But as I said, I'm lukewarm about this idea. The only reason I'm moving to Shikoku is because the young man I like is going there. I can't believe it myself sometimes that I'm doing such a bizarre thing in my condition."

"No, I'm sure you gave it a lot of thought before you decided."

The doctor smiled for the first time that day—albeit a weak smile—and saw Kizu out. Afterward, as Kizu was waiting in line one floor below to pay his bill, the doctor passed right by him on his way to the staff bathroom, his face looking unexpectedly old and worried.

16: The Clinician

1

Ikuo delivered the letter and records to Dr. Koga's clinic right away. Kizu had wanted to go over to say hello personally, but Dr. Koga was busy tying up loose ends before their move to Shikoku. Ikuo relayed a message from the doctor that he couldn't spare the time right now and would see Kizu later; holding out hope because he'd said *later,* Ikuo took it upon himself to see that things proceeded in that direction.

Dr. Koga had been raised in an area behind the Tokyo University Hospital, where his father worked, and the only traveling he'd ever done before now was plane trips to academic conferences in the Kansai region, Kyushu, and points in between. The village they were heading to in Shikoku had a clinic but no regular doctor; since he would be taking charge of the facilities, Dr. Koga had already gone there once to consult about the clinic. Since that trip was by plane, from Haneda airport to Matsuyama, when it came time to move to Shikoku he said he hoped they could make the whole trip by train.

After many years in America, and knowing he wouldn't have another chance to travel by train across Japan, Kizu also thought it would be nice to see scenery different from that in which he'd been raised as he journeyed to the site of his final abode. Ikuo picked up on this idea and arranged for Dr. Koga and Kizu to travel by train, accompanied by himself and a former member of the Izu Research Institute. They were to leave Tokyo a little before 11 A.M. on the Nozomi bullet train. Something over three hours later, they would arrive in Okayama, where they'd change to the Shiokaze; from there they'd cross over to Shikoku on the Seto Bridge and take the Yosan Line, arriving in Matsuyama after 5 P.M. At the JR train station in Matsuyama they'd meet up with Patron, who was traveling by plane, and the church members coming by minivan, and then everyone would head by car to the forest.

When Ikuo reminded him that the train trip alone would take six hours, Kizu was surprised not by the length but by how short it was. Just to get from his college town in New Jersey up to Boston sometimes took just as long, if you had a bad connection. But Kizu was a bit on edge, worrying about all the time he'd be spending together with Dr. Koga, whom he barely knew. Aware of this, Ikuo bought two sets of Green Car luxury tickets for seats apart from each other. Kizu and Dr. Koga would each have window seats, with Ikuo sitting beside Kizu and the former Izu researcher beside Dr. Koga.

Most of their luggage was being sent by rented truck, so Kizu and Dr. Koga were able to travel light, with one bag each. For their part, their seat mates had taken on the task of transporting the vacuum tube amplifier that Patron had been using for years and the video equipment of Ms. Asuka, who would be joining them in Shikoku sometime later.

While Kizu searched for the right train car, Ikuo and a man in his mid-thirties were at the front of the platform loading two crates as large as the steamer trunks foreigners travel with. By the time Kizu boarded, the two crates were already stowed aboard. Ikuo introduced the older man as Mr. Hanawa. The latter merely bowed his head in greeting and sat down, leaving the window seat open for Dr. Koga, who had yet to appear, and began reading a book in a foreign language with all sorts of formulas in it.

Three minutes before the train was to pull out of the station, Dr. Koga appeared at the front entrance of the car and strode toward them with the same firm steps he'd shown at the memorial service. Four or five rows ahead of Kizu, Dr. Koga came to a halt where Mr. Hanawa was reading and, hunting cap still on his head, greeted him enthusiastically and swung his bag onto the overhead rack. He removed his duffel coat, which was made of the same deerskin pattern as his cap, and, now in a blue long-sleeve shirt, settled down in the window seat. As Kizu watched him from behind, he worried that, like any city dweller concerned about the weather in the kind of backwoods area they were headed, perhaps Dr. Koga had brought an overly heavy coat.

Kizu was impressed by the no-nonsense way Dr. Koga didn't try to locate his other traveling companions in the flurry just before the train was to leave. Just before he put his suitcase in the overhead rack, Dr. Koga had taken out a thick book that he was now engrossed in; Mr. Hanawa didn't speak to him, and neither did Ikuo stand up to walk over and say hello. Even so, it was clear that Ikuo and Mr. Hanawa were attentive to their duties as escorts. It had been a long time since Kizu had felt so at ease in the midst of people he didn't know and he settled back, giving himself up to the motion of the train.

Even after they left the cities surrounding Tokyo, the hills and valleys were filled with houses, and in the rare patches of greenery, bulldozers were busily scraping away the last vestiges of nature. In America one would never find such uniform scenery like this. Kizu was surprised to see, on the slope of one mountain, a row of twenty identical houses. The scenery was moving by at a faster clip than he remembered. He spied some tall buildings crowded together beside a river in a valley between two steep mountain slopes and suspected they were in a region of hot springs, though he wondered whether there really was a hot springs so near to Tokyo. Meanwhile, after passing through a short tunnel they went through the city of Atami. The Bullet train lived up to its name.

Mount Fuji suddenly appeared, like a raised dark-gray plane, and three lines of leftover snow on it flowed by as streaks of dull white. After this, mountains and forests appeared only sporadically between the towns. Kizu had always had a mental image of train travel in Japan as express trains running past rice fields and mountain forests, and all the towns made him feel a bit uncomfortable. He turned to Ikuo beside him and grumbled out a complaint.

"One of my colleagues at the institute traveled in Japan and told me the whole country's nothing but cities and suburbs. I told him to try taking a long-distance train. 'You'll see some pastoral scenery, real Japanese hills and fields; once you change to a local line it'll be even more like that,' I insisted. But look at this—it's all houses or roads or construction sites for new subdivisions. And we've been traveling for an hour at least."

"On Hokkaido, though," Ikuo said, "all you'll see from the train is mountains and fields. I'm sure that once we cross the Seto Bridge and start into Shikoku there'll be a lot more natural scenery."

"You mean until then it's all like this? I was looking forward to chatting with Dr. Koga while we enjoyed looking out at the mountains or the sea. Japan's certainly not what I expected."

"Now that you've given up on the scenery," Ikuo said, in a rare joking way, "maybe it's about time to start talking with Dr. Koga? It's a long trip, and I suppose he felt in no hurry to come over."

"Maybe he's holding back on my account. We're all going to be one big happy family from now on, so I suppose it's high time I changed and stopped being so standoffish."

The relaxed feelings the trip had engendered in Kizu brought on this remark, but Ikuo's response was blunt. "You got that right. I think you *will* have to change," he said. "I'll switch seats with Dr. Koga. The scenery won't be rural for quite some time."

2

Ikuo took Dr. Koga's seat, while the doctor strode over to where Kizu was sitting. Under thick eyebrows a smile much younger than his years sparkled in his deep-set eyes; he sat down and without any real greeting launched into the topic of Kizu's physical condition.

"The doctor you consulted in Tokyo was a year or so behind me in medical school. When things got out of hand during the student movement period he transferred to a university in California. He's a man who knows how to get ahead, I'll give him that. When you look at how efficiently he handles things like getting me to take over your case, you'll see I'm no match for him.

"The place where we'll be living is an hour and a half from the Red Cross Hospital in Matsuyama—provided the traffic's light. Some areas in the Tokyo area are even farther from a decent hospital, so I wouldn't worry if I were you. I will do whatever's necessary."

Kizu didn't expect to hear anything more at this point from the doctor who'd be caring for him. He nodded, relaxed by Dr. Koga's smile.

"We'll be together from now on so there's no need to rush, but I do have some questions I'd like to ask, if that's all right?" Dr. Koga looked ready to stand up and leave if Kizu hesitated.

"Yes, I'd like that," Kizu said. "The reason I haven't come over to talk with you is that I've been looking out the window, waiting impatiently for us to get someplace where there aren't any more buildings or roads. Now that I think about it, though, it's silly to imagine they'd build a bullet train through remote mountains and valleys."

Dr. Koga settled back down in his seat and gazed out the window. He seemed to speak only when he wanted to discuss the business at hand, which Kizu found refreshing.

"Did your doctor explain the symptoms of your disease to you clearly?" Dr. Koga asked. "Typically, that only happens when an immediate operation is indicated, at which point the patient gets pretty busy, with little time to consider the situation carefully. When you were given the prognosis, though, you didn't have an operation—you didn't have any proper treatment, either. Instead, you've done what most patients don't get a chance to do—think deeply about your condition. I'd like to ask you, not out of simple curiosity but as a physician: Has this prognosis brought about any psychological change?"

Kizu mentioned what came to mind first. "My sense of time has changed," he said. "Actually, I'd been feeling that change even before this latest diagnosis—which made me realize all over again how I'd been feeling that way for some time. This might not be the answer you're looking for, though."

"No, what I wanted to find out was exactly that, whether you'd felt this way before."

"There's one example I can give you," Kizu said. "At the beginning of last week, Okinawa was hit directly by a typhoon, and it affected the weather in Tokyo, making it unusually warm. That afternoon I was resting in bed. And I felt then that the passage of time perfectly suited me. It wasn't just a fleeting notion but something I'd been feeling the entire morning: a calm sense of satisfaction, I suppose. As if the world's clock and my internal spiritual clock—my soul, if you will—were completely in sync.

"I'm sure I'm not unique in this regard, but when I first became conscious of time as a child I already felt that the world moved too slowly. Say I was told to wait somewhere for an hour; it seemed so long I couldn't stand it. And when I thought of living ten, twenty years—one hour piled on top of another—it scared the wits out of me. Then I realized I'd already lived three years, or five years, or whatever it was, and with the inevitability of death I'd already used up a measurable portion of the finite amount of time allotted me, and that frightened me too.

"When I reached my thirties and forties and was teaching in the university, however, it made me choke up when I felt how fast time raced by, particularly the spring semester. I felt this in chunks of a day or a week, and I could see the free time between teaching that I wanted to use for my own painting eroding right before my eyes.

"Time was either at a standstill or racing by, and either way it didn't fit my own internal clock. Now, though, I've come to feel that Time with a capital T and my individual sense of time are a perfect fit."

Dr. Koga was staring out the window at a line of woods streaming by that was unblemished by buildings or roads, his gaze all the more intent for the knowledge that this scene would soon disappear. And when he spoke his voice was content, not just with what he saw but with what he'd heard. "It's a good feeling, a sense of balance, I suppose," he said.

"I'm just an ordinary person," Kizu went on, "so before long my inner clock will get out of tempo with the world again, going either too fast or too slow, which makes me all the more reluctant to give up this sense of time-in-sync I've been having lately. It's the sensation that I'm less an animal and more like a *plant*."

Soon the scene outside the train window revealed a cluster of factories, all built in the same rounded-off style, bunched together in a small oasis. Dr. Koga turned to Kizu.

"What you've experienced is a sense of time that transcends the human," he said. "I may be wrong about this, but it seems to me similar to the feeling I got in meeting Patron again and experiencing *his* sense of time. It's as though he's set his internal clock to run at the same time as the late Guide."

Kizu looked out at farmhouses racing by, one after another, each home surrounded by an expanse of rice fields, each with a stand of sturdy-looking oak trees. Kizu had never seen such richly hued young leaves as filled the branches of the oaks.

"I know what you mean about Patron being unique," Kizu said. "It always strikes me that all I can see of him now is the *Patron* part of him. It's like half—maybe just a quarter—of him is on this side, but the larger portion is on the *other side,* invisible. I think there's some overlap between this and what you said about Patron being with Guide, who's gone to the *other side.*"

"I was singled out for Guide's project at the Izu workshop," Dr. Koga said, "but I belonged to Patron's church well before that. When Guide was staying in Izu and was engrossed in things he seemed pitiful, somehow, as if he and Patron, who were always together, were like twins, and Guide had been yanked away from his other half.

"Not long ago some of my colleagues took Guide captive, and you know what happened next. I think they wanted to get back to the kind of intimate relationship they had with him back in Izu, apart from Patron. Having known the kind of relationship the two of them had in the church, that was probably a move in the wrong direction. Even though I wasn't actively involved, when Guide died—like one twin forcibly separated from the other—I realized what a horrible thing I'd been a part of. And when I met Patron again it felt to me like he was now living for the two of them, for himself *and* for Guide."

Though he'd been trying to keep his voice down, Dr. Koga's clear enunciation was enough for the people seated around them to hear. However, the man across from them in the aisle seat, dressed in a blue suit and narrow necktie, had on a pair of earphones and his nose stuck in a weekly magazine; next to him, in the window seat, was one of those middle-aged matrons Kizu could never see in Japan without feeling on edge, decked out in a Chanel suit and Hermès scarf, who—and Kizu found this strange as well—like most Japanese women as soon as they sat down in a train, was napping.

"They want me to work beside Patron to help fill in the gap left by Guide, but I'm not an extraordinary man like he was," Kizu said, not worried about those around him hearing. "It's not so much that Patron has agreed to this, but more like what you said, that Guide is alive within him even now. He's defined my role as historian for the new church. The best

I can do, I think, is to keep an illustrated journal of the events that take place."

Koga gazed at Kizu, his expression filled with a kind of childish curiosity that made one think how well brought up he was.

"An illustrated journal—what a wonderful idea! One with professional drawings, no less. You know, when my shock-troop colleagues were arrested and interrogated they couldn't answer the questions well, so they handed over an illustrated journal instead, minus any text. The police leaked this to the press and it appeared in newspapers and magazines. I was taken aback by how childish and grotesque their drawings were.

"This group were the best and the brightest in the fields of chemistry, physics, and engineering, but they were part of a very visual generation, raised on comic books, that can express things more easily in drawings than in words. Guide, myself, and the other older people there treated these youngsters as true intellectuals, but when I saw those drawings I saw for the first time how immature and dark their inner worlds were.

"The media claimed that the radical faction at the Izu Institute was attracted less by religion than by the magnificent research facilities, but I'm convinced it was their own suffering and fears that attracted them to Patron's teachings."

"What about yourself?" Kizu asked. "You're well known for your medical research, and you don't appear to me to be going through any inner turmoil."

Dr. Koga didn't answer right away but, with a calm expression bordering on the gloomy, he stared down at the hands in his lap, agile sturdy-looking hands, Kizu thought. "I don't know if this will provide material for your illustrated journal, but I'm quite the opposite from what you imagine. If it hadn't been for Patron's support I never would have survived the past fifteen years. I rely on Patron totally. If I hadn't met him I never would have escaped from a horrendous situation.

"After I graduated from medical school and had just finished my internship, I found myself in a frightful state that I thought I couldn't survive. All the confusion going on with the student movement had something to do with it, but in the end it boiled down to a personal matter, which manifested itself in an inability to touch other people's skin. I was desperate. Not only couldn't I perform my duties as a doctor, I was not even sure I'd be able to go on living.

"I went to med school because of my mother. The last four generations in my family had studied at Tekijuku, and as far as my mother was concerned if I didn't go there I could forget about the future. If you look at my name it's all too clear—my given name is written with the same character as the *teki* in Tekijuku. My mother's father was a bureaucrat in the Ministry of Health and Welfare, and it was my mother who really wanted to marry my father, who was a doctor.

"I was born in Boston, where my father had been sent as a research assistant, and I lived there until I was four. So I was one of the first 'returnee children,' as we now call them. Back in Japan I suffered through all kinds of bullying. I liked languages and wanted to study literature, but when I told my mother this she exploded. Naturally she brought up all our ancestors who had studied at Tekijuku. 'It doesn't matter what language you're talking about,' she said, 'Chinese, Dutch, whatever—the only reason people should study them is to use them as tools with which to make a contribution to society. But making a career out of languages is a waste. Name one of the six hundred students at school who've made foreign languages into a useful career!'

"So there it was: I entered medical school. After graduating and finishing my internship I ran smack dab into a brick wall. The word *doomed* would be appropriate. I couldn't touch people's bodies anymore. Usually when you say *people's* bodies you mean people other than yourself. But unless I used a cloth or paper to come between me and my own skin I couldn't even touch *myself*, if you can imagine. Thin latex gloves were out because there's no resistance and it feels even more like real skin.

"After a while it wasn't just touching people that disturbed me, but also talking with them, and I became painfully conscious of other people's gazes. Being a doctor was out of the question—or even being a patient. I wrapped my hands in bandages, wore tinted goggles, and stayed shut up in a Japanese-style room. And my mother, who'd managed to have her son follow in the footsteps of his illustrious ancestors and graduate from medical school, stayed by me day and night, lamenting what I'd become. Who could stand that? Ha ha!"

A glint in his eyes, Dr. Koga laughed heartily, his sturdy teeth shining.

3

Before long Kizu began to notice that Dr. Koga's expression and forceful way of speaking was attracting other listeners. The businessman across the aisle had removed his headphones and was leaning toward them, while the napping woman, too, had woken up and was gazing in their direction. The people in front and behind them weren't visible, but the two men in suits diagonally across from them to the right, rather than trying to ignore Dr. Koga's penetrating voice, had turned around with evident curiosity.

Eventually Dr. Koga realized what was going on. Coming to a convenient break in the conversation, he stopped, returned briefly to his seat, and brought back a small booklet. The booklet had a bright resin-coated cover and a title in a foreign language Kizu couldn't read. Dr. Koga opened the book to a spot he'd marked with a colored card, and there was the heading "The Untouchable Body" and his own name.

"Since it doesn't seem appropriate to continue to talk about it here," he said, "why don't you read this? We can talk more after you grasp what an awful fix I was in. We compiled this booklet after the persecution by the authorities had calmed down and we'd rebuilt the organization. We edited this as a collection of all our testimonies of faith. The shock we got at the childish-looking pictures those young people drew spurred on all the members of the workshop to try to organize their thoughts and write them down."

"What does the title mean? It looks like German," Kizu said, before letting his gaze drop again to the pages of the booklet.

"It says *Andern hat er geholfen*. I'm not sure where this expression comes from," Dr. Koga explained, "but in English it means *He saved others*. It expresses the feelings of some of my younger colleagues who, even after the Somersault, continued to believe in Patron."

"I'd always imagined it was just as the media reported," Kizu said, "namely, that after the Somersault the former radical faction detested Patron and Guide as traitors and that Guide's death was their act of revenge. I was sure Patron was next on their hit list, which made me worry when I saw how happily Patron accepted all of you back into the fold. But from your perspective Patron was more a tragic figure, wasn't he?"

Dr. Koga squinted as if smoke from a campfire had wafted up in his face. Without a word, he stood up and traded places with Ikuo.

Feeling as though Ikuo was blocking out the other people in the train for him, Kizu eagerly read the booklet to find out what came next in Dr. Koga's story.

From morning to night, my mother mumbled some strange things. The words were directed at me, but in such a low voice I couldn't catch them. Her words leaked out like a faucet that won't stop dripping.

When my mother could still speak clearly to me, she often quoted two poems:

"I, who sleep without awakening from the world of dreams, which I clearly see to be insubstantial—am I really human?" And "When you realize that your state in the world and your mind are not in accord , then truly you will understand."

At the time I was sure my mother couldn't be quoting from classical poetry and only later realized my mistake. For her, after all, Japanese poetry was anathema, for all her ancestors who'd studied at Tekijuku viewed scholars of the classics as their sworn enemy. So I was convinced that these two poems were something she'd conjured up herself as a kind of parody of classical learning. She muttered these words over and over, never explaining what the poems meant, but her mutterings themselves had a kind of dramatic presence, and I knew they expressed a powerful idea that had taken hold of her.

"Even if I could see this world, filled with disappointment, in my dreams, that's the way it is, so why should I be surprised—continuing to sleep, that's the kind of person I'd become." And "Once I realize that my body doesn't do what my mind wants it to, then I will understand well this world, and people, and everything." This is how I interpreted the poems.

Since I was suffering because I was unable to control my own body, I found the second poem particularly unnerving. Even though I felt this deep down, though, I had my doubts about whether this would lead me to a generosity of spirit when it came to other people.

Once, and only once, when she happened to be in a good mood, I asked my mother about this mind-body question. "Your body and your mind are alienated from each other," she said. "The mind is powerless to control your body. I learned this from you. Something is fundamentally wrong with a world that compels someone to live with a mind and body like that. Now I know the world is evil and sinful. This is the wisdom these poets extol," she said.

Returning to the first poem, she went on to say that, knowing how awful and disappointing this world is, she wasn't surprised anymore to wake up and find reality as cold as the cruel dreams she had while sleeping. In short, though she couldn't put it into words, she was appealing to me to escape the world with her.

Though she was putting her fate in my hands, I couldn't murder my mother. And I couldn't kill myself either. The reason was quite simple: my phobia about touching bodies, even my own.

Before long this total despair made my mother desperate, and she committed suicide with some poison she'd gotten from a doctor relative before she was married. She took advantage of a short spell of time during which I slept—as I lay sleeping shut up in my room as always all day long, my days and nights like a line of white and black Go stones.

I continued my daily routine, awakening only to fall asleep again. But I soon felt something was wrong with my mother because she was always so orderly but now just lay unmoving in the rattan chair on the porch, with the shutters closed. The smell was what first made me suspicious. I couldn't touch other people, so I couldn't do anything myself and had to leave things as they were until the woman who brought trays of food to the entrance to our room discovered what had happened after days went by with the food untouched.

Writing about it this way may make me look quite unfeeling. But I wasn't. I was frozen; a strong sense of guilt had me in its clutches. My mother suffered, afraid to live in this world. She didn't believe in an after-life, she believed that at the end of life everything was snapped off completely and time in all its hideousness lost any hold it might have on us. She clung to the hope that everything could be reset to zero.

That's how she disappeared from this detestable world of suffering. In her final act of slamming into a wall—beyond which lay nothing—and disintegrating, all she hoped for was that her son, the last thing that worried her, accompany her. For her, the sole pleasure to be found in this world lay in vanishing from it, together with her suffering son. Did her old-fashioned sense of morality keep her from inviting me to join her?

The only way she could appeal to me was by humming those two po-ems. But I didn't understand what she wanted, which made her despair complete. And as this thought tormented me, I thought once more about the poems that my mother mumbled over and over again:

"I, who sleep without awakening from the world of dreams, which I clearly see to be insubstantial—am I really human?"/"When you realize that your state in the world and your mind are not in accord, then truly you will understand."

At this point, with a guilty conscience on top of everything else, I was at my wits' end. Totally lost, I decided to get serious about climbing out of the abyss I'd fallen into.

I'm writing this in the belief that all of you who have experienced simi-lar depths of despair will acknowledge how such a seemingly meaning-less transition can take place.

This was the kind of person I was when Patron and Guide welcomed me into their midst.

4

After Kizu finished reading Dr. Koga's essay, he was confused. He read some of the other essays that preceded and followed Dr. Koga's, hoping to find a way out of his confusion, only to feel the strong arm of each writer shoving him aside. Were these the so-called radical faction, then, he wondered, these young people who had survived such unusual misery and relied so much on Patron and Guide's church? Compared with these people, Kizu considered himself downright happy-go-lucky. Right now he had his face forcibly pushed up against the painful reality of his cancer, and he could only manage an unfocused feeling of regret.

The people who wrote these essays had crawled on all fours across their own individual wildernesses of suffering to arrive at a faith in Patron and Guide. And on their backs they struggled to carry the heavy social burden of being a member of the ostracized radical faction. As if this weren't bad enough, their leaders abandoned them, ridiculing the doctrines they believed in as laughable and meaningless. Yet for ten years they had borne it all and never lost their faith. And among them now were those who had to carry the additional burden of Guide's death.

When Kizu had seen these former radical-faction members at the memorial service—the very picture of late-thirties and forties vigor—he had already felt how soft, both physically and mentally, he was in comparison. Though he had yet to see the town in Shikoku where they'd be living together, he felt a tangible menace in the place. After they left Kyoto, the view from the train was filled with rows of houses and hills covered with thick growths of broad-leafed trees. Kizu wanted to lose himself in this familiar, nostalgic scene. He stirred and felt, deep down in his lower belly and near his back, the resistance of a hard foreign substance. So he wasn't entirely *soft,* was he, with this hard intruder in his fifty-plus-year-old body? It made Kizu want to laugh as he simultaneously gave himself credit and put himself down.

Beside him, Ikuo lay back in his seat, eyes shut, but the movement behind his lids showed he wasn't asleep but was reacting to the slightest movements from Kizu. From Kizu's viewpoint, Ikuo was a great emotional and physical support for a soft late-fifties man with a serious illness; at the same time it was also clear that he had a great interest in, and was helping to support, a group Kizu wouldn't want to get on the bad side of.

Soon after they left the New Osaka Station, Kizu stood up and Ikuo shifted his legs to let him pass, throwing him a questioning look. Kizu merely nodded and walked down the aisle to where Dr. Koga was seated. Both he and his companion were asleep. There was something about Dr. Koga's posture and expression in particular that pierced Kizu to the quick. He passed them and sat down in a vacant seat.

The window seat beside him was vacant as well, and Kizu tried to make his harsh breathing calm down. Standing or seated, Dr. Koga was clearly a person who'd done a lot of physical training, but now he looked like a strangely aged infant, his upper body collapsed diagonally across the seat, hands clutching his tucked-up knees. His broad eyelids were yellowish, his mouth open, teeth clenched. Beside him, Mr. Hanawa lay diagonally in the other direction, his dark face etched with tiredness. He too had had an extraordinary life and an accumulated exhaustion that in ordinary circumstances he willed into submission.

They arrived in Osaka much earlier than scheduled. Kizu continued to sit by himself until the announcement came that they had reached Okayama. As they changed trains, Kizu followed behind Ikuo as he carried their bulky luggage, trying not to catch Dr. Koga's eye. When the new train crossed over the Seto Bridge, Kizu pretended to be absorbed in the sea and the small islands outside.

Once their train began to run along the Yosan Line, it was just the four of them in the Green Car in the middle of the train. Despite his short unsettled sleep, Dr. Koga looked refreshed, and when he invited him over, Kizu summoned up the courage to continue their earlier conversation. Ever since they entered Shikoku the hills had taken on a decided gentleness, the forests growing thicker, no doubt helping Kizu's shift in mood, the scene outside the window growing closer to his mental picture of his homeland.

The four of them unwrapped the Matsuri Sushi box lunches Ikuo had purchased in Okayama, and when the cart came around selling drinks, Dr. Koga teasingly had Ikuo buy two cans of beer for each of them. The beer made Dr. Koga even more lively than one would expect of a man his age.

"I just want to be with Ikuo," Kizu began, "which is what's led me to participate in Patron's new church, even if I don't have much time left. I appreciate Patron's generosity in allowing someone like me in. Though it does bother me sometimes how wishy-washy I am, a follower without faith."

"I'm thankful you can be with Patron," Dr. Koga said. "I know having you with us will liven things up. But more than that, *Ikuo* needs you. If you hadn't come he never would have joined us. I've talked with him a lot recently, and one thing I can say with certainty is this: Your participation in the church is a great thing—not just for Ikuo but for Patron, and for the former radical faction too."

"For better or worse," Kizu said, "Ikuo and I *are* pretty tight. But truthfully I don't know how useful I'll be to Patron, or to you and the others."

Gazing at the peaceful line of hills and the gentle green slopes, and with the beer taking effect, Dr. Koga's expression softened, though soon a deep-seated tension returned.

"To respond to your comments in reverse order, it's very important for us to have an outsider like yourself in our midst, to give us a fresh perspective on our faith in Patron. Ten years ago, not entirely at Guide's instigation, the religious fervor of those of us at the Izu Institute reached a climax. This reached a peak with the Somersault, and of all Patron's followers we're the ones who feel the greatest gap between before and after. In terms of giving us room to maneuver, it's much more helpful to have someone from outside the faith work with us rather than just be a monolithic church. And this should be even more true of Patron, I would think."

"So I wonder," Kizu said, steeling himself to ask, "if you would tell me, an outsider to the faith, how you came to know Patron and Guide?"

Dr. Koga bent his nicely shaped head, with its receding hairline, and gazed at his hands in his lap. When he spoke, it was more slowly and with more controlled emphasis than before.

"It's always hard to tell another person about how your faith began, even to someone who shares it. . . . I think that's especially true for me. My mother and I lived alone, just the two of us for a long time, and I let her take care of everything. After she died and we had to handle the inheritance, I didn't even know where she kept her official seal or which documents were necessary. My aunt came to straighten everything out, but first we had to locate the seal and bankbook. My aunt scoured the house from top to bottom but came up empty-handed, so we ended up seeking the help of a psychic everyone said was quite good. This happened to be Patron, who at the time had a little church with some thirty followers.

"Patron and Guide were still running their fortune-telling venture on the side to make the money needed to run their church. I went to see them with my aunt, the first time in a long while I'd left the house. Patron's church was in Kita-ku, near Asukayama.

"We'd gone out merely to have a psychic help us locate our lost items, but once we met Patron he began to ask us all sorts of detailed questions about my mother's and my life together. I was pretty surprised but did my best to answer each question. It was not only painful for me to touch other people or to be touched, I said, but I also had trouble communicating, yet even though I'd just met Patron, surprisingly I had no problem at all talking with him.

"After I finished speaking, Patron said there was something my mother's great-grandfather had had when he was a student at Tekijuku, something packed away inside a large wooden trunk. Actually among our family heir-looms my mother did talk about a Dutch-Japanese dictionary, kept in a large wooden trunk. When I told him this, Patron told me that the seal, bankbook, and other important documents were all in there as well. The lost is found, he said, a cheerful look on his face. And indeed my aunt, who had gone home ahead of me, phoned to say that the psychic had been right on the money.

"So I accomplished all I'd set out to do in visiting Patron's church. I felt more relieved than I had in a long time, and should have left at that point. But I found the chair facing Patron's low armchair more comfortable than any other chair I'd ever sat in, and I sank down into it. And I thought I'd like to have him hear what's *really* important. Patron seemed willing, and at his insistence I removed my dark-colored swimming goggles and began speaking."

5

"So that's how I came to talk, with an enthusiasm I hadn't known for ages, about the predicament I'd found myself in to this plump little middle-aged man who gazed at me with this engrossed look on his face. As I talked I had an increasingly objective feeling toward what I was saying, the contents becoming so concrete I could almost reach out and touch them. By this point Patron was already healing me—in fact he was halfway there. When I was about half finished I got up to use the toilet, and when I looked in the mirror, I thought miserably that my eyes in my unshaven face had the impassioned, feverish look of some young kid in love.

"After washing my face I calmed down a bit, and now it was Patron's turn to do the talking. This was the first of many sermons.

"'We live in a fallen world,' he began. 'Everything in the world is fallen—from the earth, to the oceans, to the air itself. The same holds true for human beings, who are perhaps the most fallen of all. So isn't it natural, then, for someone who realizes this to feel it's disgusting and dirty to touch other bodies as well as his own? Even myself, for a few days after I've gone over to the spirit world through a trance, I hate touching things and people in this fallen world of ours. I even can't stand the smell of the air and can barely breathe. Since I wouldn't survive that way, I train myself to be thick-skinned.

"'Isn't the predicament you're in a lot like the one I'm in right after I return from the realm of the spirits? You're not suffering from some nervous condition, you're expressing a purifying awakening of the soul. In order to survive in a fallen world, though, you have to acclimatize yourself, which is not an impossible task. Think about it. If your own body is dirty and fallen, touching other people's bodies, still less your own, isn't going to intensify the overall level of filth, now, is it?

"'What you need to be aware of is that your soul is alive inside this fallen world, inside your fallen body. You're suffering because your soul is oppressed, because your soul is awakening. Your soul is not fallen, but as long as it's in this fallen world, because the temporary container your soul is in, your body, is dirty, and the world that surrounds that body is dirty, your soul will indeed suffer. You must not annihilate the purity of your suffering soul. It's hard work to survive as a pure soul in this fallen world.'

"I listened to Patron with an openness I'd never had before and suddenly felt liberated from the pride and arrogance that had always kept me tied down and hopeless. The world is fallen, and my body is polluted—this struck me as it never had before. Was *that* why I'd been suffering, why I drove my mother to a desperate death? That being said, how could I snuff out my fallen body from this polluted world as quickly as possible? Why was I following an animal survival instinct that kept me from doing that? I didn't think what my mother did was wrong, and on a conscious level at least I don't fear death.

"'That's because you're listening to the voice of your soul,' Patron told me. 'Extinguishing your polluted body in this polluted world does not mean your soul will break all ties with the world and return to a world before the Fall. And if that's the case, this fallen world itself has a certain significance, doesn't it?

"'As long as you don't find a solution here, in this fallen world, no matter where you run your soul will be in the same predicament. Escaping this world is not a guarantee of salvation. So you're outfitted with flesh and your soul is calling out to you. It's a tragic thing, but your mother was mistaken in refusing to listen to that voice.

"'People who hear the voice of the soul must do this: Wake up to the fact that our world is a fallen world, that humans are polluted beings, repent, and await the end of the world. Many people have heard the voice of the soul, which means the end time must not be far off. In fact, it is almost upon us. Anyone who hears the soul's voice must, as a penitent person, prepare for that coming and take the initiative to welcome it. You're not the only one who has awakened in this way, though not many have suffered as much as you. The church I am organizing is for people just like yourself.'

"And that's how I became a member of Patron's church. This might sound too simple, almost melodramatic, but from the moment I laid eyes on Patron I wanted to follow him. Patron encouraged me, so I joined his church.

This doesn't mean I was confident I'd truly awakened and become a repentant person. Once I had a chance to mull it over by myself I came to the conclusion that there is a huge gap separating an awakened person from a penitent one, and you have to leap across it. I'd been so thoroughly steeped in the notion that my body and other people's bodies were polluted that what Patron had said about the connection between this and my suffering struck me as entirely reasonable.

"Deep down a person knows that human beings are fallen creatures in a fallen world. In this sense he is an awakened person. But that doesn't mean he's necessarily repentant. So this was the goal I set for myself after I joined the church: to focus my activities in the church on making that leap from being awakened to being truly repentant.

"I set out with this resolution in mind, and from the time I worked with Guide to help set up the Izu workshop and began living with my young colleagues, I realized that all of them, too, were at the same stage—ready to make that leap. From the start it was clear this was their intention, but, being young and full of energy, their focus started to change.

"Awaiting the end time and transforming oneself from an awakened person to a repentant one is no easy task, but is that really all one should do? Shouldn't we go beyond that and actually help *bring about* the end of the world? Isn't that what's necessary to make the great leap? And didn't Patron and Guide entrust my young colleagues with the Izu Research Center in hopes that they would do exactly this—come up with a plan to bring about Armageddon? All it took was someone to put it into words, and this became the radical faction's point of departure."

Dr. Koga stopped speaking and squinted at the sun shining on the sea outside the train window; he sat on the sea side of the train and Kizu on the mountain side, each of them occupying two seats, with the aisle between them. When he spoke next, his manner had the practiced solicitude of someone in a position of responsibility.

"It might sound like the Izu Institute was a hotbed of political debate, but in the beginning it wasn't. Actually, we were far less radical than some other groups within the church, at least as far as our stance on Patron's teachings was concerned. The criticism of the radical faction by the media was off the mark. It wasn't just that grad students in the sciences were drawn by the generous funding and facilities—that's clear enough from the pamphlet you just read, right?—but that each researcher also thought deeply about his own faith.

"At a certain point the researchers suddenly forged ahead, shoring up their faith, and in the process became more politicized. They began debating how not just the research institute but the entire church could be reinvigorated, and what actions they had to take in society at large. We created a task force to investigate this, with some remarkable developments.

"Even if you don't know the whole process, I'm sure you've read and heard in the media about how it all ended up. From out of the talented young research group, a politically radical group ballooned up with uncanny swiftness. For the most part this was done in a democratic manner, though since I was one of the leaders I guess it might seem irresponsible of me to put it that way.

"Anyhow, during the past ten years I've reflected on my own role, and I've come to the conclusion that I'm not a religious activist or political organizer, merely a doctor. Now that I'm rejoining Patron, my main job will be running a clinic and overseeing the health of my former colleagues. And of course I'm very happy to be able to take on your case as well, Professor Kizu."

Outside the train window the flat calm sea spread out. Not a single fishing boat was visible. The sun was hidden behind a thin layer of clouds, the whole sea was gray tinged with brown, thoroughly diffused with a pale light. Dr. Koga sat there silently, lost in thought, the peaceful expression on his face in harmony with the placid scene outside.

Three rows away, Ikuo and Mr. Hanawa sat talking, also across the aisle from each other. Their topic of conversation was the thin little foreign book Mr. Hanawa had been reading, except for when he was napping, ever since they left Tokyo. Before long Ikuo spread out on the small table he'd pulled out beside his seat the paper that had been wrapped around his boxed lunch and, with a pencil Mr. Hanawa passed him, began scribbling formulas. Mr. Hanawa was nearly ten years his senior, so Ikuo toned down his usual rough, aggressive way of talking and treated him with the respect due a teacher.

Dr. Koga was also watching the two of them and turned a faint smile of admiration toward Kizu. Filled with pride, Kizu returned the smile.

"Up to a certain point," Dr. Koga said, his smile changing to a wry one, "our Izu workshop was a laid-back, intellectually stimulating place. Looking at the two of them lost in their calculations, you can tell we've got two spirited personalities on our hands. Makes me wonder what will happen when all that comes to the surface."

"So these young people with their idiosyncrasies, then," Kizu said, "will be linking up with Patron, whom they're no match for. And here I am with my hopeless—though fortunately not contagious—illness am about to join them. I'm trying to imagine what will come of it all."

"It certainly won't be boring, you can be sure of that!" Dr. Koga said, his eyes flashing with the message that he, too, was someone to be reckoned with.

Part II

17: There's Power in the Place

1

Ogi and Dancer had preceded everyone else to the site in Shikoku where the new church was to be established. There they held talks with the people on-site who had been taking care of the buildings and handling visitors; these meetings included a woman from an old established family in the area, the head of the Fushoku temple—a Soto Zen sect—plus a representative of the Kansai headquarters who had been instrumental in keeping the church running as a religious corporation after the Somersault.

Ogi had been in charge of laying the groundwork for the move, so this wasn't his first time in the place. Still, when he saw Dancer's surprised reaction to the scale and beauty of the chapel and the building the locals called the monastery, he was amazed all over again that such buildings, together with the large artificial lake they surrounded, had been provided for Patron's new church.

With Patron and Guide's Somersault, for all practical purposes the church's activities in Tokyo and the surrounding areas had come to a grinding halt. The Kansai headquarters alone continued its public activities, albeit on a reduced scale; meanwhile, the solidarity of their members had only grown stronger. Their leader was a Mr. Soda, from one of the leading general contracting firms in Shikoku and Kyushu. This conscientious late-forties man, accompanied by his hard-working personal secretary, had now come to the backwoods of Shikoku to attend the meetings.

Mr. Soda's secretary first passed out documents related to issues between the church and local authorities, as well as specific improvements that needed to be made to the facilities before the church moved in en masse, with

Mr. Soda giving a short explanation to clarify the documents. He and his secretary could only stay for half the first day of the talks, having to attend a ceremony marking the completion of a JR train station in Kyushu.

After the two of them left, the remaining members were given a detailed
briefing on the local area by Asa-san, wife of the retired former principal of
the local junior high school, and by the humorously eloquent head priest of the
Fushoku temple, Mr. Matsuo; Asa-san was taking care of the buildings the
church would use, and she and Dancer had been in close contact regarding
preparations for the move. Ogi was impressed by how objective these two local
representatives were regarding short-term issues involved in the church's
move. What's more, the two of them seemed to be rivals in the considerable
influence they had over those who held the political strings here. Ogi was
particularly impressed by their discussion of the background of the area and
its recent local history.

The town here was called Maki Township, in Kita County of Ehime
Prefecture. The region was on the northern slope of the central mountain
range running through Shikoku, just about in the middle; soon after the township was incorporated, in an area called the Old Town, a church called the
Church of the Flaming Green Tree rose up and, after a short time, disappeared. Fifteen years before, the leader of the church, named Brother Gii, had
been murdered. His church had built the chapel that stood on the eastern edge
of the south bank of the man-made lake in the Hollow, the chapel that was
so well known as an example of modern architecture. On the land to the west,
the church members had set up a site for tents where many of them used to
stay.

With Gii's death the church itself, to use a popular term borrowed from
the terminology of political demonstrations, just *melted away.* The church
members dispersed like so many drops of water soaking into the ground.
Actually, the final sermon to commemorate the breakup of the church had
been given by Mr. Matsuo, then a church activist who had since returned to
his role as local Buddhist priest.

"Brother Gii was a very simple man," Mr. Matsuo said, "yet one of the
most ethical people you'd ever want to meet. He always considered others'
lives more important than his own, and put that belief into practice. His influence is still felt among us here. The Church of the Flaming Green Tree is
no longer with us, but Gii's life and death are etched in our memories, not
just those of us who were close to him but other people as well. We would
like to keep the area around the Hollow as sacred ground, which is why when
you asked to take over the chapel for your own church, we leapt at the idea.
We thought, Why don't we help them make it happen?"

According to reports that Ogi had gathered, the transfer of ownership of the chapel, and the subsequent construction of the monastery, came about in the following way. Brother Gii had inherited the Hollow and surrounding land from one of the established families in the old village. Along with this, one follower, the head of another old family in the area, decided to construct the chapel and contributed the needed funds. When the Church of the Flaming Green Tree was incorporated and tax issues became moot, this particular church member donated the land and the chapel to the church.

Along the south side of the Hollow, a road sixteen feet wide had been built running the entire length of the man-made lake from east to west. This road was lined with cobblestones, modeled on the cobblestone paths that, according to the rich folklore of the region, used to be constructed high in the forest, remnants of which could still be found here and there. On the eastern edge of this road was the cylindrical chapel, constructed in the latest concrete technology, a building that at the time of its construction was a hot topic of conversation in architectural circles. After the chapel was built, Mr. Soda's construction company came up with a plan to construct a courtyard out of the road leading up to the chapel, with communal residences running along both sides. But it was at this point that the church broke up.

Many local residents didn't want the buildings to remain unoccupied, and they wanted to complete the ones that had been planned, as well. After accepting the donation of the chapel and the land along the south shore of the lake, the town decided to build a junior high school and a continuing education center there, and there was strong support for this idea. The plans fell through, though, because of the economic timing—the Bubble Economy of Japan had just burst and money was tight. In opposition to those in the Old Town who still wanted to go ahead with the original plan, a rival movement arose calling not just for a cancellation of the continuing education center but the junior high as well—there weren't enough children in the area to justify it, they claimed. In fact, one candidate for town head had run on this platform and won election, so the whole plan was back to square one.

This still meant they had to deal with the investment already made in the construction plans. With exquisite timing, just when the town authorities were racking their brains as to what the next step should be, the Kansai headquarters of the church began to show an interest in the land. Mr. Soda, the headquarters' leader as well as the one who'd been involved in the original construction, played a major role in the negotiations. Things didn't always go smoothly, but with the church now taking on the loans from the town, they were able to complete the original second phase of construction pretty much as it had been originally envisioned.

The chapel and the monastery had been kept up—not exactly in a hands-on way but regularly nonetheless—and like some recent ruins were beautiful and abandoned, and no discord arose between the local residents and church members from the Kansai headquarters during their intermittent visits. However, with a good number of people expected to move to the town as Patron restarted his religious movement, there were sure to be difficulties ahead. What's more, this was taking place soon after all the uproar involving the Aum Shinrikyo *satyan* that had been widely reported in the media.

Ogi and Dancer flew from Haneda to Matsuyama airport. When they arrived at the Maki Town JR Station and went into the business district in the Old Town to rent a car, they came across some protest banners and leaflets: *DON'T LET OUR TOWN BE TAKEN OVER BY FANATICS! WILL OUR CHILDREN SEE MURDERS ON THE STREETS AGAIN?* and *OPPOSE ARRIVAL OF PATRON'S CHURCH!*

The banners and leaflets were the work of a group called the Association to Oppose the Move of Religious Organizations to Maki Town, made up largely of residents of the Old Town. A month before they had put up their banners at the entrance of the Ohashi Bridge over the Kame River, which ran through the center of town, and plastered all the shop windows with their leaflets. Thanks to Asa-san's tenaciousness, these had all been removed a week earlier.

In trying to persuade people to accept the new church coming to town, Asa-san used the following argument. Fifteen years ago, during the brief period when the Church of the Flaming Green Tree flourished, their farm products had sold quite well in Matsuyama, and the farmers in the area had turned a nice profit. The church members' spending alone had been a shot in the arm to the local economy. After the demise of the church, the valley's economy had gone into a tailspin unconnected with the bursting of the Bubble Economy. If it was good for the economy why were people opposing another church?

Already the church had used its resources to pay off loans the town had taken for the junior high school project. And they'd hired people locally to build the monastery. Isn't it natural, now that they own the chapel and the monastery, for church people to move in? With all the benefits you've had so far, how can you possibly join a movement opposing their arrival?

Patron's church doesn't commit criminal acts like Aum Shinrikyo, she went on. According to reports on TV and the weekly magazines, Patron's Somersault took place because he anticipated the danger of his church becoming Aum-like and wanted to nip any terrorist plans in the bud. The death of

Guide reported not long ago was the work of a terrorist group that has been hostile to Patron ever since the Somersault, with the church its victim. After ten painful years of self-reflection, Patron had chosen this place to build his church anew. Why not just let it happen?

2

After Mr. Soda and his secretary left, Ogi and Dancer heard more details about all this from the head priest of the Fushoku temple and from Asa-san herself. Once this conversation drew to a close, they set off in their rental car, Asa-san leading the way in her own car, Mr. Matsuo as their guide, and drove from the temple to the Hollow. It was already late afternoon, and a strong late-rainy-season downpour was falling.

Right after descending to the river from the temple they came across the newly completed bridge connecting up to the bypass leading to the cross-Shikoku highway. Mr. Matsuo explained how in crossing it they would pass by the road leading down to the Hollow, but today, since he wanted them to remember the lay of the land as it used to be in this region, they drove along the old main road on this side of the riverbank.

The Kame River is lined with dikes now, he said, and is no longer a wild river—it used to flood its banks every year—yet if the water filling the man-made lake to its brim overflowed, Old Town would be flooded. According to Mr. Matsuo, this fact lay behind the wariness with which the residents of Old Town viewed the followers of the Church of the Flaming Green Tree—who lived, at that time, in the chapel and in tents in the banks of the lake—and also lay behind the movement opposing this newest church.

Besides introducing them to the special topographic features of the region, Mr. Matsuo also related some of the highlights of local history. Dancer didn't say anything while she sat next to Mr. Matsuo in the front passenger seat, but when she was alone with Ogi she complained. "That priest thinks that since our church is moving to these woods we have to revere their history just like he does. But aren't Patron and all of us going to create a *new* history in this region?" she grumbled.

All complaints aside, when they crossed a ridge filled with red pines, began descending a slope, and cut through a dark road filled with tall bamboo trees, Dancer looked up to the rise above her, filled with layers of wind-swept deciduous and coniferous trees, and felt her breath taken away.

The road began to climb up again. Although it was paved, it was more like a mountain path, with wild grasses on either side, and with raindrops dripping down from the thick oaks and beeches it felt like they were cutting through a deep forest. As soon as they emerged into the open, they came across a dam, like a huge wall blocking the way. Beside it, Asa-san, who'd preceded them, was parked in a flat spot and stood beside her car, umbrella open and extra ones under her arm.

They opened up the umbrellas, each of which had the mark of a tree done in the style of a woodblock print—umbrellas left over, it turned out, from the Church of the Flaming Green Tree. Asa-san told them that there were plenty of extra raincoats and high boots too, items essential to life here between river and woods, stored in the shed at the monastery, and they should feel free to borrow them. They all then trooped up a railless stairway carved out of the outer wall of the dam.

"This lake that was made when the water was dammed up was also the work of some young people in this area involved in a group called the Base Movement. They flooded the plain, leaving the trees standing to make the lake, and one huge tree we call the Hollow's Cypress rises above the water on a bit of land, like some island that's been there forever."

"Asa-san was a main actor in one act of recent history that took place there," Mr. Matsuo said, as he brought up the rear.

Asa-san, who was first to the top of the dam, riveted her eyes on the rain-pounded misty surface of the lake and the overgrown island with its huge cypress, but she didn't follow up on what Mr. Matsuo said. All of them—Dancer, Ogi, and even Mr. Matsuo, who scrambled up on top of the dam last—fell silent for a while as they gazed at the scene.

In the now unimpeded field of vision, the rain fell on the conifers, raising a mist around them and on the dark green of the broad-leafed forest, making its darkness brim with vigor, sending up splashes on the slightly clouded surface of the lake. On the small island near the north shore, the unusually large cypress towered upward, so high the top disappeared in the fog swirling about it, with only its charred trunk near the lake's surface and the thick, intertwined branches, the life force of the tree, visible.

On the east side of the lake, to the right, stood a wet, bright gray-blue cylinder with a gently sloping, conical roof: the chapel. On each side of the roof a half-globe skylight swelled out, showing a faint golden luster. To the west of the chapel an ancient-looking stone wall ran up to the southern edge of the dam, and above this loomed a Western-style shed-shaped monastery—the dormitories, in other words—a courtyard between them, with two parallel rows of roof tiles, the one nearer the forest slightly higher than the one in front.

As Ogi and Dancer stood absorbed in the scenery, Asa-san spoke contentedly to them in a way that left no doubt what a basically decent person she was.

"The huge cypress is trying its best to be as full of greenery as the stand of camphors on the slope to the north, isn't it? If you stand at a different angle, though, it looks horrible, like a blackened, charred pillar. Even from here you can see that a little. Fifteen years ago, the withered branches were burnt, you see. I find it hard to believe now, but that was Brother Gii's one and only savage act."

"There's no need to recite the whole of recent history, now, is there?" Mr. Matsuo gently chided her.

Asa-san readily turned to more practical matters. "That patchwork-colored area just in front of the camphors used to be a tangerine orchard," she said. "And do you see that prefab building off to one side? We haven't taken as good care of it as we should, so the branches all around are overgrown and you can only see the roof. I inherited that house, and your church asked to buy it from me. I've decided to accept their offer and have it fixed up so you all can use it. The monastery will have to be thoroughly cleaned, I'm sure, before it's livable. In the meanwhile you can live in that prefab building on the north shore."

"When she decides to support something, Asa-san doesn't fool around," Mr. Matsuo added, putting Ogi's thoughts into words.

Asa-san turned her face, the freckles standing out on her prominent cheekbones, toward the lake and directed a languid look at its surface. Her expression looked sad, but when she spoke her voice was full of conviction.

"I'm already old, having spent most of my life right here," she said, "and I've seen a lot of tragic but compelling things happen here in the Hollow— everything from the Base Movement to the Church of the Flaming Green Tree. After the church disappeared, though, the young workers in this area just seemed to shrivel up and die, and even a staunch supporter like Mr. Matsuo went back to his temple.

"I was worried that the local spirits might get too frustrated. That's what happened just before and after the Meiji Restoration, when the riots took place. The local spirits here have a history of stirring things up. And just while I was thinking these things, look what happened—you all decided to take over the chapel and monastery! I feel revitalized now, and I'm hoping that before I pass away something exciting will happen, just like the old days! Admit it, Mr. Matsuo, you feel the same way, don't you? The other day I stopped by the Church of the Flaming Green Tree Farm, and things seem much livelier than before. You all don't know about the Farm yet, but Mr. Soda has been interested in it for quite some time. The wife of the church's founder, who helped build the chapel and planned the monasteries, is running it with a small number of friends."

The rain continued to strike the surface of the lake forcefully, sending up a thick material, neither mist nor fog, rising up toward the dam. The splashes from the raindrops at their feet grew higher.

"Let's go inside," Asa-san said. "It's silly of me to expect you to sympathize with my feelings regarding this land. Besides, Mr. Matsuo's trying to keep me from getting too worked up."

"As if I had the strength to do that," the chief priest demurred, but this time he went first, leading Ogi and Dancer into the grounds of the compound.

At the end of the dam there was a metal staircase skirting the end of a stone wall that, old though it was, had been put to good use. At the top of the stairs a cobblestone path ran straight to the east. On both sides were Western-style wooden structures that looked like school buildings. As it had appeared from the dam, the roof of the building on the forest side was just slightly taller than the one nearer the lake. Ogi and Dancer walked around the monastery, a fitting name at least from outward appearances, and peeked into the kitchen, the laundry room, and the storage rooms.

The lakeside corner of the east dorm, the part of the building fronting the courtyard that led to the chapel, was set up as an office, while its counterpart in the forest-side dorm was a detached wing with a high watchtower-like roof. Hesitantly yet persuasively, Asa-san suggested that Patron and those who helped him might live there. A passageway connected the dorms and the chapel, covering a concrete ditch down which a roiling swath of water flowed to the lake.

Looking down at the water, Asa-san said, "It's raining a lot today, but even when it isn't there's a spring on the forest side always flowing into the lake. If there's anybody in your church who's done some farming, they could grow something there, since there's so much water. Behind the building on the forest side there's a fairly substantial piece of land running east and west. That's part of the building's grounds and part of your land."

With Asa-san leading the way, Ogi and Dancer went into the chapel. The rainy sky and the half dome on the conical ceiling were bright, but only a dim light—like a collision of intersecting prisms—filtered into the rest of the building from the windows on the wall of the cylinder that were uncovered. There was enough light for them to look around the interior, however. Muffled rain beat against the solid roof. In the faint light, over two hundred chairs lined up in a fan shape threw shadows on the floor, and at the focal point stood a solid-looking lectern. Mr. Matsuo, coming in later, appeared at the entrance.

"I turned on the electricity," he said to Asa-san. "Shall I turn on the lights or keep it as is?"

"Why don't you turn them on. We're transferring this over as a *building* I've taken care of, rather than as a church, so there's no need for us to get all pious about it."

"I just thought it would be nice to look outside from the chapel without any lights on," Mr. Matsuo said disappointedly, and threw the main switch.

Once the bright lights were on, the cylindrical building looked just like a modern concert hall. The walls were as Mr. Soda had said, lustrous from a high-tech high-pressure paint job. In contrast, from a set height up to the ceiling, the walls turned decidedly rough, with porous soundproofing boards overlying the concrete. With everything brightly lit, the windows and entrance door seemed to match, though they had had an odd look earlier in the dimness.

"What a magnificent hall!" Dancer said in admiration. She'd been silent up till then. "There's a piano, too, and wonderful audio equipment."

"The control room is next to the entrance," Mr. Matsuo replied.

"The floor is solid too."

"Most people ask about the acoustics," Mr. Matsuo said happily. "But you're right. The floor *is* solidly built."

"She's a professional dancer, you see," Ogi interjected, and Asa-san, as you might expect someone from the country to do, gave Dancer a careful once-over.

"I'm hoping you'll make full use of all the chapel's facilities," she said, a more formal look on her face now. "Will Patron give his sermons here? The other church had its sermons here, but also concerts open to the public that everyone could enjoy. Though it seems ages ago. . . . There hasn't been a single concert here in the last fifteen years. As I said before, once the Church of the Flaming Green Tree was gone, everyone seemed to shrink back into their shells. Which is another reason why I'm so happy that new people will be coming here."

The light inside hit some broad-leaf tree branches, blown by a gust of wind, scraping against the east windows. Mr. Matsuo half turned to check out the movement and took up from Asa-san, his tone changed from before.

"The Base Movement had us all excited as kids, and the Church of the Flaming Green Tree movement, too, inspired the entire valley. I was so wrapped up in it from day to day I had no time to consider how it all fit into the history of this region. . . . Now that I look back on it, though, I can see Asa-san is right—it may very well have been on the same scale as the insurrections in 1860 and 1871. Even people who weren't directly involved got swept up in it. And after things settled down everyone became indifferent to the church. If it hadn't been for the funding from your headquarters, the extension of the monastery and even the chapel itself would have gone to wrack and ruin. Despite Asa-san's Herculean efforts, it's beyond one person's strength to keep them all up.

"Asa-san, here's what I think. I understand how happy you are that new people will be using the buildings for their activities. But as of today our roles as managers of the chapel and the monastery are over. We need to accept the fact that the beliefs of the people who will be coming here are different from the other church. After everything's been handed over, I think it would be better if we take a step or two back. Of course, if you find yourself in sympathy with this new movement, that's a different story."

"I wasn't even a follower of the Church of the Flaming Green Tree," Asa-san said. "I just helped them from the outside. Have you forgotten that? The reason I was attracted by what the young people were doing in the Hollow was just what the architect who designed this chapel said: 'There's power in the place.' I believe there really *is* such a thing as the *power of a place*. People have used the expression *power of the land* down through the ages.

"Ever since I was little, whenever I climbed up to the Hollow I felt a strange power here. The Base Movement created its so-called Lovely Village here. It sank beneath the water, of course, when the man-made lake was built, and now, like an emblem, that huge cypress stands on the island.

"After that came the Church of the Flaming Green Tree. The church died out, but now, with people from the city moving here to start a new church, I feel power in the place all the more, a power that moves people to gather here. This happened in 1860, and even earlier—in the Middle Ages, in fact. Whether it was dormant or not, I don't know, but I'm happy that the *power of the place* is back. That's why I took care of these buildings for fifteen years—because I wanted to care for the *power of the land* in the Hollow. And I want to make sure the young people who'll take over understand that."

Asa-san blushed, a severe look rising to her freckled face. She closed her mouth carefully, as if she were having problems with her teeth. The chapel was again filled with the gentle yet weighty sound of the rain and wind. Ogi was impressed, and Dancer, her mouth open, pink tongue visible, looked lost in thought.

"When the church disbanded I was the one who delivered the sermon here, but I remember you gave a lovely sermon yourself on the occasion of the chapel and the monastery's being handed over." Mr. Matsuo didn't speak with his earlier easy familiarity; his tone now was more respectful.

3

Led by this middle-aged woman who seemed to glide as she walked, Ogi and Dancer followed along a narrow path overgrown with bushes that kept snagging their umbrellas, finally arriving at a lone house on the north slope. The house looked to have just been cleaned that morning. They didn't need to take towels out of the Boston bags they'd brought by car to dry their wet heads and shoulders, since freshly laundered towels awaited them in the laundry area.

For a prefab building the house was well built and was outfitted in nicely coordinated gray and light brown furniture and carpeting. Dancer took the room on the west side, with a bed and desk. Ogi was given the living room, which was across from a short corridor and had a small attached kitchen. Asa-san explained to them about the chaise longue Ogi decided to use for a bed, built in the woodworking shop of the former church, a wooden-framed affair carved with flowers and birds and covered with a cloth mat. No doubt urged on by Asa-san, Mr. Matsuo had gone out of his way on the trip up to the Hollow to stop by a small market so they could pick up enough food for dinner and the next morning's breakfast.

When the two of them were alone and had finished unpacking, Dancer invited Ogi into her room. She'd opened the shutter and curtain facing the lake, had half opened the window to let in some fresh air, and was sitting on top of the covers on her bed. This bed, set out from the western corner beside the window, apparently had also been designed for the owner of the house by the church's woodworking shop. It too was built in European folk style, a little too short to be an adult's bed, angled so one was sitting up slightly in bed. Dancer rested her elbows on the flat frame of the bed. She motioned to Ogi, and he crossed to the desk on the north side of the room and pulled over the chair to sit beside her.

The surface of the lake had turned a muddy brown in the rain. Right before them lay the island, the giant cypress rising from a small meadow like some gigantic bonsai plant lashed by rain, the cloud of fog covering its upper branches having descended closer to the ground than when they'd last looked upon it. The low fog hanging over the surface of the lake had crept up the slope on the east bank, where a stand of mountain cherry trees was surrounded by broad-leafed trees, and advanced up the north slope as well. The Hollow was wrapped in silence, but every detail, along with the sound of the rain and wind, seemed in motion. The wind fluttering the branches and leaves of the giant cypress sounded almost like an entire small forest. This sound filtered in the crack of the window, along with cold-damp air. It was only four in the afternoon, but already traces of a deepening twilight had begun to fill the Hollow, itself like the bottom of a pot.

"When a huge tree like that burned up, it must have been scarier than if a house was on fire, even if no one perished in the flames," Dancer said, as if she'd been silently mulling over Asa-san's words.

Seen from the north side of the lake, the giant cypress looked like a small bush that had been hit with a flamethrower, the surface of its trunk up to ten or twelve feet completely carbonized, just thick branches like black tusks remaining, with a wet cluster of small green branches sticking out around them. Though Ogi couldn't really picture the tree burning, just looking at the clash between the inky black and dark green made his chest tighten.

"I don't think this was a happy place for someone to live. Do you suppose the former diplomat who lived here died in this bed?"

Dancer's face was ashen as she said this. She looked sleepy. Ogi stood up and reached past her shoulder to shut the window. The outline of the chapel to the southeast was vague in the rain, and a darker gray than when seen up close, the whole structure looming up against the backdrop of the foggy forest.

"I know Patron's decided to build a new church here," she said, "but I have no idea what he actually plans to do. You have some idea, though, don't you?"

"I know about as much as you do," Ogi said.

"You're in charge of sorting out all the information coming from the headquarters."

"But I'm not bound to Patron through faith, remember."

"Professor Kizu says the same thing," Dancer said. "But both of you are very important people to him."

"And so are *you*—for a lot longer time than me."

"Compared to Dr. Koga's group, though, I'm practically a newcomer. I didn't come to be with Patron originally out of any faith. You knew that, didn't you?"

"No, I didn't," Ogi exclaimed, in surprise, ever the innocent youth. "I've never heard that!"

"I suppose only Guide knew the truth. I did tell Professor Kizu and Ikuo about it . . . but I can say it again. . . ."

As one condition of being allowed to live on her own when she went to Tokyo to study modern dance, Dancer's father made her drop by to see an old friend of his who was to be her guarantor, and then to visit him occasionally whenever she needed advice. This friend was a classmate of her father's when they were in the science department at the university, and soon after she arrived in Tokyo, Dancer went to see him. The person turned out to be Guide, who was living in seclusion with Patron after the Somersault.

Dancer had a hard time at first figuring out what sort of person Guide was, but he not only took her under his wing as guarantor and mentor but helped her find a place to live in Tokyo and even guaranteed a small income, having her do odd jobs in the office in their residence in Seijo. They had a woman who made their meals and did other tasks, but she quit after half a year and Dancer took on the job of running the household. Her dance lessons were just three afternoons a week in Shimokitazawa, so she had no trouble coping with both her studies and her work. After she graduated from her dance program she couldn't find a job in her field, so while she prepared for her own private performances she worked as Patron and Guide's personal secretary. In the beginning, at least, the office work hadn't kept her too busy.

"You started living in that house even though you didn't know the two of them that well?" Ogi asked. "Pretty courageous of you."

"I trusted Guide, since he was my father's friend. I didn't know the first thing about living in Tokyo, but I felt as long as I followed Guide's instructions I'd have nothing to worry about. . . . They hadn't yet built the annex, so the three of us lived in the main house. I stayed in the room by the front entrance that you used for a while. I could lock the door, and there was a window opening to the outside, so I figured if need be I could make a quick getaway."

"You really were on your guard, weren't you?" Ogi commented.

"I wasn't afraid or anything. In addition to the dance club, in high school I was a sprinter and middle-distance runner. Even now I'm a decent runner."

"Don't worry, I'm not about to assault you here," Ogi said, naively offended.

"At first I thought that Guide must be Patron's parole officer, keeping an eye on him. There was something about Patron that just wasn't right. The first time I saw him, he reminded me of freshly unearthed beetle larva. He had skin like yellow paper stretched over soft-looking flesh, his movements were slow and lethargic, and he spoke in a small voice in a kind of disjointed way. It felt like Guide was raising some weird creature, and I was his assistant keeper.

"Before long I found out that Patron and Guide were former leaders of a religious organization who'd done a Somersault. In magazines they have those features—right?—like WHERE ARE THEY NOW? stories. A freelance reporter writing one of those came to our place but Guide, if not Patron, saw him coming and refused to open the door, so he ambushed me when I went out shopping.

The reporter hardly let me get a word in edgewise, with all his questions. I just remember, out of a childish sense of justice, believing it was wrong of the founder and his top executive to have abandoned their followers.

"I worried a lot about what they'd done, and late one night I went to Guide to ask him about it. I think I was afraid to ask Patron directly. I was still young and kind of unstable, emotionally. Guide filled me in. I'm sure he's told you things about Patron too, and as you know he doesn't talk about something until he's come to a conclusion about it himself. Talking to an ignorant young thing like me was like pruning off all the branches, laying bare the trunk. Guide told me that Patron has mystical experiences . . . in other words, he journeys to the *other side,* talks directly with God or else has a vision from God, and then returns.

"'And I try to put these visions into intelligible language,' he said, 'not an easy job. Our reports regarding these mystical experiences have become our church's gospel. It's been through this process that we've constructed our faith.

"'The church movement that developed in this way gradually started to look outward, toward the world outside, and when this became a major component of what we were, Patron began to have doubts about whether our gospel was really giving people a true picture of God's visions. What's more, at this point some of the young people in the church began preparing to take action, and we had to stop them. It became necessary for us to publicly announce, in as dramatic a fashion as possible, that our gospel was wrong. That is when we performed our Somersault. Using TV to announce it proved a great success. Through the Somersault, our church and the beliefs of our followers became a national laughingstock. All those who viewed the broadcast must have had a good laugh. Patron and I survived, living on as we had, not without some pain. I'm sure you've sensed this?'

"Guide opened his heart to me when he told me this," Dancer concluded. "I decided, no matter what, I wanted to follow Patron, and for the first time I realized I was starting to believe in him."

4

When Ogi woke up in the middle of the night, the first thought that came to him was the naive notion that hell must be as pitch black as this. An utterly gentle, quiet hell. Not completely without sound, though, for the lake and the hills were still enveloped in rain, but it was weaker than before. At first Ogi thought his bed was narrow, but when he stretched out it supported his back nicely and made him feel secure. As he lay on this wooden box and listened to the rain, it was as if the rain had cut off all his surroundings and was slicing through his body and into an abyss below his bed.

There must have been some reason why he woke up in the middle of the night, but he couldn't figure out what it was or get back to sleep. He recalled an experience similar to Dancer's that he had soon after meeting Patron and Guide. When Ogi first started visiting Patron's head office as part of his work with the foundation, Dancer had already been working for them for three years. Even then, Patron had impressed him as being quite extraordinary.

At first Patron didn't talk directly to Ogi, so it fell to Guide to explain religious matters to him whenever he had questions. Ogi's questions weren't ones he'd been musing over for a long time, just things he burst out with. Later he found it strange that he'd even said such things. And even stranger was the way Guide answered his questions so painstakingly. At any rate, their talks were less dialogues than lectures.

They began like this. One day Guide appeared in the main house carrying two LP records, explaining that the new sound system in the annex only handled CDs. Dancer had gone out with Patron to the barbershop, and Ogi was to watch things at home while they were away. Guide listened to his two records, one after another, both performances of the same Mozart symphony—number 40 with Bruno Walter conducting—in one case the Berlin Philharmonic, the other the Columbia Symphony Orchestra. Ogi asked him if the two performances were very different, to which Guide replied in a rather curt way that they were both recordings of Walter in his final years and of course they weren't the same, but you couldn't say they were all that different, either.

Ogi suddenly felt like asking a question that had popped into his mind many times after he'd begun his regular visits to Patron's office. Guide was sitting silently at a right angle to him, and Ogi was distinctly uncomfortable at his sitting there right in front of him. He may well have been influenced by hearing the subtle shades of difference in the two versions of the Mozart symphony by the same conductor, though he couldn't exactly put into words *how* this affected him.

"In your faith," he finally managed to ask, "what is salvation?"

Guide's response was no longer abrupt; he weighed each word carefully.

"When I'm asked whether I have a clear notion of salvation, I can't say that I do. Some days I feel the need for salvation very strongly, only to find that the next day I'm not so worked up about it. It's as if the weight of my heart seeking salvation makes me sink to the bottom of a tank of water. And then I rise again to break the surface. When this happens, I think that yesterday my desire for salvation was such that my mind and body were wrenched by it, yet here I am today, so calm. Doesn't this sense of calm, though, arise from the knowledge that my strong conviction that I will reach salvation is proof that indeed I *will*?

"I suffer sometimes, writhing in pain with the need for salvation. And because of this, I don't want to try to reach some rushed, clumsy, stillborn version. I just believe that I'm on the road to salvation and carry on from there."

"What does it feel like, to need salvation so much that you're in agony?" Ogi asked.

Guide lifted his head and gazed at Ogi, the look in his eyes half serious, half amused. His expression oozed sincerity. What he was about to say spoke to the core of his being, and Ogi could see in him the selfless, caring teacher of old.

"This is just based on my experience," Guide began, letting his head hang again. "There comes a time in a person's life when he feels the *unity* of his self disintegrate and realizes he can't go on living this way. You start life as an organism that knows nothing, and when you reach a certain age (for me, it was when I was past thirty), the glue that holds you together comes undone and you have no clue how to put yourself back together. And before long you die like this, broken in bits, and that's the end of you. It's no different from a bug's life, I thought, and I suffered knowing this. Now when I think of it, though, comparing myself to a bug was bit arrogant on my part.

"You find yourself seeking salvation, and though this desire isn't always right there on the surface it never dies out and remains deep down inside you. Just when I was feeling this way, another crisis occurred in my life and I happened to run across Patron. When I began working with him later on, though it didn't take me to salvation, I did find the agony of feeling my mind and body being dismembered was, to a certain extent, alleviated.

"As time passed, I became a little independent of Patron and formed my own sect within the church. This became the reason he and I were driven to the point of doing the Somersault. Now it's just the two of us. But if you ask whether meeting Patron and having gone through hardships with him has made me reach salvation, the answer is no, it did not.

"Here you need to understand that in some basic sense Patron, too, is split in two. At one extreme there's the Patron who has mystical experiences. Before the Somersault I helped him relate the visions he had as part of this. I clung to both of these extremes in turn.

"He'd go over to the *other side,* and make a connection with God quite smoothly, but those mystical experiences were, for Patron, such a trial that it was painful to be beside him and see how much it took out of him. My role was to transmit the experiences he described in that condition, and I became his closest companion.

"Once he overcame his exhaustion, though, he'd begin to consider God on his own. This was the other extreme—the fact that he didn't think of God in personified terms—which again led to suffering. I said to him, 'But you've come face-to-face with God, haven't you? You go over to the *other side,* and you receive your visions from something that can only be called God. Never once as I've worked as your translator have I doubted that.' But Patron was unable to agree with my words of encouragement.

"Patron enters a deep trance where he's swept away to the *other side* and, through this experience that's completely out of his hands, he's with God. But once he returns to this side and his mind and spirit are back under his control and he regains his identity, he insists that the personified God he'd pictured all these years is not the way things really are. And I think he suffers mightily because of it.

"Before long Patron began to think the following ideas, which formed his basic teachings before the Somersault. 'God is in the world. If that weren't true,' he explained, 'the whole world would be as scattered and pointless as the pain you feel tells you it is. Imagine another Earth existing on the outer reaches of the solar system,' he said, 'or maybe beyond the Milky Way. A world where God does not exist. Everything on that planet is in pieces, so much so that even if human beings appeared and evolved, they wouldn't be able to maintain their civilization for many centuries. Human beings would be scattered and die out, and the world would be bereft of people. Whether this is a kind of wilderness-as-hell or a paradise for creatures other than man, I don't know. . . .

"'On our planet, mankind hasn't self-destructed but somehow continues to cling precariously to life. Somehow or other order is maintained, and it's hard to deny that this is because of God's *presence.* Millions of people— Jews, Christians, Muslims, Buddhists—have personified this God, but I don't see God this way. Though I do want to construct a theory about this God who most definitely *does exist.*' This is what Patron said.

"'Wide awake on this side,' Patron continued, 'I want to find out exactly what it is I confront when I go over to the *other side.* Once I get a clear picture of this, the world shouldn't be in pieces for me anymore. Since this conviction that the world is not in pieces is something I've created on *this* side, with my eyes open, I can feel relieved about it. Once I can grasp that sense of relief, my awakened spirit can put in proper perspective the God I see in my visions—and this should lead to a deep and profound sense of spiritual peace I can experience in *both* worlds. But if I die before I can attain that peace, then I'll be torn between the two worlds and my disintegrated body and soul will flutter down into the abyss.'

"Patron was so open to me, I believed everything he said. And I was certain that someday, through this man who himself would be saved, I would reach salvation too. But I also considered at times what it would be like if I *didn't* reach salvation through him, and intimations of that frightening thought made me shudder. Patron seemed to struggle with the idea of the need for salvation in an incomparably deeper way than I ever did. One thing I was sure of, though, was this: Apart from his intercession, I could never be saved."

As these memories of what Guide had told him came back in snatches, Ogi once again had a sense of what had woken him up. *Ah,* he thought, *this* is what I felt earlier. He opened his eyes to the dark purplish gloom and turned on the hard flat bed to face the man-made lake.

Later on, when he reviewed the order of events in his mind, he was certain this is how it happened, but soon after he turned in the direction of what he sensed, in a sky that was so jet black he hadn't closed the curtains before he went to bed, far off in the still-falling rain, he saw it happen. A large light lemon-yellow disc floated up, at the top of which were five shining hemispheres. The lower part was a giant black upright pillar in which were three shining rectangular doors. It was as if a UFO had flown though the vast darkness and suddenly come to a halt.

Ah! Ogi heard a voice call out, something halfway between a sigh and a shriek.

The cry came from Dancer's room . . . so this wasn't just some illusion he alone was seeing! Ogi looked hard into the gloom and saw the glowing saucer and the pillar with its bright doors open soon shut in the rocklike darkness.

I believe God is in this world too, Ogi thought, half asleep, but not a personified God who has the facial features of any particular race—a God instead who would appear like this structure, built of light and darkness. Ogi knew, though, that in the morning he wouldn't be able to regain this *total understanding* he now had, and that he wouldn't speak of it to Dancer. And certainly not to Patron.

18: Acceptance and Rejection (I)

1

After it grew light out and Ogi had awakened again, he lay still in his wooden box of a bed, waiting for time to pass. The night before, he and Dancer had talked until late and had made do with just a light dinner of ham and lettuce sandwiches. They'd found the sandwiches at a local market, and though the place didn't seem to have many customers Dancer declared the ham to be fantastic and showed a great deal of interest in the people who produced it locally. That was all they ate, washed down by some milk, so now, in the morning, Ogi didn't feel any special need to use the toilet. He also hesitated to use the bathroom before Dancer had a chance to.

Ogi gazed up from his bed at the foliage of the stand of Japanese oaks that cut off his view of the broad sky. From the window on the lake side, there were overly luxuriant pomegranates and camellias bursting with leaves as far as the eye could see. The trees were covered with young leaves, bright green against the cloudless sky; only the places where the leaves overlapped were dark green, like a multilayered watercolor. A childhood memory came to him—from a school outing, perhaps, he couldn't recall exactly—of lying down like this and gazing up at tree branches from this angle.

Soon the whole area was filled with a cloud of soft fist-sized little lumps descending from the sky and letting out high-pitched screeches: a flock of wild birds. Two or three of the birds, like puffy little white balls, hung upside down on the tips of the slender branches of the Japanese oaks. Before long, in search of bugs to eat, the flock flew off to another corner of the slope, and a profound silence returned.

After a while, the same shout he'd heard last night came from the next room. Ogi sat up in bed, ready to meet the intruder. Dancer came in. She had on green pajamas, and her mouth was open wider than usual.

"There's fresh blood! Just below the window!" Dancer said to Ogi reproachfully.

Ogi had slept in his underwear. He wrapped the light bedcover around his waist before going over to the window and shoving open the heavy single pane. And as he looked out, he too was taken aback. From the western edge of the house a pellucid stream seemed to meander over the grass and flow into the lake. From the stone apron where the stream turned, a red belt seeped upward toward them. Ogi took a breath and, after realizing what he was seeing, said, "They're lake crabs that've floated up because of all the rain last night."

Dancer looked back at him with a look of disgust, then took her turn looking out the window.

"They're pretty small crabs, and so many of them. They're not even boiled, yet look how red they are. Anyone would think it's blood flowing."

Her slender taut calves emerged from under her pajama bottoms. Her whole body, from her thighs, butt, and waist—trained through her dancing—to her straight shoulders and thin neck, was a strange mix of firmness and fragility.

"You spent your childhood in Tokyo," Ogi said, "and earlier in downtown Asahikawa, right? I imagine you've never seen crabs float up like this before."

"So you know all about the flora and fauna in Hokkaido. But do you know the names of the birds that were just here? The Japanese great tit."

Standing beside the window, Dancer turned toward Ogi, seated on his box bed, the color quickly returning to her face.

"I agree with Asa-san that this is a special place," she said, trying to regain the upper hand. "I guess I jumped to conclusions. I find it amazing how the abandoned followers of Patron and Guide, while the two of them were in hell, laid the groundwork right here, in this land. You know something? In the middle of the night, I saw a sign that the land here accepts our church!"

Ogi recalled what he'd seen the night before. But he'd also been there when Dancer had been handed the complete set of keys to the chapel. It was hard to imagine that someone else had gotten into the chapel and turned on the lights in the middle of the night.

Leaving Ogi to his thoughts, Dancer disappeared toward the bathroom near the entrance, her pajamas swishing like a dance costume.

As they ate a repeat of last night's supper, they heard a new disturbance from the far shore. Dancer was sitting at the dining table diagonally across from Ogi, her back to the east as they ate, and they both turned to look at the glistening trees and the building, newly washed in the rain. In the forest behind the chapel, people hidden by the stand of trees were rushing by. In the wind blowing up from the south there was the sound of feet, a line of people cutting through the forest.

"Lumberjacks, maybe?" she asked. "Heading toward jobs in the woods?"

"If that's what it is, it'd just be a couple of them. And wouldn't they use animal trails to go up the hill?"

"People hunting wild boars?"

"It sounds too orderly, like a troop of Boy Scouts out on a hike."

"I thought this was a quiet place, but I guess not."

"But at least we're not being surrounded by people with placards opposing the arrival of the 'fanatics,'" Ogi said.

Dancer said she wanted to go over that morning to see if the cottage Asa-san had suggested for Patron to use was suitable. Before she went down along the narrow path toward the dam she went out to look at the crabs close up, only to report back to Ogi they must have slipped into new holes that had opened up in the soil because they'd disappeared. Her shoes were muddy, and in one hand she held a newly emerged brown cicada on a butterbur leaf. One of the cicada's forelegs was missing its first joint, and as it tried to clamber up the higher edge of the butterbur leaf it tumbled down in a comical way.

"I imagine it must have been pretty surprised after spending a thousand days tucked away under the soil to emerge and find it doesn't have enough legs to cling to the trees. Would you choose a branch where its cry can be heard easily and put it there? The reason they cry is in order to mate, right?"

Ogi took the cicada, leaf and all, and placed the poor little creature on the branch of an oak that faced the lake, the leaves heavy after the rain.

When they stood at the entrance to the house set aside for Patron, an entrance made up of round stones held together with cement, they remembered they had left all the keys for the other buildings on top of the lectern in the chapel. Dancer went back to retrieve them.

For the five minutes she was gone, the sound of the water coursing down the channel from the forest into the lake grew noticeably louder. Worried about Dancer, Ogi peeked in from the entrance of the chapel carved into the wall. In front of the space between the lined-up chairs and the far wall, Dancer was down on her knees, leaning against the lectern. Ogi removed his shoes, went inside, and found her gazing up at him like some young girl who'd been beaten as she pointed in front of her. On the floor lay a small unblemished little skull facing in their direction. Thigh bones, ribs, and other large bones were laid out to form a complete skeleton, the finger bones and other smaller bones pushed over to one side. Next to this were fragments of bones, like small branches, laid out to spell YOUNG FIREFLIES.

Dancer's shoulders shuddered slightly, and in a tearful voice she said, "I thought that was a *sign,* but all it was was them stealing the keys to this place and doing this. In the morning we weren't likely to come over here, so they grew impatient and kicked up a racket. I can't believe how cunning these people are who don't want Patron's church here."

2

After Ogi made a call from the office beside the chapel, Asa-san got in touch with Mr. Matsuo, the head priest, and they both rushed over. They didn't think the bones had anything to do with a crime, but they didn't disturb them until finally Asa-san told Mr. Matsuo to gather them all up in a cardboard box. Ogi returned to the office where he'd made the phone call, and Asa-san told them about the YOUNG FIREFLIES.

"That's a name found in legends from the Old Town, the section apart from Maki Town. The name and practice died out long ago, but when one of the elderly people in the main house of my family passed away, they revived the practice at his funeral because he put great stock in the old customs. I think I have a good idea where those bones came from.

"I'm sure you got this impression yesterday when you looked up from the road along the riverbed, but the land around here is shaped like the inside of an urn. Young Fireflies refers to a custom where the young people of the town light torches and climb up to the top of the forest at night. The young people here just liked the name, apart from the ceremony associated with it, and gave it to their young men's association.

"Children are basically very conservative, you know. Your moving in here marks a change in the status quo, so they're against it. I'd heard rumors that they were eager to do something to express their opposition. If this is what they came up with, I'd have to say it's pretty scurrilous. *Scurrilous* is the word old people use here when something's vulgar. . . .

"Since it's come to this, I'll have my husband talk with the junior high principal.

"Be that as it may, I was in charge of the keys for this building. I thought if I let them make spare keys for the chapel, they might use it for their junior high chorus practice. But they've repaid good with evil, you could say. It's all quite scurrilous, and I'm ashamed and truly sorry you had to be upset this way."

The next day, Patron, accompanied by Ms. Tachibana and Morio, arrived at the Matsuyama airport. Twenty or so former radical-faction members joined them there, having driven down from Tokyo in a caravan of sedans and a minivan. After linking up with Kizu, Ikuo, Dr. Koga, and Mr. Hanawa, who'd arrived at Matsuyama Station on the Yosan Line, the entire group arrived at the Hollow in force.

Apart from Dancer and Ogi, this was the first contingent of the new church to arrive in the area, and a few local people waited along the road by the riverbed to watch their arrival. In the lead car Morio sat next to Patron in the backseat, dressed quite stylishly in a long midnight-blue overcoat, gray chinos, and lightly tinted metal-frame glasses. Seeing him sitting there gazing up with his splendid forehead and strongly etched nose, someone reported later to Asa-san that he was sure Morio must be the founder of the church.

Having set up his residence in the Hollow, Patron decided to meet within the week with the widow of the founder of the defunct church who had transferred the chapel to them. With so many new people coming from the outside to live in the area, the question of securing enough food for all of them had become a pressing matter, and as one practical step toward solving this, Asa-san introduced the widow, Satchan, the owner of the Farm, to Patron.

Asa-san had been hoping that Patron would talk to Mr. Matsuo, herself, and others who had been connected with the Church of the Flaming Green Tree about the new church he planned to start here. The people of Maki Town, too, had expressed the same hope, and now that the church had actually begun moving in, they again proposed such a meeting to Asa-san, who was acting as intermediary between the church and the town government.

One practical issue soon arose. The group in Maki Town opposing Patron had already published a broadside revealing that the former radical faction would be participating in Patron's restarted religious movement and that one of the leaders of this faction, Mr. Hanawa, would be living here with his colleagues to help Dr. Koga. What's more—and this was the critical point— the town would be hiring Dr. Koga to run the clinic in the Old Town. As before, objections sprang up among the town leaders that the former radical faction, the one the newspapers had accused of the death of Guide, was going to be moving into the Hollow.

These issues would normally have been discussed by the mayor and Patron, but Patron was asked beforehand to talk in an informal town hall meeting with local citizens.

Asa-san, who had already convinced Ogi that she was a person who held considerable sway locally, as well as someone who didn't beat around the bush when it came to formulating plans, proposed that Patron first meet with Satchan, and Patron agreed. Dancer took advantage of this opportunity to ask Ogi to seek a more detailed explanation than they'd heard before as to how the former radical faction was to be dealt with.

What worried Ogi most was that the widow of the founder of the Church of the Flaming Green Tree might not like it if internal affairs of the church were discussed with local people—especially in the chapel. But Satchan agreed to attend, as long as Asa-san and Mr. Matsuo were also there, and for the first time in a long while entered the chapel that her church had once owned. Town officials had also wanted to attend, but Asa-san had been able to limit their attendance to just a few of the more influential members.

"How do you feel about the religion you've created, leading people to salvation—and about your own salvation?" Satchan asked, to start off the meeting.

"Well," replied Patron, recoiling somewhat, "didn't you and your late husband also found a church?"

"Satchan merely wants to ask an honest question of someone who is involved in a similar movement—and in the same place, no less," Asa-san explained encouragingly.

"I don't feel so much that I'm continuing some teachings of the founder of our church," Satchan explained in a softer tone. "I spend more time considering how my husband felt about things himself, as a flesh-and-blood human being. I believe he tried to lead his followers to salvation, but when I remember how he died I wonder whether he cared about his *own* salvation at all. I've been pondering this for quite some time."

Patron clearly relaxed when he heard this. He also seemed to show interest in this earnest individualistic woman, well into her middle years.

"Before I did the now-infamous Somersault," Patron said, "when I was quite involved in religious activities, I don't think I really seriously considered my own salvation either. It was after I fell into hell that the question of my salvation became a pressing matter. When you lead a religious organization, you soon become terribly busy, rushing around like crazy all the time. I had no time to consider whether I was saved, or wasn't saved, or even whether I would reach salvation in the end or not. What I wanted most was to lead the suffering young people who came to us for salvation. I actually groped for ways to push them in that direction.

"What I know from my own experience—and this is the same both at the beginning of the church and when it was at its height—is that there was indeed a way for the suffering people who came to our church to find the salvation they sought. All of them were proceeding toward their own salvation. The greater their awareness that they were not yet saved, the greater their conviction that they were on the path to salvation, despite the difficulties they might encounter. In fact, it was the very awareness that they hadn't yet reached salvation that accelerated their faith.

"As I've thought about my own salvation, or my image of salvation in the ten years since the Somersault, my ideas have become simplified—boiled down to a single mathematical formula, if you will. When a person thinks about death or is actually facing death, if he's convinced that his life and death are fine the way they are, isn't he saved?

"In my new church, my followers should be able to say, when they think about death or are actually staring down death, *Let's go! Hallelujah!* is another way of putting it. The basic orientation of my movement is to lead people gently in that direction. In order to do that, though, one has to truly repent. As long as one has a true awareness that the end of the world is near, this can be accomplished.

"The new church's religious movement I've been contemplating is that simple—that naive, even. What I want to convey to you is that in the ten years since the Somersault this is the kind of simplicity, naive, unadorned, and stripped of anything extraneous, that has occupied my mind."

"The Savior of the Church of the Flaming Green Tree, that's what we called my husband," Satchan said, "if the Savior were alive now, I think he might not see what you've said as so simple or naive. Quite frankly, he wasn't very educated when it came to religious ideas, yet he was possessed by spiritual matters and in that sense was an unfortunate person. He was still a sort of lackadaisical savior when his old enemies stoned him to death.

"He was called Savior like you were, but he wasn't the *ultimate* Savior. He believed that until the advent of the ultimate Savior there would be countless saviors, that when the final Savior appeared all other saviors, being linked with him, would—in the end—become *real* saviors. He gave a sermon on this, here in this chapel. . . .

"He recognized himself as a sort of lukewarm savior, one of those countless lackadaisical saviors. . . . That's the sort of thinking he wanted to believe in. Fifteen years after his death, I've grown more sympathetic to that view.

"If I understand your remarks correctly, putting my own spin on them, since I believe my husband's one of the ones who will be tied with the real Savior, I know that even when I'm on the verge of death I'll feel saved. The details of my own personal history would surprise you, but I would like to second what you say, as far as my own life is concerned. *Let's go!* Though I have the feeling that when I'm actually on my deathbed and say that, there won't be anyone around to hear me."

"There *is* a God," Patron said, "a God who is the whole of nature, who encompasses everything, your spirit and body included. Even these ideas that have arisen from your unusual life were already included in the principles that God created for the world."

From the moment that Satchan entered the chapel where Ogi and the others were waiting, and sat down in the row of chairs lined up beside the podium facing Patron, every church member was impressed. She was a beautiful woman, but something about her also gave the impression of a mild-featured *man*. She was also quite tall for a Japanese woman. Her curly hair, mixed with white, fell in a natural way on both sides of her prominent forehead. Her face had not the slightest trace of fat. In the way she looked straight at Patron as she spoke to him, you could sense an independent tough-minded spirit but also a clear open-mindedness brought about by her experience.

"I came here because I wanted to meet the people who are taking over the building used by the Church of the Flaming Green Tree," Satchan went on, "and also because I feel responsible to the local people here for your activities. People in your group were involved in some major terrorist activities, so the mayor and members of the town council asked us to find out what sort of group was moving in here. We do recognize, mind you, that your Somersault put a stop to the radical faction's plans.

"We had a group in our church, too, that began to make waves, and as we confronted this we began to steer the church back to the small gatherings with which it began. Right at that critical juncture we lost our leader, and our church fell apart. But your church is getting back on its feet, with this region as your stage. My main concern is that this radical faction might once again play a major role."

"I quite understand your concern," Patron said. "Our church started out much like yours, and until it reached a certain size it was basically just a prayer group. There was another person who made this group with me and helped me run it—Guide, the man whose terrible death I'm sure you've heard about. His idea was to gather together young people who'd been specially trained in the sciences, and he created the Izu Research Center for them.

"While living there communally, these young people continued research in their special fields, and as they began reflecting on their own faith they started debating the entire direction the church was taking. In the end they came up with their own unique course of action, which could be summarized like this: Their faith tells them the end of the world is near, which allows them to repent and prepare themselves as righteous people. As the righteous, then, they call on all mankind to repent. But how exactly do you go about preaching repentance to the masses? The church was pretty vague on this point, and the young people needed a clear-cut model, so they began concentrating on a concrete direction their ideas could take. In the end they went past the point of no return.

"At the time I was at the Tokyo headquarters, my role that of spiritual leader for the ordinary followers in their walk of faith. Guide was in charge of keeping contact with the Izu Research Institute. Which isn't to say he was in charge of the movement that was starting there—he wasn't. The institute was self-governing.

"Guide would take the funding that the Tokyo headquarters had allotted to the institute and hand it over to their accountant. But he refused to exert any direct influence on the management of the institute. He was more like their sponsor. When things were pretty much all set up the way they wanted, he took me there to deliver a sermon, but I'm sure he never spoke to them on his own about faith. The self-governing board of the institute selected board members whose job it was to oversee everything—from all the various research projects to matters of faith.

"Guide wanted to make a research facility free of the archaic structures of universities, and by word of mouth he gathered together a group of researchers who felt stifled in their former institutions. Naturally, he also chose people who were already members of the church—people who'd graduated from college or graduate school and were already working, but suffered setbacks, either through illness or car accidents or the like. People who went through rehabilitation and then entered the church. One of those people was Dr. Koga, who'll be in charge of the clinic in the Old Town.

"Some of these people were hoping to use their research at the institute as a stepping-stone, a way to circumvent Japanese academia and obtain a position in an American or European university. If anything, Guide was happy with this sort of ambition. He often stayed over at the Izu Institute, and when he returned he couldn't stop telling me, despite my complete ignorance of all these cutting-edge scientific fields, about how well these young researchers were progressing."

3

"The people at the institute," Patron continued, "were dyed-in-the-wool scientists. Also, as I've said, there were people who, in university, graduate school, or at work, had suffered various disappointments and frustrations. But thanks to the wonderful facilities, experimental lab apparatus, and the free system of research at the institute, these people once again came face-to-face with the crisis they thought they'd solved—a more fundamental crisis, one they began to see included spiritual questions.

"They also began to take a good hard look at the religious aspect of the church. Some of the members sent me a list of requests, which made me appreciate how tense the situation was there. The members who wanted to see me were ones I had personal memories of, who after renouncing the world had joined the church before being selected as members of the research institute. And this is what they told me:

> "Our souls have been aroused, and we've drawn close to your religious ideas. Through Guide's good offices we've been selected for something that's almost too good to be true, to be able to live together with other church members and at the same time carry on our individual research.
>
> "For some time we've been meeting after work, holding discussions about the happiness and peace that come from the visions of the other side you've provided. As you preached, our prayers were based not on some outside source but on our inner selves as a source of energy, and we began to hold joint prayer sessions, with prayers that welled up spontaneously from within. Guide told us our prayer group was the best and most natural group in the whole church.
>
> "With this prayer group as a foothold, one after another of the members of the research team who weren't church members came to faith. As we met more often, we began to have doubts that our prayers would really reach the other side, just by continuing our lives as they were— supported by the church to conduct research, and praying as we did. Through our prayers we stood ready, like a sprinter bent over at the starting line. Both body and spirit expectant, waiting with bated breath for the sound of the starting gun. But was this really enough?
>
> "As we prayerfully await the starting signal, our bodies and minds tense, it's painful. That pain does not come from the feebleness of our prayers. We talked about it at our meeting, and one person said it's the

pain of our thirsting souls, and surprisingly everyone said they felt the same way. Which brings us to our requests to you.

"Patron, you give us a vision of the end of the world, of the end time. And you call for repentance. From the bottom of our hearts we feel this as we pray. You bring back words that are given to you directly on the *other side,* which Guide then helps convey to this side. Those words strike us deeply and urge us on to ever more devotion to prayer.

"So this is what we ask of you, Patron: *What does God want us to do?* Tell us straight out. Why are we at the starting blocks? For what purpose are we training our bodies and our spirits? Use your trances to find out for us, we beg of you. Perhaps you have already seen this. Is this vision so frightening you shrink away from it, not even revealing it to Guide, and claim that God has not yet spoken?

"We are waiting for you, Patron, to transmit the words of God. Prayer teaches us this—that the only thing we have to accomplish in this world is to receive these words of God and use them as our basis for action. We are scientists, which means that more than other people we can clearly hear the approaching steps of the end of the world. And we are zealously awaiting your words. Didn't you receive us into the church, and didn't Guide select us as members of the research institute because of this? Because we listen to these words? Are we really so fragile that we can't bear the burden of those terrible words? We beg of you, please accept our petition."

"When Guide brought this petition to me from Izu, it was still sealed. My eyesight is bad, so when I opened it I had Guide read it aloud. When he finished reading it Guide averted his eyes with a noncommittal look, a look that bored into me nonetheless. It troubled me that Guide, who had created the research institute and who'd spoken of the trust he felt for these young people and how much he was looking forward to their future, would be so noncommittal when he transmitted this ardent petition. These young people were pressing me to come to a decision, yet Guide kept a cool distance from things, waiting for me to speak. It felt worse than being isolated and alone—it was like I'd been completely abandoned.

"Okay! I thought, coming to a decision. There wasn't any solid basis for my decision, just a voice deep inside me saying that now was not the time to let the chance slip by, that I had to take the leap if I didn't want to be lackadaisical for the rest of my life. And I followed this voice. I said this to Guide: 'Isn't the One who summons me each time to my trances waiting to hear from me about the appeals in this petition? Up till now I've never posed any questions on the *other side* about what our church should be doing, the reason being that, as the church grew, so did my sense of responsibility toward the lives of the members on *this* side. Also it was my personal responsibility to follow the call that I hear on the *other side,* no matter how far beyond our ordinary logic it goes. Listening to that call made me start this religious movement in the first place. But with so many followers now, in order to lead the church I have to give priority to the logic of *our* world. I have a responsibility to do that.

"'But one of the things I always awaken to on the other side is the fact that the logic of this world is meaningless. As the leader of the church—and as mediator between this side and the other—I have to carry out this role to the full, not letting the pipeline between the two sides clog up.

"'Next time I have a deep trance, though,' I told Guide, 'I'm going to grab this petition by the neck, drag it along with me, and ask that very question: *What does God want us to do?* No matter how terrible the reply is, I'm going to bring that vision back with me. And you'd better steel yourself to translate it. I won't be controlled by the logic of our world. The next time a *sign* is gouged out in my soul as a fresh wound in my trance, I'm not going to equivocate. That's got to be the only way out of the split I've suffered for so long.'

"Guide took me seriously, but there was still something opaque about his reactions. Blast it all! I thought. This is the first delusion I have to overcome through my own decision. As long as this delusion remains within me, my comrade who supports me in the faith will never be free. I have to overcome this for Guide's sake too, I told myself.

"And so I waited for a deep trance to take hold of me. At the time, I went into a trance about once a month. Once I started to wait, though, four weeks passed, then five, and finally eight weeks. Nothing. This brought home to me once more that the trances came to me from the other side, they weren't something I could initiate.

"I was frantic. Irritated that so much time had passed without a reply, the members of the research institute who'd written the petition said they wanted to send a representative to headquarters. Before that, Guide said he needed to talk with them and went off to Izu. That night I pretended that a major trance had taken hold of me. I managed such an enthusiastic performance that the person taking care of me reported to Guide that my trance this time was so deep and violent that afterward he was afraid I'd be weaker than I had ever been before. The next day Guide hurried back to be by my side. And as I always did, I began to speak, so that Guide would be able to translate the visions I had on the *other side.*

"At the time I didn't think about how I was deceiving Guide. I just thought I was having the same kind of trance I'd had for years, only now I'd been able to make it happen on my own. And actually I exhausted my spiritual strength doing that. I spent the time during my false trance thinking I was standing in front of the Almighty I faced whenever I went over to the *other side,* asking a question and listening carefully to the response. And I was convinced I could hear the answer.

"I'd always received messages from the *other side,* so I was all set to listen. What I heard was a response I'd made up myself, but as I listened to it I didn't consider it different from my usual visions. Wasn't this the very first response from the *other side* that I'd consciously extracted? If the vision I received in this way ran counter to the will of the *other side,* I thought, surely I would be properly punished.

"*If I'm transmitting as Your word my own vision that runs counter to Your will,* I prayed, *then kill me. Separate me from the pain of being torn apart and turn me into a handful of dust. I can't continue as the leader of over a thousand people in such a lackadaisical state. It's easy for You, isn't it, to make my weakened heart have an attack? I am creating Your vision with my own will, but I am doing it believing in You, heart and soul. Have pity on me! No matter how it may turn out, please give me Your power.*

"As I prayed like this, I pretended to have a vision and mumbled some things, which Guide translated as this:

"*'I am standing at a point where I can see the "oneness" overflowing from the Beginning. I'm seeing this together with the young Izu researchers. Once more the entire world is flowing back to that original 'Oneness.' Think of it as the opposite of the Big Bang. As the "implosion" of the whole world on this "oneness." Help us with this infinitely huge, infinitely swift movement. God awaits a truly spontaneous call, one in response to His own call. Your call has reached God, and God's answer has come back. Now is the time—the time for the battle of repentance at the end of the world.*

"*'If you fear you won't be able to hear God's answer, concentrate on your own question. Every single perception you have within yourselves is already within God. Our calls to God are already within Him, the way we receive His message, the way each of us reacts to it—they too are already within Him. Hallelujah!'*

"Guide transmitted this to the Izu Research Institute as the answer that God gave me, and the expectant young people there abandoned their various projects and flung themselves into preparation for the end time. In this world where the unrepentant oppress the repentant, they arrayed themselves for the final battle."

4

"This is how the group of young people, later dubbed the radical faction by the press, took over the leadership of the Izu Research Institute," Patron continued. "Guide reported to me on their activities, but I never tried to alter their course or force them to slow down. If what the radical faction was doing was wrong, I imagined I would have another vision, like the ones I always had—a *real* vision—telling me to put a stop to them. But that never happened.

"So what kind of preparations did these young scientists and technicians make for the battle for repentance? They were generally divided into those working on physics and those working on chemistry. My vision encouraged the ones on the physics side. The term *implosion* coincided with the concept of the manipulation of nuclear materials to create a chain reaction. Led by a specialist named Mr. Omuro, they turned their attention to building a device, capable of being transported by a small number of people, that would transform a nuclear power plant into a nuclear bomb. The chemistry researchers were to give logistical backup. Of course, all of this was aborted by the Somersault.

"At this point I was busy with religious affairs in our Tokyo headquarters, while Guide spent all his time at the Izu Research Institute. He returned to our headquarters three times in two months. He made one trip on his own to get approval for a new research budget. They were gradually needing more and more funding for their activities. In other words, he came to withdraw some money from headquarters.

"The other times he came were to take care of me when I'd gone into a major trance and to work with me to put the vision I had into words. Through these trances the sense of mutual trust, the basic need we had for each other, was renewed. However, the days we spent together gradually produced an awkward atmosphere between us.

"Whenever he heard that I'd fallen into a trance, Guide would race back from the Izu Research Institute. Each time he'd bring the hopes and fears of his scientists with him: their burning desire to know when the order would come to take action, the hope that I would provide the vision that would make this clear. Each working at their own tasks, the physicists and the chemists were uneasy about the struggle that lay ahead.

"Once a certain amount of preparation is laid, it's hard to have to wait forever. They'd taken the first step and were fearful that the long arm of the law might reach out to seize them. Until their plan was put into action, they were anxious, too, about whether their faith would hold out. Guide reported to me that some of the female researchers had appealed to him about this.

"But when I was on the *other side,* I received no instructions. Guide pressed me, and when I was about to enter a trance I would pray to be given an order to give them, so they could take action. I wanted this so much, and I prayed as I went into a trance, and it was all quite painful and trying. In the end when I returned, completely spent, the message that Guide heard from me and reworked into ordinary language told them neither to take action nor to desist.

"After one of these deep trances, when I was exhausted and recovering in bed, Guide became terribly irritated and spoke to me more gruffly than he ever had before.

"Stop fabricating things, he told me, just because you say you can't get any orders from the other side. I'm *your* Prophet, you know—and also for those serious, outstanding young people who want repentance more than anything, I'm *their* Prophet as well!

"As I looked back at Guide, who was glaring at me as he sat in a low chair beside me, folding his long legs, I realized he'd seen through my phony vision, and I felt ashamed.

"Knowing full well that I was lying, Guide had still gone ahead and interpreted it as I wanted him to, transmitting it to the young people who'd sent me the petition. Not only that, he'd done everything in his power to aid the researchers who, encouraged by my words, had begun making concrete plans to put them into practice. He'd been so earnest about restructuring the research institute, doing all he could to accomplish this and passing along the questions the researchers had for me. And yet he knew I was lying! How did he know that?

"After all these years with me, had Guide lost confidence in the one who pointed toward the end of the world? And in desperation had he made a gamble? While fabricating a vision, I was trying to convince myself that as long as there was not a second vision that denied the first one, that meant it was confirmed. Most likely Guide, my longtime spiritual companion, felt the same way.

"After having invited the young people to take action, and having done his utmost to aid their preparations, wasn't he afraid—just at the stage when they would be putting their plans into action—to admit that whatever they did from now on had nothing to do with the will of the *other side*? Weren't his misgivings the same exact things I was afraid of? The thought made me shudder.

"Events quickly moved toward the Somersault. I assume you saw the farce on television. Here I'll just touch on the how it came about and the plan we put together with the authorities.

"The idea for the Somersault was quite sudden. Already the relationship between Guide and me was strained. One evening he arrived unannounced. He stormed into my bedroom and yelled at me that the young people had decided to implement their own insurrection. They were going to occupy several nuclear power plants. This would mean not only their own deaths but the annihilation of the church. '*They have to be stopped!*' Guide shouted. '*I don't have the power to do it, and neither do you, but we have to do something drastic!*'

"I hesitated to hear the plan Guide had already formulated. I blamed him and asked him why the young people in the research institute decided to take action unilaterally. Guide said that since yesterday they'd been insisting they also could hear—all on their own—a voice from the *other side*.

"I was frantic. I'd fabricated a message to the young people to the effect that God was ordering them to start in a new direction. But hadn't this been God tricking me into an unconscious self-defensive maneuver because I didn't want to hear His actual frightening voice?

"And now, carrying things one step further, when both my conscious and unconscious were doing their utmost to reject this, wasn't I being tricked again by a different strategy—the young radical faction's own collective illusion—that made all resistance futile?

"Guide could see how shaken I was. He glared at me; he said, 'I won't let either you or the young people in Izu destroy our church. If I have to drag you around with a rope around your neck, I'm going to make sure you take responsibility for this! Those folks in Izu will learn their lesson!'

"As all of you saw on television, I had to do some things that were far more shameful than being dragged around with a rope around my neck. The ones who suffered even more directly because of the Somersault, though, were those members of the shock corps of the radical faction, especially those responsible for the Threshold Crosser device. A hurried meeting was held between us and the police, the federal authorities, and executives of the power company. We decided that my Somersault announcement would avoid any mention of this device. Mr. Omuro, though taken into custody, not only avoided going to trial but vanished altogether. There are rumors he escaped to an American military base on Okinawa. Some say he was given a series of electroshock treatments and completely lost his memory. Others say they've seen him wandering among the homeless on the streets. Another rumor has it he was stabbed to death by the *yakuza*. This worried Guide most of all. This was the most base and cruel outcome that Guide feared would happen because of the Somersault.

"During that period I felt a great joy and at the same time a deep fear. Because I was convinced that God existed, in a realm beyond my arbitrariness. Even if it was a useless bit of resistance, I wanted to betray and deny that God. I was resolved to do that."

19: Acceptance and Rejection (II)

1

Patron's talk was serving as an inaugural sermon for their new chapel. Sitting nearby, Ogi could tell how deeply moved Ikuo was by what he heard, though he himself had a hard time following it all. At this point Dancer raised up her pale face and spoke.

"I'd like to hear from Ikuo too," she said. "You're a new member who had nothing to do with the church before the Somersault. But you'd been interested in Patron for a long time and got close to him very quickly."

"You'll have to take my background into consideration," Ikuo answered briefly, still under the spell of Patron's magnetism.

"Why don't you start there," Dancer said. "I don't fully understand the reasons why you were so attracted by Patron that you became an ardent member of the church almost immediately. I know you said you came to the office originally to see me, someone you'd come into contact with a long time ago who was now working for the founder of the church, but that's not the whole story. You knew quite a lot about the Somersault already, didn't you?"

Ikuo looked like he'd finally made up his mind to speak.

"It's true I was interested in Patron and Guide's Somersault," he began. "I was interested, as well, in the fall of Aum Shinrikyo. When their headquarters at the foot of Mount Fuji was surrounded by the police, I was glued to the TV. It looked like a gunfight might erupt at any moment. I was on pins and needles, wondering whether Aum, with all those chemical weapons, was going to counterattack and start a real revolt. At the time there was another show on TV, a special retrospective on the Somersault. I remember seeing the actual broadcasts, though I was just a child then. Watching these old videotapes they were showing as a kind of adjunct to the massive coverage of Aum made me interested in Patron and his church all over again.

"With Aum, of course, in the end nothing happened. Asahara, who should have given the order to attack, was arrested, discovered asleep next to a trunk full of money. I can't tell you how disappointed I was when I heard this!

"To tell the truth, when I saw Patron on TV, he looked insincere and aroused my antipathy. Guide, on the other hand, didn't say much and seemed more trustworthy.

"Patron explained in this singsong voice how the visions he'd had on the *other side* were all so much nonsense. 'The church's planned actions are just a joke,' he said. 'So I call on all members of the church throughout Japan to stop this farce!'

"What Guide said was a little different. He was asked whether the relationship between the two of them, Guide believing in Patron as the savior, Patron seeing him as the prophet, was also just a joke they'd come up with. 'It might very well be,' he said. 'I believe that the visions from the *other side* I've interpreted have, through our own mistakes, changed into something they shouldn't be. I hereby declare that all I've said till now is null and void. And I want each and every follower to accept this immediately.

"As for Patron, I thought that if a savior were to announce himself in this day and age he might very well be like this—a pitiful comic figure."

"I think your view of me applies before the Somersault too, Ikuo," Patron said. "Even after Guide forced me into the role of savior I didn't really have a strong sense of what it meant. At the time of the Somersault, I had to deny this idea completely, so this was probably the first time I ever really examined the notion of myself as savior.

"Until I met Guide I was more of a mystical hermit. For a long time I had my trances but couldn't put my visions into words. And that's how things would have stayed if I hadn't met Guide. Not only would I have spent the rest of my life without calling on the world to repent, I might very well have died without ever noticing all those words stored up inside me. Even now all over this planet there must be lots of hermit mystics like that.

"But once this chubby little middle-aged man was told he was the savior Guide was seeking, he was forcibly dragged out of his dark cave, redolent with his own odors. You're the savior I've been seeking, Guide told me, which may have been just a thought that occurred to him on the spur of the moment. Once he voiced it, though, and once he added that he was my prophet, Guide really began to work actively on my behalf.

"We established a set relationship after this, that of speaker and listener. I'd always treated my visions like a bout of fever, wanting only, after it was over, to escape from the aftereffects. But Guide took my random mutterings and returned them to me in the form of logically consistent statements. The words I'd mumbled, still dizzy from my trance, now came back to me, via Guide, in a very realistic outline. And reflected in the mirror of Guide's words I saw an image of myself bathed from head to foot in the light from the *other side.*

"That's how I came to think it was all right for me, the intermediary along with my prophet for these visions from the *other side,* to be called a savior. . . . Since the day I first thought that, Ikuo, I no longer had qualms about being called savior—real or fake."

2

Ikuo raised his massive head to look at Patron, and though his words were polite enough he spoke quite firmly.

"What I'd like to ask Patron is this: When you come back to this side, you speak about the visions you had. And Guide retells them. But in that process, aren't there some things that *can't* be expressed in language, certain things that get omitted in the process? When I still hadn't known you very long, Guide challenged me to ask you an important question. I think he wanted a young person to take over where he had unexpectedly been defeated.

"While Guide was raising you up he was afraid you'd run wild and be out of his control. Ten years ago, if you had enthusiastically supported the faction's plans, before Guide discarded his scientists he would first have had to figure out what to do with you."

Patron listened carefully to what Ikuo said and was silent for a while before he replied.

"One of Guide's goals in founding the research institute was to select young people who would stimulate me. But when the institute was complete, the young people all assembled, he felt he had to train them himself the way he wanted to, as a church elite. But he went too far.

"As a result, when the young people forged ahead on their own, he had to cut them off, coldly, without a moment's hesitation. That's what brought on the Somersault."

"Guide was a born teacher, I think," Dancer said. "When I first got to know him, he wasn't interpreting Patron's visions, but he did help bring Patron and us closer together through words we could all understand.

"Professor Kizu told me that people who are able to experience a relationship with God directly are called mystics. And that people like Guide who can clearly expound what the mystic is trying to convey have a completely different type of gift.

"A weekly news magazine once ran a special edition titled BIOGRAPHIES OF DUBIOUS POSTWAR JAPANESE MESSIAHS. I was secretly reading the magazine in the office when all of a sudden Guide grabbed it away from me. 'In my night school classes,' he told me, 'I was quite adept at confiscating comic books the students were stealthily reading.'" Dancer grew teary at this, but soon recovered. "And after he looked at it he made me laugh when he said how surprised he was at the number of saviors there've been in Japan. And he asked me this: 'If Patron isn't the true savior, would that bother you?

"'Real saviors are few and far between,' Guide told me. 'For people who feel the need for a savior deeply, on a personal and societal level, isn't even a *phony* savior better than none? And who's to say if a savior is real or fake? Though of course it's best for people who feel the need for a savior and follow him, repenting as we head toward the end of the world, if he turns out to be real.'

"I agreed with him," Dancer went on. "I think Guide educated me not to be some amateurish mystical type but someone who could serve as a conduit to society at large. This was the exact opposite of the challenge he threw up for Ikuo."

"Guide was a true teacher, for Ikuo and for you," Patron responded. "I too was taught by him."

Dancer waited for Patron to continue, but since he didn't, she let out everything she'd been holding inside.

"I don't know if I really understand Guide's way of thinking," she said, "but you might recall, in one of the myths Socrates discusses, how there are people who are like spheres, before people are differentiated into male and female? Guide told me once that he and Patron used to be connected like that, their bodies and spirits with one big artery-like pipe running through them. 'Our hearts are one,' he said, 'pumping blood into that pipe.

"'For Patron,' Guide went on, 'the conversion of his visions into words is like synthesis or hormone production within a living organism. At that stage the materials or hormones aren't yet complete. Those flow into the pipe in my direction. And I return this to Patron,' Guide said, 'as something solid, as hormones without anything extraneous.' The relationship between Patron and Guide, then, was as seamless as a dream.

"When I heard this, I thought that though Patron and Guide had suffered a lot, if they continued to live quietly like this until they died these would be their happy golden years. Like an acolyte in a monastery, I was happy to serve them and I completely forgot about dancing."

Ikuo was irritated at Dancer's romantic way of speaking. "But even before the Somersault," he asked, "wasn't there an attempt to sever the pipeline between Patron and Guide? I can understand the radical faction wanting to be directly connected with Patron, without Guide as a go-between. They must have dreamed of becoming mystics themselves, having the same kind of trance visions that Patron did, and then realizing them in the real world."

Kizu spoke up. "Just as with Ikuo, I had nothing to do with the church at that time. I'm basing this on church documents I've read. But didn't the church teach that believers following Patron would also have trances?"

"You have to understand there are two aspects to trances," Dancer answered. "One aspect is as part of the daily prayers of the followers who've accepted Patron as their savior; the other came about when the radical faction went off on their own and committed the mistakes they did. In a normal situation, where the church was healthy, Guide should have been able to keep the radical faction under control."

"So the radical faction short-circuited the process, lumping themselves and Patron together," Kizu said. "Guide felt he had to restore this circuit between himself and Patron, that he had to strengthen his control over their followers, right? So it was unavoidable that he cut off the radical faction—in other words, do the Somersault."

"It's a little strange to be speculating about these things with Dr. Koga and Mr. Hanawa here with us," Dancer said, "but I'd have to say I agree entirely. And in making sure that happened, wasn't Guide doing the right thing?

"The radical members who killed Guide were people who held a particular grudge toward the Somersault. They're different from the members who've moved here with us. I hope the local people will appreciate the distinction. The first group held Guide prisoner and roughed him up to the point where he died, so the whole thing had to be referred to the Tokyo DA's office. It's unbelievable how cruel they were, pushing him to the point where the aneurysm in his brain burst.

"One thing's for sure," Dacner went on. "When he was being mistreated by them, Guide maintained his dignity to the very last. Toward the end of the tape recording you can sense he has resigned himself to being killed. He stood up to them. 'Why,' he asked, 'are you using professional equipment to record all this? Are you planning to provide the courts with proof of your crime?' The radicals said, 'We're doing it so we can send it to Patron and make him suffer and die.' They loathed Patron too. They had a great deal of anger toward both men."

"But didn't Guide, who created the institute in the first place, have a pretty intimate relationship with them?" Kizu wondered. "They shelved that relationship and tried to connect directly with Patron. After the Somersault, though, the press claimed that Patron and Guide got some devilish thrill out of letting the radical faction climb to the top of the roof and then yanking away the ladder."

"That's completely wrong," Dancer insisted. "Guide translated Patron's visions back to him in understandable language, and then he transmitted them to the followers. That was Guide's role. Guide wanted to insert the reactions of this group of sensitive, intelligent young people into the pipeline between himself and Patron."

Kizu pressed on. "If anyone got a devilish thrill out of this, wasn't it those who tortured and killed Guide while recording the whole thing? But what was *their* goal? What possible significance was there in making Guide suffer, physically and emotionally, to the point where he died?"

"I don't think they acted without a purpose," Dancer said. "I think they were trying to be proactive, trying to figure out why the Somersault had to take place. Guide told me about some of those young radicals. What I got out of it was that these were young people who were trying to fill in what was missing in their own lives. They were searching for spiritual peace. They wanted the wisdom that would allow them to live in the trying times to come.

"They were bright and serious, which makes them all the more sad. These lonely, suffering young people had, for the first time in their lives, created their very own community at the Izu Research Institute. But Patron and Guide just couldn't handle them. If the control of the church was turned over to the radical faction, the ship of the church, so to speak, would have rammed into an iceberg. So Patron and Guide scurried away to safer ground. You can't deny that, right?"

"You're pretty outspoken for a young woman, aren't you?" Kizu said regretfully.

Patron, who'd let it all slide by, spoke up. "But she's exactly right, " he said, standing up for Dancer. "We not only abandoned ship, we denied that the ship ever had any use to begin with—either back in the beginning or in the future. That's what the Somersault was all about."

3

When Dancer saw that his little pronouncement was over, she spoke again, before Kizu had a chance to comment.

"Apart from their special fields," she said, "Guide was the main teacher for those young people, showing them how to live a life of faith. As everyone admits, he was a born educator. The young people's group in Izu should have been Guide's masterpiece. I don't see it as a group of sadists. These were the best and brightest of the elite university system, people used to the seminar system of training, right? They weren't about to dig themselves holes in which to ponder things alone; they were best at getting together to study and debate as a group.

"Their last seminar—with the guest speaker being held against his wishes, a dangerous thing to do—revolved around learning what, ten years after the fact, the Somersault meant to Patron and Guide.

"If you listen to the tape, you'll hear that in the beginning they were divided into two groups. One group vehemently denied Patron, saying the church was totally meaningless. They were the ones who felt abandoned and wanted revenge. The other group insisted that Patron and Guide were victims. TV had made them into laughingstocks all over Japan. Thanks to this, the underground shock troops didn't get a chance to leap into action.

"This second group viewed the Somersault as Patron's clear warning that the end of the world was near. Just as Jesus was crucified along with two criminals, letting oneself fall into the most wretched place possible meant the final stage had been reached, where the end time is announced. 'We should believe in the sullied and insulted Patron and Guide and await the Day of Wrath,' they said. 'If Guide, who suffered the worst pain in the most wretched of places, tells you to believe in him, all trials can be transformed into something positive.' That's the kind of appeal these people made.

"The two groups didn't just debate each other, they also talked about their individual experiences, the trying times they had had because of the Somersault—not just the obvious abandonment and loss of spiritual support but their need to take responsibility for the plans of the whole group, be investigated by the authorities—all of this must have been horrible.

"In the face of this horror, Guide didn't try to make excuses or explain away his true intentions. As long as the questions were straightforward, he answered them concisely and sincerely. The only time he got emotional was when he heard they'd poisoned his Saint Bernard. 'Why did you have to do that?' he rebuked them. This brought on laughter from those who were detaining him, from the first group, at least.

"Because of what they'd gone through, all the kidnappers demanded a complete explanation. I've listened to the tape many times and would sum up Guide's response as follows." At this point Dancer took out a paper she'd had ready and began to read.

"'Some people say that Patron and I did the Somersault in order to use the media to deceive the public. That's not true. We might have done something like that if the Somersault had been entirely our own arbitrary decision.

"'With a great deal of fanfare we confessed to the public that all our beliefs until then were a sham. The highlight of the whole Somersault was when Patron said that the written records of his visions—the account, for instance, of an anthropomorphic God—were completely laughable and our gospel was worse than some stupid Hollywood spectacular. But what this showed was that there is a faith that *isn't* mistaken. After the Somersault, Patron and I fell into the pit of hell. Our faith may have been in error, but this was an unmistakable sign that over the two of us and our errors towers a living God.

"'Right now Patron and I, believing in that sign, are crawling up out of hell. But the way you're acting now disqualifies you from being part of Patron's new movement. Ten years ago, like a crystal extracted from a solution, it was you, rather than our gospel, who substantiated our religious movement's errors. Our book has been trampled on and disappeared, yet still you haven't repented.'

"As Guide said this, the first group laughed in his face again. Laughing about the dog was bad enough, but this time it was even more cruel. At this point, according to what Dr. Koga told me, the only thing the second group felt it could do was get away, it being obvious that Guide was only going to be tormented further. I cried as I listened to this tape, knowing that all that was left for Guide was to be killed. Such a meaningless death. And just when he was climbing out of hell with Patron!"

Dancer turned her face toward the hemispherical light on the ceiling, her pink mouth open, and cried. Teardrops rolled down both sides of the slim bridge of her nose. Despite her tears, Ikuo zeroed in on her. "I'd say that Dancer's long tale has done what it set out to do. You've kept with the intentions of the town authorities who are accepting us into their midst, cried tears over Guide's death, all very natural as a response, making it hard for Patron to oppose this. Your goal is to have everyone arrive at a consensus to deny one party of the former radical faction—in order to accept Dr. Koga and his more 'sensible' colleagues. But is this fair? Is it right for Dancer's tears to make us agree that the former radical faction's burst of laughter was cruel and outrageous? Is this really appropriate for a new church with Patron at its center?

"According to Ogi, when he was listening to the tape with Dancer, she did indeed stop the tape and cry for a while after the second burst of laughter. But Ogi said that after this she plugged in some headphones and listened to the rest of the tape by herself.

"I don't believe Dancer is just an emotional person, let alone a sentimental one. This morning she called me over to talk with her. 'We've already decided the conditions under which the town would accept us,' she told me, 'yet you're trying to wreck it all. And even if you weren't, the antichurch movement is smoldering in the town,' she said, 'criticizing me and any plan to allow former radical-faction members who want to be accepted back into the fold.'

"Though we've only heard the church's side so far in our discussion today, we're seeing a consensus forming between the leaders of the church—apart from me—and the town. The reason you haven't heard from Dr. Koga today is that Dancer negotiated with him beforehand, as she did with me. Unlike with me, however, with him she was successful.

"After the accident with Guide, I met with Dr. Koga, leader of the former radical faction, and we spoke after this from time to time. I promised to try to persuade Patron and the other staff members to allow as many as possible of the former young radicals to participate in the new church.

"With the Somersault, Patron and Guide had broken off their relationship with the church. Ten years later they returned from hell and wanted to start a new movement. Patron's first concept of the new movement was to include only people who had had nothing to do with the first church. Until he was kidnapped, that was Guide's idea as well. But that just shouldn't be done, in my opinion.

"The former radical faction may have been split over the meaning of the Somersault, but after they were forced out of the church by official and police pressure, they continued to keep their promises. They're also a group that has the power to actually get things moving, so I don't think it's very bright to exclude them when you're trying to start over.

"Of course I wish they'd never done something as awful as kill Guide. They knew Patron had risen from hell and was starting a new movement, so in order to get a handle on what was going on, wasn't it only natural for them to want to speak to the person they had had the deepest relationship with—Guide? Dancer hinted that one part of the former radical faction was planning from the very start to get revenge on him and had no thought of reconciling. But is that really true?

"If they were just after revenge, why did they wait ten years? And why target Guide instead of Patron, the one really responsible for the Somersault? Didn't the cruel laughter we heard when Guide refused to let members of the former radical faction participate in Patron's new movement ring with the sound of their despair?

"I beg of you, Patron. Please give the people who killed Guide—who felt driven into a corner, full of despair, and who never intended to kill him— a chance to repent. Only one person can do that: *you*."

Ikuo stood up, walked over to Patron, and knelt before him. He spoke in a sorrowful, youthful voice.

"Patron, please. Tell me and those people what God says. No matter what it is, tell us what God really *wants*. I've talked with them, and I know they're hoping for the same thing I am."

Ogi watched as Patron reached out a hand, as if to lay it on Ikuo's head or shoulder, but halted in midair. In this noncommittal stance, Patron spoke to Ikuo.

"In order to do that, I first have to regain the power to hear God's voice. And without Guide's help! Only if I'm able to do that will I be able to transmit anything of any consequence. At present all I can do is seek to have all the members of the former radical faction, the ones you were in touch with at the time of the memorial service, join our church here in its new home. And. to have this communicated to them. I think Dr. Koga would agree with this."

Ikuo looked moved by Patron's words, but Dancer was indignant. Before either of them could say anything, though, Kizu spoke up.

"Patron, among this group you're thinking of having join the movement are the people who held Guide prisoner and tortured him, the ones who made him collapse and die. The main two perpetrators are in custody, but the ones who surrounded them and Guide didn't lift a finger to stop it, did they? I find what Dancer says very convincing."

"I want even the two who are in jail to return to the church as soon as they're released," Patron said. "That's what I hope for. Isn't it precisely *because* they're the ones who killed Guide that they must return to us?" Patron opened his dark eyes wide, looking even more like a bird as he fixed them on Kizu.

"Guide didn't deserve what they did to him. The power of the state is judging their guilt on one level, and revealed in the light of the new church we are creating, they are covered in the vile and abominable sin of their actions. But we couldn't be happier, could we, if, as these souls lift their faces from the dark abyss, the light reflected in their eyes is the light of our church?"

Patron stood up and bid the kneeling Ikuo to stand up as well. Ogi watched with a softened heart as Patron grew calm and gentle as he turned to Dancer. As everyone else rose, the woman named Satchan, widow of the founder of the church that had arisen here only to disappear, addressed Patron.

"I feel I understand what you mean when you keep saying you've been in hell for the last decade," she said. "I think about how wonderful it would be if my husband, who created the Church of the Flaming Green Tree, could have returned once more—as you have done. Ever since our church broke up, a handful of friends and I have kept running the Farm, and since most of the land and equipment has been dormant it would make me very happy if you could find a use for it."

Patron didn't respond aloud, but he bowed his head respectfully to her. Morio, though, who had been sitting beside Ms. Tachibana and paying close attention to the conversation, walked over to stand between Patron and Satchan and began applauding, as enthusiastically as if applauding a violin soloist and her piano accompanist on an outstanding performance. That sound, with its gentle feeling of oneness, washed over everyone and reverberated throughout the chapel.

20: The Quiet Women

1

After the meeting, Kizu was still worried about how the people of Maki Town would receive the church members. When he went to the teachers' office of the junior high school to consult with them about the art school he wanted to open, he couldn't help but raise these concerns after the preliminary pleasantries were over.

"It's strange for me to try to speak objectively about this, since I'm one of those who moved here with the new church, but I'm quite surprised at how readily the townspeople have accepted the idea of our followers—including the former so-called radical faction—coming here. I would have anticipated a stubborn conservative opposition, but everyone seems quite flexible."

The junior high art teacher was cautiously silent, but Asa-san, who'd accompanied Kizu, spoke up confidently.

"The people here don't have the generosity to debate with those who oppose them in order to arrive at a compromise. But don't you find the same thing happening in cities? The reason the town authorities and the group opposing you have basically consented is because Ogi was so efficient in passing around a list of names and explaining about the people who'll be coming here. If I'm correct, there'll be one men's group and one women's group. The men's group is the one you speak of. There are twenty-five people altogether, and though it's true they're members of the former radical faction, its core will be a level-headed group led by Dr. Koga. Dancer said that after Guide's death the more proactive group washed its hands of the church and wouldn't respond even if Patron invited them to join. The other group coming is a woman's group called the Quiet Women, as I recall. Why would anybody oppose them?

"Even so, after our meeting in the chapel the head of the town council told me that once this initial move is complete he wants to hold on-the-spot inspections. I told him in no uncertain terms that inspections would violate human rights. Just yesterday in the Old Town, the antichurch faction pasted up new handbills and announced excitedly how they'd won a victory by excluding the more extreme elements in the church from moving in, but that they mustn't let down their guard."

Kizu questioned Ikuo once more about this and was told that with Patron's lenient policy they expected a variety of people to join them. But when they sent out inquiries, many people turned them down.

"Maybe this is a good-sized group to start out with," Kizu said, encouraging the depressed Ikuo. "Even if it stays small, it's important to have the more moderate people involved."

"The local authorities say they want to keep a watch over any radical elements in the church," Ikuo said, "but I'm more worried about the opposite—that now we've finally started to get things rolling the church will turn into an old ladies' club."

Ikuo's sarcastic remarks may have been a bit exaggerated, but they weren't unfounded. Though they might be hiding some militant attitudes, the first former radical members that were coming were, it was fair to say, a group that was completely into repentance at the end of the world. Rather than theoretical researchers, they were made up of the older experimental scientists who, even at the Izu Research Institute, had dubbed themselves the Technicians.

As for the old ladies' club, as Ikuo called them, actually he wasn't too far off the mark. It was made up of about half of the women Kizu had visited in their commune along the Odakyu Line, and though they had lived together with their children there, only the women would be moving to this new location. When he heard that the women would be occupying the monastery that surrounded the inner garden, Kizu had naively assumed that this was a temporary arrangement until the children joined them. But that wasn't the case.

Kizu had a chance to talk directly with the women in the church's new office, set up in the annex to the chapel, built outside the cylindrical building itself but separate from the monastery. That afternoon, after he'd finished having an early lunch in the cafeteria—which they'd constructed by tearing down the walls between three smaller rooms—Kizu popped his head into the office, expecting to find Ikuo but finding Ogi and Dancer instead, welcoming some women Kizu remembered seeing before.

Among them was Mrs. Shigeno, the widow of the hospital director and donor of the property, who greeted Kizu very pleasantly. "How was your lunch in the cafeteria? I'm sure it wasn't anything like the faculty dining room in your U.S. university, though I daresay it compared favorably to student cafeterias over there."

"It was very nice," Kizu said. "There isn't much difference between the faculty dining room and the student cafeteria in America."

"I'm happy to hear you liked it. We'll be the ones in charge of the church's cafeteria from now on."

As he talked with her, memories came back to Kizu of the greenhouse where they had been packing lilies into boxes and of the memorial service in his apartment's basement. A vivid memory came to him of Mrs. Shigeno speaking at the service, and he clearly remembered the other two women with her from the greenhouse. One of them was Ms. Takada, the young woman with the skin covering one of her eyes; the other was one of the leaders during the prayer time at the greenhouse, a Ms. Oyama.

Vaguely aware that Kizu might already know them, Dancer still went ahead and introduced each woman in turn. She explained that Kizu had been a longtime art educator in the United States, despite the fact that when he had visited their commune he'd given them his business card, and Mrs. Shigeno, in the way she had addressed him now, was obviously aware of his background.

"I'm really happy to hear that you'll be in charge of the cafeteria," Kizu said. "I've been fixing my own meals for far too long."

Mrs. Shigeno, explaining what they'd been discussing with Dancer, said, "It seems, however, that some people have raised objections about our faith. Though they're happy we'll be running the cafeteria, they wonder why we emphasize our own sort of exclusive group prayer."

"To the point that they've even dubbed us the Quiet Women," Ms. Oyama added in a bemused way; a small woman, her build and expression suggested she was stalwart and dependable. "In political and religious movements alike, these factional nicknames usually start as a kind of insult, which then get fixed permanently. Like the names Anarchists and Quakers. The name Quiet Women, too, is somewhat negative, suggesting women who maintain a weird silence and aren't entirely to be trusted."

"When Ikuo—who's come with me here—and I visited you on that snowy day," Kizu said, "we were very impressed by your lifestyle. Your children were so quiet, it was like some nostalgic scene from the past. . . . When they join you, I imagine things will get much more lively around here."

Kizu had addressed this to Mrs. Shigeno, who looked at her two colleagues and then urged Ms. Oyama to reply.

"For the time being we're not planning to have the children join us. Maybe we will just accept the name that's been given to us and carry on as the Quiet Women."

Kizu couldn't quite follow this, but he hesitated to ask further questions.

"We've been living communally for the last ten years, deepening our faith along with the children. And after these ten years, Patron has, on Guide's martyrdom, started up a new religious movement and called us to join him. This is extremely important. Being allowed to live together once again with Patron means accepting his teachings. Which means we have a lot of learning to do to connect his denial of our doctrine and faith with the activities of his new church. We have come here with great hopes and resolve.

"We've lived together for ten years, but when this change in direction came about, differences of opinion started to surface in our group. Some women were opposed to an unconditional return. They felt that since we'd been abandoned by Patron and Guide we should continue down our own spiritual path and that remaining in the church Patron created was not the honorable thing to do. They wanted Patron first of all to give a thorough self-critique of his actions at the time of the Somersault. I can understand their reaction. This sort of opposition arose even in regard to whether or not we should participate in the memorial service, and we came to Tokyo at that time without coming to any sort of agreement. At the service the adults from our commune sat in two separate groups. Ogi kept the former Izu research group from saying anything, and we kept our opposing faction from speaking up, letting Mrs. Shigeno speak for us from the floor. This allowed the service to take place without incident.

"When we returned to our commune, nearly half the women said Patron hadn't criticized himself enough and they were against returning to the church. So we ended up leaving them behind. But we'll be sending faxes to them every day regarding the teachings of Patron's new church. We're hoping this will convince some of them, who could then form a second group and move here. . . . That brings you up to date on what's been happening with us."

"You've given it a lot of thought, obviously, and I think your response is unique—and very logical, too," Kizu said, reevaluating this Quiet Women's group, who were unlike any Japanese women he'd ever known. "But why aren't any of the children participating? Are you afraid the church will try to take over their education?"

"We listened to the children's opinion," Mrs. Shigeno answered. "Through our communal life together the children have grown very close. Most of them said they didn't want to be separated, so we decided to let the children in the two groups be entrusted to whichever side the majority of them voted for, which would then take responsibility for their education. I'm an optimistic person and I was sure the children would want to come with us. But when the votes were counted they'd decided to stay."

"But you were quite decisive about it, weren't you," Kizu said, his defenses down in the face of the elegant Mrs. Shigeno's smile.

Ms. Takada didn't let this go by. Her right eye wide open, she turned it and her blank left side toward Kizu and said, quite resolutely, "We may have been decisive, but that meant we gave our lives over to faith only to be abandoned by our leaders. From our perspective, that's what the Somersault was. Pondering this over the past ten years, our initial hatred and resentment disappeared, but to be truthful, right now we're not sure how the faith we've kept for the past decade can merge with this new movement.

"Knowing this meant risking everything, we split into two groups. If we had had more confidence in Patron's new movement, we should have been able to convince the others and bring the children along with us. We are most definitely aware of the feelings of those who had to leave their children behind to come here. We didn't do this because we wanted to. Moving here and being with Patron again represents the last chance for our faith. If Patron had been murdered instead of Guide, I don't know how things would have turned out. Is it so strange to have such desperate thoughts?"

Neither Mrs. Shigeno—her earlier smile now replaced by a look of concentration—nor the intrepid Ms. Oyama—head bowed and fingers moving ceaselessly—spoke up to help Kizu. To break the momentary tension, Dancer spoke instead.

"Professor Kizu hasn't just come here as a lark. He's suffering from a severe case of cancer, and yet he's been doing all he can. He'd been planning to teach an art class, for both the local children and the church's children, and I imagine he finds the fact that your children aren't coming a great disappointment."

"Well, then, maybe he should consider taking in older students," Mrs. Shigeno suggested, and the gentle mood of the discussion was restored.

2

Dr. Koga had asked Kizu for a painting for his clinic, based on a sketch he liked, and after it was finished, Kizu took it over himself to the riverside. He had had the frame made in the woodworking shop that, he was told, had originally been set up by the former Base Movement, a workshop that had for a time been absorbed into the Church of the Flaming Green Tree and afterward continued as an independent operation. Kizu was quite impressed that the cultural movement begun in this mountainous region by young people some forty years ago had been so carefully maintained. Apply a little stimulus, he mused, and in a short time it could easily be revived on a larger scale.

One of the Technicians who had been helping outfit the clinic fixed a nail on the freshly painted wooden wall, and Dr. Koza and Kizu hung the painting on it. Dr. Koga looked steadily at the work, a portrait of Ikuo, naked from the waist up.

"Is this work a study for a tableau?"

"I did the sketch with that in mind," Kizu replied. "I haven't done any real painting for a long time, and I haven't formed any particular plan. In my own defense I should say that I'm searching as I draw."

"As long as you continue in this vein," Dr. Koga said, "I have no doubt you'll end up with a magnificent painting. . . . Since models all have a unique shape, character, and movement, is your main focus then the *outer* surface? Or are you influenced by the *inner* world of the model?"

"I'm not sure I make a distinction between the two. Especially with this model. It's as if as I drew his shape I gradually came to a greater understanding of his inner being, which leads me to confirm how very appealing he is."

"Now that you've settled here, why not use it as an opportunity to begin a large-scale painting? There's a lot of space to hang such a work in the chapel."

"That's a thought," Kizu replied. He appeared to be considering the suggestion seriously. "A series of events happened in Tokyo, but well before that I was planning to paint a tableau based on a biblical theme. The first time I met Ikuo, in fact, he told me he was interested in the illustrations of the Bible I'd done for a children's picture book."

Although the walls and ceiling were freshly painted, the desks and chairs neat and tidy, the clinic overall had an old-fashioned look to it. Dr. Koga was seated beside the window looking out on the road, but since the Technicians had taken all the chairs for patients out to the courtyard to repair them, the only place for Kizu to sit was on the examination bed. Dr. Koga looked at him with invigorated eyes. All of a sudden, as if finally getting to the heart of the matter, he said, "How about using Ikuo as your model for Jonah? He seems to have an unusual interest in that book."

"We've discussed the book of Jonah before. He's talked about it with you too?"

"There seems to be some reason behind his interest," Dr. Koga said, suppressing a faint smile but not adding any details.

Kizu changed the topic. "Were you aware that the women's group that's moved into the Hollow does not include all the women who were living along the Odakyu Line?"

"I'd heard something about that. One of the fellows in my group is a friend of one of the women, and after they moved here they had a lot to talk about."

"It must have taken a great deal of resolve for them to break up the group they'd lived with for ten years, leave the children behind, and come here."

"It's the same with the Technicians—only half of those remaining from the former radical faction at Izu have moved here. There's another thing I've been thinking about, Professor Kizu. According to the mayor, there used to be a movement to change people's lifestyles here called the Base Movement."

"As a matter of fact," Kizu responded, "the frame for this painting came from the woodworking shop that was started by them and was later absorbed by the Church of the Flaming Green Tree."

"Don't you think what we're trying to do here is to build a kind of *base* ourselves—for a new church? There will be lots of people who don't move here but who come on a pilgrimage to this holy site to hear Patron's sermons, so in that sense this place will function as a kind of home base."

"Patron told me he's going to be busy with some sort of project here for the next six months or a year," Kizu said. "I don't think he said this just to encourage a sick person like myself."

Dr. Koga examined Kizu with the conscientious eyes of a veteran physician and then turned his gaze outside, to the peeling wall of the now-unused sake warehouse across the narrow road, a wall that had a quiet antique look.

"Ikuo has the same idea," Dr. Koga said. "He was interested in the house we had after we were forced to leave the Izu facility, less a secret hiding place than a kind of liaison office, and dropped by to see us. He negotiated a lot of things between us and Patron's office. It seemed clear enough at the last meeting that his goal was to connect up with the more radical members of the faction.

"I was surprised to find that the members who moved here as a group are all intent on working at the Farm. But that sort of thing happens, I suppose. I don't expect that'll mean they'll be going the way of the Quiet Women, praying all the time. They have a plan of action, though they're not insisting on any outward, daring type of thing. They're like a bunch of bored dilettantes, hard to get worked up about anything.

"The gathering where they debated Guide aggravated the opposition within the group and forced them to split in two. They all agreed to the debate, and even members who had never shown their faces at our liaison office showed up for it. But once the meeting started it was the more radical group that took over. The moderate faction's motivation for attending, to hear about Patron's recent religious activities, went out the window. In the recording of the brutalizing that Dancer spoke of, there was a proposal made to let Guide go. I sided with the moderate faction on this. But a dispute arose and we were kept from further participation, after which the tragedy unfolded.

"With the interrogation of Guide still continuing at that point, it's no wonder people say it was irresponsible for the moderates to withdraw. Especially for me, as a doctor. But Guide really wanted us to leave. I think deep down his attitude was similar to that of the moderate faction, myself included, who wanted somehow to express ourselves after Patron's ten years of silence. I think he let them interrogate and torment him at will because he wanted, if worse came to worst, to let them find shelter in a place where the authorities wouldn't pursue them.

"Guide accepted the invitation for the meeting, after all, but was less concerned about me and the moderate faction than in searching out some accommodation, some third way, with a group that even after ten years was still pretty radical. Wasn't it precisely because those radical members would be there that he accepted the invitation at such short notice? But Guide's third way and the expectations of the radical group were completely at odds, which explains what took place."

"The more I listen to you," Kizu said, "the more I feel the reason Ikuo got close to you all was because he was attracted to these more extreme remnants of the radical faction."

"To me," Dr. Koga said, "Ikuo is a Jonah-type personality, which leads me to hope you'd express this in your painting. I guess I'm hoping your painting will help me grasp who he really is. He's going to play an important role in Patron's new church, but there's one thing about him I don't quite understand that I'd like to—"

The two calm men at the open entrance door next to the reception area had finished their preparations for bringing in the chairs from outside. Dr. Koga's expression became brisk and businesslike as he turned his attention to the practical matters at hand, and Kizu bid him a swift farewell and withdrew from the clinic.

3

Kizu, painting in hand, had gotten a ride to the clinic from Ogi, who was on his way to the Old Town, but on the way back he had no choice but to walk home along the river. Groups of two or three junior high school students were coming toward him, the boys in matching smocks, the girls in navy blue uniforms and wine-colored mufflers. Their clothes struck Kizu as shabby.

On the heights on the other side of the Kame River was the cross-Shikoku highway bypass, with a ceaseless flow of huge trucks racing down the road. On the road on Kizu's side of the river, in contrast, there was only a scattering of cars and light trucks. With its view of the lush greenery behind the homes on the mountainside, the road was pleasant enough to walk down, but the children's rough and violent ways wiped the area's unique qualities away.

After he'd passed the T-shaped intersection that led to the bridge, Kizu located a general store that, while its frontage was the same as the stores to both sides of it, extended, as he could see through the glass door, much farther back. Thinking to buy something for the next day's breakfast, he went inside. Dancer had told him that this little market carried ham and bacon, as well as vegetables and eggs, produced by the Flaming Green Tree Farm.

To the right of the entrance was a cash register of the kind Kizu remembered seeing at the entrance to the public bath he frequented as a student, next to which squatted a person facing the interior of the store. This white-haired old woman showed no interest in Kizu as he entered. He was hit by a wave of nostalgia as he gazed at the simple displays. The shelves had the usual items—snacks, instant noodles, meats, fish, and pickled vegetables—but instead of appealing to the shopper, the products seemed shoved back in the shadows.

The fresh produce section was especially cramped, as was the meat section, with only packages of pork cut into bite-size chunks, slices of salted salmon, and half-dried, darkly glistening sardines. Every time Kizu returned to Japan he felt something akin to car sickness when confronted with the overflow of goods in Tokyo supermarkets. Used to life in America, he always found himself stirred up by the vitality of Japanese consumerism. The vast gulf between that and this village market made Old Town look like a ghost town.

However, as he made one circuit of the chilly, dusty aisles, he came across a shelf and stand set apart in one corner, the only display that seemed alive. On the shelf were packs of hams and bacon, butter in glass jars, eggs, and mounds of cabbages, carrots, onions, and other vegetables, as well as still warm-to-the-touch freshly baked bread, the kind sold in the supermarket in Aoyama as French Country Bread.

Kizu picked up a jar of butter; the label on it had a colored woodblock print of a tree and the logo FRUIT OF THE RAIN TREE. Kizu selected some meat, butter, eggs, and vegetables from that display shelf, and when he took his shopping basket over to the register the old woman lifted her gray head, her wizened face still lively, and said proudly, "You won't find roast ham better than this in the city!"

"It does look good. Why do you keep it shoved back in the corner?" Kizu asked.

"It's not shoved in a corner; it's just that only certain people buy it. Since new people are moving here from the city now, I was going to increase my order, but Satchan from the Farm—not a very friendly type, I can tell you— said she's going to negotiate directly with the new church's cafeteria!"

Kizu paid for his purchases. As he was about to collect his paper bag of groceries, the old woman lifted rheumy eyes that seemed to cling to him and said, "You're the painting teacher, aren't you? I understand you're famous! The junior high is very happy such an important person's come to town, but they also say to keep the door open when they're alone with you, Professor. The assistant principal said this, and to the boys, no less! What a distressing thing!"

Kizu was taken aback by the old woman's sudden comment. But with the good grace of a man his age, he was able to roll with the punches.

"Well, it's only natural," he said, "that people who've lived here for a long time want to keep an eye on people from the city bringing in their own religion."

The old woman suppressed a faint smile, but went with the tack Kizu was taking.

"If you go upriver from here and over the pass, just before the Hollow, where you all are, there's a house above a tall stone wall, right? We call it the Mansion to distinguish it from the other houses. A lot of unusual people have come out of that line, including one man who went on to college and became a diplomat, and then his son came back here to start a church! The ham and butter you just bought were made by people related to that diplomat's son. Their church isn't around anymore, so if you build this new church you can expect people to say things for a while."

"I suppose it's only to be expected that we wouldn't be very welcome," Kizu said, trying to put an end to the conversation. He was finding her a bit too much, but the old woman wasn't about to let him get away so easily.

"No, no. We're not that kind of people! People in Maki Town came here with handbills. I put them up for a day but then took them down. I buy goods from them, so I had to post them, but I'm not opposed to a new church being started here! All the food you bought—and you bought a lot, didn't you?— was made by former church people; this woman named Satchan who runs the Farm, they say her son got his power from his father, the one who built the old church here!"

Just then something happened that truly startled Kizu. When he'd entered the store, walked past the register, and looked around, there hadn't been any other customers visible in the three aisles. But just then, in the aisle next to the one he'd been in, from out of the shadows of the shelves of detergent and toilet paper a thin-as-a-rail middle-aged woman suddenly popped up, pointed at Kizu, and began prattling.

"They call that son of hers New Brother Gii, but where he came from is anyone's guess! The woman who gave birth to him fourteen years ago? When I used to teach at the new junior high she was a *boy* student. A womanish man!

"Is it really possible she became a *mannish woman* and had a child? You're from Tokyo—an educated man, I gather—but don't let her coax you into anything. She made my husband donate his whole estate to their church. That's one scary woman, I tell you!"

"My, my, Mrs. Kamei," the woman at the register said. "And here I was thinking you'd recovered from your hysteria. I don't believe someone from out of town would understand what you're talking about, even when you go into such detail."

The woman customer's hair was pulled back, affording a clear view of her face. Her skin had the strange look of a shriveled apple someone had forgotten in a refrigerator. She shrank back at the words of the old woman at the register but still looked up at Kizu as she continued her warning.

"You've got to watch out for that woman. She's going to be running that Farm she inherited, together with your church, isn't she? *That* woman is what I'm saying! I went to the Hollow to warn you people not to be deceived by her, but with those men guarding the buildings I couldn't get close. So I lay in wait beside the river until you came out of the clinic. I don't have any ill feelings toward you and the others. All I want is to warn you how frightening that mannish woman is!"

The old woman came out from behind the register and struck Mrs. Kamei—who was leaning against the shelf of detergent, saliva wetting her chin—on her back. When Kizu left the market he was afraid the woman might follow him, so he hurried up the slope that led to the Hollow.

4

The arrival of the first wave of new residents was finally over, the room assignments all taken care of, and it was decided to hold an evening meeting, with Patron in attendance, so everyone could hear the reports from those in charge of the various aspects of the move.

Kizu, though, hadn't heard about the meeting, since Ikuo had gone off after breakfast to take care of some matter at the Church of the Flaming Green Tree Farm without mentioning it. The first time he heard about the gathering was when he joined Ogi and Dancer, who as they were wont to do came an hour after the peak time for lunch in the monastery cafeteria. Dancer asked Kizu to report at the meeting on how his plan for a children's art school was coming along.

"If Ikuo had only told me there was a meeting, I could have finalized things with the teachers this morning," Kizu said. "For some reason they seem a little slow in responding."

Dancer found it strange that Ikuo hadn't said anything about the meeting, even though the two of them were living together.

"Ikuo's been talking about the Farm with Satchan, and they've just about reached an agreement," she said. "I expect he'll report on it tonight. . . . Professor, you bought some of the Farm's ham, butter, and vegetables, didn't you? Isn't it great? They've hired some of the local young people and have been able to continue farming the fields and running the meat plant on a small scale. The original investment to set it all up came from their church.

"Satchan told us that wages have gone up this year and they might not be able to turn a profit. They weren't thinking of scaling back to the point where the work would be done in individual homes, but she was worried whether she'd be able to pass on the factory to the children going to the junior high now and to her adopted daughters.

"When he heard this, Ikuo proposed that the Technicians be allowed to use the facilities for their own work and help run the factory with them, so it could get back to the size it was when the church was operating it. It was a perfect match. So they drew up a plan to have several people from the Technicians spend their time at the Farm."

"He hasn't told me any of these details," Kizu said, clearly full of misgivings, "but even if it's for the church could Ikuo really be so interested in the production of meats and other food? I find that hard to believe."

"He's very enthusiastic about it," Ogi said, in Dancer's stead. "He's also quite interested in the communal life the church's young people used to live at the Farm. Not long ago, Asa-san held a workshop on how they've been running the Farm, and Ikuo showed a lot of interest in something that came up; namely, that a sect in that church, people who were involved in the manufacturing process, had engaged in weapons practice in order to defend the church."

Ogi went on to explain that Ikuo's plan was to have the Technicians take over work at the Farm on an experimental basis and make it into an economic base for a second and third wave of believers. Ogi also mentioned that Ikuo had been holding talks with a group of students from the junior high in the valley and the high school in Old Town.

"After we spent our first night in the house on the north shore of the Hollow," Dancer added, "we went back to the chapel the next morning. There were human bones laid out on the floor, and though Ogi was pretty calm about it, I can tell you I was shocked. After I talked with Asa-san, I understood that those bones were a written challenge to us from this group of boys and their little detective-novel secret society. Ogi, remember how they spelled out the name of their group in the bones?"

"YOUNG FIREFLIES. According to Asa-san it's the name given to a local custom—"

"That group, then, was threatening us because we're encroaching on their territory," Dancer said. "We knew the people in Maki Town were divided into two factions, those who accept us and those who want us out. What worried me was whether those children sneaking into the chapel to play a prank were a vanguard of the group opposed to us and whether this meant a serious clash with the church was imminent.

"When he heard this, however, Ikuo went to meet with this secret society and arranged things with them by himself. I think the former junior high principal was also involved. We found out that the leader of this group is Satchan's son."

"Ikuo never said a thing to me about it," Kizu admitted.

"I'm sure the two of you have more important things to talk about," Dancer said encouragingly.

"Ikuo should be giving a report at the meeting today," Ogi said. "I think he's the person in the church who's been working the hardest, what with forging a relationship with the Farm and trying to get to know the young men in the area."

The podium had been put away to clear a space in the middle of the chapel for the meeting, with several rows of chairs set up around this space. Light filtering in from the high windows on the cylindrical walls and down from the skylight made a play of light and shadow in the empty space that Kizu found beautiful.

Whenever they had meetings in the conference room of his university and there were more people than chairs, the students and staff would spontaneously squeeze more chairs into each row, with an efficiency that always impressed Kizu, and the way the chairs were lined up here revealed an intimate knowledge of the interior of this building. Obviously it wasn't the first time they'd used the chapel for these purposes.

When Kizu mentioned this to Dancer, she told him that setting up the chapel had become part of the Technicians' day-to-day duties, just as the Quiet Women had taken on meal preparation and the daily cleaning of the inside of the chapel and its grounds.

Kizu recognized the sort of dynamic manpower that those trained in intellectual endeavors could demonstrate. It was different, though, from what he'd known at his own institute, something he realized for the first time since joining this organization of believers.

Now that he thought of it, the way the Quiet Women prepared the daily meals also ran so smoothly it was as if they'd been doing it all their lives. Every day at noon, when he went from the north shore of the Hollow along the weir to the dining hall, he found the chapel, the monastery, and the courtyard, as well, all clean and neat as a pin.

After eating lunch in the dining hall he usually went back home to the north shore. When he stopped by the office or went through the courtyard, almost every church member he ran across were people he'd seen before. Kizu got the impression that in the rooms in the monastery they were leading an equally well-ordered communal life. It also occurred to him that the lifestyles of each of these two groups, the Quiet Women and the Technicians, couldn't help but affect others who were to move here.

On this day, too, both groups took efficient charge of the meeting. Everyone found seats without any congestion, in so orderly a way you would have thought individual names were carved on the backs of the chairs. Patron, accompanied by Morio—Ms. Tachibana taking an inconspicuous spot diagonally behind them—sat down in the first row of seats on the lake side of the building. Dancer and Ogi, who sat on either side of Patron, urged Kizu to sit in the same row with them. Beside him sat Dr. Koga and, next to him, Ikuo.

Directly across from Kizu sat Mrs. Shigeno of the Quiet Women—together with their leader, Ms. Oyama—who gave Kizu a friendly nod of greeting. Among the group of Quiet Women clustered around these two were women Kizu remembered seeing in the greenhouse along the Odakyu Line. He caught a glimpse of Ms. Takada, the one with the scar on her face, her body angled off to one side, seated in the second row.

This was the first time Kizu had seen all the former radical faction, the Technicians, who were among the first to move here. Clustered in their own little group like the Quiet Women, these men in the prime of life gave the impression of being an intelligent elite group. Kizu was frankly pained by the thought that these well-educated researchers had left their fields of specialization and were now doing manual labor as members of a religious organization.

What a terrible loss to Japanese academia and industry! Kizu thought, the idea itself the product of his long years in America and an American university. He wondered if the church office had prepared a program to make good use of these men who—both as people and as highly skilled specialists— were so far above average.

Patron opened the meeting with remarks that were unexpectedly carefree.

"Well, everybody, I'm hoping, with the land and the buildings that are still being readied and through the facilities at the farm, that you've been getting an upbeat feeling about our future here. How do you feel about it? I don't think the character of our life here will be changing all that much, so if any one of you feels uncomfortable with our communal life, I'm not recommending that you just grin and bear it. There's a great number of people who've already announced their intention to move here. Please feel free to discuss this in informal groups or come individually to the office if you'd like to talk about it, but feel free to move in and out as you please. Normally you'd be hearing this sort of thing from representatives of our office, but since I don't have anything else to say today, I decided to announce this in their place."

Morio seemed so taken by Patron's casual way of speaking that he could barely restrain himself from applauding. Instead, he merely nodded, and Patron gave him a serious nod in return. Kizu was favorably impressed by their completely natural rapport. Those who lived with Patron in his detached house on the mountain side of the eastern edge of the monastery didn't take their meals in the dining hall, so it was the first time in quite a while that Kizu had seen Morio.

Soon after they'd moved to the Hollow, Patron had invited Kizu and Ikuo for dinner at his residence, but Kizu was busy with his large-scale painting—he'd finished the sketches he'd begun in Tokyo and though the main theme wasn't settled, the hint Dr. Koga had dropped was swirling around in his mind—and couldn't spare the time. The explanation the office staff had given convinced Kizu that Ikuo was busy, but day after day he'd return late at night, well after dinner was over, and Kizu, finding it too troublesome to walk alone over the weir to the dining hall, would more often than not make do with groceries he picked up at the market.

In this casual intimacy between Patron and Morio, Kizu could sense a positive mood surrounding Patron's daily life in this new location, where he now seemed to be getting back on track.

Mrs. Shigeno spoke next.

"The Quiet Women would like to get everyone's opinion about the cafeteria. Have the meals we've prepared up till now been all right? Starting this week we'll be using ham, bacon, and fresh chicken from the Flaming Green Tree Farm. We're also negotiating with a company we've done business with for a long time to buy some very fresh pork as well. As for fish, a church truck will be going to the sea to lay in a stock. The only remaining question is finding a reliable provider of beef.

"We're not doing this for all of you in the church so much as in the hope that it will help improve people's diets here in this region. Soon after we arrived, I was quite shocked at how poor the selection of goods is in the markets here, and when I went to the Old Town I found it much the same. The Era of Rapid Growth and the Bubble Economy have passed this place by with barely a ripple.

"Still, it's interesting to look at the schoolchildren here, because they're as big and strong as any kids you'd find in the city. I hope we can get the Farm completely up and running soon so we can provide these children with delicious, healthful food. According to Ikuo, the Farm has a variety of equipment so as long as we can reestablish connections to some reliable suppliers, we can leave the rest up to the Technicians."

Seated beside Ms. Tachibana and behind Patron, Asa-san hesitantly replied to Mrs. Shigeno. "In its heyday, the Flaming Green Tree Farm had a good connection with a major meat wholesaler for ham and bacon, as well as with retailers to sell the finished products. Satchan had her reasons for scaling back the Farm's operations, but maybe you could revive this connection with the supplier again. Anyhow, besides the negotiations to turn over the management of the Farm to the church, she has been putting out feelers in a few other directions."

"Thank you very much for your explanation," Mrs. Shigeno said politely. "That being the case, there's not much cause for concern. The only thing I'm trying to do is find out whether you've liked the food so far. I don't imagine you want to come right out and say you don't like it. Should we talk about whether to go along with a supplier who wants us to put in a vending machine with beer and alcoholic drinks? The Technicians, though, since they're in a field that involves calculations with equations, don't seem to drink alcohol much."

Dr. Koga spoke up briskly. "Some of them *do* drink, so when they want something they buy it from the vending machine in front of the general store down by the river. Can't they just continue to do that? That's the least we can do to help out the local economy! Speaking as a doctor, it's healthiest if the vending machines selling alcoholic drinks are as far away as possible. Good exercise, after all. Also, and the Technicians are all in agreement on this, we have no complaints about how the Quiet Women are running the dining hall. Compared to the research institute's dining hall ten years ago, Japanese food has become quite gourmet."

The calm former radical members followed Dr. Koga's pronouncement with a serious, almost solemn attitude.

Dancer spoke next.

"We've already come up with a proposal for Patron to give sermons in the chapel. We've posted the first announcement on the bulletin board in the dining hall, but this doesn't mean we'll follow the same schedule every week. Some people have gotten in touch with us at the office requesting that a regular program of sermons be set up as soon as possible. The main question is Patron's health. Patron has been mentally preparing so that the church can have a clean start. We've come this far. I ask that you be patient until he's physically and mentally ready to begin. At the beginning Patron told you some things that Ogi or I should have reported, and now I guess I've said some things that are more properly in Patron's purview."

Kizu was sure that calls—if not protests—for Patron to address them directly would arise from the assembled group, but instead a warm reaction welled up from the circle of participants. The feeling that *we've come this far* was clearly not confined to Dancer.

At this point Ikuo spoke up. To Kizu at least, his forceful words seemed aimed from the beginning at intentionally introducing something completely at odds with the congenial, homey atmosphere they'd built up.

"I think we've heard enough about the transfer of the Farm to our church," he said. "There's something else I'd like to talk about. I'm hoping Patron's new church will begin here, in this building—on this piece of land, I suppose I should say—at the earliest possible date. I can't imagine what direction the church will take, but like everyone else I trust in Patron and am looking forward to a new beginning.

"As we're waiting for the launch of the new church, all of us new residents—individually or in groups—each have our own approach to things. There's no need for us to criticize the way others are standing by, waiting for things to develop. As Patron's conception of the church takes shape, disagreements and agreements will naturally come to the surface, and we can cross that bridge when we come to it. At this stage, each group and individual must examine their relationship with the local people and ask how this might benefit the church. I'd like to mention what I'm doing myself. As this progresses, I hope you'll let me continue to act on my own.

"Right now, through the good offices of the former junior high principal and the head priest of the Fushoku temple, I've begun to meet with the local youth group. At first they were rather antagonistic to our church, thinking we just barged in here without consulting anyone. But the other side of this coin is their curiosity about us. The reason I'm interested in *them* is that they're still young—high school and junior high students, the age when people still treat them as children—but there are some real individuals among them, and as a group they're quite outgoing. About twenty or so well-disciplined members get together regularly with their leader, who himself is a unique guy. As I meet with them I'd like to consult with them and report any new developments in our church. May I have your approval to do this?"

Ikuo came to a resolute halt. Nobody said a thing. The Technicians' faces didn't show whether they approved or not, but Kizu could sense that they and Ikuo had long since come to an understanding.

"I'd like to hear Patron and the office staff's opinion, but from what I've heard here I have no problem with what Ikuo's been doing," Dr. Koga replied generously. "Nothing's more important than building good relationships with the local people. This may sound like I'm blowing my own horn, but that's why I took over the clinic. We can't give the local people the impression that we're just shut up in our buildings concentrating on our own affairs, no matter how spiritual they may be. You only have to consider what happened with the Aum Shinrikyo *satyans* to understand this.

"On the other hand, though, it was quite a lot of trouble for the Quiet Women and the Technicians to come to the decision to move here, and actually to carry it out. After finally settling in with their new church, do we really expect them all to be open to the local people right off the bat? I think we want to get deeper into ourselves and into our faith. That's how very great our expectations are of this new path Patron's taking. Which doesn't contradict Dancer's understandable call for us not to rush him.

"Our honest thoughts on this might disappoint you, Ikuo, but what I want to say is that we've only begun. I find your dealings with the next generation here intriguing. And I promise you that every one of the Technicians will spare no effort to help you make the Farm a success. That's all I want to say. Do exactly as you wish."

* * *

The next day at lunch Kizu heard from Dancer that Patron, who except for his first announcement had remained silent throughout, was quite pleased with the results of the meeting. Patron had also said something else. Dancer lowered her voice so the Technicians seated nearby, who had returned for a late lunch from working to restart the facilities on the Farm, couldn't hear.

"Patron asked me, 'What's with the former radical faction? Why is such a formerly outgoing, active group now living like a bunch of monks?'"

21: The Young Fireflies

1

Since his plan to run a children's art class would be using a room in the junior high school, Kizu needed to look into how this would fit in with the second-semester curriculum—and though he had considerable time to consider this, with the summer vacation between now and then, he went again with Asa-san, the wife of the former junior high principal, to visit the school's staff room. While they were there he asked Asa-san about the group called the Young Fireflies that Ikuo had mentioned during the meeting in the chapel.

Asa-san began by explaining the local custom of the same name. She was nearing sixty and had first heard about it as a ceremony her mother had participated in as a child. When someone died in the valley, children ages seven to ten would light torches and climb up the surrounding slopes. The children were divided into pairs, and each pair climbed to a designated tree at the top of the forest. One of the pairs carried an object, representing the soul of the departed, to bury under the roots of a tree. Several pairs would go up at the same time in order to keep the chosen tree a secret.

"My mother said her first memory of this was when she was three or four," Asa-san went on, "still too little to be a Young Firefly herself. She said that when she looked up at the forest from the back sitting room of her house she could see countless torches ascending the slopes. The number was greater than the number of seven- to ten-year-olds who lived there, somebody told her later, because they were allowing smaller children to join them.

"One other thing you should hear concerns a child named Doji, who led the second of two rebellions around the time of the Meiji Restoration. After the rebellion was a success, they say Doji returned to the forest. The name

Young Fireflies might have grown out of this, since Doji is a homonym for the Japanese word translated as *young*.

"The present Young Fireflies group that local junior and senior high school children have formed is connected with this history but has nothing to do with the defunct custom. They do, however, assemble at dawn and practice climbing up the forest, so at least they're maintaining the *form* of the ceremony.

"They're children, so they may very well be drawn to the figure of Doji, the child leader of the insurrection. Satchan told me they debate among themselves how to live in this land and how to improve the environment. Her son Gii is the leader of the Young Fireflies. When he was little he used to come to our house to talk with my husband. An odd child, I'd say, to want to spend time talking with the principal."

"Don't they say his father is the one who founded the Church of the Flaming Green Tree?" Kizu asked. "When I was buying ham and eggs at the market by the river, another odd person, a woman, told me the boy isn't Satchan's."

"Oh, that's the former music teacher at the junior high. She's been behaving herself these days, but I did hear she got worked up and caused a ruckus. A man by the name of Kamei in the former church gave his entire estate in order to build the chapel, and his wife tried so hard to dissuade him that something snapped in her and they were divorced. That's the woman you met. She still carries a grudge against the church and directs her anger against Satchan."

Not long after this, Kizu heard from Ikuo about this leader of the Young Fireflies he'd been seeing. One evening at twilight, a week after the meeting in the chapel, after a calm, sunny, though unseasonably cold day, Kizu finished putting in order all the drawings and supplies he'd sent from Tokyo and was resting on his bed, which did double duty as a chaise longue, his head propped up high, when Ikuo returned. Youthfully flushed like some formidably featured young woman, Ikuo had come back to ask Kizu to dine with him at the monastery. His voice was excited.

"The Gii of the Fireflies, who's regarded as the new Gii, is an amazing guy, a genius, in fact. Because of this, he's quite a confident young fellow. He's so young it's hard to say he has much experience, I guess, but there's a deep connection here between this land and the history of his clan.

"Gii knows everything there is to know about this area's legends and its past, recent events included. You know how we look back on things in our lives and say certain experiences were good and regret others? That's how he has considered historical events that have taken place here. He also has a good idea of what he plans to do in future; he's set on spending the rest of his life here.

"When I suggested that at least he go to college, he shot down that idea with a scornful laugh. He has a strong conviction based on the history of his family as to the path his life should take. His father got a degree in agriculture from Tokyo University and started that church here that failed. His grandfather also graduated from Tokyo University, in education, became a diplomat, and retired to the Hollow, where he died of cancer. The things he learned at school didn't help him reform anything in this small local society, let alone the nation. It didn't amount to anything. So Gii says that living here in this *anti-Center* valley in the woods he can really do something important. The legends and history of this place will be his textbook. If he needs to know anything else, he said, he'll read some books."

Kizu felt a twinge of childish jealousy, for Ikuo was full of a cheerful enthusiasm that had been missing at the meeting in the chapel.

"When I saw you last time I thought I hadn't yet met Gii," Ikuo went on. "I planned to talk to you and the church only after I'd actually met him. But now I realize I *had* met him. Whenever I went to talk with the young people at the Farm there was always one young man who, though he never looked directly at me, was unforgettable. That's Gii. They start their training every day while it's still dark, and after they're done the high school boys ride their bikes to the high school a half hour away. Today's a holiday, Founder's Day at school, so they could take their time practicing, and I was able to join them and finally talk to Gii.

"After we crossed the bridge and entered the woods, I could sense he was the leader, even though he wasn't obviously calling the shots. He has this very fetching way of walking. We followed a kind of animal path beaten down through the woods as we scaled the hill in a clockwise direction. Twice we crossed a river and a road, which they hurried over on tiptoe as if they didn't want to sully their feet with profane ground. As I tried to keep up with them, Gii told me more details about the group. Steadily climbing the steep slope, he told me all this in a very thoughtful, precise way. He's a splendid young man."

Kizu couldn't help smiling when he heard this. His jealousy had vanished, replaced by a pleasant sense of how excited Ikuo was.

When he saw Kizu's reaction, Ikuo stopped speaking, and Kizu took advantage of the pause. "Let me make a suggestion," he said. "You haven't told any of this to the office staff yet, have you? Let's invite Ogi and Dancer, and we'll all have dinner together while you tell us about it. It's a shame to not share this report with the others."

Kizu called Mrs. Shigeno in the dining hall to ask about the menu for that night—ham steak sandwiches made of ham the Technicians had helped to cure, as well as vegetable soup made of the ham bones. That sort of food was simple to transport, so it was easy enough for all of them to eat together at the office. Kizu asked Mrs. Shigeno to phone the office about his plan, and then he and Ikuo left their house on the north shore.

Mrs. Shigeno enjoyed impulsive ideas, and she packed their dinners into the cardboard boxes with the logo the Church of the Flaming Green Tree used when they sold box lunches in the hotel in Matsuyama and the shops in the airport, the one Kizu had seen in the market. When Kizu and the others heard that Patron and Ms. Tachibana and her brother had received the same dinners packed the same way, they pretended that they were all on a picnic and settled down in the room next to the office, looking out over the moonlit lake. While they were waiting for their food to be brought over, Ikuo drove over to the general store and procured some cans of beer from the vending machine. Feeling he was on the same wavelength as the Fireflies now, Ikuo continued to be in a buoyant mood.

Gii had asked Ikuo whether he thought they were all free to choose their own fate. Ikuo agreed in principle, and Gii went on to tell him how he'd surveyed the people in Kame Village, before it merged into Maki Town, to find the different paths people had chosen in their lives. When they had their school festival in the second year of junior high, Gii had made a display presentation of his findings in the social studies corner. Teachers and parents ignored it, but his display had turned out to be the impetus to forming the Fireflies. Gii had taken a copy of his findings out of the back pocket of his jacket to give to show Ikuo, clearly having prepared in advance for their talk. His list read as follows:

a. People who live in the village who have some role to play in the social system. Those who control and who are controlled. Each side views the other critically.

b. People who live in the village but have fallen out of the social system. People without any abilities: the elderly, those with severe handicaps, those who have committed crimes, children.

c. People who live in the village who tried to create their own subsystem but failed. Leaders and followers in various movements. On the surface they have no influence, but behind the scenes it is a different story.

a.' People who've left the valley to live in urban areas and have found a role to play there. These people are greatly respected in the village society, but since they live in cities they have no role to play in the village. Even if they return to the village, they aren't given a role, either up front or behind the scenes.

b.' People who've left the village for urban areas and have fallen out of the social system there. Generally they've vanished, with no reports about them. Occasionally reports surface of some of them becoming criminals.

c.' People who have left the village to live in urban areas and are attempting to create an independent subsystem. Though the possibility exists, no one has yet been victorious or been defeated in these endeavors. One example from the distant past of this would be Fujiwara Junyu from the lower reaches of the Maki River.

"Gii certainly has the ability to think abstractly," Ogi said, in innocent admiration, as he read Gii's notebook page. "If you took this to its logical conclusion, wouldn't there also be a classification in *c* and *c*' of people who were successful?"

"That's probably because there weren't any specific examples in *c* as there were in *c*'," Ikuo said. "When Gii was dividing these into groups, I understand he did have some examples in mind. It's kind of a typical junior high school way of doing things, but that doesn't mean he's incapable of abstract thought. In fact, as you say, it's quite the opposite. In this classification system, I think Gii himself wants to be a successful example of *c*. In other words, one of Ogi's missing pieces—someone who's created a successful subsystem. That's why he founded the Fireflies. Pretty bold fellow, I'd say."

As Ikuo was bragging about them, Kizu thought that if it were up to him he would have called them nice kids—and he would have included Ikuo in this category.

"Gii knows that in this region there are examples in the *c* category who've failed. First of all there's the man said to be his father, Satchan's husband, the Brother Gii who made this lunch box." Ikuo showed them the lunch box resting in his hand, the contents of which had been devoured, a box with trees painted on it with detailed green leaves. "There were still a lot of these lunch boxes left over at the farm. And Former Brother Gii, who led the so-called Base Movement. Also there are the leaders of the various insurrections and the legendary figures he's uncovered.

"Gii told me, with a laugh, that he's thoroughly investigated all these figures from the past in order *not* to follow their examples and has come up with his own idea: a plan—through his own subsystem of the Fireflies—to conquer this land. The children have pledged themselves to create this as their program for the future. This isn't to say that all the members of the Fireflies have to remain here. Most of them would go to be educated in cities. But they would never forget their pact and would return here as soon as they could. Those unable to return would support the Fireflies from the outside. It's that sort of flexible pledge.

"What I find most intriguing is Gii's notion that this land is the center of the world, and that creating his own subsystem here is equivalent to creating a subsystem in category c' in the entire society. He grew up listening to legends of this land from old people here, who in turn had learned them from their own grandparents, and that's where he came up with his worldview."

Ikuo leaned forward to pop open a can of beer, and Dancer took the opportunity to ask a question.

"Ogi and I first thought the incident we experienced was a bit of harassment on the part of adults opposed to the church taking over the chapel, but later we learned it wasn't the antichurch faction in Old Town at all but the work of these young boys. Do you get the sense that they have special feelings toward the Hollow?"

"As I mentioned," Ikuo said, "the Fireflies have gone around collecting the legends of this region, and as they've done so they've started to believe that the Base Movement and the Church of the Flaming Green Tree are historically important. The Hollow for them is a kind of sacred ground that links all these groups. That being the case, when a bunch of outsiders from an unrelated church comes in and occupies this historic building, they can't help but express how upset they are."

"It's like the Palestinians and the Israelis," Kizu added, "though naturally there are more differences than similarities."

"Actually," Ikuo said, "Gii told me that with the sacred Hollow snatched away from them by our church they *do* feel like Palestinians."

"But surely there are brighter prospects for coexistence here than in the Middle East," Dancer said.

"First of all I'd like to get them to consider our position," Ikuo said. "Also, as one member of the church, I'd like to consider what we have to offer to this land. Instead of cooperating with the village authorities to suppress the Fireflies, I think it would be much smarter to get to know them better. At any rate, Patron has agreed to my negotiating. And I want to. After all, Gii's the son of the owner of the Farm, with whom we'll be working closely."

"The more connections we have with the local people the better, I think," Ogi said. "I haven't told Professor Kizu this yet, but Asa-san phoned a while ago about the art school and said the local schools can't help. According to her, the Old Town faction opposing the church staged a comeback."

"Is that right? I suppose it's to be expected," Kizu said disappointedly. "If Aum Shinrikyo had had an artist among them who wanted to open a painting class in the village at the foot of Mount Fuji where they had their headquarters, I don't suppose the locals would have welcomed the idea."

"I thought it was going to work out, having the former junior high principal's wife pulling for you," Dancer said, a note of dissatisfaction in her voice, though Kizu was already resigned to it.

After dinner, Ogi and Dancer still had work left to do, so Ikuo and Kizu left them at the office, leaving behind a few cans of beer. When they'd left their house on the north shore of the Hollow the wind had made them shiver, and now while they'd eaten dinner the wind whipping down the north slope had gotten even colder and was accompanied by a thick fog, unseasonable even for these woods. The only light was set up where the path through the court-yard ran downhill, so the rest of the time they walked in darkness.

Kizu called out to Ikuo, who was shining his flashlight on the fog-shrouded dam as they walked along.

"They say the dam was made to collect water from the river and from natural springs, but it's really an amazing amount of water—even in the dark you can sense that. One older person who used to act as electrician at the former Izu Institute proposes to redo the lighting around the chapel and the monastery. He says he'll also put a light that will burn all night at the corner where we turn to go up to our house. Can't have anyone falling in the lake, now, can we."

"The Technicians who've moved here have really been working hard. I imagine they think that if they do, this place can become a good foothold for them. Things have gotten pretty lively at the farm since they started working there, that's for sure."

Very considerately Ikuo moved behind Kizu so as to light up the path ahead for him. With this young man so immersed in his work, though, Kizu felt more and more left behind.

2

The next Sunday, Ikuo left near dawn to join the Young Fireflies in their training as they made one complete circuit of the forest. Despite his physical condition, Kizu didn't find it hard to get up early, so he joined Ikuo for break-fast before he set off. Afterward, afraid of the dull pain that sometimes hit him right after he awoke, Kizu wrapped himself in his blanket, opened the window on the lake, and sat looking at the swirl of thin fog outside. The birds weren't yet chirping, and bees buzzed halfheartedly around the leaves of the oak trees, dripping with the fog.

Before long—from the woods that ran behind the monastery on the heights of the opposite shore, where the fog was lifting—he could sense a line of people cutting through across the woods. He could hear the sound of trees being struck and lush branches snapping—all to the accompaniment of the sound of soft-soled sneakers, so this wasn't some herd of animals. Was it really natural for people used to walking through the woods to make so much noise? Perhaps, Kizu considered, Gii was deliberately having his boys cause a commotion to advertise their presence.

Two hours later Ikuo was back, redolent of fresh foliage and grasses, and he asked Kizu if he'd noticed them passing by in the woods. Racing through the forest with a group of young men seemed much better able to revive him than spending time shut up indoors with an older man. Kizu just listened as Ikuo enthusiastically talked about what he'd found out about Gii.

"He seems to be about fourteen, though his mother has never disclosed his birth date, so even on his family record it's not clear how old he is. This is why Gii says there are people here who insist he's adopted or even stolen. Did you know that until she graduated from high school, Satchan lived as a man?

"Anyhow, Gii's only about fourteen, but he lives with a woman, if you can believe it, an old friend of Satchan's who came back here awhile back; she does dyeing. Gii helped her collect the tree branches she needed for her plant dyes and that's how they became friends. Gii says he finds it amusing how, no matter what he says, the older woman always replies, 'No way!'"

That afternoon, Kizu and Ikuo happened to run across that same woman at the crossroads at the main bridge. At first Kizu thought she was bald. The head on top of her well-balanced muscular body had sparse reddish hair wrapped around it.

Just as it had upgraded to having vending machines, the general store at the crossroads had begun to accept parcel post deliveries, and Kizu wanted to check on the art materials donated to him by the store in Tokyo. According to the owner of this local shop, a thin, gloomy man who never looked you straight in the eye, several boxes had indeed been delivered, but this was before anyone from the church had moved into the Hollow, so he'd returned them to the main office in Matsuyama, where they were in storage.

After some tiresome haggling with the owner, they agreed that he would go pick them up, provided Kizu paid for it, the owner finally coming out from the entrance of the old wooden building to accept their documents. A woman who had been in the back of the dirt-floored entrance preparing a long box for shipping ran after him.

"Hello, Professor! It *is* Professor Kizu, isn't it? I'm Mayumi, the one you helped arrange an exhibit of Japanese dyed cloth in New Jersey. I'd heard from Gii that you were here."

Kizu searched his memory as he gazed at the woman, clad in a white-and indigo-dyed dress, her face with its taut tanned leathery skin smiling at him.

"I must look very different to you, I'm sure. I used to have quite luxuriant hair, but this spring I developed a rash from the dyes, and look what's happened. I'm sorry if I startled you."

Kizu's memory was still a little hazy, but Mayumi was sure he remembered her and continued, bashful at her own recollections.

"Would you mind talking for a while? There's no coffee shop along the river, but there *is* a nice little place just right for having a talk."

Kizu and Ikuo agreed, and Mayumi led them on, a basket woven from arrowroot swinging at her side.

"Just up the river from the main bridge there's an old bridge at the next curve in the road. No one drives on it anymore, and it's perfect to sit there and have a chat or to cool off. In fact that's how the local people have been using it."

The bridge had a weathered railing made of coarse granite, with a line of logs set up to keep cars out and thick knobby stumps and short logs arranged for people to sit on, making the bridge into a small park. Mayumi led them to the center.

On the opposite shore a grove of zelkovas formed a screen with their still, soft, light-green leaves. Seeing Kizu observing the trees so closely, Mayumi explained about the zelkovas and the broad-leafed woods on both sides of them. When she moved into the small house next to the farm, construction on the cross-Shikoku highway bypass was in full swing, and the cypress and cedar woods had all been mercilessly leveled. Cracks and holes appeared all through the broad-leafed woods that ran down to the riverside. But in the years since, the forest had recovered, and looking from below, at least, greenery covered the remaining wall of the bypass that ran though it—so much so that if a major economic downturn came and the bypass were to close, trees and vines would soon cover the slope completely, returning it to the state it was in before human beings inhabited the valley.

"It's past the season for it, but when the new leaves are sprouting and the flowers are in bloom it's a remarkable sight. Over there are beeches and oaks. And just up the river a little way when the *kojii* flowers are in full bloom, a shiny golden light-green, they're absolutely magnificent. Behind the chapel it's all one line of dark green, right? Those are Chinese hawthorns, and the place where they come together with the *kojii* is beautiful. The temperature's cooler than by the river, and it's in the shade for a long time, so the flowers were in full bloom until a short while ago."

As Kizu obediently listened to her, he looked around the expanse of broad-leafed trees, and up at the cypress and cedars beginning to be shaded with an indigo that, to him, was as pleasant as the throng of young leaves. From the bright cloudy sky a layer descended—snow or fog, it was hard to tell—the tips of the pillars of fog at the top of the forest rising to touch the darker layer, the tops of this lower layer visibly blending with the cloudy sky and forming a contrast with the forest below.

"Gii formed the Fireflies in order to work out his concept of creating a community independent of the outside world, didn't he?" Ikuo ventured.

"Yes, but these long-distance trucks run day and night down that highway, with no connection whatsoever to production and consumption in this valley. And as long as that continues, the bypass to the highway won't be closed to traffic like this old bridge was. Gii's not the sort to amuse himself with the impossible. 'My daydreams aren't real,' he told me once."

Feeling snubbed, Ikuo turned his dark face toward the river's surface, from which fog was also rising. For her part, sensing distrust of what she'd just said in his attitude, Mayumi continued seriously.

"Still, Gii has a concept of what the future holds and insists that there *is* a sense of reality to it. When he says that, the only thing I can say is *No way!* to put a damper on it.

"The kind of future Gii envisions is one in which the outside world has died out and the world constructed by the Fireflies is all that survives. This goes way beyond the notion of closing down the highway, but I can tell you he's dead serious about it!

"Gii's mother, Satchan, and I go way back. When she and Gii's father were running the Church of the Flaming Green Tree, one of their supporters was a woman pianist who also worked in international exchanges of various sorts. In a storage shed at the Farm, Gii ran across a Bach CD of a Russian pianist whom the woman had invited to Japan at one time.

"Gii was moved by the performance, but he got a hint for his concept from a poem the pianist wrote. Particularly the line *Perhaps the world has already passed away*. Listen to the Italian concerto, Gii said, the second movement, the andante, and that's how he began conceiving his unique vision of the future.

"Since the world has died, the people living in it are, of course, dead themselves. They're just pretending to be alive, Gii says. But sometimes, very rarely, you'll run across someone who is truly alive, like this Russian pianist, who stands opposed to the *already dead* world. Gii decided that in the future he wants to act the same way—as someone alive in an already dead world."

"I've felt the same thing," Kizu said, "that there are two coexisting worlds, one already dead, the other living. The two worlds overlap, and the world we know is a mix of the living and the dead."

"I don't really understand it myself," Mayumi said, "but when you consider the way the future might turn out, it's not good for the dead to have too much influence on those who should be living in the future. I heard from Gii that tomorrow the Fireflies will be meeting with the leader of your church. That's had me a bit concerned, which is why I wanted to talk with you."

Mayumi stopped speaking, rested her arms against the white mica-flecked railing of the bridge, and then spoke in a changed tone of voice.

"When the fog rises from the forest and merges with the descending clouds like that, it means rain's on the way. You may not be able to walk back to the Hollow in time. I apologize for having kept you."

3

The rain continued until the next morning. Ikuo got up early with Kizu, seemingly concerned about the Fireflies' dawn march through the forest. During breakfast, undeterred by the chilly damp air coming in from outside, he opened the window facing the lake, trying to catch the moment when the shift in wind direction would carry the sound of the Fireflies' movements their way.

After they cleared away the breakfast dishes, Ikuo came over to Kizu, who was back in bed reading, and told him he wanted to meet up with the Fireflies when they emerged out of the forest at the crossroads and give them a ride to the monastery.

"Patron's going to hold a meeting with the Fireflies today while they all eat lunch. I'm sure they'll be soaked after being in the woods and if they go back home to change they'll keep Patron waiting. I'd like to have them clean up in the monastery's communal bath and dry their clothes in the dryer there. Then they can start right at noon."

"There aren't many opportunities to hear Patron directly," Kizu said, "so I suppose there'll be a lot of people, won't there? I think I'm going to go a little early."

"Everyone's planning to take their lunch trays over to the chapel. Thanks in advance for helping out."

When Kizu followed Ikuo's directions and took his tray over to the chapel it was still a while before the meeting was to start, but everyone had already taken their seats. The chairs were set in two facing rows. Seated in the row on the lake side of the chapel were Patron, Dancer, and Ogi, Ms. Tachibana and her brother, and Dr. Koga, who was able to get away from the clinic only during the noon hour. The seat beside Ikuo was left vacant for Kizu. Twenty of the Fireflies were in the other row, already eating lunch, their carefree upbringing reflected in their physiques. Surrounding them all were the Technicians, as well as all the Quiet Women who weren't on kitchen duty. The whole scene was quite lively.

Ikuo, seated beside Kizu, had already devoured his lunch and didn't introduce Kizu to the Fireflies, but Kizu could tell they already knew who he was. The Fireflies looked very different from young boys Kizu had seen in Tokyo. These boys were all dressed alike, in jeans or soft cotton trousers and T-shirts, and they all looked well scrubbed after their communal bath.

The Fireflies kept their movements and conversation to a minimum as they wolfed down their meals. They weren't the only ones making short work of their food; the people in Kizu's row of seats were nearly done with theirs, and as the Quiet Women in charge of the meal went around handing out tea in disposable cups, Kizu had just about figured out which of the young men was Gii. He was seated in the middle of their group, and in the way he moved his shoulders and hands and in the timing of his little inclinations of the head, Kizu could understand the charm Ikuo had described.

Soon the church members, too, had finished their meals, and everyone waited for Morio and Kizu to finish. Meanwhile, several of the Quiet Women gathered all the dishes of the church office staff and the Technicians onto trays and carried them out to the dining hall. Ikuo motioned to the young men not to take their trays out but to stack them instead in a corner of the church. Time was of the essence, and he wanted to get the meeting under way as soon as possible.

"We planned on having a private meeting today between Patron and the Young Fireflies," Ikuo said, "but since there were so many in the church who wanted to attend, and there's no need to keep any of this a secret, the meeting has grown to include all these other folks too. I discussed with Patron how we should proceed, and he said he'd like the Fireflies to ask him whatever they want. I think it would be best to have Gii represent the Fireflies in asking questions. First Patron has a few words he'd like to say, and if he asks any questions I'd like Gii to be the one to answer them. Just follow the same procedures we've used in our own meetings."

As Ikuo sat down, Gii stood up, the eyes of all the boys suddenly riveted on him. Gii had a high forehead but not the type of hairline you'd expect to recede when he got older, dark eyebrows, and a sharply etched nose. Apart from a slightly pronounced jaw, his tanned face overall had a classic look. With hardly an ounce of extra flesh on him, he had the sharp yet lovable look of a dog just out of puppyhood. But as he stood there, tensely waiting Patron's words, the whites of his eyes glistening like porcelain, there was a childish, fragile feel to him.

"Ikuo wants me to answer questions from the Fireflies, but first I hope you'll indulge me by letting me ask some questions of my own," Patron said, still seated, returning Gii's gaze. "How did you come to make the Fireflies? You might very well want to ask us why we came here to make a church, but first I'd like you to answer me."

Gii's face showed a boyish bashfulness and a bit of pluck, for what both he and his companions wanted was straight talk, not beating around the bush.

"It might be a little unexpected to start off answering this way, but the basic reason we made the Fireflies and the reason you have this building are the same—the declining birthrate in Maki Town.

"The Church of the Flaming Green Tree built this chapel, and right afterward the church was dissolved and the building was supposed to be donated to the junior high. The town council decided that the land where the monastery is now was to be made into new classrooms. But foreseeing that the number of children going on to junior high would decrease, the council abandoned the plan. Your church expressed an interest, and it was a convenient out.

"Since long ago in this region, second and third sons went off to the cities to find work. Because the birthrate is now low, most of us are only children and have ended up living at home. That being the case, we decided to find a positive reason for staying here. Every one of us agrees with that. And that's how the Fireflies began. Could we ask some questions now?"

Patron nodded silently.

"While we were out training this morning, we discussed what we should ask you. Most of the requests were along the lines of having you tell us in simple terms what it means to believe in God. We hope you won't yell at us and just say that's a childish question—something you can't explain in simple terms—but we'd still like to hear what you have to say."

Dancer, mouth characteristically ajar, turned her gaze to the space above the Fireflies. The overlapping new green leaves in the oblong window on the forest side of the concrete wall were, until a moment ago, clearly visible, but now they were darkly shaded, meaning that the treetops were gleaming brightly. A faint smile came to her lips. Kizu wondered whether she found Gii's innocence amusing but decided that wasn't the case. As one might expect of Patron, he neither made light of Gii's question nor did he try to side-step it.

"As you all know," Patron said, "I'm a person who's done a Somersault. I'm not the kind of person, then, who can very well use *God* and *belief* in the same sentence. However, based on long experience I can say that even if God is completely out of the picture, one can still speak of belief. This gets a little tricky, but belief involves viewing oneself *vertically,* not just thinking along a horizontal axis.

"You've seen satellites being launched on TV, right? Just as the rocket goes *whoosh!* up into the sky, your thoughts rise to be the central axis around which you live. Climbing straight down a deep root is another way of look-ing at it. They're both the same thing."

Patron was silent and bent forward slowly, as if pondering his own remarks.

In contrast to the ruddy faces of the young men, the skin around Patron's eyes flushed in his otherwise round white face, a sign that he was excitedly concentrating, as well as irritated that he wasn't able to explain things as simply as they wanted. Kizu was fascinated by Patron's words, something he shared with the Quiet Women, at least the ones in his field of vision.

"Before the Somersault they say you often went into deep trances," Gii said, "and that you'd have these terrible visions. But that once you woke up and tried to tell what you saw, you couldn't do it alone."

"That's correct. As I'm sure Ikuo has told you, that's exactly right," Patron replied.

"We understand that your helper was Guide."

"Yes. It was like two people running a three-legged race. But now he's dead."

"So do you plan to train a new interpreter?"

"If only I could, that would be wonderful," Patron said with a frank sadness, his tone appealing, but different from before. "Problem is, since the Somersault I haven't had any deep trances."

"They say that by doing the Somersault you made a fool out of God."

Patron knit his brows together in a rather feminine way at this and took a deep breath. Kizu could feel the tension, not only in the Quiet Women but in the Technicians as well.

"That's right. My Somersault made a fool of the God I'd been connected to through my trances. It's quite okay to say that. Afterward Guide and I fell into the pit of hell, and that's where Guide died. It's not entirely clear to me whether I've managed to rise up out of there myself."

"So you mean this is hell?" Gii asked. The Fireflies let go with a burst of laughter to release the tension.

Kizu listened to Gii's typical adolescent laugh. Patron, a blank look on his face, gazed around at the laughing young men, for all the world like some plump dull pigeon.

4

"Patron's been very honest in what he's been saying," Dancer said, taking it on herself to break the silence that followed the laughter. This was directed less at Patron than at the others, her voice loud enough for the Quiet Women and all the Technicians to hear. "But maybe this is something hard for young people to understand."

"Patron *has* been saying what the Fireflies wanted to hear," Ikuo answered back.

"What we don't understand right now, we'll review when we go home. Just like they always taught us at school," Gii said, in a frank yet reserved way, and his friends burst out laughing again.

"Hard to tell which are the adults here," Dr. Koga whispered to Ikuo, in an amused tone.

"I'd like to continue with our questions, since we didn't come here to study how to enter Patron's church," Gii went on. "Our plan is to take over what *He Who Destroys*—in other words, the first Gii—began in these woods so long ago. The Base Movement aimed at following his ideas in improving production in the village and in improving young people's attitudes toward their own lives, while the Church of the Flaming Green Tree concentrated on prayer.

"In one sense this man was a kind of god, so people tried to do what they did out of a belief in him. I think both movements did only half of what they should have done. Our plan's to carry out both aspects. What you've said here about prayer is very helpful. Assuming, of course, that I understood it. . . .

"So now you've come to this sort of place and are going to make your church here. Right now the Fireflies are just a group of people. Once we establish our own headquarters, we might very well have to fight you, but at present if we can join together to do something to shake up the old folks in this region, that'd make us pretty happy. Well, those are our ideas."

As Gii finished speaking and plunked himself down, there was applause. Kizu looked up and saw that it wasn't just the Fireflies who were clapping but some of the Technicians, too.

The next day Ikuo, who'd gone to ask Patron what he thought of the meeting, reported to Kizu that Patron had found these "new men" quite intriguing.

22: Yonah

1

Everyone agreed that, apart from Dr. Koga's activities in his clinic, Ikuo was the one who'd been working the hardest since the move to the Hollow.

The meeting he'd arranged between the Fireflies and Patron and the other church members was not an isolated event but part and parcel of his overall activities. During the meeting it never came up that the leader of the Fireflies was the son of the owner of the Church of the Flaming Green Tree Farm. However, Ikuo was enthusiastic about restoring the farm operations, especially by getting meat production back to its previous level. Several of the Technicians were interested in this and, with Ikuo as their leader, were on the verge of mastering the necessary skills. The office agreed to the plan and to having most of the Technicians spend their time at the farm.

Laying the groundwork for this business meant that Ikuo was on duty at the farm every day. He returned to the house on the north shore of the Hollow only every second or third evening. Seeing that the abandoned buildings that used to house the farm workers would be of use when the second and third waves of church members moved to the village, he expanded his team of Technicians engaged in carpentry to fix them up.

Ikuo hadn't forgotten about Kizu's health, however. Once the Farm's housing took shape, Ikuo brought his team, now looking like full-fledged carpenters, over to their house to remodel the interior. Kizu was using the living room, where he also had his dining table, as a work space, and the carpenters removed the wall separating this from the short hallway leading to the bedroom next door. This completed, the interior became one airy, spacious room.

The Technicians rearranged the east side of the room as an art studio and set up a box with wheels containing the easels and painting sets Kizu had sent from Tokyo. Ikuo promised Kizu that once he began painting his oil tableau, he would make time to model for him no matter how busy he got with the farm.

Ikuo brought up another point, one that had been bothering him for some time. This had to do with the conversation Kizu had had with the owner of the store beside the river that handled package deliveries. Ikuo had decided that on one of his trips to Matsuyama on business, he would pick up the stored art supplies, even though the art class wasn't about to happen. Kizu was aware that, in line with the new relationship between the church and the farm, Ikuo was shuttling back and forth in trucks and vans between the town and Matsuyama, but he'd never pressed him to pick up the supplies.

Ikuo described one of his recent trips. "Last week when I went to Matsuyama I took three of the Fireflies with me. I planned to pick up the art supplies on the way back. Since we were driving a van, I knew I couldn't just load up the supplies the way they were boxed, so I brought them along to help. Once we unpacked the boxes, and the boys were loading them into the van, they were fascinated by all the paint sets and sketchbooks, like you'd expect kids to be.

"They started talking about how lucky people in an art class would be to use all these wonderful supplies and how the town didn't show any interest in opening a class. Finally someone said that these supplies would just end up stored away in some shed in the monastery, and Isamu, a high school senior who's Gii's right-hand man, proposed that all of them who'd helped load the art supplies get a free sketchbook.

"When he heard this, Gii smacked Isamu as hard as he could, so hard the man from the delivery company who was helping us was stunned. Gii is shorter than Isamu so he almost had to leap up when he hit Isamu right above his temple.

"Still worked up, Gii turned on me. It was kind of comical, like some typical juvenile delinquent shakedown; he asked if there wasn't a plan to use the art supplies would I let the Fireflies have them.

"I asked him what he planned to do with them, and he said he'd take them to the art shop on the main street and negotiate a deal. If we showed them the form with my signature I had to sign when we picked them up, and show my driver's license, he added, they wouldn't think they were stolen goods.

"'How do you plan to use the money?' I asked him. 'You just smacked one of your friends who wanted to skim a little off the top, right?' Gii said,

'Don't worry, I have a plan all right.' He wanted to set aside the money for something he had in mind for the Fireflies. So I said okay. I know I should have got your permission first. . . ."

"So did his negotiations work out all right?"

"They only managed to get a small amount of cash," Ikuo replied, clearly relieved.

2

That weekend Kizu began officially to work on his tableau. Ikuo or Dr. Koga no doubt laying the groundwork, Patron had asked Kizu to paint a triptych for the wall of the chapel.

Kizu had already decided to use the book of Jonah as his theme for the tableau, and when Ikuo came to convey Patron's request, Kizu explained his plan for the painting.

"If it's a triptych I'd like the first panel to show Jonah inside the belly of the whale. Jonah hears the call from God and is told to proclaim the wickedness of the people of Nineveh. But he runs away. The part where he's on board the Gentile boat and the captain and the sailors berate him and throw him into the sea would be good too. But it's the three days and three nights Jonah spends inside the whale that show how the rest of the story will develop. All of Jonah's thoughts are summed up in his prayer to God while he's in the belly of the whale. There's my copy of the Bible on the shelf above the trunk. Would you read that part for me?"

> "'In my distress I called to the Lord,
>   and he answered me.
> From the depths of the grave I called for help,
>   and you listened to my cry.
> You hurled me into the deep,
>   into the very heart of the seas,
>   and the currents swirled about me;
> all your waves and breakers
>   swept over me.
> I said, "I have been banished
>   from your sight;
> yet I will look again
>   toward your holy temple."

The engulfing waters threatened me,
>the deep surrounded me;
>seaweed was wrapped around my head.
To the roots of the mountains I sank down;
>the earth beneath barred me in forever.
But you brought my life up from the pit,
O Lord my God.

"'When my life was ebbing away,
>I remembered you, Lord,
and my prayer rose to you,
>to your holy temple.

"'Those who cling to worthless idols
>forfeit the grace that could be theirs.
But I, with a song of thanksgiving,
>will sacrifice to you.
What I have vowed I will make good.
>Salvation comes from the Lord.'"

"I can tell from the way you read it that you've been studying the book of Jonah," Kizu said, impressed.

"Yes, I have read it a lot," Ikuo replied, "but I don't know where the Lord is or what he's like. And the same holds true for salvation."

"How do you envision the second panel of the triptych?"

"How about a picture of Jonah, furious as he confronts God?"

"Would you read that part, too?" Kizu asked.

"'O Lord, is this not what I said when I was still at home? That is why I was so quick to flee to Tarshish. I knew that you are a gracious and compassionate God, slow to anger and abounding in love, a God who relents from sending calamity. Now, O Lord, take away my life, for it is better for me to die than to live.'

"But the Lord replied, 'Have you any right to be angry?'

"Jonah went out and sat down at a place east of the city. There he made himself a shelter, sat in its shade and waited to see what would happen to the city. Then the Lord God provided a vine and made it grow up over Jonah to give shade for his head to ease his discomfort, and Jonah was very happy about the vine. But at dawn the next day God provided a worm, which chewed the vine so that it withered. When the sun rose, God provided a scorching east wind, and the sun blazed on Jonah's head so that he grew faint. He wanted to die, and said, 'It would be better for me to die than to live.'

"But God said to Jonah, 'Do you have a right to be angry about the vine?'

"'I do,' he said. 'I am angry enough to die.'"

Ikuo closed the compact Bible. "I'm interested in the book of Jonah up to this point," he said, "but I don't like what God says after this. It's strangely *human*."

"The part where Jonah, angry, is sitting under the vine would make a clear theme for the second panel. What about the final panel? I'd planned for it to be the centerpiece of the triptych."

"I'm really interested in how you visualize that," Ikuo said seriously. "It's important to *me* too."

"Well, what sort of mental picture do you have?"

Standing beside the window with the lake behind him reflecting the setting sun, the edges of Ikuo's bull head were tinged a reddish black. Looking down, it seemed as if he were holding his breath, gathering his thoughts before he spoke.

"What I always imagine is the huge city of Nineveh burning up, the scene of more than a hundred and twenty thousand people who cannot tell their right hand from their left, children and countless cattle, all burned up. Not that Jonah's resisting God and asserting himself would lead to God's necessarily changing his mind and going ahead with the destruction he'd canceled."

"At any rate, with your help I'd like to begin painting the first panel," Kizu said, sounding like he hadn't really grasped the direction Ikuo's thoughts were heading. "When I start on the second, I think the concept for the third one will develop. Who knows? Maybe our life in the church from now on will show me the way."

"Yeah, it might," Ikuo said, making Kizu think that his own words had flown right over Ikuo's head in the direction of the man-made lake. "Just reading the book of Jonah might not give you an idea for the third panel. I've mentioned this to you before, but ever since I was a child I've wondered if the book of Jonah in the Bible is really the way the story ended. You remember how Guide urged me to appeal to Patron, and you wrote that letter for me? One of the questions I wanted to ask someone like Patron, who's suffered in reality and for his faith, was exactly that—about what happened afterward."

"How would the Technicians respond, do you think?" Kizu asked. "Aren't they themselves like uncompromising Jonahs?"

"They've been trained by experience to be men of few words, which means that once they do decide to speak you can bet they'll say something worth listening to."

3

So Kizu began his painting. First he set up two easels in the studio next to the lake, a studio bright with the reflected light of the sky and water; then he laid out so many drawings and watercolors of Ikuo on the floor that there was barely space to walk to the part of the room used as a bedroom. As he worked on the painting he felt that, although the number of days left to him was clearly few, he'd never experienced the moment-to-moment reality of time as intensely as he did right now. Not once did he feel time hanging heavy on his hands, certainly not when Ikuo was modeling for him and not even when he was away at the farm.

In spite of a deep-seated sharp pain and a sense of wasted effort and anguish that had settled inside him, Kizu discovered that once he began his tableau his attitude toward his cancer started to change. The first panel, the depiction of the walls of the whale's stomach that surrounded Jonah, he painted to reflect an endoscopic view of the path from the esophagus to the stomach and from the anus to the colon.

Sketching with crayon or pencil the figure of Jonah lying down, sitting, standing in front of this backdrop, he experienced the feeling that the drawings and watercolors he'd drawn up till then were less studies for a painting-to-be than indexes of a completed work. Up till then he was used to his sketches not being bound by any overall concept, only connected by the fact that they were done at one particular point in his life. But now he felt a conceptual connection binding them all, something totally new and unexpected.

As Kizu quoted from these studies as he worked, he also came to sense the inner world of this young man Ikuo, yearning, as if writhing in pain, to be understood. An inner world that—just like Patron after a trance without Guide—he could grasp artistically but that refused to coalesce into words. While his fundamental grasp of Ikuo was still imperfect, just being able to spend the rest of his life alongside the young man made him feel deeply privileged. Just the thought made him blush.

But would painting this picture of Ikuo be enough to let him inside the young man's inner being? For over ten years he'd abandoned the achievements he had diligently attained. Kizu felt a helplessness come over him, and once again this brought on a deep sadness, an emotion not unconnected to his cancer. Even though he might slump dejectedly in his chair before his painting, when Ikuo returned to model for him Kizu got so energetic it made him a little self-conscious.

In addition to Ikuo there was one other person who didn't hesitate to come into his studio to talk with him while he was working—Mayumi, the dyer, who was living with Gii. Kizu saw her as an artistic colleague, not a competitor, and welcomed her visits.

Mayumi came about once every three days and told him, among other things, how she came to be a friend of Gii's mother. When she was still living with her husband, a photographer and instructor in dyeing, Mayumi got to know Satchan, who at the time had some problems with the activities of the Church of the Flaming Green Tree and had temporarily left. Mayumi soon had troubles of her own and went abroad to escape from her husband. Dyeing, though, was something she couldn't abandon.

Before long Mayumi heard that the Church of the Flaming Green Tree was dissolved, Satchan had a child and was taking care of other children too, as she took over the management of the Farm, and Mayumi decided to help. She turned out to be more of a burden than a help, though, and settled into a house on the outskirts of the Farm that she converted into her dyeing studio. She got to know Gii as he helped her collect materials to use in her dyeing, and before very long they formed a relationship.

Mayumi had Ikuo pick up some coffee beans and a drip filter coffeemaker, which pleased Kizu no end. Sensing he was in a good mood for the first time, Mayumi broached the real purpose for her coming to visit the studio, her concerns about Gii. While he was painting, Kizu couldn't face her as she spoke, but when he took a break he sat down at the dining table across from her; she did all the talking, a worried look and a tiredness befitting her age etched on her dark face.

"Gii often talks about what he heard from his mother, a line from the sermon given by one of the followers of the Church of the Flaming Green Tree at the time it broke up. Something said by the head priest of the Fushoku temple, a happy-go-lucky sort of fellow. *Wherever each of you ends up, aim to be like a drop of water soaked up by the ground* is what he said. Another line is something the Former Gii said: *Become a flash flood of concentrated hate.*

"The Former Gii started the Base Movement here and worked to improve production and living standards in this region. He's the one who built this dam and gathered all the water to make the lake. But he didn't get along with the local people, and the people from the Old Town at the lower reaches of the river were directly opposed to him.

"What happened was, in the rainy season when the lake was full of water, he claimed the water was blackish and smelled bad and announced that he was going to blow up the dam and ride the ensuing flash flood himself. The Former Gii was an amateur expert on Dante, believer in a love that would change the world, yet in the end he became the exact opposite, a flash flood of concentrated hate.

"The local people thought this was getting too dangerous, so on a night when it was raining hard and the dam looked about to split open and flood the Old Town, they murdered him and dumped his body in the Hollow.

"If Gii formed his band of Fireflies here based on that first line, I find it a little too mysterious. These days, though, when the Fireflies gather in my house it's the *second* line that he brings up. This worries me. Since Ikuo is a Fireflies sympathizer and particularly favors Gii, I wonder if he's been telling you the truth about those kids. That's why I wanted to talk with you. I hope you'll make it clear to Ikuo in no uncertain terms that he has to avoid getting the Fireflies too worked up."

"Young Gii is really quite a leader in his own right," Kizu replied, "so even if they do include Ikuo in their activities I don't think they'd be incited by anything he did."

"Gii may not be the type who's easily flattered, but you have to realize that a boy that age is bound to look up to Ikuo, since he's older and open to their ideas."

"I have to admit Ikuo seems more youthful after being with the Fireflies," Kizu said. "Today, for instance, he's having them help out at the Farm. The Technicians are moving things along there so they can use the facilities as part of their future plans, but I imagine that for Ikuo it's more fun to work with the Fireflies than those older guys."

"I've met a few of the Technicians myself," Mayumi said, "and find them a bit eccentric. They're usually much quieter than Ikuo and just concentrate on the work at hand. They could be doing something really significant, but here they are doing these little piddling jobs in the middle of nowhere."

"Some people insist there's a special *power* in this place," Kizu said. "I have to tell you I find it a bit eccentric, too, that a young city woman like yourself would come to live way out here in the country."

"Maybe," Mayumi said, "but ever since I arrived here I've been excited, as if something amazing is about to happen. Which makes it a bit contradictory for me, I realize, to tell you church members not to respond if Gii throws up a challenge."

4

Once the design for the picture of Jonah in the belly of the whale was finished, Ikuo brought around Gii, Isamu, and five or six of the older members of the Fireflies, ones who were attending high school. Kizu had called ahead to the dining hall to order a lunch of sandwiches and milk for the youngsters. They stopped by the dining hall to pick up their lunch boxes before climbing the northern slope of the Hollow.

The boys were quite boisterous until they entered Kizu's studio, but once inside they were quieter than any students Kizu had had in an art classroom on either side of the Pacific; they stood behind him, silently gazing at the easel, their eyes fixed on his palette, shining like a mirror in its center where Kizu had mixed in turpentine and, using his own special technique, resin as well. The first one to break the silence was, naturally, Gii, the boss who held the kids in order. Gii seemed to find the model for the painting, Ikuo, much more important than the painting itself.

"This really is Ikuo all right! It makes me want to call him Yonah."

"You're right about that," Kizu agreed, approving his use of the Japanese pronunciation.

"Ikuo told us that you were still wondering how to depict Jonah in the third panel of the triptych, Professor," Isamu said, "but from the looks of it I'd say you've already reached a conclusion."

"What kind of conclusion?"

"The one that Ikuo's had from the beginning."

"Ikuo hasn't said anything to me about it," Kizu said.

"But Ikuo as Jonah wouldn't obey God's suggestion that the people of Nineveh be spared," Isamu said. "Didn't Ikuo tell us it's possible Jonah wasn't convinced by the parable of the vine?"

"If he's already reached a conclusion, he wouldn't have brought us here," Gii said. "Didn't he tell us he wanted us to take a good look at the first and second panels and give our opinion about how the third one should go? He wants us kids to help figure out the conclusion he's been pondering."

"Which is why I just gave my opinion about the first panel," Isamu said.

"Oh, I see. You do have the right to say that, don't you, Isamu."

"There's no need to jump to conclusions," Ikuo broke in. "Just look at this painting in progress and tell us what you think. Professor Kizu plans to take his time to decide on how to do the third panel."

Having wrapped that up, they passed around the boxes of sandwiches. The farm had just started milk production, and cups of milk were poured out for everyone from a large glass bottle.

As soon as they all began to eat, Ikuo turned to the Fireflies and brought the topic back to Jonah.

"Ever since I was a little boy, every time I thought about my life my thoughts would invariably converge on Jonah. You might laugh to hear this, but before that my model was Gusukonbudori."

"The Kenji Miyazawa story, you mean?" Gii asked.

"Right. The story where they come up with this idea to use an apparatus to make a volcano on an island erupt and raise the temperature of the entire earth by five degrees. The kind of project that environmentalists would definitely have problems with, for sure, but Gusukonbudori helps out. In order for the plan to succeed one person has to sacrifice himself, and that's the role he volunteers for.

"When I was a child that's exactly what I wanted to do. I was crazy about the part where he volunteers, is told that he shouldn't do it, and explains himself very calmly to the professor:

There will many more people like me from now on, and people who can do much more, whose work, whose laughter, and lives are more outstanding, more beautiful than mine.

"When I ran across the book of Jonah the object of my youthful enthusiasm changed. When I first read it I thought there were connections between it and "The Life of Gusukonbudori." Specifically, the part where the Lord announces to Jonah that the city of Nineveh will be destroyed in forty days. This reminded me of the time when Gusukonbudori's teacher predicts that Samutori volcano will erupt in a month (though this isn't the volcano that he makes erupt).

"At any rate, I recommend that you read Kenji Miyazawa along with the book of Jonah."

Kizu was amused by how Ikuo took on the role of teacher. After quickly downing their sandwiches and milk, the boys gathered together all the undone paper boxes and paper cups and were preparing to take them all back with them.

"Your new friends have certainly done a bit of training as a team, haven't they," Kizu noted.

"You should see them in the woods," Ikuo replied. "Their level of organization is amazing. They keep a strict, almost military discipline."

"Is all that training done for a purpose?"

"Better to let the Fireflies speak for themselves," Ikuo said, turning to Gii. "You told me your training is to simulate how you'd protect the order found in this valley if it were under siege, right?"

Gii and two of his fellows were relaxing on the wooden frame with a mattress that was Ikuo's bed when he returned from the farm, but he was attentively following their conversation and responded right away.

"We're just goofing around. If guys our age say that's what we're doing, then it's nothing worth discussing, really."

"It might be play, but even to an outside observer something intriguing is going on. Why don't you tell us about it?"

"There are these legends," Gii said, "stories handed down in these parts. A force came from over the mountains and occupied the village. And a farmers' revolt took place here, and when they marched out every last man joined them. We made a mobile unit that can move freely through the forest—just like those groups in the old days."

"Do kids these days use the term *mobile unit* when they play?" Kizu asked.

"It's more *your* generation, Professor, that avoids using military terminology, isn't it?" Ikuo said.

Letting that little collision between Kizu and Ikuo pass, Gii picked up where he left off.

"There's one other element in our game," he said. "This is from a French play that Asa-san's older brother the novelist told me. In this play, at harvest time for a couple of days the young people in the village, who are usually belittled, grab power from the local lord. If young people were to do that, to take power, in the end they'd be hunted down and terrible things would happen to them, right?

"So this is what we thought. How about if the young people, who are always treated like idiots, train themselves so when they grab power at the festival they can attack the establishment and continue to fight on even after the festival is over? That's the starting point for *our* game, and we go on to simulate what would happen if all the authority in the village, from the local government to the police, fell into the hands of the Fireflies."

"You actually had some predecessors in this village, didn't you, people who started reform movements, churches, and the like?" Ikuo said. "There's Former Gii with his Base Movement, Brother Gii and the Church of the Flaming Green Tree. But both those Giis were killed before they could accomplish anything. The newest Gii, then, is trying to learn from the past and not copy their bad examples. And this simulated training you're into is based on that."

"Adults don't take the Fireflies seriously," Gii said. "They think it's just some childish things the kids are doing. And we've been in existence for two years now. After Patron's church came here, Ikuo was the first person to treat us decently. He listened seriously to what we had to say and even helped us out financially. I know this is also thanks to you, Professor. . . . Now the Young Fireflies movement has a real future ahead of it."

5

As the Fireflies began to leave, arms full of empty sandwich boxes and paper cups, Ikuo asked Gii to stay behind. Isamu, next to Gii, gave him a look, but he brushed this aside and settled back down on the bed. Isamu appeared hurt, but Gii looked so proud that Kizu found it delightful.

"Three days ago Patron asked to meet Gii again, and they had a nice long chat," Ikuo began, as soon as the three of them were alone. "Morio was sprawled out beside him. It sounds like you had a productive talk. Patron started out asking you about the Church of the Flaming Green Tree, didn't he?"

"My father founded the church," Gii said, "but since I was born after the church was gone, all I know is what I've heard from my mother."

"What was Patron interested in about your father's church?" Kizu asked.

"*Anti* and *ante,*" Gii answered seriously.

"Patron's talking about the antichrist," Ikuo explained. "Patron is clearly an *anti*christ, while the leader of the Church of the Flaming Green Tree, whom his followers called *savior,* insisted that he was an *ante*christ. He preached that before the real Christ returns there will be countless *ante*christs, *ante* in the sense of *coming before,* and that he was one of them. After he graduated from high school in America, he went to Tokyo University, so he had some grounding in classical languages. Maybe he came across the term *antechrist* in some reference work? I don't know. Patron was quite interested when he heard this story from Asa-san, and he asked Gii to tell him more."

"But I don't know anything more than that," Gii insisted. "When Patron asked me whether it was possible for him to be both an antichrist and an *ante*christ in the sense that my father used the term, I remembered something my mother had said and told him that that didn't jibe with what my father taught. And Patron said, 'I guess that's right,' in a such a moving way I was quite surprised."

"I think that was a very valuable meeting for Patron," Kizu remarked. Ikuo, too, considered this, and the three of them were silent for a while until Gii, youngster that he was, couldn't stand the silence anymore and raised a new topic.

"Patron asked me why my mother and I hadn't kept the Church of the Flaming Green Tree going," Gii said. "'Don't they even call you the new Gii?'

he asked. I was kind of annoyed. I felt almost like picking a quarrel with him, coming back with something like, *What if I am? If I asked you to return Brother Gii's chapel to me, would you do it?* But I kept my cool and talked about what's always been on my mind. You're asking me why I distanced myself from both the Church of the Flaming Green Tree and the Base Movement and why I had to create the Young Fireflies? Well, the reason is that I have some problems with the leaders of both those movements. I may not be using the term correctly, but I think both leaders were *defeatists*. That's what I told Patron."

Gii stopped speaking, his pale face quite excited. Ikuo, too, was silent, pondering all this.

"What do you mean by defeatists?" Kizu asked.

Gii's pale cheeks suddenly revived. He'd been afraid they'd point out he'd used the word incorrectly.

"What I mean is from the very beginning neither Former Gii of the Base Movement nor Brother Gii of the Church of the Flaming Green Tree thought their movements would be successful."

Gii pursed his lips tight and turned pale again, so Ikuo explained things to Kizu.

"You know how the Former Gii threatened the people who lived downstream, saying he was going to blow up the dam and flood them? If he'd really wanted to, he could have done it, but he didn't. When he was murdered and his body dumped in the Hollow, his own tale was finished. Hadn't he known this? He created his movement resigned from the start that it would end up this way, which is why he's a defeatist.

"Brother Gii attracted a lot of followers and got production up and running at the farm, and things would have gone well if only he'd stuck it out. But suddenly he announced that the church was over, and a handful of followers would go out as missionaries, and that's when he was killed. I suspect he had a premonition at the beginning of his missionary trip that his story was over too. Gii thinks this is defeatist, and that putting that kind of person in charge is a big mistake."

As Ikuo spoke, Gii looked at him again with trusting eyes, blushing. But a moment later Ikuo turned on him.

"I haven't asked this before, but do you think that Patron, who did the Somersault, is a defeatist too? Are you saying that Patron, without doing a proper self-critique, has come here to this region to restart his church, but he's still a defeatist? And that before anything concrete gets done he's going to be murdered or something? In other words, you guys aren't taking him seriously; you think that if you just bide your time the Fireflies will come out on top?"

Far from flinching, Gii held Ikuo's gaze calmly. To Kizu, Gii's features—the outline of his ears and nostrils, as well as his clear eyes—looked fresh and soft, like some newly budding plant. Gii chose his words carefully as he replied.

"I haven't given the term *defeatist* a lot of thought, so there may be contradictions in what I said. But I find it interesting that Patron would start his own church and religious movement and then, at a certain point, do a Somersault and announce that everything he's preached till then was nonsense. The defeatists I'm talking about never had the guts to do that.

"No, I'm not some optimist sitting just around waiting for Patron's church to self-destruct. We Young Fireflies are planning to make this region independent, and now a formidable opponent has entered the picture—your church. I don't think either Patron or Ikuo are defeatists. The Hollow's legally occupied, as are these large buildings; that's a given. What we have to do is build up our forces so we can compete with you. Anyway, that's the second thing I wanted to tell you."

Later that day, Kizu recalled their conversation and felt quite keenly that Gii was, as Ikuo had told him, an outstanding young man, the main reason being the skillful way he'd wrapped up their conversation.

"Patron told me you have cancer, Professor," Gii had said suddenly, throwing Kizu a challenging look. "The church hasn't begun any new activities, he said, but he'd like to concentrate his spiritual strength in trying to control your disease."

Looking over Kizu from top to bottom, Ikuo asked, "So has Patron's spiritual concentration had any effect?"

"The exhaustion I felt when I lived in Tokyo doesn't seem to be as bad as it was before," Kizu replied. "And I'm not as depressed."

"Yeah, but having a person's spirit soar when the founder of his religion concentrates his spiritual power for his sake does seem a *bit* predictable, doesn't it?" Ikuo said, as Gii let out a happy laugh.

23: The Technicians

1

"I heard from Gii," Dr. Koga said, "that Patron's trying to use his spiritual powers to control your cancer. Who knows but what it might be slowing down the spread of the disease."

He said this as he handed over two weeks' worth of the various medicines Kizu was taking.

Putting the question of how he was feeling on hold, Kizu looked at the painting he'd done that was hanging in a frame on the wall of the clinic, the one showing Ikuo from behind, naked down to below his waist. Ikuo's broad back was so muscular it looked like he was carrying a soft shell on his back. His overall build, with its bulging muscles, looked entirely natural, not like the localized protuberances one expects from weight trainers. Dr. Koga, putting all the medications in a paper bag, followed Kizu's gaze.

"Ikuo seems to fit right in with the kids here," he said. "The parents who use my clinic used to consider the Young Fireflies as some reserve youth corps of the *yakuza,* but with Ikuo in the picture they changed their tune."

"The art class project was turned down, though, thanks to my affiliation with the church," Kizu said. "Well, with Ikuo and the Fireflies doing so well, Dancer and Ogi wanted me to ask you something, an internal matter of the church actually."

"About the Technicians?"

"That's right. Ikuo seems to have a good relationship with them too, but there doesn't seem to be much communication between them and Patron."

Dr. Koga fixed his dark deep-set eyes on Kizu and then gave a practical suggestion, hoping to lighten the mood.

"The clinic's closed today, and it's raining a little, so what do you say we take a drive and talk? Patron's spiritual concentration aside, a drive shouldn't be bad for you. In the afternoon I'll drive over down below the dam and honk my horn."

Every two weeks, on days when the clinic was closed in the morning, Kizu went to get a thorough examination from Dr. Koga and refill his prescriptions. He'd heard that Dr. Koga had been taking drives here and there in the area, using copies of maps from the town hall, since with all the new logging roads that had been built the standard maps were of little use.

Dr. Koga showed up after lunch, early, and Kizu climbed into his car. The rain had ended but, instead of a uniformly overcast sky, clumps of dark-gray clouds scuttled across overhead. They drove up the slope toward the forest, which was chockful of lustrous leaves after the morning's rain. The slope was steep, but as long as one paid attention to the shoulder it wasn't dangerous. When they passed the T-shaped intersection below the farm that Ikuo and the Technicians had taken over, they saw a small truck that was going to pick up some materials that had come down and was waiting for them to pass when the rain had let up; some of the Technicians were aboard. Mr. Hanawa, seated at the wheel, bowed politely to them as they went by.

"As Dancer says, it's true the Technicians haven't made an opportunity to talk with Patron," Dr. Koga said, "but you have to remember their work has kept them busy. That kind of hard physical labor is good for their outlook on things, I'm sure.

"After Patron and Guide's Somersault—and this is actually something they brought on themselves, since as members of the Izu Research Institute they made it all inevitable—the Technicians suffered a lot, though not as much as their colleagues who were dragged off by the police and not taken to court.

"I was able to resume my medical practice, but the other Technicians had to hide their research and use their technical skills somehow to earn a living. With automation taking over factories, these skills were less in demand, but once they took a job at some small subcontracting factory they quickly rose to the top and could show what they were capable of.

"Some of them worked in university and business research labs, doing experiments under the supervision of people who used to be their colleagues, making one-micron incisions in the brain and so on. Universities and industries on the cutting edge needed high-caliber technicians like them.

"I think my colleagues are valuable in that they're hard workers who don't have any academic ambition. Working for ten years at the bottom of the heap has made them tougher. After I met them again, I thought that the self-ridiculing name Technicians they'd given themselves was actually a good choice."

Dr. Koga wound his blue Saab, a car that suited him perfectly, through the sprinkle of hamlets in the area that went by the overall name of the outskirts—an area along the river that stood in contrast to the highway on the opposite shore. As they drove up the rough ancient-looking road, he explained that the name outskirts wasn't a proper noun.

Kizu was impressed by Dr. Koga's explanation about the Technicians. Somewhat inadvertently, he said, "Doctor, I guess after all you're the Technicians' highest adviser, aren't you?"

"I'm not even a *low*-level adviser," Dr. Koga said. "Rather, I feel they've cut me off. They don't even let me into the rooms they share in the dormitory."

Kizu was surprised to hear this, though it did fit with what he'd heard from Dancer.

"Ogi and Dancer told me," he said, "that the Technicians won't let them into the five rooms they've taken over either. Of course Ogi doesn't go into the Quiet Women's rooms, but Dancer, too, has refrained from doing so. Ms. Tachibana and her brother are the only ones from outside whom the Quiet Women allow in, and sometimes they participate in their prayer sessions.

"So the problem the office staff has at present is this: After the first wave of people have settled in here, they have to help out the second and third waves. It wasn't the original plan to have these two sects be the first groups here; Patron was hoping that people who'd gotten in touch with him individually would make up the first group, which is why he had Ogi contact all of them. The two sects that made up the first group keep to themselves and have no interest in other followers who've moved here. The Technicians especially are like that. What can be done? Dancer asked me about this."

Eyes on the seething water rushing down the edge of the ditch beside the road, Dr. Koga managed a warm smile.

"I imagine the office staff wants the Quiet Women to open up their quarters to others—women only, of course—and want to assign beds in the housing at the Farm on an individual basis. In the beginning, though, there's nothing we can do but accept these two subgroups as the first residents.

"After this base is settled, and the second and third waves of individual believers move in, hopefully these subgroups will eventually disappear of their own accord. But this can't be done overnight, Professor. Patron has finally publicly begun his new church movement, and we can expect his influence will be felt on each and every individual here. As this starts to happen—or as it happens *once more,* I should say—won't it be possible to keep the Technicians from becoming a fixed sect within the church? The Technicians have returned to Patron's church and found a new raison d'être, so to speak, so it's not a good idea to fall over oneself trying to control them.

"This might not be the answer you're looking for, and you might be upset that you're being treated like some kid running an errand, but that's all I can say right now. I'd appreciate it if you'd convey my thoughts to Dancer."

They drove up over the ridge of the mountain chain, coming out on a gentle slope of neat harvested fields. Dr. Koga parked the car at a spot where there was a pull-off that protruded from the low point of the slope. A farmhouse sat above the stone wall high on the opposite slope, and an old man who had come out to the edge of the garden bowed politely to them. Dr. Koga gave a friendly bow back.

"Let's walk along the path through the fields to a place where you can see the entire valley. That's Isamu's grandfather by the way, the boy in the Fireflies."

Below where the path petered out was a neat little chestnut-tree orchard, and looking down through the soft green leaves they could see the modest line of buildings in the jug-shaped hollow along the river. The road leading up from the eastern edge that ran along the river valley was cut off from view by a small pass rising up like a bump, cutting off the view of the Hollow beyond. The cross-Shikoku highway bypass, too, was hidden in the shadow of a mixed cedar and cypress forest jutting out from the edge of the chestnut grove.

"It was called Jug Village for a long time, apparently," Kizu said, "and looking down at it from here it's easy to understand the legend that grew up that for hundreds of years the village was shut away inside a jug."

"I'm sure the topography *does* account for many legends," Dr. Koga responded. "But if you drive twenty minutes over to the Old Town district they're opening up a Denny's Restaurant, so it's not hard to understand why the Young Fireflies march through forests at dawn, trying to shore up their collective illusion."

Dr. Koga laid a plastic sheet over each of two black natural boundary-marker stones. As they sat down side by side, facing the valley, Kizu had the feeling that he was about to hear something more detailed than any of their earlier brief conversations. And indeed that's how it turned out.

"While we traveled here by train I confessed a lot of personal things to you, Professor," Dr. Koga began, "and I'd like to take up where I left off. I can understand why Guide had such drawing power over the researchers at the Izu workshop, but why did Patron? For one simple reason: We quite naturally believed that when he went over to the *other side* he communicated directly with God. Listening to Patron's sermons after his trances, one couldn't help but believe—the kind of belief that brings on a deep feeling of contentment. In his trances Patron and God had a genuine rapport. After returning from the *other side,* Guide's painful efforts would allow the vision Patron experienced to be transmitted in words we could understand. And this whole vision was powerfully *real.*

"The radical faction's action program was created as an extension of that reality. Especially as events sped up, as we began to swing into action, as we listened to secret reports coming in from the sites on our strategy list, we felt that *we* were a part of Patron's trance. And then—out of the blue—the Somersault came crashing down on us.

"Now we wondered what the Somersault was all about. Along with Guide, Patron led us, his advance guard, urging us to hurry and make his message from God come true. Is that what the Somersault was—the two of them standing at the head of the troops but losing their nerve at the last minute? We wondered what God would say to the apostate Patron the next time he had one of his trances: a frightful thing, if it actually took place. But an even more frightening thing happened: For ten years Patron was out of touch with God. I find the term somewhat vague myself, though the Quiet Women evaluate it quite highly, but I think this is what they mean when they say that Patron *fell into hell.* From the beginning, Guide's torture and death came about because of reports that Patron was starting a new religious movement. They drove us into a terrible predicament and left us there, with just the two of them starting something new.

"On the other hand, we thought that if only there was a convincing explanation—in other words, if Patron was able once more to have a vision and reveal what he'd seen—we could have taken the lead in the new movement. So the ones doing the interrogating asked Guide: what Patron's latest vision was. But Guide didn't answer. We thought he was hiding something, but now that I look back on it I realize there was nothing he could say. Why did Guide remain silent? I believe it's because of this: He couldn't bring himself to tell these former radical followers that Patron had been abandoned by God. Guide had an admirable reticence in him, when you come right down to it."

2

Kizu felt led to take their talk a step further.

"I've been talking about it in vague terms, and you might have guessed already—and people might think me crazy at my age—but my desire to spend my remaining days with a certain young man is why I'm here. Honestly speaking, I don't think I'm qualified to hear anything very substantial.

"My remaining days—a pretty accurate way of putting it, as you know, Dr. Koga, since I could be struck down by the cancer at any time. Cancer's calling the shots, in other words. You don't seem to think all that highly of Patron's using his spiritual power to effect a cure, but I'm not entirely dismissing it. Not that I'm clinging to it, either, as my last hope.

"Living together with Ikuo, seeing my neither-here-nor-there life as a painter to its conclusion with him, I'm doing what you suggested and starting to paint again. Painting as the Fireflies would have it, Yonah—Ikuo, this real young man, as the biblical Jonah, as the final creative work of my life. I don't have any particular dissatisfactions about life in the Hollow and my painting, but what about Ikuo? I do know he's got some plan he wants to carry out through Patron's new church, but what it is I haven't the foggiest. He's not the type of person to live a quiet life of faith, though, that's for sure. Be that as it may, I'm prepared to help him with whatever plans he has, but I don't have the courage to grill him about them. Or, more accurately, I don't *feel* like doing it. So, awaiting new developments from his end, I spend my days painting my final work.

"Seeing how much energy Ikuo is putting into his work every day, I realize that he's waiting, too, for Patron's activities to take shape. That's quite clear. On the surface, he's creating an economic base for the first wave of followers who moved here and for later waves to follow. Ikuo consults closely with Dancer and Ogi as he plans out his work, he's got the Technicians using their technical skills in starting up production again at the farm, and he's guiding Gii's Fireflies in a way that maintains the boys' independence. All well and good. Ikuo's an unexpectedly able person, and so far he's had good results. But is that enough for him? I don't think so. Since he was a young boy, he hasn't been able to live a normal life. He's become exactly what the Fireflies, with their children's intuition, call him: Yonah. And he's leaving the basic issues up to Patron, hoping through him to arrive at a clear-cut solution.

"In that respect I think he's a lot like you, Dr. Koga, and the Technicians. Why was Ikuo like that as a child, and what sort of hope does he entrust now to his relationship with Patron? I haven't questioned him past a certain point, but especially seeing him after we moved here I can understand that. I feel like I was listening to what you said in Ikuo's stead."

Dr. Koga paid rapt attention to Kizu's words. It had been a long time since Kizu had been able to talk so forthrightly with an intelligent person his own age, Japanese or foreign.

Kizu wasn't the only one who felt this way, for even after he stopped speaking Dr. Koga didn't respond; instead, he gazed at the far-off scenery. Kizu looked in the same direction.

The high sky was still white, tinged with gray, but the quick-moving low clouds had disappeared. In the unimpeded view that stretched out before them, beyond the mountain range that surrounded this land, lustrous light-purple trees continued off to the horizon.

Kizu considered the people long ago who'd followed one forest glen after another to arrive, and then live in, this dead-end valley. And their descendants. And those who trooped off in the opposite direction to find work in the Kansai area, in Tokyo, or in Yokohama, and how they might still be in the grip of vague ideas about their connection with the founding fathers of this forest village. The Fireflies made a pact that even if they went off to the cities they would still view this valley as their base and would someday return to it—a childish pledge, perhaps, but weren't they supplementing, albeit many years later, the notions that brought settlers pushing their way into this land in the first place?

"When I see the faces of the Technicians, I think the same thing you think about Ikuo, Professor," Dr. Koga said finally. "When they were given the chance in Izu to do their own research they basically followed a proper path, but once they started to get soaked in Patron's aura, they all began to view their research in a different perspective. Eventually things turned completely around, and they threw themselves into situating the church as a force to be reckoned with, one that could actually change society.

"Just at this point they were abandoned by Patron and Guide. Ten years pass and here they are, once again gathered around Patron. Which makes me wonder: Does Patron really have a new plan that will fit all they've accumulated over this painful decade? I don't have any desire to ask him whether he has any plans for action, plans that will surface in the near future to fit what the Technicians are doing. Some people might call me—to use an old union term—a corrupt trade boss for thinking this, but I think we should just let him be himself.

"The Quiet Women seem fully content just to be living in the same place as Patron and to spend their days near him in prayer. One time Morio had swollen tonsils and came to the clinic, and Ms. Tachibana told me about the way the Quiet Women pray in their rooms. It's extremely intense, apparently. The Technicians also have a quiet time of reflection after each day's work that's so intense it's guaranteed to make you feel uncomfortable."

"Both groups have moved here and settled in, and we need them both to support the activities of the church. Dancer thinks this, too—of course, all under the leadership of Patron."

"This contradicts what I said before," Kizu said, "but the Technicians and the Quiet Women are clearly different types of groups, and it'll surely be a test of Patron's leadership skills to get them to cooperate."

"I can imagine a scenario," Dr. Koga said, "where things turn hostile, with both groups surrounding Patron insisting that they be allowed to show what they're capable of."

"I don't think it's just the Quiet Women and the Technicians who'd do that," Kizu said. "You'd have to include Ikuo and those under Patron's direct supervision—Ogi and Dancer—as well. And let's not forget the Kansai headquarters, which is lying low at the moment. I wonder if Patron isn't waiting for the energy of all these people to get compressed and then he's going to leap into action all at once. If Guide were here I'm sure that's what he'd do."

Kizu and Dr. Koga looked intently at each other. Kizu felt all over again the closeness he'd begun to feel toward this other man. Dr. Koga was visibly exhausted but, with his characteristic magnanimity, was trying to follow his colleagues in their new activities. Wasn't this exactly what Kizu was trying to do with Ikuo? As was his habit after many years in America, Kizu spoke aloud what he'd already convinced himself of, to make sure of his thoughts.

"Dr. Koga, you consider the Technicians kindred spirits, but at the same time you feel apart from them enough to keep an eye on them. You want to participate with them yet keep your distance."

"That's correct," Dr. Koga replied, his eyes at once both slightly worried and filled with a sharp intelligence. "When you said you were moving to Shikoku despite your cancer, I can tell you I was envious. This is a person, I thought, who is truly free.

"I've trained with the Technicians, and as long as I can I want to help them out. The thought occurred to me that it wouldn't be so bad to end my days as a small-town doctor here in this valley, but if Patron and the Technicians get in a confrontation, I imagine I'd leave here with them.

"When I think about the future, I have the distinct feeling that someday soon I'm going to be in a difficult fix because of the Technicians: lamenting that we should just *get on with it* and ending up in some desperate struggle. Still—like you and Ikuo—the fact is, I accompanied them here. Maybe I invited you out today because of this simple yet subtle feeling of empathy? I don't know."

"I'm not saying this to you as patient-to-doctor," Kizu said, "but my intuition tells me I have a lot of time left to be with you before cancer makes me withdraw from the front lines."

Dr. Koga gave him a happy, sympathetic smile but, veteran physician that he was, he wasn't about to give any hasty words of encouragement. He urged Kizu to stand up, and when they both did he briskly folded up the plastic sheets they'd been sitting on, stuffed them in his pocket, and made a new suggestion.

"Why don't we drive upstream a little? You came into this region by going up the Kame River from the Old Town area, right? If you go upstream a bit more you'll feel you're in the middle of the main mountain range in Shikoku. It's quite interesting from a geopolitical standpoint because it's the crossroads leading to Kochi on the one hand and Matsuyama on the other.

"In medieval days the Tosa armies advanced up to that point. Asa-san told me when she was little and didn't obey her parents they'd scare her by saying, 'General Chosokabe's coming to get you!'"

Dr. Koga wasn't just knowledgeable about local history, he was well acquainted with the local topography too, and he took them down a different road through the woods, one that brought them down to the prefectural road that ran along the river. Kizu was sure the road was a dead end shut off by the mountains, but after passing several hamlets that dotted the roadside they came out onto the road along the valley that ascended to the northeast. The tree branches overhanging the road, with their green leaves freshened by a recent rain, had an animalistic power, and it struck Kizu that he really was living in deep mountain recesses.

The crossroads leading to the two local cities Dr. Koga had spoken of was a broad basin, the field there much more extensive than in anything in Maki Town, let alone Kame Village before it was incorporated. Dr. Koga avoided the road leading to the hollow where there were rows of old tradesmen's houses, and did a U-turn at one corner of the road the bus ran along. Dr. Koga hadn't said a word nearly the whole hour they'd been driving, but as they arrived at the road that went back home he finally spoke.

"What with their shrine with a huge gingko tree and their old noodle shops, you can really see the region's cultural differences here. It suddenly popped into my mind that this might lead to a bit of rivalry. Ikuo and the Technicians are coming here with a light truck today. Did you know that?"

"No," Kizu said.

"The wife of the town barber had a religious awakening and decided to move in with the church. Her little daughter has a terrible disease they've been able to control with a cortisone-like medicine, but the side effects are terrible. A doctor at the Red Cross Hospital recommended me to her, and she's been coming to my clinic every week.

"The girl's mother was quite moved by the Quiet Women's prayer meetings. Before long she said she wanted to renounce the world and move to the Hollow with her daughter. There wasn't any precedent for it—we have yet to welcome the second and third waves of followers, after all—so it's proved to be a sticky problem.

"Still, Dancer said it was better to have her there than to have to entrust Patron to some barber they didn't know anything about, so the woman was allowed in as a onetime exception. Seeing how things stood, the woman decided to work as a barber in the Hollow. The barbershop had two special barber chairs. She claimed one was hers and wanted to bring it with her, but her husband refused point-blank. Ikuo and the others are coming today to pick up that precious barber chair. They'll also bring the mother and her daughter back with them. The husband has rallied a few of his relatives and longtime customers, who are ready to stop them by force if necessary."

Dr. Koga finished his story, and some time passed. When they arrived at a spot where they could see the buildings of the elementary school on the other side of the bridge spanning the deep valley, a light truck passed them from behind. They didn't see who was driving, but in the truck bed they saw a large barber chair wrapped in quilts and tied down with rope. Kizu and Dr. Koga could see the backs of two cold-looking men huddled together; they watched until the truck and the men disappeared into the growth of trees overhanging the road.

3

Ikuo was back in the house on the north shore for the first time in quite a while and had been modeling all morning. The third panel of the triptych, the central piece, was still blank, but Kizu was working on the first and second panels simultaneously.

The day before, according to Ms. Tachibana, Ikuo and Dancer had quarreled in the office over Kizu's painting, and Kizu was concerned. He didn't mention this, though, as he painted, continuing to work silently on details until, before long, Ikuo broached the subject.

"You don't need to feel responsible, Professor, but I sounded Dancer out about having Patron model for you nude from the waist up. For whatever reason she blew a gasket. It was quite a mess."

"Patron nude from the waist up? Hmmm," Kizu mused, his brush poised in midair. "What sort of scene are you imagining?"

"Nothing definite. But if the third panel of the triptych is going to show Jonah debating God, don't you need a model for God?"

"So you're envisioning Patron as the God Jonah complains to?" Kizu asked. "But Patron raised a banner of revolt *against* God, said everything he'd done was a joke, and denied his relationship with God!

"Just as the Fireflies see you as Jonah, I've been viewing you as a Jonah-like person in my work here. But as you've expressed your doubts about it, for the sake of argument let's say that what's written in the book of Jonah *isn't* the end of the story, that Jonah rejects God's sermon to him, laughs in his face, and leaves. Isn't that close to what Patron did with his Somersault?"

Kizu laid his brush and palette aside and sat down. The reflected light from the lake was so intense he'd moved his easel farther back in the room, and Ikuo was posing near the kitchen. He went over to the leaf-framed window to retrieve his robe. As he walked in front of Kizu, the strong reflection from outside etched his profile from his nose to his chin as distinctly as if they had been made from neon tubing.

Ikuo put on his robe and turned around, his entire face one dark mass. From out of that came a voice dripping with a childish youthfulness.

"When I argued with Dancer I didn't have any definite idea in mind. But after what you said, I was thinking it made sense to have Patron in the painting as God, showing him persuaded by Jonah's protest.

"God's given up on it once but has now completely consigned Nineveh to the flames and is standing there with Jonah gazing down at the burning city. That was the vision of God I had."

"If that's the case," Kizu said, "it certainly makes sense to have Patron model for the painting. I'd say the theme for the third panel of the triptych is starting to gell."

That night, after Kizu woke up once and then fell asleep again, he had a dream. Dr. Koga always gave him a great variety and amount of medicine, and though he was diligent about keeping up the dosage of the analgesic suppositories, he wasn't very conscientious about taking the other medicines, picking and choosing the ones he wanted and taking less than the prescribed dose. Even so, he started to run a slight fever, which he put down to the side effects of the drugs. Whenever he had a fever he'd wake up in the middle of the night, confused about where he was and why he was there.

He switched on the light beside his bed, went to the bathroom, and on the way back, still doubtful of his surroundings, looked into the part of his studio where the canvases weren't covered; and as he drew back the curtain and gazed out at the far-off buildings bathed in moonlight, things became clear to him and his fear and confusion disappeared. But the feelings he had until that moment—the sense of being cut off from this scene and his surroundings—remained strong within him. He went back to bed and, after he turned off the light, was struck by the thought that what he'd just witnessed was a scene from after his death.

I'll leave behind this half-finished work, and in less than a year I'll be dead, he thought, and what will remain is that scene. These thoughts led him to consider how pointless his life had been. No, he thought, it can't be that meaningless. He struggled to conjure up significant incidents from his life but couldn't think of a single one; his chest tightened with sadness, and he turned on the light once more and gulped down a sleeping pill.

After all this, he was finally at the threshold of sleep, in the dangerous place neither on this side or the other side of wakefulness, when he saw Patron seated in the precious barber's chair, Ikuo standing beside him, and the two of them gazing down at a city engulfed in flames. Kizu felt relief wash over him. This was the long-pending theme of the third panel of the triptych.

Kizu got up late the next morning, no doubt due to the aftereffects of the sleeping pill. His house on the north shore of the Hollow was surrounded on every side except where it fronted the lake by a thick growth of beeches, Japanese oaks, and other deciduous trees. Kizu had heard that the diplomat who formerly occupied the house had planted the tangerine, citron, and lime trees in order to make a fruit orchard, but that was now overrun by the thick greenery of the camphor trees. Farther back, a layer of oaks formed a sound-proof wall.

As the greenery grew more luxuriant, the several-times-a-week march of the Fireflies through the woods grew harder to catch. Instead, every morning, not too early, Kizu heard a flock of Japanese tits, sounding like a fall rain, fly over in search of food. On this particular day the sound was like a ripple through his fitful sleep.

The strangely realistic chair he'd seen in his dream was the one he'd seen being carefully transported in the light truck on his way back from the drive with Dr. Koga. He'd seen it later on, after it was installed, so all the details had been accurate.

The chair that Mrs. Tagawa, the barber's wife and the church's first new member after moving to this place, had brought along with her grade-school daughter was set up inside the chapel. In that makeshift barbershop she started off cutting Patron's hair and shaving him. For many years Patron had had all his tonsorial needs taken care of at a shop in Seijo, and he was pleased with the results at Mrs. Tagawa's hands. Patron found the barber chair comfortable, even saying that when the church officially restarted that's where he wanted to sit to give his sermons.

Designated as the church's official barber, then, Mrs. Tagawa offered her services to all the male followers and, if they wished, to the female followers as well. So whenever the chapel wasn't in use, it did double duty as a barbershop.

The day after Kizu had the dream of the barber chair, he went over after lunch to check out how well the barbershop was doing. Mrs. Tagawa—Hisayo was her first name—was probably around her mid-thirties, and dressed in the mannish way you often saw women barbers dressed in the countryside. A large old sofa set up between the piano and the barber chair was occupied by three gloomy-looking Technicians. In the next stall the daughter sat with a Hello Kitty notebook on her lap, perhaps noting down the order of those waiting for haircuts.

Kizu stopped by the office, where Dancer was working alone at her computer. Thinking he'd like to get a haircut, since he hadn't had one in a while, he asked her if he'd have to wait long for his turn. Dancer looked up at him, mouth open, no trace of a smile on her lusterless face.

"I'll check the appointment schedule. The Technicians are all well educated, but there's a bit of a herd mentality at work. Once one of them gets a haircut they all follow suit."

Dancer's eyes gazed at Kizu from her yellow-ivory face. Kizu was silent, so once more she slowly began to speak.

"Did you know that Ikuo and I had a quarrel over his idea of having Patron model half nude for the triptych?"

Kizu found it strange that Dancer would be preoccupied all this time about her argument with Ikuo.

"Yes, I heard. I still don't have a definite plan about the third panel, but I had this fleeting vision in a dream that told me not to worry, it's all settled."

"I always thought Ikuo was more the type to stay quiet when he has an idea," Dancer said. "I imagine you've heard about the wound in Patron's body from Ikuo. I figured Ogi told Ikuo, which piqued his interest, and that's why he came up with this notion of Patron modeling nude. I couldn't say this in front of everybody, which is why our argument didn't go anywhere. If Patron models as Ikuo wants him to, naturally it would be stupid to try to hide the wound anymore. It seems like, with the new church about to be launched, Ikuo wants to put Patron in a position where he can't retreat."

Kizu knew that lashing out at him was her way of getting rid of her gloomy feelings, but he couldn't imagine what she meant by a *wound* in Patron. He brought a chair over, sat down across from her, and urged her to tell him more. Realizing suddenly that Kizu didn't know anything, Dancer balked. Still, she mustered up a determined look. He was reminded of the dauntlessness she'd shown when he'd first seen her as a young dancing girl so many years ago.

"Ogi hasn't told you anything about it because he promised me not to. Still, if Ikuo knows about it he'd use the painting as pretext for breaking that promise. In that case, I think it's better to speak of it myself.

"For a long time only Guide and I knew about the wound, but one day I got careless, and Ogi found out about it. Ogi must have let it slip to Ikuo, which led to his idea of having Patron model nude. If Patron agrees, there's nothing I can do about it. From the start he didn't plan to keep this a secret."

Irritated by how this was all coming out, Dancer closed her mouth, biting down on her thin lips. Kizu found it pitiful to watch and turned toward the lake, the surface reflecting the white cloudy sky.

"They call it a Sacred Wound, don't they? The kind Saint Francis of Assisi had, just like Jesus' wounds when he was crucified."

Kizu remembered the word *stigma,* the word he often, for some strange reason, thought of, and the way he'd connected it with the stigma of the delicate dark red flower of the slippery elm. . . .

Watching the absentminded-looking Kizu, Dancer ignored her own rhetorical question and went on.

"On Patron's left side he has a gaping wound as if he's been pierced with a spear. Technically speaking it's not a wound but more like a hole in his side that never closes up, and at the bottom you can see the color of blood. When he's not feeling well, pus oozes out and dries in yellow strands. Right now, actually, pus is coming out. In the past his doctor would always prescribe antibiotics for him without his having to go to the hospital, and he was able to tough it out that way.

"But when we moved here I didn't think about it, and the day before yesterday I asked Dr. Koga to give us some antibiotics. But he told me that if Patron needed them he'd better examine him. That's what was bothering me and why I was so cross with Ikuo."

"So Dr. Koga doesn't know about Patron's wound?" Kizu asked.

"Guide and I were the only ones who knew. And then Ogi happened to see Patron in the bath once."

"Until the Somersault, though, Dr. Koga took care of Patron, so wouldn't he have noticed this wound?"

"If it's something that appeared after the Somersault, Dr. Koga wouldn't know about it, would he? Guide never told me when the wound first appeared, and I couldn't bring myself to ask Patron directly. But now with the church starting up again, pus is coming out and it scares me. The wound shouldn't have appeared *after* the Somersault, should it? When Patron was relating his visions and calling on people to repent there was no wound, but now, after the Somersault, there it is. . . . Or maybe the wound is God's punishment for the Somersault. That scares me, too."

Her skin flushed, the color so different from before, and tears rolled down her cheeks. Her eyes, glistening with tears, clung to Kizu. Kizu didn't feel like going where the overwrought Dancer's question led. He had to shift to a different question, one with a different answer.

From his experience running seminars, Kizu knew he had to divert Dancer from the question she'd raised. Instead, using some down-to-earth language he knew would sound dubious to this young woman, he said; "Let me ask Dr. Koga about getting some antibiotics. At my age I can't claim it's gonorrhea, but if I say I have some pus coming out of my urethra, I think he should give me the medicine to help Patron without insisting on examining me first."

Dancer looked blank for a moment, but was soon her old self again.

24: Viewing the Sacred Wound

1

Kizu, however, didn't find the time to negotiate with Dr. Koga, for the day after he talked with Dancer the situation changed abruptly. Ogi was taking care of things at the office, and Dancer had gone out to the dining hall for a late lunch when an anxious phone call came from Ms. Tachibana.

It was warm that day, almost summery, and Ms. Tachibana's call was not unconnected with this rise in temperature. Patron had had a fever since morning and couldn't get up, so Ms. Tachibana had brought him breakfast in bed. When she fetched his lunch, he had thrown off his covers because of his fever and the hot weather, and the upper half of his body lay exposed. But what threw her into a panic was Morio, curled up at the side of the bed at Patron's legs, with yellow pus covering both eyes, one ear, and his nose and mouth.

Ms. Tachibana had screamed, and Morio flopped his arms and legs around like a baby turtle but was panicked, unable to open his eyes. Patron was awake and sat up in bed. That's when Ms. Tachibana saw the red hole in his chubby left side, pus oozing out.

By the time Ogi ran over, Patron had fallen asleep again, and Morio's head and face had been wiped clean. Ms. Tachibana, though, was still struggling with panic, her shoulders trembling as she insisted that Patron had a wound in his left side. Apparently wanting to take care of Patron, Morio had pressed his face against it and had gotten covered with pus. Ms. Tachibana insisted that Dr. Koga take care of Morio's eyes and his precious ears so that no bacteria invaded them, but insisted even more loudly that he come over right away and treat Patron's wound.

Dr. Koga was in his clinic. Making his excuses to his patients, he promptly boarded the car Ogi had brought around. Ogi reported to him that the wound in Patron's side was festering, and learned that Dr. Koga, Patron's longtime doctor, had no knowledge of this wound, which had not closed up for years.

"So what you're saying is that, since you first saw it, the hole in his side has remained open?" Dr. Koga asked. "And that it's festering and causing the fever? Have you taken his temperature? . . . Well, that's okay. Dancer's not there. I can imagine how flustered you were and why you raced right over."

When he entered the bedroom where Patron lay, Dancer was back from lunch. Dr. Koga handed her his medical bag and told her to open the window on the forest side to let in some cool air. Morio was up, changed into a fresh shirt and trousers, but still looking thunderstruck. After checking his eyes and ears, Dr. Koga ordered Ms. Tachibana and Ogi, as well as Kizu, who'd been summoned, to escort Morio out to the living room.

For whatever reason, Ms. Tachibana had kept the rooms shut tight while Patron was in bed with his fever, but now they threw all the living room windows wide open. Morio sat directly on the floor, choosing an FM station on the stereo, the sound of a string quartet, or perhaps a sextet, filtering out for a moment before he slipped on the headphones and went into his own little world.

Ogi leaned forward near Kizu and Ms. Tachibana, and they spoke in low voices.

"I had no idea he had that hole in him," Ms. Tachibana explained, "which is why I was so shaken. Dancer just told me about it. I can imagine how unpleasant it must be to have had that for so long! Mrs. Shigeno said that Patron's being in hell was no metaphor, and I'd have to agree."

"I just happened to hear about the wound yesterday from Dancer," Kizu said. "It's much worse than I imagined."

As you'd expect of a craftsman whose eyes are the tools of his trade, Kizu's expression showed that the afterimage of what he'd seen was still fresh in his mind.

The two of them were silent, so Ogi felt obliged to tell his own impression of the wound in Patron's side—something that was actually more Dancer's idea than his own. "Well," he said, "I certainly consider his wound rather extraordinary, though I'm not at the point of thinking of it, as Dancer does, as a Sacred Wound. Patron is certainly a man of special gifts, someone who's had great hurdles to overcome in his life. I never imagined I'd be working for a person like him.

"Even so," Ogi went on, "I don't think my devotion to him has any mystical coloring to it. Nothing of Dancer's insistence that the wound in Patron's side is a condition of his sanctification. That's been my attitude toward Patron, and I don't think it's put me at a disadvantage. Dancer, though, has a lot invested emotionally. She feels it's her responsibility that the wound in Patron's side she's been taking care of when she bathes him and so on should have started to fester; this has really upset her."

"Dancer thinks Patron's wound getting worse like this after we've moved to the Hollow might be a premonition that something's going to occur with the new church movement," Ms. Tachibana added.

Kizu looked as if he'd heard this before, but Ogi gave it some thought and, though he hadn't figured it all out himself, told them what was bothering him.

"Dancer hasn't confirmed this herself, but according to what Dr. Koga told her, that wound apparently appeared *after* the Somersault. When I happened to learn of this wound by chance," Ogi went on, "I didn't have any proof, but I was sure it must have been there ever since he started his church. You know—since people who start religious movements must be different, it was a sign that he's *chosen*. Following this logic, even after abandoning his doctrine and his church, Patron must *still* be an extraordinary person since he still has the wound. Maybe this way of thinking only goes to show why people call me an *innocent*. But don't people who are outside a religion tend to sanctify the people within it, even though they're not necessarily influenced by them?

"Once I heard that the wound appeared *after* the Somersault, though, my simplistic way of interpreting it was as God's punishment, as a sign of disgrace. Isn't that why he called himself an antichrist? But whether it's a holy sign or sign of disgrace, one thing's for sure—I can't view this Sacred Wound from a neutral standpoint anymore, as if it has nothing to do with me."

Ogi, though concerned about what was going on in the next room, had become more and more absorbed in his own impressions. He could feel Kizu's eyes on him, a leisurely look that reacted positively to what he was saying. Ogi felt embarrassed by his final, excited words, but Kizu took up where he left off.

"About this Sacred Wound," Kizu said, "to use the term you seem to have settled on: I wonder how Ikuo will react to having had this kept secret from him by his fellows in the church. That might be a problem. Just as you say, Ogi, I can't imagine Ikuo being unmoved by it. Two days ago, I think it was, Ikuo and Dancer debated whether or not to have Patron pose naked in my triptych. Dancer let Ikuo have his way without revealing a thing about an injury."

Just then Dancer and Dr. Koga emerged from the bedroom. Dancer turned to Kizu and spoke in a decisive voice.

"There's something I'd like to say. I'm the one who confused the situation, so first of all I'm going to go over to talk with the Quiet Women. I assume they've all heard the details of what Ms. Tachibana saw, and I'd like to apologize for keeping it a secret.

"Dr. Koga says the key thing is how the Technicians react. They shared a life of faith with Patron until the Somersault and believe they're somehow privileged, so we really have to put our heads together to come up with a convincing way of explaining things to them. To them, Ogi and I are just some assistants who started working during Patron's period of inactivity, so it might be better if Patron spoke to them himself."

Dr. Koga went over to take a look at Morio, who was still absorbed in his music, his head turned completely away from them; then he turned toward Dancer.

"Aren't you're being a little too emotional about this?" he said. "I can understand how seeing Patron suffer with this fever might make you react. But being overwrought and attacking the church organization is only going to lead to trouble."

"So being overly calm about it is better?" Dancer asked. "You said we need to wait until his wound is cleaned up and his fever is down, and we shouldn't let the news about the Sacred Wound spread beyond those who've actually seen it. But I don't think that's what's important."

"What *is* important?"

"How the church moves forward. After Patron suffered for ten years, he's restarting his movement—which is the whole reason why he moved here. And right afterward something happened to the Sacred Wound he's been concealing. Isn't that significant? I'd like to apologize to Professor Kizu too," Dancer went on. "I opposed his plan to use Patron as a model to help complete the painting for the chapel. But seeing how things are, I realize I was wrong. Please feel free to go into the bedroom and sketch him as he is, suffering from the wound in his side. Dr. Koga can wait a while before bandaging it up."

2

At dinner that evening, Ogi didn't run across either Ikuo or Kizu in the dining hall. Dancer went off to discuss the Sacred Wound with the Quiet Women at the Hollow and with the Technicians at the Farm, but she didn't show up later at the office. Ms. Tachibana and her brother were staying with Patron.

As Ogi ate his solitary late supper, one of the Quiet Women, Ms. Oyama, came up to him. She'd already heard from Ms. Tachibana and Dancer about Patron's fever and all the attendant happenings. She didn't, however, express any concerns about Patron's health. Instead she invited Ogi to attend the prayer meeting the Quiet Women would be holding that evening at eight in the chapel to pray for Patron's recovery.

After dinner, in the interval before the meeting, Ogi stopped by Patron's residence. According to Ms. Tachibana, the antibiotics hadn't started working yet, but Dr. Koga had been able to alleviate the pain so Patron was able to sleep. Fortunately, Morio's eyes and ears were unaffected. Dr. Koga had told her that when she found her brother by Patron's bedside, his eyes unable to see, his inert form was a sort of empathetic response to the feverish Patron.

When Ogi entered the chapel he found the piano pushed toward the front and the barber chair set in front of the rows of chairs, with Mrs. Shigeno and Ms. Takada and several of the other Quiet Women surrounding a young girl with short dark hair cut in straight bangs, deep in conversation. In the half circle of chairs sat some of the other Quiet Women and, behind them, ten or so middle-aged Technicians.

Ogi sat down in a vacant aisle chair. From there he could see the bowl-cut girl was holding a large frame that hid nearly half of her. It was Kizu's pencil sketch of Patron he'd done that afternoon, the wound colored in with pastels.

The time for the meeting to begin came, and the young girl, at Mrs. Shigeno's direction, went to sit in the high barber chair, setting the picture frame on her lap. The drawing was more visible than the girl, for only the shiny top half of her head showed above the frame.

Mrs. Shigeno went to stand by the chair, rested a hand against the high armrest, and turned to face the audience. Ogi opened his red-covered notebook. Mrs. Shigeno, aware of the fine acoustics, spoke in a subdued tone.

"We have maintained our life of faith through Patron," she said, "who connects us with the Almighty. Still, we knew nothing about the Sacred Wound. Now, though, all of us are aware of what has been happening to him physically. According to the details Ms. Tachibana and Dancer have given us, Patron has had this unhealed wound for a long while. His condition worsened recently, leading to a terrible fever. Today Patron is not yet fully conscious, so we'd like to hold this prayer vigil to pray for his speedy recovery.

"First of all I'd like all of us to consider deeply the drawing Professor Kizu did of Patron in his sickbed. We've asked Mai-chan, who's come with her mother, Mrs. Tagawa, as a new member of our church, to hold the painting in the chair her mother uses in her work."

Having taken care of the mother and daughter's official change of residence forms and the girl's school transfer papers, Ogi had heard the girl's name before. It had struck him as urban and contemporary, and Asa-san, who'd helped with the paperwork, had said, somewhat contemptuously, that nowadays in Japan the most popular names for children were Daiki for boys and Mai for girls.

"As I said at the outset, it is through Patron that we've been able to lead our lives of faith, both when we were in the church and afterward, and now in his new church. Still, until these recent events, the only ones who knew about the Sacred Wound were those who took care of Patron after he and Guide did their Somersault.

"Having this ever-open wound in one's side must be very unpleasant, especially for a man. Right now bloody pus is oozing out, which led to the fever. Patron's temperature this evening is just over 101 degrees Fahrenheit. When he was found with Morio, unconscious in bed, I'm sure it was much higher. One item on our prayer list, then, should be a prayer for his fever to go away.

"When Ms. Tachibana discovered the two of them, Morio's eyes and ears were covered with the matter coming out of Patron's wound; his head seemed to be made of yellow clay. Apparently Morio was trying to respond to Patron's suffering. Let us also pray that Morio stays well.

"As we pray, we'll be hearing some music Morio composed depicting a sister and brother being led to heaven by Patron." (This evening, instead of Ikuo playing, one of the Quiet Women sat very seriously at the piano and played the piece over and over for about ten minutes.) "Since Patron hasn't said anything about when he first had the Sacred Wound, Dancer doesn't know anything definite, but according to Dr. Koga, when he gave Patron a physical before the Somersault it was not present.

"This means the wound came about during the ten-year interval between the Somersault and the restarting of the church. Undoubtedly Patron has had it during the entire period in which he fell into hell. We recognize this hole in his side as a sign of a holy person, as a Sacred Wound, and we recognize his suffering with great joy.

"We joined this church hoping to be led to heaven by Patron. Instead, we had to go through the trials and tribulations of the Somersault. But our faith in what awaits us in heaven has never wavered. We knew in our hearts that someday Patron would appear again on the path to lead us.

"With a sense of nostalgia, and also sadness, we wonder what sort of painful place Patron is wandering in now. When we met him again and he told us about the hell he and Guide had fallen into, we could visualize this hell right before us. We have learned further that this descent into hell carved the Sacred Wound into his side. For what he has revealed to us, we are all grateful to God in heaven. Hallelujah! The wound is a sacred sign that links the Patron before the Somersault with the Patron afterward. God made him shoulder this painful wound so he might survive the hell into which he'd descended.

"Guide, who fell into hell along with Patron, did not have a Sacred Wound. If he had, the police would have made it public after his death, announcing it as resulting from the rough treatment he received. Instead of suffering from a wound, Guide's fate was—at this final stage of the descent into hell—to die. All this was God's will, just as Saint Peter was crucified upside down and the disciple John lived to a ripe old age

"Through the darkness Patron passed through, and through this wound that was a part of his suffering, Patron shouldered a mission, one we need to reflect on deeply. The day is near when Patron will fulfill this in his church of light. Isn't that exactly the message we should get from the suffering he's going through?

"Last week at our early morning prayer service, Asa-san told us about Former Brother Gii, who lived here, researching Dante, and how he was killed after starting a reform movement. After she spoke we had breakfast together, and she asked how the names Patron and Guide came about. We weren't able to give a complete answer. Asa-san told us what she'd picked up from Former Brother Gii concerning Dante's *Divine Comedy*. In Dante, Virgil is the one who appears soon after Dante falls into hell, who accompanies him to the highest point of purgatory, where he says goodbye to his disciples who are continuing on to heaven, only to remain behind himself. As Dante called him the first time he met him, Virgil is both a poet who is a *patron*, a teacher for all mankind, and a *guide* for people who are ascending from hell. Weren't the roles that Virgil undertook alone the ones your leaders undertook as a team? she asked.

"What Asa-san said made me think very deeply. After the martyrdom of Patron's indispensable colleague, like Virgil he undertook both roles—that of Patron and of Guide—when he returned to be in our midst. Did he do this to lead us to the highest point of purgatory and then say farewell and return alone once more to hell?"

Mrs. Shigeno stopped at this point and turned around to see what the audience was gazing at; the drawing of the recumbent Patron with the wound on his side on top of the barber's chair shook ever so slightly, startling her. Mai, a sensitive girl, was weeping. As if to soothe the poor young girl, Mrs. Shigeno signaled to Ms. Tagawa, today dressed quite fashionably, her hair in a mannish Takarazuka dance-troupe cut, and ended her sermon.

As if waiting for this opportunity, one of the Technicians who had been sitting behind Ogi—a scientist who, it was said, was an expert in astrodynamics and who'd done orbital calculations for NASA satellite launches—signaled that he wanted to speak. Mrs. Shigeno nodded to him, and he made the sort of comment one might expect from a rocket scientist.

"I'm sure many of you have seen, when a rocket launched toward the moon reaches a certain altitude, that the propulsion device separates and inscribes a track like a burning leaf. I can picture Patron/Guide as a rocket inscribing a huge arc as it strays away."

Mrs. Shigeno picked up where she left off, tying her sermon together with what had just been said.

"I think that's exactly right," she said. "I believe Patron is resolved to help us to the very end to reach our apogee, even if it means he'll descend to hell once again, burning up as he reenters. Doesn't this explain what he meant when, after the Somersault and losing Guide, he returned to be with us and announced he's an antichrist?

"After the Somersault, the Quiet Women resisted a host of temptations that befell them. We maintained our faith in heaven, with Patron as our mediator. And now we know, more than ever before, that this was the right thing to do! Hallelujah, hallelujah, hallelujah!"

Answering Mrs. Shigeno's almost pleading cry, the Quiet Women took up the same prayer, and then all at once switched to silent worship. Mrs. Shigeno turned toward the drawing of Patron and bowed her head.

Desperately emotional again, Mai seemed about to drop the drawing on the footstool. She grasped the upper edge of the frame as hard as she could in her little red hands and, unable to cover her face, sobbed. The Quiet Women gathered around her, heads bowed, and continued to pray.

Ogi and the Technicians around him were overwhelmed.

3

Ogi had lunch the next day in the office, during which he had a good talk with Dancer. Having been out of the office for a day, he had a lot of e-mails, faxes, and phone messages to take care of. The idea to have a meeting that summer in Shikoku to commemorate the founding of the new church was in full swing. Believers from before the Somersault who had clung to Mr. Soda's Kansai headquarters were urging Patron on now, and one of Ogi's tasks was to gather together all these communications and deliver them to Patron.

There was something else that he urgently needed to talk with Dancer about, but she didn't show up at the office until just before noon. As soon as she could, she told him that the concentration of antibiotics had reached the optimum level and Patron's fever had broken. The wound wasn't as inflamed as before. And Dancer had reported to Patron that all the believers who'd moved to the Hollow were now aware of the Sacred Wound.

"Patron didn't seem concerned about how his followers were taking the news. He did remember, though, that Kizu sat next to him and sketched him when he was half conscious, and he wanted to see the drawing. After the Quiet Women's prayer meeting, the drawing was taken over to the farm and the Technicians apparently held their own meeting in front of it. I imagine Ikuo saw it there too," Ogi concluded. "I wonder what he said about the wound being kept secret all this time."

"I haven't seen him since this uproar began," Dancer said worriedly. "I'd appreciate it if you'd sound him out about it. They're going to bring the painting back from the farm to the studio this afternoon, and of course Ikuo will accompany it. Would you stop by then? I don't think Ikuo needs to know every last detail concerning Patron, but I'm sure he will have his own take on things."

Ogi was surprised that Dancer could be so nervous when it came to Ikuo. As for himself, except for that comical and pathetic incident in the bathroom, Dancer probably would never have mentioned the wound to him, either.

"I attended the Quiet Women's meeting, and they have a pretty set way of thinking about the Sacred Wound," Ogi commented.

"Ms. Tachibana told me all about it," Dancer said. "She also talked with Patron, and said he seemed depressed. She wondered if he was feeling that his efforts all these years were wasted."

"Meaning . . . ?"

Showing her tongue, as lusterless as her skin, she returned Ogi's gaze.

"Since I only starting working for them after the Somersault, I don't have the right to say anything about that, and I don't want to either," said Dancer. "But I did read the articles in the weekly magazines about the Somersault, and they bothered me, so I asked Guide about it. The media had a field day reporting the Somersault: How Patron sat down in front of the cameras and announced that their religious activities weren't for real and it was all an elaborate joke. When I asked Guide why he did that kind of performance, he said Patron wanted to avoid having the kind of situation you have in America with fundamentalists, when overwrought followers protest the pressure brought to bear on their leader or grow too pessimistic because they were hung out to dry. Seeing Patron play the fool before all of Japan, anyone could see it was pointless to take it seriously.

"But doesn't it put Patron in an awkward position to have people who empathize with him so much thrust aside and then, as he's rebuilding his church, to find them still offering their pathetic prayers to him?"

"The Technicians at the meeting seemed to be deeply sympathetic to the Quiet Women's position," Ogi said, "but I wonder how they'd react to what you just said."

"What I'd rather do is have you sound out Ikuo about the Technicians' ideas," Dancer said. "What concerns me most is how he's taking the fact that the Sacred Wound was hidden all this time."

4

When Ogi went up the road to the north shore of the Hollow and arrived at the studio, Kizu and Ikuo were looking at the sketch that Ikuo had just brought back from the farm. Ogi stood next to them, concerned about Ikuo's reaction, but Ikuo soon cleared away his anxiety.

"When we looked at the drawing of the Sacred Wound," Ikuo said, his use of the term already revealing his reaction, "we spoke of how terrible it must have been for Patron to have had it all this time. For Dancer, too, it must have been tough. It was bound to come out—it was just a question of timing. All in all, I think this was the right moment."

The three of them turned their gaze to the framed drawing on the floor. There was the reddish-black hole that Ogi had inadvertently seen in the bath. He remembered the contrast between this hole and Dancer's protruding pudenda.

"I talked with Professor Kizu about this recently," Ogi said. "I think I'd like you to go ahead with Ikuo's plan to have Patron pose for you. There's no reason to hide this anymore, what with the Quiet Women en masse claiming it's a Sacred Wound. If this sketch helps you complete the triptych, this little affair will have done some good by having helped boot up our new church in the Hollow."

Kizu raised his eyebrows in surprise at the computer term *boot up*. "When you and Ikuo reach my age, you'll discover that not everything has to be meaningful," Kizu said, pondering the triptych anew.

"I understand Ikuo as the model for Jonah, but what theme would Patron express, with the wound showing in his side?" Ogi asked.

Ikuo was silent.

"The Sacred Wound fits in nicely with the person who acts as mediator between us and God," Kizu said. "But instead of having this wounded mediator trying to *persuade* Jonah, I'm beginning to see him more on Jonah's side, *protesting* with him, refusing to surrender to God."

"I like the ambiguity involved—having Patron model for a figure that can be interpreted in more than one way," Ikuo said. "The followers praying in the chapel can read it any way they want."

"It also gives me a certain freedom as the artist," Kizu said.

He picked up the framed sketch and returned it to the dining table as Ikuo brought over a chilled bottle of mineral water and cups, and the three of them sat down and quenched their thirst.

"Dancer said that when she went to explain to the Technicians about having kept the wound a secret, she didn't quite understand their reaction," Ogi said to Ikuo. "How do you see it?"

"Because of all that went on in the last ten years, the Technicians have become quite cautious," Ikuo replied. "It's hard to read their reactions. But they do have a definite response. Mind you, I'm still an outsider, but I get the impression that they've been able to overcome the split that began with Guide's interrogation and 'trial.' One thing the Technicians always agreed on was not accepting the meaning of Patron's Somersault, agreeing that it was the wrong way to go. But beyond that there's a difference of opinion concerning Patron and Guide's lifestyle that surfaced when Guide was put on trial and died.

"On the one hand, you have those who wanted to execute Guide for betraying the Technicians. On the other, you have those who regret that this unfortunate accident happened just as a repentant Guide was opening up a dialogue. Seen from a different angle, you have those who've come here hoping that Patron's restarting of the church will link the time pre-Somersault with the time after—as if the Somersault never took place. And you have those who want Patron to somehow make a comeback and are struggling to find a new direction, different from the way they did things before the Somersault.

"And while all this was going on, Patron's Sacred Wound became public knowledge. It shows the direction the new church will take, I think, the real nature of Patron's appeal to society and the world. Patron is always calling for those who've sinned to repent, and the wound has opened up as a sign, a constant reminder of this. If you think about it, Patron could be a suitable leader for *either* faction of the Technicians to rally around. I've also heard some of them saying that they'd like to raise up the banner of Patron's Sacred

Wound and become the strike force of the new church. I haven't seen them this excited in a long time."

When Ogi returned to the office he reported Ikuo's words to Dancer, allaying her concerns by telling her that Ikuo had not dwelled on her secrecy regarding the Sacred Wound.

Dancer was silent for a while. "I'm really happy that the Quiet Women and the Technicians are taking the Sacred Wound so seriously," she said finally, "but I don't think Patron would be too pleased, either with the Quiet Women's excessive emotionalism or the way the Technicians are already laying plans for action."

"Professor Kizu spoke with Dr. Koga," Ogi said, "who told him how surprised he was to see the intensity with which the Technicians are dealing with the wound. He also said he's concerned that they might ignore Patron's will and use this as a pretext for reviving their radical activities."

"But what about Ikuo himself?" Dancer asked. "Didn't he join this church in order to hear Patron relay the order God wants him to carry out? Ikuo's close to the Technicians in a different way from Dr. Koga. I wonder sometimes if he might join them and rush headlong into something rash. If Ikuo and the Technicians joined forces, Patron might not be able to resist them."

"Professor Kizu kids him about how training the Young Fireflies is his main thing now," Ogi said.

The wet interior of her mouth had a much healthier hue to it than it had earlier in the day, as Dancer sat there contemplatively. "Since Ikuo's childhood was so unusual," she said, "he can't restrain himself when it comes to dealing with children. Don't you think he would have made a good schoolteacher, instead of making a half-baked effort to carve out a life for himself in normal society? Not that I have any right to say that."

Ogi felt it was he, more than Dancer, who had no right to criticize Ikuo in that way.

5

Late that night another unexpected event took place, which made this the busiest week since the church had moved to the Hollow. Kizu suffered a massive bloody discharge and sharper pain than ever before and was carried to Dr. Koga's clinic.

There were portents that this might be coming, especially when Kizu told Ikuo, as he left the studio, that he was too exhausted to go out to dinner and asked Mrs. Shigeno to prepare a light meal to be sent over to his residence. Ms. Tachibana, along with Morio, had yet to see the sketch of Patron's Sacred Wound, so she brought over Kizu's meal, which consisted of the same menu as everyone else's, minus the meat.

Ms. Tachibana's face was almost frighteningly pale, but Kizu was happy to see that there was an understanding between her and Ikuo and the office staff. Kizu was also impressed at how intensely Morio studied the sketch, the same intensity he usually applied only to listening to music. It was also nice to see that his eyes and ears were perfectly fine. Ms. Tachibana was worried, though, because Kizu didn't touch his meal while they were there, and on the way home she found herself also concerned when Morio, with his perfect pitch, told her that Kizu's voice had been one note flatter than usual.

Also, in the middle of the night, as she got Morio up to use the toilet—he'd been wetting his bed since he was a teenager—she noticed a light on in the house on the north shore, reflected on the surface of the lake. She woke Dancer up, and they talked things over with Ogi. Kizu's place didn't have a phone, so they decided to go over to check for themselves. As soon as Ogi entered the unlocked house, he found Kizu collapsed on the floor in front of the toilet.

Ogi raced back to their house on the south shore, phoned Dr. Koga, and went back to help Dancer take care of Kizu. Kizu was conscious as they carried him to his bed, though he couldn't respond and just groaned. All they could do while waiting for Dr. Koga was to stand watch at Kizu's bedside. At the same time they noticed that their palms were dappled dark red, like the painting of the wound in Patron's side.

Ikuo drove Dr. Koga over. The doctor seemed more energetic than ever as he bustled around. Ikuo, in contrast, was tearful and helpless, yet somehow he blurted out that he'd like them to take Kizu by ambulance to the Red Cross Hospital in Matsuyama. Dr. Koga scolded him, however, saying that a patient in such pain might very well have a heart attack and that transporting him such a long way would be signing his death warrant. He would treat Kizu at the clinic.

The next day the Quiet Women held another prayer vigil, this time for Kizu's swift recovery. The Young Fireflies, profoundly grateful for the donations Kizu had made to them and wanting to cheer up Ikuo, put back the partition they had taken out in Kizu's house to make the studio, to partition off a living room, again, on the east side, and a bedroom on the west for Kizu to convalesce in.

Kizu came home from the clinic one week later and was carried up to his house from the car they parked below the dam. As he was carried inside on a stretcher, Kizu noticed Morio among those lined up to welcome him back and said a word of greeting to him. Morio, solemn and serious, paused a beat before replying.

"Your voice is small, but it's the right pitch now!"

The people gathered there had heard how Morio had related Kizu's physical condition to the pitch of his voice, and an animated stir rippled through the group. Ogi realized how indispensable a person Kizu had already become to those who'd moved here.

Asa-san was among the local residents who were happy that Kizu was back home. Ogi learned that, even though she was among those who smiled peacefully at Morio's words, she was also a realist unmoved by the upbeat mood of those around her.

Watching as Kizu was carried up the slope, gazing steadily at the greenery, which had deepened in color in the week of his absence, Asa-san spoke to Ogi, who stood beside her.

"I'm not saying that Professor Kizu needs to return to America, but wouldn't it be best if he chose a real hospital in Matsuyama or Tokyo and settled in there? I think coming back to the Hollow means he's resigned himself to the inevitable."

Ogi went over to the home on the east side of the monastery occupied by Patron to report to him that Kizu was back from the clinic. Patron asked about Kizu's condition and about any new symptoms and was dissatisfied that Ogi wasn't able to give more details. Before long Patron announced he'd be paying Kizu a visit. Ogi returned to the office to consult with Dancer, and in the evening, with Dr. Koga joining them, they discussed how to carry out this request.

The sky was dark and threatening rain as Ogi and Dancer walked single file through the dark silent woods to Kizu's house, shining their flashlights at Patron's feet. Contrary to the usual feeling one got that the darkness was pushing down to the lowest reaches of the woods, the chapel and the monastery across the lake seemed to recede and somehow it felt entirely natural that—despite the large number of people living there—there wasn't a sound.

Kizu was sitting in his angled bed, propped up by cushions, and in front of him were three dining room chairs. Dr. Koga was already ensconced on one of them. Patron and Dancer sat down on the other two, while Ikuo and Ogi stood at the foot of the bed, their backs to the dark window.

"I'm sorry to have caused all this trouble with such dramatic events," Kizu said, in a voice that, as Morio had pointed out, was small but lively.

"If anyone's been acting melodramatically, it's *me*," Patron said. "Once my fever came down I was back to normal, but I've stayed in my room because I was embarrassed to see all of you. Are you in pain?"

"No, not right now."

"It must have been quite painful when you collapsed."

"I didn't even have time to think about it, the pain was so bad—more than I had thought a person could endure. . . . Physical pain can make your whole world collapse. It made me think how extraordinary your Somersault must have been, as a shock to your whole person. I realized I'd taken advantage of our closeness in age and said some pretty stupid things. It's made me think about a lot of things. . . ."

Patron didn't respond directly, and everyone else was silent. Just saying that much had left Kizu gasping for breath.

"You've just been allowed to come home," Dancer said, "and I'm sure the trip has worn you out, so it's best not to talk too much."

"Don't worry," Dr. Koga countered. "Professor Kizu isn't your run-of-the-mill invalid. He's the kind of person who can take physical pain, shift it over to *spiritual* pain, and use it to bolster his creativity. I've never had a patient like him before."

"I've only been away a week," Kizu said, "but I feel uplifted to be back with all my friends again. This really has become my *home*. I got a little carried away just now and said that after all the pain I experienced I reflected deeply on things, but I can't get Patron's wound out of my mind. I had just sketched it, too. . . . For ten years, you said, you were in hell, and I was thinking about what you endured. . . . To borrow Dr. Koga's words, along with the spiritual pain, imagine such a persistent physical pain on top of it. . . . It's the kind of pain that hits you all at once, but no matter how overwhelming it is you know it will pass. If the body is killed, the pain will disappear. But that's not true of spiritual pain, is it?"

Patron was silent. Dancer said to him, "When you were in the midst of your fever you didn't get a chance to see Professor Kizu's sketch. Could we all look together at it now?"

She went to the room next door, closed off by a wide sliding door, and brought over the framed sketch. Kizu asked Ikuo to fetch the preliminary sketchbook he'd used for the final panel of the triptych. As the latter was opened onto the floor, Kizu stretched out his neck toward it like a turtle.

"The one in the frame is the sketch I did of your wound, which I colored with watercolors. The next one, and the page in the sketchbook, are sketches I did the night I was hit by that sharp pain, while I was thinking about the tableau. Both of them center on the Sacred Wound, and I did them to try to clarify my feelings about Patron's injury.

"My pain was entirely physical, but while I was racked by it, and after a week when its aftershocks continued, when I look at these earlier sketches I feel my way of thinking about the tableau has changed. Seeing as how I've come up with a new concept, I thought I'd ask Patron to come here to pose for me."

"Well, there's no need to hide my wound anymore, so why not?" Patron replied. "Somehow your painting captures a side of me that now, even at my age, I'd never noticed before."

25: The Play at the Hollow

1

In his house on the north shore of the Hollow, Kizu still felt a quiet sense of excitement after Patron's visit and lay awake far into the night. Even without the medicine Dr. Koga had prescribed, he was able to control the pain deep in his abdomen; he was beginning, in fact, to feel a kind of symbiotic relationship with it.

Kizu realized again how hard it is to call up a memory of pain once it's passed. Still, after such overwhelming agony, he was able to put the lesser pain he felt at present, and any anxiety about the future, into perspective.

The pain that had assaulted him in the middle of that night he could certainly feel for what it was, yet it went way beyond what anything within him could actively resist. He'd felt driven, spiritually and physically, into a gigantic dark tunnel of pain, violated, with no hope of escape. During the intermittent periods when the pain receded, he was surprised that an insignificant being like himself was able to put up with so much. And then the pain would flare up again and he'd be driven back, deep into that dark tunnel. What frightened him most was the fact that there was no downtime, no letup from this abnormal power. Every time he was once again spit out, alive, from the depths, only to be handed over to a different form of pain—one that was within the realm of comprehension.

The pain that Kizu felt deep in his gut was somehow now accompanied by a sense of nostalgia. Not a nostalgia based on some past event, but more like a sense of déjà vu.

Ever so slowly the pain reached its peak, and Kizu suppressed a groan. The dregs of pain floated up on his expelled breath; his feverish body began to smell.

The second or third day, when all his organs felt stiff and hard, he couldn't understand where the pain was coming from, what the dynamics of the pain and his body movements were, and how they were related. Kizu was both afraid of this unknown opponent and roused himself to resist it, shifting positions in bed to test it. He tried this even more efficiently now and was finally able to pinpoint the pain's exact locus. This time, in place of a groan, he exhaled deeply. The sound came back to him as a sigh, a composed expression of his inner being.

"Can't you sleep?" Ikuo called out to him. He had apparently been awake all the time. "Is the pain really bad?" As this familiar voice rose up like dampness from the foot of his bed, Kizu felt a childish exhilaration.

"It does hurt, but it's not the kind of pain I usually feel inside . . . more like an imaginary pain. Like soldiers who get their legs blown off in war and still complain that their knees hurt."

"Would you like me to prepare a suppository?" Ikuo asked.

"I'd rather not."

"How about a sleeping pill?"

"It's not the pain that's keeping me up. I'm just absorbing the fact that I'm actually back here."

"Shall I open the curtain?"

"That'd be nice. But let's keep the lights off so the people across the lake won't start worrying."

A large dark object roused itself and slowly drew the curtain back. In the moonlight that filtered in, Kizu was happy to see a brusque smile on Ikuo's deeply shadowed profile. Drawn by Ikuo's gaze outside, Kizu slid himself up so he, too, could see out.

The moon was in the west, hidden behind the huge cypress that filled the whole right side of the window. The shadow of the tree cut across the surface of the lake, where fog was swirling low and beginning to thicken, all the way to the forest on the east bank. The moon shone on the fog on the surface of the lake, illuminating the concrete walls of the chapel on the south shore.

Even the needles of the cedars and the tips of the leaves of the bushes in the forest behind were shining, yet the whole was pitch black. The night sky was clear, with a purity Kizu hadn't seen in some time, with thin clouds sweeping briskly and steadily across the sky like sheets of ice.

Kizu had been quiet, concentrating on the moonlit scene for a while, when he noticed that Ikuo wanted to say something but had been hesitating.

"One of my colleagues in America has traced the American sublime in Romantic landscapes of the United States," Kizu said, in a hoarse voice. "I see there's a sublime in the Japanese landscape too."

"The Young Fireflies talk of the Hollow as a special place," Ikuo said. "During the insurrections at the end of the Tokugawa period and the beginning of the Meiji, people dragged down bamboo to use as weapons from the huge bamboo grove. Right here, which used to be a basin, was where they stripped the leaves off, the ground completely covered in green and the farmers drunk. The Base Movement started here as well, as did the Church of the Flaming Green Tree. I believe there really is what everyone calls the *power of the land,* what Asa-san calls the *power of the place.*"

"Will Patron's church be able to rely on this power?" Kizu asked.

"It's like a stage where something's going to take place, where something sacred will manifest itself. . . . I've felt the same thing once before, in another place. . . . Two days ago, when the moon was full, I came back here, to see how the Fireflies had rearranged the rooms, and spent the night. I couldn't get to sleep either, and as I looked out at the bright moonlit scenery outside I remembered that other time and place."

Kizu waited for Ikuo to continue his reminiscences, but after a moment of silence the young man brought up another subject.

"At noon the next day everyone was asking me, very concerned, about how you were. With what happened with Patron's Sacred Wound, things change so fast. The Quiet Women have started to formulate some plans of their own in addition to their group prayers, while the inner circle of Technicians, who've been wavering a bit since Guide's death, are now much more focused again—as Dancer, for whatever reason, had predicted.

"I came here following Patron rather than his church, hoping he was going to take some action. So I'd like to consider these things going on among the church members as a kind of forewarning of things to come. If the internal pressure building up in the Quiet Women and the Technicians blows, I don't think Patron can just sit around twiddling his thumbs. I'm like Dancer—I much prefer to see signs that something is about to happen. Two days ago I was convinced that something important is about to take place on the stage before me now, this moonlit Hollow. People say any convictions you have late at night are illusory, but tonight I'm getting the exact same feelings. I think the reason you're back here, Professor, is so you can observe whatever it is that's going to happen on this stage.

"Whatever it is," Ikuo went on, "I don't want the Young Fireflies to fall victim to it. I bring this up because they consider these grounds in the Hollow a special place, the site where they're planning to construct their new lives. So whatever happens, they'll be involved."

Something occurred to Kizu. "Every time I talk with you about the book of Jonah, I see you standing on Jonah's side, grumbling about what the Lord wants you to do. But your attitude right now isn't just that of a Jonah."

"What do you mean?" Ikuo asked, caught off guard.

"It's a simple thing, really. Not long ago I put it this way: Jonah stands up to God, insisting that he destroy Nineveh the way he originally planned. But God, lamenting the loss of over 120,000 children plus countless head of cattle, doesn't burn the city. And the people repent. And now *you're* worried about children not becoming victims, right?"

Ikuo turned his forehead, lumpy like the surface of a pumpkin, toward the moonlight, while below his deep eye sockets all was dark and hardened.

"I'm not making fun of you," Kizu said, "merely pointing out this contradiction. A contradiction you've never had before in your life, never thought about, but one that's significant nonetheless. If you hadn't come to this place and gotten to know the Fireflies, this contradiction never would have entered your world . . . never would have grazed you conceptually.

"I began to think about this when you were staying with me in the clinic," Kizu said. "In the middle of the night when I looked out at the backyard I saw a group of Fireflies huddled together, all gazing up despondently at my window. Soon after I laid my head back on my pillow, you got up from your sofa and, thinking I was asleep, crept out of the room. Pretty soon I heard an irrepressible stir. Just seeing you made the children in the backyard so happy. You're very close to these kids, and you have a premonition that something is going to take place here. Whatever it turns out to be, you'll be a part of it, and they can't help but get dragged in. You can't shut out such devoted admirers.

"No matter what sort of amoral activity you get involved with, it's not going to shock me into retreating. This is the stage where I'll spend my final days, and no matter what takes place I'm ready for it. But I must say I don't mind seeing you agonize over how to keep the Fireflies from getting hurt."

2

Ikuo looked lost in thought. The fog that covered the lake rose up in eddies. At first Kizu thought the wind was making it swirl, but looking closely at the outline of the giant cypress he noticed the fog was still. Was it a change in humidity that made the fog form at night? Still feverish, Kizu was sensitive enough to smell the cold coming through the bare window.

"Why don't we close the curtains, Ikuo."

Silently, with unfaltering steps, the young man moved over to the window. After closing the curtains, he walked around the bed to straighten the curtains on the opposite side, through which vertical shafts of moonlight filtered in. His eyes were used to the dark, so he moved quickly and surely. Kizu could just make him out as he climbed back in bed and pulled up the covers. Drawing back slightly, he sat up, clasping his knees together.

"There is something I really wanted to tell you tonight," Ikuo said. "It's connected with what you talked about earlier. It's the most important experience I've had up till now. I was going to tell you about it once—the time that Guide urged me to appeal to Patron, when I had you write that letter for me. But I didn't have the guts.

"I told you about how I heard a voice from above?—the voice of God, I called it, telling me, *Do it!*—though I didn't tell you what I did in response to that voice, just that I was waiting to hear the voice again. I know you're tired, but I wonder if you would mind listening to me?"

Ikuo spoke politely, though clearly not expecting a negative reply.

"I feel a premonition, I guess you'd call it, that something important will occur here very soon. The Technicians are making preparations; even the Quiet Women are active. The buildings here in the Hollow belong to the Kansai headquarters, so of course they have every right to do this, but they're planning to hold a gathering here in the Hollow with Patron and a large number of their followers. After people found out about the Sacred Wound, Patron became very upbeat about this plan and told Ogi to take charge. Most likely it'll be held in the summer.

"With all these things happening and me involved, I have to come up with a plan. But what *kind* of plan I still have to figure out. One thing I need to decide is how far I should involve the Fireflies. I've been thinking about this all week. For several days running, Gii's brought the Fireflies over to stand guard over me, as it were, since seeing me just sitting silently and thinking has him worried.

"The Fireflies are kids, after all, so they're self-centered. They're enthusiastic about doing whatever it takes to establish Gii's ideology. If an emergency arises with you, Professor—or even if it's not an emergency—and you're put in a hospital in Tokyo or New York, I probably won't be coming back to the Hollow. And that's a worry for them too, from their ideological standpoint.

"So there's this basic egotism involved, but you should know that every one of the Fireflies participated in the silent prayer meeting the Quiet Women held for your recovery. Two hours without a break. It must have been pretty hard on them, don't you think? That's an incredibly long time for young kids to sit still and keep their eyes closed, but Gii made sure every single one of them took part.

"Two hours. . . . Yes, that must have been hard on them," Kizu said.

"Their goal was to keep you here and to keep me tied to this region. They came up with other plans too, including one to threaten us. This was connected with something I told Gii about my past. I thought you might not be getting back to sleep soon, so I wanted to tell you this story now.

"When I was fourteen years old I hit my tutor, an American named Schmidt, with a poker and hurt him quite seriously. And then when I was sixteen I hit him again with a poker and killed him. Behind both attacks was the homosexual relationship we had. If you and I decided to cut our ties with the Hollow and move to Tokyo or America, Gii planned to blackmail us by sending letters to the newspapers accusing us of creating a ring in which we sexually abused young boys.

"I haven't told you before about my early life, but now I'd like to. My father was a banker who was stationed abroad for many years, and my mother was a piano teacher. Through my parents' professions we got to be friends with the family of an American who ran a music publishing firm that operated in the United States and Japan.

"I was the youngest child in my family and ended up becoming closest to this family—the Schmidts. My parents were particularly keen on having me remain bilingual, since we had lived in England, Canada, and the States until I was ten, and I was fluent in English. I wasn't a particularly studious child, but I loved making models, and when I wasn't doing that I played all day outside our house in the suburbs, where the natural surroundings were still quite beautiful, so physically at least I grew up strong.

"Every weekend I was sent to stay over at the Schmidts'. His wife was Japanese, and they had a grown daughter, and Mr. Schmidt did his work at home, in a separate cottage, and that's where I slept on an army cot they set up for me. It was during this period that you and I had our near miss at that plastic model competition. What you saw there was an indication of the violence I was capable of. My sexual relationship with Mr. Schmidt started when I was ten and a half and continued until I was fourteen, when I took that poker in the cottage—the poker he used to show me how to build a fire and keep it going; he was my teacher in many ways—and I hit him in the back and thighs. He suffered compound fractures and was confined to a wheelchair for the rest of his life.

"My parents and Mr. Schmidt came to an understanding, though, and I wasn't hauled off to court. Mr. Schmidt was quite generous to me, and after he returned to working in his house he restarted our English conversation lessons. I can't believe my parents weren't aware of the sexual element in the background to all this. But my father was a self-centered, closed-in person, and he was relieved to let Mr. Schmidt's generosity and good intentions settle matters.

"So I kept going over for my lessons, though I didn't spend the night, and two years later Mr. Schmidt was going on a business trip to Vienna and Salzburg in the musical off-season—his job then involving reissuing a series of old LPs—and asked me to go with him to push his wheelchair. I think Mr. Schmidt sort of put the screws to my father to get his consent. I could tell because when we were leaving my father looked kind of depressed. Anyway, after a busy week in Vienna, on the day after we went to Salzburg, I clubbed Mr. Schmidt to death.

"I wasn't taken into custody by the police but taken to a hospital in Vienna, where one of the counselors was a Japanese specialist who was a professor appointed to the staff there and the other counselor was a professor who'd taken his degree at Stanford. I spoke a lot, both in English and Japanese. I tried my hardest to give them the impression that I'd been forced into killing Mr. Schmidt because I'd been victimized. They believed me. Later on I heard that one of the counselors had been quoted in the newspapers to the effect that the real criminal in this case was the murdered man himself!

"Police investigators dispatched to Japan unearthed another young man who'd been sexually molested by Schmidt, which was a plus for me. Naturally they asked me why I hadn't told anyone, but one commentator also noted how Japan isn't the kind of country where sexual victimization is part of ordinary discourse.

"At least I was able to lead the hospital and the police investigation in a direction that was advantageous to me, convincing them that the physical and emotional wounds I'd been carrying around for so long finally exploded, and that not only was the process whereby I was injured completely overlooked, but that no one—neither my parents nor my doctors—had detected the calls for help I'd been sending out since the first incident. In other words, I put myself forward as the tragic victim in this whole affair.

"This was the spin I put on Schmidt's death for adult consumption, but inside I had a different understanding of it—not that I was aware of it at the time—and this has been a major issue for me ever since. When Mr. Schmidt was in Tokyo he had no compunction about walking around town accompanied by a young boy playing the role of page. This turned out to be very trying for me when we were in Europe. In front of the hotel staff he treated me as he would in Japan, but when he was in a formal situation with his social betters he treated me like some Oriental valet.

"The day the murder took place there was to be a dinner with a famous conductor who would be presenting a limited-engagement series of concerts in Japan, and though someone was needed to push Mr. Schmidt's wheelchair, they assigned that job to a member of the hotel owner's family. I was ordered to stay behind in our hotel room and be content with a room-service supper.

"Mr. Schmidt was decked out in formal wear, waiting for them to come get him, and I was watching Japanese cartoons on TV when he called me to come over to the terrace of our suite's sitting room. It was still some time before sunset, and because the hotel was situated on a hillside, you could see a broad vista, including the dark sky threatening thunder.

"Mr. Schmidt asked me if I recalled the sketch of the Alpine valleys in the copy of Leonardo da Vinci's Madrid notebook he'd told me to look at before we left Japan. The place where we were headed next was the area where his parents had been born and raised, from which they set off when they moved to America. He said that place resembled the drawing, which is why he'd wanted me to see it.

"Like the view from our veranda, the drawing showed, beyond gentle hills and thickets, a sunken plain with clumps of houses and groves of trees. And beyond that a dark, rainy ravine between two mountains, with a cap of clouds like a heavy lid on top. Farther up you could see the sunlit peaks of the clouds and the Alps ranging off into the distance.

"Recalling this, what I saw before me was something with a broader façade than the drawing, a wide-angled version, with a large castle on the mountain in the middle, light on one side, darkness on the other. To the right, farther back, range upon range of the Alps sparkled in the evening sun.

"After making sure that I did recall Leonardo's drawing and that I was mentally comparing it to the scenery outside the glass doors, Mr. Schmidt said, 'My parents were born on the slopes of the mountain far back in that ravine and were raised feeling the electricity that swells up there running through their whole bodies. Every time I look at da Vinci's notebook, that electricity my parents felt shoots right through me. For the people who crossed over to the New World from here, that's what this land meant to them. And in the art that European geniuses have created lies the same effect.'

"Twilight seemed to last forever that day, and as I ate my lonely hamburger and cucumber pickle, served on the same china as in the hotel restaurant but somehow tasting different, I looked at the scene outside for the longest time and thought. It wasn't long before I came up with the idea of beating Mr. Schmidt to death. I was enraged at him for making me study that heavy book of paintings, bringing me here to see the real thing, and then implying that—with no European blood flowing in me—neither one had anything to do with me.

"As young as I was, though, I knew getting angry like that was pointless. Instead, I was taken with the idea of feeling the electricity he'd mentioned. I couldn't get this out of my head. Now I realize it was like I was aware that my soul was being charged with electricity. It was thrilling. I could see myself from outside my body, high-voltage current running through me, my body emitting a phosphorescent glow. When Mr. Schmidt returned late that night and saw me seated in front of the large fireplace (though I didn't yet have the poker in my hand), he gave a start. But he didn't say a word, just had the blond young man with him push his wheelchair into the bathroom.

"It was my job to help Mr. Schmidt out of his clothes and bathe him. But on my way there I spied a long, solid-looking poker leaning up against the high side of the fireplace.

"At the same instant, I remembered the voice I'd heard two years before, a voice from outside of me insisting, *Do it!* Why had I forgotten that up till now? At the time I heard that voice I lacked the courage to carry out to the bitter end what it badgered me to do, and I tried to escape.

"But I knew it was okay now, I remembered it clearly. I wouldn't forget. There was no need to hurry. Just take your time and carry it out. I left the poker in front of the fireplace where I could reach it in the dark and set off for the bathroom, passing the glum-looking young man on his way out.

"One of the questions I was asked by those professors at the Viennese hospital was whether or not I'd soiled my pants when I hit Mr. Schmidt on the back of the head with the poker. The Austrian professor who'd lived in the United States a long time was the one who asked me this, and seeing that I hesitated to answer, the other professor, the Japanese one, translated the question into Japanese. His face was red, whether from anger or embarrassment I don't know, but he made sure I understood that by soiling my pants I was being asked not whether I'd lost control of my bowels but whether I'd ejaculated.

"The two adults standing there together asking me this looked to me like a pair of fools. I felt this way because I was filled with that high-voltage electricity, something I now know is connected to the spiritual, and I was cunning enough to take them by surprise with my response. I managed an answer that took the wind out of their sails and made them look silly to boot.

"'Since Mr. Schmidt didn't have his hand inside my pants when I clubbed him,' I said, 'no—I didn't soil my underwear.'

"I said this directly in English, and it was the Austrian professor's turn to blush."

3

"I undressed Mr. Schmidt and carried him to the bathtub—no big deal, considering how I was built at sixteen—helped him control his limbs as he bathed, dressed him in a gown, and carried him to the bedroom. I helped him change into pajamas. Then, as I hung up his dressing gown in the closet I took the belt and tied it around my head like a Japanese *hachimaki,* something I'd never done before. I went back to the darkened sitting room and picked up the poker, which was three feet long, longer than the one I'd used before.

"I shook my head to clear it of the excess electricity buzzing around inside and awaited the sound of that voice. *Do it!* Could I hear it? My head buzzed even more, like the echo of a far-off memory. *Do it, do it!* I rubbed my sweaty palm against the *hachimaki,* adjusted my grip on the poker, and went into the bedroom.

"I wasn't sure, but I thought that maybe if I *started* to do it the buzzing would stop, and everything would become that one voice I'd heard before. But as I swung the poker I wasn't listening. The next time I thought about that voice was when the two professors were quizzing me. Since this time I really *had* done it, I felt like I'd *become* that voice. At the same time, though, I suppressed the thought that maybe I hadn't actually heard anything at all.

"Years passed, and I was in my third year in the university architecture department. In order to graduate I had to either present my own original design or write a thesis on an existing structure. I never had any problems with math or architecture theory, but when I arrived at this stage I realized I didn't know the first thing about critiquing buildings.

"I racked my brain, trying to understand why I was basically empty inside, when the events of Salzburg and Vienna popped into my head—not the murder itself so much as the way I lied to the doctors in the hospital and how they bought it so easily. Little by little, I felt this was canceling out the incident that had preceded it.

"Glibly lying day after day had turned me into a poor little youth, a victim of sexual harassment who had lashed out in self-defense. Setting myself up as a passive child who normally would not have done what he did, I was let off the hook legally. But to arrive at this point I had to set aside everything I'd experienced up till then, meager as it was. Helped along by the adults, who were trying to make everything consistent, I fit myself right into the ad hoc mold they'd created. And that's how I've lived ever since. Now I have to bring forth what is uniquely mine. But is it any wonder I'm stifled, unable to do anything?

"Once I realized this, it bothered me that I wasn't able to screw up my courage and face things head-on. And each time I felt about to do that I couldn't help but be conscious of what it was that was holding me back.

"When I was fourteen I'd heard it loud and clear, no mistake about it, a voice urging me to act; the same voice had me commit murder at sixteen. But this deception I'd pulled in Vienna made me lose sight of *the source* of that voice. When I started to think about it, I understood that it wasn't at four-teen that I first heard that voice, but as an infant. This was a voice I knew before I was even *born*.

"I used this as an opportunity to drop out of college. I gave my profes-sors and parents some hackneyed yet honest excuse that there were things I needed to do in order to recover. What I needed to recover though, was that voice, one more time.

"Wandering all over Japan, putting everything I had into a search for the source of that voice, I ended up getting nowhere. But during this long journey I happened to meet you, Professor. I knew right away that you were the illustrator of *The Book of Jonah* for children. I'd read that book before I was fourteen. I was entranced by Jonah's features and his hair, but it wasn't just that he was handsome. At fourteen and sixteen I convinced myself that I was like Jonah, hearing a voice telling me to act.

"One other thing connected with my meeting you I find very signifi-cant—the fact that after I started modeling for you we began a homosexual relationship. After the affair with Mr. Schmidt I never did that sort of thing again. It's quite extraordinary to run across a person like you, Professor, someone willing to spend the rest of his life so that eventually I can do what it is I want to do, even though I haven't revealed to you what that is.

"Other things sprang out of our relationship too. You helped me recall the way I'd crushed that plastic city model I'd made as a child. I was able to remember how even at that time I'd heard that voice. And I could meet up again with one other player in this incident—Dancer—and through her a path opened up that led me straight to Patron.

"Patron is important to me because his trances put him face-to-face with God. He didn't willfully open up this pipeline to God. This relationship appears when he falls into a trance that's more like a horrible attack. And Patron was driven to shut off that pipeline to God himself.

"Patron announced that the visions of the *other side* he'd so long trans-mitted were all just a prank. I think it's true what they say of him, that he made a fool of God. But he still continued to suffer, so much that his inner spiritual wounds became physical ones. Guide was tortured to death by his former comrades, but Patron continues to suffer, with no relief in sight.

"As long as I follow Patron, I know that someday that voice—the one I answered only vaguely, the mere memory of which made me do something totally irreversible and from which, afterward, I ran away as fast as I could—will come to me again.

"Patron has moved to this region now in order to start a new church movement, and his followers have prepared buildings, waiting with bated breath for his next move. I was fortunate enough to come here with you, Professor. Knowing that your cancer is back, you've chosen this as your place to die. And something has taken place to reinforce the truth of that idea.

"Patron's wound has come out in the open, and all the groups of believers are excited about it. And for the first time in my life I have real friends with whom to do things. And all of a sudden this vivid memory's hit me of when I stayed in that hotel in Austria, how it was so rainy that the manager lamented how un-Salzburg-like the weather was. I remember how the electricity built up until it had to explode. I feel the same electricity here as the *power of the land,* the *power of the place.*

"Professor, are you still awake?"

Kizu wasn't asleep. He just couldn't find the words to respond to such a confession.

"Guess he *is* asleep."

From out of his summer covers, Ikuo reached out a soft palm and rested it on Kizu's lower abdomen, careful to not put too much weight on it. He stayed like that for a long time. Warmth from his palm seeped into Kizu's abdomen. Kizu could sense Ikuo's tongue moving around inside his closed mouth. Finally Ikuo withdrew his arm, drew nearer to him in the darkness, and went out into the narrow space separating the two rooms. He left the lights off, but Kizu could sense him crawling into his boxlike bed.

As Kizu listened to Ikuo's monologue he'd learned one surprising thing after another. Yet somehow, as if he'd already known all this, it didn't shock him. From the first time he'd laid eyes on the boy with the beautiful doglike eyes, hadn't he felt both a connection with something higher and yet, unparadoxically, something mysteriously low and mean? Even after they'd started to live together, that sense that they were not really close continued, something Kizu had put down to Ikuo's basic personality.

After Kizu had him model for the painting of Jonah, he discovered something special in Ikuo. Kizu discovered a person who responded to God's call at the same time that he *protested* to God, a person who had a brutal streak, even. Putting together all these pieces, he didn't find it strange that Ikuo had heard a voice from heaven as a child and took a life because of it.

Kizu knew Ikuo was his better in one area—the fact that in their sexual relationship he was the novice, not Ikuo. Soon after they started to sleep together Ikuo had mentioned he'd had some experience playing the man, but despite this Kizu had carried around with him for a long time a mixture of pride and guilt at having initiated a young man into this abnormal form of sex.

After he finally fell asleep, Kizu once again dreamt of himself as nearly completing the triptych. Though he found it strange that he could do this, since his weakened condition should make working on the tableau too tiring, in the dream he overcame this obstacle and was overjoyed at being able to progress with his work on the third panel—whose composition in reality he still hadn't decided on.

In his dream, the details of the first panel, too, the one showing the inside of the whale's belly, were crystal clear. Before a backdrop of a scene from a Salzburg hillside hotel, beyond the city streets, beyond the river and a castle-topped mountain, and beyond a ravine at the entrance to the Alps, Ikuo-as-Jonah was in the process of murdering a middle-aged man. Every nook and cranny of the background—which Kizu had painted merely as the dark labyrinth of the whale's innards—was now entirely clear, and he felt a sense of artistic completion.

In the middle of the third panel he was in reality now working on, Patron, the wound showing on his side, stood next to Ikuo/Jonah. Patron was a preliminary sketch done from memory, distinguishable by the Sacred Wound, while Ikuo/Jonah was no longer an innocent youth. Surrounding the two of them was the Hollow as an abstract opera set: the huge cypress towering darkly, with the cylindrical chapel and the fortresslike monastery bordered, top and bottom, by the moonlit surface of the lake reflecting the forest and the fog.

The next morning Kizu woke up late, and as he went out into the corridor from the still-dark bedroom he saw, in a corner of the atelier, smaller now because of the new partition, Ikuo sitting on top of his boxlike bed, unmoving as a stone statue. Kizu thought he might be asleep, but when he returned from urinating, the stone statue looked up and greeted him in a gentle voice.

"Good morning! Did you sleep well? Why don't you have breakfast in bed? I'll go get it."

Kizu drew back the curtains—the sun was high in a whitish sky, yet fog and dew still clung to the lake and the huge cypress—got into bed, and pulled the wooden tray toward him as Ikuo brought in canned grapefruit juice, tea, and toast. The young man stood watching him eat, his expression more cheerful than it had been in quite some time, with no traces of the previous night's confessions.

"Individual believers have been arriving since last week," Ikuo told him, "and they'll be assigned to stay in the closed elementary school in the outskirts or in some unoccupied private homes. Ms. Asuka is among them, and she'll be taking turns helping me here. You're able to use the toilet yourself, so you don't mind having a woman take care of you, do you?"

"I suppose not," Kizu said. "I'm thinking of starting work again today on the triptych. Have you eaten?"

"I'll bring my food in here." Ikuo started out toward the kitchen, stopped, and turned around. "I got a little carried away in the moonlight last night, and I apologize for talking for so long. It was stupid of me to do that with you just out of your sickbed. It's just that when you were staying at the clinic I decided I had to tell you."

He seemed to be trying to sound out Kizu as to how far he'd managed to stay awake and what he'd heard, but Kizu gave nothing away, and they began to eat a mostly silent meal. Ikuo lined up on the tray the various medicines Kizu had to take, along with a clean cup of water, and then went off to make some coffee. Ms. Asuka had already been given a key, which she used now to open the door and stick her head in the bedroom.

"How have you been, Professor? It must have been very hard on you," she said, in her usually diffident way. "I'll be taking care of you starting today. Ikuo-san has so many other places he needs to be. Everybody on the south shore is quite energized. Quite a stir, I can tell you. The Sacred Wound has had a remarkable effect on everyone."

26: People Like Unedited Videos

1

It was a bit too much for Ms. Asuka, after she started taking care of Kizu, to carry food for them both from the dining hall, so she would go down as soon as it opened and, after finishing her own meal, bring back a tray for Kizu. The days were getting longer so she didn't need a flashlight even after dinner.

Ms. Asuka and the other individual followers who'd moved there had been assigned rooms temporarily, in the monastery along with the Technicians or with the Quiet Women, until their own lodgings were decided, but even so she didn't run across Ikuo in the dining hall. The three of them met in Kizu's bedroom, however. When she collected Kizu's dinner tray and sat down at a window seat facing the lake, there across from her sat Ikuo.

The first thing Ikuo said was that since tonight would be her first night staying over with Kizu, if she wanted he would stay over as well. Since she'd worked in the trade, Ms. Asuka replied, sharing a room overnight with a man certainly didn't faze her.

Kizu felt sorry for Ikuo and how flustered this must have made him. Ikuo's face turned red as a devil's, and he got a little overbearing, telling her that lots of different people would be calling on Kizu to see how he was doing, and they were bound to talk about all sorts of things, so she had to promise to keep whatever she heard strictly confidential.

Ms. Asuka couldn't figure out exactly what he was getting at. Gazing back at the clearly irritated Ikuo in silence for a while, she said that video cameras had become even smaller and easier to use than the stories you used to hear about French fountain-pen cameras and the like. "When I use them," she said, "I find I don't have any particular feelings one way or another about the person I'm videotaping. So I've ended up with reels of unedited material. I might overhear what visitors say when they come to pay a visit to Professor Kizu, but that'll just mean I've got one more unedited videotape in my memory."

What Ms. Asuka said struck Kizu as logical. Ikuo seemed to think so too. Ms. Asuka's words meant that whenever she was in the house taking care of Kizu, any guests should feel free to say what they wanted. She wasn't going to abuse her position.

Indeed, as Kizu continued his painting during his recuperation, one visitor after another came to see him. When he told them how Ms. Asuka, who was waiting in the next room, had come up with this metaphor about people being unedited videos, everyone had a good laugh, which loosened them up.

The first visitor was Dr. Koga, who questioned his patient and checked his vital signs and then pulled the desk chair over near the bed and sat himself down far enough away that he and Kizu could study each other as they spoke.

"Were you aware that Ikuo's been visiting the Technicians and the Quiet Women a lot," Dr. Koga began, "and carrying out an ideological inquiry of sorts?"

"I know the Young Fireflies have been questioning him," Kizu replied, "and he said he'd have to explain to them about the various sects in the church. Most of all I think he wants to clarify things for himself."

"I can see that. There are things about the Technicians that even somebody like me who's known them for years can't understand, and that goes double for the Quiet Women.

"When I went to the monastery to have lunch, Ikuo cornered me to ask me about the Technicians. 'Why are they deemphasizing religious matters?' he asked. Not that they seem to be pushing forward with some social agenda like they did in the old days, but he doesn't think the repentant radical faction—the men responsible for killing Guide—will remain in the shadows forever. He wanted to know what direction I see them trying to nudge Patron in.

"I told him that since he was so close to them I'd like to hear *his* opinion. I wasn't trying to sidestep his question but just to let him know he's much more aware than I am of what the Technicians are up to."

"What about the Quiet Women?" Kizu asked.

"Ikuo and I view them in about the same way," Dr. Koga said. "The Technicians are certainly sly old foxes as far as faith is concerned, but the really formidable ones are the Quiet Women. The Technicians are trying to incorporate Patron in their own strategies, but there the Quiet Women beat them hands down. They've *always* been using Patron for their own purposes—before the Somersault and afterward.

"This idea of falling into hell is something Patron originally came up with, but the Quiet Women made it out as Patron's atonement for everyone, and they've repositioned Patron and Guide at the center of their faith. Depending on how you look at it, it's been the Quiet Women who've kept Patron and Guide tied down. I would imagine that these past ten years it's the Quiet Women who were their heaviest burden."

"I think Ikuo's sensed this too," Kizu said. "He's formed ties with the Technicians—*cooperating* with them is another way of putting it, I suppose—to keep an eye on them so they don't go off on their own. But he's also been attending the Quiet Women's prayer meetings along with the Fireflies.

"Dancer went so far as to ask him whether he's been spying on the Quiet Women for the Technicians, but what he's really trying to pin down is what the Quiet Women are all about. Where they're coming from, so to speak. Patron is very important to Ikuo. And he figures that the Quiet Women's faith may be the path that will lead him to Patron."

"I agree with you there," Dr. Koga said. "Ikuo has his own individual feelings about the transcendental, as you've said. As someone who's been driven by inevitable circumstances to be with Patron, I can certainly understand that.

"But a part of Ikuo still hasn't decided whether Patron's the one he seeks. As things stand now, parading Patron around all over the place may not get you anywhere. Ikuo's keeping an eye on both the Technicians and the Quiet Women to make sure they don't try something like that. Favoring the Young Fireflies may be his way of introducing a third force into the equation."

"I have no doubt that Ikuo views Patron as the person who can mediate for him with the Almighty," Kizu said, "and he has an urgent reason for doing so, something I didn't know about until recently."

Dr. Koga looked questioningly at Kizu, who didn't go on. Sensing his reluctance, Dr. Koga changed the subject, though to something still related to Ikuo. "Ikuo told me once that Patron's teachings before the Somersault had a strong Christian element, especially in the personalized view of the divine—though now the notion of the antichrist has appeared. Ikuo said that when he attended the Quiet Women's prayer meeting there was an even stronger feeling of Christianity present. He wondered what that meant.

"The Quiet Women were able to make it on their own for ten years because they got deeper into their own special doctrine of faith. After the

Somersault, people from Protestant churches who specialize in deprogramming mind-controlled cult members approached them, but the women held firm. In other words, the doctrine they'd been taught by Patron was stronger than mainstream Christianity.

"And now they've joined forces with the church Patron's going to found here. They have no particular problems with Patron, even though he hasn't withdrawn his Somersault, but I'm left wondering whether at some point in the near future they might not try to drag him back into this faith-minus-the-Somersault. To truly save Patron from hell."

"Do you think this upcoming summer conference Ikuo's involved in will bring about any great changes?" Kizu asked.

"I'm sure the Technicians, the Quiet Women, and the Fireflies all have their agendas," Dr. Koga said, "which means that the office staff, too, who are at Patron's beck and call, aren't just sitting on their hands either. . . . And among the followers coming for the summer conference, the people from the Kansai headquarters already have a clear-cut idea of what *they* want: namely, that this first-ever national conference will clarify what direction the new church will be moving in."

Ms. Asuka appeared at the door of Kizu's bedroom, dressed in a jersey dress with a broad neckline. A set of headphones hung on her bare shoulder blades as if to underscore to Kizu and Dr. Koga that she'd been listening to classical music on the radio while they were talking, instead of eavesdropping. Dr. Koga welcomed her cheerfully, for all the world like some still-youthful urban boy. As usual, Ms. Asuka had a faint neutral smile on her face, and her words were brusque.

"I know I shouldn't be saying this to a doctor," she said, "but maybe visiting hours are about over?"

"You're very lucky, Professor Kizu," Dr. Koga said, "to have such independent, thoughtful people helping you. I include Ikuo in this as well. Who is this?"

"This is Ms. Asuka. She usually works in film production," Kizu said, "and is going to be videotaping the summer conference."

2

The next person to visit was Asa-san, wife of the former junior high school principal, who had helped Kizu with the aborted art school project. In the meanwhile they'd grown close.

When Kizu had moved into the house, the leaves on the maple trees jutting out on the west side were still reddish purple but had now turned a light green. In the fall the leaves would no doubt change again. Faint drops had gathered on the small leaves and were now full-sized raindrops. A gentle drizzle had been falling intermittently from morning. Ikuo had dropped by between lunch and his afternoon appointments and was sitting with Kizu, both of them gazing out at the chilly blurred surface of the lake, when Asa-san showed up. They could hear her at the entrance passing over the presents she'd brought to Ms. Asuka, explaining how her husband had raised this and caught that—vegetables, Chinese citrons, freshwater trout. Ever since the former owner of this house passed away, she went on, they'd let the vegetation around it just grow, but she'd noticed that the boundary between the trees in the garden around the house and the trees and shrubs pushing down from the lower reaches of the forest was blurring and she couldn't stand it, so she'd have her husband come over to do some serious pruning.

When she entered the bedroom, Asa-san spoke the sort of old-fashioned greetings one paid to an ailing person. She told Ikuo how adults were quite pleased with the work that the Fireflies had done in restoring the grove of low bamboo bushes and the group of red pussy willows along the original shoreline inside the dam at the Yabe River. She then turned to the matter that had brought her here.

"Since I have some connections with the church," she said, "I'm somewhat worried about where it's headed. I'd like to ask the opinion of Professor Kizu—someone living here who isn't a church member. I'm particularly worried about the direction the Quiet Women are taking. It's such a level-headed group, with highly educated people at the core, that I don't feel it's my place to say anything. But being the kind of women they are, if they do take action you can be sure they'll be quite fanatic about it. That's what worries me."

Kizu was immediately curious. Propped up in bed he noticed that Ikuo, too, sitting beyond the foot of the bed, wanted to hear more. Kizu had heard beforehand from Ms. Asuka of Asa-san's visit. Perhaps Ikuo had also heard she was coming and had been standing by.

"This is something I've been holding inside for quite a while," Asa-san went on, "but the day before you returned from the clinic, when I attended the prayer vigil with Patron, I became even more concerned. I found the prayer itself at the meeting deeply moving. Ikuo and the Fireflies attended, so you may have already heard this, but I wanted you to hear my reaction.

"Mrs. Shigeno gave the prayer preceding the sermon. Patron sat in his favorite barber's chair while we all listened, Quiet Women and non–church members alike. It was all very nice and democratic. Then it was time for a performance of Morio's music, so Ikuo got up and walked over to the piano, set up in front of where Patron was sitting. Morio went over with him, but after Ikuo had decided which pieces to play, Morio withdrew and sat down on the mechanical footrest of Patron's chair.

"I thought it was strange that Morio didn't sit beside Ikuo to turn pages—don't they do that in most concerts?—but pretty soon I realized why. When the music started, Morio buried his face in Patron's shins, which were stretched out on the footrest. Ms. Tachibana, afraid maybe that her brother was having an attack, crouched down beside him. Before long Patron rested his hands on the tops of their two heads, both of which had the same round shape when you looked at them from behind.

"When the music was over, before they went into the silent prayer time, Patron gave a short sermon from where he sat. He said that Morio had said the music they'd just heard 'captured on paper the sound that echoes in the ears of one's soul when it ascends to heaven at the end time.' He said he heard this from Ms. Tachibana, 'but as we listen to this music aren't we all sharing the experience right here and now of ascending to heaven? This is a wonderful prelude to our prayers.

"'It's meaningless,' he went on, 'to ask which is more real, the experience of ascending to heaven at the end of the world or what we've experienced through this music. Ms. Tachibana has taught me that the end time is both experienced countless times, and as a onetime event. I'd like you to really feel this, think deeply about it, *live* it.'

"After Patron said this, a rustle of agreement rose up, especially from the Quiet Women, and the meeting moved into the prayer portion. But you know what? I couldn't *stand* it!"

Kizu and Ikuo were both startled and stared at her. Undeterred, everything about Asa-san revealed the unyielding stance of an old woman determined not to compromise. Despite the rainy-season cold blowing down from the forest, the skin around her eyes was flushed. Clearly struggling to suppress her emotions, though, a different sort of expression came over Asa-san's sunburnt, freckled face.

"I've worked hard to get you all accepted here, so I think I have the right to oppose something I don't like that's about to happen. And as someone who convinced the faction that opposed your move here, I'd say I have the *duty* to do so too. No doubt my husband would say that if something bad happens it's due to my hastiness, but before it does I have to speak out. Professor, you keep your distance from the various groups within the church, so I thought you're the best one to talk to about this. I'm sure Ikuo has a different way of looking at the situation, but I'm happy at least that you heard me out."

She was already getting to her feet. She didn't seem to be expecting any quick and easy answers.

A moment earlier they had heard Ms. Asuka welcoming a new visitor at the door. Kizu soon realized it was Gii. Ms. Asuka seemed to be holding the young man back until Asa-san stopped speaking.

Asa-san turned to Gii, who was still standing in the entrance. (He had driven himself up, and Asa-san, as the wife of the former principal of the junior high, was about to give him some candid advice).

"My, you certainly got up to the Hollow quickly!" she said. "Didn't you just finish school? No matter how much you might want to see Ikuo, you young people are our future, you know, so you'd better be careful!" Then she left.

3

It was obvious that Gii wasn't old enough to have a license, but everyone who mattered, from the authorities along the riverside to the patrolmen in the police station, turned a blind eye to the young man's driving. Coming from the city, Ms. Asuka found it amusing that this little local community made an exception for Gii, though she was also, naturally enough, worried. As Gii walked into the room, her voice could be heard from behind him.

"Don't forget what Asa-san told you. Remember that council member who said if he gets on the bad side of you and your friends, the adults who have a weakness for children won't support him in the election? It scares me to imagine what you'll be like when you grow up."

"If I *do* grow up," Gii said pointedly. "My mother apparently told Asa-san not to let me become too attached to Ikuo," he went on to tell Kizu and the others as he came into the bedroom. "But she isn't very logical most of the time."

"Asa-san's logic is fine," Ikuo scolded.

Despite the scolding, Ikuo motioned Gii over to the seat vacated by Asa-san and turned to speak with Kizu, ignoring Gii in a relaxed guys-only way.

"Early this morning," Ikuo began, "I went to check out the extension to the piggery they're building at the Farm. They've had to build it in the highest spot around because of the foul odor, and with the rain I wasn't sure our little truck would make it up the slope. Right after I got there, one of their leaders, Mr. Hanawa, who accompanied those of us who came by train, asked me a question. I was impressed then by how attentive he seemed, but he also is a bit uncompromising, the way he won't say a word to the Fireflies, for instance, even when he has them help out."

Gii nodded in agreement.

"What he asked me," Ikuo went on, "was this: 'Why is Patron so special to you? Here you are, building a barn for pigs up on the top of a ridge, but is he really worth all this?' 'How about *you*?' I shot back, and he said that they've long seen Patron as their intermediary with God and they don't recognize the Somersault as valid.

"'The first time you met Patron,' he said, 'was after the Somersault, when he wasn't having any deep trances and was just an ordinary person, and even after you moved here with him all he's done is give these evasive, fuzzy sermons. So where is the charisma to rouse people to a new faith? Except for the Sacred Wound . . .'

"As I listened to Mr. Hanawa's questions," Ikuo said, "it struck me that maybe he thinks I'm a spy. All I could do, I figured, was tell him the truth.

"'When I was a child,' I told him, 'I heard a voice that had to be that of God. And when I was fourteen I definitely heard God's voice, though my reaction to it left something to be desired. And when I was sixteen I thought now I would respond to it, and I did something that couldn't be undone.

"'But now I don't think I really heard God's voice when I was sixteen; I've never heard it since. Perhaps this was for the best, since I was able to go on without it, but with graduation from college at hand, and my life's work set out in front of me, I sensed that I couldn't go on any more. If I didn't return to the call I heard at fourteen, my life would be a sham.

"'When I awakened to this, I struggled with the idea, but I had no way of making the voice of God appear again. Established churches and cults were no help to me in my quest. Either they kicked me out or laughed at me, or else I was the one to wash my hands of *them*.

"'Just by chance, I ran across Patron and Guide, and here I am. I came here because I have the hope that Patron—connected to God until the Somersault—will be, to borrow your words, the intermediary for me with God. If it doesn't work out, it wasn't meant to be. But for me there's no other choice.

"'I'm particularly drawn to the way Patron—all by himself—cut off the pipeline connecting him and God. For the past ten years all he's done is suffer, as much as it's humanly possible to suffer. Sometimes I think maybe this suffering has taken shape as his Sacred Wound.'

"Once I'd finished saying all this, Mr. Hanawa asked me another question. 'After the so-called Somersault, Patron apparently didn't have any deep trances that brought him face-to-face with God. But from the beginning we didn't accept the Somersault. We're confident that before long Patron will become the mediator for God once more. We base this on our long experience living in the church. But how do you know,' he asked me, 'that the voice of God that Patron might transmit to you, and the voice of God you heard when you were a child telling you to do *something that couldn't be undone,* are really one and the same?'

"'I learned that from all of *you,*' I answered. 'When you pray, you Technicians always have religious texts from a lot of different religions with you; sometimes you even quote from books by scientists—in your case, Mr. Hanawa, it was a mathematics book, wasn't it? Dr. Koga told me that this stems from your conviction that, quite simply, God is *one.*

"'I feel exactly the same way. They're all one and the same: the God whose call messed me up as a child, Patron and Guide's God whom they made a fool of and yet clung to as they suffered. And the God that Jonah debated thousands of years ago.'"

"How did Mr. Hanawa react? And the Technicians?" Kizu asked.

"They just laughed."

"Damn them!" Gii said angrily.

Ignoring this, Ikuo went on. "If they don't kick me out as a spy, the preparations for the summer conference should go smoothly. I just hope the Quiet Women see things the same way."

That evening, as she served dinner, Ms. Asuka butted in, something she rarely did. "I think Ikuo went into such detail about his conversation with the Technicians because he wanted to educate Gii," she said. "I think he's quite considerate in that way. Mr. Hanawa might be too, for all we know."

"When Ikuo came to work for Patron at the Tokyo office," Kizu said, "and even when he moved here, I don't think he knew *what* it was he sought from Patron. It was still taking shape within him. He gets worked up; that's why he talks so much."

"But if you go to the dining hall," Ms. Asuka said, "you'll find out it's not just Ikuo who's excited. It's like everyone's a smoldering fire. Patron's wound was what started it all, though your symptoms, too, Professor, were a factor. There's a palpable urgency in the air.

"Asa-san seemed tense too, today, when she came to see me. She had told me that the first thing she wanted to talk to you about, Professor, was her worries over the Quiet Women. I think you need to talk one-on-one with Patron about this excitement that's taken hold of the Hollow. I've just moved here, so everything is quite strange to me, but I agree with Asa-san. There's something about it I just don't like."

Ms. Asuka looked down as she refilled Kizu's coffee cup on the tray, and as she did so her profile, now cleansed of the greasepaintlike make-up she used in her former life, looked graceful. Her usual smile was missing as well, the smile that downplayed whatever she'd just said.

"I'm afraid I don't have the strength to make it over to the south shore," Kizu said.

"Then let's have Patron come over here. When I pressed Dancer about when Patron would be posing for you again, she said it all depended on your condition."

"Have you been able to meet with Patron directly?" Kizu asked.

"I'm sure people will think I'm a hopelessly pushy woman, but I asked permission through Dancer and was allowed to videotape Patron's Sacred Wound. It was my first job since I came here. On the tape, Patron is naked from the waist up and Morio is wiping the wound with gauze that has a penicillin ointment on it. The outlines of the Sacred Wound are quite distinct, kind of a kitschy color, and the whole thing's quite wonderful. As I filmed I was able to talk with Patron and learned something surprising. I thought he'd already started the new church, but he said he hasn't yet."

"Since we moved to the Hollow, Patron's said quite a lot about the new church, though," Kizu said. "The Technicians are busy with their own work, the Quiet Women are getting deeper into the sort of prayer meetings that have Asa-san worried, and I must admit I interpreted all this activity in the same way as you—that the new church had already been established."

"Patron seems to want to use the summer conference as the venue for officially launching the new church," Ms. Asuka said. "The office has the same idea, and Ikuo has talked with me about recording the whole conference on video. Though we'd have to budget for people to handle the sound and the lights."

"There aren't many days left, but maybe Patron's planning something really remarkable for the summer conference," Kizu said. "Maybe all the excitement that's swirled up since people found out about the Sacred Wound has had an influence on him. I guess I'd better hurry up and finish my triptych."

"I'll go talk with the office staff, then, about having him come over to your studio to model. This Sacred Wound fever even seems to be getting to *me*, doesn't it?"

4

*If tomorrow there's a break in the rainy season and it's warm and sunny,
I'll come to your studio to model for you.* Patron had entrusted this message
to Ms. Asuka, on her way home after lunch the next day, much to Kizu's
surprise. The weather was fine the next day, and though the surface of the
lake, bloated by the rains, was a dirty brown, it clearly reflected the cylindrical chapel and the long walls of the monastery.

Early that morning a large ruddy-faced man with cropped white hair
showed up on the north shore and with steady strides made a circuit of the
grounds around the house. He seemed to be appraising the trees, washed to a
brilliant green by the rains that had only ended two days before, and when
his gaze met that of Kizu, who was reading in bed, they nodded a greeting to
each other. The man was Asa-san's husband, the former principal of the junior high school, who'd come to trim around the house. He looked a little chilly
in his long-sleeved high-collared shirt, but once he started working he had to
wipe the sweat away with the towel draped around his neck.

He started by pruning the trees visible from the window that faced the
lake. As he trimmed, the rich white flowers of the camellia and the pome-
granate, the latter a faded light purple due to lack of sunshine, emerged from
the overgrown clump of greenery. Next year, Kizu thought, I won't be around
to see these flowers. He turned his gaze outside from time to time, to find the
petals of the camellias, wrapped in pods and now exposed to the sun, trimmed
in a neat horizontal line that was attractive enough, but lacking its previous
otherworldly feeling.

In the afternoon Ms. Asuka threw open the window facing the lake to
see how warm it had gotten, and the room was filled with the volatile fragrance of newly cut branches. For the first time since his most recent illness,
Kizu had on the jeans and loose cotton shirt he favored when doing some
serious drawing.

Patron arrived at Kizu's house at two-twenty. It had taken exactly twenty
minutes for him to go from the south shore along the weir and up the slope
on the north shore. Patron had been less concerned, it appeared, about his own
physical condition than that of Morio, whose legs were slightly impaired.

Patron was in the best shape he'd been in in quite some time, and emotionally upbeat as well. Kizu had always thought of himself and Patron as
virtual contemporaries, but now he had to admit that he was no match for
Patron when it came to vitality. Patron had changed into summer clothing,
which also added to this impression. Below the stiff collar a deep U-shaped

depression was visible, and his maroon shirt stood out under his ice blue jacket. Morio wore an identical set of clothes.

"I've really been looking forward to modeling for you," Patron said, by way of greeting. "Now that I see you I realize you're fit enough to go back to painting. Shall I sit down here? The sun was so warm I'll be glad to get out of this jacket and shirt. You don't want me completely nude, do you?"

Morio smiled happily as if he'd just heard an amusing joke. Ms. Asuka took Patron's jacket to the bedroom and then adjusted the chair and footstool for him. As he checked the reflected light off the lake, Kizu adjusted the cushion at Patron's back, while Ms. Asuka brought in another chair for Morio.

Preparations went smoothly, but when they reached the point where Patron was about to remove his shirt and tank top, Kizu couldn't help but tense up. Patron, though, cheerfully stripped down, removed the palm-sized gauze covering his wound, wrapped it up in fluttering strips of surgical tape, and tossed it on Morio's lap. Morio took out a plastic bag from his pocket and stuffed the gauze inside.

"This is the first time I've been able to get a good look all the way to the bottom of the wound," Patron remarked. "The antibiotic Dr. Koga gave me seems to be working. Before, I just had this vague notion of the hole being a certain size, wider than it is deep, but now I can see it's heading straight for the heart. I asked Dr. Koga about this and he said it's only to be expected— seeing as how it's a *sacred* wound.

"Well, how would you like me to pose? I understand I'm supposed to supplement Ikuo's Jonah."

"Just sit facing me is fine," Kizu replied, and began sketching. Ms. Asuka stood behind Kizu, videotaping the proceedings. The video camera was completely silent and didn't bother Kizu. After some twenty minutes Patron spoke up.

"Modeling's hard if you don't talk. The last time you sketched me I was only half conscious. Is it all right to talk?"

"That'd be fine," Kizu said. "Though I'll mostly listen, if you don't mind."

"Seeing you after such a long time reminded me of something I'd wanted to tell you," Patron said. "It's delightful to have such a diligent listener."

Patron spoke smoothly and cheerily, though his topic was quite serious. Kizu had somehow sensed that it would be.

"At the memorial service for Guide, I announced I was starting a new church. You'll recall how I also said that I'm one of the countless antichrists who will appear at the end of the world and vowed to oversee this new church as one of these antichrists. I didn't just blurt this out. It's something I've been pondering for the past decade. It's not surprising that I restart my church as an antichrist, but I was pretty worked up when I said it, and it's placed me in quite a predicament. It would be a lot easier if I'd kept this idea of being an antichrist to myself.

"So I had to think and think about the best way to rebuild the church. The process of moving here after the memorial service, getting everything ready, is very likely the final obstacle in my ten years of being in hell. Guide isn't with me, yet things are moving forward. I felt driven into a corner."

Listening to all this as he sketched, Kizu noticed Morio, seated diagonally in front of him, begin to stir. His whole body, not just his legs, was impaired, but his movements were always natural. Kizu was a moment late in sensing that something was wrong, but Patron responded immediately.

"I'm afraid I've said something to worry you, Morio. I'm just remembering the suffering I've had and am telling Professor Kizu about it, that's all."

"You've posed long enough—that's plenty," Kizu said, for the sake of Morio, who still looked up worriedly at the half-naked Patron. "I'd be happy if we could discuss how this sketch might be incorporated into the triptych."

As Patron slipped down from the high chair, Ms. Asuka passed him a freshly laundered dressing gown, helped Morio up, and led them to the dining table, which had been set up in the bedroom. Tea and pound cake awaited them. As the guests settled into their seats, Ms. Asuka brought the hot water for tea, while Kizu took the triptych panels down from the easel and lined them up in front of the partition. As he did so, Ms. Asuka said, "Why don't you lie down on the bed and talk? Painting wears you out. You look pale."

Looking back on it later, Kizu realized it was at this point that something strange was starting to take place in his body. He reluctantly did as she said, though he wasn't about to let go of the excitement he'd felt since morning or this chance to talk with Patron.

"The foreground of the middle panel shows Ikuo as Jonah. Are you planning to use my image in the open part on the left?" Patron asked.

"That's right."

"In other words, I'll be depicted as the Lord?"

"Since that's who Jonah quarrels with, yes, it would be the Lord, though my conception has changed a little since I first started. It doesn't have to be the Lord, exactly, though it *does* have to be someone who transmits God's will to Jonah."

"And he goes to all the trouble of showing this wound in his side to convince Jonah?"

"Rather than the biblical Jonah, I'm starting to see it more as the Ikuo-as-Jonah image the Young Fireflies have, Ikuo as the young man awaiting God's intermediary to give him the word to act."

"Since I'm less a model for God than for an antichrist," Patron said, "even if I tell him to act it makes it a complicated sort of instruction, doesn't it? If you show the antichrist here with a wound in his side debating with Jonah, it's like you're depicting this young man as seeing beyond the antichrist to God. This Jonah gives you the feeling that's entirely possible, what with that inscrutable look on his face."

"You're very perceptive," Kizu said, his comment heartfelt.

"This is changing the subject," Patron said, "but when Dr. Koga came to check on me, Asa-san came with him to see how I was doing. This was when you were in the clinic, Professor. I mentioned earlier about the depth and width of the wound, but Dr. Koga said this: There are still reports of women and children in Mexico and the Philippines having these kinds of spontaneous wounds, but they're always superficial. In my case, though, less than half an inch deeper and it might have been fatal.

"And then Asa-san told me this: Brother Gii was an amateur scholar of Dante's *Divine Comedy,* and he told her there were all sorts of issues involved when the heretic Cato the African committed suicide and was then appointed gatekeeper of the island of Purgatory. According to Plutarch, Cato cut open his own belly and then had a doctor friend sew it back up, only to cut it again himself and commit suicide.

"'I can't explain it well,' she went on, 'but for Patron to make his own wound worse in order to die—it's doubly, triply wrong. You can't let that happen!' Once she decides to say something, Asa-san's the kind of person who can get pretty adamant."

Patron laughed out loud. Unable to join him, Kizu turned a confused smile toward Ms. Asuka. He couldn't even give a forced laugh, for he was already feeling the rumblings of something uncontrollable happening inside him.

Finding it impossible to follow Patron's loquaciousness, and so that Patron wouldn't misinterpret his tense expression, Kizu turned to look out the window. The white camellia flowers were in full bloom, but with the yellow pistils jutting out, as if seeking something, the flowers struck him as disagreeable. He could no longer deal pleasantly with people and things outside him; his entire world was measured solely by the tension rising up in his gut. . . .

Memories of his recent bout with disease let him know what to expect next, though he knew this time the pain would be even fiercer. Kizu turned his restless eyes back to the room and saw that only Morio, silently, was watching him closely. Patron was deep in conversation with Ms. Asuka, but to Kizu their voices blended into one.

Feeling desolate and isolated, already in the throes of nausea, he thrust his throat out in anticipation of the groan the first wave of pain would drag out of him. *It's almost here.* Yellow liquid dribbled down his lips. Kizu saw Morio reach out a hand to Patron's thigh.

It had come.

27: Church of the New Man

1

Ogi learned about the awful pain Kizu was suffering when Ms. Asuka called him on the cell phone she'd brought from Tokyo. She'd phoned Dr. Koga as well and asked Ogi to take the car to his clinic. There's apparently no danger of heart blockage, Dr. Koga had told her, adding that this time he wanted to admit Kizu into the Red Cross Hospital. I'll have Ikuo arrange for the ambulance, Ms. Asuka replied.

When Dr. Koga and Ogi arrived at the home on the north bank of the Hollow, they found the patient curled up diagonally on the raised bed, half his body draped over the edge. Ms. Asuka was kneeling on the floor, clearly drained of energy, while Patron was seated at the desk in the rear of the room, patting Morio, who knelt at his feet, on the back.

"Except for Ms. Asuka, I'd like everyone to leave the room, including Patron," Dr. Koga said firmly.

Retreating dejectedly to the studio, Ogi couldn't help but notice that Patron, and even Morio, looked terribly worn out. Patron had Morio lie down on the sofa but was unable to calm himself; instead of taking a seat in the armchair, he looked through a few of Kizu's books and picked up and examined the sketches that lay scattered about. Soon he went up to Ogi.

"Would you mind going into the bedroom for me and bringing back the middle painting of the triptych?" he whispered. "Without disturbing Dr. Koga, of course. Bring the drawing he made of me a while ago, too. I think it might give me a hint I've been needing."

Ogi peeked into the room, fearful of disturbing Dr. Koga's examination, but neither the doctor, looming over the nearly naked patient, nor

Ms. Asuka turned around. Ogi lifted up the middle painting, which was leaning against a divider—the drawing Patron spoke of was taped to it—and when Ms. Asuka finally turned to face him, Ogi nodded to her and withdrew.

Patron took a seat in the backless chair Kizu had set before his easel and gazed at the painting. Morio, too, got up from the sofa, sat down at Patron's feet, his knees up, and examined the painting. Elbows out, he plugged up his ears with his fingers, perhaps disturbed by the voices coming from the adjoining room.

Ogi himself concentrated on the painting, the largest of the triptych. In the right foreground was a nude, which Ikuo had posed for. On the space to the left was a large sheet of sketchbook paper, a rough sketch Kizu had drawn of Patron from the waist up, the wound on his side clearly visible.

The painting was a painstakingly done portrait of Jonah, and a rough sketch, on the same scale, of a figure facing him. Ogi surmised the two persons were confronting each other.

Ikuo and Ms. Tachibana arrived, and when Ogi went out to the foyer to greet them he experienced a mild disorientation gazing at the real Ikuo so soon after seeing the painting. Tell Dr. Koga the ambulance is here, Ikuo told Ogi. He continued, in a voice audible to Patron, who was looking in their direction from a corner of the studio, "The last time, Kizu put up with the pain alone for so long it affected his heart, but with Dr. Koga coming over so soon they can take him to the Red Cross Hospital this time, don't you think?"

Dr. Koga stuck his tense face out of the bedroom. "Yes, we should get him to a specialist," he said. "I'd like Ikuo to come along. Everyone else just wait here until we get in touch."

Patron's response seemed a bit of a non sequitur. "We'll leave it up to you. Professor Kizu is going through a major transformation now, which may very well be a transformation for the good."

This made Dr. Koga so upset he thrust his gloomy face toward Patron, but he swallowed whatever he was about to say, turned to Ikuo, and asked him to have the stretcher brought in. After Ikuo left, since Dr. Koga didn't give Patron, Ogi, or Morio permission to come in the bedroom, they could only return to the studio. Ms. Tachibana, though, went along with Dr. Koga and made preparations for moving the patient.

Ikuo led the emergency personnel inside, the work proceeded apace, and the group soon set off for Matsuyama. All the while, Patron and Morio stayed glued to the painting. Ogi saw off the stretcher as far as the ambulance, parked below the weir, his mind filled with what Patron had said. *A major transformation . . . possibly a transformation for the good.* What did he mean? That Kizu was undergoing the inevitable as he faced death, his body racked by the agony of cancer? When Ogi got back to the house, Patron was just as he'd left him.

Patron stayed that way for a while and then turned, as if awakening, and opened his mouth. He said nothing about the departed Kizu; instead, he asked everyone to assemble in the studio.

"What I'm going to say is something I should tell all the members of the church, but first I'll say it to you. I'd like you to pretend this is the chapel and I'm delivering a sermon."

Each of the four people picked out spots in the studio, redolent of oil paint, sitting on the boxlike bed or pulling chairs from the bedroom, settling down to listen to Patron's words.

"Since moving to the Hollow," Patron began, "everyone here, including the Technicians and the Quiet Women, has been steadily making preparations for the future. As I watched all this, I felt it was urgent for me to settle on a schedule for officially rebuilding the church. As I said to Professor Kizu just before he fell ill, quite honestly I've felt, at times, driven into a corner.

"This is not just a spiritual question; it has surfaced in a physical way as well. The wound in my side—the one you call the Sacred Wound—has remained unchanged for the past ten years, but recently it took a turn for the worse. I came down with a terrible fever and felt the kind of pain I haven't experienced in a long time.

"I'd never thought of comparing the two, but the notion occurred to me not long ago that the physical pain I suffered was similar to the agony I felt when I used to fall into a trance. The question is, This time did I bring back a vision from the *other side*, as in the old days? And if I did, with Guide dead, who was going to interpret it?

"My thoughts hit the usual dead end, but suddenly an idea struck me: No, things are different this time. I not only brought back a vision but was able to translate it into the language of *our side*. The one who played the role of Guide this time was Morio. I'd like to thank him for all his efforts while I was suffering.

"I'll get to the details of how this came about in a moment, but what I brought back to this side, and was able to put into words with Morio's aid, is something I didn't comprehend until quite recently. I wasn't able to see it for what it is: a message directed at the founding of our new church.

"As recently as this afternoon, while Professor Kizu was sketching me, I told him the problems I've had restarting the church after declaring that I'm an antichrist. Professor Kizu captured that aspect perfectly in the triptych. It's still a rough sketch, but he's done a wonderful job of depicting me as the Old Man confronting Jonah, the New Man, and the world they are about to create. The painting helped me envision how my revelation would take shape, a revelation, as I said, that Morio helped me interpret.

"The painting portrays the confrontation between the antichrist sponsoring the church, the Old Man, and Jonah, representing the New Man, and the two of them facing the body of believers. The painting boldly depicts the basic misconception I had up till now about the difficulties I've been facing. My mistake lay in thinking that *I* should be the one to build the new church. But now I know that's wrong.

"Right after Guide's death, I asked Professor Kizu to assume the role of Guide for me. And as an artist, he has fulfilled those duties admirably. Just as Morio, in his own way, has done the same.

"Getting back to where I started: The night before my wound started to ooze, I came down with a fever; the pain hadn't yet made itself fully known but was beginning. I woke up in the darkness and felt an excitement in my chest—whether from pain or joy I wasn't sure. I don't drink, but I wondered if that was what being drunk felt like. Very soon, I became obsessed with this thought—that for the first time in ten years I was about to fall into a deep trance. But Guide wasn't here. I would suffer, and after all that pain there would't be anyone to interpret the vision I brought back from the other side. It would be lost forever.

"I was desperate. I remembered the story Guide told me of the drowning child grasping at a straw. I reached out my hand in the darkness and my fingers brushed the Bible by my bedside, Guide's old Bible. Morio noticed something amiss in the dark, and I passed the Bible to him. I don't care where, I told him, just open the Bible and mark a passage with your fingernail. Morio took the Bible and did as I said, but it was dark; he fumbled with it and dropped it under the bed. This bothered him, so he picked it up again and marked a second passage. I was already coming down with a fever, and could only sense Morio moving about in the dark. The next morning the fever was worse and I couldn't get up; later that day there was all that fuss about my Sacred Wound, so I couldn't very well check out what I'd asked Morio to do the night before.

"Time passed. I noticed that Morio seemed concerned about the Bible, and finally I remembered the exchange we had had the night my fever began. I immediately looked through Guide's Bible. There were two passages Morio had marked, and as I carefully read through them, I discovered that they both contained the expression *new man*. I had Mrs. Shigeno check into it for me, and can you imagine—in the entire Bible, Old and New Testaments, those are the only places where that expression appears!

"Ever since my Somersault, what I've been thinking about is something along the following lines, not exactly verbatim from the Bible, but something like this: As this world approaches its end, *a savior must appear who will make one the two that stand opposed, destroying in his flesh the dividing wall of hostility, abolishing the law with its commandments and regulations.* And I believe that such a savior will surely come.

"*He will create in himself one new man out of the two, making peace, and in this one body reconcile both of them to God through the cross, putting to death their hostility.* This too, I believe, will come to pass.

"That being the case, what role will an antichrist play? Precisely this: He is the Old Man who acts as herald for the savior. All sorts of antichrists will appear—strange, comical types of heralds who clown around and make fun of God. All antichrists, though, are united in the role they play as Old Man and all that term implies. They are the ones who pave the way for the savior. I am firmly convinced of this, which is precisely why I want to construct my new church as an antichrist.

"I also appeal to you through the second passage Morio marked in the scriptures: *Put off your old self, which is being corrupted by its deceitful desires; be made new in the attitudes of your minds; put on the new self, created to be like God in true righteousness and holiness.* I appeal to you as an antichrist, as one who will forever remain an Old Man. Even though I'm such an Old Man, one thing I *can* do is challenge each of you to become New Men! As the painting shows us, the time is ripe for our new church. Morio handled the Bible in the dark and fulfilled the role of Guide, and Professor Kizu, through his own pain, has done the same.

"To commemorate the start of our Church of the New Man, let us pray for Professor Kizu's speedy recovery!"

2

Ogi found it too difficult to ask Patron directly about the two quotes, so he searched the Bible himself. He pored over scripture, searching in vain, until Mrs. Shigeno pointed out the passages. Some of her fellow Quiet Women, and some of the Technicians, had come to her with the same question, so she went over to the main office to make copies of the selections and distribute them. There, Ogi along with Dancer, learned about the passages.

Mrs. Shigeno gave Ogi and the others their own copies of the passages, which turned out to be from Paul's letter to the Ephesians. She couldn't understand, though, she told them, why Patron chose the term New Man from this letter of the apostle Paul. When she used to attend meetings of the Non-Church Movement and there were talks on Ephesians, they always dealt with such topics as predestination and the role of the church, never anything to do with the expression New Man.

The lecturer in her former church, a famous economist, began his talk with the question of why Paul, who was imprisoned at the time, would write a letter to the Ephesians in the first place. He explained that the reason lay in the fact that among the Christian believers in this Gentile land there were those known as Judaizers, who wanted to maintain the Jewish nature of Christianity. There was even some influence from the East, from Persia. Gnostic heretical beliefs arose about the nature of the soul and the body, as well as heretical opinions about angels.

"Now that I think of it," Mrs. Shigeno said, "it does make sense for people like Patron and Guide, who basically have a syncretic view of religion, to be interested in the letter to the Ephesians. Patron can insist that Morio marked these spots in the dark, but that Bible was the one Guide was constantly reading, so I suspect these pages, ones he came back to over and over, naturally fell open. I have a feeling Patron senses that too, which is why he places such emphasis on them."

Ogi merely listened in silence, but Dancer voiced her opinion in no uncertain terms.

"Unless I have some time to read these passages carefully and digest them," she said, "Ogi and Ikuo are going to be miles ahead of me. Still, I feel energized somehow, knowing that Patron is taking positive steps to rebuild the church. No matter what, I've decided to follow him, but I am a little worried about how we're going to build the church in this new setting. I'm really happy, though, that the day is approaching when he'll reveal our future plan of action."

"If that turns out to be the day you find true faith, it'll be a happy day indeed," Mrs. Shigeno said. "The first happy event of Patron's Church of the New Man."

After Mrs. Shigeno left the office, Dancer turned to Ogi.

"Mrs. Shigeno is shrewd enough to see that my working in the office here and following Patron like some groupie doesn't add up to real faith. She might look like some sweet old lady, but don't let looks deceive you—with all the struggles she's weathered before she became a member of Patron's church, and after his Somersault—there's a lot more to her than meets the eye."

Mrs. Shigeno had rather casually used the term Church of the New Man, and Dancer and Ogi soon realized that she'd wanted to test their reaction to the name, already the Quiet Women's expression of choice.

With this pronouncement of Patron's, the meetings of the Quiet Women began to take on a different character. They'd always allowed the Technicians and the Young Fireflies to participate freely and join in their prayers, but now they limited attendance to their own members. Still, Ikuo and Morio and Ms. Tachibana, who was close to the Quiet Women, were also permitted to attend.

The rainy season had once again set in when Ms. Tachibana showed up in the chilly dim office to report on one of the meetings. At the morning prayer meeting, she said, Mrs. Shigeno had repeatedly used the term Church of the New Man in her sermon. Ms. Tachibana was unclear whether this was a new idea Patron was pushing or was something limited to the Quiet Women; at any rate, she took copious notes.

First, she reported, Mrs. Shigeno read aloud one of the passages from Ephesians that Patron had discovered with Morio's help: "*In this way Christ's purpose was to create in himself one new man out of the two, thus making peace, and in this one body to reconcile both of them to God through the cross, by which he put to death their hostility.*

"As a member of the Church of the New Man," Mrs. Shigeno had said, "I've begun to see this passage in a new light. It's so simple I don't need to interpret it, but it's saying that on the cross Christ created a new man out of the two. In building his Church of the New Man, Patron must be considering the cross as the place where he is heading too. Now that the end of the age is approaching, he has decided to take up his own cross. That's the idea he's building on, the cornerstone of his new church. He will mount the cross as an antichrist and in so doing will show us how to confront the end of the world. After his Somersault—a trying time for all of us—Patron descended into hell and returned to move forward. Now it's up to us to define the roles we should play in the new church and move forward ourselves. Hallelujah!"

Ms. Tachibana's thin-skinned oval face had lost its luster, as if she were suddenly preoccupied by some gloomy thought. She didn't put her thoughts directly into words but circled around what really bothered her.

"Mrs. Shigeno also told Morio she'd like Ikuo to perform his composition, and he did. Morio and I were quite moved. But afterward, during prayer time, Mai was sitting right beside me and I couldn't concentrate. I was concerned about all the talk about the children we'd left behind when we moved here joining us during the summer conference. . . . I worked for many years at a girls' school affiliated with a university, which might account for how I feel when I think of the children like Mai I saw at Guide's memorial service. I can't help but fear that something terrible is going to happen. Will the children get caught up in some disaster? I have no idea what kind of disaster, but all the same I worry about it."

Ms. Tachibana looked at Dancer and Ogi, her normally pale cheeks turning a livid rose red with her violent emotions; she said nothing more and abruptly left the office.

Dancer tried to go back to her work, but she was too upset to continue. Before long she turned to Ogi, himself unable to concentrate, and said angrily, "Ogi, don't you think Ms. Tachibana contradicted herself? She said she was moved by Morio's music after Mrs. Shigeno's sermon, the theme of which is the ascension to heaven at the end of the world. Yet she saw the children's participation in this heavenly ascent as *unhappy,* as being caught up in a disaster."

"How is that unnatural?" Ogi replied. "Even if what she says seems contradictory, if somebody sees children getting caught up in mass suicide as a disaster, to me that's a healthy attitude. Though she never put it in such bald terms. People like Ms. Tachibana have their feet on the ground. If things ever get out of hand, you can count on her to put a halt to it."

"You really think Ms. Tachibana would stand up like that?" Dancer asked. "Morio might be mentally handicapped, a child, really, but he's already quite grown up. He wouldn't get involved in anything dangerous connected with the children. Mrs. Shigeno is certainly a sophisticated woman, but don't underestimate Ms. Tachibana and Morio—they're more complex than meets the eye. Personally, on an emotional level I can't relate to either Mrs. Shigeno or Ms. Tachibana. So until Patron defines the role of the Church of the New Man, at least while you're in this office I'll thank you not to use such careless terms as *mass suicide.*"

3

The next day that the rain let up, the temperature, rising since morning, had such energy to it that the soft leaves of the oaks and camellias—pruned under the direction of the former junior high school principal—wilted in the sunlight.

That day Ogi led a group around the chapel and the monastery. The group consisted of local sake and pickle makers, as well as an environmental group organized to protect the confluence of the Kame and Maki rivers. The group also included the editor of a local magazine produced in Tokyo—a woman who was writing a piece on the former residences of a Meiji literary figure—as well as the editor of a magazine in Ehime.

Dancer took care of all the arrangements through the town hall, part of her plan to forge a good relationship with the next generation of civic leaders, the pro-growth faction. Many activities the church was involved in had helped lessen the suspicions of the townspeople: the fact that the church did not proselytize locally, the starting up of production at the Farm again after a long period of dormancy, the leadership role the church was taking with the Young Fireflies, and, most of all, Dr. Koga's medical practice. None of this escaped Dancer's attention.

What most interested the local authorities and businessmen was the upcoming summer conference, with church members scheduled to come from all over the country. The business leaders saw it as an excellent chance to advertise local goods and sell their farm products.

Ogi met the study group as they alighted from their minivan to view the chapel and the monastery. It surprised him that, for the short distance between the Farm and the Hollow, Ikuo volunteered to drive. The group, talking merrily among themselves, apparently mistook Ikuo for the church's full-time driver.

As the group listened to Ogi's explanations, the woman intellectual, the leader of the group, sounded as if she were familiar with other buildings designed by the architect of the chapel and monastery; the rest of the group seemed somehow proud of what she said. I'm not speaking about these buildings, the journalist from Matsuyama began transparently, his remarks directed at the woman, but you remember how last night at the party at the sake factory we were talking about the imbalance between the poverty of ordinary people's homes in the provinces and the ultramodern government buildings in the same locales? The two of them chuckled to each other and exchanged knowing winks.

Ogi rode back with the group to the Farm, where they boarded cars brought up from Old Town and left; Ikuo, seated next to Ogi in the driver's seat of the van, had been silent all along but now spoke up.

"That skinny Olive Oyl woman and those guys from Matsuyama made me want to puke! Man, am I glad I dropped out of architecture school. If the Young Fireflies had heard them there would have been hell to pay. But it does seem that after Mr. Hanawa and the other leaders of the Technicians explained to the locals how they were using the Farm's land and equipment to revive production the Church of the Flaming Green Tree had begun, they got high marks for their efforts. With the success of food production at the Farm, people are expecting they can work with growers in Old Town and sell their products—not just in Matsuyama but in the whole Osaka–Kobe district. When people come to the summer conference from all over Japan, it'll be a good opportunity for the locals to gauge their reactions too."

Ogi set out some folding chairs in the clearing where the Church of the Flaming Green Tree once erected tents and held meetings, and he and Mr. Hanawa and Ikuo sat down and talked. Ogi had only seen Mr. Hanawa in the dining hall and around, but it was obvious how close he and Ikuo had become.

"Right now in Maki Town," Mr. Hanawa said, "one of the more expensive products is the sake the sake maker says you can freeze for ten years, thaw out, and it'll start fermenting again—that'll run about ten thousand yen a bottle. If you use refrigerated trucks you can deliver anywhere in Japan, so they're thinking ahead to make this kind of product. Though I don't imagine it'll be easy to sell in bulk a brand of sake produced in the backwoods of Shikoku.

"What do you think about making up a gift set combining the sake with the best ham we make at the Farm and some fresh pickled vegetables? Charge maybe fifteen thousand yen a box? We could start by having Mr. Soda's company buy them as New Year's gifts. According to what I've heard, there're quite a few manufacturers around here producing quality goods. You've got to connect with the right distribution system if you want to survive. We really should hook up with them."

"The group that toured here today," Ikuo said, "will learn about our church's abilities at the summer conference. Come fall, and they'll get serious about working with us."

"I may be naive, or they wouldn't have nicknamed me Innocent Youth," Ogi said hesitantly, "but are you saying the local people will start cooperating with us more actively starting in the fall? So the summer conference is the first step toward opening those doors for us?"

Instead of a typical *of course, what else?* look, Ikuo turned deeply suspicious eyes toward Ogi. Ogi felt an instinctive defensive reaction welling up, but before anything developed, Mr. Hanawa intervened.

"I know you're concerned about what the Quiet Women might be preparing to do. After the Technicians were barred from their meetings, you went there to play the piano, didn't you, Ikuo? And you said things were pretty tense. The summer conference is the top priority for the Quiet Women. They're not thinking about fall or anything beyond.

"A little self-criticism here, but in the final days of their activities in Izu the Technicians drove Patron into a corner as he agonized over how to keep the church from self-destructing—which resulted in the Somersault. The Technicians didn't learn a thing; they went ahead and killed Guide. So I can't just sit back idly in regards to what the Quiet Women are up to.

"Now that Patron's awakened from his long hibernation, for our part, we have to work steadily, starting in the fall, to build his new church: the Church of the New Man."

Ikuo studied Ogi as he listened to Mr. Hanawa. Thin clouds covered the sky, and the pale light brought out Ikuo's high cheekbones and deep eye sockets in stark comic-book fashion.

Once he opened his mouth, Ikuo's words were measured. "The Quiet Women are on fire after Patron's announcement, but I don't think they've settled on a definite program. According to Dancer, Asa-san and Ms. Tachibana have misgivings. Since the Quiet Women lived so long in an isolated environment, it's understandable that their sermons tend to be narrow and obsessive. But we've also got to give them credit, as a group of women who've gone through a lot."

"Well, if you put it that way," Mr. Hanawa said, "the Technicians are a closed-off, self-righteous sect too. That's something they'll have to be aware of as they participate in the construction of the new church. They'll have to let Patron's intentions seep into their consciousness and get feedback from the entire body of the church; otherwise it'll have been pointless for Patron and all of us to have come to live in this place. . . . At any rate, until Patron points us in the right direction in his sermon at the summer conference, we need to concentrate on building up the farm as our economic base. I'd appreciate it if you'd let the office staff know this."

"The Quiet Women aren't here right now to defend themselves," Ikuo said, "so let's be fair when we discuss them. I'd like the office staff and the Technicians not to be too eager to interfere as they formulate their program. I really hope *all* the groups gathered here will do their own thing. Otherwise, the summer conference will be a complete bore."

"Not that you're Napoleon at Moscow or anything, Ikuo, but you do tend to set up camp on the high ground and watch the battle develop—with your private little army. Is that how you consolidate an overall strategy?"

"That's what Patron wants me to do," Ikuo replied.

"But you're the one who someday will protest against Patron, right? You're Jonah, as the Young Fireflies call you."

"If I can make a request about *your* strategy, Mr. Hanawa, I'd just like you not to lynch Patron at the summer meeting. That's all I ask."

"That would be totally boring!" Mr. Hanawa answered.

In the west corner of the broad rectangular grounds, a refrigerated meat truck pulled up in front of the processing plant next to the dorm where the majority of the Technicians lived. Mr. Hanawa looked over at the truck and, with an easy dignity, brought their conversation to a halt.

"The only thing we're interested in is Patron's plan for the Church of the New Man," he said. "Some of the Technicians are laying everything on the line for that." And giving Ogi a short wave of the hand, Mr. Hanawa rushed off to join his fellows in white work clothes at the processing plant.

4

"Would you come with me now to see the Young Fireflies?" Ikuo asked Ogi. "Some of the leaders among them—I don't want you to hear what they have to say secondhand, from me, but have them talk directly to you, as a member of the office staff."

Ikuo strode ahead, not waiting for a reply. The two of them cut south across the clearing, toward the Farm, which jutted out among the trees on what looked like a peninsula, the slopes steadily getting steeper. Huge poplars and equally large weeping willows lined the path as they descended. On a rise far away, thin poplar branches jostled one another and angled inward, and the leaves of the willows sparkled like gold leaf in the sunlight. The poplars and willows were no doubt leftovers of a windbreak for the Farm set up near the ridge line.

Following the road as it twisted down through the wet broad-leafed forest, they came upon a stand of natural oaks and headed toward a house with a brick-colored slate roof where Mayumi, the dyer, lived and worked. Along the way Ikuo told Ogi how the Fireflies were planning a performance at the summer conference, with Mayumi in charge of the costumes.

In this region's folklore, the legendary figures were unique characters. Among the area's traditional events was what was called the Spirit Festival, performed for souls that had not yet reached their final resting place. The participants dressed as spirits, slightly larger than life size, and formed a procession that wended its way from the woods down into the valley. Except for some small props, the special dolls and costumes they used would be burned on the shores of the Kame River and created anew the next year. As with the Young Fireflies, the Spirit Festival had been discontinued, but the young people were planning to revive the custom as an attraction at the upcoming summer conference.

At Mayumi's pine-log-and-earthen-mortar entrance, a dyeing kettle lay beside the door on the narrow landing. Just as Ikuo and Ogi arrived, the grass-colored front door opened up as if waiting for them, and a woman with an egg-shaped head and a halo of hair leaned out.

"Gii and the others haven't come back yet. Would you mind coming in through the veranda?" she asked.

Ikuo, shoes on, climbed up onto the narrow veranda that jutted out toward the steep slope down to the mountain stream, and Ogi followed after. The veranda stretched to the southwest corner of the house; below it was an uncut lawn and, far below a sheer cliff, a branch of the Kame River.

Ikuo and Ogi went inside. The house was small, but the room facing the veranda had the generous feeling of a craftsman's workshop. A loom was set up in the back, with a bolt of indigo cloth in the process of being woven.

In the corner opposite the loom, Mayumi stood at her sink and stove, preparing tea, wearing a T-shirt and long canvas apron, a thoughtful look in her round eyes. Ogi noticed some photos behind Plexiglass that dotted the pine board walls. One sepia photo, when he took a good look at it, showed a house next to a round bayberry tree and the open interior of a second-floor room where two naked women—one of whom looked like a young boy, her breasts small—lay on a blanket sunning themselves.

Mayumi brought over a tray with herb tea to Ikuo, who was sitting at a low table leafing through a sketchbook that lay there.

"These sketches look like they're for the Spirit Festival," Ikuo said to her. "I like this one—is he the spirit of the trees or of the forests? I can't tell. The one covered with twigs and leaves."

"They're not finished yet," Mayumi replied. "The one that looks like he should have been born a tree is the spirit called Gii. In this region a person who is equally eccentric is given the name Gii. Right now it's our tender young leader who goes by that name."

Ogi had Ikuo pass the sketches over to him. One of them was of a very unusual-looking person, part old man and part toddler taking his first steps; the cocoon-shaped figure was covered from head to toe in twigs and small branches.

"Gii likes the idea of dressing up like that. I'm sure he'll play the role of the spirit."

"I was imagining he'd play the role of the founder of the Church of the Flaming Green Tree," Ogi said. "When Asa-san came to the office to explain about the Spirit Festival, I heard that that spirit was the very newest one."

Mayumi looked at Ogi for the first time with any interest.

"Do you see on the next page the spirit with wounds on his head and chest and blood flowing down?" she asked. "In a wheelchair? That's the founder, Brother Gii, who closed the church and was about to go out on a world missionary trip when he was stoned to death. Gii feels it's too simplistic, too cartoony."

"Gii must view his father as a very complex figure," Ikuo said. "Most people in this region don't seem to believe that Gii's mother is Satchan and that his father is Brother Gii."

Noticing that Ogi wasn't quite following them, Ikuo pointed to the photo Ogi had been wondering about. "Those women in that voyeuristic photo are Satchan, when she was younger, and Mayumi. You see that thing between Satchan's legs? She has male genitals, as well as a woman's, and is able to give birth. Actually, when she was young she was raised as a boy."

Hesitating, Ogi looked again at the photograph, and Mayumi immediately lost interest in him, turning her attention back to Ikuo.

"Gii's unwillingness to see his father reduced to some simplistic image is the same way he feels about the faith of the Church of the Flaming Green Tree. He doesn't want to trivialize the doubts the local people have about his mother. Whenever I read the transcripts of Brother Gii's sermons, he starts out with the Old Testament, the New Testament, or early Buddhist scripture, and so on, but he always takes off from there in his own direction and ends up emphasizing God and mystical experience. Don't you think Brother Gii and Patron have something in common? After his Somersault didn't you hate how the weekly magazines reduced Patron to a comic-book figure?"

Footsteps sounded outside, rushing down the slope with firm sure strides. Mayumi went out to greet the teenagers, who piled in the front door, not the veranda, and could be heard cleaning up in the bathroom and sink.

Ogi looked around again. The ceiling was cheaply painted and starting to show sooty cracks, but the room's contents—from the panel photos on the wall to the hanging calico curtain, the nostalgic colors of the binding of the books on the narrow bookshelf, and the heap of cloths of different sizes and materials—all gave the interior a special atmosphere. It was an atelier that obviously belonged to a mature woman engaged in creative, artistic work.

Now the youthful bodies of all the Young Fireflies entered the room, bringing with them a sense of unrestrained roughness. Ogi and Ikuo, both young men themselves, were part of the scene as well. Ikuo's reserved attitude from when he was driving the minivan with the guests from Old Town vanished now as he talked freely with Gii and the others.

In Mayumi's expression and movements, too, as she bustled around, one could detect a different kind of happiness from moments before. Ogi could see she treated Gii as a special person. For some reason, fleeting, intimate images of Mrs. Tsugane flashed through his mind.

"We've been going around collecting material for the Spirit Festival, and it took a long time," Gii said, impetuously greeting them before his older colleague, Isamu, could say a word.

"It's definitely a good idea to study how they used to perform the festival," Ikuo replied, "but since you'll be doing it at the church's summer conference, if you try to stick too close to local customs the whole point of what you're after will vanish."

"You're right about that," Gii answered docilely. "We only have faint memories of seeing the festival ourselves, so we're a bit jittery about it."

"What's important for you isn't the superficial aspect of the festival but what it stands for. The adults have stopped thinking about what the festival really means, which is why you took it upon yourselves to revive it, right? I think you should just go ahead and put on a performance that's different from the festivals of the past."

"We think so too."

"I've been looking at the photo collection that Asa-san lent me," Mayumi said, "but instead of trying to reproduce what's in there, I've done sketches of images that came to me as I listened to the legends Gii told me."

"Are all the children here raised on these stories?" Ogi asked. "It's strange for me, because I'm from a place where we don't have those sorts of legends."

The young men ignored his question.

"In order to perform the Spirit Festival," Ikuo answered in their stead, "the Young Fireflies compared all their personal memories of the festival. There were several places where Gii's memory was different."

"That's right." Isamu nodded.

"I saw your house over in the outskirts, and it seemed like an old home with a long history," Ogi ventured, but Isamu didn't reply.

"Gii's case is a bit special," Mayumi said. "Satchan was taken in as an orphan at the Mansion and was raised by Granny, who was something of a *kataribe,* a storyteller, though Satchan says she didn't hear all that many legends growing up. Granny taught Brother Gii all the legends. Satchan was his successor and passed them on to Gii. That's the line of descent here."

"We can just go ahead and use the dolls, clothes, and props of the spirits that are stored in the shrines and temples," Gii said. "Those'll do fine. Though I imagine Mayumi will think that's boring. Talking to people who were alive when the new spirits lived and trying to put all that together and create spirits isn't easy. If you oversimplify them, they'll turn into caricatures."

"You don't want to be the Spirit of Brother Gii?" Ikuo asked Gii.

"I just told you, didn't I? It might turn out as a caricature."

"Would you rather be the Spirit of the Hermit Gii, who refused military service and hid in the forest?"

"Yes, everybody thinks he should be He Who Destroys," Isamu said, but Gii ignored him.

Ikuo explained all this to Ogi. "He means the pioneer who came in when this region was a wilderness surrounded by forest and opened it up for settlers. The cliffs and rock-hard soil had dammed up stagnant water, and gas had collected. He blew it all up with explosives, so he was both a creator and a destroyer."

"If I do play He Who Destroys, one of my friends asked if I'll do it dressed up as a giant who opened up the land here," Gii said, in a calm voice surprising in someone so young. "I was born at the Farm after my father died an unnatural death, and for a long time they wouldn't let me play with the other kids. All I heard was stories about my father that my mother told me, so when I started going to school I was so far behind I had a tough time keeping up.

"People at school treated me like I was a freak, and neighbors used to taunt me as I walked home to the Farm along the river. *Must have been tough to squeeze out of your mom's cock when you were born, huh?* Things like that. Anyway, having heard all the stories from my mother, ever since I was little I've viewed the local people as *doubled.* I got this vision of a world where the living and the dead coexist from a poem by the pianist Afanassiev. And I believed that as a child I'd actually experienced it.

"I'd pass by people along the river, adults and children, and realize that some of them—people who looked just like everybody else—were people who had *come back.* The souls of the dead would go up to the forest, rest for a long time at the roots of trees, and be reborn in the bodies of newborn babies. Those are the people who've *come back.* My mother said that, in principle, all the people in the valley have *come back,* but some people stood out more than others.

"I found it terribly exciting to see the people who'd *come back* living together with ordinary people. That doesn't happen to me anymore, so what I hope is that the Spirit Festival can re-create that feeling: the people who've *come back* descending into the midst of a group of ordinary people."

"So as a child you felt the mythic heroes of this land being reborn?" Ikuo asked. "That's pretty amazing. Growing up like that must have given you a more objective view of special figures like He Who Destroys—and your father too. I can understand now why the character covered with branches and leaves has so much appeal."

"The way you put it, Ikuo-san, does sort of capture the way I felt," Gii said. "But even though I had those fantasies as a child, to look at me you wouldn't have thought I was anything out of the ordinary. I was just a little neighborhood brat with a blank look on his face."

"But that blank-looking little urchin *was* something special," Mayumi insisted. "And the fact that you have such a clear recollection of the way you felt then makes you pretty special even now, Gii."

For Ogi, this unabashed admiration from an older woman once again called up disjointed memories of Mrs. Tsugane.

28: A Miracle

1

In the Red Cross Hospital, Kizu asked Dr. Koga about something that had been bothering him for quite some time.

"When I was taken from the reception desk at the outpatient part of the hospital and up in the elevator I was fully conscious, though it felt like everything was taking place in a dream. It was like I was a shallow bay in which the tide was receding. It had a strange physicality. The thought struck me that soon I would be empty—in other words, I was going to die—and I was scared and confused. I couldn't move, and I'm sure I looked quite ugly."

"Not from the outside you didn't," Dr. Koga replied. "Though Ikuo told me that when you started looking around so nervously he wanted to do something for you but had no idea what to do."

"I was struck by the feeling," Kizu went on, "that my body was about to rise up horizontally, and I was flustered, thinking I was headed straight for the coffin. There was only one thing I could cling to—the thought that before long the pain would hit me with a thud. And then I would crash and die and life would come to an end. Besides the fear and confusion, I had a cynical premonition that if someone told me now I was under the wrong impression and things weren't as they seemed, I wouldn't have had any objections.

"Yesterday, when Ikuo came to visit me, he told me what young Gii told him about having often seen *people who've returned* living together with normal people. Right now I really feel, talking to you like this, that I am one of those people."

"I think that if the next *thud*, as you put it, had come, you really would have died," Dr. Koga said. "As your doctor I was trying to forestall this, but it was risky to take you all the way to Matsuyama. I took the risk partly because Ikuo insisted but also because I believed you were going to pass away from cancer anyway before much longer. I was anxious, thinking we had to take you to Matsuyama, otherwise you'd die the way you were, though I know this isn't exactly logical. . . . If you had died on the way—well, I figured that would be unfortunate but not the worst sort of death. I did still feel responsible, though, even if you'd passed away after we took you out of the ambulance and turned you over to the intensive care unit."

The sense of fear and confusion Kizu felt at that time was no longer near, though it was bound to overwhelm him again. He didn't feel like complaining to Dr. Koga, though, and confined himself to a sigh.

"It was all pretty strange the way it worked out," Kizu said.

"It was a *miracle*!" Dr. Koga exclaimed. "As your attending physician I've made one mistake after another. When you had your first bout of pain and bloody stool, I just went on the assumption that you had terminal cancer and should be given medication to alleviate the pain. But you recovered quickly, so I designed a program both to control your pain with medication and to allow you to recuperate at home. People your age are wary of being overly dependent on drugs, not to mention being pretty stoic, so you were a model patient.

"The thought didn't occur to me of trying to locate the origin of your pain. A complete cure was out of the question. That's the situation when you had this recurrence and all the terrible pain involved. I imagine Ikuo's told you all about this, but on the day you went into the hospital Patron used that as the impetus for launching this notion of the Church of the New Man. It had a tremendous impact on everybody—from those in the Hollow to those out at the farm.

"Patron says that the concept of the Church of the New Man is expressed in the painting you were doing at the time of your collapse, so I went over to your studio to check it out. If only I'd seen it beforehand I would have definitely taken another look at the source of your pain. There's a power in that painting. I don't care how much technique and experience an artist might have, there's no way a person taking drugs to suppress the pain of terminal cancer could draw something with the kind of power I saw in that painting.

"In actual fact, it turns out you don't have terminal cancer at all. So where was the pain coming from? Well, now we know. Eight years ago you had the viscous matter they discovered in an X-ray cleaned out. The material that collected once again in your gallbladder was rather tenacious, and the gallbladder was just about ready to burst. The young doctor at the Red Cross Hospital opened you up, removed it, and that was that.

"'The pain he had before was accompanied by jaundice, right?' the doctor asked me, 'so why didn't you suspect gallstones?' He treated me like some ignorant intern. I'd heard it was untreatable intestinal cancer. I asked the young doctor what he thought of the bloody stool. He said it's no longer a concern. And he was exactly right. The fiberscope showed no bleeding in your intestines and of course no sign of cancer. As far as we could see during the gallbladder operation, no cancer had spread to any other organs. 'Which isn't strange because there wasn't any cancer to begin with!' the young doctor said, in high spirits."

"So there really wasn't any cancer?" Kizu asked.

"The doctor who examined you in Tokyo is an outstanding physician with a great deal of experience. Terminal intestinal cancer isn't that hard to diagnose. It is a bit strange, though, that he didn't do a biopsy."

"Maybe that's because the physician who introduced me to him is a renowned diagnostician," Kizu said. "Patron once said he'd do something for my cancer. Do you think he really did what he said he would?"

"All my belief rests on him," Dr. Koga said. "Which doesn't hold true for you, Professor. I can't deny what you say, but it makes me wonder. Naturally, I'm happy that things have turned out as they have. Something bothers me, though, about that high-spirited young doctor. 'The cancer identified by the former attending physician has completely disappeared—yet the patient didn't follow up with any standard anticancer treatment. And he's living with the leader of a religious life. Can we ignore these facts?' That's what he said.

"Ambition might get the best of him and make him talk to the media, and then Patron will be drawn into the spotlight all over again. It's an unpleasant thought, especially when we're in such a critical time for the church."

2

Over and over Kizu kept thinking about what it meant that the cancer he'd been aware of having invaded his entire body—though if asked how he was aware of this he could only give an uncertain, vague reply—had completely vanished. The conclusion he arrived at was pure nonsense.

A *fluid life force* inside me, he thought, something I've never felt before, arose, moved through me, eradicated the focal point of the cancer deep inside, gathered it all at a spot where it could be expelled from my body, and then discharged it very painfully as that bloody stool!

Before the first wave of pain hit, while he was sketching the feverish Patron, Kizu had felt a tremendous force poured into his body. He recalled this when he was in the hospital. And while he had been sketching Patron naked from the waist up, this came back even more forcefully, which is when he started feeling bad and this latest episode had occurred.

When the next wave of pain hit him, the cancer had gathered in one place and came out in the bloody stool! Kizu knew this was an audacious fantasy, yet his insides retained a firm memory that this fantasy had actually happened.

Kizu proceeded to tell his story to the "high-spirited young doctor," as Dr. Koga called him, who was named Dr. Ino.

"I'm not saying this is how it happened," Kizu said. "But if you think about it, the relationship between what happened to my body and the power I received from Patron can explain it."

The doctor's face was round and fat, but the skin looked dirty. A nasty-little-boy smile came to his lips and he rejected this suggestion out of hand.

"If the doctor tells you it's colon or rectal cancer, well, if you're going to have cancer those are good places to have it. . . . At any rate, that's a sweet fantasy for a terminal cancer patient. I suggest you confirm this with Dr. Koga."

Kizu felt the smile of pity was directed toward him because of his chronic immaturity, and he accepted the doctor's designation of it as a fantasy. Still, he had to raise a mild protest at the way the young doctor treated Dr. Koga as an accomplice in the misdiagnosis.

"I'm overjoyed, of course, that I *don't* have cancer," Kizu said, "but my doctor in Tokyo was quite sure he'd discovered cancer, and Dr. Koga based his treatment on what the doctor passed along to him. Not noticing that the cancer has disappeared, though, perhaps is a slipup on his part as my attending physician—"

"*What?* Cancer doesn't just *disappear!*" Dr. Ino said, his expression even more spirited. "If a sample of a person's cells are taken to a diagnostic lab and they discover cancer, then he's a cancer patient pure and simple. You'd resigned yourself to being killed by those cancerous cells, and now, finding out that you aren't going to die, of course you feel great. But aren't you forgetting how you suffered when you were told you had incurable cancer?"

Every time Dr. Ino visited Kizu—as follow-up care after his routine gallbladder operation—he asked him when and how he'd started to suspect that his cancer was recurring. Kizu told him he'd grown aware that his physical condition was getting worse over the past three or four years but had put it down to his body's slowing down as it aged. After he'd talked with a renowned diagnostician he no longer doubted—on an emotional level—that his cancer was back, and so he'd returned to his native land.

As if this weren't enough, Dr. Ino prepared a questionnaire for Kizu.

What tests did the doctor in Tokyo run before he concluded it was cancer?
What words did he use to explain his findings, and how did you react?
After you were told you had cancer, didn't you refuse not just an operation but also radiation treatment and anticancer medicine because, in the back of your mind, you had doubts about whether you really had cancer or not?
If you did have doubts, what prompted them?
Or, on a more positive note, did you think maybe the diagnosis of cancer was a misdiagnosis?
If so, what did you base this on?
Why didn't you discuss these doubts with your present attending physician, who also happens to be a friend of yours?

Most of the questions were irrelevant because Kizu had never had any doubts. Still, Dr. Ino read the entire list of questions aloud. Some of them *were* relevant, however. When asked: *Thinking that you had cancer and that death was not far off, did you put your affairs in order?* Kizu just answered truthfully.

The final questions were different from the others, which made them all the more interesting: *When you told your friends and colleagues that you had cancer, was there a change in their attitude toward you and in your attitude toward them? Did your attitude change toward yourself?*

Kizu had done his best to respond honestly. And afterward, as he lay alone in bed, he mentally reviewed his responses.

What kind of examinations had the doctor in Tokyo done to arrive at the conclusion that he had terminal cancer? What Kizu remembered—it was only six months ago but the details were so fuzzy it seemed a lifetime, which only irritated Dr. Ino, and the more Kizu tried to recall the vaguer it all became—was that when the doctor in Tokyo questioned him about his condition before examining him, Kizu reported his bloody stool, but this didn't cause the doctor's mood to sour. They'd taken X-rays in Tokyo and done a CT scan and ultrasound. And drew blood. With the bad experience he had before with a fiberscope, Kizu didn't feel much like having it done again. But he couldn't recall whether the doctor asked him if he wanted to go through that procedure. Perhaps by this time the doctor wasn't under any illusions? Whether you're talking about the stomach or the intestines, if the patient's the type who doesn't like examinations, what's the point of making him suffer only to discover cancer in yet another part of his body?

After he was told he had cancer, the most important person he talked to about it had to be Ikuo, and this had been the spark that led to a deepening of their sexual relationship, a private preserve he wasn't about to get into. Instead he had told Dr. Ino how Patron had told him that as long as Kizu had life within him he would clarify his own mission as a religious leader, and how after Kizu accepted his role Dr. Koga began to show greater interest in him. Further, he talked about how everyone here in this area knew he was a terminal cancer patient, but it didn't seem to make people any more or less interested in him and he was able to lead a happy life and get along well with others.

After all these questions, Dr. Ino had asked him this: In weekly magazines and on TV shows you often see reports of how patients everyone has given up on were cured by such folk medicine as Chinese chi therapy or eating mushrooms from South America, right? Do you understand your own cure as the effects of Patron's mystical powers?

"When Patron's longtime companion fell ill," Kizu had replied, "not just Patron but everyone around him hoped he could save him through some mystical forces. But it didn't happen. So I don't believe Patron has mystical healing powers. However, while I was drawing the wound in Patron's side, what members of the church call the Sacred Wound, I felt a tremendous life force welling up within me, so powerful I wondered whether I'd be able to get through the session all right. The second time I was drawing was when I collapsed, but the terrible pain I felt came from that tremendous life force.

"As I usually do when I'm drawing, and as I sketched Patron with his side exposed, my eyes and hands functioned to connect up the inner and outer worlds of my model, and it was as if I suddenly got plugged into Patron's soul. This touched off a kind of uncontrollable life force that welled up in me, a force was so overwhelming that I thought, If this is a display of Patron's mystical healing power, it might very well lead to that *thud* I was talking about and kill me. But I accepted that.

"After my first operation, my cancer—assuming for the moment that what I don't have now I *did* have then—having lain dormant until then, started to be active again, and who knows but maybe this too was due to the stimulus I got from encountering Patron. At least that's the way I'd like to think of it.

"When it was discovered I had a relapse of my cancer—and I was told there was no chance of recovery—I surprised myself by how industrious I became. I got deeply into things I'd never done before, gave up the teaching position I'd held for years in America, and moved here to the woods of Shikoku. Understand that I wasn't thinking of my relapse of cancer as a negative thing. I knew I'd die before too long, but that didn't frighten me or make me feel regretful. I recognized that the *basis* for my life had changed. Isn't that what happens? I didn't see it as a terrible *end* to my life."

"Now that you know you *don't* have terminal cancer," Dr. Ino ventured, "do things seem new to you in any way?"

"The symptoms I noticed myself haven't changed," Kizu said, "except that the dull pain I had for a long while is gone. I don't feel the overflowing life force that filled me while I was drawing Patron. I don't think this is just postoperation weakness.

"If there *is* something new, it's a sense of anxiety. I came here with Ikuo, who wanted to be with Patron. To me, Patron is a special person, of course, but so is Ikuo. Wasn't it the knowledge that I had cancer and didn't have long to live that led me to be with them without worrying in the slightest? On an unconscious level, wasn't I hoping I'd spend the short time left to me for their sake, without thinking about anything else? With my crisis past, how can an unexceptional person like me possibly associate with the likes of *them*? Frankly speaking, it frightens me."

Once more a faint smile came to Dr. Ino's face, and Kizu was left feeling there was something he didn't get, something that had nothing to do with the young physician's usual high spirits but reflected an ulterior motive at work.

A week after this conversation, on the day before Kizu was to be released from the hospital, a special scoop appeared in a weekly magazine—the magazine itself wasn't to be found in Matsuyama so they were relying only on the ads in the newspapers—that was based on the exclusive account of his attending physician. The headline ran: RELIGIOUS LEADER WITH SACRED WOUND CURES TERMINAL CANCER WITH HIS HEALING POWER! CANCER THROUGHOUT THE BODY EXPELLED IN ONE LUMP!

3

Kizu left the hospital accompanied by Ms. Asuka, with Ikuo doing the driving. A minivan was to follow them with his belongings, with Mayumi at the wheel until they reached the mountain pass, after which Gii was to take over driving. Several members of the Fireflies were with them.

Escorted by Ms. Asuka, Kizu walked out to the carport at the front of the hospital and waited for Ikuo to bring the car around. As they passed by the elevator hall and front desk, Kizu sensed a flurry of activity around him, but Ms. Asuka didn't slacken her pace. As they walked by they heard a woman call out "*Mr. Kizu!*" in a thicker dialect that that used by the residents of the Old Town in Maki Township, but before he could respond, Ms. Asuka gently pushed him out the door and they were outside in the summery sunshine. The car pulled right up, Ikuo opened the door from the inside, and Kizu and Ms. Asuka climbed in.

Nobody mentioned the woman calling out to them, but after they'd wended their way through heavy city traffic for forty or fifty minutes and had begun to climb the slope up to the pass that formed a major crossroads for all of Shikoku, Ikuo turned to glance at the minivan following them and said, "I'm glad we could get rid of those pests. It would have been more trouble than it's worth if the Fireflies had come to blows with them right there in front of everybody."

"I was more worried that those boys would get in a quarrel after you and the TV reporter clashed," Ms. Asuka said to Ikuo. "Seems all those marches through the woods have made them respect your physical prowess."

"Was all that something to do with me?" Kizu asked.

"The TV and newspaper reporters have been trying to get near you since last night, and the Fireflies have been standing guard."

"Ikuo's role in the summer conference is crucial," Ms. Asuka said, "so we can't have him getting detained for disturbing the peace."

"It's not the weekend, and summer vacation hasn't begun yet, so is it really okay to have the Fireflies helping out like this?" Kizu asked.

"The boys in Gii's van are new members, older than the others," Ikuo said, "young men who are going to take over their families' businesses in shops along the river in the Old Town. One of them has a job in Matsuyama and took time off from work. Once the Fireflies started getting noticed more they asked if they could join. At first Gii hesitated, but since one was the older brother of a guy who was already a Firefly he gave in."

"The Fireflies is an association with a plan for the future, correct?" Kizu asked. "Which should make it especially meaningful to include boys in this age group, I would think."

"They'll all work together," Ikuo said, "to help prepare for the summer conference. I imagine Gii will consider afterward whether or not to reorganize them. . . . First the news got out about Patron's Sacred Wound, plus a sense that the Church of the New Man was finally organized. And now come reports that your cancer, Professor, has disappeared. People way beyond our little valley are starting to show an interest in our church."

Their car headed up the increasingly treacherous and windy slope, the foliage on the hillside across the deep valley now a luxuriant dark hazy green. The large greenhouses on the slope, as well as the remains of the local construction projects, all had a calm, antique look to them. Kizu felt he was returning to an imposing and stable land.

"The news that my cancer, or what all the doctors thought was cancer, has disappeared was in a weekly magazine, apparently. Have people also been talking about it in the Hollow and in Maki Town?"

"There's nothing we can do about that," Ikuo said.

"While we were checking you out of the hospital, Ikuo went over to a large stationery store to have a copy of the magazine article faxed from a friend in Tokyo," Ms. Asuka said, turning around in the passenger seat. She'd put a pillow and blanket on the backseat and told Kizu to lie down if he felt tired. "I ate alone in the hospital cafeteria," she went on. "At the next table was a group from one of the afternoon talk shows who'd come to do a story on you, Professor. I couldn't believe some of the things they were saying. They were even talking about how Ikuo had hit Gii."

Ikuo shifted in the driver's seat, his body language sending out a message to cease and desist, but strong-willed Ms. Asuka, not about to be deterred by any man trying to restrain her, brushed this aside.

"When Dr. Koga called us," she said, "to tell us that after your gallbladder operation they had started to think you didn't have cancer after all—they'd be running some tests, but it didn't look like cancer—Ikuo and Gii were both in the office. Everybody was overjoyed, until Gii made some flippant remark about how he found it disappointing. 'Why's that?' Ikuo shot back, the situation already getting tense because Gii is still, after all, a child. 'When someone who's dying from cancer shortens his life even further to work for our upcoming conference,' Gii remarked, 'it's a *much* more interesting story.' Ikuo walloped him but good on the back of his neck; the poor boy got quite a bruise. That's why Mayumi didn't even say hello to Ikuo today.

"The TV people must have heard about this from somewhere. One man suggested that if they got on the good side of this boy he might give them a tasty interview. Another man, a real hardliner with this affected made-for-TV voice, said that considering all the families in the country who have relatives with cancer they could really crank up the ratings. A guy from another group, a cameraman, said he wished he could get a shot of the toilet with that lump of cancer in it, and a woman reporter, a sort of geisha-with-a-brain type, knit her brow and laughed."

"We got rid of them once, but I'll bet they'll be back, this time at the Hollow."

Kizu looked concerned when Ikuo said this, so Ikuo continued.

"We're setting up tents we borrowed from the farm down below the dam that we'll use to register people during the summer conference. I found out from the town office that Satchan owns that land. Someday Gii will inherit it. We've arranged to park our car and the minivan not in the parking lot but on land that's already been cleared. So if those reporters follow us and try to corner you, Professor, we'll have the right to get them to leave since it's private property. Gii came up with this strategy."

"So you have a faxed copy of the magazine article?" Kizu asked.

"Shall I read it? I'll skip the boring first part," Ms. Asuka said, wasting no time.

"The doctor who performed the gallbladder operation on Professor Kizu stated that this is nothing short of a miracle, if the patient indeed had had terminal cancer as his personal physician said. He went on to say he expects to receive faxes of the CT scan and X-rays of the affected parts from the doctor who made the original diagnosis of cancer, after which he plans to make a presentation at a medical conference.

"The church leader who performed the miracle refused to make any comment. This leader, who now goes by the name of Patron, is one of the men who did a Somersault eleven years ago in the face of violence on the part of a radical faction within their church. His confidant, known as Guide, was subjected to a kangaroo trial earlier this year and ended up dead, news still fresh in our minds.

"The way a politicized radical faction planned indiscriminate terrorist acts foreshadowed what happened with Aum Shinrikyo. And now with the founder apparently able to cure terminal cancer, are we again seeing a harbinger of things to come?

"The local authorities declared that there were many opinions regarding this group of believers moving in, but from the standpoint of protecting religious freedom they had no fundamental opposition to the church. . . . Just as many former radicals have turned to running natural foods cooperatives and leading local environmental groups, several of these radical religious groups have switched to emphasizing healing."

Ms. Asuka stopped reading and returned the sheaf of faxes to her lap.

"It's better than what I expected from the headlines," Kizu said. "Though I know you've only read the choicest parts. But I can't see that Patron has changed his doctrine to emphasize healing. As he builds his Church of the New Man, I imagine that along the way he'll heal some incurable diseases, but that's not central to what he's doing."

Kizu suddenly felt exhausted, so he placed Ms. Asuka's pillow in one corner, pulled the blanket up over his stomach, and lay down. His cancer might be gone, but his energy level was still low.

Kizu closed his eyes. Instead of relief at having avoided death, a palpable unease rolled over him as to what he was supposed to do once he returned to the Hollow. All sorts of movements were afoot now that they were moving toward the launch of the Church of the New Man. Was there a role for him to play?

Completing the triptych to be hung in the chapel: That was the main thing. After his stay in the hospital, he was again assailed by doubts that he really understood the relationship between the two figures facing each other in the middle panel. In the midst of doing preliminary drawings, something about Patron's body—his wound exposed to view—struck him, though he hadn't had the leisure to reflect on what it all meant.

A new personal issue had also been raised. The excitingly charged sexual relationship between Ikuo and himself—a man who didn't have long to live— was now reduced to nothing more than a senile old man, who might hang around forever, infatuated by a young man's charms. . . .

The car bounced over a rough spot of road, which roused Kizu from his gloomy thoughts. He had a bitter taste in his mouth. After rattling around for a while, he was fully awake and he gazed out the window of the car, as it rolled to a stop at the clearing below the dam, at a huge wing jutting up above the manmade lake, blotting out the summer sky. This was the reviewing stand for the summer conference, a symmetrical structure projecting out to the edge of the lake. Something in the scene brought back memories of long ago.

4

That evening, at twilight, Kizu had an early dinner, a habit acquired in the hospital, sat down in an armchair by the window to enjoy the cool breeze, and gazed out at the Hollow, with its expectant air of activity as the summer conference approached.

One level below the stone wall surrounding the chapel and monastery on the south shore, the path leading to the edge of the lake had been trimmed clear of bushes and summer grasses and now lay exposed. Identical wooden stands had been constructed there and on the east and north shores of the lake—the bleachers for the summer conference. Even the path that led to Kizu's residence, running straight east from the point where it narrowed and went uphill, was under construction.

Now, though, as Kizu gazed out at the scene there was no heavy construction going on, just a placid view of men putting the final touches to the work. The sun was already down, but a line of cirrocumulus clouds had begun to spread quickly over the clear sky, their thin folds aglow in the gentle evening light and reflected in the perfectly still surface of the lake.

Hearing that Kizu was to be on the six o'clock Matsuyama evening news, Ms. Asuka had brought over a TV set for them to watch. Earlier, while Kizu had been watching the grandstands with their fragrant scent of freshly cut timber as they made their way up to the dam from the open space set up for the tents, Gii and his minivan had done their best to keep back the taxi that had been tailing them. So the TV crews hadn't been able to interview Kizu directly and had to content themselves with scenes of Kizu at the dam, apparently taken out of the taxi window.

From the way the announcer spoke, it appeared that this coverage of the "miracle man" whose cancer had completely disappeared had already been broadcast a few times. Kizu was shocked at how unsteady he appeared, standing there. He was also surprised by the film of him making his way through the crowds at the hospital, how very sad his slack, lined face and neck looked.

He remembered how, as a child, he'd thought it one of the mysteries of life how the faces of old people normally had a sad, depressed expression. Now that face was *his,* and he couldn't bear to look.

Ms. Asuka's dinner schedule was reversed now; she took her own meal at the dining hall *after* returning Kizu's dishes. This evening as she ate she was told that Patron would be paying Kizu a visit that evening between seven and eight. Though a deep exhaustion still had Kizu in its grip, he had slept soundly all afternoon, thanks to the dry air of the woods, and now stayed in bed to await Patron's visit.

When Kizu had arrived back at his house on the north shore he sensed the same woody fragrance he'd smelled at the dam. He thought at first this was because the window facing the Hollow was open, but actually the wood smell came from a newly constructed additional room just off the kitchen. The canvas partition that had separated the sickroom from the studio was gone. Ms. Asuka didn't stride into the kitchen as briskly as she had before, but after she changed her clothes she reported the news about the visit.

"The doctor who performed the gallbladder operation didn't hesitate to say that there wasn't any cancer," Kizu said, "and did these thorough tests. It's only been a week since the construction started? It's amazing they could add on this extra room by the time I came home."

"The day after you went into the hospital, the Technicians' carpentry team came over. Patron had them start work because he was expecting great things of you, Professor, in the Church of the New Man. Some people say Patron foresaw all of this. Still, though, when we heard the news that you didn't have cancer, Patron was the only one with a strangely pained look on his face."

Kizu was listening to the voices of the cicadas and, interspersed, the calls of birds as they echoed, a split second later, off the surface of the lake—all part of something vast that converged on the forest and spilled down from it. Soon he heard the sound of music, amplified through a speaker though still subdued: two or three short piano pieces; he wasn't familiar with the melody, though the chords and accompaniment were pleasant enough.

While the foothills surrounding the Hollow still echoed with the music, Ms. Asuka gracefully appeared from the kitchen to explain.

"Every time Patron leaves his residence, they use piano music to let people in the church know. It's one of Morio's compositions. When they hear that music, people who have things they want to ask Patron leave their work or meditation and come out looking for him. He's left his residence now and I imagine, since someone has stopped to talk with him in the courtyard of the monastery, it'll be another thirty minutes before he arrives. Shall I turn on the light?"

"He can see this window as he comes here, so if we turn on the light it might appear we're rushing him," Kizu said. "Let's leave it off until he arrives. Patron seems to be really enthused about the activities of his Church of the New Man, doesn't he?"

"He's leading a more formal lifestyle now, as befits the leader of a church," Ms. Asuka replied. "You'll see soon enough when they get to the top of the dam. Morio waits on Patron like a page—or a court jester, if you will— and Gii has organized a squad to guard him."

A clump of people moved out of the monastery courtyard, went up to the dam, and passed through the reviewing stands, their faces unclear in the gathering gloom as they approached. Morio fluttered around next to Patron, who looked a bit unsteady on his feet, and they were both surrounded by young men walking with measured, determined steps.

Keeping up with these trained strides must have been difficult, but the bodyguards looked fairly relaxed, and Kizu imagined that if, for instance, Morio were to fall into the lake, they'd be able to effect a well-organized rescue.

Watching the little band until it turned into the newly reconditioned path leading to the north shore, Kizu retreated from the window. How should he best greet Patron? Should he thank him for using his spiritual powers to rid him of cancer?

Honestly, though, Kizu didn't feel he could attribute the disappearance of his cancer to anything Patron did. Once it was gone, even the pain that had held his entire being in its crushing grip was hard to remember as something real. Similarly, though the doctor who declared he didn't have cancer didn't say it had disappeared, right now that seemed like a reasonable way to think about it.

As they heard Patron and his group approaching up the slope, Ms. Asuka opened the window to catch the cool breeze, switched on the light, and went to the front door, taking care that mosquitoes and other flying insects didn't invade the house through cracks in the shutters.

Patron and Morio came in and Ms. Asuka called to the young bodyguards to do likewise, but they were determined to remain outside. As Kizu greeted them from where he sat in an armchair from the bedroom in the large room, now one big studio, Morio called out *"Ah!"* in a loud voice.

"What's the matter, Morio? Don't be rude, now," Patron said reprovingly.

From behind Patron, Morio put his right arm on Patron's shoulder and half hid behind him, held his left hand in front of his face, and said in a pitiful voice, *"Ah! Ah!* He's supposed to be dead!"

With Morio leaning on him, Patron swayed a bit and turned his now somewhat thinner and less conspicuous double chin toward Kizu. His eyes, with their heavy folds at the outer corners, might look weak at first, but Kizu could detect a thorough egocentrism at work in them that was calm and yet concealed deeper currents of emotion.

"In the sermon I gave telling how you recovered and returned to the Hollow," Patron said, "I said you'd died once and been reborn. I also said that because of this, in your body with its *new* life dwelling in it, it was only natural for the cancer of your *old* life to disappear without a trace. Morio was quite moved by this. He likes to paint mental pictures of what life is like in heaven, and he came up with the vision of the soul first taking the form of a simple grouping of sounds. I think that led to the notion of a more concrete vision of *something*—not a person exactly—that's walking the earth."

Patron removed Morio's arm from his shoulder. Then, holding his quaking companion, he turned to Ms. Asuka.

"Bring a chair and place it beside the desk next to the wall on the north side. Do that and he'll calm down. Morio, you need to pull yourself together, okay? So be brave." He watched Morio carefully.

After Ms. Asuka made the space for Morio, Patron asked Kizu to stand up and adjust his chair too, so it faced the studio part of the room. Ms. Asuka brought over a chair for Patron from the studio and set it down on the lake side. Kizu and Patron settled down, sitting diagonally across from each other, about three yards apart. After regaining his cool, Morio was able to lift his face from his arms to discover Patron straight across from him.

"I'm happy to see you looking so well," Patron said, in a renewed greeting.

"You look well too," Kizu said fervently. "You seem to have gotten slimmer. The line of your chin is different from when I drew you."

Patron fixed his gaze on the drawing Kizu had attached to the middle panel of the triptych. "I feel like my face *has* gotten thinner, though I haven't been moving about any more than usual, even with starting the Church of the New Man. I'm expecting great things from you now in our church, but at the same time I feel a bit sheepish saying this. After all, you'll be going through rehabilitation for some time."

"Morio's reaction was quite honest," Kizu said, "saying he thought I was dead. That really struck me. I'm sure your sermon convinced all the members of the church. I *do* feel like I died and was reborn, though I didn't notice my rebirth when it was happening."

"That's a pretty common reaction, I think—the way most people deal with death," Patron said. "We don't have the strength to go through the dramatic kinds of death and rebirth you find in the Gospels . . . but it certainly is excellent news that all your symptoms of cancer are gone."

"I'm very thankful."

As if to let Kizu's words, unexpected, and entirely natural, pass by, Patron turned to gaze at his portrait. He remained silent, as if waiting for Kizu to continue in another direction. But Kizu had nothing left to say. When the young doctor at the Red Cross Hospital told him it was strange he didn't make absolutely sure about the existence of his cancer, he'd replied that he never doubted that he did have cancer, though he had to admit that his actions had been ambiguous. Even now, he couldn't wipe that ambiguity away.

"With the rehabilitation you need to go through, I know this will seem like I'm rushing you," Patron said, "but when will you be able to start work again on this large oil painting? I know it must be physically tiring to paint a large tableau."

"Admittedly, the operation has taken something out of me, but I should be back on my feet soon," Kizu replied, although he knew this was pushing things. "I should be able to start again before long."

"Can you finish it before the summer conference?"

Kizu nodded.

"One of the reasons I came over tonight was to ask you that, even though I know you're very tired," Patron said. "Ikuo very much wants to show the triptych to people who will be new members of the Church of the New Man who come to the conference from all over the country. He's also thinking of opening the chapel to local people and tourists who want to see it. There are a lot of people interested in the miracle that took place in your body, which they connect up with my wound. Nothing could satisfy them more than seeing the painting you did of my bare torso.

"Ikuo sees the summer conference as the national debut of our Church of the New Man. He's been working with the Fireflies on a plan to help make it a success and says he'd like to make viewing the triptych part of the orientation for the participants. I have one more related request: Before you begin work on your painting again, would you take a look at my body one more time? Right now. I know it's sudden—"

"No, not at all," Kizu said, trying to compensate for his surprised expression. "If anything was sudden, it was me collapsing when you were modeling."

Still seated, Patron very carefully began to unbutton his brand-new shirt from the top. The fact that he wore no undershirt struck Kizu as odd, since men of their age usually did. Patron sat up in his chair, and when he finished removing his shirt completely this feeling of oddness grew even greater. Kizu gazed at Patron's side and got the same impression one gets looking at the face of someone with thick glasses who's just removed them.

"*Ah,*" Kizu sighed. The Sacred Wound was *gone*! He stared hard at Patron's flank. Patron twisted his shoulder in response, slightly rotating his chest. There was a round rose-colored spot on his side. It was a smooth mark, as if left by a heated cup pressed against the skin and not released until the air inside had cooled.

"I'd like you to complete the triptych as you've done in the drawings," Patron said, "with the hole still open. I know you're still trying to get used to the idea that your cancer has disappeared, and likewise I'm still unsure what my wound's closing up means. Though in the part of the triptych where I'm confronting Ikuo, I think it makes more sense for the wound to be open." He rubbed the now-healed smooth skin where the wound had been, as if he were massaging his tired eyes.

"I should be able to complete the painting based on the sketches I made when the wound was oozing and you were feverish," Kizu said. "The ones I did before I collapsed. But there'll be a lot of people coming to the chapel who've been moved by the legend of the Sacred Wound. If by chance they find out the wound has healed, won't there be trouble?"

Because he was thin and drawn, Patron's profile as he gazed at the painting had a sober coldness to it. "The only trouble I can think of is when those veteran journalists trumpet their scoop. I learned a lot about reporters during the Somersault. But I'm too old to worry about what they think. Within the church itself, the Quiet Women see the wound in my side as a *sign* of the sin of having done the Somersault. Having the wound disappear right now, at the point where I've decided to build the Church of the New Man, would fit right in with their doctrine. However, I'm not building up the Church of the New Man in order to directly praise the power of the transcendent. I'm doing it as one of many antichrists. So I'm certainly not planning to reverse the Somersault.

"Having said that, the transcendent has, as I inaugurate my church, chosen this time to heal the wound that has troubled me over the past decade. Considered in that light, the significance of your cancer suddenly disappearing becomes clear. You're painting what will be the central icon of our new movement. As you neared completion of it you were overwhelmed by pain. And once you recovered, your cancer was gone. The transcendent smiles down on your work, Professor, and in order to lift you up so you could complete the painting, it took away your cancer. That makes eminent sense. In the building of the Church of the New Man we'll be engaged in from now on, the transcendent is indifferent about whether I'm a faithful follower or whether, as an antichrist, I'm trying to regain the will I had in the Somersault. The transcendent is absolutely self-centered. It doesn't stand on the side of those who are trying to do good.

"Just like the journalists I mentioned, the Almighty is bereft of imagination. Spinoza's completely right on this point. If you call the transcendent God, then you're saying God has no imagination. Every time I read the section of the Gospels where Jesus is crucified, I find myself thinking that God's son has no imagination. For Christ, there is only this world God made—that is, God itself and His designs. 'My God, my God, why have you forsaken me?' Jesus cries out, but he accepts everything that happens to him.

"The antichrist, in contrast, *does* have imagination. Imagination, in fact, is *all* he has. And my Church of the New Man will be built in this way—as the church of the antichrist. Once you've grown used to the cancer's having left your body, Professor, I ask that you do your utmost for our new church."

Morio stood up from his chair over by the wall and with small steps slowly made his way past Kizu to stand in front of Patron. Then he sat down at Patron's feet and laid one hand reverently on Patron's left knee. Patron gently brought his fingers together and tousled Morio's hair. Patron turned his gaze from the portrait of himself to the still incomplete full tableau.

"But there's no need for me to preach to you about the transcendent," Patron went on. "You've gotten close to us through Ikuo. And I suspect you'll continue working for his sake. That being the case, I don't need to be too concerned about this. To tell the truth, Ikuo's still something of a mystery to me. But I do know he's putting everything he has into our church, doing all he can to pave the way for the summer conference that will decide our future.

"And in your triptych, won't you be showing the relationship between Ikuo and myself, the antichrist of the Church of the New Man?"

29: Lessons Learned

1

The Technicians' carpentry team was up on stepladders, pounding thick red concrete nails into the wall of the chapel. It was something any amateur could do, and Kizu found it amusing that they approached the task as some specialized, highly complicated assignment. No matter what was going on these days, you could count on a Technician to be there.

The completed triptych was being mounted on the narrow wall near the piano. There were two chairs beside the piano, one the performer's seat occupied by Ikuo, the other by Morio, as they sat there expectantly. At some distance away from them, in the front row of the chairs used for meetings, sat Gii and Isamu, as well as a third Firefly, who'd helped Ikuo transport the painting from the studio, all of them watching the Technicians go about their job.

For the time being bereft of work, Kizu sat there looking at the antique silver spirit level, decorated with line drawings of lilies, that Gii had brought over. Gii had casually mentioned that it had been handed down to him by his mother and was part of the legacy left behind by the diplomat who had lived in the house on the north shore, the one who'd designed the beds in the style of rustic Eastern European furniture.

The Fireflies were called over to carry the triptych to just below where the nails had been set. Gii leaped nimbly on a stepladder, set the level on the top of the painting to be sure it was hanging straight, and signaled to the Technicians. The way Gii maneuvered the little tool had all the winsomeness that Kizu had sensed the first time he met the young man, and he could feel the pride Ikuo had as he looked on.

When they'd set the painting right where they wanted it, Ikuo returned to the piano. A sheaf of copies of Morio's compositions lay there. Ikuo chose one piece and began playing, freely changing the speed, emphasizing the lower register as he played it through twice. Instead of sitting beside Ikuo as one might expect, Morio was up and moving about, silent and agile despite his impaired legs. Absorbed in the music, he moved in diagonal lines, tracing a pentagon in the circle of the chapel walls, as if stepping on the shadows cast by the aerial dome of the ceiling.

Since the chapel was built as a perfect circle with a radius of fifty feet, ordinary sounds would focus on one point and a flattering echo would be produced, which originally made it impossible to hold concerts. All sorts of changes had been made to modify this since the building was first built—porous boards placed to absorb sound on the ceiling and up to about twelve feet above the floor; the walls all redone to diffuse sound evenly. Even the windows and the entrance door were set slightly out of alignment with one another to improve the acoustics. But now in the midst of this carefully designed space they were about to hang a six-by-sixteen-foot painting, plus two side panels each half again as large. So the first thing they wanted to do after hanging the painting was to have Ikuo play the piano while Morio, with his sensitive ears, checked for a flattering echo.

Soon Morio, his whole body showing a sense of relief, went back and sat beside Ikuo. He tucked his legs up under him like a monkey settling in and listened to the rest of his composition. He couldn't have been happier. The rest of the people standing about here and there in the chapel also turned their attention to the music, all the while gazing up at the triptych.

Gii came over next to Kizu and said, "Morio doesn't hear any echoes."

One of three Technicians sitting nearby said to his companions, "If they put it in a heavy frame with glass it might have a different effect altogether."

"We won't be using a frame," Gii said, speaking as an equal to the older Technicians, "so go ahead and attach it permanently."

The three of them watched as the painting was being moved, and everyone could hear Gii express his unease to Isamu and his other companion.

"Why do they have to say such pointless things?"

"It's not pointless, is it?" Isamu was concerned that Gii's voice might carry to those in front.

"It is *too* pointless," Gii insisted. "We know that sound isn't reverberating. What's the point of suggesting we put it in a frame and glass and see if we can make it echo? Let's go," he said decisively.

As Gii, Isamu, and the other Firefly got up to leave, Ikuo, who was straightening up the copies of Morio's music, called out to them. "Would you please go over and tell Dancer to come and take a look at where they've hung the painting?"

"Will do," Gii replied. He'd been twirling the silver spirit level in front of him, between his thumb and middle finger, but stopped as he answered.

The Technicians' body language, too, showed how close they felt to Ikuo, and they politely acknowledged Kizu as they departed. Thanking them, Kizu could tell—compared to before he'd gone into the hospital—that Ikuo had come to play a much more vital role in running the church.

Dancer appeared, accompanied by Ogi and Ms. Tachibana. The people already there, and these newcomers, all gathered in front of the turpentine-redolent triptych. Kizu was worried about how people would react to the first work he'd done after being discharged from the hospital, the two portraits in the foreground of the central panel. The screech of cicadas, which he'd forgotten about while Ikuo played the piano, now came back in full force.

Dancer gazed up at the painting. "If you look carefully you'll see that Jonah and Patron are not really facing each other directly. I was expecting them to be questioning each other, trying to persuade each other."

"Maybe they've been debating but haven't arrived at a resolution, so they're looking off to one side and thinking things over," Ms. Tachibana commented.

Kizu had been waiting for Dancer or Ms. Tachibana, who knew about Patron's side being healed, to say something about his portrayal of the wound. But neither one of them seemed about to touch on it. Before long Ms. Tachibana spoke up.

"The piano a while ago was simply lovely," she said to Morio.

"There weren't any echoes at all," Morio replied.

"At the summer conference we'll use a microphone and play it over speakers, but when we play it like this without any amplification, can people really hear it all over the Hollow?" Ikuo asked.

"We were in the office," Dancer said, "with the windows on the lake side open, and we could hear it echo off the north shore."

"At first we played with the windows shut," Morio said, "but then we opened them."

"So we must have heard the last half," Dancer said.

"The Quiet Women requested that at the morning meetings we just let the piano sound all over the Hollow, without using any speakers," Ikuo said. "Morio, why don't you go back to Patron's place with your sister and tell him the acoustics in the chapel are fine. And then take a rest; you've worked hard today."

"Can I take back all the sheet music?" Morio asked.

"Of course. And thank you."

2

After Ms. Tachibana and her brother left, the others all sat down around Kizu, who'd stayed rooted to his chair, and gazed up again at the triptych. Kizu could feel them holding back any comments on the painting. A faint whiff of turpentine wafted toward them.

Dancer was the first to speak.

"In the right part of the painting, in the upper right corner, do you see that strangely balanced girl wearing tights? I think Ogi's the only one I need to explain this to, but this young lady—young girl, really—is modeled on me. That's how old I was when I met Professor Kizu and Ikuo. If I hadn't encountered Ikuo, and Professor Kizu hadn't observed it all, I wouldn't be here with you today.

"The events of that day long ago threw me off track of being a *normal* girl, so I didn't care anymore that I wasn't a quote-unquote average Japanese. Which makes me all the happier that that memorable day has become part of the painting."

Ikuo sat there in a depressed silence. Ogi naturally couldn't grasp the whole context, so Kizu explained.

"Dancer, in tights there," he said, "and Ikuo, when he was a young boy, had a bit of a collision that I witnessed. A long time after that, when I met Ikuo, I remembered what had happened, and that led to our getting in touch with Dancer. Through this we got to know Patron and finally ended up moving here."

"Ogi needs a little more explanation than that," Dancer said. "There was an awards ceremony sponsored by a newspaper, and as one of the attractions I was hired to dance while a children's choir sang. I put on my costume and was about to appear onstage when I got entangled in one of Ikuo's creations. He was one of the candidates for an award. It went right up inside my little skirt, so I was sort of hanging there in midair, hurt and embarrassed, and the boy glared at me with his puppy-dog eyes and I wondered how angry he'd be if the model was wrecked.

"The way I was standing was quite bizarre, a much harder pose to hold than a plié, but child though I was I decided to tough it out. We were backstage, but it made me wish we were out *on* stage, under the spotlights.

"This painful yet wonderful situation was resolved when Ikuo threw his model on the floor and destroyed it, but I was left with regrets. Someday, I thought, I'd like to reenact that scene in front of an audience. I think that was the reason I continued dancing even after we moved to Hokkaido.

"After I moved to Tokyo, and Patron and Guide began looking after me, I had the feeling that eccentric people like them would understand my idea. That's the reason I continued working in Patron's office. When Professor Kizu showed up with Ikuo I was certainly surprised, but happy too. I felt sure that my premonition was entirely correct—that being with Patron and Guide would open up a path for me. With Guide by his side helping out, Patron's power had made my dreams come true. . . . And now in this triptych Professor Kizu has painted the day it all began."

Dancer stopped speaking and held her left hand, as if pushing against something heavy, out toward the small painting on the right side of the triptych. Everyone's eyes were drawn upward. Only Ikuo, after looking, turned his large, sunken eyes toward the nearby window and the trembling oak leaves with the sun shining through them.

"I'd heard from the young boy what that day meant to him," Kizu said, "but this is the first time I've heard what was going on in the young girl's mind. I was just an outside observer, but it really *was* a special event, wasn't it. . . . You've been able to meet again with Ikuo, but what do you think—would we be able to prepare a stage for you to use to finally express yourself the way you'd like?"

"I think you and Ikuo have already begun to do this for me," Dancer replied. "I'm an adult now, and I don't fantasize about being in the spotlight anymore. I just want to walk, once more, toward that great light I saw as a child.

"Now that you've recovered from your illness, Professor, I know you're doing everything you can to move in that direction—the summer conference, that is, that Ikuo's working so hard for. I have a feeling that Ikuo's going to make that event into something quite incredible. Patron's anticipating this, trying to figure out exactly where he stands. I don't think Ikuo's plans for the conference are entirely set, but they'll definitely include the Fireflies, right? And won't the Quiet Women and the Technicians be in the mix as well?

"Even with the way you've built up the Fireflies, Ikuo, I don't think you'll be able to redo the Church of the New Man according to your own color scheme. Which means we have something quite extraordinary to look forward to, but what it is no one can say. So there's something I'd like to say to you, Ikuo, in front of everybody here.

"Ogi and I and the church office will do whatever we can to help you carry out your plans for the summer conference. We're in charge of taking care of all those who'll be attending, which includes staying in close touch with the Kansai headquarters, dealing with the media, negotiating with the town, consulting with the police about security—we're handling all of that. So even with the Fireflies on your side you won't succeed without our help. If Patron asks us to oppose your unilateral activities, we already have enough participants that you'll be expelled from the Church of the New Man. As long as you understand this, we'll help you."

Ikuo bowed his large head, the shadows of the setting sun etching the tension on his darkly chiseled face. Very slowly he opened his mouth, only to say a few words. "I'm not planning anything with the Fireflies."

"We don't know what Patron's planning," Dancer shot back, "so we need to stay receptive, right?"

"That's right," Ikuo said.

"But you *have* found out more than anyone else about the Technicians and the Quiet Women. And you've been giving a lot of thought about how to deal with them, correct? I only hope you're not thinking of some stupid plan such as throwing your weight behind one side, or getting the two powers to compromise their positions. That's why I'm talking about *your* plans. I'm only going to say this once. That's where we stand."

Dancer's lips were slightly open in her flushed face. Ogi was silent, but his expression showed he agreed. Kizu was impressed by Dancer's frankness, though he detected a hole in her logic.

"I understand Dancer's intention of supporting Ikuo without taking sides with either the Technicians or the Quiet Women," Kizu said. "And I'm sure Ikuo is encouraged by this. But what would you do if, say, Patron agrees with one of these sects and throws his support behind them?"

Ikuo glared at Kizu, his eyes fairly burning. "You really think that's why he proclaimed his Church of the New Man?" Ikuo asked.

Just then Dr. Koga came in, banging the door shut behind him. While this conversation had been going on, the breeze from the lake had grown chilly, so Ogi went over to close the oblong windows. The windows weren't latched, so they each made two separate sounds as they shut, making a nice airtight seal.

In his usual youthful way Dr. Koga was wearing a T-shirt, one of the shirts Mayumi made to sell at the summer conference that had a print on it of Kizu's sketch in red and yellow of the wound in Patron's side. Dr. Koga strode right over to the painting on the wall, looked up at it, and then turned to express congratulations to the artist.

"It's amazing how well you were able to complete it, even though you're still recovering. I noticed the Technicians had a satisfied look on their faces after they helped hang it up."

"Every time they set up some new equipment somewhere—be it the Hollow or the Farm—they think they're racking up points, don't they?"

Dancer's face was still flushed, but her voice was calm. "It makes me wonder whether they think they can take charge of *everything*."

"It's the democratic way, though, isn't it, for people to step to the plate and take responsibility?" Dr. Koga said, parrying her remarks. "And you have to admit it's nice they're happy about it. Professor Kizu, I'm not up on art very much, but isn't this a rather ambiguous design?"

"Before we hung it on the wall, Mrs. Shigeno and Ms. Takada came to see it," Ikuo said. "The Quiet Women seem rather cautious in giving their opinion."

"What about Patron?'

"When he went to the studio to see it before it was completed," Dancer replied, "he said that the painting is the starting point of how we're going to create the Church of the New Man."

"Before long we'll need to have you paint another triptych for this wall, Professor," Dr. Koga said. "One that looks back happily on how the Church of the New Man was built."

"You're pretty optimistic sometimes, aren't you, Doctor?" was all Kizu could say.

"I don't know, it just makes me excited seeing people get together like this and get going," Dr. Koga said. "The enthusiasm of the religious/social movement we had at the research institute is still with me, I suppose. I know this is the exact opposite, though—I guess I was brainwashed in Izu."

"What you're saying is that Guide was quite the educator," Kizu said.

"He certainly was. But don't forget Patron's role. Sometimes he looks like he's not doing anything, but don't be fooled into thinking he's passive. Even now that's true, right, Ikuo? In your own preparations for the summer conference, and in what the Technicians and the Quiet Women are doing, you're all working together for Patron's new church, aren't you?"

"For me, too, everything depends on how Patron wants things to develop," Ikuo said, sounding much older than Dr. Koga.

"I'm sure Patron has an idea of how the Technicians and Quiet Women should fit in and what roles they should play, but I'll have to admit that when I compare those two sects there're some things I just don't understand," Dr. Koga said. "What do you think about the secrecy the Quiet Women have in regards to the Technicians? I don't want to be one-sided in my criticism here, though; the Technicians have been having their own closed meetings to decide what tack they're going to take."

"Since last week Ms. Oyama has asked me not to attend the Quiet Women's prayer meetings," Ikuo said. "Including playing the piano. I find it encouraging, though, to see how excited they are about the conference. The

Quiet Women want to meet the whole lot coming from the Kansai headquarters only after they're good and ready. But isn't that a natural attitude to take? The Technicians feel the same way."

"Along with your overall preparations for the conference, I imagine that you and the Fireflies are laying out some plans of your own?" Dr. Koga asked. "Still, I'd have to say you've been dealing fairly with both the Quiet Women and the Technicians. The Technicians trust you, at least."

"The Quiet Women trust him, too—according to Ms. Tachibana," Dancer put in.

"That being the case, I hope you'll reveal all the information you get to us," Dr. Koga said. "How about it, Professor Kizu? Apart from any sects in the church, wouldn't you say older fellows like us are the church elders? Not that we'll be doing anything unilateral either. We'll clear everything with the office first, of course."

"That's what I'm hoping for," Kizu replied, and then asked, "I was wondering, when you're treating Patron does he talk about whether he sees the Fireflies as—to use your terminology—a third sect in the church?"

"I think the Somersault is still critical to Patron," Dr. Koga said. "On principle he's doesn't want to undo his previous apostasy by apostatizing again. Which means his stance toward building this new church should be quite simple, shouldn't it? This new church will be a church of the Christian God-the-Father, right? With Patron insisting he's an antichrist, there's really no outward position for him in the church.

"In building up this Church of the New Man, he's resigned to the fact that he himself is an Old Man. So for him it's actually a positive sign for the church to be run by many different sects. Competition between different sects will help it develop into a multifaceted entity. He'll be watching all this from the sidelines, but not taking a leadership role.

"Getting back to your question, Patron told me that when he and Ikuo talked, Ikuo came to an understanding of Patron's position and said he'll support Patron's relativistic way of doing things while they build up the new church. Patron told me, quite happily, that Ikuo said he wants to work so Patron can be unencumbered."

"I don't remember being so high-and-mighty in the way I phrased it," Ikuo said, "but basically that's what I said. I've wanted to speak with Patron for a long time, so I spoke directly to him. I have no doubt whatsoever that he was in face-to-face communication with something very special—God, if you will. I only met Patron for the first time after the Somersault, but I feel more and more sure of this every time I talk with him. But he ended up making a fool of this very transcendental partner he was so deeply tied to. And now he's building a new church, without having erased the Somersault, and I find that intriguing. So people could understand where's he coming from, he gave himself the title of antichrist. It's a refreshing attitude.

"You'd better believe that when Patron talks about this in his sermon at the summer conference, it is going to turn off those who followed him from before the Somersault. There'll be a lot of people coming from the outside, the media included, and I'll bet there'll be some reporters who'll mock him just as they did at the Somersault, calling it all *antichrist syncretism* or something. Still, I find a reality in him as a religious figure, a reality that includes the feeling that—before much longer—he's going to find himself in a bind all over again. He's an extraordinary person. And basically I think that the Quiet Women and Technicians sense the same thing. At the summer conference it'll be those people who really believe that the new church will produce New Men who will get the ball rolling. Isn't this exactly what Patron's hoping for?"

After Ikuo finished his deliberate explanation, Kizu felt a rush of pride. Dr. Koga turned his deep set, darkly shaded eyes, with a glint of the impish in them, toward Kizu and said, "Your painting predicts this new relationship between Patron and Ikuo. I can't think of anything better to have hanging in our chapel!"

3

After the "miracle" of his cancer disappearing, and after having completed the triptych, Kizu became aware of a harsh reality: He had a massive amount of time left to live. He still remembered how, after he was told his cancer was back, he had felt the richness of each and every moment. But what he felt now was something else again, a complete powerlessness in the face of all this newfound time. He'd felt the same thing on sleepless nights, but this was much more overwhelming. The sense of confusion hit him most in the early morning and late at night.

In the mornings, the sound of birds chirping from behind the house was enough to wake him. And at night he felt oppressed even more when he'd awake soon after going to bed. Though he knew it was a strange reaction, he found that at times like these the most appropriate attitude was to pretend he was already dead.

In the early morning all he had to do was stay in bed, half propped up, for two or three hours and wait for the first stirrings of activity in the monastery across the lake. The retired diplomat who'd designed his bed might have spent the early hours of each day in much the same way, he mused. When there were still four or five hours left till dawn, though, Kizu fell into a space where he couldn't just leave everything up to the passage of time.

He started going to bed early, as the church members in the Hollow were wont to do, except when he'd sat awake until late reading a critical work on Dante, donated to the junior high by the later Brother Gii, which he'd borrowed from Asa-san.

For times like these, when he went to bed late and woke up after sleeping only a short while, he kept the shutters open, of course, but also a space between the curtains so he might gaze out at the lake right after awakening. When he woke up he'd take the conductor's baton the former diplomat had used to practice with, spread the curtains wider apart, and spend his time gazing at the chapel and monastery on the far shore.

Ever since the night when he and Ikuo had talked for hours, Kizu had a special affection for moonlit scenery, but even on moonless nights the chapel and monastery floated up faintly in the lamplight, and he found it enjoyable to drink in this scene with the eyes of an artist.

This particular evening, Kizu woke up in the middle of the night, checking the long, narrow fluorescent clock face sunken in the headboard of the bed, itself another leftover of the late owner. He propped himself on one elbow and pushed the curtains aside to get the widest possible view of the dark scene outside.

A light was on in the chapel across the lake, and something was moving inside. Kizu peered intently through the two oblong windows with their glass slightly out of alignment. He saw shadows of a person moving up and down. Kizu remembered that stepladders had been placed there; the shadows seemed to climb up, then down, then move the ladder, then climb up again. The shadows were of two people merging together, only to break apart.

Kizu's heart beat violently. Was it two people about to hang themselves? One of them helping the other get to the proper height to do the job, then once the first person was dangling from the rope the second person follows suit? Is that what was going on? The movements seemed furtive yet bold.

Kizu had been holding his breath; and now he let out a ragged stream and pondered the situation. If he got Ms. Asuka up, she could call the office on her cell phone. But the office beside the chapel was dark, the monastery a pitch-black mass rising up in the lamplight.

Kizu adjusted the shade on his lamp so the light would shine straight down and switched it on. He got up from bed, but in the small circle of light he couldn't locate his underwear. Flustered, he pulled on his trousers right over his pajamas. If he raced over to the chapel, yelled out to wake up somebody, they'd be able to get the person down from where he was hanging by the neck. If only he was in time to revive him!

Even if there wasn't any emergency, they couldn't blame him for hurrying over to the chapel simply out of fear that his newly displayed painting was about to be stolen.

Kizu shone his flashlight before him as he cautiously walked down the hard dirt and gravel path; then, as he came to the newly paved road from the dam to the north shore, he went faster in the lamplight. He was filled with a sense of gratification that he'd regained his strength so quickly.

He took the walkway behind to the back of the bleachers, ascended a short staircase, walked through the hushed monastery courtyard, and found the door of the chapel half open, light spilling out onto the base of the big cylindrical building. If there really were thieves inside about to make off with his painting, they'd make short work of an old man showing up out of the blue like this, but this didn't deter Kizu.

Still, he trembled as he leaned forward in the open space and peered inside. Two beings were there, like big and little stuffed bears, one crouched at the top of the stepladder, the other clinging to the ladder supporting it. A moment later, Patron, who was standing on the floor, turned to face Kizu, while Morio, on top of the ladder, very carefully turned to gaze down. The two of them were dressed in identical thick yellow and dark green striped pajamas.

"It's dangerous to turn around like that when you're on a ladder, so face the wall again and climb down," Patron said, his voice echoing in the chamber, and Morio, ever faithful to instructions, did exactly that. Then Patron spoke to Kizu for the first time.

"You're up very late, aren't you? Were you worried about your painting?"

Kizu waited until his heart stopped pounding before he replied. "From where I sleep I could see people moving around in here. . . . So you were examining the painting up close, you and Morio?"

"Yes, both of us have bad eyesight, you see. We were discussing the painting as we were getting ready for bed and decided to take another look. So, Morio, what do you think?"

"Ikuo in the painting looks just like the painting in the book."

Kizu couldn't understand what Morio's slow, confident words meant. As Patron held on to the ladder and Morio climbed down, he thrust out his firm jaw and pointed to a faded old book on top of the piano. Kizu walked over and picked it up. It was Wolynski's *Das Buch vom Grossen Zorn,* translated by Haniya Yutaka: an edition put out during the war, apparently, with a crudely done cover.

"Do you see the page slipped in as a frontispiece?" Patron asked, his voice gentle again. "Long after the war they came out with an edition that includes that frontispiece, and it's important to have that frontispiece in order to understand the text. The edition you have there, though, is not bad, and ever since I first found it on my father's bookshelf it's been a favorite of mine, so I made a copy of the frontispiece in the revised edition and stuck it in."

Kizu looked at the print. The background was a sculptured group like a relief of a scene from the Bible, and in the foreground there was a dark standing figure, a man facing forward, arms stretched out. His eyes were brimming with despair and rage, his mouth like an open hole, the barely suppressed outlines of his face with its broad manly forehead and strong jaw, all of which clutched at Kizu.

"The painting is Watts's *The Prophet Jonah*. When I heard you were going to use Ikuo as your model for Jonah, I immediately remembered this drawing. Because before this, even, I'd projected Ikuo onto that drawing by Watts.

"You were released from cancer, Professor," Patron went on, "and completed the triptych. And when Morio saw it he said that the face in the painting was the same as in *The Prophet Jonah*. After dinner this evening he didn't seem to be able to get this out of his mind, and as we talked about it we decided, finally, to go over and see the painting again tonight. I think Morio's right. Ikuo's features do look exactly like that, but that's not all there is to it. Morio understands things through hearing, rather than visually, and he says he hears the same chords, the same dissonance, emanating from both paintings. You, on the other hand, Professor, are a visual person, with a painterly intuition that sees down to the core of Ikuo's being. That's where you and Watts have something in common.

"Actually, I've wanted for some time to talk with you about this. And here you are in front of us in the middle of the night. It's fitting, don't you think, to say I summoned you here? If so, Professor, then I think your—"

As if noticing that he wasn't making much sense, Patron stopped speaking. Kizu thought, *That's right! It* is *right to think of him as the one who made my cancer disappear!* Patron made Morio sit down on the barber chair set back near the light on the wall, and stroked back the sweaty strands of hair clinging to his forehead. Kizu found the scene of the three of them—two in matching yellow and green pajamas, one sunk back, face up in a barber chair, joined by Kizu himself in a pink and gray striped pajama top—like clowns in some old woodblock print. *And,* he thought, *my painting of Jonah is definitely like that frontispiece of the prophet Jonah.*

Before speaking, Patron waited for Kizu, who was poring over the book, to look up.

"When Ikuo first came to see me, just before I got to know you, Professor, I thought that the Jonah combined in Wolynski's words and Watts's drawing had come to life right before my eyes. When he started talking about the book of Jonah I was less surprised than struck by the feeling that it was meant to be. . . . Ikuo's question was quite simple: Was it right to repudiate God's decision to destroy a city and his order to carry that out? He asked this as if he were taking Jonah's place. As the Fireflies say, it was *Jonah-like*.

"When Guide was still alive I couldn't understand why he didn't handle this troublesome young man himself. But what Guide did was coax Ikuo into questioning me. And you wrote the cover letter for his petition to me, didn't you, Professor? I'm not sure I gave him a satisfactory reply, but at least he's still with me, trying to get his questions ultimately answered. Didn't you paint this picture sensing all this from the sidelines?"

This question—though not entirely unexpected—left Kizu at a loss for words. Patron didn't pursue the point further. The topic was deep, but his manner was serene.

"At the summer conference where we launch our new church, Ikuo isn't the only one who'll press me for an answer," Patron said. "The Technicians, who wanted to reverse the Somersault so much they ended up torturing Guide to death, are now helping me, the one who played dumb about the whole Somersault. I have to steel myself to the fact that they're now going to turn the questions they had for Guide on *me*. And of course, there are the even more potentially troublesome Quiet Women ready and waiting in the wings."

Patron said all this in a burst of speech; then he stopped and, pondering something, ran his fingers through Morio's hair.

"Ah, Professor—could you pass me that book? I marked some lines in it. Jonah's finally come to Nineveh to act as a frightening prophet. Jonah curses them in the name of God, saying they will all be destroyed, so it wouldn't be surprising if they tore him limb from limb. But what about Jonah, who dared do something like that?

"However, here a great disillusionment lay waiting for him. When he saw the people of Nineveh repent, and God forgive them, he couldn't grasp the complex elusive nature of the heavenly dialectic, the workings of divine wisdom, so filled with a mysterious dissension, and the infinite, all-encompassing divine nature—so Jonah was spurred on to resistance and anger.

"And thus he spoke to God this way.

"'Now, O Lord, take away my life, for it is better for me to die than to live.'"

"Aren't Ikuo and the Technicians and Quiet Women pressing me hard with that very same cry?

"There's another thing I'd like to say, taking off from Wolynski's theme, about Dostoyevsky. I find it fascinating that Ikuo is driven by these Jonah-like thoughts and takes so much time looking after the Fireflies. What I recall is a passage written by Wolynski's translator, Haniya, about Aloysha's love for the boys, and the boys' 'Hurrah!' in response to this. I copied this down in the margins of this book.

"Not just Aloysha, who thirteen years hence is supposed to be crucified for being an assassin of the Tsar, but the lustful Dimitri, who carries the burden of a crime he didn't commit, as well as the Grand Inquisitor Ivan, who cries out in his thirst for life—all of them make a complete change from their positions and reach the sublime at the chorus of shouts from the boys of 'Long live Karamazov!'

"Into what terrible state will our country's people have to descend in order to spark a worldwide repentance?" Patron said. "How far will Jonah have to step forward? . . . Oh no—this won't do at all. I've gotten so excited, Morio's having one of his attacks! Professor, let's call it a night. You can borrow the book if you'd like."

Patron offered the book, then put his hand on the footrest of the barber chair and turned it around. He knelt down on the floor in front of Morio, who with a sweaty, stern look on his face lay slumped over, limp in the chair. Sweat trickled down from Patron's pale neck to his back, and though he faced away from Kizu, unmoving, Kizu knew he was being urged to leave.

4

As Kizu cut across the courtyard's flagstone path, he saw a slim woman standing erect under the lamplight beyond the reviewing stands. A strange sight to see, considering the hour. Taking care not to startle her or take her unawares, Kizu deliberately rattled the loose iron railing on the stairs as he descended, and as he did so he realized that the woman was Ms. Asuka, who must have awoken at the sound he made going out and come to look for him.

Actually, when Ms. Asuka came out from behind the reviewing stands to where the lamplight reached and turned toward him, though she didn't show a bewildered smile, her body language showed she was, indeed, flustered, and she reluctantly raised a hand in greeting.

"Well, imagine a young woman standing all alone like this in the middle of the night, beside a mountain lake," Kizu said, answering her gesture. "Nobody just saunters up here—aren't you afraid of wild animals?"

"Wolves are extinct here, and otters don't attack people," Ms. Asuka replied quietly, her voice mixed in with the hearty sound of cicadas. "I was worried about you."

"I saw a light in the chapel and went to investigate. Patron was there and we talked for a while. Ah . . . I see. You were imagining a depressed old man jumping in the lake? But I'm a lucky old man, whose terminal cancer has disappeared!"

"These past few days, though," Ms. Asuka said, "this lucky old man has been a bit gloomy."

Something black moved at Ms. Asuka's feet. Looking carefully they saw three or four small frogs at the base of the streetlamp.

"At any rate it doesn't look like I'll be drowning myself anytime soon," Kizu said. "Once you understood this you turned your attention to observing these frogs, didn't you? You're quite the visual artist."

"Once I came down, the thought of climbing up into that shadowy grove of trees gave me the creeps. I heard voices from the chapel so I decided to wait."

The frogs sat there silently, heads up, the pulse in their necks visible. Bugs were descending toward them in black streaks or flashes of iridescence. One frog closest to the bugs suddenly moved, gulping down a bug from the air. Looking up at the streetlight one could see a clump of bugs like a single dark spot. Only a few of them were swooping down toward the frogs, perhaps finding the strength to fly again once they descended to the top of the light, or maybe being wafted away on a breeze rising from the lake.

Out of the group of frogs, all neatly maintaining their positions, one frog held a small gold bug that had fallen and lay upside down on the dam and, suddenly agitated, clawed at its throat with his front legs; one of the other frogs turned to face the spit out bug, but before it could anything about it the bug spread its wings and inscribed an arc into the dark night air.

Ms. Asuka, a smile clearly showing on her long face now, started to lead the way.

"What did you talk about for so long?" she asked, shining a flashlight to light the way for Kizu.

"We talked about how the Jonah in the triptych looks like the Jonah drawn by an artist named Watts. Patron showed me the book and I think he's right. It was Morio who originally pointed it out."

"I'd like to hear more and don't plan to go to bed right away," Ms. Asuka said, "so how about joining me for a drink?" And by the time they arrived at the home on the north shore, they'd agreed to do so.

They pulled two chairs over to one end of the study desk in the bedroom, and Ms. Asuka brought out two cans of cold beer and two double shot glasses of whiskey. They each mixed the beer and the whiskey in whatever proportion suited them.

Ms. Asuka spread open the book Kizu had borrowed from Patron and, sipping her drink with her thin lips, gazed at the copy of the inserted frontispiece. She read a little of the text, her smile replaced by a serious, almost sullen look.

Then she raised her face. "My, did the prophet Jonah really end up doing all these things? It's different from the book of Jonah that Ikuo doesn't like, the one that ends with Jonah accepting the Lord's harmonious sermonizing."

She passed the book over to Kizu, who read aloud a part that Patron had underlined.

"The theologian Gregorius recognized one more special characteristic of Jonah, saying that 'Jonah foresaw the fall of Israel and sensed that the blessings of the prophets would pass to the heretics. He withdrew from evangelizing, questioned the state of his church, discarding the ancient high place and position of the tower of rapture, and threw himself into the sea of grief.'"

"No matter which Jonah is the real one, persons named Jonah are born to suffer," Ms. Asuka said, holding the copy of the frontispiece between her slim fingers. "This drawing really shows that kind of Jonah. Almost *too* clearly, in fact. . . . The part about the heretics is pretty important too, don't you think?"

Kizu couldn't grasp the point of her question.

Even before the medical researcher at the institute in the United States had pointed out the possibility that he had cancer, Kizu had felt something not quite right inside him and wasn't able to take strong drink anymore. Now, in the feeling of relief after being liberated from the disease, he was drinking whisky cut with beer, but he knew he couldn't hold his liquor like he once could. Ms. Asuka's face, though, took on a nice rosy color, an uncharacteristically youthful clinging gaze in her eyes as she forcefully made her point.

"Ever since Patron quoted from the letter to the Ephesians, everyone's started studying it. While you were in the hospital, Mrs. Shigeno's study group was particularly popular. I'm not a Christian, but even I joined in. According to what I heard there, what's important about this particular letter, one of the epistles attributed to Paul, is that it's a letter aimed at proselytizing the Gentiles—heretics, in Jewish eyes. The New Men at this time were the ones who were able to overcome the discord between Gentiles and Jews. Jonah ran counter to this trend.

"Deep down, Ikuo may very well not agree with the direction this Church of the New Man is taking. Though as the twentieth century draws to a close, the Japanese are still all heretics."

"If the prophet Jonah were alive today," Kizu said, "he'd say the whole planet's run by heretics. With groups of heretics attacking each other, skirmishing over who's more legitimate. And even among the heretics in this little out-of-the-way mountain area we find groups like the Technicians, the Quiet Women, and Ikuo and the Fireflies trying to establish themselves with Patron."

"The summer conference promises to be stormy, doesn't it?" Ms. Asuka said, pouring the last of her whiskey into her glass of beer. "Also while you were in the hospital, Professor, I heard a lecture by Asa-san about this person called the Former Gii and how he was stymied at every step. Which is why when I saw you go down to the lake tonight I had some troubled notions about what might happen."

"I heard the same thing: that Asa-san pulled up Brother Gii's body from the surface of the lake the day after a storm."

"I wouldn't have the strength to do something like that," Ms. Asuka said pensively, "but at least I'd have wanted to video it. In the morning, as long as there was enough light."

Kizu poured the remaining whiskey into his beer. "The corpse, you mean? It *does* seem like it's true what they say about the *power of the land* stimulating the creativity of newcomers!"

The two of them were silent, drinking their whiskey-darkened beer, draining their glasses in time with each other. The area around Ms. Asuka's eyes grew faintly pink, something Kizu found erotic.

"I apologize for going on about my own personal fantasy," she said.

"That's all right. I'd have to say I have even more intense fantasies than that," Kizu said, feeling his face flushed with drink. "Once I found that cancer was no longer controlling my destiny, it made me feel uneasy, as if the bottom had dropped out of my life. If Patron hadn't been in the chapel and I'd made my way back here—and with the Fireflies looking after the dam the water's filled it all the way to the edge, well . . ."

"Sometimes the water in the Hollow turns black, which Asa-san says is an evil omen. And the water does seem darker than when I arrived." Saying this, Ms. Asuka gave her usual close-lipped smile, shook her head, gathered up the glasses on the tray, and withdrew.

A lot of lessons learned today, Kizu mused. All he had to do was remove his trousers. Back in his pajamas, he laid his drunken body down to rest.

30: Memories of Guide

1

It was decided to hold the summer conference the first week of August, with registration beginning on Friday morning and the conference running through Sunday at the Hollow. A preliminary meeting was scheduled for July 10 at the lodge run by Maki Town to explain the plans for the conference to the local authorities and some of the young leaders of the area, particularly those involved in the river preservation movement. Newspaper and TV reporters from Matsuyama were also slated to attend.

On the day of the meeting Ogi remained behind in the office, though he and Dancer were the ones in charge of arranging the meeting. New members of the Fireflies, who had helped out the day Kizu was released from the hospital, were formed into a security squad, which was also put in charge of transportation to the Old Town. It took less than thirty minutes to drive from the Hollow to the lodge in the hills surrounding the basin where Maki Town lay. Still, with Patron participating, the security squad left nothing to chance and came up with a detailed plan.

The car with Patron and Dancer was sandwiched in between two others, this followed by a minivan carrying Ms. Tachibana and Morio, Ms. Asuka, Dr. Koga, Mrs. Shigeno, and Mr. Hanawa (who was in charge of production at the Farm) and, bringing up the rear, Kizu in a car loaded with security squad members and with Gii in the front passenger seat.

Maki Town had already had a hotel at the time a national soccer tournament was held there but built this lodge in addition; the word was that after that one tournament the place had never again been full. Now, though, all two hundred and fifty rooms were booked solid for the three-day conference.

The head of the Kansai headquarters of the church, Mr. Soda, had been in charge of construction of the lodge and had close connections with the town leaders.

A banquet hall, spacious enough for a wedding reception, was set aside for the meeting. In front of the chairs lined up on the main floor was a low raised platform for the church members to sit on. The media were assigned seats behind the town authorities and other interested parties.

The mayor made a few opening remarks, and then Dr. Koga, seated on the dais between Patron and Dancer, took the microphone.

"Ladies and gentlemen, we are the Church of the New Man, the name given to the church by the leader we call Patron. This summer conference has given us the opportunity to meet with the town authorities and future local leaders. We are grateful to you, Mr. Mayor, and all of you, for taking time out of your busy schedules to join us today; we're also joined today by members of the media.

"We'd like to proceed with a question-and-answer format. However, please be advised that Patron will not be directly answering any questions. In his stead, each of us will field questions based on our own area of expertise. Now I'd like to turn things over to the young woman called Dancer, her professional name within the church, who works most closely with Patron."

Dr. Koga started to pass the microphone to her in front of Patron, but she leaned back to take it from behind, and the audience burst out laughing. Kizu understood what a popular local figure Dr. Koga was through his work at the clinic in town.

Dancer's hair had been dyed by Mrs. Tagawa with brown mixed in with the natural black, and she had on an open-collared floral-print blouse.

The comic role Dr. Koga had just played in this mix-up, and Dancer's calm reaction, underscored all the more the dignified way in which she prepared to speak.

"There is a reason Patron has on sunglasses," she began. "Those of you in the media taking pictures, please refrain from using a flash.

"The upcoming summer conference will be the first national meeting of the Church of the New Man, as well as an opportunity for the local community to get to know us, so Patron is preparing a sermon for the occasion. The concentration required for this is the same needed for the trances that used to be at the core of his religious activities and is one of the ascetic practices he's engaged in at present.

"Those of us in the inner circle of the church are eagerly anticipating Patron's sermon, which will be the climax of the conference. We have the deepest gratitude and respect for Patron for undergoing the emotional and physical strain involved in concentrating as deeply as he is now. This intense concentration every day makes his eyes overly sensitive to light, thus the dark glasses. Despite this sensitivity, Patron has been kind enough to join us here today. He's doing this because there are two points he'd like to make clear to you. They are as follows:

"Item one is that our church is not being threatened by any opposing groups. I'm sure all of you have read this in the newspapers and elsewhere, but a combative stance by a radical faction over certain issues led to the sacrifice of a person very dear to us, Guide; these issues, however, have been partly resolved.

"The so-called former radical faction, people who were at the Izu Research Institute, are here now, devoting themselves to building our new church. Dr. Koga is one of these people, which should give you an idea of the sort of group we're talking about. So rest assured there's no danger of any attack by an opposing group that will throw the summer conference into confusion. Nevertheless, we do want to take precautions regarding security. In this regard we're receiving help from a local organization called the Fireflies.

"Item two is that we do not intend to use the summer conference as the opportunity to proselytize or expand our church. The members who attend from all over Japan will not be remaining here after the conference.

"Now I'd like to turn things over to Dr. Koga, who will handle the question-and-answer session."

"I've been working with the church's farm production and Maki Town special products to come up with a plan to sell our goods in Matsuyama and the Kansai region," said the first person to stand up and ask a question, a man Kizu had seen visiting the church. He owned a sake brewery and had participated in the movement of the Fireflies to restore the natural environment along the banks of the Kame and Maki rivers. "I've talked to quite a few people in the church, and I get the feeling that I can work with them. It felt like a regular church, with the Fireflies that were just mentioned often attending. Some parents were concerned about this and came to discuss it with me, so I checked things out. The conclusion I reached was that the Fireflies and the church are two independent groups that have an amicable relationship. My opinion of the Fireflies went way up, in fact, and we're actually considering some joint projects.

"What I'm hearing now, though, is that the church is solidifying itself around its existing core. Doesn't this mean that it will exclude outsiders? And if that's true, won't this cause difficulties between the Farm and all of us? Instead of being cut off from their present loose connection with the church, won't some of the Firefies think it'd be better for them to join an increasingly exclusive church? That's what worries us."

The whole time she listened to the question, Dancer fixed her eyes on Patron. To Kizu, it didn't appear that Patron was sending out any instructions. Dancer turned to face the questioner and, carefully choosing her words, replied.

"Instead of expanding the church," she said, "what we'd like to do is firm up our base, but we certainly don't intend to get tied down by any kind of secretive way of doing things. In order that people can see this, we're prepared to open our church conference to anyone.

"We have great hopes for your joint work with the Farm. You've already taken a step in that direction, haven't you? It's true that the Fireflies and some of our members have a good relationship, and we're thankful for that. The Fireflies don't live in any church residences with us, though. They live at home, where they all have plenty of opportunity to speak freely with members of their own families. Not one of the Fireflies has approached us about joining the church."

One of the participants from the town, a lively, ruddy-cheeked young woman who edited the town's bulletin, *Leaves from Maki,* had a question.

"In the program of events we received, the composer of the music for the conference is listed as a Mr. Morio Tachibana, is that right? I understand he's mentally challenged, so who would be the arranger?"

"Since the composer is right here, why don't we have him answer that one directly?" Dr. Koga said, handing the microphone over to Ms. Tachibana.

"Well, the arranger . . ." Morio muttered, the undulations in his gum line behind stiffened cheeks looking curiously small.

The young woman inclined her flushed face, pondering how best to continue this conversation with a mentally challenged person.

"No one has added anything to my brother's music, nor does he allow anything to be taken out," Ms. Tachibana said, point-blank.

2

Showing his irritation at the young woman editor's attitude, one of the leaders of the TV crew that Kizu had encountered when he left the hospital broke in. "I'd like to ask about some of the church's ideas. Patron created a church based on the notion that we must prepare for the end time. At the Somersault he denied this doctrine and declared it all a joke. Now that he's creating a new church, does he still view the end of the world as a joke?"

They had already decided who would field which questions, so Dancer stood up and changed seats with Mrs. Shigeno. With a composed, serene air, Mrs. Shigeno picked up the microphone.

"Patron's call for repentance in the face of the coming end of the world remains unchanged from before the Somersault," she replied. "If this wasn't so, how could he possibly build this new church? Correct me if I'm wrong, but I think that Patron does not believe now that the end of the world is coming on one particular day in one particular month in a set year in the twenty-first century.

"Before the Somersault, Patron had divined that the day of wrath was to come on a fixed date, not unlike Nostradamus. And with this in mind he felt the need to call everyone to immediate repentance. Within the church some people appeared, saying that we should draw the day of wrath to us; we should work to bring it on. With the Somersault, though, Patron made it clear how erroneous this way of thinking was.

"Still, the group in the church that I belong to, the Quiet Women, doesn't discuss things in terms of the world gradually collapsing to the point of no return. The end of the world *will* take place on a single day sometime. As we pray for this day, that day will certainly become known to us. And that prayer itself is an act of repentance. We feel that the Church of the New Man must become a place where that sort of repentance can take place."

"What is Patron doing to prepare for the end of the world?" the reporter asked. "And how do you think about this as you pray?"

"Patron may be trying not to *lessen* the pain of human beings on the day of wrath but to *increase* it," Mrs. Shigeno said. "I think he'll be active that day, gaining power from the source of that wrathful ether filling the air. Patron has declared that he is not the savior, something that must be painful in the extreme to say while he still has the Sacred Wound in his body. It was through the hell he fell into after the Somersault that he was able to establish this faith. Even now he is concentrating very hard on being the mediator for everyone as we approach the end of the world. And he's created the Church of the New Man as the venue where this takes place.

"The mistake that the radical faction committed, the ones who drove Patron to committing the Somersault, lay in their attempt to cause the end of the world to happen sooner, through their own efforts. But that's not something human beings can or should do. The world itself will create its end. God, who *is* the whole world, will take care of this, rest assured. We learned this from Patron's sermon, when we were able meet him again after the Somersault. Does this mean there's nothing we can do for the sake of the end of the world? Of course not. We ourselves are a part of the world, and what is in our hearts is also part of God's design. And through this we can actively participate in the end of the world. That is true repentance.

"After Patron's Somersault, we Quiet Women were struggling to find a way in which we could participate. We've been able to meet up with Patron again and live under his guidance, which has borne fruit in this new Church of the New Man. We feel blessed to be included in this official launch of the new church at the upcoming summer conference."

Mrs. Shigeno gave a charming little gesture, and a burst of applause followed. The applause came from the floor, from a group of interested local residents, but several of the church members sitting across from them also joined in, including Kizu. Dr. Koga, who didn't join in the applause, leaned over to Kizu and said in a low voice, "Let's not forget that the Quiet Women were also one of the sects that drove Patron to do the Somersault."

Dr. Koga then turned to face the audience and said, more loudly, "Our meeting here to discuss the upcoming summer conference of the Church of the New Man is now concluded." He ignored a few raised hands from the reporters. "Details of the program for the conference are as stated in the handout.

"Next on our schedule is a visit to the basement hot-springs pool, which had been closed and is now reopened for the use of our guests. It's just been cleaned, and we've been invited to try it out today. Getting a little carried away, perhaps, we'd like you to see for yourselves Professor Kizu's miraculous recovery that I know you're all interested in. As a special favor to the TV crews, we've arranged to have Professor Kizu swim in the pool.

"One other point. During the conference, the triptych that Professor Kizu painted of Patron's Sacred Wound will be on public view in the chapel, and we encourage you to visit it."

Kizu preceded the participants, who had begun to get up, down to the basement. The pumped-up feeling he got he took as another sign of his recovery. As he was changing into his swimming suit, Ms. Tachibana came in, dressed like a woman swim-team member of a generation ago. She was guiding Morio. Unusually for her, she was telling him to get a move on. As Kizu scrutinized the scars from his two operations in the mirror, Ms. Tachibana said encouragingly, "If you keep a towel wrapped around your shoulders until you get in the pool, you'll have nothing to worry about. You're not planning on doing the backstroke, are you?"

As he came out of the changing room and walked across the concrete floor where the shower nozzles were lined up on one side, Kizu recalled how the first thing he did when he came to stay in Japan was join an athletic club, and how it was at the drying room of the club that he had run across Ikuo again. So much had begun right there—and brought him *here,* to this point.

The pool was in the basement, but since the lodge was on a slope the five lanes of the pool looked out a window to a stand of trees, and the cloudy sky still let in a lot of sunshine. Dr. Koga was already at poolside, having passed through the shower and the small pool one rinsed off in first; he carried a portable blood pressure monitor with him. Kizu wiped his dripping chest with his bath towel and Dr. Koga measured his blood pressure and heart rate. A long narrow row of seats along the mezzanine was filled with reporters and curious onlookers.

After Dr. Koga reported that all the readouts were within normal range, Kizu did a few warm-up exercises and got in the pool. The water was warmer than he was used to, either in the on-campus pool in America he'd used for many years, or the pool in the Nakano athletic club. He adjusted his goggles and started doing the crawl, and though at the first turn he stopped momentarily, resting his hand on the edge before turning, his body took it all in stride and at the end of the next lap he changed to a quick flip turn.

Kizu swam up and down in his lane. With a twinge of nostalgia he recalled how the term *flip turn* was actually an Americanism, something in keeping with the American character, he mused, while in French the same move was called *saut périlleux*—in other words, a somersault. Kizu was taking Patron's place, performing one somersault after another to entertain the crowd, but he didn't mind.

On his way back, as he turned to breathe he caught sight of the crowd of onlookers and Dr. Koga talking with the leader of the TV crew, who was leaning forward from the railing. He looked around for a moment at Kizu, then looked up again and shook his head decisively. The TV crew reacted casually to that and started to pack up to leave, though the rest of the crowd, including the young editor of the local bulletin, remained behind.

Beside the pool Ms. Tachibana was still running Morio, palely chubby like a sweet rice cake, through some warm-up exercises. Kizu could tell that Ms. Tachibana had been on the swim team in both junior and senior high school, but actually what she ended up doing, after leisurely getting Morio in the water up to his shoulders and instructing him to walk up and down the lane, was begin swimming the breaststroke herself in the nearer lane, her form and powerful strokes impressive.

Kizu stood up at the end of his lane and watched her swim. Dr. Koga was struck by her swimming too. After four or five laps, without missing a beat, Ms. Tachibana changed over to Morio's lane. She skillfully had Morio float up, securing his body with a thin but muscular arm held around his chest up to his shoulders. Paddling with one hand and doing a scissors kick, Ms. Tachibana carried Morio over to the side. As if they were watching the masterly practice rescue of a drowning man, a stir of admiration rose from the mezzanine.

3

When August rolled around, the number of people coming to visit the Hollow suddenly shot way up and Kizu hesitated to leave his house. Mostly men and women in their late thirties, these newcomers would appear at the dam like a sudden summer rain, clamber up the flagstone pathway, and disappear into the monastery courtyard. Then they would walk back down to the east shore down the tunnel formed by the overhanging young leaves of the cherry trees at the eastern edge of the chapel, and along the corridor that had been made there. Some of them would look up at the summer sun reflected off the plastic globular canopy that had been attached to one side of the chapel's dome, some would gaze off toward the giant cypress in the island on the lake, and others would slowly make their way closer to the studio window where Kizu stood observing them.

Some of the visitors ate a light lunch looking down on the nearby tents set up in the square below the dam. Even from a distance you could make out their Fruit of the Rain Tree lunch boxes and plastic bottles of Rain Tree Water, bottled from the spring behind the chapel—evidence that the visitors had gone to the Farm first and bought lunches and water bottles at the little store run by Satchan's two adopted daughters.

According to what Ms. Asuka had heard, the majority of these visitors were believers from the Kansai headquarters. They all had their own jobs but were taking a week's vacation in order to visit this holy place and enjoy breathing the same air as Patron. Some of them had volunteered to work at the Farm in exchange for room and board. Others had booked rooms well in advance at the lodge where Kizu had put on his swimming demonstration, while others, unbeknownst to Kizu, who had any number of times walked along the path below it, were using the Mansion that now belonged to Mr. Soda of the Kansai headquarters. Through his long-term relationship with those in the Hollow as the builder of the chapel, Mr. Soda had purchased the Mansion, which had been slated for demolition, and rebuilt it so that it was once more livable.

Kizu had been in charge of any number of symposiums at his research institute and knew firsthand the troubles involved, so he had a vague anxiety about the summer conference. But Ms. Asuka, who started to help out at the office after the middle of July, reported to him that the participants were extremely cooperative and the outlook for the conference was bright.

The believers who came early to the Hollow didn't make many demands on the church; indeed, they volunteered to help out, and at the dining hall they were allowed to use, they renewed old friendships—admittedly not very deep ones—with people they knew in the Quiet Women and were happy when they spotted faces they recognized among the Technicians.

According to Ms. Asuka, the office's efforts in organizing the conference were paying off. The grounds of the elementary and junior high schools in the Old Town were being used as parking lots from Friday to Monday. The Fireflies, organized as a security squad, were busy too, with preparations for their Spirit Festival, and didn't have the energy left over to take charge of the parking lot, so the task fell to some older youths who were continuing the local Village Association group; they too were unpaid volunteers.

The Kansai headquarters leader, Mr. Soda, arrived in the Hollow at the end of July. He invited Dr. Koga, Ms. Asuka, and Kizu for dinner at the Mansion, where he was staying during the conference. On the day of the dinner there were none of the city folk around the dam or on the flagstone path, and in the midst of the loud buzz of cicadas and the cries of wild birds, Dr. Koga and Asa-san appeared in the parking lot from the road leading to the prefectural highway. Rather than turn to wave to Kizu in his studio window, they looked out at the giant cypress tree, its leaves stirring with the faint breeze blowing in from the woods around the lake.

When Kizu saw the well-bred city boy Dr. Koga with a linen sports coat on, he put on a lightweight jacket himself. As a present for Mr. Soda, he took a watercolor he'd done of the view of the chapel and monastery from the north shore, put it in a frame, and left the house.

When Kizu got down to the dam, Dr. Koga and Asa-san—the latter all dressed up in a summer-weight wool skirt and navy blue blouse—were talking with one of the Technicians, who was setting up the microphones in the reviewing stands. Several of the Fireflies were sitting on the dam itself, undoing a huge coil of cable and threading it through plastic tubing to keep it waterproof. Apparently they were going to run an electric line underwater out to the island with the huge cypress.

Kizu and the others walked down to the tents, crossed over the surging waterway, and took a flagstone path that ran all around from the traditional gate in the long wall to the main house. When they arrived at the main gate, shaded by the lush overhanging leaves of the camellias, a smaller side door in a corner of the main gate was open to the inside.

With Asa-san leading the way, they ducked through the side door. On the broad concrete floor was something they'd heard about from Asa-san on the way over, a gold-and-copper alloy pipe—a *fuigo,* as they called it—to carry smoke from the sunken hearth that now was faintly glowing. Mr. Soda was standing on the wooden floor below that and led the three of them over to the natural stone flooring, where they removed their shoes. With his pinstripe dress shirt and gray vest, all Mr. Soda needed was a coat and jacket and he'd be ready for a business meeting, though his collar was casually open.

"Hey, looks like your blood pressure's not acting up," Dr. Koga said, as if speaking to a good buddy. "So you prefer staying in the annex more than the main building? I guess this was originally a place for people to live in, wasn't it. You have a large kitchen, too. This *fuigo* pipe running out of the oven is nice.

"It's like a pipe in a pipe organ, don't you think? It was specially ordered, and since Former Gii named it, I've respected his wishes," Mr. Soda responded, turning to greet Kizu and Asa-san. "I'm glad you could come. Koga and I were in the same class for our first two years of college. The guys who were going on to medical school were all kind of snobbish and someone like me in engineering found it hard to get along with most of them, but Koga was okay."

On the left-hand side, in the back of the concrete floor, set off at a gentle right angle, was a sink and a stove. A large man was working there, bathed in the reddish light coming in from the west window, but Mr. Soda didn't introduce him, instead leading his guests to the side around the sunken hearth.

Kizu passed the watercolor painting to Mr. Soda, who turned his stylishly crew-cut head and taut face toward it with a word of thanks. He didn't give any opinion about the painting, though, which Kizu found totally refreshing.

Mr. Soda told about how as a young man he and Dr. Koga were on the same rugby team at the Komaba campus of Tokyo University and how Koga was fast enough to break through his opponents easily but wasn't brave enough to attempt a goal and would just keep running, all bent over.

"The first one to make a touchdown in the church, though, was Koga, who was the one who invited me to join," Soda went on. "He had those troubles with his mother, and went through a terrible time until his aunt took him to see Patron."

A complex expression showed on Dr. Koga's face, but he said nothing.

They could hear the sound of the cicadas that came out at twilight, and a twilight bird call Kizu was familiar with: a gray thrush, perhaps. The naked beams of the building loomed darkly above them; beyond the packed dirt floor of the proportionally large kitchen was a long window from which one could doubtless see the waterway they'd crossed on their way here. The wind blew in through the shutters. The air was moving enough to raise a sound from the gold-copper alloy *fuigo*.

The man who'd been working in the kitchen preparing dinner brought over a series of small plates on a shallow wooden box, something Kizu knew was called in the local dialect a *morobuta*. The man, past middle age, wearing a white collared shirt and cotton khaki trousers, turned out to be the former principal of the junior high school who'd done the trimming around Kizu's house. Asa-san hurriedly brought over the lacquer trays stacked up in back and lined up on them the dishes that her husband passed her.

Mr. Soda stood up and went over to the kitchen to a bucket of water and lifted up one of two bottles of sake inside it, provided by the activist sake producer whom Kizu and the others knew. The four-*go* bottle appeared to have been frozen and then thawed out, and the label had come off, the only bit of decoration the wire cap that held down the pressure built up by the fermentation.

"Tonight we have steamed chicken with a sesame sauce, chilled tofu with grilled eggplant, which we eat here with soy sauce, and then chopped bonito," the former junior high principal said, sounding as if he was someone who liked to talk a lot but was purposely keeping his words to a minimum. "I'll be preparing some salt-grilled fresh-water trout as well, and for the final dish a specialty of this region, grilled sea bass in chilled miso paste. You eat this over rice, so I brought over mortars along with the rice."

"He's been studying cooking shows on TV to prepare for tonight," Asa-san explained as she laid several small dishes of condiments beside each of the trays.

"Please have as many helpings of rice as you'd like," her husband said. "The sake tastes really good when it's like sherbet so we kept it in the freezer, but the mouth of the bottle sometimes gets stopped up—that's why I've laid three chopsticks at each place setting, so you can use one to unstop the bottle if need be."

They watched his broad back as the former junior high principal went back to retrieve the trout.

"My husband has some curious ideas," Asa-san said. "Believe me, we don't ordinarily put three chopsticks down for each person."

4

What Kizu found interesting was that Mr. Soda and Dr. Koga, seated respectively on the north and east side of the sunken hearth, said a silent prayer before eating. Since he'd come here and had meals with church members, Kizu had never noticed this custom before. Perhaps the Kansai headquarters was actively preserving the way things were done in the church before the Somersault.

Next Mr. Soda poured a good amount of sake, now melted into something less viscous than sherbet, into each of their matching cups, cups used for dipping sauce for *soba* noodles, a set he'd purchased as part of what came with the Mansion. After they'd downed this he filled each cup again, and everyone understood that was all they were going to get.

Asa-san took away the two sake bottles and went over to her husband, seated in the western corner of the room eating the same meal as the others, and refilled the cup he was just draining. She didn't, however, come back with any new bottles.

"This is a lot different from the usual way people drink in the country-side in Japan, isn't it—drinking themselves into a stupor," Kizu said, impressed.

"At the time he started the Base Movement in the Mansion, Former Brother Gii transformed the way drinking bouts are held among the young people," Asa-san explained. "Tribes in Africa do the same, he told them, drinking till they pass out, but things aren't so tough here that you need to do that." Her eyes, with their dense layer of sunburned wrinkles, turned red as she said this.

"The young local fellows I used to help in the construction of the chapel and monastery followed Brother Gii's custom," Soda put in, "and I'm trying to emulate that."

The former junior high principal brought over the rice, still in the rice cooker, and Kizu was amazed by the main dish in a large mortar. Asa-san scooped rice into each bowl, added some thick pieces of grilled sea bass and crumbled tofu, finally pouring over it the chilled miso paste the former principal had made, then passed a bowl to each of them, noting that they should add as much of the thinly sliced condiments—scallions, green shiso leaves, ginger buds—as they wanted. The former principal took his own large bowl back to his spot, and when Dr. Koga said in admiration, "This is fantastic!" he smiled happily and motioned to him to help himself to another serving.

Mr. Soda was the first to finish, and, as if planned ahead of time, he launched into a long-winded but organized monologue about Guide. Kizu was surprised by his frankness.

"I became a member of the church a little while after Dr. Koga, by which time the church was pretty well established. For me, though, the church was more Guide's than Patron's. Patron went into his trances, was able to open a corridor to the *other side,* and then related the visions he had there. This was the religious foundation we all relied on. As we stood on this foundation, though, it was Guide who urged us actually to go out and *do* something. Without Guide the church's activities never would have gotten off the ground. I'm not saying there could have been a coup d'état with Guide as the chief instigator, because Guide really needed Patron. Without the two of them in partnership, neither Patron nor Guide alone would have been able to do a thing.

"So both of them were our leaders, though in actual fact we looked to Guide. One time, when Patron wasn't there, we all gathered around Guide and peppered him with questions. We were very earnest about this. 'Why do you put Patron ahead of you when it comes to running the church?' we asked. 'What he says may be profound, but it's equally vague, isn't it? We need someone like you who has clear-headed ideas leading us if we're actually going to *do* something. To borrow terminology from the Japanese Constitution about the Emperor, isn't Patron better as a *symbol* of the church, a symbol of unity for the believers?'

"Guide spoke quite openly to us then, and I thought it must be true. 'I had strong feelings toward my father who disappeared,' Guide said, 'so ever since I was a child I wanted to participate in a religious organization. I was kicked out of a lot of churches, though, and with no clue as to how to proceed I reached adulthood, and when I was teaching in night school I happened to run across Patron. His habit of falling into these trances convinced me he was a unique fellow. I knew he was the *one,* and that's how it all started.

"'Patron had nothing to do with ordinary people and eked out a living as a clairvoyant, but when I started living with him,' Guide said, 'his trances were on a different level from what I'd been led to believe. He'd come back from the *other side* more dead than alive and would mumble something incomprehensible. As soon as I started being his listener—not just a listener but his adviser—I started getting actively involved. I'd gather together all his rambling statements, contextualize them, and give them back to him, and this formed the basis for some of the mystical things he then said. Gradually a clear narrative developed out of this. I had no doubt that on the *other side* Patron had otherworldly visions, and I became a loyal follower. In short order I began to tell all the followers what Patron had communicated to me. That's how I became Guide.' But did Patron have the ability to lead these followers in the kind of organized activities you expect of a church? 'Sometimes I had my doubts,' Guide told us.

"Once we heard this, those of us sitting around debating with him got all excited. Patron's visions had led all of us into a deeper spiritual understanding, but there were bigger trends to consider. As repentant souls we wanted to actually *do* something. Unless we prepared for the end of the world that Patron envisioned, there would be no reason for us penitents to live. 'These thoughts are making us suffer,' we complained to Guide.

"Our suffering boiled down to the same sort of frustrations that Guide had. 'Just as you take Patron's incomprehensible mutterings and convert them into intelligible language,' we told him, 'why don't you set up a springboard and make him take a huge leap off it? Once he jumps, we'll all leap off behind him!' That's as far as we took it that particular time, but this led to the creation of the Izu Research Institute. You were part of this, too, weren't you, Dr. Koga—you who ran and ran but could never score!

"As for me, I had a pretty responsible position in the company I was working in. Putting aside the question of whether I could score a touchdown, from the get-go I wasn't the type to run full speed and break through the other team's defense. Also, once the Izu Research Institute was launched and grew by leaps and bounds as an elite group, I became more involved with keeping the whole church organization up and running. Once I even went to speak to Guide to complain about how high the institute's budget was. That was when we started to think about letting Kansai headquarters make independent financial decisions. I'm a conservative person, and quite persistent.

"In the end the radical faction was completely betrayed by Patron and Guide's Somersault. It wasn't just the radical faction that suffered because of this, of course. The Quiet Women would be a typical example. As I indicated in my talk with Guide, we had a plan to keep going and decided to let the church survive centered on the Kansai headquarters."

"I can see you're a person of vision, but at that stage did you think your plan would be the basis for building a *new* church someday?" Dr. Koga said.

"At the very least, we always thought Patron would return."

"And what *we* did was kill Guide for nothing," Dr. Koga said.

"But you're not just some ordinary member of the radical faction," Mr. Soda said soothingly, but Dr. Koga remained with head bowed.

Kizu intervened bravely. "There's something I don't quite understand," he said. "Something Ikuo doesn't understand either. I know he's talked with Patron about it a few times. . . . There's always something missing from everything you've just been saying: namely, the actual strategies and tactics of the radical faction that were called off on account of the Somersault. There've got to be things that haven't been publicly discussed yet. If these tactics really existed, what were they? *That's* what *I'd* like to hear."

Mr. Soda hesitated. Once he began, though, he didn't hold anything back.

"What they had in mind was the same sort of terrorist assassinations the right wing carried out before the war, plus a postwar phenomenon: deliberately causing an accident at a nuclear power plant. And if they were to survive that, they planned to create a millennial reign of repentance.

"After Chernobyl the Japanese government and the power companies announced that such a large-scale accident in a power plant could never happen in Japan. NHK and the major newspapers all agreed. A national consensus grew up, in other words, that a nuclear power plant accident could never be a likely scenario in Japan. The Japanese people had too much belief in the information and technology the system controls. I'm sure someone like yourself. Professor Kizu, who's lived abroad, would tell us it's the same in other countries as well.

"Anyway, it was left to the experts on nuclear issues at the Izu Institute to figure out how to shake Japan and the Japanese people's fixed ideas about nuclear power by figuring out which nuclear plant they should target and what scale of accident they should cause. The radical faction's plans weren't just some pie-in-the-sky idea but went as far as suggesting a complete destruction of all the nuclear power plants concentrated on the Japan Sea coast—in order to set off the end of the world.

"The assassinations were a much simpler affair. Members of the radical faction planned to assassinate top leaders in the government, the bureaucracy, and the financial world. The assassins would all officially resign from the church so they could take individual responsibility for their acts. They did, though, curry favor with a citizens' relief organization by making contributions so they'd help out in court. They came up with a long detailed list of targets. The list of bureaucrats was compiled by a fellow who graduated from the law department at Tokyo University. The list was confiscated later, but the authorities and police never made it public. They were afraid of the effect it might have if the media ever got hold of it.

"A hundred assassins murdering a hundred leaders in a short space of time. Accidents at two or three nuclear power plants. Once this was done the church members would all take to the streets to announce the coming end of the world and set off an all-out insurrection. Imagine how dangerous it would be, and how much courage it would take, at a time like that to be out on a street corner seeking repentance. Insurrection wouldn't just be some vague term anymore. Then, with no leadership in place and the government paralyzed, they would establish their millennial reign of repentance. Actually, one or two years would be enough, because it wouldn't survive Armageddon. In the final analysis it would be a reign of repentance that focused on the end time: in other words, on dying and ascending to heaven.

"Since the Kansai headquarters followers were to be mobilized in this all-out insurrection too, I didn't know what to do. This morning I looked at the triptych hanging in the chapel, and I know it's based on the book of Jonah, but looking at the background of Nineveh up in flames I remembered the fear that gripped me back then.

"The whole church felt cornered by this crisis, because if you followed the church's doctrine you couldn't very well oppose this plan. That was the situation. In my opinion Patron's Somersault was the appropriate response. The reason the followers at the Kansai headquarters didn't feel their faith shaken was because we made sure all our members understood that the drastic reaction of the Somersault was necessary to put an end to the radical faction's violence. Patron and Guide, who made this painful decision and thereby saved the followers from being entangled in the radical faction, would take responsibility through the Somersault but would, after a time, rebuild the church. This is what we all believed."

5

Just as a chilly damp wind blew in through the window on the valley side, raindrops began to pound on the slate roof. In the far corner of the wooden floor, the former junior high principal stepped down to the dirt floor and shut all the windows he could reach and, turning a handle, shut the windows higher up as well. From deep inside the *fuigo* the roar of the wind from the forest flowed back in. As the former junior high principal approached the dirt floor, he came over to the piece of wood along the entrance, one step lower than the sunken hearth, and waited for the four people seated around the hearth to turn their attention to him.

When they did, he pointed toward the little *kamidana* shrine farthest back in the dirt-floor kitchen above the stove with its old-style tiles. A moment later he called their attention to a kind of box like a sea chest in the shadows of the shrine.

"This is where Meisuke-san is enshrined," he told them. "A second *kamidana,* as we say here. You'll be seeing this in the Spirit Festival procession, but there are two *kami*—gods—one in a light place, the other in a dark place, and Meisuke-san represents the second kind. He was the leader of the first of two insurrections around the time of the Meiji Restoration, died an untimely death, and was enshrined here.

"I think it's significant that a person like that can become a *kami,* so I don't feel like criticizing the extreme tactics your church was unable to put into practice. Truthfully, when you get to my age the idea of a millennial kingdom that focuses on repentance is quite an attractive notion. However, there is one practical fact I'd like you to be aware of. Not far from here is the Agawa nuclear power plant. I have nothing to say about some new blood brotherhood pledged to carry out terrorist assassinations, but if the remnants of the radical faction dust off their plans and try to blow up the Agawa nuclear plant, I don't care what it takes, I will stop them. It's only twenty-five miles from the power plant to Maki Town. As the crow flies—but radiation won't neatly follow all the winding mountain roads in order to get here!

"The buildings in the Hollow were first built by the Church of the Flaming Green Tree, which was quite active for a short time. The peak of their activity was when the congregation all marched out of the Hollow to this very nuclear power plant. When they arrived, all of them, from the Founder down, prayed, and the plant suddenly shut down. There must have been some small malfunction or something.

"In your case, those who were followers before the Somersault make up the core of the new church. I heard from my wife that Patron's policy is to accept even the former radical faction. Most churches end up excluding a minority. They push one group to the point where they end up creating a small extremist faction. This sort of intolerance is a common fault of movements in this country, so my wife was quite impressed by your church's level of forbearance. I'd like to be a tolerant person myself. But there is an absolute line beyond which tolerance is impossible.

"I respect people who are preparing for the end of the world, I really do. And I feel the same way about believers who value a millennial reign of repentance more than their own lives. I'd like to return the vegetation and plant life around here to the way it used to be and put a brake on the decline in the local people's diet. I'm just a simple old man, but in a way I do think about the end of the world. But if the former radical faction attempts to collect on their old IOUs, then as I just said you can be sure I will put a stop to it."

His hair was white as an old man's but full, and he shook his head to punctuate each phrase. Her prominent freckled cheeks shining, Asa-san took up where her husband left off.

"My husband did the cooking tonight in order to let you talk freely without being under the watchful ears of the local women. Another reason was he wanted the chance to tell you his opinion—as he just did! He's had a bit too much to drink, but it hasn't affected him, and I know he gave this some careful thought. Even if you hadn't come here, there still would be a history of Patron, Guide, and the church, wouldn't there, before and after the Somersault? My husband and my history can't be separated from this land here.

The Former Brother Gii's Base Movement, the New Brother Gii's Church of the Flaming Green Tree—these are all part of the history of this land."

"Don't forget Meisuke-san's insurrection," her husband added, now definitely showing signs of drunkenness.

"There's this history that clings to the land," Asa-san went on, "but this doesn't mean that history repeats itself. My older brother, who's a novelist, has written that most things people do is a kind of repetition-with-slippage. Not just a simple repetition, in other words. Starting with the two insurrections connected with Meisuke-san, through the Base Movement of Former Brother Gii to New Brother Gii's Church of the Flaming Green Tree, each one was a *repetition-with-slippage.* The slippage, then, is productive.

"And now here's Patron and all of you about to build your new church in this land. It's possible to see it as a repetition of previous events. Or maybe a repetition of things you all have done elsewhere. Either way, it will end up a repetition-with-slippage. In other words, there will be new elements in whatever you end up doing. As my husband was lamenting, your church shouldn't just have to repeat what it was trying to do before the Somersault."

An emotion appeared in Dr. Koga's eyes, now even more dark and shining than usual, and as Asa-san paused he called out to her.

"Ma'am, I think the principal and you are truly outstanding people. When I opened the clinic here I had the same misgivings the principal spoke of. But wouldn't it be a little too obvious if the remnants of the former radical faction tried to deceive Patron once again into doing what they planned before the Somersault? For the time being I'm relieved that Patron has put forth his concept of the Church of the New Man. That's the slippage you spoke of. He's an obstinate person. He isn't criticizing his own role in the Somersault, nor is he going to set the clock back to before the Somersault. He's trying to introduce some *slippage.*"

"The liquor's gotten to me, I'm afraid," Mr. Soda said, "and I can't make any proper comment, but I do agree with Dr. Koga that the slippage that Patron has carved out over the past decade is powerful. As long as that holds true, we at the Kansai headquarters made the right decision to lay the groundwork for him here.

"What do you say we follow the principal's lead and go down to the floor level? The space below Meisuke-san's *kamidana* was wasted space, so we made a cellar for storing sake. It's a wine cellar, but we also have some very nice whiskey there. It would appear that we haven't maintained the good drinking habits of the Base Movement, after all. Would you join me for a drink? Koga, be a good guy and bring some glasses for us. There's water in the cellar."

"I'll take care of the glasses," Asa-san said in a spirited voice. The former principal told her to rinse them out first, so she went over to the sink to do what he said.

Mr. Soda turned on a light in the dirt-floored area and the four men, looking down through the window that looked out over the valley and the shiny rain-dewed leaves of the nearby branches of the birches and elms just outside, sat down in a row and began to drink their whiskey and water. The former principal expounded on the topic of the island region where this malt whiskey originated.

For the first time Mr. Soda expressed his reaction to seeing Kizu's triptych. "Dancer sent me an e-mail saying that Patron quoted from the letter to the Ephesians. I reread it myself, and it says, 'He has made the two one and has destroyed the dividing wall of hostility through his own flesh,' right? When I saw your painting in the chapel, Professor, I thought it shows exactly that: the Old Man and the New Man in one painting. Old Men like us still want to have hope, don't we?"

"That's right, Mr. Soda. Guide died as one of the Old Men, and even though we're all Old Men ourselves, we want to believe we can coexist with the New Men."

Dr. Koga, too, was starting to show signs of being drunk, and when Asa-san, who'd quickly finished the dishes, slipped on her sandals and joined them, he reverently poured out some whiskey into a new glass for her, asking how much water she'd like.

31: The Summer Conference

1

Registration was to begin at 10 A.M., on the first Friday in August, at the temporary office set up below the dam. Under the clear sky a line had already formed before seven. Kizu heard that by the time the official registration began, the line extended all the way to where it could be seen from the Mansion, where Mr. Soda was staying.

The temporary office was set up in the square below the dam with two red and green vertically striped tents that looked like overturned bowls. A festive summery feeling swept through the line of people, making the atmosphere all the more lively.

Ms. Asuka brought over a Fruit of the Rain Tree lunch box and soup in a paper container for Kizu and was uncharacteristically excited as she reported that by afternoon the number of registrants had topped five hundred. Events planned included the Fireflies on Friday night and their Spirit Procession on Sunday afternoon, followed by Patron's public sermon, all of which could be seen from the bleachers set up on the newly prepared path around the lake in the Hollow. Plans for the conference were based on the number of seats there, including areas for people to stand. Sightseers from Maki Town and surrounding areas, however, were allowed free entrance without registering.

Registration cards with numbers were distributed that allowed participants free access to the dining hall in the monastery and to the chapel to view Kizu's triptych. Having people register was a way for those who'd dropped out of the church after the Somersault to declare their intentions now that the new church was about to be launched.

The office estimated that over seven hundred people would register on the first day, and since they'd all come from far away there was a need to find lodgings beyond what had already been arranged. They checked at the Maki Town Inn and other Japanese inns that they'd originally left off their list because of the price. They also had to increase the number of shuttle buses taking people from their lodgings to the Hollow. Followers who'd arrived ahead of time helped out as volunteers at the temporary office, but the whole first day was chaotic, to say the least.

"Patron's public sermon of course will be one of the highlights, but the small-group meetings tomorrow and the next day at the monastery, where people will talk about their sufferings over the past decade, seem quite popular as well. The Quiet Women are running those.

"Other followers who haven't gotten in touch with us have talked with their former fellows in the church and will be holding their own independently organized small meetings," Ms. Asuka added. "The office has to find rooms for the meetings, so we've asked the Farm, the Mansion, and Fushoku temple to provide space, and we've had to increase the number of smaller gatherings. Dancer's been very quick to take on this task and is quite the negotiator."

There was one more important reason that brought Ms. Asuka to walk up to Kizu's house on the north shore of the Hollow. Among the people who registered were those with no previous or present connection with the church, she reported, but who were cancer patients or family members of those who were too ill to make the trip. They wanted to be cured by Patron—or at least have him agree to try—and also hoped to hear directly from Kizu about his miraculous experience.

It would be impossible to have Patron do anything like that while the conference was in session, and Kizu couldn't be asked to participate in all these small-group meetings. Patron wouldn't be participating in the press conference the following day, but could Kizu attend and say a few words? He couldn't say no.

Ms. Asuka did everything with great enthusiasm. Undaunted by the heat, she was dressed in short-sleeved khaki work clothes and high laced shoes. She also talked about how she'd been allowed to videotape the Fireflies' procession scheduled for that evening.

"Asa-san told me that the Fireflies are children who carry lanterns with candles in them, and other children carry extra candles, and they all climb up into the woods with some object that a soul has been transferred into, which they lay at the base of a selected tree. These small lights moving through the forest are hard to see, and it would take a lot of time, so I'd given up on trying to film it.

"But what happened was the Maki police and fire department said they wouldn't allow children to play with fire like that, so Gii drew up a revised plan, and they were given the go-ahead. Which also made it possible to video-tape it. I can really see why Ikuo expects great things of Gii!"

The twilight sky was still brightly reflected on the lake's surface, though the woods were completely dark, when Kizu heard Dancer's voice from speakers on the island in the middle of the lake giving an explanation of the Young Fireflies. Kizu sprayed insect repellent all over his arms and legs, turned out the houselights, and sat down in front of the open window to watch the proceedings.

Before long, as the sky was just losing its reddish tint and the chapel, monastery, and dam sank into the gloom, two groups of children, one quite young, the other junior high age, appeared in front of the reviewing stands, where they put lighted candles inside lanterns. As they descended from the stands, illuminated by the lanterns, the bobbing lights flickered on the lake's surface, drawing a sigh of admiration from the crowds of onlookers on the darkened shores.

The two groups with their lanterns made it safely up the stairs from the dam. Just as they were about to step onto the flagstone path, though, the lantern lights disappointedly vanished. A sigh went up again from the crowd, along with laughter. A moment later, though, lights reappeared, the same lanterns as before, it seemed, on the slope in back at the same height as the chapel roof; they moved horizontally toward the east, dipping in and out of view in the thick foliage. As soon as it seemed they'd vanished completely in even denser foliage, they'd pop up a few moments later at the same height, farther along the course they were taking to the slopes of the east bank, like some persistent beast moving in the night.

Fellow Fireflies no doubt awaited them farther down the path they all followed in their morning training sessions. The leader of the whole procession, situated in a spot where he could see all the proceedings—Gii, who had crossed over to the island with its cypress tree—would signal to all the kids on the ubiquitous beepers junior high school children all carried, and have them remove the covers from their lanterns and set off once again.

Kizu was interpreting the proceedings this way when the Fireflies procession turned to the north slope and left his field of vision. He groped his way to the kitchen, opened the fridge, found a can of beer in the lighted interior, popped it, and returned to his chair. As he drank, he waited for the procession to arrive back at the dam and again make its way to the reviewing stands. Gii must have found it too simple to have them settle the soul at the base of a tree way up in the forest, everything taking place in the dark.

Even though the lanterns were far away, whenever they disappeared the dark forest and lake slipped back into monotony and the passage of time slowed down. As the crowd surrounding the lake looked up at the movement of the lanterns cutting across the north slope and descending ever lower, an occasional child's shout could be heard, but otherwise no loud voices at all. The crowd of onlookers wasn't just being patient, but awaited further developments with an air of great expectation.

High up on the eastern slope a cuckoo called out, and another cuckoo answered. A *kyororon-kyororon* melody of some other bird Kizu heard quite often recently—a call that reminded him of a Vivaldi guitar concerto— echoed loudly across the still lakeside.

Finally the lanterns began to ascend from the north corner of the dam. The young children holding the lights, and the junior high school pupils with them, lantern light glittering in the high water along the shore, marched on toward the reviewing stands. They turned their backs on the lake as they began to climb up the wooden stairs above the reviewing stands, and after a moment of darkness, the space above the stands was filled with the light from all the lanterns held by this crowd of children. Right above them was a banner, illuminated by their lanterns, that read: Church of the New Man.

Music came from the speakers on the island, a melody Kizu recognized as Morio's "Ascension," parts 1 and 2. The burst of applause of the onlookers at this display of light quickly faded out of respect for the subdued music. Lights went on in the chapel and the monastery, and the lamppost outside went on as well. It was already past nine.

2

Friday night's Fireflies procession was a resounding success. From early Saturday morning on, the people who gathered around the Hollow were abuzz with talk of how much they'd enjoyed it.

Ogi was in charge of public relations for the conference, so he heard a lot of these opinions from people outside the church. One fiftyish man from the Old Town introduced himself, undaunted, as someone who'd been active in the movement opposing the move of the church to the Hollow, and came out with the following ambiguous words of praise:

"I asked the deputy mayor why they allowed a procession like that carrying fire over such a wide area, and he said that although it was well planned by some young guy, the important thing was that one of the young people from the fire department was in charge, so they couldn't very well call a halt to it! You all are very calculating in what you do, which I find rather frightening!"

On Saturday at 9 A.M. a press conference was held in the dining hall of the monastery for all reporters, including foreign correspondents. Dancer got in touch with Ogi, underscoring her desire for all the leaders of the church, with the exception of Patron, to attend. Dancer herself would be busy at the office, responding to faxes and e-mails and anything unexpected that arose, and wouldn't be able to participate.

Ogi was to be the emcee at the press conference. The church representatives all sat together, their backs to the window looking out on the lake. Ogi was in the middle, Kizu on his right, and next to him was Ikuo, thin and haggard, who sat with his chair pushed back a little. He looked as if he wasn't planning to make any comments but, if need be, was ready to help out.

Next to Ikuo sat Dr. Koga and Mr. Hanawa of the Technicians, while on Ogi's left sat Mr. Soda, Ms. Oyama of the Quiet Women, and finally Gii. Before the press conference began, Ms. Oyama was speaking with Mr. Soda in a low voice, but Kizu could catch what she said. Mr. Soda's reply was to the question of the canceling of the Quiet Women's children's participation as a group. The women had been looking forward to spending the summer vacation with their children, but with the unexpected problems in finding lodging for all the conference participants, they'd decided at their prayer meeting to give up the idea of having their children join them.

One of the people attending the press conference was Fred Parks, the reporter for the New York newspaper who'd originally told Kizu about the modern buildings in the Shikoku woods. In order to keep reporting from Tokyo, Fred was now a freelance journalist and had expanded his areas beyond the architecture and art fields.

The middle-aged woman Fred had hired as an interpreter turned out to be Ogi's old friend Mrs. Tsugane. Ogi was surprised to see her, but tracing back the connection it made sense that she was here. Ms. Asuka, official videographer of the summer conference, had invited members of the Moosbrugger Committee, and Mrs. Tsugane had answered the call. But since Ms. Asuka already had two assistants handling lighting and sound, Mrs. Tsugane had to find work elsewhere and had replied to a notice on the bulletin board in the monastery courtyard from a reporter seeking an interpreter. Since Ogi had last seen her, she'd divorced her architect husband, and she thought this would be a good opportunity to make some money to cover her traveling expenses.

Just before the press conference started, as Ogi settled down in his emcee's chair, a letter arrived for him, the envelope written on the Japanese *washi* paper that was a specialty of the Old Town, decorated with a woodblock print. The letter read:

> After not having seen you for so long, I'm so very pleased to see you're doing well. I'm with a foreigner here to check out the local legends. I'm looking forward to the Spirit Procession today. I understand that if you go deep into the woods on the north side of the valley there's a place called Sheath. In the local legends they say that's another word for vagina. As the name implies, when young men and women go in there they can't help but give in to sexual passion. Putting aside the question of whether I'm young enough to belong there, what do you say? It's been a while. Why don't we give our passions a run for their money? I was divorced not long ago, so any moral issue that might restrain you has vanished. I have some free time before Patron's public sermon.
>
> You Know Who.

The press conference began, the opening question coming from a female reporter, a third-generation Japanese named Karen Sato from the *Los Angeles Times* who was also helping a TV team with its coverage. She was in her mid-twenties, and her question was directed to Kizu.

"Professor, since you've given lectures on cross-cultural symbolism, there's something I'd like to ask you," Ms. Sato said, in rapid-fire English, relying too much on what the publicity pamphlet said about Kizu's background and his abilities in English. (Ikuo, who had sat beside Kizu for this very reason, could tell how nonplussed he was and explained basically what the woman had asked. Kizu was typical of his generation in that he could speak English but often had trouble catching what others said.)

"I heard that the children carrying the *chochin* lanterns last night," the woman continued, "went up into the woods carrying the souls of the dead. And that these souls return to the valley and enter the bodies of newborn babies. The souls, in other words, in a Neoplatonic way, travel back and forth between the profane world of the valley and the spiritual world of the mountains. But if the souls keep on doing this over and over, it reminds one of Buddhist transmigration. So do you interpret it, Professor, from a western or an oriental viewpoint?"

"I know a little about Neoplatonism from the commentaries on Blake's paintings," Kizu replied, "where the soul when it ascends to heaven returns to God's presence and a community of souls. According to the legends of this region, the soul rests in solitude at the base of the selected tree until the time comes for it to be reborn. In Buddhist transmigration, human souls are also reborn in *animal* bodies, which is different from souls being reborn inside newborn babies. I see the Young Fireflies' view of life and death, based on the premodern life of the people of this region, as something quite unique.

"Imagine, if you will, a solitary village springing up in the midst of a vast forest and coming up with its own legends as if it were a remote island. The souls of people who live in the village after physical death still remain in the forest that overlooks the valley. And they come down to the valley any number of times. I interpret it as the world of the living and the world of the dead forming, in this topography, a single unit."

"If it's that unique a view of life and death, then I guess it *is* a religious philosophy, isn't it?" the woman said. "As people with an anti-Japanese religious philosophy coming into the area and building a church, didn't you experience opposition?"

Ms. Sato's question seemed to want to probe further. Ogi picked up the ball and responded.

"I've heard that there was a movement among the townspeople to oppose our move," he said, in the English he'd learned in college, "but since we've actually moved here there's been next to nothing in the way of harassment."

"Your statement implies there *was* some. Could you give us some examples?"

"Young people from along the river in the valley, and from hamlets in the forest, had formed a group to revive some of the cultural legends of the area. One element of this group made a sort of . . . *installation* in the chapel designed to menace us. But that was the end of it. There are almost no local people participating in our church, nor have we been proselytizing in the hope that they would join us. In fact, this conference is the first official opportunity for us to get together with the local community."

"I heard that last night's wonderful demonstration was done by young people from the community," the woman reporter went on. "Is this an exception, then, local people who participate in the church?"

"That's correct," Ogi said. "And they aren't members of the church, mind you. As you know, last night's demonstration was a revival of an ancient rite. Actually they're the group I was talking about that confronted us early on. The church is very pleased that now our relationship is on the right track. A representative of that group is here today, so why don't you ask him directly?"

Gii made an endearing yet not frivolous move, as if he were caving in and wanting to flee, which brought on a sympathetic burst of laughter from the others. Kizu wondered whether he was just pretending to have such a negative reaction to English, but Karen Sato accepted this at face value and added a final comment in Japanese to wind up her questions.

"Your demonstration was—*subarashikatta*—wonderful!"

3

The next person who stood up to ask a question was a Japanese woman who looked to be in her late forties. She was dressed stylishly, but her manner was unassertive, and when she began to speak Kizu was struck by her tone of voice, deeply dyed as it was with an emotional and physical exhaustion resulting, no doubt, from the hardships she'd gone through.

"Patron's teachings have sustained me over the years," the woman began. "So much so that at the time of the Somersault, when many people were all upset and left the church, I couldn't understand why. After his trances, Patron and Guide would craft a message for us. Just hearing a fraction of this I knew how beautiful a person Patron was, how lovely his soul was, and I became a believer.

"Then Patron announced that, though he'd been preaching repentance, he'd been mistaken, that the people of this country had no fundamental relationship with the God who was in charge of the end of the world. Borrowing the God that Westerners believe in, and thinking that we too must do something in order to show our repentance, was no different from children dressing up as adults and putting on a play. You can't take it seriously, in other words. 'And all I did,' Patron went on, 'was enjoy directing this little children's play.' He also said it was laughable that we thought— by acting out some cute little children's play—that *their* God would deign to pay us a glance. When I saw this announcement on the TV news I thought, *Ah, so that's what's been going on!* Because I'd never felt comfortable with the western God, either.

"Despite all this, though, I saw him—the laughingstock of Japan—as still a beautiful person, with a beautiful soul. Could anything be as painful as this: denying everything about yourself?

"I accepted what he said, that everything he'd told us up till then had nothing to do with God. That being the case, a thought struck me. If those weren't the words of God, they were still the words of a beautiful person, of a beautiful soul. Even if he said he'd only been fooling around, he had the right to do that. He said he knew he was crazy but he still kept on talking and talking, and if that's the case I think he had even more right to fool around like he did.

"I thought, it's okay that I was so struck by this unsurpassed, even painful joking, by the words of this unhappy, crazed person. I even felt that what this world needs is a beautiful person just like him, a beautiful crazed soul. Once I'd decided that, my heart melted, and all I hoped was that Patron would be able to find a place where he could be free. And the Somersault no longer bothered me. I stayed in the church, holding dear to me the words that he'd given to us.

"And now, just a little over ten years later, Patron is back. Guide met with a painful death, but that makes it even clearer to me how precious a person has returned. I'm so happy he's survived to this point. The reason I could be so calm back then, I think, was because I had a premonition that, happily, things would work out as they have.

"I don't really have a question; I just wanted to tell you all of this. There *is* one more thing I'd like to say, though. Patron has come back to the Church of the New Man and we're all together again, yet I find the attitude of some of the Quiet Women quite incomprehensible. Yesterday they all gathered in their rooms in the monastery and prayed. The curtains were all shut, the place was dark, and even if you wanted to talk with them you couldn't because there were men standing guard at the door.

"The same thing's happening today. And tomorrow evening, when we'll all be sitting around the lake listening to Patron's sermon, aren't the Quiet Women planning to take over the chapel to hold another prayer meeting?

"The Technicians, who also moved here along with Patron, will be listening to the sermon along with everybody else in the stands around the lake. Why do the Quiet Women alone have these special privileges, and why do they ignore their former colleagues who've come from so far away? With the Church of the New Man about to be launched, is this really a good idea? I'm asking this for all the women believers from the Kansai headquarters, all of whom have their doubts about this."

Her question finished, the woman remained standing, awaiting a reply, and Ms. Oyama, who'd been taking notes, raised her head. Normally what struck Kizu about her was her strong-looking body and her no-nonsense look, but now she and the woman asking the questions seemed to share a common fatigue.

"I'm not sure if I can give a satisfactory answer as a representative of the Quiet Women," Ms. Oyama said, "but I'll go ahead and try. Ms. Kajima, it's so nice to see you after so long. I understand how you were able to maintain your religious life at the Kansai headquarters, and it's through the efforts of you and others like you that we're able to open our new church in such wonderful facilities. Seeing as how you're the ones who've stayed in the church all along, it might be strange for me to say that I'm happy you've come here, but I do want to convey my heartfelt thanks to everyone who's participating in the conference.

"When those of us who share the same faith left the church and made the decision to live collectively, we were counting on your joining us. When, at the last moment, you decided not to, I must say we were quite bewildered. After the Somersault, when we were confused, doubting our faith, and suffering, it was *you*, Ms. Kajima, who encouraged us. With Patron and Guide no longer in the church, we were trying to live on our own, relying solely on our faith. Everyone believed you were crucial to our success. When we learned that you wouldn't be joining us, several people actually dropped out of our group, and even after we started our communal life together as the Quiet Women, we never forgot you. We were distressed and talked over why you didn't join us."

"I'd like to be allowed to explain," said Ms. Kajima, who had remained standing. "Just a moment ago I said I felt it was completely up to Patron where he would go after the Somersault. Truthfully, though, I still had an attachment to him, which is why I grew close to your group, Ms. Oyama. I was convinced that you were still in secret contact with Patron and Guide and that, with no other place to go, they might join you at your commune.

"The last day I was with your group, Mrs. Shigeno gave a sermon—I haven't had a chance to see her here yet, but I'm happy to hear she's well. I can never forget how she said she would never forgive Patron and Guide for having done the Somersault. She said that through their communal life they would get an even firmer grasp of the God that Patron and Guide rejected and would show them a thing or two. Everyone was quite stirred up by this.

"I had no ill feelings toward Guide, of course, nor toward Patron. Even having done the Somersault, he was still a beautiful soul. At the same time, I saw him as someone forced to suffer to the point where the Somersault was unavoidable. But someday wouldn't he come back to us? I kept the words he had told us in mind and tried not to be self-destructive. He said himself that it was all a joke, but once the words were out there, in the public domain as it were, they were mine to deal with as I felt best. . . . Just around that time I met Mr. Soda and heard that the Kansai headquarters was planning to keep the church organization going.

"I'll rephrase my question so a practical and bright person like yourself, Ms. Oyama, can answer directly. This is what I want to know: After the Somersault, what kind of spiritual process did the Quiet Women go through to forgive Patron and be able to rejoin him here and become part of his new church? Unless I know this, your secrecy will continue to bother me. I'd also like to ask the Technicians a similar question."

"We've managed to live our communal life for more than ten years now," Ms. Oyama replied. "As you said, at first we *did* hate Patron and Guide. The power of hatred, in fact, helped bind us together. But in time we overcame those ill feelings, though I'm afraid it's beyond my ability to analyze the process of how this happened. I say this because each person conquered her feelings in a different way, consistent with how she became converted and the way she had lived her life since.

"Still, there was one impetus all the Quiet Women shared that helped them overcome their feelings of animosity. This was the information that Mrs. Shigeno brought to us—the report that after the Somersault Patron and Guide had descended into hell. We too felt we'd been abandoned, left in a place where we were anxious and suffered. When we heard this information we thought, very naturally, that it made perfect sense. That being the case, we also clung to the hope that Patron and Guide would someday climb up out of the hell they were in and lead us in a new direction.

"Then a terrible thing happened: Guide was murdered, a truly awful event, but we received the notice of the memorial service for Guide, sent from Patron, and for the first time in ten years there was something hopeful to cling to. It was a straight path from the memorial service to this present conference from then on.

"This only means that we Quiet Women need to talk together even more. These past ten years we've been in the habit of holding some deep discussions to come up with a group consensus. We're supposed to see this conference as former church members overcoming the Somersault to launch a new church, right? In our decade of communal living this has got to be the most critical situation we've faced.

"That's why we hold our discussions. And these discussions—of people who've lived together for ten years, sharing their pain—we like to hold in private. We really need to talk together—just *us* and no one else. I hope you'll allow us to do so. And when we meet by ourselves next time, I'm sure one of the topics we'll be discussing is this very question you've put to us."

"Still, though, I find it ironic that we're excluded from your discussions," Ms. Kajima commented.

"Once again, I ask your indulgence," Ms. Oyama replied. "The Quiet Women will be working, though, at the party being held tonight at the Farm. So if you'd like to talk with us individually, that would be a good time to do so."

Ms. Kajima didn't pursue her questioning any further. Instead, she turned her attack to the Technicians.

"The Technicians were the elite at the Izu Research Institute, people I never met or spoke to directly. Which led to me having a one-sided view of all of you. Forgive me for saying this, but the extreme tactics of some of your colleagues pushed Patron and Guide to the wall, forcing them to do the Somersault. That's the view of those of us who remained in the church. And then later some of your colleagues—I'm not saying *all*, mind you—put Guide on trial and ended up causing his death. To us it seemed that the years after you left the church didn't change your way of thinking or your tactics one iota. That made us disappointed and angry.

"Now, though, we find the Technicians in charge of everything at this conference for the new church. Mr. Soda, the head of the Kansai headquarters, discussed this with Patron and agreed to it, and since he's our leader we accept it as a fait accompli. But there are many people in the Kansai headquarters who feel the way I do—that there's a lot going on here we can't understand. Some people say they find it outrageous. So I'd like to hear from some of the Technicians as to how they feel about this."

A piece of paper was passed to her at this point, and she sat down, and a small stir went through the audience as they speculated as to what was going on. This soon calmed down, though, as the American reporter Fred Parks, who was sitting beside Ms. Kajima, stood up and asked a question.

"I'd like to ask a follow-up if I may," he began.

His question was translated into Japanese by Mrs. Tsugane.

"As you can gather from my asking in English, I'm a foreigner, but at the time of the Somersault I was especially interested in the Izu faction that you just mentioned, because they had a plan for radical social change. Until just before the Somersault, neither Patron nor Guide seemed opposed to this and provided funding for their activities.

"Still, Patron and Guide eventually negotiated with the authorities and sold out the radical faction. I wonder how the remnants of the group, the Technicians, feel about this. How do all of you evaluate the killing of Guide and Patron's return to the church? Thank you."

4

Kizu knew only that Mr. Hanawa was a research scientist. In Mr. Hanawa's attitude as he silently surveyed the audience, all the while taking notes at the long table, Kizu was reminded of the head of the student council in his college days, a group under the sway of the Communists. This impression was reinforced when Mr. Hanawa spoke.

"It would take quite some time to discuss how we felt at the time of the Somersault, and since I don't think that's particularly relevant at this point, I'll talk about how we feel about it *now,* ten years down the road.

"We were completely turned inside out by Patron's Somersault, but we already knew at the time that our plans would have been a total failure. So we were betrayed by Patron and Guide through the Somersault, which was okay because it helped avoid a massive blunder, right? People might say that, but if you look at history you'll find that even in what appears to be stupid, failed insurrections, often something significant emerges. *Aborted* insurrections, however, lead nowhere.

"Even now we wonder whether the Somersault was really the only option open to Patron. In a similar vein, we talked over what Asahara, the leader of Aum Shinrikyo, did or didn't do when the police raided his hideout at the base of Mount Fuji, and we all agreed that was Asahara's own Somersault.

"If Asahara hadn't done a Somersault, what options did he have? Assume the lotus position, back straight and eyes closed, leap out of the highest window in the *satyan,* and levitate toward Mount Fuji? If he really couldn't fly, he should have just leaped out the window and crashed to the ground. With his senior disciples already shot, the CIA or the Japanese police or religious organizations antithetical to Aum would insist on shooting Asahara—floating in a lotus position toward Mount Fuji—out of the sky. Like a single fish egg in a stormy sea, this may very well have led to a single grain hatching and a new Aum myth. For the church that remained behind a new history would be born.

"We haven't wavered from our conclusion that the Somersault was a mistake. But we also recognize it was a mistake to have driven Guide to such a tragic death. In other words, we won't be pushing Patron anymore to take responsibility. The reason we've returned to be with Patron and help him build a new church from the ground up—and please note that we're not managing things in the Hollow; we're providing security for the Quiet Women's prayer meetings, at their request, and will be helping out at tonight's party at the Farm—is because we have great hopes for the new church and for Patron, whom we know is an outstanding, inspiring leader. We're not asking that he reverse the Somersault of a decade ago. We're hoping for a *brand-new* Somersault."

The next question didn't come from the reporters and TV crew occupying the front half of the audience but from a man, sitting with some others, apart from the ordinary participants, along the aisle on the west side of the hall. The man stood up. These people had come in late, and Kizu had seen Ogi ask the Technicians, already helping out here at the press conference, to move some extra chairs in for them.

The middle-aged man who wanted to speak had a deeply lined, receding forehead, a penetrating look, and a very poor complexion. He was very low key, with a hoarse, muttering way of speaking; Kizu realized it had been some time since he'd met a Japanese person like this. The question, it turned out, was directed to *him*.

"The questions I'd like to ask may have nothing to do with the launching of the new church," the man said. "Still, I hope very much that you'll understand why I have to ask them. Professor Kizu, did you come back to Japan because you heard that the Founder had the power to cure cancer? Did you not get any modern medical treatment because the Founder instructed you not to? How did the Founder treat you, and how long was it before it started to take effect? My next question is best directed at the Founder himself: Is this treatment also available to people outside the church?"

Ogi passed along a piece of paper with these questions all neatly printed out. Up till now the church members responding to questions had relied on the notes they were taking.

"I don't know if this will help you or not, but I'll tell you about my experience," Kizu began. "While I was living in America, a professor of medicine in my institute told me he suspected I had cancer. He recommended a complete examination and said he himself would do the pathology. I resigned myself to this being what I'd been fearing, a recurrence of cancer, and using the sabbatical leave I had coming I scurried off to Japan.

"Five years ago I had an operation for colon cancer. And this last year and a half I haven't been feeling well. Seven years ago my older brother, who also had had colon cancer surgery, found it had spread to his liver, and two years later he passed away. When I came back to Japan to see him before he died, he told me about the symptoms, and they were the same symptoms I was having, so I resigned myself to suffering the same fate. Still, I didn't go into the hospital for all those tests, because I remembered all too clearly how awful the ones they'd run on me before had been, the abdominal artery contrast test and all the rest.

"My U.S. specialist had referred me to a clinic in Tokyo, and I consulted with the doctor there about how to deal with the disease as it progressed, particularly how to deal with the pain. After doing a CT scan, this doctor concurred with my own assessment of my condition. I thought a biopsy was pointless so I refused to have it done. And when we moved here, the Tokyo doctor passed along all his information to Dr. Koga, who was traveling with me.

"After that, on two separate occasions the pain became so unbearable that the second time they put me in the Red Cross Hospital and removed my gallbladder. I thought the cancer had spread—only to be told that it never was cancer to begin with, which reminded me that I'd never had another biopsy done after the first operation. The doctor at the Red Cross Hospital told me the pain must have been from gallstones and not from any recurrence

of cancer. But looking at the symptoms my late brother had, there was definitely a reason for me to think the cancer had recurred and I didn't have long
to live. Even now, after doubting it many times, I always come back to that
belief.

"Since I moved here I've been living communally with Patron—the
Founder, as you call him. I'd met him—and Guide—about a year before in
Toyko, and we'd had a number of chances to talk. After we moved here our
relationship has gotten closer and Patron modeled for my painting. Still, I
never felt he was intentionally treating me. I remember once he told me he'd
take responsibility for my physical condition, but he never did anything that
made me feel he was consciously working on it, and I can't say that Patron is
prepared to treat anyone, either those in the church or those outside. Even so,
to answer your question, I feel I *did* have a recurrence of cancer, which is now
cured. And I've found myself believing that moving here and becoming closer
to Patron had an effect on what has happened to me."

Kizu stopped speaking, and though he thought nothing he'd said was
very well put, the man who'd asked the questions and those around him unexpectedly broke into applause. And then, from beside them, standing because
there weren't enough seats, an elderly man, slightly built, but whose chest
under a dark blue shirt was unusually muscular, spoke out loudly without
waiting to be called on.

"I don't have one of those tickets you need to ask a question, but I'm
a blacksmith and farmer from the outskirts, and I think people from outside might not fully understand what Professor Kizu's saying unless I add
something!"

Ogi went over quickly to have a few words with this man who, although
it wasn't yet noon, was obviously a bit tipsy. He didn't make him leave but
made it quite clear that certain guidelines had to be followed.

"Okay, I get it!" the man said. "I'll cut to the chase. My son Kaji died of
lung cancer and a brain tumor. At one point, though, Brother Gii, who built
the chapel in the Hollow, used his touch to heal my son's liver cancer. The
doctor at the Red Cross Hospital said the cancer had shrunk an incredible
amount.

"I believe there's a power in the Hollow that raises people up who have
a healing touch and draws them in from elsewhere. Wasn't it this *power of
the land* that brought out the Founder's healing power? In this new church,
too, you should make this healing power available to all those suffering from
cancer! From his grave I'm sure Kaji would want this."

The man who asked the first questions, not paying any heed to this second man, interrupted. "We're really counting on the sermon tomorrow. But

if at all possible, either before or after the party today, can we meet with Patron? We've all come a long way, hoping we could." And he bowed his head, as did the tipsy blacksmith-cum-farmer whose pronouncements had been cut short.

That was the end of the press conference, and in the stir as the reporters, TV crews, and participants all stood up, the American reporter, Fred Parks, who was accompanied by Mrs. Tsugane, came over to the long table where Kizu was still seated.

"I think it's very wise the way you've allowed the interested parties to debate the internal issues of the church in front of foreign reporters," Parks said. "I've attended Aum press conferences, and they never let any problems they might be having among themselves see the light of day."

"That's right, Fred," Kizu replied. "Our church is different from both Aum Shinrikyo and from your country's insistence on sticking to principles no matter what."

"Those cancer patients are so sad," Fred said. "It struck me that maybe you never had cancer to begin with. If that's the case, you're one sly fellow—sitting there with a straight face like one big billboard for the church."

While the two of them were talking in English, Mrs. Tsugane tilted her newly permed head toward Ogi and whispered something. Kizu had wanted to ask Ikuo if there was anything he could do to help out between the afternoon program and the evening party at the Farm, but Ikuo had disappeared while Kizu was talking with Fred.

After Mrs. Tsugane left the dining hall with Fred, Kizu went over to where Ogi was standing with Dancer—who'd come in near the end of the press conference—facing the window on the lake side, deep in conversation. Despite their intense tête-à-tête, Ogi saw Kizu, turned around to him, and said, "Would you talk with Dr. Koga for us? He has a problem the office can't deal with."

Ogi was so tense as he said this it made Kizu turn to look around him. With a worried look, Dancer glanced up at Kizu but didn't say anything and looked away. As Kizu walked over to where Dr. Koga stood, surrounded by cancer patients, and others who were no doubt family members, Dr. Koga cut off his talk with them and made his way out of the crowd toward him. Kizu had never seen such a serious expression before on Dr. Koga's well-formed features.

Ogi went out ahead of them. In the courtyard between the two buildings of the monastery there were enormous mobs of people, not just those leaving the press conference but other participants, talking in groups, strolling the grounds. Kizu and the others headed toward the chapel. The necks and arms of everyone they passed were sweating profusely. Dr. Koga, too, walking just in front of Kizu, kept wiping his neck with a soiled handkerchief. The sunlight was dazzling, and the clamor of cicadas poured down on them from behind Patron's residence.

Ogi unlocked the door to the office, let the two of them in, told them to lock the door behind him, and left.

Dr. Koga cut across the first room to the room nearest the lake, and was standing by the fax machine, a pile of faxes beside it, about to reach out for them automatically when he stopped short and fixed an unsmiling gaze on Kizu.

"Ever since he saw the Fireflies last night, Patron's been quite frightened and not himself. Ikuo restrained him and calmed him down, but Patron's quite strong and gave him a hard time. And that's not all."

5

Dr. Koga explained that the night before, as the Fireflies were performing, Ikuo had visited Patron to show him the plan for enlivening Patron's sermon on the final day.

A ceaseless line of people, headed toward the chapel and back, was passing in front of Patron's house, and the constant stir had Morio on edge. Two Fireflies stood guard outside the front door, which stood about five yards up a slope from the courtyard, and with people posing one after another in front for souvenir photographs, the normally unflappable Ms. Tachibana, too, was uneasy.

Patron spent quite some time preparing for his sermon on the final day. He wasn't scheduled to appear at any other functions until then, but at that time he would be speaking in front of an expected crowd of some one thousand people, seven hundred registered participants plus casual visitors from Maki Town and its surroundings. Even during the heyday of the church before the Somersault, Patron had only spoken to such a large crowd a handful of times.

The plan that Ikuo brought over to discuss with Patron was a proposal he'd received from Gii's mother by way of Gii. Satchan was grateful to Ikuo for taking the Fireflies under his wing and helping them expand to the point where adults in Maki Town approved of the group. She was also allowing the church to use the cypress island in the Hollow, land she owned, in their conference and had made the church a proposition.

The giant tree, half destroyed, was awful to look at, even though new leaves appeared on it every year. The cypress was the remains of what happened when Brother Gii, planning to dissolve the Church of the Flaming Green Tree and leave the area with his wife, Satchan, burned down the tree in place of the chapel. The next morning, as Brother Gii set off with a small group of pilgrims, he was stoned to death by attackers.

Fifteen years later, it still pained Satchan to look at the horrible sight of this burned and mangled tree still standing. "If you cut down the tree and use the land as a small park," she said, "I'll give the island to the church."

Gii added his own idea, saying that if the tree was to be cut down they should incorporate this as a rousing end to the conference. How about burning it down completely? Since it was on an island in the middle of a lake full of water, the fire department shouldn't have any objection. They were planning to burn all the spirit dolls anyway, once they'd been used in the procession; if they piled the dolls up at the base of the cypress and burned them together, two birds with one stone, it would be a spectacular finale.

Patron immediately approved of this proposal when Ikuo presented it to him. After they finished discussing it, Patron, Ikuo, and Morio went over to the window that looked over the lake to watch the Fireflies as they were just setting off in their procession. The three men soon moved over to the east window and followed the children with their lanterns as, the older boys accompanying them, they swiftly walked up the forest slope that, in the darkness, seemed all the more close. A second group was waiting for the procession, and the first group lit the second's lanterns and then began to run toward the eastern bank of the Hollow in a large curve.

Ikuo had already sensed, along with Morio's being on edge, that Patron had lost his composure when all of a sudden Patron turned to them anxiously and began to speak. Weren't the Fireflies preparing to spread kerosene all over the area along the animal trail they'd been taking, he said worriedly, a *lot* of kerosene? Weren't they all set to light the kerosene that was running down the forest slopes, and weren't the boys running with the lanterns already setting fires in places you couldn't see from here and then passing the batons one after another to the next groups crossing the forest?

At first Ikuo thought this was some kind of joke. But Patron's insistence wasn't normal. All of a sudden Patron leaped up and yelled for Ms. Tachibana, who was downstairs. When she showed up, a worried look on her face, he ordered her to get his clothes ready so he could go outside. "Morio's coming down with his shoes on," he yelled out, "so get the same clothes ready for him!"

Though there was no need to, he shouted at Ikuo in the same fearful voice. "If the Fireflies set fires and the whole forest surrounding the Hollow goes up in flames at once," he shouted, "there'll be a panic among the thousand spectators! We have to do something to stop this tragedy!"

Ikuo tried to calm him down, telling him this was just a ridiculous fantasy. But Morio was even more hysterical than Patron, and as Patron was being dressed by Ms. Tachibana, his vehement words pouring out unabated, Morio clung to his waist, crying. Patron upbraided him, urging him to change his own clothes as quickly as he could.

Seeing that Ikuo was still seated calmly, Patron had changed his tack, announcing that he was going down to the reviewing stand to take the microphone and urge the spectators to evacuate the area. "You and Ms. Tachibana take Morio, he can't walk well!" he shouted, "and run past the parking lot and escape to the bypass!"

Patron had pulled on his shoes right on top of the rug and was about to head downstairs alone. Not knowing what else to do, Ikuo physically restrained him. If Patron's call was amplified by the microphone and rang out in the darkness, imagine how much more of a panic this would throw the spectators into, Ikuo argued. "People will be thrown into a worse panic, thinking they'll be burned alive in a forest fire," he said, trying to calm Patron down.

Although usually mild-mannered, Patron had become like a frenzied child, foaming at the mouth, his face bright red and swollen as he resisted, trying to wrench himself free of Ikuo's grasp. When he couldn't, he twisted to one side and boxed Ikuo on the ears. "*Satan, Satan!*" he screamed.

Likewise, Morio jabbed at Ikuo's thighs, yelling out the same thing. With Morio wrapped around his lower half, Ikuo grasped Patron tightly so he couldn't pound him anymore and dragged him backward toward the bed in the next room, faintly visible in the gloom. The momentum sent Morio tumbling down the hallway that led to the staircase. He let out a cry, and Ms. Tachibana came running.

Ikuo had finally managed to hold Patron down in bed, but he kept on resisting, spitting out hard flecks of foam as he shouted, "You faggot Satan, you!"

As Dr. Koga was leaving the chapel annex with Kizu, Ogi, who had the key with him and was waiting for them, called out. Ms. Tachibana wanted Dr. Koga to come over to Patron's place right away. Kizu watched him walk up the short slope to Patron's residence, raise a hand in greeting to the Firefly security guards, and, looking down, walk inside. As Kizu turned his gaze toward the overflowing crowds of people, Ikuo showed up, his sweatshirt and corduroy trousers sweaty and smelly.

"I'll take you over to the north shore," he said.

Leaving Ogi behind, Kizu and Ikuo walked off, a two-man security guard from the Fireflies clearing a path for them through the milling crowds. As they got to the narrow place where the lunch menu was posted, the blacksmith and a woman who looked as if she were fighting illness were waiting in ambush. They passed so close to Kizu and Ikuo they could smell the liquor on the man's breath, but Ikuo ignored the man when he called out to them and put his thick arm protectively around Kizu as they strode away.

The smell of Ikuo's sweat made Kizu feel calm and protected. A fear still lingered, though, as to what the blacksmith might say to the woman— perhaps not ill herself but with a husband ill with cancer—as they stood bathed in the direct sunlight beside him.

The security guards led them from the crowded dam, along the broad road connecting to the north shore of the Hollow, to the path leading up to Kizu's house. Ikuo was in a hurry but he was careful to go in first, and as Kizu headed straight for bed to lie down, he opened up the windows from the studio to the kitchen to disperse the heated, stuffy air.

Kizu laid his head back at an angle on the high part of the bed and watched. Ikuo sat down at a chair in front of an empty easel, picked up a drawing of himself and Patron on top of a box of paints, and gazed at it. The strong light shining in from outside emphasized the contrast even more, but Kizu had already noticed how haggard and beastlike Ikuo's face looked, compared to the sketch.

Ikuo didn't look back at Kizu. He hadn't said a word on the walk over to the house, but now he spoke.

"I went over to see the triptych again, and I'll tell you it's a big hit," he said. "Of course, the part showing Patron's wound is the main thing people are interested in."

"You knew the wound in his side has disappeared, didn't you?"

"Yes, Dancer told me. Just as she hid its existence from everyone for so long, now she plans to keep the fact that it's gone a secret from everyone."

· "It must be tough on Patron, too. . . . Do you think things just built up inside him that led to last night's incident?" Kizu asked.

Ikuo was silent, but he came over to stand next to Kizu, the drawing still in his hand. "I knew the way I felt about the triptych was different from everybody else, and now that I see this preliminary drawing I know exactly what I *was* feeling. About what kind of Lord that Patron is to me—me as *Jonah,* as the Fireflies call me."

Ikuo was silent, sunk in thought. Kizu thought he caught a glimpse of a dangerous imbalance between the expression on Ikuo's face, all bones and dark skin, and the look in his unmoving eyes.

"I've gone any number of times to see the painting. After the press conference this morning, when you and Dr. Koga were talking, it worried me, so I went to see it again, and now I finally understand what it all means."

Ikuo drew his eyebrows together over his penetrating, still unmoving eyes. It was his habit, after examining what he wanted to say in his mind, to push aside any hesitation or doubts about whether his listeners would understand what he was getting at and just forge full steam ahead, speaking like some fanatic.

"Even after last night's incident I still believe Patron is a very special person. He's an extraordinary person, one who definitely journeys to the *other side* and has mystical experiences. I think that characteristic of his came out in a strange way last night. What happened last night was quite out of the ordinary.

"Even after he was no longer able to sink into a trance, he's continued to suffer as the mediator between the world and his own special God—whether a personified God or something else, I don't know. He's resigned to never escaping that role. What I find more extraordinary is how he made a fool of the God he had such an intimate relationship with and abandoned his followers. And now, without thoroughly reflecting on what he did, he's welcoming back these hundreds of people.

"But what was even more of a shock for me was how crazed with fear he got, positive that these believers and onlookers are going to be burned to death. That's a *human* way of looking at things, but since I'm the one they've dubbed Jonah, I'm not expecting ordinary human behavior from him."

"Since I drew both of you in my painting," Kizu said, "you as Jonah, Patron with his wound as the Lord, I suppose I could be accused of having a hunch that your relationship with Patron would follow the lines of the book of Jonah, with Jonah being persuaded, in the end, by God. This has bothered me for a long while.

"When Morio and Patron went in the middle of the night to see the painting, Patron told me the person you're modeled after, according to Wolynski's book, never gives up protesting to God, ends up in despair, and leaps into the sea himself. When I heard this, I felt freed from the concerns I've had for so long. Your relationship with Patron might very well develop in a different direction from that of Jonah and the Lord in the book of Jonah. Not that I had any idea what path this particular Lord would lead Jonah in. . . . At any rate, Ikuo, you are a person who has led a consistent life. From day one you've been the Jonah who protests."

"I suppose you're right," Ikuo said, turning his face to the surface of the lake, glittering in the noon sun, and once more squinting his eyes shut in the brightness. "I felt the same thing about Patron last night. He's a person who's been consistent his whole life, and always will be. Even after the Somersault, he suffered because of a very human sense of integrity. I don't think calling what he experienced a descent into hell exaggerates the kind of suffering he endured. Still, he insisted on being consistent with what he had done in the Somersault. He never attempted a Somersault in reverse."

"And now you've given up hoping for Patron to be the mediator for you and the Almighty?" Kizu asked. "Though you're still quite young, you've lived your whole life seeking God—who will tell you, *Go ahead and do it!*— and the mediator between you and that voice. And now you've found that Patron isn't the one.

"Does this mean you'll wash your hands of him? That you'll return this Founder, overflowing with love for humanity, to his followers at this conference, and make a clean break with him? Whatever your decision, I want you to know I'll follow you—wherever you go. If that's how things end up, though, with Patron curing my cancer I'd say I was overpaid for the triptych."

"No, I'm not planning to leave right now," Ikuo said. "After our struggle last night, Dr. Koga rushed over and gave Patron a shot to calm him down. He was probably still feeling the aftereffects of this, but this morning before the press conference he called me over and asked me to exert still more effort to help him with the final event in our program, his sermon.

"He had called me Satan and worse, but he didn't take it back or apologize. He had a new idea for the direction of his sermon, connecting up with the pageant on the cypress island we'd talked about last night. He told me he got the idea from a strangely realistic dream he had, and he'd like me to help him make it happen.

"Patron's going to deliver his sermon from the reviewing stand, and he wants to do this wearing a doll made to look like Guide. The other new dolls for the Spirit Festival he wants taken over to the island and burned up with the giant cypress. Guide's doll should be burned there too, so he wants another Guide doll, a much larger one, made for him to wear. His concept is to have himself wearing the same sort of thing as these dolls that are burned up in a requiem ceremony.

"I said I'd help him. As we speak, the Fireflies are out in the hot sun now working on the island, constructing a wooden frame in front of which we'll stand the doll of Guide and a microphone, the same way Patron will be standing in front of a microphone, and placing several kerosene tanks among the cypress leaves.

"They're putting everything they have into the job. Since it'll be a public demonstration, a continuation of last night's Fireflies procession, I'll make sure they do a great job."

A beat or two of silence ensued. Then Ikuo turned his back to the bright window. For the first time in quite a while his expression was gentle, even bashful, as he said, "How about a shower? I'm all sweaty from last night and I'd like to take one myself. Let's take the afternoon off, in preparation for tomorrow. Pretty soon we're not going to have much to do with them anymore, so let's skip the party at the Farm tonight and leave everything up to the Technicians and the Quiet Women."

32: For Patron

1

On Sunday morning the green leaves of the trees and the summer grasses sparkled in the strong fresh sunlight, and clouds reflected whitely on the surface of the lake. Ogi was out with some young workmen sent over by a local company that had contracted to build additional temporary toilets, trying to decide where to locate them. From their experiences on Friday, the night of the Fireflies procession, it was clear that the portable toilets provided by Mr. Soda weren't enough. So they set out to dig out holes in six spots around the grounds that would then have a wooden framework built around them— knowing they had to finish in time for tonight's meeting.

They selected a relatively flat spot, on the mountain side of the path through the grandstands that circled the lake, and set to work. Once the conference was over they'd wait until the ground at the bottom of the holes had absorbed all the liquid before filling them in. The holes the motorized shovels scooped out were deeper than Ogi had imagined. Once they'd decided on the locations and work had begun, Ogi was left with little to do. As the shovels continued their loud clang, he walked down the path from east to north, to the point closest to the island with the giant cypress in the middle of the lake.

The branches of the giant cypress had been trimmed back to a height of about twenty feet. The lopped-off larger branches and the smaller ones with green still on them were piled up on a two-tiered wooden frame surrounding the trunk—the middle of both the upper and lower tiers left empty for the dolls to be added—and leaned up against the lower tier. Along with the stack of firewood in the island meadow, this was enough to make a spectacular firestorm.

The entire structure was like some sturdy square building. Even if kerosene was poured on and lighted, it wouldn't collapse to one side but would end up a huge bonfire, safe for all spectators to enjoy.

Another wooden frame was set up apart from the one around the cypress but of the same height, made up of two or three logs with speakers set on top. Beside it lay a sturdy bamboo ladder, the kind used by lumberjacks, to be used later to place the dolls that were going to be burned on top of the wooden frame.

Sensing someone behind him, Ogi turned around to find Gii, his suntanned face looking much older now, leaning against the tiny light-green leaves of a maple and watching him. Gii said, unhurriedly, "Yonah's going around this morning, talking to everyone to make sure everything's set for the evening meeting. He'd like you to go with him; he's already settled the matter with Dancer."

"Right this moment?" Ogi asked.

"My truck is in the little park beyond the parking lot."

They turned back to the east shore, greeting the young workmen they passed, and walked down the aisle, a little shoddily laid out, below the chapel and the monastery. Unconcerned about all the trampled-down spots on the path's shoulders, Gii strode on.

"Where did he say we're going to talk?" Ogi asked.

"We'll be meeting the first group, representatives of the Quiet Women, in the hills. After the party last night, some of their friends stayed at the monastery, and we can't very well make them leave so early in the morning. The women will drive over in Yonah's car."

"You drove over here, right? So I'll drive from here. The prefectural police haven't shown up yet, have they?"

"They don't view the church as dangerous enough to warrant sending the riot police here this early."

As Gii had said, there weren't any other cars at the little park. Despite Ogi's insistence, though, he didn't make any move to hand over the keys. Ogi caught a glimpse of a doll wrapped in cloth bags in the loaded truck bed.

"I'd heard about these dolls, but the ones used in the Spirit Procession are really big, aren't they?" Ogi asked.

"The one in back was made to Patron's special order; Mayumi had to stay up all night to do it. It's the Spirit of Guide. She said it wasn't so hard since she'd already made one, though the larger size did cause her a little trouble."

They drove down the Shikoku highway bypass, down to where the older district road leveled out, and crossed the bridge over the Kame River, the water sparkling below.

"We're going to drive up to a piece of worthless meadow my mother inherited," Gii explained, "at the intersection of two logging roads. One road goes up past the entrance to the Farm; the one we're going to climb goes past the junior high."

As the truck turned the corner and entered the glen, a woman teacher from the junior high, out sweeping the decorative shrubbery in front of the school, looked up in surprise at Gii, driving without a license. For his part, Gii remained totally cool and collected.

He parked the truck at the base of a red pine tree, branches trimmed back to quite high up, the greenery near the top shining in the brilliant sky. A red Ford Mustang was parked in front of a clearing leading to another logging road. As Ogi stepped down the narrow path down the short slope, clutching at branches to steady himself, Gii said to him, "Better not touch the wax trees. He Who Destroys planted wax trees from here up to the ridge to use as raw material for the Fireflies' candles. Do you suppose he really planted them so he could pour hot oil over his enemies?"

At an unexpectedly steep slope where they could look down at the villages and the river in the bottom of the valley, there was a square meadow jutting out like a stage. Ikuo was standing there, talking with three of the Quiet Women.

To the left below them was a sparse stand of red pines, a path cutting through it that went down to where they could see—through a large bamboo grove just before the path went uphill again—half of the lake in the Hollow and the Plexiglas skylights on the roof of the chapel reflecting the sunlight. In the midst of this wonderfully placid scenery, the bypass to the cross-Shikoku highway cut through a mountain one hill over. The whole scene was so bucolic it made Ogi want to tell Gii that he understood the feelings of the Fireflies, ready to fight to defend the legends of their land.

Before he could say anything, though, Ikuo saw the two of them approach and abruptly waved Gii off.

"Go guard the car," he told him abruptly. "The key's in it, so if a truck comes and wants to pass, move it so he can!"

Ikuo led Ogi and the three women over to an old tree in the west corner of the meadow, bursting with dark green berries hanging down on long stems. There was a place constructed out of thick logs where they could sit.

Ogi found Mrs. Shigeno and Ms. Takada, whom he hadn't seen in a while, full of the same sense of incongruity he'd felt yesterday morning in Ms. Oyama, who rounded out the threesome. Their skin was equally pale and lusterless, but what was even more noticeable was the clumsy, amateurish way the Quiet Women had done up their hair. The hair behind their ears and at the napes of their necks was newly shorn. What's more, a dark, solemn shadow had fallen over their expressions.

As the three sat side by side on the log seat, with the river on their right, Mrs. Shigeno, at the end, looked up at the small orange-red berries on the branch above her and said, "Whenever I see this many berries it always makes me think of when the Chinese matrimony-vine wine we used to make was ready to drink. But that doesn't move me anymore. My interest in trees and plants is entirely practical."

Ogi was the only one who responded to this by gazing up at the thin stalks of the matrimony vine and its bell-like berries. He realized that her statement was merely a prelude leading up to the main theme of their talk.

"Ogi is helping Professor Kizu write a history of Patron's church, and I want him to witness all the decisions that are made and the events that take place," Ikuo said, as if making sure the Quiet Women understood. "I'll be talking with the Technicians next, and he'll be accompanying me there as well. . . . Ogi, I'd like you to remember that the Quiet Women were followers of Patron years before we first came across him. As junior members, then, you and I have to do whatever we can to help them, no matter what they ask of us. They're not looking for our input, and it would be out of line to object to anything they say. Okay, this being said, we'd like to hear what sort of program the Quiet Women propose."

"Do you understand, Ogi-kun?" Ms. Oyama said. "Ikuo's told us you're the church's chronicler, but *we're* the ones responsible for the events you'll chronicle. Before Patron's sermon, after seven P.M., we'd like to have the whole chapel set aside for us to use. At yesterday's press conference there were people who said that was unfair, but I'd like you to give your word one more time that you won't say anything. In terms of time, this should overlap with part two of the Spirit Procession.

"I'm sure there'll still be people who want to come see Professor Kizu's triptych or who'll want to take refuge inside the chapel to listen to Patron's sermon without all the bugs flying around them. Our old friends might insist on coming inside. Despite this, just before seven P.M. the Quiet Women will enter the chapel and barricade it from inside. The Technicians will be outside, standing guard."

Before Ogi could say a thing, Ms. Takada, who ever since moving to this area no longer seemed bothered by having only one eye, and who was in charge of business affairs for the Quiet Women, spoke in a calm, composed voice.

"At that time, blessed by Patron's sermon, we will ascend to heaven. In the sacred ground of the church, listening to Morio's music, the Quiet Women will pass away."

Aghast, Ogi turned around to look at Ikuo. His rough-hewn, brawny face stared straight ahead, his expression unchanged. Only Ogi's heart was pounding, his face flushed. The blood pounding in his ears drowned out the cicadas screeching all around them. Mrs. Shigeno tried to explain things further.

"After Guide passed away, Patron announced that he would be returning to his religious activities. At that point we took this to mean that he was laying the preparations for ascending to heaven. That's why we had our children sing 'Hallelujah!'—to praise Patron's decision. We were so happy he allowed us to move here right away, thinking he was giving us the go-ahead sign. After moving here and getting to know Ms. Tachibana and Morio better, our resolve is firmer than ever.

"As it turned out, though, we were leaping to conclusions. The confrontation two days ago between Patron and Ikuo convinced us of this. Patron was afraid that more than a thousand people would be burned to death. He was going to make an announcement over the speakers to tell everyone to flee, but Ikuo stopped him. It was like he was insane. We think he was merely afraid.

"When we heard this news, we thought *Hallelujah!* as a scene flashed through our minds of seven hundred believers all passing up to heaven along with Patron in this glorious holy place. But Patron was afraid. He lost consciousness and had to be comforted by someone of limited intelligence. When we heard this, we decided we'd have to do things *our* way.

"The Passion in this holy land that seven hundred couldn't realize *we've* decided to carry out with *twenty-five.* Wasn't the illusion Patron had—that the Fireflies were about to burn to death a thousand people, curious onlookers included—something that bubbled up out of his dread, out of the depths of his very being? If Guide were alive I know he'd correct Patron's mistake. But the only way *we* can correct him—and educate him—is by *taking action.*"

Mrs. Shigeno's confident tone quickly drew Ogi's imagination away from the three women seated in front of him to a place, some ten hours later, where he was dealing with the dead bodies of all the Quiet Women. Strangely enough, this made him picture, quite intimately, the face of Mrs. Tsugane, her features, perhaps because of her age, sharply outlined, as she arranged a tryst between them deep in the woods of this very same north slope. Ogi sought refuge in the scent of her living body, so very different from the smell of death.

As he thought all this, Mrs. Takada, totally indifferent to the smooth skin covering the spot where her right eye should be, said, "I've had this for quite a long time." She pulled out a thick glass bottle, four inches high, from a paper bag. "They told me it's enough cyanide to kill fifty people. I'll divide it into twenty-five portions. Dr. Koga would help me, don't you think?"

Ogi flinched from the proffered bag, but Ikuo stretched out a long manly arm and snatched it up.

Ogi, feeling helpless and alone, couldn't stay quiet any longer. "People call me an innocent youth, and I'm not sure but what you're pulling my leg here, but why do all of you have to *pass away*? Can you imagine the impact it's going to have if all the Quiet Women commit mass suicide right when Patron's about to launch his new church?"

Ikuo and the three Quiet Women all looked disgusted. Even so, Mrs. Shigeno tried to respond.

"I'm getting on in years and I want to settle things while I'm still in my right mind, while my body still is able to function. I'm not speaking for all the Quiet Women, though. . . . To put it in a more general way, don't you feel that the world is fast falling apart? In twenty years it will be even worse, and everyone then will have to consider the problems I'm thinking about *now*. When you picture this, you realize that the coming end time will be just like Patron used to preach about before the Somersault. What we're going to do is revive the message of Patron's old sermons and pass away first.

"From the bottom of our hearts, we wish Patron well in establishing his Church of the New Man. Some of the media reported that after he and Guide left the church we lost all hope and Patron feared we would commit mass suicide. So he made statements making fun of our belief, saying it was ridiculous, so we no longer seriously considered dying. That was his plan all along, the articles said.

"When we read these articles we couldn't believe them. It was just too simplistic. We were outraged, because if what they said was true, it was an insult to the Quiet Women. But after what just took place, we've had to re-think our position. Patron didn't calculate anything. He was simply *afraid*. . . . This time *we're* going to take the initiative and pass away. After that, if Patron makes another calculated Somersault, it won't have any meaning."

Ogi was at a loss for words. He felt hopelessly naive and impotent. He told himself over and over he couldn't cry in front of Ms. Takada, with her pale smooth skin over one eye.

Giving Ogi's shoulder an almost cruelly strong thump, Ikuo addressed the three women. "The sun's getting a little hot, and I think we're about finished here, so we'd better be getting along. Please excuse Ogi for not keeping

his promise about not interrupting. As everyone says, he's terribly innocent. . . .
Please take Gii's car back to the Hollow. I'm going to go with Ogi to the Farm.
Don't worry, he won't break your trust anymore."

"At last night's party, backstage, we settled things with Mr. Hanawa,"
Ms. Oyama said. "If they were really to oppose us, our occupation of the chapel
wouldn't last very long."

Mrs. Shigeno turned to Ogi, who was flushed and completely unnerved
by what he'd heard. "Trying to get in touch with the police would be even
more futile," she warned. "We've given a lot of thought to the arrangements
for our ascent and have come up with several possible scenarios. If you try to
do something, first of all Ikuo will stop you. But even if you get through to
the police and they show up, we'll just hole up in the chapel that much earlier, with the Technicians standing guard. If there isn't time for the poison to
work, the windows in the chapel are just the right height for hanging. There
are footstools in the chapel already, and we've laid in a stock of rope."

2

Many cars were parked inside and outside the Farm, cars not left over
from the party the previous night. Three RVs were parked in the meadow
opposite the entrance, all with curtains drawn. Activity had begun at the
Farm, with nothing left over from the party. Some young people in the open
space in front of the buildings were cleaning up, others were transporting
mountains of garbage bags, while still others were removing the party deco-
rations from the roof and side walls of the barn. Technicians were supervising each of these groups. Visitors were walking around, looking at the
meat-processing plant from outside, checking the enlargements being made
to the chicken coops.

Before Ikuo and Ogi could get out of their car, a young Firefly whose
face Ogi remembered came over, eager to carry out his assigned duties.

"Mr. Hanawa is working behind the warehouse," he said, "and told me
to tell you to meet him over there." On the north side of the grassy meadow,
where all sorts of activities were going on, stood a food manufacturing facility, but Ikuo and Ogi walked on the west side, which was deserted except for
two large warehouses, and continued down a narrow path between them,
coming out to a spot like a garden in a mountain retreat between a quiet grove
of oaks and beeches. One could sense the calm life of the person living there.

On the north side stood an old two-story western-style house, which was
where Satchan, the farm's owner, lived. The well-tended land sloped gently

down from west to south to a woods with evergreen oaks, and in the midst of the dark foliage they could see the roof of the house where Gii and Mayumi lived.

Below the eaves of the house was a pile of thick pine logs, each about twenty inches in diameter. On their near side, Mr. Hanawa was working. *Working* might not be the right word for it, for there was a calm about him as he squatted there, as if it was his habit to be lost in quiet contemplation. From the slope there was a line of thick birches and oaks as a windbreak. The foliage of the trees, higher than the roof of the house, cut off the sunlight, making a cozy little spot just perfect for Mr. Hanawa to do simple tasks and to meditate.

Before Ikuo and Ogi approached him, Mr. Hanawa stood up, holding a wooden-handled tool with a metal Y at the end. At his feet in their canvas shoes, long stumps of finger-width-size roots lay scattered.

"A motorized weed cutter would make short work of these. Mountain azaleas put out buds again before you know it," Mr. Hanawa said, explaining what he was doing. "Yesterday and today we have guests staying at the Technicians' office, so let's talk here." He threw Ogi a look.

"I want Ogi to know everything that's going on," Ikuo explained. "The Quiet Women are on track with their plans, though they may occupy the chapel a little earlier than planned. If they have to do that it'll be a bit troublesome to kick out any visitors who might happen to be there."

"If the police find out we'll have to mobilize the Technicians," Mr. Hanawa said. "The Fireflies will have their hands full with the Spirit Festival."

At this point Ogi couldn't help but break his promise again. Standing beside Ikuo, who was so businesslike, Ogi said, his emotions bare, "The Technicians aren't going to intervene in what the Quiet Women are planning to do?"

Mr. Hanawa clearly shrank back from Ogi's words, but Ogi didn't flinch. He waited, making it clear he wanted an answer. Finally Mr. Hanawa settled down enough to respond.

"I never really knew the Quiet Women until we moved here," he said, "but during these past ten years aren't they the ones who're most exhausted by it all? Even if we try to prevent them by force, I think eventually they're going to do what they want to do, so they might as well carry out their plan at the same time as the inaugural sermon announcing the Church of the New Man. It's ideal timing for them. Who are we to mess it up?

"With the Church of the New Man as our base, we Technicians plan to reconsider what we tried to do in Izu. Patron and Guide's Somersault made those earlier plans fizzle out, but we don't think we should simply abandon the idea of a millennial kingdom to follow or our plan to bring the Japanese people to repentance. Patron has his Church of the New Man, and likewise we have our plans that we've reworked over the past ten years. Their Somersault gave us time to let these ideas mature. Since we've faced these issues head-on, we want to respect the freedom of the Quiet Women to take whatever actions they've thought long and hard about, so we're going to help fulfill the atonement of these twenty-five women."

"You idiot!"

Groaning this out, Ogi lunged at Mr. Hanawa, who, with his free arm—careful not to touch Ogi with the metal-tipped tool he held—lunged back and blocked him.

"Hear me out," Mr. Hanawa said, not at all out of breath. "At the time of the Somersault we were going to blow a nuclear power plant to kingdom come, and we didn't mind passing away in the process. Why should we cling to this degenerate world? But we couldn't just abandon the plan for a millennial kingdom of repentance. So we were exposed to ridicule.

"This shows how innocent we are, perhaps, but we believed that our decision and Patron's plans deep down had something in common. Once we had that troubled meeting with Guide, though, our illusions vanished. The only option left for us was to lead the Church of the New Man as a starting point for our reign of repentance. We're going to have Professor Kizu paint a fourth panel depicting the atonement of the Quiet Women."

This time Ogi lunged at Mr. Hanawa without a word. Never having fought anyone before, he missed, punching the air, while his exposed neck was slammed with a cudgel-like fist and he collapsed to the ground.

When he opened his eyes, his saw Mr. Hanawa's canvas shoes moving right in front of his eyes. He hunched his neck to avoid the kick he thought was coming, but the boot tips were merely poking at what looked like an inlaid bat in the short cut grass. Once he realized that dark object was a neatly cut stump, Ogi staggered to his feet.

Rubbing his upper right arm, Ikuo calmly assessed the situation. "Another promise down the drain. . . . Mr. Hanawa, we're going to go speak with Patron. That's the only way Ogi will be convinced, don't you think? I'll have the Fireflies report in detail on the Quiet Women's movement up until they enter the chapel. Thanks in advance for your help.

"Before we see Patron, though, there's something the Quiet Women asked me to do," Ikuo said to Ogi. "First we'll stop by Dr. Koga's clinic. He's working independently here, though of course he's originally a colleague of the Izu research guys, and I know he keeps in close touch with Mr. Hanawa, not to mention the Quiet Women. So no more going out on your own and breaking your promise, okay?"

The reception area in the clinic was empty. Dr. Koga was sitting alone in front of a desk in an examination room, the one with Kizu's watercolor. He watched Ikuo come in with his paper bag and then frowned when he saw Ogi bringing up the rear. Hesitantly he said, "Mrs. Shigeno called me."

"Ogi knows what the situation is," Ikuo began. "I came over to leave this with you. Ogi is opposed to the Quiet Women's decision, and opposed to having the Technicians guard them, but he's not going to be scheming to outmaneuver them or anything. Could you take a look at his head?"

Ogi was once more aware of the pain in the back of his head, but he remained seated. Dr. Koga came over to look at him from behind and touched the tender part.

"This is pretty bad. Hit by a fist, were you? You have an abrasion."

Ogi had thought he'd been sweating, but it was blood dripping down. Dr. Koga brushed aside Ogi's hand as he reached out to touch his head, and after applying pressure for a time he took the bottle Ikuo had given him and disappeared into the deserted pharmacy.

Dr. Koga came back with some antiseptic and treated Ogi's wound; then, as if suddenly remembering something, he asked Ikuo to show him his right hand. Ikuo ignored him.

"Do you *really* think this is for the best?" Ogi persisted, but he was so upset he choked up and couldn't go on.

"The Quiet Women have given it a lot of thought," Dr. Koga replied, sitting down at his desk again. "The Technicians have had some bitter experiences these past ten years too, but I'm not about to make any presumptuous remarks. Don't you think we should respect the intentions of people who deserve our sympathy? What should the Technicians do? If the Quiet Women ask them to stand guard, that's all they *can* do. . . . When all's said and done, I'm going to stick with whatever Ikuo's planned. This isn't just some spur-of-the-moment idea, mind you. Not that the Technicians would allow me to act on my own, anyway."

"I don't know the legalities of it, but can't you be charged with aiding and abetting a suicide?" Ogi asked.

"With these women putting their lives on the line, would that really be such a big deal?" Dr. Koga asked. "Ikuo, haven't you talked with our innocent youth here about the other path?"

Ikuo turned to Dr. Koga and let his large head slump forward. When he spoke, he seemed to be feeling his way through what he wanted to say.

"I don't think I have the right to express any misgivings about what these church veterans—both the Quiet Women and the Technicians—are planning," Ikuo said. "The same holds true for Dr. Koga. But I do still believe that what Patron decides is even more important. If there's another option based on what Patron wants, I'd hope we can get the Quiet Women to switch over to it in time. I'll be the one who does that—with your help, of course, doctor. As for you, Ogi, I'd like you to watch from the sidelines. There's no need to explain every detail."

"That's exactly right, Ogi," Dr. Koga said. "I'll bring over the package at exactly noon, Ikuo. . . . And whatever you do, don't mix up the two bags."

Ogi noticed that the way Dr. Koga carried himself, his expression, and the tremor in his voice were all something new. Ogi also caught a whiff of distilled spirits. On Dr. Koga's desk he saw a flask and an empty glass. Ikuo stood up. Ignoring this, Dr. Koga reached out for the flask. Standing up himself, Ogi couldn't help but say something.

"The Quiet Women say that they've seen now what a coward Patron is. If that's true, why don't they just leave and go back to their children? If they feel they've seen through him, why in the world do they feel they have to take poison? What good will *that* possibly do?"

"What's important for them isn't Patron's character but his *being*," Dr. Koga said enigmatically. "Though I'm sure there are still some women in the Kansai headquarters who don't think that way."

3

As Ogi sat next to Ikuo as they drove off toward the Hollow, the sky, which had been clear all morning, suddenly grew overcast. With one part of the Spirit Festival scheduled for that afternoon, the road going down to the Hollow from the Shikoku highway bypass was already crowded. Ikuo chose the road that went up below the Mansion. The cloudy sky looked ominous, and the road below the pass, covered with its thick canopy of overgrown branches of evergreen oaks and beeches, was gloomy and dusky. Finally, heavy raindrops began to fall.

Headlights were coming down toward them, but they couldn't very well pull off to let the vehicle pass with the shoulder on the river side so obviously uncertain. The lights turned out to be those of a truck that had gone to dump some of the garbage containers hastily set up below the dam. Ikuo docilely reversed the car. After backing up for a long while, he stopped against an old horse chestnut tree to let the truck pass. The driver, a town employee Ikuo knew, had his window rolled down despite the rain, and he shouted out to Ikuo that another truck was following him, so Ogi and Ikuo waited under the shadows of the large branches.

"You're pretty deeply involved with the Quiet Women and with the Technicians now, aren't you?"

When Ogi said this, Ikuo made an unexpected face. "Even though I was told not to," he replied slowly.

"But even if you hadn't gotten involved, you can't say the Quiet Women wouldn't have gotten that idea in their heads or that the Technicians wouldn't have helped out, for whatever ulterior motives they might have. All I'm saying is that you got deeply involved with them."

Ikuo was quiet for a while, before responding patiently. "I was interested in the Technicians from the first," he said. "I did have a very strong impression of the Quiet Women, though, from when Professor Kizu and I visited their commune and saw how pious they are. I developed a close relationship with them because that's what Dancer told me to do. It wasn't some office consensus but more Dancer's own idea. I realize now she was right to do this; she'd foreseen danger for Patron in opening a new church here, so she ordered me to get a handle on the two groups. Dancer's top priority is and always will be Patron's safety. That's just the way she is."

A second identical light truck came down the slope toward them, gave them a wave, and passed by. Ikuo pulled their car out from under the shelter of the horse chestnut tree and drove off uphill in the blinding rain. When they arrived at the square below the dam they found conference participants crossing over on flagstones since the ground had been flooded by water that ran from the lake and overflowed the watercourse. Some people had small umbrellas, but the majority just held plastic sheets or cardboard boxes over their heads. Everything was finished at the red and green tents, so these people were making their way to the chapel.

Gii, who apparently had been waiting for them all the while in the parking lot in front of the tents, ran over with two umbrellas. Dressed in a raincoat and rain hat, he was oblivious to the downpour, and as he walked beside Ikuo he reported that the Spirit Festival would go on as planned. No problem, he said, summer-morning rains blow over soon, and since Ikuo looked doubtful he reassured him that in this region that was indeed the way it was.

Gii managed expertly to protect Ikuo and Ogi from the crowds of people in front of the dining hall, and they soon arrived at Patron's residence, where some of the Fireflies were standing watch. Gii wanted to go inside with them, but Ikuo asked him to take a message to Ms. Oyama to the effect that Dr. Koga would do what they had asked and would deliver at twelve; showing no regret at not going with them, Gii retraced his steps.

The temperature had dropped quickly because of the rain, but when she opened the front door Ms. Tachibana's hair was plastered to her pale forehead. The house had been shut up tight and was humid with a close lived-in odor.

Since the incidents two nights ago, Patron was holed up in his bedroom on the southwest side, unchanged from when Ikuo had been summoned to see him the day before. Ms. Tachibana showed them into the shadowy room, where they were met by an even more musky animal smell.

Patron was lying in bed. He sat up and opened the curtain on the southern window. Light spilled into the bedroom through the rain-swept foliage of the oaks outside. Morio was curled up like a dog at the foot of the bed and didn't acknowledge the newcomers. A sense of the dark confinement he'd shared with Patron still clung to him.

Ikuo sat down in the low-backed armchair brought from Patron's Tokyo home, while Ogi sat down in a straight-back wooden chair and faced Patron, whose cheeks were sunken.

"Late last night after the party, Dancer stopped by and told me about the Quiet Women's plans," Patron said in a low voice. "This morning Ikuo was to hear their final intentions and make certain of the Technicians' response. There's been no change. Am I correct?"

"Yes, that's right," Ikuo replied.

"Ever since I announced at the memorial service for Guide that I would be restarting the church, and I decided to allow the Quiet Women and the Technicians to join first, Dancer has had her doubts. If after they returned to the fold the Quiet Woman and the Technicians recognized the Somersault—and recognized the new church as developing *out* of the Somersault, rather than out of a *denial* of it—these groups would be powerful allies to have. But that's not the case, she said. We moved here to Shikoku with all that still up in the air. So I entrusted you, Ikuo, with the task of getting to know both groups better and trying to discover what's really going on with them."

Patron's speech was getting noticeably slower.

"That's right," Ikuo said. "My two responsibilities since coming here have been that and supervising the Farm. Meeting the Fireflies, admittedly, led to other activities."

"Knowing now what the Quiet Women are planning plus the fact that the Technicians will be indirectly helping out, I can see that Dancer was right to be suspicious," Patron said. "The Quiet Women and the Technicians immediately denied the Somersault that Guide and I did, and nothing's changed. They haven't altered their stance in ten years. Dancer tells me that at the meeting where I'll announce the launching of our Church of the New Man, they're planning to take me captive and act as if the Somersault had never taken place.

"After the Quiet Women have made sure that the Somersault has been canceled, they plan to pass on joyously. They'll be the martyrs who saved the church, and a great Hallelujah! will ring out. And the Technicians, bearing the atonement of these twenty-five saintly women, will take over the church and run it the way they have always wanted.

"If that happens, it doesn't really matter whether I truly canceled the Somersault or not, does it? All they have to do is take care of me until the day I die. Our summer conference would then be remembered as the time when Patron canceled the Somersault and the Quiet Women ascended to heaven and became divine. Dancer told me she could already sense this at the party at the Farm. Is that a good summary?"

"Gii told me he felt that too," Ikuo said. "As far as the order of events is concerned, it wouldn't really matter if you deny the Somersault *after* the Quiet Women passed on, would it? Applauding the atonement of the Quiet Women, God would—Hallelujah!—forgive you for making a fool of him.

"Before they pass on tonight, the Quiet Women are praying that they can atone in your place for what you did. They're also praying that you're repentant after having fallen with Guide into hell and after Guide had to atone with his death. They're cleansing your image so you can be an appropriate leader for the new church. They've already typed up a prayer on a word processor and prepared a thousand copies. It's a direct prayer to God but also an appeal to their former colleagues in the church and an announcement aimed at the media. To the Quiet Women you are no longer the Patron who mediates between man and God. They're trying to reestablish the bond between you, repentant, and God.

"In their discussions so far, the Technicians recognize how inscrutably adroit you were in doing the Somersault. They're optimistic that after you hear about the Quiet Women passing on you'll deliver a sermon responding to that and cancel the Somersault once and for all."

The window started to get lighter. The leaves were still dripping, but the rain had let up.

Patron closed his eyes and lay back down, while Morio, who was awake all this time, didn't move a muscle. Ogi felt sorry for both of them. But Patron's words after a long silence didn't reflect any of these empathetic feelings.

"Dancer feels very strongly that this is beyond her," he said. "I'm afraid I've dragged her into some foolish things. And you too, Ogi. I imagine that the church from now on won't be the same Church of the New Man that I was hoping to make with you two. When you leave the Hollow, Ogi, I'd like you to take Dancer with you."

It bothered Ogi that Patron hadn't mentioned Ikuo, but Ikuo didn't respond to this. Instead, he spoke of other things, his tone changed.

"Friday night convinced me that the popular interpretation of the Somersault in the media was absolutely correct," Ikuo said. "In other words, you feared the mass suicide of your followers, so you took humane steps to prevent it. But if the Quiet Women commit mass suicide now, that will just add insult to injury. So I'm going to make sure that not only will their plan fall through but also they'll be so sick they'll give up any alternate ideas too. I've got it all set to go.

"Dr. Koga will be helping me, but I don't think I'm making him feel he's a traitor to his fellow Technicians. I have two plans, Plan A and Plan B. Which of the two it'll be is up to *me,* not Dr. Koga. While the Quiet Women are recovering, I'll put one of those plans into effect. All you need to do is persuade people in a humane way. Once the Quiet Women abandon their mass suicide of atonement, I suspect the radical elements of the Technicians will be so deflated they'll leave. Then the followers reunited at this conference will support your humane church, with the Quiet Women, who've given up on passing away, at the center.

"In order for all this to happen, you'll need to use the sermon today to set the direction you'll be going in. Emphasize this humane approach. The name of the church, Church of the New Man, should help."

"This Plan A and Plan B you mentioned, let's say what you do tonight is Plan A. Well, what is it?" Patron asked, sitting up in bed. Morio sat up too and gazed at Ikuo with the same expression on his face as Patron.

"It's as much of a farce as your Somersault. Dr. Koga's going to give me twenty-five doses of a powerful laxative."

At this Ogi couldn't help but let out a high-pitched giggle.

"Dr. Koga will also prepare twenty-five doses of a second kind, as part of these two plans. There's no toilet in the chapel, so they'll have to break their siege. But after they've had such terrible diarrhea, they won't have the strength left to climb high enough to hang themselves, will they?"

Patron and Morio both looked as if they loathed the faint smile that played around Ikuo's now-silent lips. But this didn't bother Ikuo. He turned his gaze first to Patron, then Morio, and finally to Ogi—who was holding his tongue after his previous slipup—as if appraising their reactions one by one.

"I'd like you to make sure that plan succeeds without fail," Patron said. "On your way out, would you ask Dancer to come in here? If Ogi takes her place, I think she can leave the office for a while."

"I'm going to let Ogi go for the day," Ikuo said. "Even if he were to go back to the office, we're not expecting any important calls today, so I think it's okay for him to sneak off for some R and R with his friend."

Once more Ogi was flabbergasted.

"There's something else I'd like Dancer to tell you," Patron said, in undisguised disgust for Ikuo. "She's the one—not Professor Kizu—who has the greatest influence on you now."

4

Late in the afternoon—in another little innocent tale—Ogi, thinking he might as well go along with what Ikuo suggested, vanished for a while, and then, after he got back, received a proposal from Ms. Tachibana, who'd been awaiting his return. She wanted to tell him that she wouldn't be able to take Morio to hear Patron's sermon in the special seating set up between the grandstands and the area below the monastery.

The music played for Part One of the Spirit Festival was captivating, with its exaggerated changes of rhythm, but there'd been some capricious disparities that Morio, with his sensitive ears, couldn't stand. (During Part One of the Spirit Festival, innocent young Ogi, too, had heard the music loud and clear as he and Mrs. Tsugane were trysting deep in the forest.) Ever since the incident, two days ago, Morio had been upset and didn't seem able to recover. Ms. Tachibana said that during Part Two of the Spirit Festival she was going to make him lie down in Patron's bedroom, ear plugs in place. Right after Part Two was finished, Patron would begin his sermon, but by that time it would be impossible for them to push their way through the dense crowds to get to their reserved seats.

Even after the rain cleared up it still wasn't very hot, and the evening was pleasant. Just before Part Two of the Spirit Festival was to begin, Asa-san and her husband, the former junior high principal, had planted themselves in the special roped-off seating, where Ms. Tachibana and Morio would normally be, and the principal was explaining to Ogi about the music used in the Spirit Festival. The rhythm was the same you'd find in boat dances in fishing villages along the Shikoku coast and on the islands of the Inland Sea, he said, which lent credence to the legend that the pioneers who settled this land had rebuilt the boats that used to sail down the Maki and Kame rivers to the sea and used them to sail upstream.

Since he'd left the office untended during his afternoon R and R, Ogi was busy until Part Two of the Spirit Festival began. With the Quiet Women using the chapel exclusively after 7 P.M. on this, the last day of the conference, he was inundated with one complaint after another.

The conference participants were planning to enjoy watching Part Two of the Spirit Festival from the seats set up on the path that circled the lake and then listen to Patron's sermon. After that, some of them complained, shouldn't all the believers be given equal access to the chapel for prayer? Another complaint came from a group that had been lined up in the court-yard, talking and waiting their turn to view the triptych, when the Technicians roughly pushed ahead of them.

Ogi also had to listen to one well-intentioned report. When Mr. Matsuo of the Fushoku temple heard that Ogi hadn't seen Part One of the Spirit Festival, he described the whole thing to him from start to finish. Mr. Matsuo was in charge of lending out dolls, costumes, and props to the participants from his own temple and the Mishima Shrine, and he'd observed every detail.

Just as the Fireflies procession had been changed to a course running through the forest surrounding the lake on three sides, the procession in Part One of the Spirit Festival that started at 3 P.M. was also a revised performance. They took the path the Fireflies had run down from the western heights, cut across the northern slope to arrive at the eastern slope, and then came down the glen to arrive beside the chapel on the western slope. They then passed right in front of the spectators and went up to the dam. Once they'd climbed up to the grandstands, they descended again to the dam and the performance came to a conclusion, the participants disappearing off in the direction of the Mansion.

Those who'd dressed as Spirits were now waiting in the Mansion for Part Two to begin. The Fireflies transporting the good Spirits would, following the legend, go clockwise up the forest. And the bad Spirits, again following the legend—since they were ominous souls who had met untimely deaths—would descend in counterclockwise fashion. The Fireflies who would be playing the Spirits had done their homework.

Mr. Matsuo went on to describe each of the Spirits in detail, in particular the one called He Who Destroys, the person who first settled this area, and his woman companion, also a gigantic figure, named Oshikome. And the giant named Shirime—"Butthole Eye," literally—an ostracized figure who, as his named implied, had a single eye looking out from between his buttocks. These were the Spirits handed down as myths, while the Spirits recorded in history included Meisuke-san, the one who led a peasant rebellion and was executed; a postwar woman in the village named Jin who, because of Okura disease, weighed 300 pounds; then Former Brother Gii; and last New Brother Gii, who founded the Church of the Flaming Green Tree. The papier-mâché dolls this year were particularly well made. The brand-new doll of Guide was especially impressive.

Part Two of the Spirit Festival began at 7 P.M., right after the Quiet Women, ignoring all the protests, locked themselves in the chapel. In the Hollow, the twilight forest was dark, the sky alone painfully bright.

As the procession set off from the Mansion, the rhythm started up that had pained Morio earlier—*dan! dan-dan! dan! dan-dan!* beat out on gongs and drums of different sizes—and as the musical part of the procession leading the way made its way up to the dam, the flutes, which had been out of sync, played in a lovely unison.

The musicians were dressed in ancient kagura court-musician costumes with headgear—green and yellow, red and silver—and coronets on their heads. Their feet, though, were in canvas shoes, and the faces of the boys looked familiar. When they got to the grandstands they went beside them, lined up in a crescent shape, and continued the performance.

Next, the Spirits came up the dam, each half again larger than life size. Eye holes and breathing holes were cut out of the chest area of each of the papier-mâché dolls. Clothes were put on over this, and some of the dolls carried spears and swords. Mr. Matsuo didn't explain why, but Ogi could guess the stories behind them.

After a while the Spirits, which had appeared at the dam in groups of three, passed in front of the grandstands, each with a unique way of walking that was part of the performance, and came down to the reserved special seating. Western-style boats and Japanese boats used in river fishing had come up beside the highest step, which was submerged in water, leading down from the dam. The Fireflies reached out to steady the boats, as the Spirits climbed aboard, and then got in too, pushed off with poles from the dam, and rowed over to the island. Several bare lightbulbs were lit around the giant cypress, which was surrounded by its wooden frame, but they weren't enough to illuminate the tree. In the midst of that dim light the Spirits took off their papier-mâché coverings. Using the bamboo ladder, they carried up the papier-mâché and laid it on both sides of the upper and lower levels. The former Spirits, now young men in T-shirts and jeans, returned to the water's edge and were rowed back to the dam.

Now a gloomy pall settled over the events. The music filtering down from above the stands was growing monotonous and lonely and, even worse, boring. Finally, though, a papier-mâché figure of Guide appeared, remarkably larger than any of the previous dolls, dressed in the clothes of a Southern European farm woman, and a cheerful stir swept through the onlookers once more. This Spirit, gesticulating in an exaggerated manner, was rowed out alone to the island.

Right after this, a papier-mâché figure of Guide, somewhat smaller than the one on the island, appeared in the grandstands where the musical procession had made its exit. Some of the Fireflies brought a microphone over to where that figure was standing. Another mike had been set up right in front of the papier-mâché figure standing in the middle of the top level of the wooden frame on the island. The Spirit of Guide at the grandstands lifted the microphone up to his chest and stepped forward. He thrust out his chest and the stir among the crowd quieted down.

It was quite an unexpected entrance, but the thousand or so people surrounding the Hollow quieted down. This was Patron, dressed up as Guide, about to begin his keynote sermon. Speakers on either side of the stands and on poles on the island carried Patron's voice to his rapt audience.

"It's been a long time since I've seen all of you," he began. "I imagine you former members of the church who've come from so far away will understand why I'm inside this doll made up to look like Guide to deliver my sermon. As I need not remind those who are from this region, this papier-mâché covering is called a *shell* in the valley. Wearing this *shell* to talk is in keeping with your legends. . . . Whenever Guide related my visions, I was in a sense clothed in his body. The *shell* covering my spirit was his flesh. Now that I've been left behind by Guide, I'm trying to re-create the past, at least on the surface.

"I would like to speak with all of you about the Somersault. And I'll begin by talking about a young man who was the first one to evaluate the Somersault in a positive light. He's the model for Jonah in the triptych in the chapel I'm sure you've all seen. He's so perfect a person to serve as the model that the Fireflies, following Japanese pronunciation, have dubbed him Yonah.

"After Guide and I did our Somersault and left the church, many people discovered the place where we had taken refuge and came to ask us what the Somersault was all about—its present and future meaning. But only one person and one group understood it as an inescapable calling. The person was Yonah, and the group was the remnants of the Izu radical faction. This group was essentially negative toward the Somersault; Guide was killed by them in place of me. The reason I'd like to begin with Yonah, as I said, is because he viewed the Somersault in such a *positive* way.

"Before that, though, let me speak of the interrogation that group did of Guide. They questioned him, grilled him, and he answered—or at least he tried to. I couldn't share in his pain; I could only listen to the recording made of this kangaroo trial. But throughout it, Guide never once lied, I can guarantee that. And after a long interrogation, Guide was tortured to death.

"This evening Guide has joined the procession of Spirits—those who have died untimely deaths in the midst of this forest. We will burn up all the *shells* on the island so the Spirits can return again to the forest. The real shell of Guide's Spirit is exhibited there on the tower. The papier-mâché I'm wearing is thus nothing more than a shell of a shell.

"Guide, who died this untimely death, thus joins the procession of Spirits in this land where our Church of the New Man will be built. He was an extremely responsible man, who even took responsibility when *I* made mistakes, and I know that whenever the Church of the New Man goes through trials he will be there to help us. I am grateful to the Fireflies for letting Guide's soul join the Spirit Festival. And I'd like to express my respect for them for having the sense to come up with the name Yonah."

Applause rang out from three sides of the lake. On the wooden scaffolding on the cypress island, Guide's Spirit thrust out his papier-mâché chest. Once more the Guide doll at the grandstands lifted up the microphone, and the crowd became so quiet one could hear the cries of insects for a moment.

5

"Now, this young man who first viewed the Somersault in a positive way came to me, as you see him in the triptych in the chapel, as Yonah. In addition to what he's actually said to me, I have also imagined the appeal he's making to me silently. What he really wanted to ask me, I think, was whether I did the Somersault in order to be the kind of Lord who could rewrite the ending of the book of Jonah. Even if I wasn't that sort of Lord, he wanted me to know that I *could* be—I *could* rewrite the book of Jonah.

"Here I'd like to re-create what I imagine Yonah's words to be.

"Since you are a person who can communicate directly with God, he'd say, isn't it possible for you to become another Lord yourself? You're the person who made a fool out of God. Even after God decided against destroying the people, children, and cattle of Nineveh, you're the Lord who can raise his voice in protest! You're the Lord who can call not just on Nineveh but on the whole world, to repent as it faces the end time—the Lord who can defend the original calling.

"When I was a child, Yonah would continue, I heard the voice of God telling me to take action! And I obeyed this voice. But afterward I never heard the voice of God again. I suffered, thinking the reason must lie with me. But it was God who erased this call. Just like Jonah, I have the right to protest.

"Transmit this protest to God for me! If God still continues to cancel out his call, then I want you—as someone with the courage to make a fool of God—to give me your own special call. Tell me to take action!

"Because you had done a Somersault, when I met you I thought I'd finally met a person who could rewrite the ending of the Book of Jonah, something I've longed to do for such a long time. Let me and my friends stand by, awaiting your call.

"I think this was the young man's appeal to me as *Yonah*.

"Yonah knew that the Somersault Guide and I did was a decision we were forced into by the tense situation between the Izu radical faction and the authorities, and that carrying it out, we knew, would have great after-effects on church members throughout the country. Over the past ten years this has become public knowledge through reports in weekly magazines and other media. Yonah had to be aware of this.

"But Yonah saw a relationship with God in this very dilemma Guide and I found ourselves in. If Guide had shot back the following question to Yonah, this would only have created the grounds for Yonah to question us:

"*Yonah,* Guide might have said, *have you considered one other possibility? That even before the Somersault neither Patron nor I ever believed in a transcendental being? Just like most Japanese! Still less did we believe in the possibility that we were mediating for God. That this whole setup of Patron's coming into direct contact with God through his trances and me relating the visions he had is nothing but a bunch of nonsense we made up ourselves?*

"Yonah would be shocked at first on hearing this. No doubt, though, he would come back with his own fearless response. *By your Somersault,* he'd say, *you made a fool of God, Patron. But can you make a fool of something that doesn't exist? The fact that you had no choice but to do the Somersault is inescapable proof that God appeared to you. Patron acted as he did in front of the TV cameras at the time of the Somersault, but if you think he did it for the viewers, you're greatly mistaken. He did it for the sake of God, a God who is real.*

"Yonah's positive questions have made me ponder things, and I now recognize that I made a fool of a God who is real though silent, a God who is definitely keeping watch on me. And because this is so, the descent into hell awaited me after the Somersault. If Guide and I really broke all connections with the *other side* through the Somersault, why in the world would we have to suffer in hell?

"What was it like to live as Patron? I'd like to review this very briefly for you. Through the trances—that I couldn't willfully produce or distance myself from—I had visions that became a part of me. That's how I spent the better part of my life. Still, though, if people ask me if I saw God's face or heard his voice, or ask me what the face and voice of God are like, I can't say.

"I was asked this once by a lady who helped pave the way for our move here. The former diplomat who spent his final years in the Hollow after retirement tried his hand at writing a science fiction story. The plot apparently involved a being from another universe that covered the planet like a weather system and sent out messages. When I was in the midst of a trance it was like this—as if I were a mushroom in the middle of a wind stream.

"Friends, after I moved into my residence here in the Hollow I've been scattering sunflower seeds under the eaves of the second floor. The nuthatches have taken over, chasing away all other little birds. They eat a few of the seeds right there and take some away to hide for later. While they're gathering their sunflower seeds they're quite bold, but just as they're about to fly away they do a complete about-face, screeching as if they've been overcome by fear.

"When I awoke from my trances, the kind of mutterings I spewed forth were just like the screeching of those birds. Guide was the one who made them intelligible. That's how I became a mediator for God's word. Guide devoted his life to it. Then came the Somersault. Yes, Guide and I were driven into a corner, put in a real fix by the radical faction. But did I have to go so far as to make a fool of the God I was intimate with? It's become clear to me as I've mulled over Yonah's questions that this was absolutely necessary. There was no other choice.

"By making a fool of God, Guide and I made a *confession of faith*. It's clear to me now that fear of our followers committing mass suicide was just an excuse. If that's all it was, there would have been other ways out.

"Using that image of God as expressing himself through the weather, Guide and I, like tiny mushrooms shaking in the wind, had to suffer. But by making a fool of God, the existence of this wind-stream God took on an even greater reality.

"Before Guide was murdered, when he and I were living in seclusion, I had a pitiful little dream about the future. Time would pass, I dreamed, and the world would forget about us, and just at that point my trances would return. I would go over to the *other side* with a sense of nostalgia, I'd come back in a weakened state, and while I recovered Guide would explain what all my senseless mutterings meant. And weren't we, at this moment, even more deeply, even more *really,* just small mushrooms in the rush of wind that is the Lord?

"Before this could occur, though, Guide was killed. Truthfully, I only made up my mind to rebuild the church after this happened. With Guide gone, I announced the rebuilding of the church to all of you—for all the world like one of those little birds giving out a scared, flustered screech.

"But having done the Somersault, and now without Guide by my side, would I really be able to lead the church? It was Yonah who made me push aside my hesitancy. This was the calling I got from him, to be the one who made a fool of God, the one who, still protesting against him, could continue to be a mediator. After Guide was murdered, I was searching for a new Guide. Professor Kizu, Morio, and our young Yonah himself may all have been new Guides. That being the case, the triptych in the chapel is the most suitable painting for our church.

"Well, I don't have much more time. I've told you my story up to this point, but the story from this point on will be told by all of *you.* Launching the new church means its can't just be a continuation of the same old story. We need a story that's entirely *new.* The Quiet Women are hoping I'll do a backward Somersault. Yonah was anticipating a Somersault that went even farther forward, done by another Lord who would make a fool of God. But even if that weren't as boring as going backward, I wouldn't do it. Even if I were trying to pretend to be another Lord, the Sacred Wound in the painting has now vanished from my body. I imagine that Yonah no longer has the illusion of setting me up as another Lord.

"So now I want to deliver my message as a person who can only stand on his own, who isn't the puppet of any sect or individual. All I can do is put the finishing touches on the launching of our new church, the Church of the New Man.

"At the end of the sermon it may confuse and anger some of you if I suddenly add a scatological comment, but even those of you without good hearing or sense of smell will detect—as sort of a basso continuo to my speech—the sound and smell of a group of women unable to hold back their farts and diarrhea, lending an earthy sort of foundation to my philosophy. I don't want these poor but wonderful women to have to hold back any longer, so their very human sounds will blend with Morio's music that points toward a pure ascension to heaven.

"Fireflies, you may begin your ceremony of returning the Spirits to the forest. I will pray now that the Old Man is sloughed off. With the end time upon us, I call on all of you to repent and to embark on becoming New

Men. Finally, I leave you with the words of a foreign author, his earnest prayer for New Men: *Three cheers for Karamazov!*"

Right as Patron's sermon drew to a close—the moment when, clearly pressed for time he added this sudden prankish comment that threw his listeners off—one after another, clumsy-looking women, obviously in too much of a hurry to remove the barricades at the front entrance of the chapel, leaped out of the low open windows on the lake side of the chapel. As soon as they hit the ground some of them, either having sprained their ankles or just drained of energy, squatted there like hens. Of those who didn't, others sprinted straight for the temporary toilets set up on the eastern slope. Most of them, though, raced off to the dark thickets and shrubs. From the stands, where a stir went through the perplexed spectators, a call rang out, chorusing Patron's final words.

"*Three cheers for Karamazov! Three cheers for Karamazov! Three cheers for Karamazov!*"

Morio's piano piece "Ascending, Part One" spilled out from the speakers on either side of the stands and on the island.

The bare lightbulbs hanging down from the grandstands illuminated Ikuo's thick features as he stood up beside Dancer. The rest of his massive head, like a darkly shaded bull's, swayed violently, catching Ogi's attention.

Dancer was pushing something onto the back of Ikuo's left hand, which hung down straight. A gust of wind shook a hanging light that briefly lit up what it was: a box of matches. Ogi could tell that the matchbox, soon sunk again in darkness, was being forced on Ikuo. Holding one end of the matchbox, Dancer was twisting the other end onto the back of Ikuo's hand. At the same time she stretched up on tiptoes toward that massive black head, whispering something. . . .

As the bare lightbulb lit them up again, the back of Ikuo's left hand still didn't budge, but finally he reached out with his right hand and snatched the matchbox away. He then set off for a boat lying in the shadow of the Japanese-style boats floating beside the stairs filled with dark water. The boat rolled as Ikuo got on board, and one of the Fireflies quickly shoved off and set the oars.

Dancer slowly moved backward to where Ogi stood. With a fierce look, she watched the boat set off. The darkened island was lit up by a floodlight from the stands. The floodlight lit up the Spirit dolls piled up on the wooden framework surrounding the giant cypress, particularly the conspicuously larger papier-mâché figure of Guide.

The doll that Patron was wearing above the grandstands, where he had now finished speaking, was closer, but strangely enough seemed smaller than the one on the island.

Ogi realized he'd forgotten the order of the program. Was Patron supposed to remain standing with the costume on by the grandstands, or was Ogi supposed to take him behind the curtain and have him rest on a chair there? Dancer leaned over to whisper, so close to him that her skull banged his temple.

"*Go ahead and do it!* I told him," she said in a strong voice, like some angry young girl. "You're always bragging about how you'll do it if you hear the voice telling you to. Can't you hear the voice now saying *Do it?* That's what I told him! Even if you don't hear the voice, afterward you can always claim you did! That's exactly what I told him!"

Led by the floodlight, the thousand people surrounding the lake fixed their eyes on the island, their attention turning from the slapstick confusion still going on around the chapel to the papier-mâché Spirits that were about to go up in flames. No one wanted to miss this, the finale of the summer conference. Everyone anticipated that Patron, still above the grandstands, would once more call out in response to the conflagration.

The Firefly manning the oars in Ikuo's bow rowed strongly, the prow of the boat running up onto the shoreline of the island, a meadow inundated with water. The rower stepped into the water up to his knees and held the boat steady. Ikuo plunged decisively out of the boat and with the momentum of the landing ran toward the giant cypress, his head bent forward. He came face-to-face with the giant doll of Guide, standing behind the bamboo ladder and the wood frame it was leaning against.

"Isn't he telling you to *Do it?* Up on the frame of the cypress. *Do it!*" Dancer's hot breath brushed Ogi's cheek.

"That's not what's supposed to happen, is it?" Ogi responded, holding his rising anger in check.

"*Do it! Do it!*" Dancer said vehemently, ignoring Ogi's protest.

Morio's piano music had changed to "Ascending, Part Two" and then went back to Part One. It wasn't a simple tape loop but the recording of a performance that played the music in that order. The massive body of the skillful performer of this music now clumsily approached the wooden frame. Before long this dark figure, his large head hanging down, slowly began to move. Finally he took something out of his pants pocket—Ogi knew it was the matchbox—and laid it on a low wooden bar on the wood frame.

Then, as if he'd forgotten something, he quickly retraced his steps. Even before the Firefly standing in the dark water could pull the boat closer, the dark figure stepped into the water and almost collapsed into the boat, the Firefly shoving off the edge with both hands. As the boat rowed back, the dark figure on board sat there unmoving, like some bulky cargo.

A moment later two more dark figures stood up at the water's edge on the chapel side on the island. Water dripped from both of them. One of them supported the other as the figure struggled to walk in the soft sand. The two figures stood side by side in front of the wooden frame around the cypress. The upright slim figure looked around a bit—Ogi realized it was Ms. Tachibana—and reached out a thin arm to the wooden bar on the frame. A match flared, and the wavering flame reached out toward the papier-mâché Guide that draped down from the lower level of the frame.

As soon as the flames lapped up the lower edge of the frame, a wide swath of red flames raced up to the wild hair of the doll's head. All at once a round of applause rose up from the broad circle of onlookers surrounding the Hollow, drowning out the piano music. The larger of the two shadows turned to face the grandstands and gave a respectful bow as if it were a performer on a stage acknowledging the audience. The applause roared up cheerily, and the flames made small exploding sounds as they covered the entire wooden frame.

At the grandstands, the boat passed around the Japanese boats to arrive at the inundated steps, and Ikuo walked up them alone. Dancer ran up to him with such force she almost sent him falling back into the water.

"Murderer! Did you hear the voice telling you, *Do it?*" Dancer cursed him, slamming her body into his.

Probably no one else heard that besides Ogi, who'd come running after her. Now a different kind of stir swept through the crowd, mixed in with screams here and there, and the stir rose even louder. Seeing that Dancer was being restrained, Ogi turned to look back at the island, where the surprisingly high flames illuminated, at the base of the wooden frame, which itself was ablaze, the two shadowy figures from before crouched down, hugging each other, their free hands held up to shield their faces from the flames.

The papier-mâché Guide on top of the burning frame seemed to leap and, together with the other dolls around it, went up in flames. The fire now reached to the cypress branches piled there, to the luxuriant leaves of the smaller branches; then even the thick trunk of the tree, like a pillar rising up through all that was piled around it, began to burn.

In the midst of new screams, the mass piled up on the upper level that covered the wooden frame collapsed in a shower of sparks onto the two prostrate figures. In the reddish glow of the flames things collapsed one after another. Shouts and crying voices rose up. The roar of the flames was rivaled by the sound of the wind rising up from them; the entire area around the lake was like a strangely clamorous festival.

Like the agitated crowd around him, Ogi's eyes were riveted on the flaming giant cypress, but he sensed some disturbance, spun around, and saw the Technicians' security detail grab the person wearing the papier-mâché figure of Guide and roughly rip off the disguise. Gii emerged from it, dressed in T-shirt and jeans. The young man was limp and dripping sweat as if a bucket of water had been poured over him.

An even greater scream went up as the papier-mâché Guide on the island fell to the ground from the blazing frame and bounced up, and out of the wreckage appeared a human body.

Epilogue: The Everlasting Year

1

Young Ogi, accompanied by the American newspaper reporter Fred Parks and Mrs. Tsugane, visited Maki Town for the first time in more than a year. In the intervening time Ogi had married Mrs. Tsugane, so it was strange to keep calling him by his old appellation, though that's what he planned to go by with everyone in the Hollow. The three of them landed at the Matsuyama airport, transferred to the express train, and by the time they got off at Maki Station a December snow was steadily falling, something Ogi had never experienced in Tokyo. The man-made forests that made up most of the mountain ranges surrounding the Maki basin looked as if a brush had been used to sweep polishing powder over the blue-black earth. Despite the heavy snow the air was filled with the approach of a gentle twilight. Snow had piled up in the square in front of the station, and the roads leading out from that spot were already covered in white, with not much traffic at that time of day. No taxis were waiting outside the station.

They'd called ahead from the Matsuyama airport to say they'd be taking the last express train of the day, and since no one was there to greet them Ogi considered phoning again. He wasn't at all sure, though, whether at this time of day Dancer would still be working in the office next to the chapel. She'd gotten married too, to Ikuo, and was now in overall charge of running the Church of the New Man. It was windy as well as snowing, and Fred, who wore only an old trench coat, was grumbling about the cold.

Before long a brand-new Nissan President luxury sedan went past the prefectural road and then turned back toward them. The car scattered newly fallen snow in the intersection in front of the square as it made a wide detour back, coming to a halt in front of the windswept station exit where Ogi and the others were waiting with their luggage.

Mr. Matsuo of the Fushokuji temple opened the driver's door and leaned out to greet them. Then he said, emphatically, "This looks like it'll be the first major snowfall we've had in some time. Even if it weren't snowing so much, taxis don't like to drive to the Old Town. With the recession they've cut back the number of cabs, plus the drivers are still a little bit shy about picking up foreigners. I'm not saying they're prejudiced or anything, it's just that they can't speak English."

Mr. Matsuo got out of the car, dressed in a dark navy-blue jacket, and darted about, helping first Mrs. Tsugane and then Fred into the backseat; he stowed their luggage in the trunk and motioned to Ogi to sit in front. The passenger seat, like all the other seats, was quite plush.

"Weren't you on your way downriver?" Ogi asked hesitantly.

"I was supposed to attend a meeting of the River Conservancy group at the sake manufacturer's place. With the Fireflies busy running the Farm, the Village Association group and I have taken over these duties. But with all this snow, it might be smarter to skip the meeting, don't you think?"

They passed by the newly built overpass at the confluence of the Kame and Maki rivers and then drove upriver along the prefectural road, already covered in four inches of snow. As they drove, Ogi reintroduced Mr. Matsuo, whom he remembered meeting at the summer conference, to Mrs. Tsugane. Mr. Matsuo went back to talking about the snow.

"Driving through the snow like this makes me think of Morio's music. He was a very special and pure person, his sister too. Even now the church plays his music all day long to mark events in the daily schedule. Every time I go over to the Hollow to see Ikuo about something, it always amazes me—"

"He composed pieces about the snow?" the always level-headed Mrs. Tsugane interrupted.

"I think he must have, since he composed lots of short pieces," Mr. Matsuo said kindly to her, following the deferential way Ogi treated his older wife. "But there's something throughout all of Morio's music that conveys a kind of snowy feeling. There's a saying by the famous Buddhist priest Dogen that one should always be in harmony with the melody of the snow. I think it means that snow is silent, and one should play in concert with that.

"Morio was mentally challenged, but he made up for it with a keen sense of sound," Mr. Matsuo continued. "When he composed his music, I imagine he put things in the real world and things he felt and thought on an equal footing. That's how I feel whenever I hear his music and look at the falling snow. Even if we know we're supposed to be in harmony with the melody of the snow, clever musicians never take it that far, though for Morio that was the most natural thing in the world."

"Fred wants to know which text that quote is from," Mrs. Tsugane said, after she had explained in English to Fred that they'd been talking about the monk Dogen.

"I don't know if there's a translation of it, but it's from the *Dogen Osho Koroku*."

"He wants to know if this is different from the *Eihei Koroku*."

"It's the same."

"He says that maybe snow is often mentioned in Dogen's sermons because of how cold it was in Kyoto and Fukui, where he lived."

"Fred, I underestimated you," Mr. Matsuo said. "I trained at the Eihei Zen temple, but I've never really read the entire text. Learned it instead by ear—in Dogen's teachings there's the term a *sixth ear*. Do you say that in English? Six ears?"

Fred Parks laughed and didn't pursue the subject any further. In a fine mood, Mr. Matsuo went on about the snow.

"When's it's snowing this hard, the local people know just how much it's going to accumulate. They used to be quite nervous about it, knowing how many days the delivery trucks wouldn't be able to get through. The produce grocer along the river used to put chains on his truck and dash off to buy supplies and be buried in snow on the way back. Sometimes the fire department would have to be called out.

"Now, though, it's different—see that car coming from the opposite direction? Since the church is doing such a great job of running the Farm, there's no need to get concerned about where the vegetables or eggs are coming from. They're even raising char in the spring behind the chapel. So people feel much more secure. Now people along the river and those in the Outskirts as well don't mind if the road's closed.

"That gives you an idea of how much the church has influenced life around here in the past year. Simply put, we don't have to worry about getting a steady supply of inexpensive quality items. I'm sure this is obvious to you, coming from the city, but regional cultural differences show up in the distribution of goods; in backwoods places things are shoddy and expensive and you have to wait forever to get them. That's been reversed here. In the bazaar held here every other week you'll find not just folks from the Old Town but even people from Matsuyama coming *here* to shop instead of the other way around."

Fred was quite interested in all this when Mrs. Tsugane translated the details for him.

"Fred wants to know, after such a tragedy, with children present to witness it, whether the church didn't become alienated from the local people." Ogi conveyed the question, letting Mrs. Tsugane translate Mr. Matsuo's reply.

"That shows how wise the people in this region can be," Mr. Matsuo said. "Having the Farm is advantageous to them. There was going to be a mass suicide in the chapel, but in the end nothing happened, so the local people aren't going to harp on that forever. The east slope of the Hollow is a center for butterbur, and when it's in season hordes of people come from the river basin and the Outskirts. The people in these parts like to give names to places based on some event that occurred there, and they've given a new name to the mountain stream where they pick these butterbur. They call it Mountain Stream Where Twenty-five Refined Ladies Shat, and they say it's a particularly tasty crop of butterbur this year. Ha ha ha!"

Nobody laughed along with him, so the head priest changed to a more prudent topic. "As time passes, just as the achievements of He Who Destroys and Oshikome are now distant events for us, the summer conference will fade into the past and—who knows?—perhaps the only thing to remain will be that place name."

"Much like the Buddhist concept of the evanescence of life," Mrs. Tsugane suggested.

"The *power of the land* counts for a lot, they say," Mr. Matsuo went on. "The cypress island's been cleaned up, and that's where Patron and Ms. Tachibana and her brother are buried. The memorial was done in relief by the architect who built the chapel and has one of Morio's scores carved on it. The tombstone is surrounded by the lake and faces the chapel, but now it's all covered in snow. In harmony with the melody of the snow, you might say."

By then they'd left the district road, passed over the main bridge, and started down the cross-Shikoku-highway bypass, looking down on houses along the river that, in the snow, had already turned off their lights.

"Are Professor Kizu's remains buried on the island as well?" Mrs. Tsugane asked. This time Ogi fielded the question.

"He wasn't a member of the church. And Ikuo in particular insisted on wanting Professor Kizu's soul to be free from the realm of God."

"But isn't Ikuo the one who took over as leader of the church after Patron?"

"He's leading the church, having separated the managerial aspect of running it from the spiritual," Mr. Matsuo said in a serious tone. "Ikuo himself seems to be free from the voice of God. Gii's been selected to take over the spiritual side of the church eventually, and the Quiet Women and the Technicians are teaching him. Gii will be inheriting the Farm from Satchan, so it'll be convenient for the Farm to merge with the church, but I don't think that the managerial side—Ikuo and Dancer, in other words—did this purely out of self-interest.

"Gii has some religious element in him that connects him to Patron, don't you think? And half his genes are from the founder of the Church of the Flaming Green Tree, let's not forget. It's a little tricky to guess how Satchan feels about all this, though Gii's own choice is pretty clear. This spring he didn't go on to high school. The Technicians designed a curriculum they say can take him through high school and college in six years. And Ikuo is apparently drilling him pretty hard in English."

"Fred wants to know what you mean by saying that Ikuo is free of God's voice," Mrs. Tsugane said.

"That much English I can understand," Mr. Matsuo said, summoning up his dignity as head priest. "There's no easy answer, though, even in Japanese. . . . If tomorrow it looks like the snow won't be letting up, you'll most likely be staying four or five days. Why don't you ask Ikuo himself? One other thing you should know is that, now that Gii and the other Fireflies are part of the church, they no longer call Ikuo *Yonah.*"

Mr. Matsuo drove the car through the entrance to the parking lot, completely white in the darkness, and all the way around to the exit. Ogi helped him get their luggage out of the trunk. After quickly thanking Mr. Matsuo, Mrs. Tsugane and Fred hurried into the courtyard of the monastery, trying to avoid the thick flat snowflakes. Anticipating their arrival, the church members had swept the walk clear of snow. Just then music played, signaling the end of all official activities for the day.

Mr. Matsuo turned his snow-covered head toward the chapel. "Hear that? It's Morio's music."

The music's quiet echo was one with the snowdrifts and the snow falling on the surface of the lake.

2

The next morning it had stopped snowing. Ogi and Mrs. Tsugane had used the oversized bed that Patron and Morio had pretty much lived in, while Fred happily made do with the Japanese futon they'd laid out for him in the living room on the south side of the house. In the dinette, filled with the lively calls of birds from the snowy woods, Mrs. Tsugane prepared a breakfast of bacon and eggs from the Farm, which had been put in the refrigerator for them. An hour after they heard the music announcing the opening of the dining hall, Fred still showed no signs of getting up, so Ogi and his wife lay in bed waiting for him.

Getting up was all the harder since they'd stayed up late in the heated dining hall talking. The late-night Hollow, lost in snow, had been as soundless as the bottom of the ocean; the guests were startled each time they heard a piercing crack ring out in the woods. They'd been told what it was—branches of the bamboos in the large grove on the right-hand slope on the way to the Mansion cracking under the weight of the snow—but still it made them jump.

The little banquet held by the church members to welcome Ogi and the others, held two hours after their usual dinnertime, was hosted by Ikuo, Dancer, Dr. Koga, and Gii, and, from the Quiet Women, Ms. Oyama and Ms. Takada. Mrs. Shigeno was away in Chiba visiting her daughter, who had married a physician.

All the Quiet Women had remained in the Hollow, and now most of the children they'd left behind when they moved to Shikoku had joined them. Half of the Technicians had left, but in addition to the Fireflies, who'd been moved by Patron's sermon and were now enthusiastic supporters of the church, there were a number of other young people who'd joined, and production at the Farm was right on schedule. After attending Kizu night and day in his final illness, Ms. Asuka was now back in Tokyo editing the video of the summer conference.

As for Ogi, he had gone back to work at the International Culture Foundation and was planning in his spare time to write a book on the establishment of the Church of the New Man. He was preparing a first draft based on notes he'd taken from the time he first started working for Patron and Guide at the office in Seijo up to the hectic summer conference at the Hollow. Mrs. Tsugane had used a word processor to make a fair copy of everything he had written so far.

As everyone involved pondered things anew after the events of the summer, Kizu had felt a renewed sense of the mission Patron entrusted him with—namely, to be historian for the Church of the New Man—and had begun filling sketchbooks with memos of events. After his death Dancer put it all in order. Hearing of Ogi's plan to write a history of the church, Ikuo contacted him by phone to offer the materials for his use.

This is why Ogi and the others had come to the Hollow. Ikuo read over the fair copy of the first draft Ogi brought with him, while Ogi read through Kizu's memos. Afterward they discussed things, and after outlining a general plan, Ogi went ahead with reworking his first draft, laying great emphasis on Kizu's records and incorporating Ikuo's explanations as well. This was Ogi's own personal project, but once complete it would serve as a good introduction to an official church history.

Actually, the groundwork for this agreement had been laid by Mrs. Tsugane. At the time of their marriage, in place of a wedding ceremony they held a reunion dinner with Mrs. Tsugane and Ogi's family. Ogi's elder brother and his wife, who had introduced her to Ogi in the first place, ordered a cake decorated with a ribbon saying FIFTEENTH ANNIVERSARY OF THE PANTIES OF PURE LOVE, in order to tease Ogi. If their trysts deep in the Shikoku woods had come to light, there's no telling how carried away Ogi's brother and sister-in-law would have gotten.

After dinner at a modest Italian restaurant in the Imperial Hotel, Mrs. Tsugane made a firm resolution. She would help her young husband—the one member of the Ogi family, renowned in the medical field, for whom no one had any expectations of success—to achieve his long-held plan, at the same time sweeping away the chagrin she'd felt at being treated so lightly by his family. She'd convinced herself that it was entirely due to the promotion campaign she'd run that her former husband had achieved international recognition, but when it came to Ogi the more relevant question was not *when* he'd complete the project but whether he'd ever get *started.* So at this point Mrs. Tsugane suggested that he begin his "History of the Age" by writing a first volume tracing developments from the Somersault to the founding of the Church of the New Man.

At the same time she urged Fred to write an article about the now year-old church, including the horrifying events of the summer conference. Fred was assigned to do this by an American news agency and then asked Mrs. Tsugane to travel with him as his interpreter to gather material, and that's how the plan to visit the Hollow near the end of the year came about.

After ten that morning Dancer called Ogi's residence with an invitation for Ogi, Fred, and Mrs. Tsugane to gather at the chapel with Ikuo and Gii to continue last night's conversation. The slope leading from Patron and Morio's former residence down to the chapel was less than sixteen feet, but as soon as they pushed open the front door they hesitated, looking out at the mound of white glittering in the flood of light. Even if they were to plow their way through it, the snow would come up to Fred's thighs, and he was the tallest of the group. The path had been swept clean the night before, but still it had accumulated this much.

Just then Gii, attired in a sturdy-looking outfit of boots and windbreaker, appeared, snow shovel in hand. Wielding the shovel in the painfully bright light, he was clearly more physically developed than a year before. As he gallantly shoveled his way up to the entrance Gii greeted Ogi and his wife in Japanese and Fred in British-accented English. In between shovelfuls he advised them that it would be wise to wear overcoats when they went to the chapel since it was cold inside. He added that Ikuo—he didn't call him Yonah as in the past—didn't want to meet in the dining hall because other church members could eavesdrop on their conversation there.

"Since you're able to speak directly with Fred, he doesn't need my poor interpreting skills," Mrs. Tsugane said, turning on the charm as she spoke to Gii, who was flushed from his exertions clearing the snow.

As Mrs. Tsugane repeated in English to Fred what she'd said, Gii gave a reply in English that revealed how undaunted a fellow he was.

"If you're investigating a *native* religion here in the Hollow, instead of having an English-speaking *informant* it would be better, wouldn't it, to use an interpreter and have one *native* speak to another?"

Mrs. Tsugane went inside to collect her overcoat, and while she wrapped herself in a scarf that her ex-husband had designed, she showed her displeasure.

"What a charmless young man we have here. Much better to be labeled an innocent youth."

Ogi pretended not to hear.

Fred, who seemed to understand Mrs. Tsugane's Japanese quite well—in fact, Ogi suspected he had a better grasp of the spoken language than he made out—said in his characteristic grumbling way, "Pretty amazing to find such a complex intellectual environment so far out in the snowy forest! A priest who drives an expensive Nissan and quotes Dogen, and on top of that a fifteen-year-old who's got a good grasp of the imperialist aspects of cultural anthropology!"

Dancer had brought a kerosene heater with a built-in fan into the chapel. But when Ogi and the others came inside, what caught their attention was less this than the thirty guitars lined up neatly along the wall behind the piano. Last night they'd heard about this, that the junior high school, which had turned down Kizu's idea for an art classroom, was now using the chapel for music classes. So not only did one of the more prominent wind instrument groups in the district use the chapel for practice, it was also being used regularly by local students for their guitar lessons.

From the darkly shadowed triptych with its Renaissance-style scenes, one by one the three newcomers found themselves drawn to the sparkling long window set in the cylindrical inner concrete wall of the chapel. Surrounded by snow-covered forest, the lake in the Hollow reflected back the blue sky that looked like the bottom of a hole. In the midst of this diffusely lit scene, the square enclosure on the flat white stand that was the cypress island showed as undulations in the sparkling snow.

"It's too bright without sunglasses," Fred said. "I heard that because Japanese people have dark eyes they can stand bright light, but I don't really understand why. They say the older you get the less sensitive you are to light. Is that really true?"

"I'm fairly old and wear bifocals, but they're tinted, so don't treat me like some insensitive *native!*" Mrs. Tsugane said.

Fred replied, "What a grump!" and shrugged his shoulders in an exaggerated way, more put off than ever; Ogi, though, was impressed by her gallant response.

Ikuo came into the chapel lugging an old leather briefcase Ogi remembered seeing Kizu using. Dancer brought over chairs around the heater, now blazing away, and they gathered around. Out of the leather case, which seemed to radiate cold, Ikuo took out a couple of sketchbooks and copies of other documents and laid them on an empty chair.

Next to these he laid down the typed first draft that Ogi had given him, and said, "Maybe it's the snow, but I felt as impatient as a child this morning and got up early and read the whole thing. Your descriptions are great; it reads like a novel. And I'm impressed by how you've remembered the details of conversations, even though I saw you always taking notes. But if you flesh this out, covering everything from Patron's Somersault through Guide's torture and up to the summer conference and the Church of the New Man, won't the whole thing be enormously long?"

"I told Ogi that if you don't carefully write all the details," Mrs. Tsugane replied, "it won't be much of a history of the age. We experience things without really knowing what they mean and how they'll end up, right? That being the case, all you can do is write down as much of what you saw and heard just as you experienced it. Maybe it's a case of God being in the details."

As if to forestall any quick reaction from Ikuo, Mrs. Tsugane translated her remarks for Fred, who blinked his chestnut-colored eyes as if, even inside, it was too bright, and sighed. "It's amazing the amount of intellectual information that flits back and forth here."

As if this was the opportune moment he'd been waiting for, Gii said, in English, "I think Ikuo and Ogi have some things they need to talk over by themselves, things that don't need to be translated for Mr. Parks's article. I mentioned being an *informant* before, but I'd be happy to answer anything I can as honestly and accurately as I can. I won't just butter you up with things

I think a foreigner might want to hear. So why don't we find a corner that's out of the sun, and you and I can talk?"

Fred Parks liked the idea. He and the Gii quickly moved over to the space between the piano and the wall where the triptych hung. Ikuo placed two chairs for them, his actions showing that he was quite used to being the one in charge now.

When it was just the four of them left, Mrs. Tsugane said, "Ogi resisted the idea of including in the record of the church such things as what he'd written down in his notebooks about the two of us doing *that*. Though he wrote it down at the time as if it were an important matter. I insisted that he put it into his first draft. It's a history of the church, but you also have aspirations to write a History of the Age, right? Unless you decide to write down *all* the details, including the ones that are hard to reveal to others, the amateur writer tends to leave out what's important. It's also good practice for describing the facts."

Ogi, of course, but also Ikuo, who'd read the typed first draft, were both unsure how to respond. At this point Dancer spoke up, her way of speaking unusually gentle now, something Ogi had picked up on the night before.

"I think I understand what Mrs. Tsugane is getting at," Dancer said. "The same applies to the summer conference and my life up till then, even before I started living in Tokyo. When I try to remember things that happened when I was a young girl in ballet tights, I can't distinguish between what was important and what's just extraneous details. During this past year since you left the office, Ogi, almost every day I've been mentally reviewing everything that happened, and it feels, like you say, that the key to everything lies in the details. . . .

"Ikuo, don't you need to tell Ogi how Professor Kizu passed away? Just as Mrs. Tsugane said, try to conjure up the details of what happened. Professor Kizu's parting words might seem like he was making fun of you, but aren't they important too? If you include them, and Ogi writes down all the details as he does in his notebook, who knows but that you might find yourself reaching a deeper understanding of what it all meant. I've only read a portion of the first draft, but it's clear Ogi is no longer just an innocent youth.

"On the other hand, I don't think there's anything I can say that would be of help. I won't be upset, though, if—to borrow Mrs. Tsugane's term— Ikuo tells everything about *that* which took place at the time of Professor Kizu's death. This might be hard to talk about in front of us women, so why don't I take Mrs. Tsugane over to see what the children of the Quiet Women have been doing? I think it'd be worth your while to see our fish pond, too, though with all this snow it might be like looking down a well."

In Dancer's now-mature voice and mannerisms there was something that made Ogi feel—in a complex way he'd never felt before—that she was truly an extraordinary woman. With Patron now gone, she'd been handling all the church members and the facilities for the last year and had, despite the events of the past, rebuilt relations with the town and local schools. As Dr. Koga had remarked the night before, there was a relaxed dignity about her now.

When the two women left the chapel, Gii raised his head like a weasel and looked over. But since the American journalist, puffing away despite the ban on smoking, was scribbling in the small notebook spread on his lap, Gii went eagerly back to talking with him in a low voice.

3

For nearly five weeks after the summer conference, both the Hollow and the Farm had been in turmoil. Below the surface confusion, though, something deeper and more persistent was taking place.

The media's concern had been with the so-called FIERY SUICIDE AND LOYAL DEATHS of Patron and the Tachibana siblings; starting with intense TV coverage, specials appeared in the weekly magazines covering an overabundance of material in a typically unfocused way. The illustrated weeklies ran color photographs of the sprawled, naked body of Patron, like some dry-lacquered image of Buddha, with the nude, charred bodies of Ms. Tachibana and Morio reaching out to him.

When the church made its official response, which included dealing with the police, Ogi had been in the thick of things. So there was no need for him to hear once again from Ikuo about all this. Still, Dancer had prepared a file of clippings from the local press on this period for him to peruse.

As he was talking with Ikuo and leafing through these clippings, though, Ogi noticed that in the middle of September, just after he moved away from the Hollow, Kizu had finally opened his art school for junior high students. As one of those involved, Ogi knew that the church had tried to repair its relationship with the Old Town and Maki Town. Guessing from his experience at the time that Kizu himself wasn't pushing the project too hard, Ogi deduced that this must have been the doing of Asa-san, the wife of the former junior high principal. And this art school in the Hollow in turn had led to the present healthy relationship with the junior high and to their using the chapel for their music classes.

Another article discussed how Kizu's falling ill again had led to the closing of the art school after a short time. Along with the article was a color photograph, about half the size of a postcard, of a landscape Kizu had painted of the fall foliage around the chapel and the monastery. Ikuo explained to the tearful Ogi that since the leaves didn't turn that well last fall, the painting must have been done in the beginning of December when Kizu took his students to the north shore for outdoor sketching instruction.

Soon after closing the art school, Kizu went into Dr. Koga's clinic. Ikuo speculated that the local reporter didn't touch on the events of the summer conference, or on the "miraculous" disappearance of cancer from his body, not just out of respect for Kizu's international standing as an art educator but because of his contributions to the town.

The previous night Dr. Koga had described in detail how Kizu had died of a cancer that, for his age, had spread quite quickly. The cancer, which Dr. Koga deemed a new occurrence of the disease, started in the liver and spread to his lungs, and the autopsy revealed some brain tumors as well. In the year that had passed, Dr. Koga had taken on the look of quite the country doctor, his skin, including the bald spot now at the crown of his head, a sunburnt brown, his mannerisms deliberately exaggerating this role, referring to himself, in imitation of Gii's childish way, with the rough pronoun *washi* instead of the normal *watashi;* Dancer gently ribbed him about it, and though his observations on the symptoms were quite pointed, his look was the same as always, a mix of gloom and urbane cheerfulness as he recalled what had happened.

"Some people say the cancer that was removed in the United States came back, but since a fair amount of tests concluded that he didn't have any cancer before this, I'd say cancer snuck up on him for a third time and this time got the better of him. Kizu was in my clinic until spring. Since he was resigned to what was going to happen, he really wanted to go back to stay in his house in the Hollow, so Ms. Asuka devoted herself to nursing him. Former Brother Gii had planted a lot of cherry trees on the east slope as part of his Beautiful Village project, and Professor Kizu passed away when they were in full bloom.

"The Red Cross doctor and myself were both convinced that when Professor Kizu came here to live with Patron his cancer had disappeared. Opinion is divided, though, about whether he had cancer from the beginning or not. But once Patron was gone, the cancer rallied for a full frontal attack and did him in. After he returned to the Hollow, Professor Kizu didn't fear his cancer; death didn't bother him anymore. It was as if he'd conquered cancer and wanted to die. The cancer ravaged all his organs, and it was a pointless struggle.

"I'll let Ikuo tell you how Professor Kizu spent his final moments, since I wasn't there at the very end. Ms. Asuka seemed at a loss as usual, but also quite in control, and reported that she thought Kizu might not make it through the night so Ikuo should come attend to him. She doesn't have an ounce of sentimentality, though when Professor Kizu was in the hospital she stayed in his room the whole time. She's an unforgettable person, Ms. Asuka. Professor Kizu too, of course."

The story of Kizu's final moments that Ikuo told to Ogi—not at all what Ms. Asuka anticipated, with Dancer there as well—he said he'd add later on. Ikuo's later letter, written on the model Ms. Tsugane set for first drafts in that it left nothing out—proved helpful in this regard.

This letter contained details that Ikuo found hard to talk about that day in the chapel especially since all this became the basis for a turnabout in Ikuo's life. Even as an outside observer Ogi could sense, in this visit to the Hollow, how much Ikuo had gone through in a year's time, and this made him realize how in his own past year with Mrs. Tsugane he too had changed.

After Ikuo and Ogi had talked together for nearly an hour, Gii came over to the space heater with Fred and said that he and the Fireflies had to do some snow removal so he'd await their visit in the afternoon, and left the chapel alone. Fred seemed to be dying to tell Ikuo something about what he and Gii had discussed, so Ogi left his talk with Ikuo for later.

Ikuo spoke in English with Fred. The type of English they spoke— Fred's, of course, but also Ikuo's, who had been bilingual since childhood— was not the type of English Ogi was used to hearing. But once the conversation had settled down on track and he retrospectively picked up on what they'd said and outlined their conversation in his notebook, he was able to follow the general drift.

At first Fred seemed to be sounding out Ikuo, holding some mysterious trump card in reserve. Repeatedly he asked Ikuo whether there'd been any changes in Gii's way of thinking or his actions since the summer conference. At last night's discussion, everyone seemed to take it for granted that Gii was going to be the successor to the Church of the New Man. But wasn't Gii just being pushed forward like some automaton? After Patron's death, among those influential in the church, the hard-line remnants of the radical faction left the Farm together with Mr. Hanawa, and the police and the media had sounded a warning about allowing the Technicians who remained to hold any power in the church. Wasn't the way the church dealt with this—having a young boy like Gii as the front man—just a smoke screen?

Ogi couldn't catch all of what Ikuo replied in English, not because he spoke too quickly but because of the content. Still, he could tell that Ikuo, very patiently and meticulously, was responding to Fred's provocative questions. But what really remained with Ogi was the change in Ikuo since they'd last met. He'd swept away the dangerous instability of old, the rebelliousness and negativism, the violence that even he himself couldn't control. Very clearly Ikuo was Yonah no more.

Since the summer conference finale ended as it did, Ikuo said, Gii and the Fireflies, who were deeply involved, were naturally shaken. Especially Gii, who showed his own unique reaction to events. He was furious that the performance with which the Fireflies had planned to wrap up the summer conference was upstaged by Patron's and Ikuo's plans. The reconciliation began only when Ikuo explained to the Fireflies how at the very last minute Patron had turned the tables on him.

After this, nestling up close to where Gii's thoughts took him, Ikuo opened up an even deeper dialogue with the boys. The first thing Gii said was this: His principle for living was to deny defeatism. In this point he evaluated Patron's church more highly than Former Brother Gii's Base Movement or the Church of the Flaming Green Tree. But in the end wasn't Patron the most defeatist of all? He didn't seriously ever plan to set up and run a church here in the Hollow. Instead, didn't he just use this whole thing as a public spectacle to finally do what he couldn't at the time of the Somersault—commit suicide? "I find it hard to forgive him for using our legend of the Spirit Festival the way he did," Gii said.

But Ikuo patiently went on explaining things and finally Gii and the others admitted that, yes, before Patron had the idea of committing suicide at the finale of the summer conference, they'd been able to carry out the Spirit Festival, with Guide's spirit included, and that performing this Spirit Festival in front of so many people from all over the country was the plan they themselves had so strenuously pushed forward. And it was true that Patron, when he felt he had no other way out and reluctantly made use of the Spirit Festival, did it in a way that showed great respect for the Spirits.

As for defeatism, since Patron actually did commit suicide I can't defend him, Ikuo went on, but can't you young people be a little more generous? Consider this: When people who've passed a certain age think about how they can wind up their affairs as best they can—and you could see in Patron's final sermon the effort he made to do this—and then commit suicide, this suicide may be just like the heroic but miserable and comic suicide of the African Cato that Patron spoke of, a variation of an honest and real effort at life.

It was Patron's fervent hope to build his Church of the New Man here, in this land. And hasn't that been accomplished? The Quiet Women were bent on their own plan to take the cyanide, but look at them now—they've accepted Patron's final request and are doing their utmost to help run things at the Hollow. There's no hint now of something happening like with American cultists who all want to make a beeline to heaven en masse. These women have an experienced, healthy, realistic view of things and have developed a good relationship with the local women. Right now they're so close they go off together to the Mountain Stream Where Twenty-five Refined Ladies Shat and have a good time together picking butterbur.

It's true the Technicians split in half, and one faction left. But the other faction stayed, abandoned the agreements made by the leaders of the Technicians before the summer conference, and formulated a new policy of full cooperation with the church. Aren't the Technicians friendlier and nicer to us and to each other than ever before? Look at the way we're working together to teach you and the other Fireflies.

After listening to these details, Fred asked a question. "With the Church of the New Man starting off as it did, the position of leader, Patron's replacement, is vacant. And everyone—the office staff, the Quiet Women, and, more strongly than anyone else, according to Dr. Koga, the Technicians—agrees that Gii will assume that responsibility. How did *this* happen?"

Ikuo fielded this one. What Patron built is the Church of the New Man, so doesn't it make the most sense for those who lead to be the ones who have, in many senses of the word, the greatest possibility of *becoming* New Men?

After hesitating to ask again the reason why Ikuo didn't see himself as that kind of person, Fred asked, "Do you really believe young Gii is the right person to be the leader of the church?" And for the first time, Fred revealed his trump card.

In their little tête-à-tête in the corner it was obvious that Gii had been pestering Fred about something, which turned out to be whether Fred knew of any GI group in Okinawa or on the mainland that sold contraband machine guns out of the bases. Once he got hold of these high-powered weapons, Gii said, he'd have some Americans who fought in Vietnam train the Fireflies in their use. If they reinforced the ceiling of this chapel with steel sheets and the armed Fireflies holed up inside, they should be able, for a while at least, to hold off an attack by the riot police and military helicopters.

As if he were re-creating a battle scene from a Coppola movie, Gii described the Fireflies battling it out from their chapel stronghold—all the while making sure that everything he was saying was off the record. "I just want you to understand," Gii went on, "when you talk with those groups I mentioned earlier, the level of resolve the Fireflies have as a part of the Church of the New Man. We're ready to take on Japan and the world!"

Gii was very much drawn to the same concept of a postinsurrection millennial reign of repentance that the Izu radical faction had had before the Somersault, something that people now knew was clearly different from the Aum concept of a self-centered Armageddon. Having an insurrection lead straight to the end of the world, to nothing but death, was a defeatist attitude. "Through an insurrection based on using the Church of the New Man as our foundation," Gii told Fred, "I want to make the millennial reign of repentance a *reality*. Even in the European idea of the millennium, a millennial reign isn't seen as such an impossibly long time. If we turn the chapel into a fortress with the weapons that spill out of the American military bases—even if we only hold out for ten days—our call for repentance will reach the ends of the earth. We've already started our own Web page. And the memory of what we do, like that of He Who Destroys and Meisuke-san's uprising, will remain forever in the realm of myth. The next New Men who arise will carry on where we left off. In other words, through the Church of the New Man we will become one with the legends of this land."

"What do you think about these ideas of Gii's?" Fred asked Ikuo. "You still plan to hand the church over to him?"

"Since more than anything else Gii hates a defeatist attitude," Ikuo responded, "he won't rashly start an insurrection. For the longest time I've been mulling over Patron's final words in his sermon—the call of *Long live Karamazov!* When Dancer was going through Patron's effects, she found a dog-eared copy of the novel with the following commentary circled in red pencil. I read this over so many times I can quote it verbatim:

> "Not just Aloysha, who thirteen years hence is supposed to be crucified for being an assassin of the Tsar, but the lustful Dimitri, who carries the burden of a crime he didn't commit, as well as the Grand Inquisitor Ivan, who cries out in his thirst for life—all of them make a complete change from their positions and reach the sublime at the chorus of shouts from the boys of '*Long live Karamazov!*'"

Ikuo translated this very deliberately into English. After this, when he spoke next, Ogi felt he was seeing the Ikuo of old, as if a bizarre, out-of-control Yonah had removed his mask. And what he remembered later with unusual clarity was the strong feeling that Ikuo had a beauty not in keeping with his face—no, more accurately even his face was part of this now. Yet despite this he was someone who might very well be Ogi's lifelong adversary.

All the while, a faint smile rose to Ikuo's lips, *inscrutable* but quite the opposite of the meaningless smile that Japanese display when talking with foreigners—the adjective that Fred used when, days later, he was going over with Ogi his notes of his conversation with Ikuo—and Ikuo said that when Patron shouted out *Long Live Karamazov*! he had to have been thinking of those here, the Japanese version of young men full of possibilities for the future.

"No matter what frightening things the young people in the church do over the next ten or fifteen years," Ikuo continued, "as long as they're New Men I'm not going to drive them out. I imagine that from now on Gii will, in both what he says and does, be the one who fluctuates the most violently, but right now in the church he's our number-one New Man. I want to educate him to be the one who shouts *Long live Karamazov!* and succeeds the dead. I want to raise him up in our church—and *outside* it, too."

Days later, when he was reviewing his conversation with Ikuo, Fred Parks asked Ogi whether, on that day in the chapel, Gii and Ikuo hadn't planned out all their answers ahead of time–at Gii's instigation, mainly—and were pulling his leg. But Ogi was less inclined to think about that than the crystal-clear memory he had of Ikuo that day—a memory that in later years often came back to haunt him.

4

On his final day Kizu had clearly been growing weaker, but he had his pillows piled up high on his bed and, with the lightweight opera glasses Mr. Soda had brought over as a gift when he came to visit, was gazing at the wild cherry blossoms on the east shore. Ikuo had been watching over him all night, and Dancer had joined them. The night before was a full moon with only a thin scattering of clouds, and Kizu had tried to view the cherries in the moonlight but couldn't see them so well, he said. Checking to see that he'd be all right for a few moments, Ikuo had walked down to below the dam where Gii and some of the Fireflies were parked and asked them to take care of something.

Gii had uncoiled a long line they'd used in the summer conference from a covered outlet at the foot of the outside wall of the chapel and shone a floodlight on the wild cherries on the jutting crags where the bilberries grew. Ikuo was happy that the attempt was a success. But Kizu had been too worn out to lift his head from his pillow.

With no way for Ikuo to signal Gii and the Fireflies by the crags, the young men could do nothing but remain standing next to the floodlight. Concerned about how things were turning out, Kizu fell into a comalike sleep for ten minutes, then opened his eyes and asked three times whether the floodlights were still lit. Ikuo looked out at the moonlit ink-colored forest and the cherry blossoms looming up palely in the floodlight and said yes. With the dark gray of the grove of cherry trees just outside the ring of light, the whole scene was one of great depth. But since there was no way they could even get Kizu's head raised up to look out a little, Ikuo asked if he'd like the curtains closed, to which Kizu responded in a listless, muffled voice—Dancer had skillfully helped him get up the phlegm—that it wasn't good to keep the young boys out there if they were still standing by the crags.

As the moon shifted, the surface of the lake was thrown into dark shadows and Kizu awoke from a lengthy sleep and asked Ikuo to pose for him. Dancer acted shocked, thinking Kizu was hallucinating and thought he was painting, but Ikuo knew differently. An easel stood next to the bed, with one of the drawings Kizu had done for the triptych, a sketch of a nude Ikuo he particularly liked. Ikuo stripped off his clothes and struck the same pose. Slowly tilting his head on the pillow, Kizu gazed intently at him.

"Can they see you from the crags?" Kizu asked, somewhat embarrassedly, his voice again muffled.

"Even if they can, Gii and the others don't have binoculars," Ikuo replied.

"Can that . . . stand up, do you think?"

Ikuo looked down. It came to him what Kizu wanted, but he couldn't think of what to do about it. Quick-witted, Dancer got up out of the low chair, moved forward and got to her knees, held Ikuo's penis directly against her lips, and then put it inside her mouth. The penis immediately rose up magnificently, and with the momentum as she drew her open mouth back, glistening with a line of saliva, it smacked once against her small nose. Kizu, breathing lightly, watched all this.

"So that's what it was like. . . . That's enough, you must be cold."

"No, I'm okay," Ikuo said, but, concerned about his shriveling genitals, he was relieved to put his clothes back on.

"Actually, I can't see too well. That's enough," Kizu said. After a while, he turned to the now-dressed Ikuo and kidded him with a question. "So— the two of you are pretty close now? I'm happy for you."

"Thank you," Ikuo said.

He was afraid Dancer was going to deny it, but she merely glanced up, saliva glistening around her half-opened mouth.

After dozing for an even longer time, Kizu woke again and said, in the same tone as before, "Ikuo—is it really so bad that you can't hear God's voice? You don't need God's voice, do you? People should be free."

Ikuo couldn't just say what popped into his head. A dark yet gentle emotion permeated him, as if the darkness covering the black lake had risen up and seeped inside him.

"You say . . . God's voice . . . told you that . . . but I think . . . even with-out God, I want to say *rejoice*. To me, and to . . ."

Kizu let out a ragged breath, fell asleep, and then suddenly sat up and vomited dark blood and began to writhe. His upper body, supported by his strong waist, trembled like a caterpillar searching for a leaf. Ikuo was flus-tered, unable to react. Kizu's head fell heavily onto the window frame, and he nearly fell off the bed in the space between it and the window. "*Professor Kizu!*" Dancer shouted, as if scolding him. Kizu stopped moving and turned in their direction; his head plopped down on his chest, and he breathed his last.

Dancer called out again, leaning forward with her thin shoulders, but Ikuo had already made certain that Kizu was dead. He walked around the bed, pushed open the window, stuck the floor lamp outside, and waved it a couple of times. Because this was what Kizu had been most concerned about.

The light illuminating the wild cherry trees above the crags went out. What looked like a black smudge appeared in the center of the now pale grove of cherry trees. Once again the top of the forest was under the moonlight, the smudge was soon gone, and a wind they couldn't feel down low rustled the light-reddish and milky-white heaps of flowers.

"The last thing he asked was whether it was really so bad not to be able to hear the voice of God," Ikuo said. "And just before he died he used the word *rejoice*. To himself, and to . . . *something else,* he said."

Ikuo scowled fiercely. Perhaps irritated at his own vague words, Ogi thought, large teardrops began to course down his face.

Ikuo shook his huge head, wiped back the tears, and said, "That was half a year ago. . . . It's been a long year since the summer conference. I've thought about it a lot since then, and I agree with what Patron said. Gii's taken by this idea of a millennial reign, but Patron said he would lead the church as an antichrist. As a free man, I plan to stand beside Gii until he takes over the church."

"I've no doubt Gii is the sort of young man who can become a New Man, but he never told me he believed in God or stood on the side of the antichrist," Fred said. Then he closed his notebook and asked very calmly, "Has this become a church without God, then?"

On Ikuo's brawny features a truly beautiful expression arose as he pon-dered this. From the bottoms of the domes on the ceiling, snow melted in the sun and fell off with a thud. The large cylindrical space was surrounded by the sound of water. Between the question and the reply enough time passed that the direct relationship between the two grew fuzzy. When just enough time had passed for Ogi to feel this, Ikuo finally replied.

"For us, a church is a place where deeds of the soul are done."